Daughter of Thunder

By
J. A. Aarntzen

PublishAmerica
Baltimore

© 2007 by J. A. Aarntzen.
All rights reserved. No part of this book may be reproduced, stored in a retrieval system or transmitted in any form or by any means without the prior written permission of the publishers, except by a reviewer who may quote brief passages in a review to be printed in a newspaper, magazine or journal.

First printing

All characters appearing in this work are fictitious. Any resemblance to real persons, living or dead, is purely coincidental.

At the specific preference of the author, PublishAmerica allowed this work to remain exactly as the author intended, verbatim, without editorial input.

ISBN: 1-4241-6986-0
PUBLISHED BY PUBLISHAMERICA, LLLP
www.publishamerica.com
Baltimore

Printed in the United States of America

To my dad,

*You have always been there standing behind me
Now I want you to step forward and stand beside me
For there is no one worthier than you*

Acknowledgments

I want to thank all those that read my first two books with PublishAmerica, *The Little Boy of the Forest* and *Corman the Carp*. You have made a lifelong dream come true.

Special thanks go to Karen Gallant (author of *The Betrayal of Cerridwen*), Jim Spence (author of *The Herman Effect*) and James Duncan (author of *The Book of Legends* series). Thank you for the encouragement, the input and the camaraderie. My skills at this craft have been enriched because of you.

Other Books Available by J. A. Aarntzen through PublishAmerica

The Little Boy of the Forest
ISBN 10 1413780555
ISBN 13 978-1413780550

Corman the Carp
ISBN 10 1413781802
ISBN 13 978-1413781809

Please visit www.storytelleronthelake.com for more details on J.A. Aarntzen

Prologue

"They should have returned by now. More than three moons have passed since they left the village," the tribal elder remarked. A party of younger men that had grown concerned about the missing father and son requested his advice.

Gray Ashes and his son Rautooskee had departed on a pilgrimage to the sacred lake of Jibatigon shortly after the trees had blossomed and the frogs began croaking in the rivers and bays. It was now the season where the leaves were afire and the lakes grow silent. They should have been back by now. A journey to Jibatigon and back should not entail such seasonal stretches in time.

Something must have gone amiss.

A search sortie had gone to the holy waters a month earlier. When they returned the only news they had was that they had seen some burnt blankets caught in a weed bed along one of Jibatigon's many inlets. Although badly charred, the weave in the blanket did seem to bear the markings of the Hendorun house to which Gray Ashes and his son belonged.

"They are not coming back," an older man said from the rear of the open-air enclave set in a natural amphitheater amid the shade of the surrounding Jack pine. This man was normally silent and was regarded with little respect in the tribe.

He was the brother to Chemung, father of Gray Ashes. His name was Madoqua. He had been very marginal in the affairs of the People since he had slandered his respected brother's name and reputation many years ago. Chemung was highly regarded by the tribe. When he died at the waterfall entering the sacred lake all those years ago, Chemung was revered as a noble spirit in the eyes of the People for he fought bravely and defeated an evil spirit that sought to claim the lake for his own. The great Chemung saved his son's life but was mortally wounded in the encounter with the demon beast. Before he died he pulled his *boy from the water and showed him the way out of the magical lake. This was what Gray Ashes had told the tribe when he had come back to the village without his father. The People embraced the lost boy and mourned the loss of the man that rescued him.*

But Madoqua told another story of Chemung. He said that his brother did not behave according to the traditions of respect and reverence that the great Rabbitman, Chendos, demanded the People display towards Jibatigon. Madoqua said that his brother openly challenged the time-honored mores and flaunted his arrogance in the face of the enchanted lake. The lake rose up in anger and smote this upstart and claimed his body and spirit.

This was the true story that Gray Ashes had brought back from Jibatigon when he was in his youth. It was a story that he told his uncle but would not tell the rest of the tribe in fear of being chastised as the son of a heretic.

Gray Ashes would not tell the tale but Madoqua did and when Gray Ashes would not second the uncle's allegations, Madoqua's status in the tribe became peripheral and he was cast to the shadowy perimeter of Hendorun society. There he resided for a generation. His fellow tribesmen treated him with disdain. They would not eat with him. They would not give him a share of their meat. He had to fend for himself but he never left the village. He had as much residence there as the rest of the dirt from which the forest grew.

Then a few weeks after his nephew left on his own pilgrimage to Jibatigon with his son, Madoqua had a dream about his relatives. He dreamt that after a confrontation with the spirit of Chemung, Gray Ashes had unintentionally violated the sacred laws of the lake and its surrounding land.

The lake and the land exacted its punishment upon Rautooskee, leaving the boy near death. The laws of the lake and the land were inviolable and possessed no measure of mercy. Jibatigon went to war on the man and his son and in the end had claimed the life of Gray Ashes. His son Rautooskee was permitted to live but live only under the severest of conditions. A sleep had gripped him and would not let go of him until the time that he was woken up by a stranger that would cry out his name from a distant land.

Once risen, Rautooskee would enter the body of another, a son of a usurping people and will live the consequences of this other. He may finally perish or he may live and restore the world to the way that it should be had not Chemung angered the spirits and set the Earth upon an evil course. This all depended upon this stranger from a distant land and a far off time and on the spirit that hosted him.

The host must cry out Rautooskee's name while the distant stranger must dance the Dance of Petition for not only Rautooskee but for all those others that were instrumental in setting up the conditions for the readjustment of events.

This Dance of Petition, which was a sacred rite of the People to call out to the departed ancestors to come and greet a new arrival on the shores of Jibatigon and allow the newcomer entry into the land of the spirits, must not be danced for Rautooskee until his spirit was ready to enter those lands. If a Dance of Petition were to be danced for him before he was ready, the Hendorun people would pay severely. They would lose their lands to strangers and be scattered and never again know the quiet of their souls. They would be miserable and shadows of what they were and what they could have been.

It was this dream that Madoqua announced to the council of elders when the people had given up hope that Gray Ashes and Rautooskee would return. Almost at once, the others mocked him. They asserted that he was once again only trying to undermine the noble memory of his brother Chemung and his descendants. They demanded that he forget his dream and that as the oldest living member of Chemung's house that he must initiate the Dance of Petition for Gray Ashes and Rautooskee. He cried out that he would not but he was overpowered and administered powerful medicines that made him forget his dream. He underwent the one-month long cleansing rituals that would allow him to dance.

Then after a month of fasting and meditation, Madoqua was ready to begin the ritual. But before he commenced the dance, the great Chendos visited him and told him that his dream was true. A dance for Rautooskee would bring the ruin of his people.

Madoqua announced what Chendos had told him but the people would not believe him. They would have someone else dance for Gray Ashes and Rautooskee. They banished Madoqua from the tribe forever. They put him into a canoe and sent him on his way. He was never to return to the People.

The banished man spent many moons traveling on the streams deep in the bountiful forests of the land. He kept away from all others. His life was that of peace although he was still disturbed by his dream. Then after so much time went by that Madoqua had never measured, he discovered that he had become a spirit, a roaming spirit that was not permitted entry into the land of the ancestors. He was doomed to remain in his canoe and paddle in solitude through the lakes and rivers until time came to an end or until someone danced the Dance of Petition for him. The latter was unlikely since his people had long ago disappeared. Strangers from a far away place had usurped the land.

But still Madoqua continued to paddle. The first part of his dream had come true in the form of distant men with lighter skins and darker hearts. They had come in vast numbers and soon uprooted not only Madoqua's people but also all the other people that lived under the great forest. The forest, itself, was beginning to disappear just as Chendos had foretold. It was now up to the lone spirit to see that the rest of his dream comes to fruition as well. No one else would do it for him.

CHAPTER 1

Fiasco at St. Andrew's

"That lake in Canada is a curse to this family," Aunt Myra said as she stood amid a throng of mourners on the stately stairs in front of St. Andrew's Church on that beautiful July 1929 morning. The sun was catching the ivy that climbed along the steeple's red brick and gave it a resonance that truly made it feel that this was God's house.

"Mr. Meadowford is not the first to die up there," a younger lady responded, while nervously clutching to an inappropriate white handbag with her satin gloves and squinting her eyes in the glowing Grappling Haven sunshine. Her nervousness could obviously be attributed to her error in dressing for the weather rather than the occasion.

Aunt Myra laughed, "He's not the first but I think that he will be the last. My sister Cora told me that just before Mr. Meadowford died there was a big family ruckus and that in her eyes there will be no way that any of them will reconcile with each other."

"It's just the two of them left though now, isn't it?" the younger lady asked. She seemed more composed now. She had not been rebuked for her bright attire. "Just your brother-in-law Langley and that Faye Thurston, right?"

"You're forgetting that old coot, Thaddeus Meadowford. He's still a part of the picture. He has not given up the ghost yet. Now that Sambo's gone he's the sole family patriarch. Not that anybody will listen to him."

"He isn't here, is he?" the younger lady looked surprised and climbed up onto the toes of her ivory sling back shoes and scanned the crowd of people that had come to pay their final homage to Samuel Angus Meadowford the Second or Sambo as he was known to his friends.

"No," Aunt Myra responded. "He could not be dragged away from the family holdings in Michigan for his brother's funeral. There seems to be some form of labor dispute there that demands his attention. Business before family, that is the Meadowford way."

When her mother's older sister made the remark, Thora could no longer eavesdrop on the conversation. She turned to her twin sister Rebecca and said, "That's not going to be my way!"

Rebecca looked at her with a lifted eyebrow. "What are you talking about Thora?"

"Weren't you listening?" Thora scoffed. "Auntie Myra says that we Meadowfords place business before family!"

The two sisters were standing on their own amid the hundred or more people that had come for the church service. It seemed that none of them wanted to pay their condolences to the two girls dressed in black that had lost their grandfather. They had all been here only a year earlier when services were held for the girls' cousin, the little boy Jack Thurston. That service was a very sad affair that was made all the more troubling in that the coffin was empty. Little Jack's body was never recovered from that lake that held a curse upon the family.

Besides Jack and Sambo, Pioneer Lake had also claimed the lives of Sambo's wife, June Meadowford, and Jack's older brother Percival. Sambo was the only one that was not a drowning victim. The twin girls, Thora and Rebecca, were too young to remember their paternal grandmother and their cousin Percy. These two had died while the girls were still toddlers in their swaddling clothes.

Many of the people here though would remember June Meadowford and Percival Thurston and would have attended services here at St. Andrew's for them. They would recall that those services also were more memorials than funerals. Just like Jack, the lake that had taken June and Percy never gave up their bodies. Sambo's service was the first to actually possess flesh that could be interred into the ground.

"I was thinking of Grandfather lying in that coffin," Rebecca answered. "He looked so cold. He did not seem like he was at peace."

"I think that we Meadowfords never can be at peace," Thora said to her sister. "There is something about us that is restless and refuses to stand still."

"Do you think that he liked us?" Rebecca suddenly asked. She gave no regard to Thora's gloomy comment.

"Whatever do you mean?" Thora was shocked by what her sister said.

"I don't know," Rebecca smirked. "It seems to me that he at best only tolerated us. I saw him out of the corner of my eyes roll his eyes in the direction of Aunt Faye and Uncle Tom whenever Mother had us playing at the piano upon the lake. It was like he was saying to them, 'Here we go again with another show by Cora and Langley's trained monkeys!'"

"I never noticed," Thora answered, although she had glimpsed the same thing too on many occasions up on Pioneer Lake. It had never been truly comfortable up there for her. She sensed the covert but deep-rooted hostility that existed between her parents and Aunt Faye and Uncle Tom. There was sibling rivalry present with all of its ugly ramifications. She had sworn to herself that she and Rebecca would always keep their relationship loving and warm.

"Do you think he liked us or not?" Rebecca repeated her question.

"In as much as he could show it I think that he did. But more than that, I think that he loved us," Thora asserted although she felt that her words were empty. Grandfather never gave any clues as to his affections or disaffections with the twin girls. He acknowledged them but never sought to ingratiate them.

"I think that he liked and loved Jack best, if you ask me," Rebecca said. There were tears forming in her eyes.

Upon seeing these tears, Thora could feel her own vision become clouded by droplets of her own. She knew that Rebecca was right. It was clear that Grandfather's favorite was Jack. The boy was so full of life and energy and carried a disposition that was most charming and genuine. The day that Jack died was a day that she was sure that she would never forget. It had been such a typical day at first, a day that would have got lost in that fuzzy mire of fond recollections of their times upon the lake. Jack and his father, Uncle Tom, were playing in the water. They were carrying on with that tiresome game of siege engine when the accident happened and Jack was thrown into the rocks where that spike had been lodged. Jack died instantly. How the family mourned that tragedy! It should have been a typical day that should have been lost in the fuzzy mire of fond recollections of their times upon the lake. Instead it was a day for mourning.

Aunt Faye was so distraught over the accident that until this very day the family was under strict instructions from Grandfather that they should not make mention of the boy whatsoever whenever any of them were in her company. Thora had always thought that that was an unwise decree and that it would only foster deeper psychological trauma in the woman.

"Do you think that it was perhaps because Jack was a boy and the only living grandson that Grandfather had?" Rebecca asked while pulling out a handkerchief from her purse to wipe away the tears that had formed.

"Jack did not have the Meadowford name," Thora said while taking her sister's cue to fetch a handkerchief of her own to be ready for any deepening tears. "He was a Thurston. And I don't think that gender played any part in Grandfather's choices. He liked Aunt Faye much more than he liked Father."

"The name Meadowford will disappear as soon as you and I are married," Rebecca said as she rubbed the handkerchief to the corners of her eyes. "It is rather sad, isn't it? Especially when you think that our great grandfather possessed the dream of a Meadowford dynasty upon Pioneer Lake."

"Becky, you are forgetting about the line that descends from Uncle Thaddeus. He had several children. Some of them were boys. They are now all old enough to have children of their own and I am willing to bet that there is at least one of them that carries the Meadowford name."

"But they all moved away to Europe and have disappeared from family memory. We don't even know their names!" Rebecca protested rather loudly.

"We don't know whose names?" the girls' mother, Cora Meadowford, said. She had come out of nowhere and joined her daughters. She was dressed in a dark brown outfit with a floral imprint and was wearing a veil over her face that concealed her eyes and nose but drew accent upon the heavy red lipstick upon her mouth. To Thora her mother was not properly attired for the funeral of her father-in-law. Her clothing did not seem to convey a message of respect for the old man.

"The names of Uncle Thaddeus' children!" Rebecca said.

"Heavens, why would you concern yourself with a subject such as that!" Cora remarked. From the way that her lips moved, Thora guessed that she must have rolled back her eyes behind the veil. "Really, girls, it makes no difference who they are. None of them have shown the decency to attend their uncle's funeral or even send flowers or letters of condolence. They are nobody to us and as nobodies they should remain nameless."

"Maybe they don't even know Grandfather is dead?" Rebecca put in. "Has anybody thought of sending them a telegram with the news?"

"News as such has a way of finding the ears that it is meant for," Cora said. "I am sure that your Aunt Faye managed to get the word out to them."

"Aunt Faye managed to get what out to whom?" Cora's sister Myra remarked. She had pulled herself away from the group that she had been standing with and slipped into the company of her sister and nieces.

Thora did not like Aunt Myra. She was a busy body and a gossip and was always quick to rebuke anyone that did not meet her standards.

"Get word out to Thaddeus'..." Cora started.

Myra broke into her sister's comment. "Did you see what Margaret Whattam is wearing? The dizzy woman must have thought that this was a wedding and not a funeral!"

Thora looked across the stairs to the other group of women. There, standing like a brilliant macaw amid a flock of crows, was Margaret Whattam. Margaret's husband, James, was the chief legal and business advisor to Thaddeus Meadowford. He was not here at the funeral for he was away in Dearborn, Michigan along with Uncle Thaddeus trying to rescue the family business.

"At least she had the decency to pay her respects to Grandfather!" Rebecca said in a rather terse tongue. "I don't think that she should be mocked for what she chooses to wear. Grandfather led a happy life. It should be something to be celebrated and not be sad about."

Thora was still staring at Mrs. Whattam when Rebecca had raised her voice. It was plain that the woman in bright clothing heard what was being said. She turned her head away sheepishly and seemed like she pretended that she did not hear anything.

There was shock on Aunt Myra's face at the remarks made by the girl.

"Rebecca Meadowford, you mind your manner!" Cora said in defense of her sister. "You apologize to Aunt Myra and pray that she has it in her good heart to forgive you!"

"I won't do anything of the such!" Rebecca would not back down. "Aunt

Myra has poisoned many a thing in our lives with her vile assertions. I am not going to let her poison a day that should belong to the memory of Grandfather with her snobby critiques of the apparel of others!"

"The girl is obviously upset over the loss of her grandfather," Cora said to her sister. What could be seen of her face had taken the rosy hue of someone in a compromised position. "She doesn't mean anything that she says."

"What's gotten into you, Rebecca?" Thora whispered to her sister. "This is no place to be causing a scene!"

"Don't worry Cora, I take no offence," Myra said. "Your girl is thirteen. She is obviously entering a change of life and hormones are getting the better of her." With that said, the woman haughtily returned to her other group and was undoubtedly relaying her latest adventure to them, Margaret Whattam included.

"The funeral is over girls. The two of you can go home now, if you like," Cora said in an icy voice. It was more of a command than a request. The house where they resided was just over a block away down the shaded elm street from the church.

"But what about the burial?" Thora spoke up. "I want to go to the cemetery!"

"And I want to have some words with Aunt Faye," Rebecca added. "I have not spoken to her since being up at the lake."

"You are not to speak to that woman ever again!" Cora pulled the veil from her face revealing bulging eyes. "After all those filthy things that she said about your father and I, I consider her dead and you should do so as well too!"

Thora remembered the filthy things that Aunt Faye had said about her parents. She had said in no uncertain terms that her father, Langley, had been pilfering from the Meadowford business and that he had not only kept a mistress in New Hampshire but he had placed her in the unforgivable position of being with child. Naturally, Thora could not believe those things about her father but she knew that Rebecca had secretly questioned his integrity.

During the service Aunt Faye had sat on the opposite side of the chapel from Langley Meadowford's brood. Thora had glanced over at her several times, sitting by herself. She felt some pity for the woman for she had nobody to sit with her. The two sons that came from her womb were both dead and gone. The man that she married was also gone. And now her father had departed as well. There was nobody left for Faye Thurston. Not once during the hour-long memorial to Samuel Angus Meadowford II did Faye cast an eye over to the opposite side of the chapel. Thora sensed that as far as Aunt Faye was concerned Langley, Cora and their twin girls were dead too.

"Where's Dad?" Thora demanded. "I want to speak to him. You are not going to deny us the chance to say our final farewell to Grandfather!"

"Your father is still in the church."

"What's he doing in there? Everybody else is outside! Even Grandfather is gone!" Thora responded. Grandfather's coffin was in the black Hearst at the bottom of the steps. The car was running. Its headlights were on. Soon the procession to the cemetery, Silent Hills, would commence.

"Your father is in a very deep state of grief. He loved your grandfather dearly and has such profound regrets that the last time that he was together with him had to have been such an ugly occasion, thanks to that psychotic sister of his!"

"Dad's not in the church, Mother!" Rebecca said out loud. "He's standing over there with his hunting friends."

Thora turned and spotted her father. He was wearing a snug fitting black suit with an oversized gray felt fedora that sat tilted on his head. The expression that Langley Meadowford bore on his face was anything but morose. He was smoking and laughing and carrying on. Although Thora could not hear what he was actually saying her ears did unerringly pick up the guttural chortle of his wheezy guffaw. He certainly was not in the throes of any state of depression brought on by regrets over his final relationship with his father.

When Cora saw her husband acting like today was just any old day, she grimaced. "So he is. Grief is such an odd emotion, girls. It comes out of us in different ways. You can be sure that behind that handsome smiling face is a man deeply plagued with profound feelings of depression."

"You are wrong, Mother!" Rebecca snapped. "Dad never cared for Grandfather. He did everything that he could to undermine the old man and try to pull the business out from under him. Today is a day of celebration for him and not one of deep sorrow."

"Rebecca Meadowford, how can you say such things!" Cora glowered. "A daughter should be more respecting of her father!"

"Why? He never showed any for his father!" Thora's sister spoke so loudly that heads all over, including that of Langley Meadowford, turned to look at her. "Look at him over there! You say that you see a handsome man? I see only a sniveling rat out only to aggrandize his meager measure of self-importance!"

Thora was absolutely shocked by the words coming from her sister. Not even Faye Thurston could have said such harsh things. Langley Meadowford was not the ideal father, Thora would be one of the first to acknowledge this fact, but he did what he could to try to keep the family happy and would often lavish his girls with expensive gifts and fantastic vacations such as the promised one later this summer to New York City where they would stay in a fancy hotel and shop from only the best clothing stores in Manhattan. Thora could never see her father as a sniveling rat.

"Langley, can you come over here for a moment!" Cora cried out in exasperation. Thora knew that her mother did not know how to handle this situation on her own.

All around them any conversations that may have been taking place had all been put on hold as the observers wanted to see how this dramatic scene in front of the church would play itself out.

"Can it wait, Cora?" Langley called out to them. He had not budged from his group of friends. "I am in the middle of some important negotiations with the gentlemen present!"

"You are no doubt trying to settle on what golf course you are going to play this afternoon after the funeral!" Cora growled.

"Now Cora! Don't be so silly!" Langley responded. "We are discussing sensitive affairs that will have a direct impact on the way that we live our lives."

"Such as the one that you had with Lena Taylor!" Cora snapped.

Thora was surprised that her mother would bring up that name. That was the name of the house servant that her father allegedly had clandestine relations with up in New Hampshire. According to Aunt Faye, her father had impregnated the young woman who was still in her late teens. Thora thought that her mother had forgotten that story after her father did so much to prove it wrong on their ignomious return trip from Pioneer Lake. She thought that her dad had managed to convince her mother that everything Aunt Faye said was a gross misinterpretation of the facts. Yes, her dad had met with this Lena Taylor in New Hampshire but it was all business. Lena had contacted her dad to ask for a loan to start up a restaurant along a busy highway. Her dad at first agreed to the business venture and had given the woman several installments to get the restaurant going. But he soon learned that Lena was not using the money for such an endeavor. She was using the money to pay for an expensive suite instead. When he discovered this he cut off the funding and demanded repayment but received instead a notice that she was with child and that he was the father. It was an outlandish assertion, her father claimed. The real father was some drifter that had come through town and deposited his seed before moving on. Langley Meadowford's dealings with Lena Taylor had always been above board and there was never anything circumspect about them. "Besides," her dad had said, "Lena's far too skinny. I prefer my women plump!" If this was meant as a compliment to her mother, Thora could not see it, but her mother somehow accepted it and all of Langley's informal deposition of the events behind the lavish apartment and Lena's pregnancy. Cora had been convinced that everything that Aunt Faye had said were lies.

That was why Thora was so taken aback by what her mother just said. She had believed that the ghost of Lena Taylor had been exorcized.

Langley waved his arm downward at his wife as if he were dismissing what she said as nothing but the ravings of a stressed and berserk woman. "You know the real story there, Cora!" he said, shaking his head in disappointment and looking to the men that surrounded him for support.

"The real story is that I soon will have a half-brother or half-sister that I will never know!" Rebecca cried out. Rebecca was the only one in the household that had not accepted her father's version of events. She saw him as a cad and someone that was capable of disgusting acts that would demean the foundation that he rested upon.

"Langley, this has gone out of control!" Cora whined out loud and struck Rebecca across the face. The sound of the slap echoed against the steeple of the church.

Everybody assembled was silent as the Meadowford clan displayed their dirty laundry for all to see.

"You bitch!" Rebecca screamed at her mother before she stormed away. Her path led directly through Aunt Myra's group. Aunt Myra tried to grab her but Rebecca pushed her aside and landed her against Margaret Whattam who managed to keep the startled woman from falling to the cement.

Thora never felt more embarrassed in her life. Her family was acting like they were hillbillies just descended out of the Ozark Mountains. To see her father, mother and sister behaving so disgracefully in public at an occasion meant to show reverence to Grandfather gave a marked impression to the thirteen-year-old girl. She no longer was sure that she wanted to share her future with any of them.

"Why can't you act like a man for once in your life, Langley Meadowford!" Cora hissed venomously to her husband. "None of this would have happened if you would have just come over here when I asked you!" There were tears streaming down her face. A portion of her veil became glued to the running mascara.

"You never knew how to control those spoiled brats!" Langley shot back. "You let them do as they please like they were raccoons at a dump! I have had it up to here with you and them, Cora!"

Thora could see that her father was livid. The veins at the side of his head were bulging so much that they were visible the more than thirty feet that separated him from her. His words hurt her very much but they did not surprise her. He no longer held a vaulted status in her eyes. He was more the sniveling rat than a grand duke. Anything that had been said about him in the past seemed now much more likely. Even his cronies looked at him with non-condoning expressions.

All of a sudden there was a piercing pain emanating from her ear. Her mother had seized her by this organ and was dragging her away. "You can bury your father by yourself Langley Meadowford! I never cared for the old man anyway! He never liked the girls and me and never did anything to make us feel a part of the family. And when you are finished burying him, don't bother coming home because as far as I am concerned the doors to that house are forever locked to you!" Cora spat out as she pushed her way down the stair with Thora in undignified tow.

Thora did not want to lift her eyes as she was being led down the stairs like a cow ready for the slaughterhouse. This day had descended into the darkest day that she could ever recall. Her family had disgraced her and she had determined that as soon as she could she would leave them and have nothing to do with them forever.

As they moved down the stairs, their progress was suddenly stopped. A man was blocking them from going further. Thora lifted her eyes and looked upward to the chin and face of Tom Thurston, her former uncle.

"Cora, get a hold of yourself," Tom said calmly to her mother.

"I am only doing what you did!" Cora replied to him. "It was the smartest move that you ever made getting out of this family!"

"Now, now Cora," Tom cooed as he gently took her hand away from Thora's ear. "The family is not all that bad."

"Oh, yes they are! And you know it!" Cora spat.

"If they were all that bad then I would not have shown up here now, would I?" Tom responded.

Thora looked at the man that at one time was married to her Aunt Faye. He was a very handsome man with his broad shoulders neatly wrapped underneath a black suit that was not cut from as an expensive a cloth as her father's but managed to make the man appear more elegant than her father could ever hope to be. She always liked her Uncle Tom despite all the disparaging remarks made about him from the likes of her father and Uncle Thaddeus. They saw him as a gold digging playboy with the intelligence of a zoo creature. They had been proved wrong about Tom's aspirations for wealth and status for after he and Faye parted their ways he never tried to stake any claim to the Meadowford fortune.

"Although Sambo and I had our differences, I respected the man and felt that I owed it to myself to say good bye to him," Tom continued. Thora had seen Tom sitting at the back of the chapel during the service. She had thought that she had seen tears glistening from his eyes. She remembered all his tears a year earlier at the memorial service for his son Jack. She wished that she had a Dad that could love her as much as Tom loved Jack.

"How can you say such things Tom? You should have heard what they said about you behind your back!" Cora snapped back. Thora remembered these things as well. She remembered that her mother was often the most vocal in finding ways to undermine the character of Tom Thurston. Thora knew that her mother's verbal torpedoes were meant to sink Tom as she saw in him a direct adversary in trying to win over the hard to gain Meadowford affections. And now her mother was acting like she had been

Tom's champion all along. Her mother sickened her as much as her father did.

Before Tom could reply, Langley had descended upon them. His face was raving. He grabbed his wife by the shoulder and pulled her away. He was hauling back his fist ready to strike Cora in the head.

Tom's hand shot out and clutched Langley by the wrist. "You had better think about what you are doing!" he warned.

"Come on Langley hit me in front of all of these witnesses!" Cora bellowed. Her face was leaned forward into that of her husband's. The veins in her neck were so stretched and tight they could have been used in a piano. "You lay one finger on me and I will leave you as penniless as poor Tom!"

By now everybody had circled the fighting couple. Thora slipped to be among them. She did not want to be part of the center of attention. Her parents were behaving like idiots. Why did they save all their pent-up hostility for each other for this moment in public? Why couldn't they have aired their differences behind closed doors and out of view of assessing eyes? She could well imagine what Aunt Myra would have to say about this later on.

"You are not going to see one penny from me you social climbing whore!" Langley blurted. "I know that you and Tom have always been scheming to strip we Meadowfords from our money. I know that you are secretly in cahoots and that you have always had eyes for each other!"

Even Thora knew that the claims were outlandish. Her mother never liked Tom and she had good reason to believe that Tom never thought much of her. Her dad was just trying to provoke a fight. He and Tom had sparred before and Tom had laid such a licking on Langley that it took weeks for him to even show his face around the dinner table at Pioneer Lake once more. But this time her dad had his friends with him and they would be there to help him should a physical fight commence.

"Tom is more man in his baby finger than you could ever be Langley Meadowford!" Cora rasped. "You are a lowly coward. How I ever said yes to you is beyond me!"

"You said yes to me because you wrapped me in your spell, you gold digging witch!" Langley shouted, shaking his hand free from Tom's, and grabbing her by the veil. He yanked hard on the light fabric. Some of it tore but enough of it held to pull Cora's head forward. This landed it in a tight hold between Langley's clutching arms and his soft belly. Cora tried to break loose but Langley had her overpowered.

At once Tom took Thora's mother by the waist and pulled her free. He let go of her and immediately went to manhandle Langley. But before he could get a hold of the man, Langley's friends had stepped in and quickly forced Tom to the ground. Once Tom was on the cement Langley swiftly and unceremoniously kicked him in the face.

"For God's sake Langley can you for once show that you are a product of the expensive education lavished on you!"

Thora turned her head and saw her Aunt Faye standing with her clenched fists resting on her hips two steps above her brother and ex-husband. Even though Faye's eyes burned with anger Thora never had seen such an icon of dignity. "This is Father's funeral, Langley. Show him the respect that he deserves!" she said in a slow authoritative schoolteacher manner.

Despite the fact that Aunt Faye was speaking to Langley, Thora saw that the woman's eyes were upon Tom Thurston, her ex-husband. Blood was trickling from his mouth where Langley had kicked him.

"I ask you to kindly leave," Aunt Faye said to him. "This is meant to be a private family function open only to family members and close friends." Her words were sculpted out of ice. It was hard to believe that this woman would have ever felt any affection for the man. "As for the rest of you will you please go to your motor cars so that we can finish this somber ceremony? The Hearst is waiting!"

Aunt Faye was not a large woman by any means but she was able to marshal respect out of the assembled as if she were a club-wielding Titan. Upon her words people began moving towards their automobiles in silence. If they had any comments to be made about what had just happened they would save them for the privacy of their cabs.

"You heard the woman! Go!" Langley said to the still prostate Tom. "You have done enough to drag this once proud family down!" He gave in to temptation and once more kicked his foot forward towards Tom's face.

But this time Tom was ready for it. He caught Langley by the ankle and jerked it so hard that Langley fell unceremoniously to the cement. There was a low thud sound as the back of his head made contact. When Langley did not immediately get up, Thora felt her stomach tie up in a knot. Her dad was hurt! She ran to him at once scared that her father might have died.

When she was upon him she saw that his chest was heaving up and down and that his face was slowly moving in contortions of pain. Her father was alive. Before she knew it she was shoved aside by her mother who hung over her unconscious husband stroking his face and sobbing her own tears of anxiety over Langley's health.

It was such an about face from moments before. Thora could not understand her parents. They were so mixed up. They were love and hate contained in the same jar. The concoction that came out was sweet and vile and although it had sustained Thora throughout life she was now beginning to realize that it was inedible.

With hateful eyes Cora turned to Tom Thurston and said to him, "How could you do this? You are nothing but a brute from the lowest order of society!" she hissed at Tom.

Tom Thurston paid his ex-sister-in-law no never mind. He got up to his feet and brushed off the dust on his pants. Holes had been torn into his suit's knees and elbows from his fall. A better-made suit would have been able to sustain the rough and tumble incident. Thora's father's suit as ill fitting as it was, proved to be more durable as no thread upon it became undone.

"Will you kindly leave Tom!" Aunt Faye said once more to him. She was still a cold bastion of strength. She showed no concern for the well being of her brother.

"I will leave, Faye, but before I do I just want to tell you that your father has always been a man that I admired. It was an honor to me to be able to spend some time with him and I will miss his wisdom and his candor dearly."

For a moment Faye's face softened but she was able to quickly summon her Meadowford guard to retain her stern posture. In that brief moment Thora believed that Faye was going to rush to her ex-husband and embrace him and allow all of her pain and anxiety to pour out into him. He would have been the pillar of strength that she needed. But that moment never came to pass. All that Faye did was nod her head in appreciation of Tom's comment on her father and then she said, "Good bye, Tom."

But Cora Meadowford was not through with him. She screamed at Langley's friends to jump the man and beat him to an inch of his life for what he had done to her husband.

"Let it be, Cora," one of these friends replied to her. "There has been enough damage done already."

"We can't wait any longer," Aunt Faye said to her sister-in-law. "Langley is in no condition to go to the cemetery. Get him to the hospital. I will bury Father on my own."

Thora did not know what got into her at that moment. She had not planned to do this. It just spontaneously sprung out from her. "Can I come along with you, Aunt Faye?" she cried out. "I want to be there when Grandfather is placed in the ground."

"You will do nothing of the such!" her mother immediately responded. "Your place is here with your family."

"But Aunt Faye and Grandfather are my family too!" Thora retorted. She tried to keep her volume and her emotions under control. She did not want to be seen by the others as another trashy member of the Langley Meadowford clan.

"It is only right that a girl be present at the funeral of her grandfather," Faye responded. Thora could see that the woman was not keen on the idea but immediately recognized the reasonableness of the request.

"I say no!" Cora said once more. "You have to help me get your father to the hospital."

"Dad is going to be all right! He's just going to be a bit woozy for a while! He's had hangovers worse than this!" Thora said. She saw that her father was already starting to open his eyes and take in his surroundings. She knew that he would milk as much sympathy as he possibly could out of the situation. It was his way. He was a sniveling rat and not a man of character such as Grandfather or Uncle Tom.

"If you are going to come you had better come now, I can't wait any longer!" Aunt Faye set down the ultimatum and began walking towards the lead automobile behind the Hearst.

Thora did not allow her mother to say anything. She made up her mind for herself. "I'm going!" She ran and caught up to her aunt.

Chapter 2

Silent Hills

Aunt Faye had not said a thing to her at all during the seven-mile drive that separated St. Andrew's Church from Silent Hills Cemetery. Thora did not find the excursion uncomfortable though. She had too many impressions from the incident at the church to work through and try to consolidate into a "her" worldview.

As the scenery of the peaceful and lazy town of Grappling Haven slowly displayed itself out of the windows of the car, Thora found her eyes focused on the Hearst that was in front of her. Inside that morose black vehicle was her grandfather, Sambo Meadowford. He was now finally on the last leg of his journey to his grave. It had been such an exasperating and tiring route that started with his heart attack in the canoe on Robinson Bay. Aunt Faye had been there with him when the fatal seizure took hold of him. She had to return him to the cottage at Black Island and from there set out across the lake to Mount Horeb in a motorboat where they had to telephone the village of Riverwood to dispatch an ambulance. That ambulance took nearly three hours before it reached the isolated Mount Horeb resort. The medics on the ambulance officially declared Sambo dead although the man was probably dead before Aunt Faye embarked on the slow boat ride between Black Island and Mount Horeb.

From the posh yet rustic surroundings of Mount Horeb, Aunt Faye made all the arrangements for the funeral over the telephone. The woman was thorough and thought of everything, planning the somber ceremony to the minutest detail. She had some time to spend at the resort before the bus arrived the next day. Yet for all her planning and all of the time that she had, Aunt Faye forgot about somebody that was left behind at Black Island. She had forgotten about Capers, the family cat. With all of the stress about Grandfather's funeral, nobody could truly blame her. But of course both Thora's mother and father were in a furor that the woman could have made such an oversight. They did not realize that they had made the same oversight themselves. Capers was ultimately their responsibility and not Faye's. They should have placed the cat in the cage and carted him off when they so swiftly and summarily fled Black Island after the big argument with Sambo and Faye.

Thora wondered how Capers was doing. It sickened her to think that the feline was left on his own up there. She had pled with her mother and father to arrange for somebody to go to the island and take Capers back. But her parents said that that was too expensive. Capers would be all right. There were plenty of mice up there to keep him well fed and he would be there in the spring happily mewing when the family returned. In the meantime her parents offered Rebecca and Thora a new kitten that they would get as soon as they return from their New York City vacation. Thora had not warmed up to this idea at all. Nobody could replace Capers.

Nobody could replace Grandfather as well. The man had the most fatiguing journey after his death. Once the bus arrived at Mount Horeb at noon the following day it started the long trip home through Ontario's wild hinterland to the bustling and clean city of Toronto. There, Aunt Faye had a layover to the next day for the first train to Pittsburgh that left Toronto's Union Station at 2:00 p.m.

That was a six-hour route that was interrupted at the border station at Niagara Falls. The U.S. customs agents were on a campaign to stop the illegal importation of alcohol into America. The Prohibition Laws were being routinely violated and the rumrunners were making use of any avenue to get their spirits from Canada into the country, including using the rail system. The customs agents even had the audacity to open up the box that Grandfather was in to ascertain that it was indeed a coffin with a body inside rather than a container full of whiskey bottles.

When Faye finally reached Pittsburgh, she was only a hundred miles more or less from Grappling Haven. She had hoped that there would have been somebody from the family waiting for her there but nobody showed up. Langley had said that the family automobile had no room inside of it to carry a casket. When Faye said that the casket would be shipped the following day and all that she needed the ride for was to just get herself home, Langley had coldly dismissed her by saying that it was not appropriate that she leaves her father's body alone and unattended in the strange city.

So Faye had to wait another day before the first bus for Grappling Haven, Pennsylvania left Pittsburgh.

Four days had elapsed since Grandfather's death to the time that his smelly body at last arrived in the town that he called home. He was immediately brought to the funeral home where the undertakers had considerable work trying to restore his already decomposing form into something presentable for the funeral services.

Now it was three days later. Grandfather had been dead for a week already and now finally he was going to his final resting spot on the immaculate sloped green lawns of Silent Hills that sat peacefully just outside of town.

It may have been easier for his body just to disappear in the lake in the same manner as what happened to Grandmother, Percy and Jack. But it was comforting to Thora to realize that the lush and serene Silent Hills would hold his body for eternity rather than some feral and cold lake five hundred miles away. There were plots at this cemetery for the Meadowford dead that had been left behind in the wilds of Canada. The family, especially Grandfather, had always hoped that one day the remains of his precious June and his two grandsons would be found and laid to rest here.

Grandfather was to be buried beside the empty plots set for these missing members of the family. His was to be right next to that of June Meadowford's. It was too bad that she would not be there with him but maybe in a way she would be there. Grandfather often seemed to talk to his dead wife. Thora had many recollections of seeing him engaged in conversation with the air. It was very peculiar behavior and behavior that her father Langley had picked up upon and made him question whether the old man was capable of running the business.

The Hearst pulled into the open gate of Silent Hills Cemetery. The black iron rods of the gate pointed upward and were joined by an arch of the same wrought iron that spelt out the words 'Silent Hills'. This place had always been both creepy and comforting to Thora. Her mother and father had told her that someday she and her sister would be here as well. It was nice to know that such a lovely site would be her resting place for eternity yet it was also disquieting. She was only thirteen. She did not need to think of the other end of life as of yet. There was so much living to do before that.

As the funeral procession drew to a stop, Aunt Faye rolled down the tinted windows of the limousine to draw in some of the fresh air. She acted as if Thora was not even there. She tidied her hair and adjusted her gloves and waited for the driver to open the door for her. Thora copied her aunt's example and for the first time felt that she was a budding woman rather than just a girl. Her parents had refused to recognize that she and Rebecca were growing up. They treated them as if they were six-years-old still.

Once the door was opened for her, Thora stepped outside and noticed the long train of automobiles behind her. People were pouring out of the cars and stretching and looking about their new surroundings. All of them were here to say farewell to Samuel Angus Meadowford II. But amidst all of these mourners there were only two actual members of Sambo's family present, herself and Aunt Faye. Thora was sure that many people noticed this and that there were many impressions being made about the dysfunctional status of the family.

The Hearst was stopped beside a mound of earth that had already been dug up. This somewhat surprised Thora. This was her first real funeral. The one for Jack was just a memorial. There was no body to be interred. She had imagined that the ceremony at the cemetery would involve the pallbearers doing some shovel work to dig out the plot while the others in attendance would say prayers.

The minister from St. Andrew's came up to Aunt Faye and took hold of her hand and escorted her to the side of the grave. A deacon that Thora recognized from the same church strode somberly up to her and took her by the hand. He whispered to her, "Where is the rest of your family?"

"They are not coming," Thora admitted to him and felt shame for them in not making an appearance.

The deacon gave her a peculiar look that said that he needed some form of explanation.

"Father fell outside of the church and my mother had to take him to the hospital."

The deacon shook his head. "I hope that he is going to be all right," he said in soft, reverent tones.

"I'm sure that he is going to be fine," Thora said as the deacon proceeded to lead her towards the gravesite. He took her hand and Thora felt like a woman of dignity. She felt like she was a younger version of Faye Thurston.

When they reached the side of the grave Thora could not help but take a peek inside. It looked so refined and professional. It did not have any semblance to being just a hole in the ground. The sides were neatly and squarely bored out. Not a grain of dirt popped out from the manicured walls. There was not an empty pocket in these walls where some earth had fallen down. Everything was as tidy as if it were a wall in a house. At the bottom of the tomb was an open cement sarcophagus. Its lid was nowhere in sight.

Upon seeing this grave Thora did not experience any horrific feelings. It exuded an atmosphere of peacefulness and tranquility. It did not seem to be the horrible place that she imagined.

When she lifted her head she saw that most of the mourners had formed a semi-circle around the grave. Standing next to her was Aunt Myra. She was sobbing noisily and it got onto Thora's nerves. As far as Thora knew Aunt Myra did not know Grandfather very well at all. They did not travel in the same social circles. The only occasions where Myra and Sambo would have met would be at extended family functions such as weddings and funerals. Yet here she was crying as if she lost her best friend. She was so much like her mother that Thora resented her and wished that she were not present. This service was meant for Meadowfords and not the crass lower classes such as Myra Murphy.

Thora felt a tap on her shoulder. It was the Minister, Reverend Barton. "We are going to ask you to perform a function at this ceremony. You will be the representative for your family."

A nervous feeling took hold of Thora. She had sudden images that the Reverend was going to ask her to make a speech eulogizing her grandfather. What would she say? She had no idea. She hated public speaking. It scared her to death. But when Reverend Barton explained what she was required to do, the nervousness went away. She knew that she was fully capable of doing what he wanted her to do.

"Are we ready then?" the Reverend asked Faye.

Thora saw her aunt clench her fists and take a deep breath. "We are ready," she said softly, looking at Thora for support. Once again Thora felt like she was a woman and not just a little girl. She was very glad that she asked her aunt that she could come along. Rebecca was missing so much here. But then again if her family had shown up she was sure that she and her sister would have been shuffled off to some second row and made to appear like a matching set of juveniles not to be seriously taken.

The Reverend made a hand signal towards the Hearst. The six gentlemen that acted as ushers back at the ceremony at the church walked in what appeared to be rehearsed steps towards the back of the funeral car. There, like well-trained soldiers they ceremoniously pulled the glossy pine casket from the Hearst. Aunt Faye had chosen the casket. She selected the pine because it was reminiscent of the great white pine trees of Black Island. Thora's father thought that the choice was inappropriate. Pine was a pauper's wood. It did not bear the dignity and rich eloquence of oak or the imported mahoganies from Venezuela.

Once Grandfather's coffin cleared the Hearst, the six men began a slow procession towards the graveside. The men that carried Grandfather were all younger members of the Lion's Club. None of them knew Grandfather very well since Sambo was quite often absent from the regular club functions, especially during the summer when he was up on Pioneer Lake. But these young strong men were always there to lend their thick arms at the passing of any of the old guard. They were in a sense professional pallbearers. There was no wonder that they were so well choreographed.

When Grandfather's casket was placed upon a neatly packed mound before the grave, Reverend Barton cleared his throat in preparation for a speech and some final rituals. At the sight of the clergyman getting ready to say his words, Aunt Myra began to wail out loud. She set off others amongst the gathered to follow suit. Like a chorus of bullfrogs from Pioneer Lake the women were weeping their laments for the passing of Samuel Angus Meadowford. Even Margaret Whattam bawled her eyes out.

The only two not crying were Aunt Faye and Thora. The daughter of the deceased never lifted her eyes away from the casket that contained her father. She stared at it as if she were transfixed by it—as if there was something inside of it that was actively captivating her. Thora watched her and she could almost swear that she saw Aunt Faye's lips moving as if there were silent words spilling out of them. Thora thought about how often she had seen Grandfather talking to his departed wife, June. Did the Meadowfords leave ghosts behind that dwelt the land rather than the heavens?

"Dearly beloved, we are gathered here to say our farewells to Samuel Angus Meadowford, son of Samuel Angus Meadowford and Julia Whitney, brother to Thaddeus Lloyd Meadowford, father to Samuel Angus Meadowford the Third, and Faye Thurston, grandfather to Rebecca and Thora Meadowford and Percival and Jack Thurston." Reverend Barton paused to look at Aunt Faye to make sure that he had not forgotten any of the immediate relatives.

Aunt Faye did not respond. She seemed to be in her own lost world and was not aware of what was happening around her. Thora slightly waved her hand to draw the Reverend's attention and to let him know that he had provided a complete listing of the family members.

Reverend Barton gave her a small smile indicating acknowledgement and thanks for her input. He continued, "The people that surround us at death most often are not the people that surround us when we are born. Those have passed on to the greater kingdom of the Lord and there they wait for us on our triumphant return to the realm that is truly our home. Sadly for Samuel, or Sambo to his dear friends, there are two souls waiting for him that should have been here at this gathering saying farewell to him instead. Sambo had the greatest misfortune to untimely lose two grandsons, Percival and Jack, as well as his partner in life, June Ritchey. The bodies of the three were never to be found while Sambo was alive. But today Sambo has found them and I cannot think of what would comprise a happier moment than this."

He stopped. His words had prompted many cries of "Amen" amongst the crowd. Thora found his words extremely liberating. She had not thought about this aspect of death, that it was a reunion for the ancestors. It made her feel happy for her Grandfather. When she looked over at her Aunt Faye to see her reaction, she was startled to see that the woman appeared to be oblivious to what had been said. She still seemed to be engaged in her own private dialogue with her dead father.

"This day is a celebration. It is a confirmation of family—not the family that we sit ourselves down with at our daily repasts but the family of humanity. We are all descendants of Adam and Eve. We all share their blood. We are all brothers and sisters, sons and daughters, fathers and mothers. We are all kin and I want you to think about this and think about those special feelings that you experience whenever you are in the company of family. I want you to extend this feeling to every man, woman and child that you encounter. We are all family. We all are special to others. Take a moment and embrace the person that is beside you and say onto him or her that he or she is special and that you are his or her brother or sister."

Once again the Reverend Barton stopped. The mourners obliged his request and began hugging one another and telling each other that they were all family. Thora saw Aunt Myra and Margaret Whattam locked together in an embrace. This was the woman that had only an hour ago rebuked the other for her choice of somber attire.

When Thora turned to Aunt Faye to give her an embrace, she saw that her aunt was unaware of what was happening. Thora brought her arms down; somewhat disappointed that this opportunity was lost to make amends to this aunt of hers that was at war with her parents. But she did not interpret Faye's reaction as an act of animosity in the continued hostilities between the two lines that descended from Sambo. Rather she saw that her aunt was genuinely engaged in something real with the casket of her father.

"Is he talking to you?" she quietly asked her aunt. She did not expect a reply.

"He is speaking to me and he has a message for you," Aunt Faye answered. Her eyes never met those of Thora.

"A message for me?" Thora was so startled by this admission. Rather than being frightened by the thought that a dead person was trying to talk to her, she felt important. Her being, her essence, was being aggrandized by this inclusion in the dialogue from the two sides of the grave. "What does he say?"

Aunt Faye was about to speak, when Reverend Barton started up his sermon again. "Family," he said. "That is what it is all about. What is the meaning of life? The meaning of life is being a part of God's family. I need not say a cherished member for that goes unsaid. We are all cherished because we are all God's children. Now, some of you may have noticed the absence of Sambo's eldest son at this celebration of the old man's life. I know your nature and you are conjuring many conjectures of the relationship between the two Sams. Let me say this. As family we cannot always get along. We all see different routes to salvation for there are many paths to righteousness and we try to persuade each other that the path we select is the correct one. This leads to conflict for we do not want to see our loved ones go astray. We fight because we love. In the absence of love, there is indifference and indifference leads to ignorance and it is ignorance that is the fodder for the diabolical one that resides in the netherworld. Langley Meadowford is absent from the services today not because he is ignorant and a pawn for the Devil. Langley is absent since he had fallen and required medical attention. His loving and caring wife, Cora, has taken him to the hospital. I assure you that there is nothing to be concerned about here. Langley will survive. In their proxy, Langley and Cora have sent their wonderful daughter Thora to represent them at this service."

At the mention of her name, Thora was given a start. Once more she was frightened that she was going to be asked to make a speech. But when the Reverend continued speaking, she sighed her relief.

"It is a difficult thing for a girl to let go of a cherished family member such as a Grandfather," Reverend Barton said, while placing his hairy hand on Thora's shoulder. "Our hearts go out to this girl and we all wish that we could make the world a better place for her. But as soon as we go home, we forget these noble feelings. We allow the common place to take priority over our commitments. It is our nature. Or let me revise that and say that it was our nature. For today, rather than go home and do the dishes and cut the grass, let us remember that enlightenment we received here today witnessing the departure of Samuel Angus Meadowford the Second to everlasting life, and let us remember his granddaughter, Thora. Let us remember the commitment that we have made. Let us all adopt young Thora into our respective families and by doing so become part of our communal family under the grace of Our Lord Jesus Christ. Before you go home today, I want each of you to personally present your condolences to young Thora and to set aside a date in the future where you will entertain Thora as a guest of your household. In so doing we will keep this spirit of humanity in tact."

"Thora can be my guest tomorrow evening!" Margaret Whattam spoke up. The woman looked around at the other mourners. She seemed more surprised by what she said than the others. Her face reddened as she guessed that she might have spoken out of turn.

Reverend Barton chuckled, "Is tomorrow evening good for you Thora?" he asked.

Thora did not know what to say. She wished that someone had advised her earlier that she would be put in this situation. A large part of her felt wary about being the Church's mascot going around from house to house being the ambassador of good will. She thought the idea inane. How did she get compromised into such a position? And now here she was on the spot. She could not publicly rebuke the idea for it would swell up wrath in the assembled and it would be a slight to the character of Margaret Whattam. She liked the woman and wanted her to be given more respect by the others here. But still she could not picture herself sitting at all the dinner tables in Grappling Haven. She would feel so awkward and clumsy. She would have to keep her manners in check.

"Thora, is tomorrow evening good for you?" Reverend Barton repeated his question.

"Tomorrow is fine," she said even though while she spoke she was not sure what answer would come out of her mouth. But once it was said, she lifted her head and smiled to Margaret Whattam. The woman seemed relieved by Thora's answer. Her face began beaming and the first person she sent her rays towards was to Myra Murphy, Thora's aunt.

"Then I want her the night after that!" a gentleman in a Lion's Club's jacket announced. He seemed to be a widower and was likely next in line for the pallbearers' services. Thora did not know the man by name but knew that he lived by himself. She frequently saw him standing outside the schoolyard staring through the fence while the children had their recess. Something about the man sent shivers down Thora's spine.

The Reverend Barton must have sensed Thora's discomfort for he said, "We are digressing from the purpose of why we are gathered. Arrangements for Thora's visits can be made afterwards and through the consent of her parents. Family not only connotes love but it also connotes rules to live by. Samuel Angus Meadowford II would have been one of the first to tell you this."

Thora's mind drifted away from the Reverend's sermon. She was now wishing that she did not ask to come along with Aunt Faye. What was supposed to be a tribute to the outstanding character of her grandfather had now descended into a morass of commitments that she was not willing to make. She did not want to go from house to house being the representative of the Church's silly notion of family. She was not even sure if she bought into the religion that the Church espoused. Somehow she felt that the world and the universe operated differently than what was expressed in the Bible. For some reason she thought of that book kept at the lake, the Black Island Log. She thought of one of the early entries made by her great grandfather concerning an Indian spirit that had visited him while he was hunting a stag through the thick snows on Pioneer Lake. That story had frightened her but also intrigued her. Her family had dismissed the tale as either a prank or delusion by the first Samuel Angus Meadowford. Thora, herself, was not so sure. The Indian spirit seemed to come from a place that was very real to her—much more real than Heaven could ever be. Heaven to her always sounded too good to be true.

"Sambo was an upstanding member of the community. He and his brother Thaddeus were always generous contributors to not only this Church but to the hospital as well. The Board of Directors at the Grappling Haven General Hospital wanted to name a wing after the Meadowfords but Sambo preferred to keep his generosity anonymous," Reverend Barton was still conducting his sermon upon the gentle slopes of Silent Hills.

Thora could see that he was losing his audience. Many bore trances upon their faces. They had drifted as she did. Yet the good Reverend continued to prattle. She had heard her father Langley say that the contributions made to the Church and hospital made good business sense at income tax time. He never saw charity as a means to help people. It was only a means to help oneself. He somehow got it in her head that that was the motivation behind Grandfather's giving. She was sure that had her father been here, he would have groaned at the Reverend's remark.

And he would have grown impatient with the length of the eulogy and he would have allowed his discomfort to show. He was always making a spectacle of himself. Her sister Rebecca truly despised this aspect of their father. She saw him as a worthless conniver that one day, if there were any justice in this world, would get his reckoning. Thora always chose to cast a blind eye towards her father's ventures into greed and poor community conduct. He was her father and somewhere in that jumble of sin there must have been some saving graces. When she defended him to her sister, Rebecca was very quick to point out that she had never seen any evidence that there was anything good about the man. Sadly, Thora had to admit that Rebecca was right. But this did not stop Thora from hoping.

"If birds do not migrate north and south, then you shall nest in the west."

Thora was pulled out of her reverie. It was her Aunt Faye that said those words to her. The woman's head was bowed forward as if she were staring at the ground but Thora could see that Faye was staring at her through the corners of her eyes.

"Pardon me?" she asked Aunt Faye to repeat herself.

"Grandfather's message to you is 'if birds do not migrate north and south, then you shall nest in the west.'" Aunt Faye whispered.

"What does that mean?" Thora could not help but ask.

"Ssshhh!" her aunt placed her finger before her lips. With her eyes she indicated that they should be listening to Reverend Barton.

When Thora glanced at the Reverend she saw that he noticed her talking. Like the teachers at school Reverend Barton silently cautioned her that interruptions were not to be tolerated while he continued with his tribute to her Grandfather. Thora was not upset by the Reverend's reaction. She was more perplexed than anything. If birds do not migrate north and south, then you shall nest in the west. Those were the words that her grandfather wished to impart to her from the other side of life? She did not have the slightest inkling what those words were supposed to mean. The nest in the west bit seemed to indicate to her that she would be moving to the west of the country, California perhaps. She always wanted to move out there. The new talkies that were coming out of Hollywood had fascinated her and she possessed a secret desire to one day maybe become a motion picture actress and be the sweetheart to the nation. Was Grandfather telling her that this was going to be so?

It was the first part of his message that was throwing her. If birds do not migrate north and south? She just could not understand what that was supposed to mean. Birds do migrate north and south. It is an indelible part of their nature and birds never swerve from their nature. They always migrate north and south. Was Grandfather telling her that she was not to go out west? Was that his message? Why would he give such an absurd message? It just seemed too weird.

"Samuel Angus Meadowford the Second," Reverend Barton raised his arms in the air with his hands outstretched to the clear skies above him. "I commit ye to the Earth and from the Earth you shall journey to the salvation that the Lord Jesus Christ has promised you with His death and resurrection. You shall rise from the dead and enter the Kingdom of Heaven."

The Reverend nodded to Faye. She was paying attention. She stepped forward and took some of the dirt that was piled in a mound under the casket. She looked upward into the heavens and said in a clear voice, "From the daughter of your loins I commit ye to the Lord's grace." She spread the silt in her hand over the casket and then after kissing the coffin she reverentially stepped back to her place.

Thora knew that this was her cue. This was what the Reverend had asked her to do before the burial ceremonies commenced. She paused for a moment to make sure that this was the right time for her to do so. Reverend Barton winked at her. This was the right time.

She took several steps forward and like her Aunt Faye she reached down to scoop some earth from the mound below the casket. As she lowered her body, her ear was next to the coffin. Her heart jumped. She could have sworn that she heard breathing emanating from inside of the pine box. They were deep breaths and very distinct. She looked back to her Aunt Faye in disbelief. Aunt Faye twitched her finger. It was a sign for Thora to continue with the ritual.

She felt the cold ground in her hands. It tingled in her palm as if it were a living organism. She fought hard to suppress this feeling. In the meantime she could still clearly hear the breathing coming from inside of the coffin. She was terrified but she managed to keep herself under control. As she stood up to her full length and her ear was no longer in close proximity to the casket she could no longer hear the breathing. She sighed with relief. Maybe she was hearing her own breathing echoing from the pine boards of Grandfather's coffin.

But the dirt in her hand still seemed to burn into her skin. Was this some special soil that was used only in cemeteries to help speed along the decomposition process? She was new to funerals. She did not know. She had to keep herself composed. Others were watching her.

She reached her hand over the coffin and at once was stunned to feel the heat rising out of it. The air above the casket was very warm as if some spiritual force was radiating it. She forced herself to ignore what she was experiencing. She had to remember the words that the Reverend had instructed her to say.

She cleared her throat and began dropping the dirt upon the casket. "From the son of your loins I commit ye to the Lord's grace," she said. She had to use the word 'son' as she was the representative of her father, Langley, in this service.

As the silt began to fall onto Sambo's casket a sudden gust sprang up and some of the dirt was blown into her eyes. A fierce burning sensation ensued and she rubbed at her eyes feverishly to try and get the stinging earth from them. It hurt so much that she was sure that she was going to scream in pain. But she managed to control the urge and as her eyes cleared she thought that she saw the wispy form of an Indian paddling a canoe ten feet in the air into the trees. Above the trees a flock of blackbirds were flying towards a setting sun.

The image quickly faded. She felt her Aunt Faye's arms around her. "Are you alright?" Faye asked.

Thora did not say anything. Her sight had been restored and everything was as it was. There was no Indian paddling a canoe. There were no birds in the sky and the sun was high in the air approaching its midday zenith rather than its day's end slip beyond the horizon.

Reverend Barton was now reading a passage from the Bible. Thora recognized it as the 23rd Psalm. All around her the mourners held their heads down and the bullfrog chorus of weeping started to resound again as the cries of one woman were answered by the cries of another and so on and so on until it seemed everybody was sobbing.

"It's time for us to go," Aunt Faye said to her, pushing Thora against the upper portion of her back.

As she started to walk away from Grandfather's grave, Thora took one last look at the casket. There was something very strange going on here. It scared her and she was glad that she was getting away from it. She could not picture herself ever coming back here to visit again. If she did she was sure that she would be asking for trouble.

They were most of the way to Aunt Faye's car when Reverend Barton stopped them in their tracks. "The child has to remain behind," the minister said to Aunt Faye. "She has promised to listen to the offerings of condolence from the gathered."

"Will someone give her a ride back to her home?" Aunt Faye asked. She appeared upset that she had been stopped. "I can't stay here any longer." She did not offer any excuses why she was in such a rush to get away from the cemetery.

Thora smirched. She was hoping that her aunt would rescue her from this stupid obligation thrust upon her. She did not want to meet these people and be treated like she was part of their kin. But Aunt Faye was not being her champion. She had to rescue herself. "I never made that promise!" she cried out loud more to Faye than the Reverend.

The two adults acted like they did not hear what she said. "I'm sure that there is somebody here that will make sure that the girl gets home. If not I will assure you that I will take her home myself."

"Then I will hold you to your word, Reverend. Good day Thora," Aunt Faye said coldly and disappeared in her car where the driver was waiting and already had the engine running.

When the car did not leave right away, Thora saw her aunt inform the chauffeur that the child was not coming home with them.

Thora was numb. She could not believe that her aunt was leaving her to the wolves like this. She had thought that she had bridged that gap that separated Faye's side of the family from her father's side. Apparently not. She realized that this was very convenient for her aunt. She no longer had to meet Langley and Cora when she dropped one of their girls off at their house.

As the car drove off, Thora turned around and saw a host of friends and associates of her Grandfather descend upon her. She wanted to scream and tell them all to go away and leave her alone. But something inside of her told her not to do that. That would be behaving the way the rest of her family behaved. She wanted to rise above that.

For the next half hour she listened to many sobbing faces spout out their laments about how sad they were that she no longer had a grandfather and what a good man he was. Very few of them actually expressed any interest in having her over for dinner. Apparently they did not take everything that the Reverend said to heart. They all wanted to return to their own private cloistered lives and did not want to be part of the bigger community.

Aunt Myra was one of the first to offer her regards. "Sorry about your Grandfather, dear." Thora knew that her aunt could not tell her apart from

Rebecca and that was why she chose the word 'dear'. "But tell me what was that fight all about back at the church. What made your father and your Uncle Tom get into that scrap?"

"There are other people waiting behind you Aunt Myra," Thora said. She possessed no desire to be part of the gossip mill. She was not going to smear her father's and even her Uncle Tom's reputation by giving her interpretation of the events upon the stairwell at St. Andrew's for she knew for certain that they would be misconstrued.

Aunt Myra's face dropped and Thora knew that the woman interpreted what she said as a slur against her. "So, they are. Don't let me get in your way as your star rises in this community," she said with a pout and walked haughtily away.

Thora did not feel bad about the way that she acted. She never liked her mother's older sister. She always saw her as a troublesome, meddlesome character that she had to put up with since she was technically family. She never wanted to include the woman in that special group known as kin.

After Aunt Myra stormed away, Margaret Whattam came up to her and held her by both hands. "So tomorrow night at six, if that is okay with you Thora?" she said nervously. "It will be just you and me. James is still in Michigan with your uncle as you probably already know."

Thora saw this as her opportunity to get out of the arrangement. "I have to make sure that I receive my parents' approval before I make any commitment, Mrs. Whattam."

Once again a face fell into discord as Margaret Whattam realized that there was still an important step to get past before she would have any guest at her house. Thora guessed that the woman must have been very lonely with her husband out of town. The Whattams did not have any children or possess any extended family in Grappling Haven. They moved here about five years ago. Thora was not sure where they came from.

"Of course, you must get their approval. I would not have you if it were not such," Margaret said to save dignity and face. "But I would truly appreciate it if you were able to show up. There are some important matters that I wish to discuss with you."

"I will do what I can," Thora promised. She knew that her mother would not approve. Cora Meadowford had often commented on the apparent instability and lack of maturity in Margaret's personality. She was sure that Margaret was only one telephone call away from an asylum.

After Aunt Myra and Mrs. Whattam disappeared, the rest of the assembled quickly passed on their condolences. Some did suggest that they would like to have her over for dinner some day but these commitments were always left vague and more likely would never happen, much to Thora's relief.

When the last family extended their feelings of sorrow for her and then departed, Thora was left with only Reverend Barton. "That appears to be the last of them," she said, feeling good that it was all over.

"Did you not manage to get a ride with any of them?" the Reverend asked. He seemed somewhat disconcerted.

"I never asked," she responded. "I thought that you promised to give me a ride." She found it odd that the minister would have forgotten his commitment to her Aunt Faye over this arrangement.

"How am I to get you home, girl?" the Reverend raised his voice.

The answer startled Thora. "Well how are you getting home?"

"I am home my dear!" the Reverend responded. "I live in an apartment above yonder building." He pointed to a distant stone structure that had two levels. Thora had seen that building many a time and had been informed by her parents that it was a mausoleum where some bodies were kept.

"You live in there?" she said with amazement. How could anybody live anywhere where there are dead people about?

"It is my home. It is peaceful and quiet there and I am able to offer up my prayers to the Lord in solitude and quietude," the man replied.

"But you must have a car, don't you?"

"A motorcar is a luxury that is well beyond my meager means, young lady."

"Then how do you get about to do your work?" Thora found it absolutely incredible that an adult could live without an automobile. Cars were a necessity. They were not a luxury.

"There are plenty of good people in our ministry that are quite happy to give me a ride when I require one," the Reverend said. "But on those occasions where I cannot get a ride or when the weather is nice such as it is today that I just simply walk into town."

"But that is seven miles away!"

"Such a distance is nothing to our forefathers. And that distance is paltry to our Lord and Savior and his disciples. The Lord did not have an automobile as he wandered the countryside of Galilee. He had to walk. And if He had to walk then I have to walk as well."

"But it is seven miles!"

Reverend Barton shook his head and sighed. "You young folk truly are far too pampered! You are young and vital, Miss Meadowford. The day is beautiful and there is plenty of time before dark for you to arrive home. I suggest that you start walking now and not only enjoy your stroll through the beautiful hills and farms that separate us from town but to take the time to pray to the Lord and give him thanks for all the blessings in your life."

With that said, Reverend Barton started to walk away towards the stone mausoleum.

Thora watched him stride past the myriad of tombs towards his home. The man did not seem holy and a worthy servant of his Jesus. He had just broken a promise to her Aunt Faye. Her father had often said that he believed that Reverend Barton was a boozer. A man does not get the extended belly such as the Reverend possessed through simply eating. Thora wondered if the Reverend was rushing to a bottle that he kept in his apartment above the cadavers. Was he mixing his spirits with theirs?

As she saw him disappear into a valley, she suddenly realized that she too was alone with spirits. She was by herself in the middle of a cemetery. An extremely eerie feeling crept over her upon this realization. She remembered that wispy Indian in his canoe. She remembered the breathing that she heard inside of Grandfather's coffin. She had to get out of here at once!

She set foot on the road and began the seven-mile walk home. She prayed that she would be able to finish it.

Chapter 3

The Road Leads Two Ways

Thora had walked perhaps a mile along the dusty gravel road as it wound its way down the hillside towards the town of Grappling Haven below. Her community sat in a valley that was surrounded by verdant uplands that were in their own way every bit as evocative of the splendor of nature as Pioneer Lake. At one time this entire area was lush in a tall mixed Carolina forest with mighty oaks and glorious elm trees dominating the arboreal canopy. Most of these trees had been cut down as the white man settled the hills and placed upon them their crops and their cattle. What was left of the forest sat in occasional clumps and copses that gave border and definition to the farmlands. They delineated where one man's property started and another man's ended.

But Thora did not concern herself with the geographic history of the countryside. She was kept by the protestations of her body as she strode along this interminable lane. Her feet were sore from having to engage repeatedly the unforgiving hard gravel roadway. Her shoes were of an open concept. She frequently had to stop to remove some hitchhiking pebble that managed to find its way into that cramped space between her sole and leather instep. Her feet were also beginning to sweat and she could sense the deterioration of that instep. Soon the leather would be stripped away and her feet would have to contend with all of the cobbler's nails and stitching. Then she would really suffer.

Beautiful day or not, she was not dressed right for it. She was in a black dress that soaked up the heat pouring down onto it from the relentless sun. It clung to her in all the spots where perspiration had been formed. She was sure that indelible stains were being born all over her dress. When her mother sees how she had ruined her clothing she was sure that she would fly off into a tirade. She would curse Aunt Faye for failing to take Thora home. She would be in an uproar over Reverend Barton's broken promise. But most of all she would be angry at Thora for abandoning the family to be at the side of Aunt Faye to pay tribute to a man that never cared for his son and his son's wife and children.

Thora realized as she waddled with yet another painful stone caught in her shoe that she was not going to be walking into a pleasant situation when she finally gets home. There would be hell to pay when she got there. She was paying hell already.

Two weeks ago she would never have believed that she would find herself in such an awful situation. Two weeks ago she and Rebecca were upon the Grappler sailing in the Upper Pioneer Lake Regatta. Their father and mother accompanied them. While her parents fidgeted with the rigging and lines, she and her sister hung over the sailboat's bow and laughed heartily. They thought that they were in an excellent position. The summer was just starting and they had what they believed to be almost three months of uninterrupted joy ahead of them. The only thing that they had to contend with was grumpy Uncle Thaddeus but they knew how to keep out of the old codger's way and assure themselves nothing but bliss.

How that had swiftly changed! First, there came that telegram delivered by the steamship the Madoqua Empress that informed the two senior members of the Meadowford family that a major labor dispute was about to erupt at Dearborn Cable, the family's factory in Michigan. Thaddeus and Grandfather had determined that the best plan of action was for one of them to personally make an appearance in Dearborn and to take an active part in the negotiations with the employees that were threatening to join forces with the autoworkers union in Detroit.

When Thora's father, Langley, had heard about this scheme he tried to persuade his father and uncle that it should be him to go. Thaddeus and Grandfather quickly dismissed Langley's offer by saying that the laborers would not be satisfied with his presence. They wanted the real owners and the real power behind the company and not its dandy heir whom in their eyes knew nothing about the business. This was a true blow to Langley. Even Rebecca felt bad for her dad. His ego was severely bruised by the incident but at the same time the scheming part of his persona was kicked into high gear. He had decided that it was time for him to undermine the two old men and usurp control of the company.

But before he could do anything, Aunt Faye had appeared and made her wild accusations about Langley's corrupt past. This led to the bitter argument that conveniently gave Langley his excuse to leave the island. He was planning to go to Michigan shortly after depositing his wife and daughters back in Pennsylvania. But then word arrived that Grandfather died. The family discovered what happened to Sambo as soon as they got home in Grappling Haven. It was Aunt Myra that told them. Aunt Faye, while she was at the Mount Horeb resort, had phoned Cora's sister with the news.

Thora remembered her father's reaction upon the word that his father died. It was hardly what one would describe as shock and grief. It was instead an odd combination of celebration and anger. Langley seemed glad that his father was now out of the way but he was also bitter that he had to put his trip to Michigan on hold in order to bury Sambo. This morning when he discovered that Uncle Thaddeus had not returned home for his brother's funeral, he went through the roof. He had lost valuable time while Thaddeus was making his negotiations. Langley's plan was not to get involved in any arbitration with the frustrated group. He was going to fire the lot of them and hire new men to do the job. There was a large black population in the Dearborn area from which he could draw from. He would be able to hire them for about half the wages that the company was now paying its white workers. Thaddeus had liked the idea of a wholesale change in personnel but he was reticent about replacing them with the sons and grandsons of former slaves. To Thaddeus they were a shiftless, lazy lot that lacked the intelligence to perform the tasks that the factory required of them. Thaddeus saw no alternative but to try to come to terms with the present employees. This satisfied Grandfather. The old man recognized the changing world of manufacturing and that to get a premium product one had to have a premium labor force. Grandfather would have given them everything that they wanted. But not so with Thaddeus. He remained stingy and would only concede as little as he could.

Three different points of view with only one outcome. And it seemed that the outcome was going to be the one that Uncle Thaddeus picked much to the chagrin of his nephew Langley. Thora's father cursed and swore the morning long while the family was getting dressed for the funeral. He ranted and raved. He had scowled so much that he cut himself shaving. Finally, Thora's mother could no longer tolerate Langley's steam. She suggested that once the funeral was over that Langley should make travel arrangements for Michigan and be on a bus or train this evening for Dearborn. That had served to cool Langley down somewhat. As one of the heirs to Sambo's fortune, Langley was now in the position to exercise more power but maybe not enough power. He needed to attain Faye's cooperation before he could be on equal footing to Uncle Thaddeus. Then he might be able to coerce his uncle into trying his plan.

But his plan had now changed. After the fight with Uncle Tom this morning at the end of the church service, Thora was sure that the doctor would order Langley to stay in his bed for at least a few days to recuperate from what was probably a concussion. Her mother would cater to him in bed. She would minister to him everything that he desired. She would have forgotten all the vicious words that flew between them upon the stairs at St. Andrew's. She would do everything that she could to make sure that he stayed in bed and not permit him to board any transportation bound for Michigan. Of course, Langley would play out the role of his character. He would be despondent and surly and protest against being bedridden and do what he could to make an effort to reach Dearborn as soon as possible. This would be a half-hearted effort since Langley was a lazy man at heart and could never pull himself away from all the pampering that he was receiving from his dutiful and faithful wife.

Thora knew her parents well. Whatever troubles were between them would be put to the side when they discovered that their daughter was forced to walk seven miles on her own because of the negligence of Aunt Faye. They would phone Faye and give her ear such a blast of invective that the woman would have to have it flushed to get rid of all of the poison. A further wedge would be driven between the two halves of Sambo's feuding offspring. Thora was also sure that the schism between the Meadowfords and Thurstons would widen when her father brought assault charges against Tom Thurston. No doubt there would be a civil suit as well for the damages that Langley sustained in the attack. And this would include an attempt to seize Faye's assets, as she could be held responsible for Tom's presence at the funeral. If by some wild chance this would happen then Langley would have fifty percent ownership of Dearborn Cable and he would be then in a position to deal with Uncle Thaddeus.

Yes, Rebecca was right about her parents. They were a shiftless, capitalizing lot that cared only for themselves and nobody else. How she hated the idea of walking home to them! She had half a mind to turn around to see where this road eventually leads. That direction would be to the west. The west is where she will nest when birds don't migrate north and south.

It was a hot summer's day. The heat was growing unbearable to her. But as she sweated in the grueling solar radiation she realized that birds don't migrate north and south in the summertime. They stay put. She stopped in her tracks. Was Grandfather's message telling her that she would be traveling to the west in the summer? Was he telling her that she should not go home but rather strike off to California?

She removed the pebble from her shoe. It had been digging into the space between her smaller toes of her right foot. The discomfort at first was tolerable but with each step it had grown and grown and changed from discomfort to pain. She held the small little stone in her hand. It was a gray, indistinct thing of no special shape. It probably existed here on the Earth since the beginning of time and had gone unnoticed through the eons even though it clamored for recognition. Finally it was given its opportunity when the girl's shoe had inadvertently scooped it up. There it began to shout and it got heard. For it now resided in the fingers of a girl who studied it for a moment before flinging it to a roadside ditch where it would then go again unrecognized and unnoticed to the end of time. But it would no longer be bitter. It had its moment in the sun.

Was life like that? Thora had to wonder. Do we all just have a few brief seconds in the limelight before we drift off into obscurity? Were the atoms that composed William Shakespeare's body still drifting about the planet unseen and fitting together unimaginably beautiful verse? Were the remnants of Isaac Newton still obeying the laws of the universe that they had at one time discerned and disseminated? Did we all leave ghosts?

She knew that if this road that she strode stretched out into infinity, she would still not have enough time to discover the real answer. The real answer would have to come from some other source. All that she had was her herself and she was smart enough to know that if she worked her brain as hard as she could it would not spit up the answer. The reason being that the answer was not in there in the first place. She had not experienced and tasted of the world much in her brief years of existence.

Should she turn in the opposite direction and walk away from home? Going that way, toward the setting sun, would augment her life with experience and kindle a world-smart savvy within her that would give her answers to her questions. Yet to go that way would be running away from home. Was she ready to truly embark on such an adventure? She did not even have a dime in the small little change purse that she carried. With no money how far would she get? Where would she spend the night? She was not one to sleep under the stars. Back at the island on Pioneer Lake, Rebecca had often suggested that the two girls sleep on the rock and take in the myriad of constellations and the overpowering presence of the ceaseless heavens. Each and every time Thora balked at the idea. She had lots of excuses why they should not do so. There were too many mosquitoes. The rock was too hard to sleep upon. Fishermen would see them in their pajamas. It would be too cold. They never slept outdoors back at Black Island.

To go down that road to the west would in all likelihood mean sleeping outdoors. There were dozens of new reasons why not to pursue the highway and the high life that it entailed—the main one being that there were dangerous men known to wander the roads who would look upon a thirteen-year old girl as their perfect prey. These predators would strike day or night.

Suddenly, Thora started to get scared. She was out here in the great wide open by herself. She would be defenseless against any man that takes a not so kindly interest in her. Her mind was quickly made up. She would not run away. As problematic as it was, home was a far better and safer place to be than to go out and carve her presence upon the world at her wee age. She was still a child and a child needs the comfort and nurturance of a home. Even if that home was not going to be the nicest place on the Earth. She could not get home fast enough.

She put her shoe back on and began walking at an increased gait. She was wary of all the sounds around her. The crickets creaked constantly. She heard the electric buzzing of cicadas. Now and then her ears were treated to the trill of a meadowlark or the chattering of a flock of starlings that were working the cornfields scouring them for anything edible.

Then there was an explosive flutter that emanated only feet away from her. Her heart was given a start but it quickly found relief as she watched the feverish flight of a male ringed neck pheasant trying to escape from her. It must have been hidden in the taller grasses along the roadside and grew uncomfortable about the closing proximity of the young human walking on the gravel.

Her view still revealed the town of Grappling Haven down in the valley. It was not getting any closer. Why did Grandfather have to be buried so far away? There were scores of locations much closer to town. Why did he have to go all the way out to Silent Hills? Silent Hills was for the elite in town. The poor people were not buried there. They were put in the ground right in town. Thora recalled many evenings when she and her sister would stroll past Memorial Gardens and the unease that the two of them felt as they went by that deteriorating graveyard. They would try to scare each other in an attempt to mask their own fear. Thora was always worried that she would see a corpse climb out of its grave and come after them with a depraved grin upon its partially decomposed face. It never happened yet but that did not mean that it was not going to happen one day.

She hated cemeteries. She hated death.

Why could not have God created people directly in Heaven rather than have them spend a lifetime on a proving ground that was filled with frightening things? Why wait for the soul to perfect itself upon the Earth? If God was perfect why did he create imperfect beings? It made no sense. It was one of the many reasons that made Thora Meadowford question the veracity of what was being taught in the Church. Surely, there was a better way of explaining the purpose of existence than it just being a school where morality and ethics were taught.

What morality and ethics was she being taught out here? She was walking the road between the cemetery and her house out of no fault of her own. She was out here due to the negligence of adults, people who should have known better. Jesus spent forty days in the desert and came out of it a better and stronger person. Was this her desert? Was this where she would come out of it a stronger person? Like Jesus, she had already fought temptation when she briefly entertained the notion of running away to the west. But her resistance to the Devil came out of fear of sleeping under the stars. It did not come from any internal championing of good over evil. What was she being taught out here then?

The only answer that she could come up with was not to rely on adults. They were every bit as strewn with personality flaws as the children that they were rearing. Once again Thora's mind turned to the inadequacies of character in not only her mother and father, but in her Aunt Faye and Reverend Barton as well. And once again she rehashed the events that led her to this lonely road on a hot summer afternoon.

The road was truly a lonely road. It had many farm fields. But it had no farmhouses. It had a route but nobody traveled it. No one had gone by her. She was not good at reading the time from the sun but it seemed to her that at least an hour had gone by since she left the cemetery. She was guessing that it was around one in the afternoon but it could have been much later. It could not have been any earlier. The services had to last until at least noon. She wished that she wore her watch this morning. She normally did not go anywhere without it. But this morning with the rush to get ready for the funeral plus the dueling temper tantrums of her mother and father she had forgotten to put it on her wrist.

She was now approaching a field where a dozen or so Holstein cows were huddled under a drooping willow tree taking advantage of the shade that it offered. The cattle were smart enough to get out of the sun. They knew that the shade would give them relief from the overbearing heat that the solar orb inflicted upon the tortured land. She envied them. There were no willows or boughs from any tree hanging over the road. All of it was under the relentless sun. All of it was slowly roasting.

Thora began to realize that she was thirsty. Her throat was parched. She longed for a sip of anything that was cold. The only water nearby was a pond in the cattle field. She knew how fetid and disgusting that water would be. Yet it was still water and her body craved the liquid. Before she knew what she was doing, she began climbing over the cedar railings that separated the field from the road and began walking toward the pond. She had given the cows no second thought.

But as she neared the pond and saw how absolutely filthy the water was, she heard the sounds of turf being torn from the ground. She turned around and saw a huge, fat Holstein cow with udders that practically dragged on the soil coming towards her. The cow's eyes were bulging indicating its displeasure that the girl had trespassed upon her territory. It came to a stop not fifteen feet away from Thora. There it snorted several times, while scratching its front hoof on the dried ground. Then it let loose a deep bellow that sent shivers up Thora's spine.

The girl did not know if the animal was going to attack or not. She was not familiar with farm animals. She did recognize however that the cow was at least ten times her size and that if it really wanted to there would be nothing to stop it from trampling the girl to death.

"Good Bessie," she said to the cow in as gentle and comforting a voice as she could muster while she slowly began to shuffle her feet in an attempt to increase the distance that separated her from the creature.

The beast showed that it was not appeased by Thora's soft blurting. It also seemed aware that the girl was trying to escape. It lowed once more and lowered its head to the ground while keeping its eyes firmly affixed upon Thora. It made sure that Thora did not increase her distance. It matched every step Thora took.

The other cows that were under the willow suddenly came running up to join the big one. It was like their mother had summoned them. There, they huddled with the cow Thora had called Bessie and formed a semi-circle, each cow facing towards the little girl that dared step onto their pasture.

Thora was overrun with deep waves of terror. She was so scared that she was sure that she was going to release her bladder. How she wished that she could have bought back the last few minutes and not made the silly mistake of transgressing a well-guarded field just for a chance to sip at some water that in all likelihood would have made her sick for a week.

"Go away!" she cried, waving her hands at the creatures in the hope that this would shoo them off.

The animals did not understand. They held their ground and continued to stare at her through huge eyes that Thora could only see as being malignant.

"I said go away!" she said in a more forceful voice. She did not know how she was going to get out of this mess. All that she really knew about cows were that they supplied her with the milk that she enjoyed at the start of each day. She had petted several of them at the Grappling Haven Fall Fair. Those had been tied up. These ones were loose.

The cattle took several steps forward as a group. The smaller ones seemed to look at the big one for cues on how to respond.

Thora had no idea how fast a cow could run but surely she could run faster. She could no longer hold her stand. It was time to take action. The bovines blocked her path to the fence and road. Her only route of escape was to the pond itself. She did not know if cattle were water-loving beasts or not. She prayed that they weren't.

She rushed toward the waterhole. Behind her she saw that the cows had become mobilized and were making chase after her like a thundering herd escaping from inexperienced drovers. She reached the pond's edge and without any hesitation took a step into it. The bottom was a slippery, slimy ooze that flung her leg out from underneath her and sent her face forward into the remarkably chilly water. This pond must have been spring-fed for it to be so cold.

As she righted herself, she found that she was over her head. This waterhole ran deep. Her feet could not make purchase with its bottom. She began treading the water feeling the weight of her dress trying to pull her down. She did not concern herself with this for the moment. She had to see if the Holsteins came into the pond after her. To her relief they were standing at the water's edge staring at her with their expressionless faces. They were not coming into the pond.

But they were not going away from it either. They stood there looking at her. She had no idea what was going on in their cow brains, whether they were amused by this silly girl dressed in her Sunday's best taking a dip in the drinking hole or whether they were daring her to take a step out.

All that Thora knew was that her arms were getting tired and that she could not stay in this pond forever. She would have to get out of it before she drowned. She started toward the opposite side of the pond from the cows. As she treaded, she saw some motion on the water's surface that indicated that something was there just below it. At once she felt creepy and terrified and let loose such a scream that it startled the cows momentarily. They made a hesitant step away from the pond's bank before they stopped once more to ascertain if there was any danger present. They seemed to be satisfied that they were not at risk and they quickly returned to the edge of the pond.

The stream of water that coursed upon the pond's top took Thora's attention. Thankfully, its path was not directed at her. It was moving away from her and towards another spot within the waterhole. And then it surfaced. It was just a turtle. Not even a snapping turtle, but just a run of the mill, everyday box turtle. Thora felt silly that she had reacted so severely to the presence of such a mundane creature.

She started towards the opposite end of the pond once more. Her feet began to touch bottom. Although it was an icky surface it held her weight and she was glad for its presence. She no longer had to tread and tire out her arms. As she took a moment to catch her breath, she saw that some of the cows were on the move. They had read her intention. They had now scattered themselves and positioned themselves around the entire circumference of the waterhole. They were not going to let her out.

She screamed and ranted at them, trying to scare them away, but these were animals that were not going to be spooked by the vocalizations of something that was much smaller than they were.

Thora saw no recourse for herself but to wait them out. She looked down at her soaked black dress and saw that its smartly-tailored shape had given way to loose shapeless cloth trying to float on the pond's surface. This dress will never be worn again. It was ruined. Her mother was going to kill her.

She was not sure how much time drifted by as she sat waist-deep in the cold pond hoping that the cows would take interest in something else other than her. There was nothing else interesting out there for the Holsteins. She was the main attraction and the bovines remained at the pond's edge despite the hot sun burning down on their patchy black and white bodies. Some of them occasionally took a drink from the water and others periodically nibbled at the chutes of grass that stuck out from the parched ground. But they did not leave the vicinity.

Thora's legs were beginning to feel numb from the prolonged exposure to the frigid water. Her top half was roasting while her bottom half was frozen. It was an odd and extremely uncomfortable condition. Finally, she decided that the cows were not going to do anything. They were tame, domesticated herbivores afterall. They were not a pride of wild African lions. She started moving towards the nearest bank. But as soon as she took one step, all the Holsteins lifted their heads and looked at her. The one called Bessie lowed a deep warning to her that she had better not try it.

The girl cursed the fat animal and began to cry. How did she end up in such an awkward and extremely stupid position? She didn't care how her parents would react when she finally got home. She would yell at them if they dared say anything. None of this was her fault!

The afternoon was drifting by. Each passing minute Thora began to realize would mean the increased likelihood that she would not get home until after dark. That is, of course, if the cows ever relented. Don't they usually go to a barn in the evening? She was pretty sure that they did. When that happens then she would finally have her opportunity to escape. But that would then force her out onto that road in the black of night. It would be the time of the notorious, depraved men that wandered these dusty paths in search of little girls. This idea depressed Thora all the more.

Her only hope was that someone would come down that road soon. Yet nobody had done so in all of the time since the mourners had left the services for her grandfather. Thora could not believe that a road could be so quiet. The streets in town were often described as being quiet when they were compared to the avenues and thoroughfares of Pittsburgh. But the streets of Grappling Haven did have a steady stream of traffic upon them. Not a minute could go by without at least a motor vehicle or pedestrian traveling upon the pavement.

Here hours had gone by. And nobody had gone by.

And then finally, after Thora began to wonder if she had not died and was now residing in some forlorn spot in Purgatory or Limbo, the sounds of a humming motor and displaced gravel came to her ears.

Her eyes went to the road watching for the approaching vehicle. It was coming from town and heading up into the hills. Thora began jumping up and down, waving her arms back and forth, and whistling and crying, trying to draw the attention of the driver. It was a black car made dusty from the dryness of the road. It drove past the cow field without slowing down. It continued its way up the hill.

Thora's heart sank to its lowest point yet. Nobody was going to notice her in this pond. The lay of the road did not give a very good view of the pond. At best what any driver would see would be a bunch of cows lazing away a hot summer's afternoon by a dank waterhole. They would see similar sights all along this bucolic road. There was nothing extraordinary here that would stand out and make them take notice.

The cows did not take any special note of the vehicle either. They did not seem to even bat an eyelash at the passing car. To them the only thing interesting here was the little girl trapped in the pond.

More time went by and then another car came down the hill. Once again Thora tried to catch the driver's attention and once again she was thwarted in her attempts. It did not appear that anybody was going to come to her rescue. And what could a driver do to help her anyway? It was not like the road was a main thoroughfare for daring young matadors that would leap from their vehicles with their red cloth in hand and begin taunting these bovines into attacking them.

The only person that could rescue her, she grimly realized, was herself. She would have to challenge these curious beasts and show them that despite her diminutive size it was she that exercised command here and not they. All she had to do was draw up the nerve to put this plan in action. The nerve was a long time in coming. Several times she felt that she had sufficient gumption to take the cows on but something trivial would sidetrack her and her gumption levels would fall. One time all that it took was her shoe being nestled a bit too deeply in the mud on the pond's bottom. When she went to take a step her foot would momentarily not come with her. By the time her foot was released from the bottom her will to challenge the cows had weakened.

One thing that she did do to lessen her ordeal was to find the shallowest spot within the pond. Less of her body was now submerged in the chilly waters and more of her was allowed to soak up the heat of the sun. When those parts of her body that were exposed to the ceaseless solar rays became too hot all that she did was draw some of the water from the pond up onto them and immediately cool them down.

An idea had come to her. She was surprised that the notion did not come to her head before. She forced her cupped hand across the surface of the water and sent a spray of water at the nearest cow. The water splashed the unsuspecting beast in its face. It jerked back in surprise and then shook its head trying to dislodge all the errant droplets that were resting on its thick snout. It did not run away however. Splashing the cows was not going to be her route of escape. But it was fun. And it was a way to disperse some of the pent up anger residing in her over her situation. She sent more spray at any of the cows that she was able to reach. They all reacted the same as the first one. In a way they seemed to be enjoying it as well. She was cooling them off on a hot afternoon.

"Want to splash me? I surely can do with some cold water on my face."

Thora jumped. She had not expected to hear a voice out here. She immediately turned to find the source of that voice. There, standing by the cedar railing fence along the roadside was an old man. Behind him on the road was a small wagon with a pair of hitched horses. Thora squinted her eyes to give her clearer definition of the man. It was the fellow that she recognized from the funeral services earlier this day. It was the man that offered to have Thora come over for dinner two nights hence. She did not know the name of this fellow.

At once she felt a wave of caution come over her. There was something about the old man that she could not trust. She had felt it back at Silent Hills and she was feeling it even more here on the cattle field. But help was help. She could not stay in this pond forever.

"Can you help me?" she said to the man. "They are not letting me out."

Some of the cows saw the man as well. One of them started to go towards him.

The old man laughed. "They are not going to hurt you!" he chortled. "They are just curious about you, that's all."

Thora felt extremely silly. She had never heard of Holsteins attacking people before either. The newspapers were not brimming with stories of yet another life claimed by surly aggressive territorial cattle. Yet despite her rationalization that she was not going to get hurt if she stepped out of the pond, she could not force herself to climb out from the protective waters.

By now the one cow had reached the fence. The old man had stuck out his hand and the beast began licking his fingers. "See," he said. "These are very gentle creatures. They are very smart as well. Smarter than your dogs and cats that you keep in your house and they are all a whole lot more gentle!" He reached his other hand out and began scratching behind the cow's ears.

"You are safe. You are on the other side of the fence where they can't get at you!" Thora protested.

"Do you want me to come and get you?" the old man asked.

"If you don't mind," Thora replied.

She knew that she was making a request that she should not have been making. When she saw the old fellow begin to scale the fence and saw how this feat was not coming easy to the man with his wobbly knees and his frail frame, she started to feel bad about asking him to do this. Yet, despite these feelings, she did not recant her request.

When the old man finally got on this side of the fence, the cow took several steps away from him. It was not challenging him for the territory. It had conceded the ground and only watched the man from a safe distance.

The old fellow strode across the field that separated him from the pond. His gait was rickety and his steps were unsure. This was no easy task for him. Thora knew that she should get out of the pond and meet him and not force him to walk all that way. But she would not. Her body was petrified and was unwilling to respond to reason.

When the old man reached the side of the pond, the cows that had been there had dispersed to clear a place for him. They did not run away however. They remained nearby and seemed curious about what he was going to do.

"You are not going to force me to go into the water to get you, are you?" the old fellow wheezed. "These are my good clothes, the same ones that I wore at the funeral this morning."

Thora looked at the man's clothing. To her eyes they were barely a step above rags in the hierarchal scale of apparel. The dress that she had on was countless rungs on the ladder above the tattered jacket and slacks that the old man wore. If she sacrificed her dress then surely he could sacrifice his? Then she told herself to smarten up. She was behaving like a Meadowford. Her parents would have such reactions. She had sworn that she would no longer have such reactions. "You stay on the bank. I will come to you," she said.

She began striding towards the pond's edge. Her eyes were ever watchful on the cows. Bessie was not too far off and she was keeping a very wary eye on her. And then Thora took another step and suddenly found herself over her head. The water got deeper before the bank side. When she went down, her mouth and lungs filled with water. She came up gasping and coughing for air.

She heard a splash and before she knew it, she felt a pair of hands on her shoulders dragging her towards the banks. Through her drenched hair she saw the old man struggling to keep his head above water while he towed her the few yards to the safety of the banks. Even though she was a good swimmer Thora did nothing to help the old man along. Her legs and arms remained motionless, allowing the old man to create all the momentum to pull their two bodies out. She should have been the one putting out the effort.

When they reached the banks, the first thing that Thora did was to look about to see where the cows were. The Holsteins had all pulled back away from the water hole and were standing several yards away, watching the two humans climb out of the pond. Thora felt very ill at ease. She could still only see distrust and naked hostility towards her in their huge bovine eyes.

The old man began coughing. He was sprawled on all fours along the pond's banks. It seemed that he did not have enough energy to get himself up. The clothing that he wore, his Sunday best, were knotted up about him. They were dripping water at a rate that no faucet could match.

"Are you okay, Mister?" Thora asked, not daring to move any closer to him and to give him a much-needed slap on the back to clear his chest.

The old man answered her only through his continued coughing. From her angle, Thora saw the gooey stretch of elongated phlegm that joined his mouth to the ground. It would be all that she needed for this old man to die right here leaving her alone to fend with the cows.

To her surprise, she saw the huge cow she called Bessie saunter up to the man. The big Holstein brought her massive head down against the old man's back in a heavy nudge. The old man's arms collapsed from the push. When his head reached the ground, his coughing had stopped. Bessie gave Thora a glance that said that you should have done this, not me. And then Bessie waddled away to stand with the other cows.

The old man's breathing was loud but it was strong. He lifted his head. He had some of the mucus that had fallen earlier from his mouth now sitting like a greasy spider web on the grizzled grey hair on his temple. Thora had to avert her eyes from him or else she was going to be sick.

"Are you okay, Miss Meadowford?" the old man spoke as he glanced over to Thora who was sitting on the sides of her thigh in a three-point stance along the pond's side.

"I'm alright," Thora answered, still not being able to look at the man for the sloppy mess at the side of his head.

He seemed to understand the problem or he felt its presence. He drew his hand through his hair, drawing out the mucus. He immediately plunged his hand into the pond water to clean it up.

"Come, let's get you out of this field," he sighed, gathering himself up on his unstable knees and then reaching a hand, the same hand that he had fouled earlier, out to Thora to help her.

Thora did not take the hand. She got herself up on her own strength. As she stood she saw the cows hovering nearby. She noticed Bessie. The fat beast snorted and shook its head in a display that Thora could only interpret as a threat and a prelude to a charge.

Her first inclination was to run back into the pond but before she could do so the old man grabbed her by the wrist. "Don't let the old girl bother you," he said. "She is just trying to tell you that this is her domain and that as long as you reside here you have to abide by her rules."

They were not comforting words and Thora could tell by the old man's expression that he did not trust Bessie much either.

"Just walk with me and whatever you do, don't look them in the eyes," he said. "They read that as a threat."

He put his arm around Thora's waist and began leading her slowly towards the fence. Behind her Thora was sure that she could hear the soft thuds of hooves falling into place as the herd of Holsteins were beginning to follow her and the old timer.

"Just keep walking," he warned. "Don't turn your head and look back at them."

It was hard not to do that. She was certain that the cows were narrowing the gap that separated them. The cedar rail fence just did not seem like it was getting any closer.

"I said don't look around!" the old man said in a louder voice. "I don't know what it is about you girl but those cows just don't seem to like you."

The words sent shivers through Thora. She didn't know what it was about her either. Her relationship with animals, although not extensive, had always been on friendly terms. Capers the cat preferred her company to everybody else including her sister Rebecca. Back at Pioneer Lake, the chipmunks and red squirrels were hardly leery to take a peanut from her fingers. But these cows did not like her. They did not like her from the very first moment that they set eyes upon her.

The fence was now just ten feet away. It seemed so close—close enough to make a run for it. Thora broke free from the old man's arms and she made a mad dash towards the cedar railings.

As she did so she could hear thunder being released from the ground.

Flinging her head back, she saw that the cows were in a full run racing towards her and the old man. He was directly in their path.

Thora threw herself onto the cedar railings and wildly began to scramble up them. She was over on the roadside when one of the cows bashed into the upper railing and snapped it in half. It would go no further.

Out of breath and panting, Thora crawled onto the road. She turned around and saw the herd of Holsteins standing at the fence. They were mooing loudly. She was sure that they could be heard for miles around. Yet as angry as they were they did not try to take a step beyond the fence. They were satisfied to stay in their territory and did not want to stake claim to anything past that.

But where was the old man? The last Thora saw of him he was about to be trampled by the wild stampede of cattle. She could not see him at all. She tried peering through the legs and udders for a sign of the man underneath them. In all likelihood he should have been on the ground. But there was not a trace of him there at all.

She called out to him, "Are you there? Where are you?"

There was no answer.

The only replies she got came from the bovines and what they said to her in their deep lows was that she had better get away from here as soon as possible before they decided to make a foray past their borders.

Thora did not feel threatened for some reason. She realized that the cows were not going to breech the cedar railings. If they were going to do so they would have done it by now.

She continued calling to the man while her eyes scoured every inch of ground that separated the pond from the fence. There was not a sign of him. It was like he had never been there at all.

It suddenly occurred to the girl that there was something missing on the road here with her. The old man's cart and the pair of horses that hauled it was no longer present. Even the grooves that the wagon would have dug into the dusty road were gone. There was no evidence of any horses being here recently either. Thora studied the road as carefully as she could and she could not see anything. It was like the cart and horses had never been here at all either.

The girl started to feel very eerie about all of this.

She returned her gaze to the cows. They were still standing by the section of fence where the upper railing had been broken off. Did they see the man? Did they know what became of him? If they did they were not telling her. That knowledge would be forever trapped in their brains and never be revealed to anything under the sun.

Who was that man? Thora had seen him before. She recognized him. Yet she never had a name for him. She recalled him standing by the perimeters of the schoolyard on several occasions. He never said anything. He just stared into the yard as the children were having their recess. Now, as she thought about it, it seemed that he was not looking at the other children. He was looking at her.

This morning at the service at Silent Hills he offered to have Thora for dinner. The girl now realized that that was the first time that she ever heard the man speak and yet his voice was deeply familiar as if she had known it all of her life. It seemed like he was always there in the background and never did anything to draw himself into the foreground.

Until now.

He had saved her from the cows. He had come out of nowhere to rescue her. It now seemed to Thora that he did come out of nowhere. She had not heard him coming when surely a pair of horses and a creaky old wagon would have made enough noise to be heard a long time before it arrived. She had not known he was there until he spoke.

This unnerved the girl. It was like the old man was her guardian angel. As soon as her need for his presence dissipated he was gone. There was not a trace of him anywhere. She was sure that there was no dead or dying body on the cattle field.

Bessie suddenly let loose a very deep low from the fence side. Thora lifted her eyes and saw that the animal was telling her that she had better get moving along or else they were not going to honor her territory any longer.

It was enough to send the little girl walking at a swift gait down the road and to the town of Grappling Haven at the bottom of the valley. She could not get there fast enough.

When the sun started to sink past the hills, Thora Meadowford found herself walking on the streets of her town. For the first time in hours she felt safe.

Chapter 4

"Where Have You Been?"

"And where have you been?" the voice of her mother shot out like an assassin's knife across the room to hit Thora in the throat. The girl had just stepped through the door. Outside the skies darkened sufficiently enough to be called night. She was tired and spent. All that she wanted to do was crawl up the stairwell to her room and climb into bed. She had a feeling that her wish would be a long time in coming before it became reality.

Cora Meadowford appeared at the corridor that led to the kitchen. She was already dressed in her pajamas and had a light satin cap wrapped around her head. In her hand she held another form of nightcap.

"I've been worried sick about you! I was just about to call the police! Where have you been? It's that bitch aunt of yours, isn't it? Has she been poisoning you with lies about your father and I?" More words spilt from her mother's mouth as she stomped across the house towards her.

Thora flinched for she did not know if her mother was going to hit her or not.

"Oh Mother, I am so tired and all that I want to do is go to bed! This has been the most terrible day of my life!" the girl bawled.

"Terrible for you? What about us? What do you think it is like not knowing where your thirteen-year old daughter is? Not knowing if she is alive or dead! And what a day it has been for your dear father! You haven't even asked about him! Some daughter you are! You don't care about the well being of your parents!"

"I just came through the door for crying out loud!" the girl cried and then ducked. She instinctively knew that it was now time to lower her neck and wrap her shoulders around her head. The swats were going to fly.

Cora began flailing her hands upon the back of her daughter's head. The drink that she held was throwing up waves that splashed onto Thora's neck. Thora could feel its coldness and smell its stale alcohol aroma. She knew that her mother had several of these already this evening and that she was now drunk.

With her hands pressed against her mother's ribcage she pushed her away and out of reach. "Mom, I don't need this right now!" she said as calmly as she could. She knew that if she raised her voice it would heighten her mother into the next generation of violence. "I've had a terrible day! I had to walk home all the way from the cemetery!" she exclaimed.

Cora's eyes opened and closed slowly in an exaggerated blink brought on by the drink. It almost seemed like she was actually listening to what her daughter was saying. But before she could reveal if she made sense of what her daughter said or was just in a reptilian torpor, Rebecca appeared at the top of the stairwell.

"You're back!" Thora's twin sister said. "Where were you Thor? We were getting scared that something bad has happened to you." Rebecca, also in her pajamas started down the carpeted stairwell towards her.

"Becky, it was bad! I had to walk all the way from the cemetery!" Thora could feel relief pour out of her. If there was anybody that she could confide in and trust it was her twin.

"Didn't Aunt Faye give you a ride home?" Rebecca asked with consternation on her face.

"She was in a hurry. She did not want to wait while all the people wanted to wish me their condolences about Grandfather," Thora answered, throwing her arms around her sister and locking her in an embrace.

"That woman can be so strange at times," Rebecca said. Her arms were wrapped around Thora's waist. "You had to walk all the way back from way out there! That's practically in the next county!"

"I know," Thora sniffled. "It was so hot! And I had on this dress!"

"Look at that dress! You've ruined it!" Cora came back to life and like a veteran boxer not knowing that it was time to quit came in for another round of close proximity fighting.

This time Rebecca shielded Thora from her mother's blows. "She's drunk," she said to Thora. "She's been drunk every day now since we came back from Canada." Rebecca's words were dismissive of her mother. She accorded her mother no respect and talked about her in the third person, not granting her any iota of personhood or being a human being.

Cora tried to grab Rebecca by her braids but the girl neatly stepped aside and allowed her to stumble against the wall. "Pretty pathetic, isn't she?" Rebecca said. "Come Thora, let's go outside and we can fill in each other about what happened today."

Thora saw her mother lean against the wall, still clutching at the remnants of her glass of sherry. There was hardly a sip left but her mother gulped it in like it was an overflowing stein of beer. "You will not take a step out of this house!" she roared. "You are going to tell me why you were gone all day!"

"I already told you Mom!" Thora said in exasperation. "I had to walk all the way from Silent Hills!"

"It doesn't take all day to walk from there! A one-legged man could have gone that distance in half the time! Now, where were you?"

Thora entertained the notion of telling her mother about the incident in the cow field but thought better of it. Her mother would never understand and would only think that she was really pulling at straws trying to come up with a believable lie. It suddenly occurred to her how she could get out of this. "I already told you. But enough about me. How is Dad?" She switched the topic.

"Your father has a concussion. He is up in the bedroom trying to sleep. He couldn't get any because of you! He has been lying there awake worrying about you!"

For someone concerned about the well-being of her husband, Cora Meadowford was not going to any lengths to ensure the man the peace and quiet that he needed for sleep. Her voice was loud and demanded attention.

"Well, he doesn't have to worry any more. I am home now safe and sound!" Thora said, taking her sister's hand and going to the door.

"You stay right here! You are not going outside!" Cora barked, snatching Thora by the ear. "You are going to tell me exactly where you have been today! Don't give me any crap that you were walking home from the graveyard because I am not going to buy it!"

Thora squinted from the pain that her mother's sharp little fingers inflicted on her lobe. She could feel the rage well up in her. She had been demeaned enough already this day. She did not need any more abuse. She threw up her arm and knocked her mother's hand away. "You don't touch me, you drunken hag!" she spat at the woman. "I have told you several times already where I have been today and if you can't get it through that thick skull of yours then I'm sorry but I'm not going to tell you again." She stormed out of the door.

Rebecca followed her.

The Meadowford house possessed a huge cedar wrap around porch that was furnished with a swinging couch. The two sisters flung themselves onto this verandah furniture and set in motion its creaking hinges. Crossing her arms around her waist, Thora said to her sister, "I can't stand that woman!" Her body was still infused with all of the powerful emotions that had swept over it due to her encounter with her mother.

"She has become a veritable ogre since Aunt Faye flung those allegations about Father's conduct. Even though she denies them I know that deep down she knows that every word Aunt Faye spoke is true," Rebecca said, putting her arm over Thora's shoulder.

Through the walls of the house they could hear their mother raving. They chose to drown out her words. They knew that they were safe out here on the porch. Even drunk, Mother would never come out in her pajamas lest the neighbors see her. She was all about keeping up appearances and managed to hold onto that ideal even when her mind was saturated with liquor.

"Do you really think that Dad knocked up Lena?" Thora had asked her sister this question dozens of times and knew her sister's answer but this conversation never grew tiresome to the two girls. There was the very real possibility that they were going to have another sibling. The potential mother, Lena Taylor, was the eighteen year-old former housekeeper that looked after the Meadowford house before she moved to New Hampshire.

"Dad's always had an eye for other women," Rebecca started the response that Thora knew so well.

"But Lena was hardly what I would call attractive. She had a rump on her as big as a cow!" Upon saying the word 'cow' Thora suddenly decided to turn the topic of the conversation around. Before Rebecca could say anything about her impressions of Lena's appearance, Thora sparked, "You are not going to believe what happened to me today!"

"You did something different than just walk home from the cemetery?" Rebecca answered. "I knew something else had to have happened. Mom is right on that aspect. It doesn't take all day to walk home from the cemetery."

"I was walking down the road past these cows. I was really hot and thirsty and I saw this pond sitting in the cow's field. I just had to go there and cool off." Thora proceeded to tell Rebecca about everything that happened along the road.

When she was done, Rebecca shook her head. "I'm afraid that I don't know who that old man is."

"You've seen him at the schoolyard during recess. He is that pervert that hangs around the fence looking in at us while we are playing hopscotch or skipping rope."

"I don't remember anybody like that," Rebecca said.

"He was there at the funeral service this morning too," Thora added. "He offered to have me over for supper two nights from now."

"I don't know who you mean."

"Do you think that maybe he is my guardian angel or something?" Thora dared to ask the question.

To this query, Rebecca started to giggle, "Your guardian angel? Oh Thor, you don't need a guardian angel. You have got me, remember? I often think that the only purpose to my life is to support your life, just like a guardian angel!"

Thora smiled. Rebecca had always been there for her her whole life. It always seemed that when trouble was out looking for someone to malign it always picked her and not her sister. And it always seemed that it was Becky who went after this trouble, chasing it away and telling it to leave her sister alone. "Yes, you have always been my guardian angel. But then who do you suppose the old man is? I know that I am not making him up. He was very real. I felt his hands on my shoulders when he dragged me out of the pond. I saw him puking his brains out afterwards."

"Thora, do you need to be so graphic?" Rebecca winced.

"Well I saw it Becky. Phantoms of the imagination do not do that kind of thing. And then when I finally got over the fence I saw him amidst the cows.

He was about to be trampled and then I saw him no more. He saved my life and then he disappeared. I got to know who he is."

"You were hot and you were thirsty Thora. Those two conditions can play the devil to the mind," Rebecca answered. "I think that you were hallucinating and that you saved yourself from the pond. As for the cows chasing you? Another instance of your delirium. They were dairy cattle, Thora, for crying out loud. They were not African water buffalo. They don't stampede and try to kill people. You imagined the whole thing."

It hurt Thora to hear her sister undermine her profound experience as if it were evidence that she were going mad. "Listen, Becky, I know what is real and what is not. I can take you up that road and show you where the cedar railing was knocked down by that cow bashing against it." She pulled herself away from her sister's arm. "I'm going to bed," she announced. "I have had enough of this stupid day!"

"Sleep is exactly what you need Thor. You will feel better in the morning," Rebecca started to yawn. "Sleep is what I need to. Let's just hope that the old bat is not in there waiting to attack us again."

Thora never answered. She was apprehensive that her mother would be standing on the other side of the door, equipped with a new drink in her hand, all ready to raise Hell once more. They had not heard her for several minutes. They did not know what she had been up to.

When the twins entered the house again, all was silent. The lights were on throughout the house but there was not any sound indicating the presence of a lurking mother.

As they stepped onto the first stair of the staircase leading up to their rooms, they heard the mucus lining of their mother's nose as it vibrated with her deep snores. They quickly spotted Cora, lying out cold on the sofa. She was passed out from drink.

"I have got to get out of here," Rebecca sighed.

Without saying it out loud, Thora agreed. This house was no longer her home.

Chapter 5

Morning's Glory

The night raced by. When Thora opened her eyes and saw the brilliant sun coming through the window and targeting her retinas, she immediately squeezed them tight. Morning already. Where did the night go?

Her ears were being well exercised by the hundreds of songbirds outside all announcing their glee at being free on a glorious summer's morning.

What was so glorious about it? It meant nothing more than just another day trapped as a captive in her parents' home here in Grappling Haven. There was nothing to look forward to in the day. It would be a continuous struggle to fight the tedium and to find the means to avoid her Mother and Father who would be on her case about her whereabouts yesterday and demanding her to do her fair share of the work around the house.

If this had been a morning at Pioneer Lake things would have been different. Back there, she would have hopped out of bed and have directly jumped into the lake and felt its coolness envelope her and tickle out the final remnants of sleep that resided in her. She would not have been bored the entire daylong. There were plenty of things to keep herself amused—swimming, sailing, fishing, and watching for boys along with her sister.

Here, she couldn't do any of these things. She almost found herself wishing that school had started, as incredible as that may seem. It was counterintuitive to the way she thought in April and May. When she was at school and in particular when the spring months started to reawaken the land, all that she could do was wish for the summer and the idyllic lifestyle.

But now that it was summer and she was stuck in a small town with nothing to do, she was beginning to find that the sedentary life bestowed a heavy tax on her well-being. She started thinking of the events of yesterday, the day that her grandfather was buried. She started thinking of that road. It had seemed so endless. She had thought that she would never arrive at its end. She had thought that she was stuck there for eternity, forever wandering down it and forever discovering that it was longer than she feared.

She was surprised that she had not dreamed of the road. As far as she knew her sleep was dreamless. She was glad that it was for she knew that if she dreamt she would have dreamed of that road and that familiar but vague old man that she discovered along its path.

She still did not know who he was. She tried to go through all the different scenes in her life trying to see if somewhere amid all of these places she could find that man. But other than the schoolyard, the cemetery, and the lonesome road he was not there in any of those places.

How was it that she knew him? Why did it seem like he was someone that was there her whole life? She just did not know. She had not entirely dismissed the idea that he was her guardian angel.

"Cora! Is the morning paper at the door yet?" Thora heard her father bellow from his room.

"I can't do everything at once!" Thora's mother cried out from somewhere downstairs. "I wish that somebody here would give me a hand!" From the tone of her voice it was clear that her mother was not in a cheerful mood. She was probably deep in the throes of too much alcohol last night and too little sleep.

Thora knew that the comment was directed at her or her sister. She felt tingles travel the length of her spine. The war was already beginning and she was not even out of bed yet.

"Thora, can you get the paper for your father!" Cora demanded, violating the sanctity and sanctuary of the girl's room.

"Just a second…"

"Can't a man get any God damned attention here? All I ask for is a chance to read the newspaper!" Langley's voice boomed louder than the other piping that was bringing the house alive.

Thora did not know what time it was. She had removed the alarm clock in her room at the start of summer. She did not want to be reminded of schedules and timetables during the languorous months of idle pleasure.

"Thora, get the paper now!" Cora roared.

"Will everybody just shut up!" Rebecca cried out from her room. Thora could tell that her twin probably had the pillow over her head trying to drown out all of the yelling that was taking place. Long ago Rebecca established a working rule in the household that she was not to be disturbed until she chose to step from her room. Some days that moment was a long time in coming.

"I don't take orders from sniveling little brats that should be out of bed helping their mothers!" Langley crowed. "Is anybody getting the paper?"

"I'm going! I'm going!" Thora called out, throwing the covers from her and dropping her legs to the floor. She hated this place. She even hated this room even though she selected every piece of furniture in it and every wall hanging and every carpet on its floor. Somewhere between her selection of these items and their placement in this room they all became contaminated by her parents' presence. They dickered with her with where to place them and they always used them as something to throw back in her face whenever she stepped out of their clearly defined bounds of expected conduct from her. They would remind her of how expensive they were and that she was not worthy to possess them.

As soon as she stood up and slipped on her housecoat she felt the need to relieve her bladder. She stepped out of her room. All the ambient sounds of the house immediately were magnified and took on a more real presence than when they were muffled by the walls of her room. She could hear the electric fan coming from her parents' room. Her father had an insatiable need to have blowing air pass over his face. She could hear the sound of running water coming from the kitchen where her mother was no doubt doing dishes that should have been done the night before.

She saw that the washroom door was open. It was a relief to know that she was not going to be challenged for its use. As she walked past the other open door, the door to her parents' bedroom, she saw her father, Langley, sitting up on his bed. His eye was black and he had a nasty contusion on his forehead. Even though he was injured she still could feel no sympathy for him. He brought it on himself. Uncle Tom was not the man that initiated the scrap in front of the church.

"You get the paper first before you take your leak. I know how long you can be in there," he said to her, while looking out of the window and not turning an eye to see her pass by.

"But I need a pee!"

"For crying out loud!" Langley exploded in a booming voice. "Can't I get any obedience in my own house from my own children! Cora, do something about that daughter of yours!"

Thora bit down on her teeth. "All right, already, I will get you your God damned paper!" She had not meant to add the color to her sentence. It had just come out of her mouth on its own accord.

"What did you say?" Langley's two eyes were bulging. He was not going to let the slip pass.

"I said that I will get you your paper," Thora said, keeping her anger in check and she proceeded down the stairs to the front door where the Saturday paper would be waiting jammed between the screen door and the main portal.

As she was about to open the door, she was suddenly pushed aside by her mother. Cora grabbed the newspaper. It crinkled in her hand. "Do I have to do everything around here!" she grumbled.

"But Mom, I was just getting the paper!" Thora complained.

"Don't talk back to me, you traitor!" her mother hissed at her. Thora saw the bags under her mother's eyes and the long drawn out face. She was hung over.

"Traitor? Why do you call me a traitor?" the girl demanded. She was not ready for any of this. She wished that she still were in her bed like her sister and not have to be exposed to the cruelty and wrath of Mr. and Mrs. Langley Meadowford.

"You abandon your father in his time of need and go running off with his sworn enemy, that witch Faye!"

"Can I get my paper? Now!" Langley's voice reverberated down the stairwell.

"I did not abandon anybody. I went to bury my grandfather!" Thora replied, feeling that she was at the edge of tears.

"You did not have to go. You already said your goodbye to him at the church service. You saw the vicious attack that your father experienced at the hands of Tom Thurston. You saw him lying out cold on the cement. Yet instead of showing concern for him you run off with the wife of the man that did this to your father. And then you are gone the rest of the day without letting us know of your whereabouts! You could have at least called to ask how your father was doing and to ask us for our permission for you to stay out late."

"Mother, there are no telephones on the road from the cemetery!" Thora responded. Her hands were shaking and she could feel that she could hardly hold in her pee any longer. She started up the stairs.

Her hair was grabbed and she was pulled back down to the landing. "Where do you think that you are going?" Mother hissed. "I am not finished with you yet!"

"I'm going to pee my pants Mom!" Thora cried.

Cora thrust the newspaper into her abdomen. "Take this to him first!" she ordered.

The newspaper was in a tattered condition. Her father was not going to like it. When she handed it to him, he bellowed, "What have you done to this paper!"

But Thora was out of the room and heading towards the washroom. The door was shut and locked.

"Just a minute!" Rebecca snapped from inside of the washroom. "Can't I get any peace in this house at all!" As her sister spoke, Thora heard the telephone ring downstairs. Her mother answered it before it rang a second time.

"Hurry Becky!" Thora said. "I'm going to explode!" She put her hand down onto her crotch trying to alleviate some of the built-up pressure in her bladder.

"I'm going as fast as I can, Thor," Rebecca answered. "You should have gone earlier when you had your chance."

"Thora!" her mother called out from the first floor. "There's a telephone call for you."

Who would be calling her at this time of the morning? She had no idea. She wanted to tell her mother to take a message but she knew that her mother would refuse to do so and demand that she answer her own call at once. Her pee was going to have to wait. She hoped that the call would not be long.

As she started down the stairs, she heard her father say, "Once you get off the phone you came back up here. I want a word with you about this newspaper and where you were yesterday."

Thora nodded. She wanted to say to him that he could kiss her behind. She went down the steps and saw the telephone hanging by its cord against the hall wall that led into the kitchen. Her mother was standing beside the dangling phone. There was a very angry look on her face. The expression told Thora that she had better not ask who was calling.

She took the phone. "Hello."

"Good morning Thora!" a bright and chipper female voice spoke. Thora recognized it but could not place it. "It's Margaret Whattam. I just want to confirm with you that our dinner plans are still on for this evening. Can you make it to my house, say around five?"

Thora did not know what to say. Her mother was hanging over her like a hawk. She was not going to give her any privacy. She stuttered on the word, "I" several times before she said, "I still have to get my parents' permission."

"Permission for what?" Cora's eyes widened.

At the same time, Mrs. Whattam said on the phone, "Yes, it is important that we get their blessings. I should not want to..."

"I said permission for what!" her mother reiterated her earlier question.

Thora took a deep breath. She did not want to go to any dinner at the woman's place. She knew that her mother would go through the roof when she heard the request. Her parents did not like the Whattams. They were in too much cahoots with Uncle Thaddeus. Mr. Whattam was the old man's chief attorney and financial advisor.

When she expelled her breath she said, "Mrs. Whattam has invited me to dinner at her house this evening."

Her mother's eyes opened extremely wide. "She has, has she?" Cora blew out her held breath. "And why would Mrs. Whattam be interested in having a little brat like you over at her house? Is she going to try to poison you against your father and I?"

Thora's hand was over the receiver. Even so, she knew that the woman at the other end of the line could hear what her mother said. The woman was very fragile and sensitive. She probably hung up when she heard the hatred spew from Cora's mouth.

"No, it has nothing to do with anything like that," Thora answered.

"Yesterday at the funeral service, Reverend Barton suggested to everybody there that they all invite me for supper and that way the congregation can feel more like a family." She knew that her mother was going to think that this was nothing but hogwash.

"And since when are you so interested in feeling like being a part of a family? You are barely a part of this family! You abandon us in our time of need and you associate with those that are our enemies!" Cora answered with clenched fists. She took the receiver from Thora's hand and icily said into it, "The answer is no!" She slammed the receiver onto its cradle.

For some strange reason Thora felt glad about what her mother just did. It took her off the hook. She was no longer obliged to make that visit to Mrs. Whattam's house. Yet, she would not reveal this relief to her Mother. "Mother, that was rude!" she exclaimed. "Mrs. Whattam is a sweet, gentle person that would not harm a fly and would never say anything bad about anybody!"

"Mrs. Whattam is a spineless, gutless creature and has the maturity of a baby baboon! If you would have gone there you no doubt would have been playing dolls or tiddlywinks with her!" Cora replied. "I don't want you carousing with any adults unless you have my expressed approval, do you hear me!"

She needed a pee. She knew that her father was waiting for her. She was glad that she did not have to go to the dinner today. Despite all of this and with her mother scrambling to stop her, Thora picked up the phone and dialed 0 for the operator. "Yes, can I have the number for the Whattams?" she asked the woman that came on the other end.

At the same time her mother was reaching over her body and began trying to wrestle the phone cord from her. Thora blocked her attempts while memorizing the four-digit number the operator provided. "Thanks," she said to the operator and put down the receiver onto its cradle once more.

"You are not going to call that woman!" her mother rasped. Her face was only inches from Thora's. Thora could smell the sherry from the night before still on her breath. Her mother's eyes were red. There hardly seemed to be any human being at all sitting behind them.

"I will do what I want!" Thora responded. She could feel the muscles in her face tighten. "I have the number memorized here in my head and I am going to call Mrs. Whattam some time today and apologize to her for your shameful behavior and tell her that I will be happy to attend dinner."

"You will over my dead body. Get up to your room and you stay in there until I say that it is time for you to come out!" Cora grabbed Thora by the bicep and thrust her towards the stairs.

Thora stumbled from the unexpected shove but managed to maintain her balance. She twisted her body around and in her anger she pushed hard against her mother's shoulder. "Don't push me around, Mother!"

Cora Meadowford fell forward, bumping her head against the wall, and knocking over a small table with a potted plant upon it. The clay flowerpot shattered all over the hardwood floor. The dirt and vegetation were scattered everywhere. Cora was able to stop her tumble before she hit the floor herself. With fire and venom spewing from her narrowed eyes, she said to her daughter, "You are going to pay for this, young lady. Nobody treats their mother like this!"

She picked up the telephone and dialed 0. "Yes, this is Mrs. Meadowford on Pine Street. I would like to be patched through to the Reform School on Adelaide Street."

Thora was extremely sorry for what she did. When she heard her mother mention the reform school she at once began crying, "Oh Mom, please don't! Please, I promise to be good!" She could hardly see out of her eyes there were so many tears obscuring her vision. Her mother had threatened to send her and Rebecca to reform school in the past when the girls transgressed against the rules of the house but never had she gone so far as to actually dial up the number.

"You had your chance!" Cora barked at her. "I'm not going to feel sorry for you again! 8-2-6-7. Thank you," she said to the operator. "If you don't mind, could you patch me through? My hands are rather busy at the moment."

Her hands were busy trying to push the pleading Thora away from her. At the same time Thora could hear someone stomping down the stairs. The weight of the sound told her that it was her father.

"What in God blazes is going on down here!" he bellowed, as he entered the hall where Thora and her mother were tangling. Langley was in his striped housecoat and his hair was standing on end in disarray. He reached over Thora and ripped the phone away from his wife and hung it up. "No daughter of mine is being sent to reform school," he said in a tight, angry tone.

Never before had Thora thought of her father as her hero and champion. "Thank you, Dad, oh thank you Dad!" she wailed throwing her arms around him in appreciation.

Before she knew it she was flung to the floor and landed amid the shards of broken pottery. One piece wedged itself in the palm of her hand. She looked up at her father in dismay. She had not expected to be treated in this manner.

But her father was not even paying attention to her. He was fixated upon his wife. He had pushed Cora so hard that she was going backwards trying to maintain her balance before she ended up falling all the way back in the kitchen. "I will do the disciplining around here, Cora!" Langley commanded. "Do you understand me? You are not to do anything without my approval!"

Thora saw her mother's bare legs through the doorway to the kitchen. They were pointed upwards and kicking defensively as her husband was coming towards her for some more manhandling. As abusive and terrible as her mother was to her, she still was not going to have her soundly thrashed by this man. She got up to her feet and dashed through the hall and jumped onto her father's back and started beating against his shoulders. "Leave her alone!" she cried repeatedly.

Langley reached backwards and got a hold of her hair. He yanked fiercely at it and Thora once more found herself on the floor. She saw her mother still kicking towards her husband while shrieking hysterically. Her father, however, had given up the physical fight. He stood over her and was saying mocking things at her. Thora was able to take small satisfaction that she had stopped her father from beating her mother.

"This family is disgraceful!"

Behind her she saw her sister Rebecca standing in the hallway shaking her head. She was no longer in her pajamas. She was wearing an old summer dress. In her hand was a neatly packed bag. "I have had it with all of you," Rebecca continued. "I just want you to know that I am moving out and that I am not going to return!"

Rebecca turned around and went to the front door.

"No wait!" Thora cried out. "Becky, don't go! Don't leave me with these monsters!"

"You are not going anywhere, young lady!" Langley boomed. "Put down that stupid bag and clean up the mess in the hall!"

"I don't take orders from a man that I do not consider my father," Rebecca said calmly. "You are no more than a petty criminal and everybody knows it. I am not going to be blind to your deceit and lies any more. You are despicable and loathsome."

Her father's face, as beaten up as it was, managed to look even more pained. "I repeat you are not going anywhere!" he thundered. "I am not going to have you be a source of embarrassment to me."

"That's what it is all about, isn't it?" Rebecca cried. "You don't want to admit to your friends that you are unable to rule over your roost. You don't want to tell them that you have a runaway for a daughter and that your other daughter is locked away in a rehabilitation school," Rebecca looked directly at Thora. "It has nothing to do with either mine or Thora's welfare. It is all about you, Samuel Angus Meadowford the Third! You are not worthy of that name. Grandfather, God rest his soul, was twice the man on a bad day than you could ever hope to be on your best!"

"Rebecca Meadowford, you take those things back!" It was Cora speaking. Once again after her husband had brutally treated her she had risen to his defense.

"Oh Mother, you are so weak-kneed and drunk all the time. You would be pathetic if you were not so bitter!" Rebecca responded. "I have had it with all of you!"

When she said the word 'all', Thora felt shivers run through her. Was her sister also dismissing her as well? What had she done wrong to be grouped together with the miscreants that claimed to be her parents?

"Go then, you little brat!" Langley barked. "See how long it takes before you come crying back here again! Just to let you know though, if you step out of that door you are not going to be permitted back!"

"Even if I end up in the worst foster house in the State, I will still be in a better place than this!" Rebecca responded. She remained calm. Her face would not betray the feelings of hurt that must have been welling up inside. "I'm going now! Farewell, dear family and all of that rot!"

She started for the door. "No, Rebecca, wait!" Thora spoke up. "I am going with you!" She could not believe that she said it. It felt so liberating and yet so final. She saw pain in her father's face with the announcement. But she knew that that pain was that he would have to admit to his cronies that he had two runaways in his family and not just one.

"Thora, I am not sure that you are ready for this," Rebecca answered. "It is not going to be easy out there. You won't have the safety of your bed at night. You will have to sleep under the stars."

Those talks back at Pioneer Lake came back to Thora when Rebecca tried to coerce her into sleeping outside on Black Island's rock. She didn't realize it back then but she was casting an impression on her sister that she was weak and the more immature of the two.

"I can sleep under the stars now!" Thora responded. "After what I went through yesterday in the cow field I can do anything. Nothing scares me any more!"

Rebecca's face showed nothing but disappointment. Thora knew that she did not want her to tag along. But that was too bad. She was going to tag along. She was not going to stay under the same roof of Langley and Cora Meadowford another night.

"Tell you what," Rebecca began. "You catch up to me. I will meet you tonight at our secret place." With that said, the girl opened the door and stepped through. She was gone.

At once Cora began crying while her husband looked like he had seen a ghost. Thora hardly noticed them. She was lost in her own state of anguish. She and Becky did not have a secret place or at least she was not sure of having one. She ran to the window and watched Rebecca with bag in hand turn to the right at the end of the yard. That was the direction towards the center of town.

At the same time that Thora watched her sister disappear, she heard her father stomping up the stairs. She heard the sounds of things being thrown around in his bedroom. "God damn it!" he bellowed. "The little bitch took it!"

"The little bitch took what, my dear?" Cora answered from the bottom of the stairway. She seemed to be acting dutiful and caring for the man. One would hardly guess that that man had only minutes before thrown her hard against the floor and was about to beat her. One would hardly guess that the woman just watched her thirteen-year old baby step out of the door to never come back.

"She stole the money out of my wallet!" Langley bellowed.

He came racing down the stairs, pushing Cora and then Thora out of the way. He went through the door and began chasing after Rebecca. Rebecca must have heard him for at once she broke into a run.

Langley ran after her for a while but his belly and his years of smoking soon took a toll on his endurance. He stopped in his path and stooped over with his hands on his knees while catching his breath. Shortly thereafter he returned to the house.

"Get the police," he said to his wife. "That girl is going to reform school."

Once again, Cora did as she was told. She was a whipped puppy that could no longer growl back at its master.

"I have the police on the line, Langley," she said.

The expression on Langley's face suddenly changed with his wife's announcement. Whether he genuinely cared for his errant daughter or he was not prepared to admit to his friends that his girl was a jailbird, he said to Cora, "Never mind. We can deal with this issue ourselves."

Cora apologized to the police department while Langley went to the window and was looking down the street in the direction that Rebecca went. Whatever his motives, Thora could still see that there was love in his eyes and pain in his heart. He had lost a daughter on this morning. Thora was now not so sure if he would lose another.

As terrible of people as her parents were they were still people. They still had feelings although they did not know how to express them and often were at odds with them. Langley and Cora Meadowford were not placed on this Earth solely to terrorize their twin daughters. They were here to try to provide for their girls and to create the best life possible for them. Her father's greed and seemingly self-serving behaviors were aberrant manifestations of that desire to be a good provider.

In this moment as she watched Langley look longingly outside for his disappeared daughter, Thora decided to say, "Dad, I am not going anywhere today. I am going to be here for Mother and for you." She reached out a hand to pat him on his back.

He looked over at her and smiled. "Your hand is bleeding, girl! Don't get that blood on my new pajamas! Go upstairs and wash your hands at once!"

Thora looked at her hand and saw the shard of clay still pierced in her palm. She did as he asked. She was not provoked by what he said. That was simply the way that he was. He was a mixed up man with pent-up emotions yet had a heart that was good. When she got to the top of the steps she saw that the washroom was empty and realized that this much sought after room was going to be more available from now on seeing that there was one less person living in this household.

    She started to cry. Her Rebecca was gone! She wondered if she would ever see her again. She wondered what would become of her. She prayed for her safety and well-being. Yet, as she finally sat down and had that much needed pee, there was a part of her mind that kept exploring its hidden storage vaults for any information regarding a secret place.

Chapter 6

The Motorized Egg

Thora looked at the clock in the dining room. It was a grandfather clock. Dad had imported the ornate walnut piece from Switzerland several years back. She did not know how much that it would have cost him (or Dearborn Cable if Aunt Faye were right in her allegations), but she imagined that it could not have been cheap. The clock read 4:00 p.m.

There was still no sign of Rebecca. Thora had hoped that her sister would relent on her adventure and come back home to the house that she belonged. But Rebecca still had not returned. She wondered where her sister was. Would she be in town or would she have hit the road and be bound for some big city such as Pittsburgh or Philadelphia? Or perhaps leave the state all together? Even though she spent her entire life with her sister she had to admit that she did not know Becky's mind very well.

It was not that Rebecca was secretive. It was rather that whenever the two girls were together they tended to talk about Thora's problems and not Rebecca's. There was a great deal of truth in Rebecca's comment that it seemed that she was here to serve as a guardian angel to Thora.

But now that guardian angel was gone. Thora had nobody to look out after her. She would have to do the looking out for herself. She wished that she knew her sister better. Perhaps she would have gleaned some clue as to where their 'secret place' was. Did Becky have an actual place in mind or was it just a ploy to give Thora the message that she did not want her to tag along? Thora did not know for certain. But she was leaning towards the latter interpretation. One is usually aware of the secrets that one keeps with another.

About an hour ago her parents went out in the car to ostensibly visit the doctor for her father's head injury and to do some shopping. Thora knew that although they would carry out these obligations they would have their eyes wide open searching for their runaway girl. She hoped that they would find her.

While they were gone they gave her some chores to do around the house. There were weeds daring to rear their ugly little heads in the flower gardens. Thora was to remove them, roots and all. It was a chore that usually was allocated to Rebecca. Becky was the offspring with the gardening trait within her. Thora's household duties tended to be indoors. Dusting was her charge and it became her forte. Even at her tender age she had developed a keen sense of cleanliness and tidiness. To see a thin layer of dust on a piece of furniture would eat at her craw and she could not rest easy until that coat was removed with some good furniture polish.

As for the garden she really had no relish. Many of the plants that her mother identified as weeds seemed to her to be as lovely a piece of creation as the nurtured and spoiled leaves and flowers of those that her mother deigned as worthy to be in her garden. To Thora it seemed at times somewhat arbitrary and she actually felt sorry for the little plants designated as undesirables that were trying to eke out a living in some groomed soil where they did not belong. She could not help but think that perhaps society itself made similar decisions of the worthiness of the individuals that comprised it. Some were to be nurtured and given everything they needed to develop into valuable and elite members of the society while others were to be disregarded and uprooted and left to the elements to decay into nothingness. She knew that she and Rebecca were considered to be part of the elite. They were born into a well-to-do family and they were bestowed with all manner of privilege. They were given the proper grooming that should have steered them onto a course that would have led them into adulthoods where they would have either married tomorrow's leaders and/or perhaps even be leaders themselves, given the vast strides the suffragette movement had attained in even their short years of life.

Yet, something went wrong. They were both showing that they were weeds at heart. Thora was constantly getting into trouble and was not fulfilling the role that she was born into while Rebecca fulfilled the role but had chosen to throw it all away. There was no reason why she should have chosen the desperate and tenuous lifestyle of a runaway. Runaways usually do not make it in society. They are among the first to be plucked by the weeders. Thora thought of the stories that she heard regarding the rural roads and the bad men that travel them. Her sister was at their mercy. Why would she put herself in such a position? Thora prayed that Rebecca would come back.

She was stooped over the front garden picking at something that looked like clover growing amidst the daisies and petunias when she heard the familiar sound of the family car coming up Pine Street. The vehicle was painted yellow and white. Coupled with its oval-shaped cab the car gave Thora the impression of a motorized egg. As soon as she heard it, she jumped up and ran to the driveway. Maybe Rebecca was in it? Maybe Mother and Father had found her?

But when she saw only her parents sitting in the front seat of the motorized egg and nobody sitting back in the rumble seat, her heart sagged. They did not have Rebecca with them. Langley had a patch over his eye that he did not have before.

"You look like a pirate!" Thora exclaimed as the car came to a stop.

Her father grimaced at the remark.

"Your father has a detached retina," her mother explained.

"I will sue that bastard!" Langley growled.

"Uncle Tom?" Thora enquired.

"Don't call that man uncle!" Cora said. "He is no longer married into the family."

"He's a penniless pauper and will not get any of the Meadowford treasure!" Langley added. "But what is the purpose in suing Tom? There's no money to be had from him. But his ex-wife, my sister, will pay for this!"

Rebecca had predicted that her father would act this way. The girl was right on the money.

"You didn't see Becky, did you?" Thora asked.

Neither parent answered her question. They got out of the car and marched inside of the house. Langley was acting like he did not want anybody to see him with the patch. Once they were inside, her father said, "No, we didn't see your sister. Had we seen her we would have dragged her back with us!" He went to a mirror and looked at himself. He adjusted the angle of the black fabric that covered his eye. A small smile came to his face when he had it just right. He stood erect and proud in front of the looking glass.

Thora now understood why her father had acted so clandestinely when leaving the car to get in the house as soon as possible. It had nothing to do with the patch. He was proud of the patch. He wanted to look like a pirate. It was the badge of a warrior. It was something that his friends would admire and appreciate. Her father acted furtively because of her question. He did not want the ears of any prying neighbors to learn that one of the twin girls had chosen to run away from the domestic paradise that he had built.

"That patch looks very dapper, Dad," Thora said, playing up to her father's vanity.

"It makes me look like a buccaneer, doesn't it? Pirate Sam of the H.M.S.S. Grappler!"

"Oh Langley, grow up! You are a flabby, balding businessman. There is as much of the pirate in you as a girl's play doll!" Cora laughed.

Her father did not like the comment. He stroked his hand through his thinning hair and then gave his head a good robust shake to make his hair look thick. "I am thirty-seven years old. I still have hair! If I were to go bald I would have lost it by now." He suddenly lowered his head and his shoulders slumped.

"What is it Langley?" Cora said with concern.

"I shouldn't have done that," he said softly. "I feel dizzy."

Cora stepped up behind her husband and helped support him on his legs. "You are still recuperating from that concussion, my dear. I think that we should get you up into bed."

Thora's father slowly nodded his head in agreement. He allowed his wife to start leading him to the stairs. But before the two of them took the first step, Langley stopped. He slowly lifted his head and looked over at his remaining daughter. "By the way, girl, you had better start getting ready for your dinner appointment."

"Dinner appointment?" Thora said with surprise.

Her mother answered for her father. "We bumped into a few people while we were uptown. I will tell you all about it after I get your father to bed."

As her two parents waddled their way up the stairwell, Thora wondered about her mother. This was a direct about-face from the position that she held this morning. Back then she was vehemently opposed to the idea of Thora visiting with Mrs. Margaret Whattam. She even hung up the phone on the woman. What had made her change her mind? Her mother's face betrayed no sign that she had eaten crow. Yet she must have. One does not make a 180-degree turn in opinion without eating some black bird.

When her mother came back downstairs she was holding a handkerchief to her eyes, as if she were expecting some tears. This disconcerted Thora. "Is everything all right?" she asked. She was immediately worried about her father's health. She wondered what news the doctor had given her parents besides that Langley had a detached retina.

"Everything is fine," her mother sniffled as she walked toward the dining room and sat upon one of the sturdy chairs. "Your father is not well, Thora. He was weakened by the injuries he sustained yesterday by that hooligan and now he has to cope with the heartache and distress of a daughter gone awry. I have seen this kind of thing before. It can reduce a strong hale man to a weak, frail creature at death's door so fast that it would make your head spin."

"My goodness!" Thora blurted. "Is Father dying?" She had not expected that such a possibility could be looming so closely.

"Not yet, he isn't," Cora said. "The doctor said that in a matter of a week your father would be back on his feet and as healthy as ever."

"Then why do you say such a thing?" Thora cried. She tried to control her emotions. She did not want the fiasco of this morning to repeat itself.

"It's because I don't trust doctors. They have no understanding of all the damage a broken heart can do to a body. Your dad's life has been shattered because of all the stress you and your sister have inflicted upon him. First, it was yesterday when you were missing the entire day. And now it is Rebecca who has decided to become a vagabond. These things take a toll on a man's health. A part of his heart was dying yesterday when you were gone. It did not have a chance to fully recover before that unappreciative sister of yours so selfishly decided to fly the coop. That part of his heart is now dead."

Thora realized that her mother was talking melodramatically and that all of her suppositions did not hold much basis in reality. The only real thing happening here was that her mother was building up the rationale for why she would soon be getting a drink. Yet, there was no reason to provoke her mother with accusations that she was being too nonsensical with what she was conjecturing. "I miss Becky too. I wish that she would come home as well," Thora said, putting her hand on her mother's back and gently patting it.

"If she comes back things will not be the same," her mother answered. "The rules are going to change around this house. You and your sister have been given way too much freedom and in appreciation for the liberties that we have given the two of you all that we get in return is distress and turmoil. It is enough to drive a person to drink." She suddenly got off the chair and went to the dark oak cabinet where her decanter of sherry sat begging for her attention.

When Thora saw this her heart sagged. The cycle was set in motion again. The sherry glass would not leave her mother's hand until she was so intoxicated that she could no longer remain conscious. But today she did not have to watch this ritual into deterioration. Today she would be able to leave the house for some time and perhaps by the time that she got home her mother would be in her stupor blaring her snores on the sofa in the living room.

"I'm sorry for having to put you and Dad through the trauma yesterday. Much of it was not my fault but I should have demanded that Aunt Faye drive me home," Thora said as she watched her mother pour her glass.

Cora acted like she did not hear the apology. She took a sip from the glass and smacked her lips before replacing what she removed with another pour from the decanter. "Yes, the rules are going to change around here. From now on any daughter of mine that lives under this roof will never be away from the house more than two hours without at first reporting to us her whereabouts and then asking our permission for any extension in the absence. You are to be home before dark."

In the back of her mind Thora thought that these new rules that were nothing but a reiteration of the old rules were not so bad. It was summertime. It stayed light out to almost ten o'clock at night. Yet, she knew that her mother was expecting some sign of disappointment in her, so she did let loose a heavy sigh that conveyed this notion to her mother.

"These rules go into effect as of now. You will be back from your dinner with that woman by 8:00 p.m.," Cora said as she returned to the dining room table where Thora still sat.

Thora noted the term 'that woman'. It told her that her mother had not warmed up to the idea of her daughter spending time with Mrs. Whattam. The permission to attend this dinner must have come from her father. Her mother was only bowing to the seat of authority in the household.

"If you want to know the truth, Mom. I don't really want to go. Mrs. Whattam is a stranger to me and I don't like being in the company of strangers," Thora said.

"Well, it is a little too late for that, young lady!" Cora snapped. How her personality changed whenever drink touched her lips! "You are going and that is that!"

"Tell me, how did this come about?" Thora asked, reminding her mother that she had promised to give an explanation upon her return from getting Dad to bed.

Her mother rolled her eyes. She took a sip from her sherry. "We bumped into Reverend Barton at the clinic. He told us about his sermon of family at the funeral service and how he has asked you to become representative of this in our congregation. How you get yourself into these kind of things, I don't know!" Cora shook her head. "Your father, being the decent man that he is, told the Reverend that he thought that it was a wonderful idea and that the Meadowford clan were proud to be chosen in this endeavor into community."

Thora could picture the scene clearly in her mind. She could see her father kowtowing to the Reverend and behaving that there was nothing more important in the world to him than the Church and the well-being of those that attended it. She saw the hypocrisy in his face. Had she been there she would have hung her head low in shame of him.

"The Reverend then told us of how Mrs. Whattam immediately demanded that she be first in line for these social visits. He asked your father if he approved of this engagement and your father at once said that he did," her mother smirked. She too must have recognized the phoniness in her husband's behavior.

"But you told Mrs. Whattam that I would not be going," Thora cut in. "I thought that the dinner plans were off."

"I'm getting to that Thora! Don't be so impatient!" Cora sizzled, shaking her head and mumbling something to herself that Thora could not quite hear. She took another pull from the sherry. "After we parted ways with Reverend Barton, we went for a drive to the market to pick up a few things. Who should we bump into but Mrs. Whattam herself! Langley at once asked her if she were shopping for items for tonight's dinner. She answered that she was not aware that the dinner was still on. I had to tell her that there must have been some confusion because I had believed that you were talking to one of your less reputable girlfriends who had called requesting that you sleep over at her place this night."

Thora wondered if Mrs. Whattam bought into the lie. The woman would have overheard all the talk that went on between mother and daughter before the unceremonious hang up. If Mrs. Whattam did accept Cora's version then she was more of the fluffy-brained fool than Thora would have believed.

"So you better start getting ready for dinner, Thora. You will be there precisely on time. You will not be late. You will be an example to the rest of the congregation of how seriously we Meadowfords observe our obligations. Now start getting ready!" Her mother gave a peremptory signal that this conversation was over and that Thora had better not say another thing.

Thora did have other things to say. She observed much. She knew that her mother was not telling her the truth. If her parents went to the market how is it that when they returned home there was nothing carried out of the motorized egg? But Thora chose not to say anything. It was best to live the lie and get prepared for an engagement that she could hardly wait to be finished and over with.

Chapter 7

Apple Grove Court

From the outside the Whattam home displayed all of the accoutrements one would expect from a couple that could be described as being part of the 'Nouveau Riche'. James Whattam was Uncle Thaddeus' chief legal advisor and apparently prospered quite nicely from this relationship with the old man judging by the brand new house that he had built on an empty lot on Apple Grove Court. The neighborhood was reserved for Grappling Haven's well-to-do. Uncle Thaddeus himself lived on this cul de sac. But Uncle Thaddeus' house was austere in fitting with his miserly character. It was nothing compared to the sumptuous estate erected by his legal advisor. The house was twice as large as the residence owned by Langley Meadowford. Thora recalled how this used to irk her father but now with her grandfather dead, she knew that her dad had his designs on inheriting Sambo's regal residence once the will was read. Sambo also lived in this neighborhood but he lived on Cherokee Hills. Cherokee Hills was where the cream of the crop of the town lived. Thora was not so sure that she wanted to live there. Grandfather's house always felt intimidating. Some said that the ghost of the original Samuel Angus Meadowford, the man that built the house on Cherokee Hills and the summer retreat on Black Island, haunted it. Ghosts scared her.

She walked up the marble path through tall stands of yellow flowers and azaleas to the double doors surrounded by opaque glass. Beside the twin doors was an Oregon bench neatly decorated with morning glories winding their way through the narrow slats. Thora took hold of the brass doorknocker and let it rap out its sound inside.

A moment later Margaret Whattam appeared at the door. Upon seeing what the woman was wearing, Thora immediately felt overdressed. Her mother had forced her to wear a long navy skirt with a white blouse and a necktie. It was a very warm outfit and unsuitable for the temperatures of a Grappling Haven summer's evening. Mrs. Whattam on the other hand wore only an orange bathing suit under a white terry cloth cover. On her head she had a huge straw hat with a strawberry print upon it.

"Well hello Miss Meadowford," the blonde-haired woman beamed as she opened the door. "I am very honored that we can have this visit afterall."

Thora never liked being called Miss Meadowford. At once she wanted to set the record straight. "Please call me Thora," she said.

"And you can call me Margaret," Mrs. Whattam responded with a smile revealing a set of teeth that were impeccable in coloration and dimension. "There is no need for formalities here. I believe that formality is what forces people to stay apart. We need more familiarity in our lives, not formality. That is what I hope to gain through this visit. If everybody became friends there would be no such thing as enemies."

Thora could see that the woman was eyeing her clothes. "Mother, forced me to put these on," she said defensively. "They are far too hot for such a day."

"They are not what I would wear in a swimming pool," Margaret commented, still smiling and being overwhelmingly friendly.

"You have a swimming pool?" Thora was surprised. Not many households in town possessed such a luxury. Her awkward feelings were quickly diminishing. She was beginning to feel that she was going to enjoy this visit rather than just endure it.

"We do and you and I are going to go swimming!" Margaret smiled. "I think that I might have a bathing suit that will fit you! Come in and take a look around while I dig up something for you to wear while we swim!"

Thora stepped through the door and found herself in a hall that she could swear would be able to fit her entire Pine Street house. The Meadowford home was by no means small. It was grand in scale when compared to the clapboard shanties in the working districts of town but it was dwarfed by this gigantic house that bordered on being described as a mansion. Where did the Whattams get such money?

"Some people find my house imposing because of its size but to me I like airy places and I hate to feel cramped," Margaret admitted. "Sometimes when I look around this hall I get the feeling that I am outdoors."

Thora knew what the woman meant. The walls were painted in an evergreen shade and the high ceiling bore the color of the daytime sky. There were even wisps of white through it giving the illusion of light cirrus clouds. The sparse furniture in this greeting room was comprised of a series of intricate tables with twisting, almost eldritch legs that gave the impression of gnarly mangrove roots. Upon these tables were a variety of plants of differing size. These were not tropical in nature but rather seemed to be the ferns that one would find in the forests of Pennsylvania. The hall truly was an extension of the outdoors.

"Follow me," Margaret said and she proceeded to give the girl a tour of the home. The woman was bubbling with pride in her decorative accomplishments and seemed to have forgotten that she was going to try and find Thora a bathing suit.

Even though she really did not want to be guided through this domestic museum, Thora did find that she was quite enthralled by what this woman had accomplished in here. She had managed to create a whimsical fairyland within this structure. It was divorced from the customary formal settings that one was to find elsewhere in the stuffy homes of the Grappling Haven ruling class. In many ways this house was what one would expect in the land of make believe and not in the world of cold hard reality.

"Where do you get your ideas from?" Thora asked. She had never seen anything quite like this. She had never even believed that such poetry could exist within the interior of a house.

"I go with my moods," Mrs. Whattam responded. "Nature is not about right angles and rectangular shapes. It is not even about perfect circles. Nature is about flow and weave and that is what I want to capture within my home. It gives me a very primordial comfort. I think it must reach back to our arboreal roots in our deep primitive past when we were tree dwellers."

Thora nodded. She did not really know what the woman was trying to precisely say. All that she knew was that the house exuded an atmosphere that was unlike anything that she experienced before. The walls oozed with nurturing comfort. She was quickly realizing that they were an extension of the character of the woman herself. Mrs. Margaret Whattam was not like the other adult women that she met. There was something different about her, something that did not make her better than the other ladies, but something that set her apart and made her seem that she did not quite belong in the crusty society that she was forced to endure given her husband's drive for upward mobility.

"Tell me Thora, do you believe in evolution?" Mrs. Whattam suddenly asked.

Thora was surprised by the question. She had not expected such a topic. It seemed to her that it came out of nowhere. "I haven't given it much thought," Thora answered. "Why do you ask?"

"I really don't know why I would ask," Margaret replied. "I just get the feeling from you that you are not fully given over to the convictions that others possess at the Church."

"What's this got to do with Church?" Thora was beginning to get confused.

"Church tells us that God created the heaven and the earth and mankind. It says that God made man in His image." Mrs. Whattam seemed a little uncomfortable in broaching the subject.

"Yes, yes, I know that from Sunday school. What does this have to do with evolution?"

"How old are you Thora? Thirteen? You are coming into your adulthood. Adolescence is a time to ask questions and come up with your own decision on what you accept or reject."

Thora did not know where the woman was going with this conversation. She seemed as fluffy-brained as her mother had described her.

"Evolution does not say that we were created in God's image. Evolution says that we are the descendants of monkeys and apes. It does not give any room for divine intervention in our design. It says that we are of Nature and not of the ethereal heavens. When I am outdoors in the forest or even when I am here in my house, I can feel nature running through me. The leaves of the trees and the flowers of the fields call to me in such an intimate way that I know that I must be rooted in them rather than in some perfect paradise that feels very alien and contrary to my inner self. If life in the clouds listening to angels play harps is the quintessential description of Paradise then I feel that I must belong elsewhere than there. Give me a life amid the trees and I will not beg you for more. That is my heaven. What is your heaven Thora?"

The girl did not know what to say. She had not expected to be placed in the position of having to describe her perfect world. But then images of Pioneer Lake started to creep into her mind. The majesty of Black Island standing as a pillar against the relentless waves that pounded its shoreline seemed to be an enduring symbol to her of what eternity should look like. The peacefulness of the evening sitting upon the great dock in the lee of the island watching a family of geese quietly swimming along the shoreline conjured such warm feelings in the girl that she could not think of anything more idyllic. To know that her grandfather and her departed cousin Jack were sitting on the Adirondack chairs behind her made the image all the more meaningful and poignant to her. And to have her sister Rebecca beside her made the image the ultimate expression of what Heaven was all about.

But Thora chose not to reveal these images to Mrs. Whattam. All that she said to the woman was that she had never given Heaven much thought.

"Well, you are young. Heaven should be a long way off for you, yet," Mrs. Whattam responded. "There is one more room in this house that I want to show you. I saved it for last as it is a special room to me."

"And then we can go swimming?" Thora answered. She was not much in the mood to see more in this house. It was cast too far adrift from her conjectures of reality.

"And then we go swimming," Margaret Whattam said with a smile. She opened a door and Thora saw the stairs that led to a basement. She could feel the chill in the air rush up to her.

"We are going to the basement?" she asked. It was a very peculiar place to be taking a houseguest. The basement back home had a cement floor but that was as far as it went to addressing any amenities of comfort that a normal person would desire.

"It is down there where I feel my creative energies flow," Margaret said, flicking a switch to light up this downward stairwell in the house.

With the flood of light Thora noted that this was just not another concrete basement. The winding stairwell leading to it had wood paneling with a huge angled mirror upon its bend that previewed what to expect when one reached the bottom. From what Thora could see in the mirror was a place lit by dozens of candles. It possessed a very bewitching and ominous atmosphere that was extremely incongruent to the light airy feeling of the floors above it.

"I am an artist at heart," Margaret said, taking the girl by the hand and leading her down the steps. "I love to paint."

Indeed as they descended further into the cellar, Thora could start to see the canvases being lit by the candles in the mirror. The paintings appeared to be dark, somber portraits of people. They were not the kind of art that she would have expected from this woman.

The first picture that hung at the bottom of the stairs was of a gray-haired woman with as many wrinkles upon her face as any street map of New York City. Her beady silver eyes appeared to be crying yet there was a mysterious smile pursed on her lips. "This is my grandmother, my mother's mother," Mrs. Whattam said. "I painted this portrait of her just two months before she died. She was not very comfortable posing for the picture. She said that the little stool that she sat upon was giving her piles." The woman laughed.

"You painted this!" Thora was astounded. The work had almost a photographic quality to it. The girl was very impressed with the realistic detail that Margaret went to. She would never have expected the woman to possess such talent.

"It was my third attempt at trying to capture Grandmother's essence. I still don't think that I did a very good job. There was something about Grandmother that remained beyond the brush. Come, let me show you others," Mrs. Whattam walked deeper into the candlelit cellar.

Thora saw that she was in a huge room as large as the living quarters upstairs. The air was cool down here. It was a welcome relief from the foreboding heat that the Pennsylvania summer was inflicting upon the land outside. The cellar was finished. All the walls possessed dark wood paneling and upon most of them were portraits of people that were illuminated by a series of candles beneath them. Most of the paintings were of relatives of Mrs. Whattam. Her mother and father were there. Three of her grandparents were represented. The fourth one was not there since he had died before Mrs. Whattam was born. She was trying to find a photograph or image of him so that she could paint him as well.

There was a painting of an Indian man wearing a tuxedo and top hat. The man looked very strange with his long braided gray hair hanging over the black lapels of the topcoat. "Is he real or did you make him up?" Thora asked.

"Oh, he is very real. He was a full-blooded Micmac that lived in Antigonish, Nova Scotia. Would you believe that he was a well-respected banker in that town? But on the weekend he would return to his reserve and participate in rituals that the townsfolk would absolutely think of as pagan!" Once again Mrs. Whattam chortled. "He was an inspiration to me."

"You lived in Nova Scotia?" Thora asked. She had always noted that Mrs. Whattam spoke somewhat differently than the rest of the people here in Grappling Haven. Her cadence was a little faster and a little more difficult to discern. "That's in Canada, right?"

"I was born and raised there," Mrs. Whattam said. "A part of me will always be there. I'm a Maritimer at heart, Thora."

"How did you end up in Pennsylvania?"

"I met my husband. He was stationed in Halifax when he was part of the U.S. Navy. We fell in love at first sight and before I knew it I was following him all over the country as his Naval career blossomed. We got married in Annapolis while he completed his degree in Law. Eventually we ended up here in Grappling Haven after Thaddeus Meadowford, your great uncle, took James under his wing."

Thora knew from her time at Pioneer Lake that both her grandfather and his brother Thaddeus were Navy men. Her grandfather fought in the Spanish War and took part in the battles in Cuba during the Presidency of Theodore Roosevelt. It was something that he was always very proud of. She recalled seeing him on the rock at Black Island all dressed up in his white uniform. She did not know much of Thaddeus' career. She knew that he was in the Navy as well but he never spoke of it. Perhaps his career was not as distinguished and inspiring as that of his brother. Yet the Navy must have been important for him if he had gone out of his way to hire an ex-sailor as his chief financial advisor.

"I think that we are ready for that swim now," Mrs. Whattam said.

With the coolness of the basement the notion of swimming had all but left Thora's head. She was now more ready for a cozy couch, a fuzzy blanket and a hot cocoa than a plunge into water that would suck out any remnant warmth that she had left in her body. She knew, however, that as soon as they went outside the heat would quickly grow unbearable and that every bone and every ounce of flesh in her would crave the cooling relief of the pool.

As they started towards the stairs, Thora suddenly noticed a picture that she had not seen earlier. Her mouth dropped. She could not believe the subject of the portrait.

"It's him!" she cried out loud.

She must have startled Mrs. Whattam for the woman gasped at her cry.

"It's who?" Margaret said, once she was sure of her breath.

"I don't know who he is but it is him!"

Hanging on a support post in the basement was a portrait of the old man that had rescued her in the dairy field. Thora could recognize that thin, haggard face anywhere. The painting's eyes were as real as the orbs in any living human's face. They seemed to be staring directly into Thora, past her heart and directly into her soul.

Mrs. Whattam lifted her head to gaze at the work of her hands and imagination.

"He's the man that was at Grandfather's funeral and that had offered to serve me dinner just like you did!" Thora said. She could feel her hands trembling. The picture was having a most disconcerting effect upon her.

Margaret released a nervous giggle. "I don't know how that could be, my dear. That man has been long dead."

The basement suddenly became extremely frigid as Thora allowed Mrs. Whattam's words to enter her reasoning faculty. "You painted this picture, didn't you?" she asked.

"Yes, from a photograph given to James by your Uncle Thaddeus. I found the character most intriguing and beguiling. The photograph practically begged me to reproduce it in oil."

"Who is the picture of?" Thora was almost afraid to ask.

"I thought that you would recognize him since he is a relative of yours."

"He is very familiar to me but I cannot place him," Thora admitted, as she studied the features of the portrait's face. She started to see recognizable signatures in it of the Meadowford bloodline. She had not noticed these before. Still she had no idea who the man was.

"From what James tells me that is a picture of your Uncle Thaddeus' father, your great grandfather, I would imagine," Mrs. Whattam announced.

"Samuel Angus Meadowford the First!" the name came out of her mouth in chunks, each one gut wrenching and unbelievable.

Her great grandfather had been dead a very long time. Thora was not sure if the original Samuel even made it to the 1900's. How could she have seen him at the schoolyard, at the cemetery and along that lonely road? He had been dead so long. It could not have possibly been him.

"Are you absolutely sure that is him?" Thora wanted certain confirmation that the portrait was indeed whom Mrs. Whattam purported the picture to be.

"That is who James said it was. I can find you the original photograph and show it to you. I think that someone scrawled the man's name on the back of the photo. I think that I still have that picture. It would be upstairs in a box where I keep all my photographs," Mrs. Whattam said. "You stay here and I will be back in a jiffy."

"No, don't go!" Thora cried. She did not want to be left alone in this basement with that portrait.

"You must have seen pictures of your great grandfather before, haven't you Thora?"

The girl searched her mind. She was not sure if she saw pictures of her great grandfather. Samuel Angus Meadowford the First was the man that had not only built the family retreat on Pioneer Lake but he also had erected that huge estate on Cherokee Hills where her grandfather, Sambo, had lived. When she was younger she had been to that mansion frequently. They had not been there much in more recent years as her father Langley and Sambo's relationship had deteriorated. She knew that there were paintings and pictures in that house and she was pretty sure that some of them were of her great grandfather. But what she seemed to recall was that these were portraits and photographs of the original Sam when he was a younger man and not when he was very old. Some people's appearances change drastically when the years start piling up on them. "I just can't remember," Thora answered Mrs. Whattam. "All that I do know is this is the man that I saw yesterday at the funeral services. You must have seen him too. He was the man that spoke right after you when Reverend Barton began speaking of our Church as family."

"I must not have been paying attention, Thora, for I do not recall anybody speaking after me," Mrs. Whattam responded. "As far as I know I was the only one that took the Reverend up on his offer."

"You had to have!" Thora asserted. She did not want any suggestive insinuation left in the air that she was plagued by demons. "After the old man made his offer Reverend Barton said that before any arrangements could be made the people would have to get my parents' permission."

"He said that after I made my offer," Margaret sighed.

Thora could tell that the woman was questioning her sanity. This did not sit very well with her. She distinctly heard and saw the old man make his offer. Nobody was going to tell her that he was a figment of her imagination. Why would she make up such a character? If she were to make up somebody it would be someone young and dashing like Rudolph Valentino, not some old frail fellow that gave her the willies.

"But then again maybe I was too excited by the notion that you were actually going to be coming to my place and I may have failed to notice what had happened next!" Mrs. Whattam spoke enthusiastically. She was trying to give Thora the unconscious message that she need not concern herself about her delusional state. "As I am excited about going swimming!" she continued. "Let's get out of this cold place and return to the light!"

Thora took one last look at the painting. The face was hauntingly familiar. Could he actually be her great grandfather? The man was creepy looking. She hated to think that someone with such a gloomy atmosphere could be part of her bloodline. Yet this too was the man that she had thought of as her guardian angel. He had saved her from the cows and then disappeared mysteriously. She could hear herself groan. She wished that the supernatural elements of the universe would just leave her alone and allow her to live out a normal life.

As they climbed the stairs, Mrs. Whattam suddenly asked her if everything was all right back at home.

"What do you mean?" Thora asked. She sensed that the woman was about to delve into her family problems. Maybe she thought that Thora's hallucinations were the result of parental abuse?

"I am thinking of when I phoned this morning. I could detect some very tense vibrations coming from your household. Are things between you and your parents good?"

Thora decided then and there that she would not take the woman under her wing. It was none of her business what happened under the roof of Langley and Cora Meadowford.

"Things are great," she said. "I am blessed with the most amazing parents. I count myself lucky to be their daughter. We live in a beautiful home and none of us go for want. Nothing could be better."

They were back on the main floor of the Whattam house. The sun was coming through the large bay windows. Through these windows Thora saw the swimming pool. It was begging her to enter it. It promised her that it would purge her of her troubles. It would cleanse her world and make it anew.

Thora took the pool up on its promise.

Chapter 8

A Moment with Dad

She arrived home at two minutes before eight, two minutes before her curfew. Her hair was still dripping wet from the swim at Mrs. Whattam's. She couldn't remember much of that swim or the frankfurters on the grill that she had afterwards. The conversation that ensued on the patio was an uncomfortable affair where she dodged Margaret's prying questions. The woman seemed to know that things were not quite right in the Meadowford home and that Langley and Cora were tyrants in the house, relentlessly invoking endless cruelty on their two whipped daughters.

But Thora held her ground and did not reveal anything. She championed her parents as pillars of strength, virtue and kindness and truly deserving of the respect that they unquestionably received in the community. She did not tell Mrs. Whattam anything about her missing sister.

And as the girl stepped on the front stoop to the Pine Street house, she made a little wish that Rebecca would be inside. She dared not think that her twin was waiting for her in some place that the two of them deemed as secret. It was so much of a secret that it was a secret to her as well.

She opened the door and announced her return in the hall. She was hoping that her mother would appear from the kitchen with an apron wrapped around her waist and with flour upon her nose. She was hoping that her father would come down the stairs with a big smile on his face and with open arms to give her a grand embrace. She was hoping that Rebecca would call out from the backyard asking her if she wanted to play some croquet. These hopes were the painting that she illustrated to Mrs. Whattam what the Meadowford home was all about.

Yet when there was no return answer to her announcement, she knew that nothing at home had changed. The swim had not cleansed her world and renewed it with love. The silence in the house told her everything. She did not have to go to the living room to see her mother lying drunk in a stupor upon the couch. She knew that she was there. She did not have to go up the stairs and peek into her father's room to see him sleeping in a slouched position. She knew that he was there. She did not have to go to the backyard to look at an empty lawn strewn with croquet wickets beginning to slump. She knew that her sister was not there.

She sighed with disappointment. Life was no longer what it used to be. It had taken some turn along the road. It was no longer heading towards the sunny skies. It seemed to be on a course towards the storm clouds that lie upon the offing.

She slipped off her shoes. It all started to change with the accidental death of her cousin Jack last summer. She missed the lad. She and Rebecca doted over him ever since he entered their lives as a happy, bouncing baby boy. She remembered how her twin and her would dress him up in their clothing and made him do the silliest of things. He never complained and actually got just as much of a laugh out of the antics as they did. He was never cross. He was never given to fits of temper. He was always the same and he could be depended upon to find ways to cheer the two girls up whenever things got uncomfortable between them and their parents. Jack was a blessing in their lives and the day that he died had to be the most painful event that Thora could ever remember. The boy was taken away from them. God must have seen what a delight he was and claimed him for His own. She could imagine Jack up in Heaven amusing Jesus with his good spirits and penchant for making even Paradise a better place.

She smiled walking towards the kitchen as she thought of her cousin. After he left the world began to turn bad for Thora and Rebecca. First was the news that her Aunt Faye and Uncle Tom had split up. Even though her parents were jealous of the Thurstons Thora had to admit that she always admired the couple. She saw that the pain of Jack's death had driven a wedge between Faye and Tom. The splinter grew wider and wider and finally they gave up on each other and decided to go their separate ways. Aunt Faye was never quite the same. She had become eccentric, complicated and dour. She no longer was a sanctuary where the girls could run to whenever they needed somebody, whenever their parents became unbearable with their autocratic and arbitrary rule. The old Aunt Faye would never have left Thora to walk home from the cemetery.

She opened the cupboards looking for something light to chew. Although the frankfurters were filling at the time, she now found that her mouth was craving some change in taste to weaken the overpowering aftereffects of the meat and mustard. She looked into the cookie jar and found some remnants of a batch of butter cookies that her mother must have made recently. She took two of these chunks and bit into one. At least her mother's baking had not soured in the past year.

After the breakup of Tom and Faye the next disaster was the fiasco at Black Island last week. She could not believe that it was only a week ago. She was sure that the big fight between her father and Faye would reverberate for years to come and that the two siblings would never reconcile. Thora could not live a day knowing that there was bad blood between Rebecca and herself. She felt a tremor in her chest cavity for she realized that she was not certain that such hostile conditions did not indeed exist at present. Becky was gone and may have said to Thora that she did not want her in her life any longer. And if they did not exist at the moment, then they surely would come into fruition when Rebecca learns that Thora did not show up at their secret place, wherever that was. Thora took another bite into her cookie to try and chew away this bad feeling.

But bad feelings were everywhere. Her grandfather died. Her mother and father would move closer to divorce if there was a child to be born in New Hampshire. Her sister Rebecca had runaway. And Capers was gone.

The house was very empty without the presence of that pampered tabby gliding from room to room looking for someone to play with. Everybody loved that cat. Even her father did. She remembered how angry he used to get when Capers was a kitten and getting into things that he shouldn't have. Capers had torn apart several of Father's ties and had ripped down the new drapes in the living room that her father had so meticulously hung. But as Capers grew up and slowed down the cat would often perch himself on

Father's lap while he read the Sunday paper. Thora could recall her dad's hand scratching the purring tabby's skull and ears while perusing the business and sports pages.

The girl squeezed her eyes tight to prevent tears from rolling down her face. She could not understand why the family would not go back up to Black Island to retrieve the cat. It was only the second week of July. They had all summer still ahead of them. There was plenty of time and they would have the cottage to themselves. Grandfather was gone now and Uncle Thaddeus and Aunt Faye would not return. Why couldn't she and her parents head back to Pioneer Lake?

She heard a creak on the stairs. She recognized the step as that of her father's. He must have sensed that she had questions for him.

He rounded the corner and came into the kitchen. His hair was frazzled and his housecoat was frumpy and slightly open. Thora could see his boxer shorts peeking out from underneath. His eye patch still gave him the bearing of a buccaneer.

At first he did not acknowledge the presence of his daughter. He seemed fixated to go to the same place that she went to when she entered the room—the cookie jar.

"Hi Dad," she said to him to gain his attention.

"Rebecca?" Langley said with a start that seemed to wake him up from his somnambulism.

"No, it's me Thora," she answered. She was used to people mixing her sister and her up even when the people were her parents. She noticed the disappointment in him when he made the realization that his errant daughter had not returned home as of yet.

"How was your dinner?" he said while biting into a cookie. Before Thora could answer he said, "Your hair is wet."

"We went swimming!" Thora responded in a chirp. "Mrs. Whattam has a swimming pool."

"Some day we will have one too girl," Langley sighed. "We will have a bigger and better one than the Whattams! I promise you that!"

"Our backyard here is hardly big enough for one, Dad. Mother's gardens take up almost all of what little space is there."

"I am not talking about here, girl. I am talking about Cherokee Hills where your grandfather lived. That house is going to be ours some day soon!"

Thora was not so sure of that. She had overheard her parents talking about the legal battle that would occur between them and Aunt Faye over the possession of the estate left by her grandfather, Sambo. Her father believed as he was the eldest of Sambo's children that the house would naturally be left to him and that Faye would get the cottage in Canada. Her mother was not as confident as he was. She believed that her sister-in-law was a bloodsucking vampire that would not rest until all of Sambo's holdings were exclusively hers. She was not comfortable with the knowledge that the final time Langley and Sambo were together happened to be the day of that big fight. Langley scoffed at the idea saying that his father did not have the time to change the will in the few hours that remained to him after the argument.

Grandfather had left a final will that was kept in the offices of his attorney, William King. Mr. King at present was on a Californian vacation but would be back at work by July 18th. Today was July 10th. At the earliest the will would be read in eight days. Thora knew that these would be eight days of torture for her parents as they fretted over the will's contents.

"There's plenty of room there that is for sure," Thora said. "That house is big enough for all of us."

Langley's face beamed at the comment. His mouth was full of cookie but despite this he still said, "Once I get a hold of Dearborn Cable and carry out a few business arrangements the house on Cherokee Hills would be nothing to the mansion that we get afterwards!"

Thora could not imagine a house bigger than her grandfather's place. Moreover she could not see why anybody would desire to move into anything palatial. When it came right down to it this house here on Pine Street was plenty big enough for the family. If she really wanted to go swimming there was always the public pools in town. Besides, to Thora, swimming in a pool could never match swimming in Pioneer Lake. That was the only place that she wanted to swim.

"Are we ever going back to the lake?" she asked, abruptly changing the subject. She did not want to hear about her father's dreams of greed and lust for power.

Langley swallowed the cookie. The smile disappeared from his face. "I told you already girl. Not this summer any more. I have too many things to do. Your grandfather's death has made it an even more complicated summer for me than it originally was."

"But we are still going to New York City, aren't we?" Thora tagged on the heels of her father's answer.

"We'll see. It depends on what happens in Dearborn and the contents of the will," her father said through a yawn.

"But you and Mom promised!" Thora cried out. She did not want to get emotional but found that the emotions were being drawn out of her regardless of what her will decreed.

"That was before your grandfather died. And before Rebecca left. Things have changed, girl. We can't be living by plans set before these events occurred. If there is time and there is money, we will go to the Big Apple, but for now I just can't promise you anything."

His response was reasonable enough, Thora reckoned. She still felt a residual anger dwelling within her. The only thing that would salvage this summer and give her some pleasant memories from it was now an uncertainty. In fact she knew that it was even less than an uncertainty. It was null and void. This was her father's way of telling her to forget about New York City. It wasn't going to happen.

"The cookie is good, isn't it Dad?" she once again changed subjects.

"So good that I am going to have another," Langley answered, digging his hand in the jar once more. "Not many left here, though. I'll have to get your mother to make another batch in the morning."

Thora was finding her little visit with her father comforting. Although he had relayed some upsetting news about the cancellation of the holiday in Manhattan, he had done so in a non-confrontational manner. He seemed somewhat civil. Maybe that concussion had softened his personality?

"Here's one for you," he said, giving her a chunk of a crumbling butter cookie.

She took it from him even though she had her fill of snacking. She knew that it would not be often that her father would act so kindly towards her. "So we are going to move to grandfather's place?" she said, before taking a bite.

"If all goes well, we should. Maybe even before the summer is out!"

"What room would I get there?"

"There are so many there, Thora, you could have two rooms if you like!"

"Your grandfather built that house, didn't he?" Thora realized that she was segueing to a topic that had become vitally interesting to her of late.

"He did not so much as build it but had it designed," Langley answered. "It's the retreat at Black Island that was actually built by the hands of Meadowfords."

"What kind of man was he like?" she asked. "You knew him, didn't you?"

Langley smirked. "What kind of man was my grandfather like? Well," he shrugged his shoulders. "He was a grandfather. He was a man of his times."

"Was he a friendly man like my grandfather or was he distant and aloof like Uncle Thaddeus?"

"He was a little of both, I guess. Why all these questions about him?" Langley asked. He seemed somewhat disturbed. Whether it was the subject that was bothering him or whether it was being forced to have to delay the gratification that his cookie would give him Thora was not sure.

"Just curiosity I guess," she responded.

"Is it because of the rumors that Cherokee Hills is haunted by his ghost?" Langley showed a rare sign of insight into his daughter's motivations.

"I never really thought of that," Thora lied. "I don't really believe in ghosts, anyway."

"Nor do I, girl. Remember we are Meadowfords. We didn't get to our station in life by being superstitious. We are practical people with keen business savvy and a fine finger on the pulse of enterprise. We are not given in to such sensationalized prattle that serves the masses. We are above it. My grandfather certainly was above it. He was the man that raised us above his common peers and built a dynasty that has lasted the generations. He was far too pragmatic of a man to spend his eternity wandering the halls of a house trying to scare the living. There is nothing to be gained by that."

From her father's words Thora began envisioning a man that seemed closer to Thaddeus than Sambo. Langley was painting a picture of a shrewd character that did not do anything unless there was opportunity invested into it. That kind of person seemed incongruent to the self-sacrificing old man that had saved her from the cows. Perhaps that wasn't Samuel Angus Meadowford afterall.

"How long ago did he die?" she asked, just to keep the conversation going.

Her father lifted his head upward to the right as if he were trying to find the answer in that direction. "I wasn't much more than fifteen or so, I guess, when Gramps died."

"You were right around my age then!" Thora said with a stir. "We have something in common then, Dad. We both lost our grandfather at about the same age in life!"

"I guess that we did," Langley smiled.

"Was it tough on you, Dad? I know that it is sad for me to lose my grandfather but in a way you kind of expect these things because they are old."

Langley nodded. "To be honest I hardly remember Gramps' passing at all. One day he was just dead and life carried on from there. But don't get me wrong. I am not belittling the importance of Samuel Angus Meadowford the First. He left a proud legacy in our family. If it hadn't been for him none of us would be where we are right now." He paused and took a nibble at the chunk of cookie in his hand. "Let me reword what I just said. We probably would be in the position that we are in whether the original Sam was a success or not. My father and uncle and I guess I can include myself are driven men that strive to become the cream of the crop. Each one of us would have made it to the top on our own. But thanks to Samuel Angus Meadowford the First we did not have to make that struggle for he placed us at the apex already."

Thora thought that all that you can do once you are at the top is to go downhill. She did not give it voice. It would have stirred up hostility. She kept it silent. "Do you think that Rebecca and I have what it takes to stay on the top as well? We are the next generation."

This question must have caught her father by surprise for he did not expect it. To answer that the girls did not possess that trait that makes a person want to be the ultimate expression of himself or herself would be to admit that he was a failure as a parent. But to answer the question the other way around and to say that the girls had the gusto and the intelligence and the wherewithal to be captains of industry would be an open lie for in the past Langley often made reference to their apparent lack of savvy when it came to venture capitalism.

"Rebecca has thrown it all away," Langley finally said. "By running away and becoming a vagrant dependent on the charity of others, Rebecca has jumped to the bottom of the pool in our culture. It is a long way back to the top and there are so many other swimmers above her that would do anything to keep her down and not allow her to climb above them that I'm afraid that your sister's future is grim."

Thora nodded. She had to agree with her father's assessment. Yet she did not want to give up hope on Rebecca. "Maybe she will be back before too long and before any damage has been done."

"If she were to come back she would have been back by now," Langley said.

"But yesterday I was gone as long as Becky has been but I came back!"

"You never asserted that you were running away like your sister did. The circumstances were different."

"It is not even dark outside yet. Becky could come walking through that door any minute."

"Don't hold your breath, girl. Your sister is not coming back!" There was such finality in Langley's words that Thora immediately recognized that he knew something that she didn't.

"You know something," she said. "You learned something today that you have not told me."

Her father took the last bit of cookie that he had in his hands. He brought it up to his mouth. But before he placed it inside he said, "Today your mother and I went to the train station and made a few enquiries. We learned that a girl fitting Rebecca's description boarded a train today bound for Phoenix, Arizona. Becky is gone!"

"Phoenix, Arizona!" Thora cried out loud. "Why there?"

"You tell me why there," her father responded. "You know your sister better than anybody in the world. Why would she choose to go to such a frontier town?"

Thora had no answer for her father. She and Rebecca had never been to Arizona before. The furthest west that they had been was St. Louis, Missouri on a Christmas vacation a few years back. That was the time when her father was exploring the possibility of buying a warehouse there. That deal fell through when Uncle Thaddeus would not give his nephew the financing. It was the first financial recommendation made by his new advisor, James Whattam.

"Is it that secret place that your sister mentioned to you just prior to her leaving?" her father asked another question before Thora could address the first.

"Our secret place?" she said out loud.

"Yes, your secret place!" Langley's demeanor became more forceful and more tinged with anger. He was becoming himself again.

"We don't have a secret place!" Thora responded. "When Becky said that I had no idea what she was talking about! I have been searching my mind all day long trying to figure out where she meant."

"So that you can run off and join her!" Langley's face was growing downright ugly.

But Thora could see that this anger was based on the man's pain inside. Langley Meadowford may be a cad and a self-serving opportunist but he loved his daughters. "No!" she crowed. "I was not thinking of joining her. I just was trying to figure out where she meant!"

She threw her arms over her father's shoulders and embraced him tight. "I would never leave you and Mom, Dad! This girl is happy right here! I don't need to go to Grandfather's house or to Phoenix, Arizona!"

Langley could have held his daughter tight and could have thanked her for her display of devotion and commitment to the family. But he didn't. He pushed her off. "You're lying to me! You are conniving! You chose to be with my sister rather than me in my hour of need! You got yourself involved with my scourges, the Whattams! And I know that as soon as you get a chance you will fly off to join your sister in that forsaken desert!"

"If you keep acting like that, Father, you will drive me off to Arizona!" she hissed. She felt terribly rejected and could feel scorn grow like a cancer within her heart. This man was impossible to love. Yet, she knew that flying off into a fit would not improve matters here. She had no desire to leave. She wanted to stay here with her parents until the day she gets married. "All I am saying to you Dad is that you brought this girl up right. I have a good head on my shoulders and am not given to flights of reckless behavior. Please don't push me away. I am on your side." She knew that she was crying. She could hear it in her voice. She knew that her father looked upon tears as weakness and that they would only serve to make him more aggressive and hurting.

"My head is killing me," he mumbled through his cookie, placing his hand on his temple. "I've got to get back to bed." He never addressed her comments. He walked past her and a moment later she could hear him plodding his way up the stairs. He was saying something to himself but she could not distinguish the words.

She stayed in the kitchen a few moments longer and rehashed the conversation in her head. Where did it go wrong? It had started gentle enough. It even showed promise of becoming a special moment that she would remember the rest of her life as the day that she and her father finally communicated. But then it all deteriorated and fell apart and became yet another ugly incident in a string of many that displayed the inadequacy of character in him. There was something inside of the man that made him choose to act reprehensibly and to shun any affection. She hoped that whatever it was that it was not inside of her as well.

She went up to her room, leaving her mother snoring on the couch. Cora would eventually find her own way up. She would cough and stumble and wake up the household. That ugly thing in Langley was the thing that made this woman drink.

Chapter 9

Family Photos

    The next four days were quiet in the Pine Street house of Langley and Cora Meadowford. The three remaining occupants that resided here did much to try to avoid each other and stay out of each other's hair.

    Cora never showed any curiosity on how Thora's night with Margaret Whattam had went. She just asked a few cursory generic questions and never sought to probe deeper into the matter. It was like she just wasn't interested or rather she did not want to know lest she opens up some skeletons in her closet. The woman was aloof and kept to herself. She tended to her husband's needs but hardly interacted with him. Thora could not overhear any secret, quiet talk that occurred between the two.

    Langley, as well, did not say much. He never brought up the argument that he had with Thora on that night after the visit with the Whattam woman. He spent most of his time cloistered in his room going over the business pages and jotting down notes. The only time that he showed any kind of character above that of a slug was when his cronies would call over the telephone to see how he was doing. When they called, Langley would suddenly become animated and seem as spunky and vibrant as an energized salesman ready to make the big sale. Thora would hear him boast about how he had successfully read the trends in the Stock Market and that he was predicting that there was going to be such an economic boom in the fall that the nation would see years of unimagined prosperity ahead for itself. Her father lived for the Stock Market. Its pulse was more vital to him than anything that occurred under his roof or under his skin. She knew that he was secretly waiting for a bonanza of cash to come his way as part of the settlement of Sambo's will. This money he was looking to invest and to become rich beyond his dreams, beyond the dreams of any Meadowford. Yet, as soon as his telephone conversation would end with his friends, he would return to his dark, pensive character and shun the others in the house as if they were the plague.

As for herself, Thora spent most of her time doing the chores around the house. Her mother did not even have to ask her to do them. She just proceeded to dust, wax and polish on her own. It was a routine, a comforting routine that allowed her to try and forget the overwhelming sadness that was veiled over the house.

Everybody was missing Rebecca but no one said it. Thora felt incomplete without her sister's presence. Had Rebecca been here things would not have ostensibly been that much different but the emptiness would not have been as pervading. Every item in the house was colored by Becky. Everything could somehow be associated with her. The telephone that hardly rang any more, outside of the few calls for Langley, used to be constantly in use as Rebecca made her daily round of phone calls to her network of friends. These friends did not call here for they were all afraid to get Mr. or Mrs. Meadowford on the line. Her parents had a reputation in Grappling Haven of being nasty and prying when it came to the affairs of their daughters.

Thora was not as gregarious as her sister and was not apt to make calls on her own. She allowed Becky to be the twins' social convener and to allow her to make all the arrangements for activities and amusements. Thus, she did not call upon or be called upon by the assortment of similarly aged girls in the neighborhood. She spent her time by herself. It did not bother her to be alone. She found that her thoughts often were all the company that she needed. They could take her to places that her friends would never go.

One thought that was recurring over and over again was that of her great grandfather, Samuel the First. She had come across a photo album that her parents kept in a drawer in the living room. Although she had studied the pictures many times before she never tired of gazing upon them. It seemed that each time that she looked her goal was different. She never made it her purpose to seek images of her great grandfather before. She decided that she would put down her dust rag and seat herself on the sofa and hunt for some pictorial evidence of Sam the First.

But as she went through the fifty pages of photographs all neatly held in place by corner fitters upon thick charcoal vellum she discovered that most of the photographs stemmed from her mother's side of the family, the Wrights. The Meadowford pictorial history was hardly present at all. She knew that it was not that these pictures of her father's side did not exist for she had seen lots of photographs both at her grandfather's place and at Aunt Faye's. It seemed that Langley was left out of the loop when it came to photographic heirlooms. There were perhaps only a handful of pictures in the album of her father when he was a boy and most of these were taken at Pioneer Lake.

He was a gangly lad with awkwardly stretched limbs. He seemed to be the kind of child that could race up a tree with the agility of a spider but Thora knew different. Her father was not athletically inclined. He was accident-prone and had broken his legs twice before he was twelve-years old. His gait to this day still bore testament to improperly healed bones.

The Black Island retreat was under construction back in those days when these pictures were taken. The marvelous additions that Sambo and Thaddeus constructed were just framed timbers and studs that were erected around the existing building made by Samuel the First in these photographs. In the pictures Thora could identify her grandmother. She hardly knew this woman as she drowned shortly after the twins were born. Although Thora would never admit it to anybody, there was something about Grandmother Meadowford, June Ritchey was her maiden name, that made her feel creepy. Perhaps it was nothing more than the fact that this woman was dead most of her life that made her feel this way. She lived in the realm of the afterlife, a place where Thora was in no hurry to reach.

She could also recognize the two young men in the pictures. Both had bushy hair and powerful physiques. These were the brothers Sambo and Thaddeus. They looked so young and strong back then. They were so full of life that it saddened Thora to think of where they were now—Sambo freshly in his grave and Thaddeus, a weary spent looking man still struggling to build his empire.

There were children in the pictures as well. She could easily identify her father and her Aunt Faye. Faye appeared like a fairy princess back then. She seemed to always be dressed in wonderful clothing that gave elegance to the feral landscape that surrounded her. The other children she did not know and could not lend names to their faces. These were the offspring of Thaddeus. All that she knew was that by the time that they reached adulthood they all had moved to Europe with their mother and were not heard of again. Thora had learned through her mother that Mrs. Thaddeus Meadowford, nee Barbara Truscott, had met a man named Higgins and quickly fell in love with him. Barbara dropped Thaddeus like a glove and was whisked off to Germany where Mr. Higgins conducted his business. This was prior to the Great War. Although no one knew for sure it seemed that the newly married Higgins and her brood of children had fled Germany prior to the breakout of hostilities and that they made their home in Ireland during the war years. That was all that Cora knew about the fate of Uncle Thaddeus' missing family. It was assumed that most if not all of them were still living.

The only person that was missing in these pictures of that bygone era was Samuel Angus Meadowford the First. Perhaps he was the photographer and it was his eye that captured these images.

Her purpose for studying the photographs was unsuccessful but as often is the case another mission came into existence. Thora became engrossed by the pictures of the Wright family, her mother's side. They did not come from the same high pedigree of the Meadowfords. In fact they were little more than commoners with a strong will to climb using the most expedient methods. Cora and Myra, the two daughters of Alan and Helen Wright, both married for money. At least that was what was claimed by their brothers Brent and Carl. Brent and Carl Wright both now lived in Pittsburgh and worked at the steel mills there. They hardly associated with their sisters whom they looked upon as nefarious gold diggers. The sisters in turn looked upon their brothers as pariahs and did as much as possible to dissociate themselves from them.

The photographs revealed that Myra and Cora were lookers when they were young and that they could easily catch the eye of any young man with their beauty and their charm. Grandmother and Grandfather Wright had made sure that their daughters were given all the grooming that they required to permit them to comfortably enter the world of the well to do, much to the chagrin of the two boys, both of whom were forced to leave their education early despite promising academic records. The girls were sent to expensive finishing schools and acquired all the social skills that would make them much sought after debutantes.

Myra, the older of the two, was an exceptional and rare beauty. She was so gorgeous in fact with her flowing raven hair that her parents arranged for her to travel to New York City where she spent two years as a fashion model. Her face adorned several of the magazines of the era, as she became the visual representative of companies hocking a variety of wares mostly in the home appliance industry. Indeed, one of the pages in the photo album was a cut out of a Harper's Bizarre magazine from 1908 where Myra stood with a big smile on her face in front of a kitchen counter where she was inserting some bread into a brand new toaster. The motto beneath the picture read, "Toast In Two Minutes!"

Myra's career as a model was cut short when she had become pregnant out of wedlock. She swiftly married the father, a New York City police officer, but the marriage was annulled after Myra had miscarried. With her career tainted by the scandalous pregnancy, Myra returned to Pennsylvania with her tail between her legs. Thora and Rebecca were not to know about this grim period in their aunt's life but their mother revealed it to them on one of those many occasions when the two Wright sisters had a falling out. Cora demanded that her girls never let Aunt Myra know that they were aware of her earlier life. To Aunt Myra the only history that her nieces knew of her was that after her highly successful career as a model on Fifth Avenue she came back home to marry her childhood sweetheart, Stuart Murphy, Uncle Studz to the girls.

Uncle Studz was every girl's dream of the ideal man. He was athletic. He was rugged. He was smart. And beyond this he was rich. Uncle Studz came from a family of old money. His grandparents were pioneers in the steel industry. In fact the two Wright boys, Brent and Carl, worked in a mill owned by the Murphy family. It was Myra who got her brothers jobs in the Pittsburgh foundry but she would not do anything more for them. They could not be automatically given positions in management despite the fact that their brother-in-law was sitting on the Board of Directors by the time he was twenty-five.

For the first five years of their marriage no couple could be happier than Stuart and Myra Murphy. They had it all. They had lavish vacations on both sides of the Atlantic Ocean. They did it all. They saw the seven wonders of the Earth. Then when Myra had her third late-term miscarriage by Uncle Studz and she failed to drop the weight from the pregnancy things started to change for the couple. Myra fell into a deep depressive state due to the miscarriages and was sent at her husband's behest to a sanitarium for a period to help her recuperate. By the time that she returned, Uncle Studz was openly cavorting with other women and showed no signs of trying to make his marriage work. Shortly thereafter the couple parted and went their separate ways. For some reason Stuart and Myra Murphy never divorced and Aunt Myra still carries his name and still lives well off of his beneficences.

Thora had met her Uncle Studz many times. He was one of her father's friends and golfing associates. He lives on Cherokee Hills in a house that would rival Sambo's in grandeur. His relationship with Myra had not entirely cooled. Thora heard her mother remark that her sister was one of many women in the stables of this womanizer. In fact the twins were not to call him Uncle Studz to his face. It apparently was a derogatory nickname that Cora had concocted for him due to his carnal proclivities. The girls were to call him Uncle Stuart or just Uncle Stu whenever they were in his company or even when they talked about the man with their father. Langley would not have approved of his daughters calling his friend a stud.

After her second failed marriage no one courted Aunt Myra again. Her looks were long gone. She was on the verge of being described as stout. Her long raven hair of her youth now was cropped short and was more gray than black despite the fact that she was only forty-years old. She was well on her way to becoming one of those blue-haired society women that travel the charity and church circles sticking their noses into the business of others.

Thora did not much like her Aunt Myra. This was an attitude that she did share in common with her mother. Cora secretly and sometimes openly despised the woman. The woman had always told Cora that she could do better than Langley Meadowford. Langley may be from a rich family but he was the kind that would soon squander everything that was given to him and then Cora would be forced to wallow in the mire, as the man's weakness and ineptitude would sink them further into poverty. Cora believed that her husband was of better stock than that. She took no time at all to tell her sister upon her return from the sanitarium to find Uncle Studz roaming with other women that Langley would never do such a thing to her. Langley possessed character. He was not depraved like Stuart.

Thora closed the photo album on her lap and thought about the allegations that Aunt Faye made at Pioneer Lake. If they were true then Langley was no better than Uncle Studz. Who knows? Given their friendship, maybe it was Uncle Studz that encouraged her father to go after some stuff on the side. Like her sister, Cora had lost some of her qualities that made her fair and beautiful in her youth. Age took its toll. Her hips were excessively wide and her bottom bulged out like she had a pair of pillows sutured in her buttocks under her skin. Her face still retained traces of the fine features of her youth but the increasing years and her addictions to alcohol and tobacco had hardened these features. She hardly represented the attractive trophy her husband wanted to flaunt into the faces of others as evidence of his success in life.

Did age have a similar fate in store for her, Thora wondered. She was now a blossoming woman and she saw how the boys in class now seemed to pay her more attention than they did a few years previously. She knew that she and Rebecca were pretty. But how long would that last? Cora and Myra were pretty as well but now they had faces that looked tired and old sitting on top of misshapen and flabby bodies. Was this what she had to look forward to in twenty years?

Before she could give the matter further thought the telephone rang. Thora lifted her head to see if either her mother or father were making their way to it. Neither were anywhere in the vicinity. Reluctantly, the duty to respond fell upon Thora's shoulder. She got up and placed the photo album upon the seat that she occupied.

The phone rang a third time.

"For crying out loud Thora! Would you answer that damn thing!" her mother's voice shouted from the top of the stairs.

Thora picked up the receiver, "Hello."

"Is this Thora or Rebecca?" an ancient hesitant voice said from the other side. Thora immediately recognized the voice as that of Uncle Thaddeus.

"It's Thora."

"May I speak to your father at once?" Uncle Thaddeus sounded demanding and showed no inclination to talking nicely to his grandniece.

"Just one moment," Thora said. She pulled the receiver away from her mouth and called out in a loud voice, "Dad, it's for you!"

A second later she heard her father cry out, "Who is it?"

"It's Uncle Thaddeus! He wants to talk to you."

There was the grinding sound of some furniture being dragged along the bedroom floor upstairs. Shortly thereafter came the familiar thumping cadence of her father's steps.

He came around the corner and even though it was four in the afternoon the man was still dressed in his pajamas and housecoat. He no longer was a pirate as the doctor removed the eye patch the prior day. A moment afterwards Cora rounded the corner. She was tightening up her housecoat. She looked almost as messed up as her husband. Thora wondered what the two of them were doing upstairs.

Langley pushed his way past his daughter and grabbed the dangling phone. "Uncle Thaddeus?" he said. "Are you back from Michigan?"

Thora watched her father's head nod. She could faintly hear Thaddeus' voice come through the tinny speaker of the telephone but she could not make out anything that he said.

"That will be fine," Langley said. The complexion of his skin had paled. Something disturbing must have been said. "We will see you shortly. We will have dinner ready for you. Bye bye."

As he hung up the phone, Cora immediately said to him, "What was all that about?"

"Start cooking woman," Langley said. "We're having two dinner guests."

Cora lowered her eyebrows in a disapproving response. She was disheveled and as awful looking as Thora had ever seen her. "Who's the second guest?"

"Jim Whattam," Langley gritted his teeth. It was no secret that he despised that man. Uncle Thaddeus' advisor had thwarted him many times in the past.

"What time are they getting here?" Cora appeared restrained as if she were assessing all of the damage that the phone call created.

"In about an hour," Langley responded, his eyes roving as if he too were trying to get a measure of what was coming their way.

"You can't expect me to cook up a feast in such short notice!" Cora suddenly blurted. "And look at me for crying out loud! It looks like a tornado hit me. It is going to take me at least that long to get ready. Thora, go into the kitchen and start cooking!"

Thora gulped. She had a feeling this was going to be thrown her way. "Cook what?"

"I don't know!" Cora seemed exasperated. "Just pull out something from the fridge and start cooking! I have got to get ready."

Thora went to the kitchen and looked into the refrigerator. She had no idea what she was looking for. She was sizzling inside. She only rarely had been called upon to make dinner in the past and on those occasions she always had Rebecca to help with the duties. And now her mother was leaving her with the awesome responsibility of fixing up a hurried meal for family and guests! And one of the guests was the most discriminating and opinionated man that she had ever met. Uncle Thaddeus would find fault with the finest of meals from the menu at the Park Plaza Hotel in New York. He would declare holy war on any of the meager offerings that this fridge before her contained let alone the sophomoric cook who had to improvise the dinner.

The only meat that she found suitable and that was in sufficient quantity to serve was the spicy sausage that her father liked. Even though her mother and her stomach would greatly protest the aftereffect of the meat, she saw that she had little choice. It was the only meat that could be cooked still frozen. Everything else would require hours of thawing.

She went to the vegetable pantry and pulled out what she deemed to be enough potatoes, beets, onions, carrots, green beans, and cauliflower. She had no idea what she was going to concoct but she believed that whatever it was it would be made up of these ingredients.

She turned on the stove elements to their highest setting. She threw the sausages into a frying pan and placed them on the burner. While they started to cook she set about the task of peeling the potatoes. She never was any good at this. She never developed the knack in slicing the skins closely. She found that she was chopping off great pieces of edible potato as she peeled. But it would have to do. She was nervous and she was rushed. And she did not know how many potatoes that she needed. After peeling the third one, she believed that she had enough. She threw a large spoon of butter onto them and put them on another element.

She started to work at the beans, clipping their ends and tossing them into yet another pot. This chore she was good at. She had done it many a time for her mother. When she got to the cauliflower she came to a complete standstill. She had no idea what to do with the plump vegetable that looked like a brain wrapped up in leaves. She knew that it was normally served with melted cheese upon it. Perhaps that was all that needed to be done. She found a chunk of old cheddar and she began slicing it into strips that she placed overtop of the cauliflower. She placed the cheese-covered head into a frying pan and set the element on high. She wanted to make sure that she had the meal ready by the deadline.

The sausage was beginning to smoke. It must mean that it was time to flip them. She took a fork and began jabbing into each tube to try and rotate them. The hot juices within the sausage sizzled out and poured onto the frying pan sending off hot vapors into the air that burned into her fingers. She had to pull her hand away.

As she did so she saw that the potatoes were beginning to smoke. With her bare hands she lifted the pot from the element and saw that the butter was melting but the three potatoes still looked raw. Then it suddenly dawned on her that you are supposed to boil potatoes. She had forgotten the water. She took the pot to the sink and a moment later a singing cloud of steam rose upward enveloping the skin of her hands and producing an agonizing pain that caused her to shriek.

As she opened her eyes she saw that smoke was rising from three of the stove's elements. The only thing that was not burning was her beans. This meal was going to be a fiasco she realized. She wanted to run away from the kitchen and sink her head into her pillow and cry. But she could not do that. She recognized that she had a potential fire in the works here on the stove. With her stinging hands she turned off the elements before returning to the sink and dousing her fingers under the coldest water that she could summon from the taps.

"What in God blazes is going on in here!" her father boomed from the entrance to the kitchen. "Are you trying to burn down the house!"

Thora turned to look at her father. He had a white shirt in dire need of a pressing half done up. Overtop of it he had a loosened tie. He did not have any pants on.

"Just making supper Dad!" Thora answered, knowing full well that she was upon the verge of being ridiculed.

"Just shut everything off!" Langley shook his head. "We are going out for dinner!"

"Everything is off Dad!" Thora began to whimper.

Langley opened the back door to let out the smoke. "Hasn't your mother taught you how to cook yet girl? A three-year old child would have done better than this!" He began emptying the contents of the pots and pans into the garbage can. He did it in such a hurry that half the contents missed their target and spilled on the counter doors and the floor. The only thing that he did not toss was the pot of cauliflower. "Such fine food being wasted! You are not to cook a meal in this house again until you get proper education! And if your mother cannot provide it for you then you will obtain this skill at summer school!"

"They don't teach cooking at summer school, Dad," Thora sniffled. She realized that her father was not being as terrible as she had believed. He was not being nice about it but at least he did not swat her or become extremely volatile in his verbal abuse.

"Well, they ought to! This is a disgrace!"

"The whole house smells like smoke!" Cora suddenly appeared in the hall leading to the kitchen. She was only in her bra and slip. Her hair was pulled back and her face was covered in a milky cold cream.

"Uncle Thaddeus is going to think that we are inept and incapable of even running a household let alone a major business," Langley groaned. "How come this daughter of yours knows nothing of cooking? She doesn't even know that in order to boil potatoes you need water! And look at the cauliflower! What in the dickens kind of dish is that supposed to be?"

"I've tried to teach her things about the kitchen," Cora said defensively, "But she just is unwilling to learn! She has a rebellious streak in her. She will never make a man a good wife!"

"We should be Catholics. If we were we could send her to a nunnery and get her out of our hair!" Langley answered.

Thora never felt more dejected and rejected. It was clear that she was not measuring up to whatever standards her parents had set for her. She started to quietly slip out of the kitchen.

"Where are you going, girl!" Langley shouted. "You are going to clean up this mess that you made!"

"What about supper, dear?" Cora asked. "Uncle Thaddeus will be here in less than half an hour."

"You and I will take them to a restaurant," her father answered.

Thora focused on the 'you and I' emphasis in the sentence. Her father was saying that she was not invited. She knew that she should be silent but she found herself protesting, "What about me? Don't I get any supper?"

Langley lifted the pot of cauliflower towards her. "This is your supper!" he scoffed. "You are not going anywhere until this kitchen is cleaned and the house is aerated!" He walked out of the kitchen mumbling to himself.

Before Cora left the room she said to her daughter, "I hope that I can trust you to clean this room without having to worry that the walls are going to cave in!"

Thora did not dignify that remark with an answer. Cleaning house was a task where she was an expert. She was hurting by the comments made by her parents. No one knew how to get at her more than them. They could have handled the situation a little more delicately and they should have realized that they should not be asking her to create a rushed impromptu meal with the minimal training that she received in the kitchen. They were not very good at being human beings. They lacked sympathy and compassion and they held unrealistic expectations. Maybe Rebecca did the right thing in fleeing this house. Maybe a nunnery would be a better place to be than here living with Langley and Cora Meadowford.

She looked at the counter and saw the pots and pans strewn about. She saw the discarded potatoes and sausage grease on the doors and the floor. The stovetop was smeared. It was going to take hours to clean up the mess. She felt like crying some more.

Without realizing it she sat at the kitchen table and shut her eyes and listened to her parents arguing upstairs. Her father was taking it out onto her mother for her failure to teach the girl how to cook. Her mother was defending herself saying that it was not her fault that Thora showed no inclinations towards the culinary arts. There was something defective about the girl and that they should have done something about her a long time ago once they realized that their daughter did not have everything that it takes.

Thora had no idea what she meant about that. The only thing that she did know was that she hated the both of them upstairs. They were weak yet they did not know that they were weak. The whole world could see that they were weak and the world felt sorry for their daughters. Perhaps it was in recognition of this observation that Reverend Barton wanted Thora to go to the other houses in the community so that she could feel that love can truly exist within a family and that she was worthy of being loved.

She suddenly noticed that the sound of the tap was running from the kitchen sink. Hadn't her father shut it off? When she looked that way through her tears, she saw a pot lift off the counter, pause a moment under the hot running water, and then settle into the sink. This was followed by another pot and then another pot.

For some reason this did not frighten the girl. Soon all the pots and pans were in the sink, clunking and clinking together as they jostled for space within the confines of the hot water.

Then overtop of the errant sounds of the dishes she could hear whistling. It was a calm, ambient tune with no specific recognizable melody. She could not see the whistler but she knew that he was there and she had a good idea who he was.

One by one the pots, pans and utensils came out of the hot water and placed neatly on the drying rack. There was something very peaceful and serene in watching the dishes being done. Thora chose not to question her eyes or to challenge the reality that they were displaying to her. She felt a calming of her frayed nerves. She no longer thought of her parents. Her ears were shutting them out as they continued to bicker upstairs.

The whistling continued as the dishes were dried and returned to their allocated places under the counter and in their shelves. The grease and spilt food gradually disappeared from the floor. The stovetop started to shine.

All the while the girl watched. She was not in a state of disbelief. There were no primal emotions being stirred. She sat in acceptance of what she was witnessing. She possessed a good idea who the whistler was. For some reason her guardian angel chose not to reveal himself. He stayed in an invisible state as he set about looking after the chores Langley had left Thora to do.

She began to notice that the air possessed a fragrance like a wind over a field of grass. It was so fresh and invigorating that Thora realized that for the first time in a long time she was able to breathe cleanly as wholesome air filled her lungs.

Then when everything was spotless and clean the whistling stopped. A voice that she heard on the cow field said to her, "Get dressed my child for you are going out for dinner."

At the same time her father came downstairs and saw the kitchen cleaner than it had ever been. "My, my!" he said approvingly. "You really know how to work when you set your mind to it!" He was tightening his tie. His hair for the first time in days was combed and he looked as good as he could. "Get dressed my child for you are going out for dinner!"

Chapter 10

Cristo Pando's

Uncle Thaddeus and James Whattam did not even have a chance to get out of their chauffeur-driven car before they were informed by Langley that they were going to meet at Cristo Pando's for dinner. Thora saw the old man at the rear of the black Bentley frown in disappointment. He must have been tired. Yet he relented to his nephew's request and the two automobiles, the Bentley and the Motorized Egg drove the town streets towards the restaurant.

While riding in the back seat of the Motorized Egg Thora's mind kept going back to what she witnessed in the kitchen. What exactly happened there? She knew that it could not be a figment of her imagination since there were tangible results from it. No hallucination can alter a room from a disaster area to a setting worthy of gracing the pages of a modern homes magazine. There was no way that she could have done it herself under a trance. It was done too quickly. It was done at a speed beyond human capability. Intervention from some other place had to have occurred. It had to be her guardian angel and her guardian angel had to be that old man, her great grandfather Samuel Angus Meadowford the First. That was twice now that he had come to her rescue. Why was the old man so drawn towards her and so concerned about her well-being? She did not have an answer to this but she did possess a new confidence in life. If the ghost was going to show up and set things straight every time things go wrong then she really did not have anything to fear.

As they drove up State Street towards the restaurant, Thora wondered if the old man were not indeed riding in the Motorized Egg with them. Was he sitting in the empty seat beside her—the seat that used to belong to her twin sister Rebecca? Her eyes drifted to the black leather cushion and saw the rip in the fabric there that had been created when they had that accident last winter in the ice storm. Rebecca's fingers had torn that hole as she dug them into the leather as the car slid into an electricity pole. No one was hurt in the mishap but the Motorized Egg did sustain some serious front-end damage that cost her father a fair dollar to repair. The cost of reupholstering the backseat was prohibitive and Langley chose to hide the rip by placing a blanket over it. The blanket was removed several weeks back when the family made their annual drive to Pioneer Lake. It had proven to be too uncomfortable for the girls to sit upon.

She missed her sister fiercely and in her mind she asked the old man, her guardian angel, to return Rebecca to them. She was not really expecting an answer and it came as no surprise to her that none came.

Cristo Pando's was located along a strip of stores and shops on State Street. It was found between a dry goods store and a bicycle repair shop. It was one of the most popular restaurants in Grappling Haven. Of course there were only two other restaurants besides Pando's in town. The other two specialized in home cooking while Cristo Pando's cuisine was cosmopolitan, featuring both French and Italian dishes. The well to do and those that wanted to create the illusion that they were well to do frequented this restaurant. Most often a reservation was required. This was a Thursday though and was not a premium night for the place. Or so Langley speculated. He had not bothered calling ahead to arrange a table much to the chagrin of his wife.

When the two cars came upon the restaurant they saw that all of the parking places in front of Cristo Pando's were occupied. That was not a good sign. A quick glance at the dry goods store and the bicycle repair shop showed that neither premise was overloaded with an abundance of customers. The passengers of the parked cars must have been in Pando's.

The car being chauffeur-driven for Uncle Thaddeus and James Whattam stopped in the middle of the street and the two gentlemen stepped out.

Thora could see her great uncle rubbing down the folds in his suit that the automobile inflicted upon it. He looked back at the Motorized Egg and indicated that they would meet them inside.

Langley drove on.

"See, I told you we should have called ahead!" Cora complained. "They are probably packed."

Her husband did not answer. He often did this when he was in the wrong. He was often in the wrong. There was not a parking spot available for almost a block. For some reason it was busy in town tonight. "It never used to be like this," Langley commented. "Too many people own cars nowadays if you ask me! They should make these things out of reach for the regular man's pocketbook and then we would not have to park so far away."

"But you want automobiles to be affordable to the masses, Langley," Cora responded. "It is the masses that keep Dearborn Cable afloat."

"I can only hope so," Langley mumbled. "I wonder what the old coot accomplished in Michigan. I don't have a good feeling about this. That jackass has screwed up opportunities in the past with his strict adherence to failed nineteenth century business acumen."

He parked the car in front of a Laundromat. Inside were at least twenty of the masses taking advantage of the fancy coin-operated washers and dryers. As the Meadowfords crawled out of the Motorized Egg one of the occupants inside of the laundry place stepped out. He wore a snug cap pulled tightly over his forehead causing his eyebrows to furrow. All that covered his chest was his white Italian undershirt that hung loose and wrinkled over his thick cotton slacks. There was a toothpick sticking out from his lower lip. Thora recognized the adolescent thug as Rory McQuoid, a boy that would have been a grade ahead of her had he not dropped out of school.

"Still a Daddy's girl, eh Thora?" Rory smirked. "At least your sister grew up!"

Thora tilted her head downward and tried to ignore the boy. She hated being seen in public with her parents. It made her feel like a little child. Rory McQuoid was always considered a troublemaker in school and for this reason he was looked up to by most of the kids. If you were part of his gang you were considered to be the cat's pajamas. Thora had tried to infiltrate this clique in the past but she did not have the street smarts and the lack of respect for authority that were required. Her sister had always shunned Rory and his ilk. She had told Thora that these boys would go nowhere in life and that in ten years the bulk of them would be in penitentiary.

"What do you mean by that comment?" her father suddenly snapped. He grabbed Rory by his undershirt and drew the surprised boy close to him.

Thora never realized how small Rory was until he was next to her father. He looked like a pipsqueak yet back at school he was considered quite big. Rory still had a lot of growing up to do.

"Let go of me you galoot!" Rory rang and spat on the concrete sidewalk.

"What do you mean that my daughter has grown up?" There was fire in Langley's eyes. "Do you know something about her?"

"Langley, let the delinquent go!" Cora demanded. "All that will come out of him is a pack of lies!"

Her husband did not listen. "Answer me, boy, before I knock your head through that window!"

Rory's face was growing red. The veins in his neck were popping. "I meant nothing by it, Mr. Meadowford!" he said. "I was just having a bit of fun with Thora!"

Langley pushed the boy aside. He placed his palm behind Thora's back and escorted her along.

As they walked past the Laundromat Thora could see many of its occupants had come up to the window to watch the potential altercation. When nothing came of it they returned to their washers and their dryers.

From behind her she could hear Rory yell out, "Some day you are going to pay for this!"

Her father ignored the threat. He said to his wife, "It must be common knowledge now that Rebecca has flown the coop. I don't like this at all."

"Maybe we should get the police involved and have them find our girl," Cora huffed as she tried to keep pace to the quick gait of her husband.

"We're not going to have the police get involved!" Langley boomed. "We do not need that kind of attention drawn onto our family!"

As they moved swiftly along Thora was caught up in a wave of self-pity. Her social status among her peers was going to be seriously compromised by that incident in front of the Laundromat. They would not only see her as a Daddy's girl but they would also see her daddy as a prime target for any rebellious lashings out at authority. She was sure that Rory McQuoid would not forget the incident and that the Pine Street house would be vandalized someday soon. Rory was a punk and he was no good but he was good for his word and he said that someday her father was going to pay for this. Yet as awkward as the situation had been Thora could not help but feel some admiration for her father. He was not afraid of the street toughs. He stood up to them and made them cower. Make an enemy out of Langley Meadowford and you will have hell to pay. The only problem was that Rory did not mind paying hell.

When they got to Cristo Pando's and opened the marvelously scrolled door with the stained glass they immediately saw Uncle Thaddeus and James Whattam. They could not help but see them. The two men were standing in line, waiting to be seated.

As soon as Uncle Thaddeus spotted his nephew he complained, "You did not make reservations?"

Langley scrambled for words. "You gave us such short notice," he replied.

"A home-cooked meal would have sufficed," Thaddeus grumbled. "Frankly, Jim and I have had our fill of restaurant meals being on the road for more than a week."

"Just a moment," Langley said to his uncle. "Let me see if I can do anything about this." He slipped past Thaddeus and Mr. Whattam and then tried to get by the people ahead of them, a family of four.

The man in this group, a fellow in the uniform of the U.S. Army grabbed Langley by the shoulder. "Where are you going, Mac?"

"Excuse me," Langley responded, stroking the soldier's hand away.

Thora was not sure if her father had more words to say to the fellow. If he did they never had a chance to be spoken as the soldier said, "You wait your turn in line. I got here first."

Langley paid the man no mind. He was waving his hand to draw the attention of the maitre' d. "Harvey! Harvey!" he called to the old chap that stood at the head of the line.

The soldier and his family—a pregnant wife and two girls about half her age, obscured Thora's line of sight. She recognized the girls from school. They were many grades behind her and she did not know their names. All that she recalled about them was that they were always poorly dressed and had bad hygiene. They were obviously from the poorer end of town.

"Good evening Mr. Meadowford," Thora heard the maitre d' Harvey say to her father.

"Any chance of getting a table right now for a party of five?"

"All the tables are occupied at the moment, Mr. Meadowford. I don't see your name on the list. But the next table that comes up will be yours."

The soldier suddenly lunged forward and took Langley by the arm and swung him around. "You wait your turn, Mister! My family was here first! I have to be back on base by nine tonight and this is my only chance to treat my family to a classy meal like they deserve!"

Langley smirked at the man, "You should have made a reservation!"

"A smart aleck, are you?" the soldier grinned, moving his hand upward so that it cupped Langley's chin. "I did make a reservation! Blenham, party of four. The waiter will confirm that my name is on the list. It's you that did not make the reservation."

"We will tolerate no fighting in Pando's," Harvey said in a loud, firm voice. Even though he was in his sixties he was not afraid to exercise authority over younger, bigger men.

"Then tell this pip to wait his turn in line. We got here first and we have a reservation!" Private Blenham retorted. "Doesn't this country respect its fighting men, any more?"

"Langley, just come back here and wait your turn," James Whattam said. "Allow the soldier to have a nice dinner with his family!"

Thora knew that Mr. Whattam should not have said that. Her father despised the man and would not take any direct orders from him. Had James not said anything then Langley may have backed down. But now his back was up. "This restaurant does not cater to the plebian class," Langley said to the soldier. "You could not even afford a cup of coffee here. Why don't you take your smelly brood to Potato Pete's where they belong and eat the greasy slop that they serve there! You do not have the palate for the fine cuisine of Cristo Pando's!"

Potato Pete's was a diner at the other end of State Street. It was always jammed pack with the kind of people her parents would call rabble.

"You are an asshole!" the soldier said. "If my family were not here I would…"

"Sir, we do not tolerate foul language on these premises!" Harvey spoke up. "I must ask you to leave at once!" Although the maitre d' had a gentle demeanor about him there still was something that glowed in his eyes that told you that if you did not heed his words trouble of the worst kind would quickly follow.

Private Blenham had his arm pulled back ready to punch Langley in the face. "If I weren't such a gentleman I would rearrange your noggin!" he said through gritted teeth. "Come on, Marie! Let's get out of this hellhole and get ourselves some real food!"

The two little girls that watched their father get humiliated looked quietly at each other and then to Thora. When they saw that she was looking at them, they turned their heads away and walked quietly past the Meadowford party.

Thora felt so bad for them. They were nice girls and they deserved to have had a special meal with their father in a special place like Cristo Pando's. She was ashamed at the way that her father behaved here. The description that Private Blenham provided for her father was very apt.

As the Blenham family left quietly and with dignity, Harvey the maitre d' announced to Langley that a table of five had just become available.

"Well, it's about time!" Uncle Thaddeus mumbled lowly. Thora, standing next to the old man, was the only one to hear him utter the words. She was still thinking of the Blenham family. What made her family more special than theirs? It had to be only money for it certainly could not have had anything to do with the social graces. Uncle Thaddeus' comment was rude and uncalled for. They had only been here a matter of minutes. It was not like they had been waiting around for hours. She knew that once Private Blenham and his family arrived at Potato Pete's they would likely have to wait more than an hour before they finally get something to eat. She was ashamed of her family and the privilege that they received. They were entirely unworthy of it.

Harvey led the Meadowford party to a table in the center of the room. Other patrons sat in every direction from this hub. As Thora walked through the dimly lit room, she could feel the chill of air conditioning. The cool air was a welcome relief to the oppressive heat outside. When she seated herself she saw that not everybody in the family had made it the distance. Her father and mother were delayed at a table where some of his friends sat. She could see her parents smiling and laughing and behaving like they were right at home here in Cristo Pando's. She started to realize that the Blenhams would have been a poor fit in this place. Everybody here came from the upper echelons of Grappling Haven society. They would have all looked down upon the soldier and his brood.

Uncle Thaddeus was detained at another table. His manner was not cavorting in the way that her parents behaved. He held a serious demeanor and his countenance was rather dour. The old man looked tired to Thora. She sensed that the purpose of this get-together was not going to be a jovial reunion with his nephew.

The only other person that came to the table with her was James Whattam. He sat at the opposite side of the round table from Thora. Given the general din in the room he was a bit too far away for her to engage in any quiet conversation. She would have practically had to shout to talk to him. He was not even looking her way. He was trying to read his watch but there was not sufficient light in the room for him to do so. He seemed to be in a hurry. Thora guessed that he was itching to get home and be reunited with his wife. He had been on the road a long time with Uncle Thaddeus.

The man suddenly got up and went to a nearby waiter. Thora watched the waiter point towards the lobby. Her eyes followed the handsome man in the splendid suit as he crossed the room. There she could see him pick up a pay telephone. He was probably calling home and telling his wife, Margaret that he was going to be late.

Thora was all by herself. She did not mind this at all. On her own, she would not have to deal with her embarrassing family especially her pugilistic father. He had already been in two altercations and they had not even sat down together as a group yet. She was sure judging by his aggressive manner and Uncle Thaddeus' somber countenance that the words at the table would be more heated than the food.

Everybody returned to the table seemingly on cue. Mr. Whattam had completed his phone call and the social visits of her parents and Uncle Thaddeus came to an end. Thora sat in between her mother and father. Uncle Thaddeus and Mr. Whattam were on the other side. A waiter was bringing another chair. As he placed it beside Mr. Whattam, the legal advisor said, "I hope that you don't mind but I have asked my wife to join us. She should be here shortly."

None of the Meadowfords said anything. Thora sensed the invisible eyes rolling back in her mother. She detested Margaret as much as her father detested James.

"I understand that you had dinner with Margaret earlier this week Thora," Mr. Whattam said. "She said that you were delightful company and that you are a very good swimmer."

Thora was thrown on the spot. She felt awkward having to speak at the table. She was hoping that she could have remained silent and not have her presence felt. But it was too late now. She was thrown into the fray. "Yes, it was very nice," she said. "The swim was very refreshing."

"Some day we will have a pool of our own girl," Langley said.

"If we do I want to make sure that you wear a bathing cap at all times," Cora said to Thora. "It took hours for you to work out the tangles caused by your wet hair."

"Either that or we cut your hair short," Langley added. "Long hair is so passé nowadays. You should have a nice bob."

Thora knew that she grimaced. The thought of chopping her hair short was alien to her. She needed it to hide behind.

"Where's the other one?" Uncle Thaddeus asked as if he were only now recognizing that one of the twins was not present.

Simultaneously Langley and Cora dropped their heads as if they were ashamed to admit that one of their daughters found living with them so overbearing that she preferred the danger of the road to staying at home. "It's a long story," Langley said. "But Rebecca is not…"

"She no longer lives with us," Cora interjected and finished her husband's sentence.

"Those things happen," Thaddeus responded. It seemed like he did not want to hear the details. In fact it seemed like he did not care at all that one of his kin had disappeared. His face was in a menu. "I wish that they would provide more light in these places. Forget the ambience and let an old man see!"

Cora and Langley's heads were lifted. They were reprieved from having to admit that they failed as parents. They should have expected Thaddeus' response and covert approval, Thora thought. Afterall all of his children fled from his house as well.

"I know what you mean Uncle Thaddeus," Langley said. "I have a hell of a time making out the words on these menus."

"That's because they are in foreign languages, my dear. You know how bad you are when it comes to them!" Cora chuckled. "You should have seen Langley in Berlin trying to order a beer at a boulevard café! It was hilarious! He…"

"Please, Cora, I am tired and I have no desire to listen to your cackling about matters that I will not find amusing," Uncle Thaddeus rudely chopped into her mother's story. He threw the menu down onto the table. It slid forward and caused a glass of water to momentarily teeter. "I wish that you would have provided us with a meal at your house!" he continued. "I just am not in the mood to make any decisions at all!"

"Had you let us know that you were coming beforehand we may have had something prepared for you!" Cora answered in a very bitter tone. She was reeling from his acidic dismissive remark. "But you caught us unprepared and there was nothing worthy in the house to serve our long lost dear sweet Uncle Thaddeus!"

Thora could almost taste the sarcasm coming from her mother's lips. At least it was sarcasm rather than blame being thrown at her inept daughter. That was about the only thing that Thora was thankful for here at the restaurant. This was going to be a long difficult dinner. The firewood was dry and there were plenty of matches around.

"Are things that bad in your household Langley that you cannot scrape together a meal from your empty pantries?"

"Tomorrow is shopping day," Langley answered. "Had this been tomorrow then…"

"Are you becoming a Democrat?" Thaddeus once again cut in.

Langley smirked and cleared his throat. "Goodness no! What is that supposed to mean?" The Meadowfords had a long tradition of being staunch Republican Party supporters. The term 'Democrat' was considered a dirty word in the extended family.

"You are shopping like one! A Republican buys his meals daily and that way always is well stocked. A Democrat waits for the larder to run bare and then goes running in a panic to the store and pays exorbitant prices for what he could have had cheaper the day before!"

"You just caught us at a bad time Uncle Thaddeus! What with burying Dad and then dealing with Rebecca flying the coop, we just did not have the chance to go shopping," Langley said in defense of his family. "Believe me our shopping habits are normally very Republican."

"I don't even know why you concern yourself with such trite and trivial matters. You should have servants attend to these mundane chores. This will free you up for items that are more worthy of a Meadowford's attention."

Uncle Thaddeus was such an old coot, Thora thought. He was even less likable than her parents. His rigid upper crust attitudes should have gone extinct with the turn of the century. Did he really think that the Meadowfords were an evolutionary rung higher than everybody else?

"It would be nice to have servants," Langley said. "But the fact of the matter is that we cannot afford them."

"Plus, I take a joy in cooking," Cora said. "It is an excellent vehicle to steer my creative energies. I…"

"And the reason why you can't afford them is because you squander your money, Langley!" Uncle Thaddeus interjected, lopping off Cora's remark before it could even be formulated in her mind. "I received the auditor's report on unnecessary expenditures within the organization and I have found that the majority of these involve you. We do not possess any interests in New Hampshire and we are not in the market to pursue any but for some reason we have some holdings in that state and that these regularly recurring expenses are endorsed by you."

Langley's face was once again changing color. Thora saw that he was watching his wife out of the corner of his eyes. "There are opportunities there that I believe to be very worthwhile."

"Then you pursue those opportunities with your own finances, Langley, and not with company money!"

The waiter chose that moment to come to the table. "Are we ready to order?" he asked.

Before anybody could say anything, James Whattam said, "We are waiting for another person to join our table. She should be here shortly. When she arrives then we will be ready."

"I'll have the Veal Alfredo," Cora said. "Could I also have a Caesar salad and perhaps some garlic bread as well?" She was looking directly at Mr. Whattam. It was her way of saying that this was a Meadowford dinner and that the Meadowfords do not wait for any upcomers.

James Whattam looked the other way. Thora could detect a change in his brow that probably indicated the existence of some not very pleasant thoughts regarding her mother.

"Anybody else ready to order?"

Cora turned her eyes towards her husband. Her eyes were telling him that he had better order or else he was in some very big trouble.

Langley cleared his throat. "I'll have the thickest steak that you have. Never mind any vegetables, salad or pasta. All that I want is the steak."

"Keep eating like that Langley and you won't be alive in ten years time," Uncle Thaddeus remarked. The old man then looked at the waiter and asked him what he would recommend this evening.

The waiter started reciting some items on the menu. He spoke with a flourish as he rolled his r's and elongated his l's and modulated his vowels through the use of nasal effects. Thora could tell that the young man probably did not have a command of the foreign languages that he pretended to know.

"Just get me a steak too!" Thaddeus answered. "I doubt that I will be around in ten years time so what does it matter to me."

"What do you mean that you won't be around in ten years, Uncle Thaddeus!" Langley remarked. "You look as young as I have ever seen you!" He was being blatantly ingratiating. In fact he may have been acting sarcastically for all that Thora knew.

"Give it up Langley. You are counting the days to my demise. Don't try to fool me with any false fealty. I know your heart and your motives," Thaddeus answered. "You are no different than me!"

"Is the young lady ready to order?" the waiter asked Thora. He was trying to get his words out overtop of those of the two men. Thora could see it in his young face that he found this table very disdainful and distasteful. The Meadowfords were not who they thought that they were. They were not the cream of society. They were the fat that the cream of society produced. They were the unwelcome derivatives that living well produced as a side effect.

"I'll just have spaghetti," she said as quietly as she could.

"And how about you, Sir?" the waiter asked Mr. Whattam.

"I will wait for my wife, thank you," James said. He gave a condescending look across the table at Cora Meadowford. Thora could recognize that he did not think much of her at all. Perhaps he detested the Meadowfords of Pine Street as much as the Meadowfords of Pine Street detested him and his wife.

"Really, Uncle Thaddeus, I do admire you and the way that you have been able to keep your head straight even when your personal life was falling apart," Langley said. He and Uncle Thaddeus did not allow the waiter's business to interrupt their conversation.

The waiter left the table jotting down some notes on his pad. Thora could sense the relief the fellow experienced by getting away from this table of ill manners.

"You kept Dearborn Cable running even when your wife and children left you," Langley continued. "I admire you for that. Not every man could do that. My father, rest his soul, would not. When Mother died I believe that Dad was ready to sell the business and live out the rest of his life in mourning. It was you that persuaded him not to sell and to keep Dearborn Cable afloat."

"I did that for selfish reasons," Thaddeus answered. "I did not have the finances back then to buy him out. If I did I would have done so immediately. I wish now that I did. But at the time I resolutely believed that I was unable. I also did not want any new partners who would bicker with me every step along the way. For that reason I talked Sambo into staying with the company. Better the devil you know, as they say."

"Well it looks like now you will have new partners Uncle," Langley produced a large, generous smile that was hard to read as being genuine or fake.

"That may not be necessarily so," Thaddeus remarked. "There is something that I want to talk to you about." He looked around the table. His eyes fell upon Thora and she felt a sudden discomfort. She was not used to Uncle Thaddeus looking at her. She was not sure if he ever had done so before. She and Rebecca were part of the background as far as Thaddeus was concerned, she was sure. They had as much physical presence to him as a distant crow cawing upon the island.

Thaddeus' eyes moved on to Cora. The woman would not back down her gaze from the old man. She sat there naked and defiant in his eyes, daring him to say one thing wrong.

"I truly wish that we had this dinner at your place Langley," Thaddeus continued. "I could have spoken to you privately there in your study."

"Langley shares everything with me," Cora said. "Anything that you would have told him there he would have told to me immediately afterwards."

"Cora, be quiet!" Langley hushed his wife. "Maybe we could go sit at a private booth and you can tell me there," he added to Uncle Thaddeus. He did not glance over at his wife. Had he done so he would have seen glaring eyes focused upon him.

"Look around you, man! There are no booths free here! The restaurant is packed! I am afraid that I am going to have to postpone our discussion until some later occasion."

"Anything that you want to say to me you can say out in the open!" Langley proclaimed. Thora could sense that her father believed that what Uncle Thaddeus was going to say could only be interpreted as good news. He held the air about him of a child about to open a Christmas present.

She thought that this was entirely inappropriate. This was the first time that the two men met since the death of Sambo. One had lost a brother. One had lost a father. Yet neither man lamented their loss with the other. They both were looking past Sambo as an obstinate obstacle that has finally been surpassed. This was very very wrong in the girl's eye. Her grandfather had been good to both men yet now they acted as if he never existed.

"I'm not sure if this is the right place," Thaddeus grumbled.

"Well my, my! Here she is!" James Whattam said. His teeth gleamed as he smiled at the approach of his wife, Margaret.

Margaret walked through the maze of tables towards them. Her gait was elegant. She was impeccably attired in a cheerful sundress with matching purse. She held her head high and she was not afraid to display her pleasure at seeing her husband.

James stood up and stepped out towards his wife. They embraced each other tightly and kissed each other on the lips. Out of the corner of her eyes, Thora saw that the rest of the occupants of the table looked away with disgust at the show of affection in a public place. Thora did not do so. She thought it was tremendous the way that the Whattams were in love and not afraid to display it.

"You know everybody here, don't you Maggie?" James said as he pulled out a seat for his wife. She was placed directly beside Cora.

"Of course I do, Jim! You know that!" Margaret giggled. "Hello, everybody!"

From across the table Thora could smell Mrs. Whattam's perfume. It had a comforting effect upon the psyche. Perhaps its soothing would find a way to defuse the latent anger that had nestled upon the group.

Mrs. Whattam snuggled herself in her seat and rubbed her hands up and down her bare arms. "That air conditioning in here is a rather drastic change from that horrid heat outside, isn't it?" The woman was amazingly cheerful. Thora knew that it would not be contagious. Her family seemed to be immune to cheer. "So how was your trip?" Margaret asked her husband directly.

"The heat is everywhere Maggie but not near as oppressive as it is in Michigan," James responded. "They may be leaders in the auto industry but they do not seem to be aware of air conditioning. The rooms that Mr. Meadowford and I stayed at were little more than furnaces with views upon a river."

"It was not all that bad James," Uncle Thaddeus said. "I prefer the heat to this dastardly cold in this room. Your house isn't air conditioned, is it Langley?"

Thora once again recognized a stab at her father. Uncle Thaddeus was not going to be satisfied sitting here at Cristo Pando's. Her mother also noted the implicit message in the remark. "Give it a rest Thaddeus! We are here at the restaurant and that's that! Stop your bellyaching! Stop acting like an old man!"

Mrs. Whattam lifted an eyebrow at the sudden display of hostility. She at once took it upon herself to be a peacemaker of sorts. "I hope that you did not wait for me to order your meals."

"They all ordered," James said with a frown, showing his disapproval in the Meadowfords' lack of manners.

"I see. That is good," some of the cheer had been let go out of the woman. "You haven't ordered, have you?"

"Would I do that to my beautiful wife?" James said with a robust smile, reaching his arm out around her shoulder and dragging her for a kiss.

"For God's sake, man! Don't you have any scruples!" Uncle Thaddeus blasted. "You are acting like libertines!"

"Listen Thaddeus, you may employ me but you don't own me!" James immediately retorted. "If I want to kiss my wife I will kiss my wife. I don't need or want your consent!"

Uncle Thaddeus grumbled something. It was said in such a low voice that there might have not been any words contained with it.

Thora could feel that a smile was beginning to form on her face. She bit hard on her cheek linings to prevent the display of teeth. She had never seen anybody speak so boldly to the man. She remembered how meanly Uncle Thaddeus treated the help back at Pioneer Lake. They were dirt in his eyes. Yet none ever had the audacity to speak back at him. She knew that they wanted to. Her admiration for the Whattams increased once more by what had just happened.

The waiter came to the table and asked the Whattams for their order. Margaret ordered just a salad and water while James ordered fish. By the time the waiter left there was a silence on the table. It seemed like nobody dared say anything lest they would be torn apart by the others there.

Thora started getting a mental nudge that maybe she should take the onus upon herself to break the quiet. She was quite nervous to do so but the uncomfortable stillness of the table was too overbearing making the icebreaking seem as an attractive alternative. "Did you find the photograph that inspired the painting?" she asked Mrs. Whattam.

Everybody looked at her, including Uncle Thaddeus. They all in their own way seemed somewhat thankful that she spoke and broke the stalemate.

"What are you talking about Thora?" her father asked. "Are you asking me something?"

"No," Thora responded. "I was talking to Mrs. Whattam. She has a portrait in her basement that might be that of Uncle Thaddeus' father, Samuel Angus Meadowford the First."

Uncle Thaddeus at once looked at James with an expression that asked why would he possess a painting of his father.

James took it upon himself to reply. "Maggie enjoys using oils to paint pictures. She is quite good. I have a portrait that she did of my father hanging in my office. You must have seen it Thaddeus?"

Uncle Thaddeus nodded. "A husband always possesses a certain blindness when it comes to his wife," he said.

"What is that supposed to mean?" James suddenly became fierce.

"I mean that the painting is quite amateurish. If you want my advice, I would suggest that you take that portrait down. It gives your clients the wrong impression of your worthiness as an adept lawyer. I know that when I first came into your office and saw that child's sketch hanging upon the wall I felt the inclination to turn around and seek advice elsewhere."

Before James could lambaste him, Margaret spoke up. "We are all entitled to our opinions, Mr. Meadowford, when it concerns art. I also think that that portrait is not very well done. It is not representative of my talents, as they have progressed since then. But James likes the picture and will not have it replaced."

"You have a sensible wife, James," Uncle Thaddeus answered. "Maybe you should listen to her. I would like to see that portrait of my father someday."

Thora felt some internal glee that Margaret was able to prevent an outlash of emotion between the two tired travelers. She truly was a remarkable woman.

"You are more than welcome to have a look anytime that you want, Sir," Margaret replied with a smile.

"It has been some time since I have seen his face," Thaddeus said. "In life we clashed like titans but after he passed I have come to value much that he has said."

"What kind of man was he like?" Thora found herself addressing her great uncle directly. This was something that she rarely did and when she did she always felt huge trepidation.

At first she believed that the old man was not going to deign her with an answer but then he said, "My father was a builder. He not only built houses and businesses. He built family and he built friendships. Sambo possessed that trait as well. I fear that this quality is lacking in Langley and I. We are the scrappers and we know how to fight to retain what is ours and to take what is not ours and to make it ours. But yet we do not inspire loyalty the way that my father and brother did. This might make us better fighters as we have to always protect what belongs to us but it always leaves us targets as well. And frankly as you get older you get tired and you don't want to be fighting all of the time but our pasts leave us little choice but to continue to do so." He looked at his legal counselor, James. "That is why Jim and I want to have this talk with you Langley. I just wish that it could have been in a private location and not here in this public house."

"If you like we can return to my house after dinner and we can have that discussion there?" Langley said. He looked momentarily over to his wife before adding, "In my study of course!"

"And in private if you so desire," Cora said. She seemed to accept the needs of the old man.

For some reason Thora could feel that everybody was thankful towards her for getting the conversation rolling. She could no longer sense the pall of an impending melee hanging over the dining Meadowfords.

Shortly thereafter the waiter started carrying the meals to the table and setting them down. The largest plate of spaghetti that Thora saw in her life was sitting in front of her. She did not know if she could finish all of it but she was sure eager to give it a try.

Chapter 11

Overcooked Meat

"This meat is overcooked!" Langley said through a stuffed mouth. He lowered his head and spat its contents onto the plate.

"Langley, that is disgusting!" Cora remarked. "Where did you acquire such boorish manners?"

"I can barely chew it! I didn't order it well done. How is yours Uncle Thaddeus?"

Uncle Thaddeus' jaws were working vigorously, masticating the steak in his mouth. He lifted his finger in an indication to wait a minute. He was unable to answer at the moment.

"You didn't tell the waiter how you wanted it done, Dad," Thora said, while rotating a swirl of noodles above a spoon. Her spaghetti had been very tasty until her father spat out his food. Now her appetite had disappeared. "You just said that you wanted a big steak."

Langley's nostrils flared slightly at his daughter's comment. "Stay out of this girl! When a man orders a steak in a restaurant the waiter is supposed to ask how he wants it done!"

"Maybe he was too busy!" Thora said in defense of the young man. "And maybe when he didn't, you should have spoken up." She could not believe that she was acting the way that she did. The peaceful umbrella that had settled over the table disintegrated and the rain of deep-rooted anger was beginning to fall upon them again. Her father had broken the peace and maybe that was why she was being so spiteful.

"And maybe little girls should keep their mouths shut if they want to do what is best for them!" Langley mocked her. "Garcon! Garcon!" he began to crow like a dissatisfied rooster.

Thora glanced around the room to find the waiter. She could see a lot of people looking over at the Meadowford table. Their expressions all conveyed a 'Here we go again. The Meadowfords are once more being miscreants' message. She spotted the waiter serving another table. He lifted his head towards Langley and then seemed to return his attention to his customers.

Langley must have noticed this as well. He at once rose from the table and stormed across the room. "Boy, I was calling you!" he shouted.

Thora could not bear to watch. Or to listen. She placed her hands over her ears hoping that she could drown out her foolish father. As she did so she saw that Margaret Whattam was watching her. There seemed to be sympathy oozing out of her eyes, telling her that she was part of the extended Church family now, and that she did not have to suffer the excesses of her parents if she did not want to.

There came so much shouting at the other table that Thora could no longer shut it out. Her instincts forced her to turn around. A patron from that table was standing up and haranguing her father. She did not recognize the man. He was wearing a Hawaiian shirt overtop of Bermuda shorts. He was obviously a tourist in the Grappling Haven community.

Upon seeing her husband in potential trouble, Cora immediately dashed from the table to be by Langley's side. Uncle Thaddeus continued chewing his meat but he watched with what appeared to be a keen interest. He did not seem to be in any hurry to protect his kin. James Whattam shook his head and whispered something to Margaret. There was pain etched on the woman's face and her eyes continued to bleed towards Thora.

The waiter had pulled himself away from the hot spot and was dashing towards the kitchen. A moment later, a man dressed in a cook's outfit complete with towering cap came stomping through the swinging stainless steel doors. He was not a very big man. His skin was that of a swarthy Mediterranean and he possessed the fiery disposition of someone born and bred from the hot countries. It was Cristo Pando himself, the Macedonian owner of this prestigious restaurant.

Pando stepped in between Langley and the tourist and demanded to know at once what was going on here. Both Langley and the tourist simultaneously shouted out their respective gripes.

"One at a time!" Pando blared in a voice loud enough to wake up the dead. "You go first!" he said to the tourist while holding his hand over Langley's mouth so that he would not say anything.

"My family and I were placing our orders with your fine waiter when this fat buffoon comes plodding in like a rogue bull elephant demanding that the waiter cater to him first! I know that from where I come from people have manners and they wait their turn!" The man had an accent. It was not a European one. It was a tongue nurtured on American soil but Thora could not pinpoint where.

"And you choose to invoke a war over such a minor incident?" Cristo Pando said, shoving the man away in a manner that said that he was master of his domain. "Now you tell me your side of the story!" He took his hand from Langley's mouth.

Langley wiped his lips and made a grimace. Thora guessed that there must have been something foul tasting on Pando's hand. There was still plenty of fire in his eyes. "We were here first," he said. "And we demand satisfaction from our host before he goes sauntering off catering to the petty tourist trade!"

Cristo Pando looked over to the Meadowford table. He was acquainted with the family although had never had any opportunity to ingratiate himself with them. Even though the Meadowfords usually loved his food they bore no fondness for the man. He was an immigrant making him an untouchable in their eyes. "I see food on your table," Pando said. "I would think that my boy has completed his job there."

"I wouldn't dignify that crap on the table as food," Langley shot back. "My steak is as tough as an old football. I wouldn't even give it to my dog!"

Her father had said the wrong thing. First off, the family did not have a dog. But the damaging aspect of his remark was that he criticized Cristo's cuisine. That was a fatal error. Nobody criticizes Cristo's cuisine. The little Macedonian in the chef outfit at once was transformed into a Minoan bull. "There is nothing wrong with that steak!" he bellowed. "I prepared it very nicely for you. I made sure that I was generous with my spices to give it that special tang that makes people rave about it for days after!"

"It was overcooked!" Langley said flatly.

"If you want barbecue food then go to Potato Pete's!" Pando retorted. "That steak was made precisely the way that a steak is to be done according to the philosophy of my restaurant. I am an educator of the palate. I refine it and make it civilized. I don't cater to canine appetites. If you want to eat like a dog, go to Potato Pete's!"

The man was very demonstrative in gesture. His command of the language was faultless although it was spiced with a thick helping of the seasonings of his home country. It was apparent that his audience was not Langley Meadowford. He was speaking to all of his assembled patrons.

"Well this is America, Mister! This is where the individual can get what he wants and not have others dictate to him what his choices are!" Langley retaliated. "In America if I want my steak medium rare then I get my steak medium rare!"

"You have freedom of choice, my friend! If you want dog meat then go to Potato Pete's! Here at Cristo Pando's I offer an alternative for those of more exacting tastes, for those who want to climb above the masses and to show others that they are not just another barking mongrel at the dog pound! I am making America a better place, are you?"

Cora had been silent through all of this. She could not be silent any longer. "Do you know who you are talking to?" she said to the restaurant man. "He is Langley Meadowford. He is one of Grappling Haven's finer sons. I am sure you have heard of the Meadowfords. If you haven't then you obviously do not belong here!"

"The Meadowfords?" the tourist chimed. "I have heard of you folk! You run that steering cable company in Michigan, don't you?"

"Why, yes!" Langley answered. He was obviously taken aback that the man would recognize the family name and business. "How do you know that?"

The tourist smiled smugly. "It is my business to know," he said. "I'm Art Rozelle. You might have heard of me too!"

Thora could see that her father had no idea who the man was but there was a definite reaction by both Uncle Thaddeus and James Whattam. "Holy Christ!" Mr. Whattam sighed.

"I'm one of the chief legal counselors for the auto workers' union. I have a stack of grievances upon my desk yea thick regarding Dearborn Cable! Your company is going to go tits up, buddy!"

"No dirty talk in my restaurant!" Cristo Pando exclaimed. He signaled over to the maitre d', Harvey.

At the same time Uncle Thaddeus raced across the room. "I have addressed all of those issues on your desk," he said to Mr. Rozelle. "As far as I am concerned we have a working agreement with the union and that the union will honor its commitment to stay out of Dearborn Cable."

"Well, if it isn't Thaddeus Meadowford himself!" Art continued to smile. "I thought I recognized that haggard face sitting over there. Yes, we have a working agreement to stay out of Dearborn Cable but we also have agreements with the auto manufacturers in Detroit that they have promised to honor. They have sworn that they will only accept their parts from unionized shops. Any arrangements that you have with any of these companies will soon come to an end and that is why your company, Mr. Meadowford, is going to be going the way of the dodo!"

Harvey, the maitre d' arrived at the table. The tough old fellow was ready to oust anyone that Cristo Pando decreed as an undesirable. At the moment Cristo was not giving any direction.

"That is unethical! And it is a breech of the anti-trust laws!" Thaddeus stormed.

"You were the one that brought this upon yourself, Meadowford," Rozelle answered. "This is a new century. The economic landscape has changed. Labor has staked its claim on the prosperity enjoyed by industrialists like you from the old century. You should have accepted the new order Meadowford and your company would have stayed afloat. Now, it is too late. Your workforce has been promised positions with your unionized competition but I am afraid that there is no place for anachronisms like you and your cheese ball son!"

"He is not my son. He is my nephew," Thaddeus responded.

Even from where she sat, Thora could see massive dejection and defeat upon the brow of her great uncle. The words of Art Rozelle must have ringed as true as a death knell in the old man's ears.

"And I am not a cheese ball, you shyster!" Langley bellowed. "We will take this all the way to the Supreme Court if need be. You cannot dictate whom a man or company can buy their supplies from. People and companies have the right to choose to buy what they want from whom they want! This argument sounds very similar to the one I am making with this Greek monkey in the cook's get up! If a customer wants his steak medium rare you give it to him medium rare! If a manufacturer wants his steering cables from a non-unionized shop then he has the right to do so!"

Her father could not have chosen poorer words.

"Greek monkey?" Cristo Pando screeched, throwing his hands in the air. When they came down they rested on his hips. His body was slightly tilted forward. He was about to release a salvo of spicy Mediterranean temper upon Langley. "I am no Greek monkey! I am Macedonian! I am a direct descendant of Alexander the Great!"

"Greek, Macedonian. Same thing to me!" Langley spat back. He had adopted a similar posture as Pando.

"That is it! I want you and your Irish cronies out of here right this minute!" the cook demanded. He nodded to Harvey.

"We're not Irish! We're American!" Langley steamed. His hands were held out by his side, ready to take on the old man Harvey.

At the same time Cristo Pando stomped across the floor to the Meadowford table. "You people out!" he squawked, taking the plate of spaghetti away from Thora.

"Mr. Pando, please reconsider your actions," Margaret Whattam said to the man. "Anything done out of anger is usually regretted the next day."

"I only regret that I cater to bigots like you!" Pando responded while stacking more plates in his arms. He was leaning over Thora in such a manner that his weight was pushing her from her chair.

Thora was scared. There was no telling the end result when adults fight. She slipped off her chair. Instead of running to be by her parents' side she stayed close to the Whattams. The couple begrudgingly rose from the table without saying anything more to the irate restaurant man.

"These people have a propensity for getting into trouble," Margaret said to her husband, while placing her hand on Thora's shoulder.

"It's a thing that we won't have to worry about much longer," James said softly to her. "By the end of the summer our relationship with the Meadowfords will come to an end."

The last remark may not have been meant for Thora's ears. She heard them anyhow and she felt a pang of angst grab her abdomen. The Whattams were going to abandon her.

"What's that mean?" Margaret asked.

James looked down at Thora and must have realized that she was taking in what he was saying. "I will tell you later, when we are alone."

"Okay, out out everybody!" Cristo Pando was waving his arms once more. The waiter had relieved him of the plates from the Meadowford table. Pando was pushing his small chest against James while nudging Margaret and the attached Thora along.

"Take it easy, Cristo," James said. "We get your message!"

Harvey, the maitre d', had Langley in a headlock. Her father was throwing his hands up at the old man but was being entirely ineffectual in his struggle to break loose. He was crying out slurs at the man but the words were lost and muffled in Harvey's red jacket.

Cora was screaming at the man and throwing punches of her own upon his back. But Harvey was undaunted by the attack. He was walking Langley towards the door where Uncle Thaddeus stood with his head held low.

Thora felt the same shame towards her kin that the old patriarch must have been feeling. Her parents were pathetic. They believed themselves to be the finest that Grappling Haven could offer when in reality they were the town's laughing stocks. They possessed no dignity. She was sure that Art Rozelle's belly was moving up and down in a chuckle over the matter. She dared not look back at the table where the tourist and his party sat. She was ashamed to show her face. She wished that she were out there with her sister. Rebecca no longer had to share in the embarrassing moments created by her parents. She was free to be herself and not to have the tag of her family name draw her down.

When they reached Uncle Thaddeus the old man looked at James Whattam. "You Judas," he said to him. "I saw what you did."

Thora threw her head around to look at Mr. Whattam. He had fallen back a few paces behind them.

"I saw you give that man your card," Uncle Thaddeus sighed and started out of the door.

"You shouldn't have done that in front of his face," Margaret whispered to her husband.

"Don't worry about his feelings," James Whattam replied. "He doesn't worry about ours. Besides he won't be needing our services soon and we need to find another way of getting the bread on the table."

Thora did not understand any of this. She could not construe anything meaningful in the words that Art Rozelle had bandied. Unions and union shops might as well have been Macedonian words for all the semantic detail they gave the thirteen-year old girl. All that she could sense was that big changes were going to be coming her way soon.

The group of six people that had sat at the table inside Cristo Pando's now was standing on the sidewalk outside of the restaurant. The restaurant owner appeared at the doorway. "None of you are ever to come back!" he roared. "If I see any of your faces in here again I will immediately throw you out!"

"Don't worry you smelly little monkey we have no intention of ever coming back!" Langley shouted back at the man.

"Not until you hire somebody that knows how to cook!" Cora added.

Thora saw Uncle Thaddeus shake his head in despair over the remarks made by her parents. He could see that they were very much what Private Blenham had called them. She felt no sympathy for him for he had been one most of his life as well.

Cristo Pando gave the couple the finger and stormed back into his restaurant.

"Up yours too, buddy!" Langley rasped, lifting his middle finger high into the air.

"Now, that's very dignified," James Whattam commented to him.

"What's that supposed to mean?" Langley growled.

"Honey, don't start," Margaret whispered to her husband. "Let him cool down."

The financial advisor nodded to his wife. "You are right. I won't let them drag me down to their level."

"Come on James, time to go home," Thaddeus said. It was plain that the old man wanted to get away from his family as fast as possible. "Now, where did our chauffeur get at?"

The Bentley and its driver that had dropped Thaddeus and Mr. Whattam off were nowhere to be seen among the parked vehicles along State Avenue.

"He was probably not expecting us for another half hour or so and he must have gone to get some gas," James answered his employer. "I saw the gauge and it was running a little low."

"I saw it too and it was not that low. The man is probably cruising the streets trying to impress women with my car," Thaddeus said. "Make arrangements for his immediate dismissal." The old man sighed deeply.

"If you want I can drive you to my place," Langley offered. "Afterall, that's where you are going to anyway, isn't it?"

Thaddeus pinched his nose in a display of disapproval over the suggestion. "I'm tired. I want to go home," he responded.

Disappointment showed on Langley's face. "I thought that there were some matters that you wished to discuss with me?" he asked plaintively.

"Those matters can wait until another time."

Langley paused for a moment. He was staring down at his feet as if he were thinking about something. And then his head lifted, "How about if I drive you home and you can tell me the gist of it while we drive?"

"And what about my chauffeur then, boy? Is he to sit here all night under the misconception that I am still dining and enjoying a wonderful meal which I was until you opened your big mouth?" Uncle Thaddeus finally gave his appraisal of the steak. He liked it.

"Maybe Mr. Whattam can wait here for him?" Langley offered. There was a trace of wicked intent in his eyes. The remark about enjoying the steak appeared to drift over his head.

"I'm going home with my wife!" Whattam replied immediately. "We don't live that far away. We will walk."

"It is a wonderful night for a stroll," Margaret said with a smile as she placed her arm through that of her husband's.

"Then Thora can wait!" Langley retorted. He was acting with desperation. He wanted to hear what his uncle had to say to him. He was unwilling to wait any longer.

Thora looked at her dad in amazement. She could not believe that he was willing to let her stand alone in the middle of town to wait for a young man that Uncle Thaddeus had branded as unsavory in character. "I don't think that that is a very good idea," she said to him.

"You have nothing else to do and you will do as you are told," Langley replied with an authoritative snap. "I will fetch the car, Uncle. You wait here with Cora."

Thaddeus did not have a chance to say one thing or another before Langley went galloping off towards the Motorized Egg that was parked in front of the Laundromat. Thora did however hear her great uncle mutter, "Jerk" as her dad moved down the street.

"Well, Mr. Meadowford, it looks like all arrangements have been made," James Whattam said. "So unless there is anything else that I can do with you I will bid you an adieu and I will see you tomorrow."

The Whattams were about to walk away when Thaddeus said, "Not so fast James. All arrangements have not been made."

The couple stopped in their tracks and turned around in a finely choreographed maneuver that displayed that they were a team.

"I want you to draw up the papers tonight and have them ready to be signed in the morning," Thaddeus said. "After what I have learned here tonight we must move in haste if we want to see our plans come through."

"You don't think that he is going to go for it still, do you?" James seemed somewhat surprised. He looked over at Cora to see if she was listening.

The woman was not. She had gone to take a peek inside of the dry goods store.

"I think that he will go for it now more than ever. He thinks that he will be getting a bargain."

Thora did not know what the two men were talking about but she sensed that they were going to play her father as a sucker. At the moment that was all right by her. Her father behaved like a boor this evening and he deserved to be given some of his own medicine.

"I'm not so sure about this one," James said. "At any rate, I better get going now. I have a lot of work to do. See you in the morning."

Just as Mr. Whattam was saying his farewell to Uncle Thaddeus, Margaret Whattam stooped forward toward Thora. "We can stay and wait with you, if you like," she offered. "I know how scary town can be to someone your age. It is still frightening to me at mine."

"I'll be fine, Mrs. Whattam," Thora responded bravely. She wanted to beg the woman to stay but she knew that if she did her status in her family's eyes would be greatly compromised.

"As long as you are sure about this," Margaret answered.

Thora could see in the woman's eyes that she was seeing right through her. But it was too late to change what she said. "I'm sure," she smiled.

James and Margaret Whattam walked away, arm in arm, down State Street and towards their beautiful home about a mile's distance from Cristo Pando's.

The Meadowford party waited several minutes before Langley finally appeared on the road. The Motorized Egg looked like it had drove through a mile of barbed wire. There were scratches everywhere on its yellow surface. At once Thora realized that Rory McQuoid had wrought his justice upon her father.

"What happened to the car!" Cora cried out when she saw the condition of the family vehicle.

Thora was one step ahead of her mother. She saw the condition of her father. His nose was bleeding and his shirt was torn. He must have gotten into a scramble with the juvenile delinquent. "Dad, are you okay?" she called out to him. Even though he had behaved horrendously during this outing, he was still her father and no daughter should tolerate seeing her dad so beaten up.

"The little bastard! I am going to kill him!" Langley roared. "We'll see who gets the last laugh on this one!"

"Shut up Langley," Uncle Thaddeus growled. "There will be no last laughs until after you get me home." He climbed into the back seat of the car and grumbled something. He no doubt saw the torn leather.

Thora got the distinct impression that if Langley had not been his nephew, Thaddeus would have absolutely nothing to do with him. She also had the feeling that their days of interacting with one another were numbered and that as soon as Uncle Thaddeus hatches his scheme, whatever it was, that would be the end of any semblance of fealty between the two men.

Uncle Thaddeus hung his head out of the window. "Now as soon as that thief arrives here, dispatch him home with my car at once," he instructed Thora.

"Can I get a ride home with him first?" Thora asked, not sure if that was part of the arrangement she was making with her great uncle.

"Don't be silly, girl!" Thaddeus snapped and pulled his head back into the window.

Thora was at a loss to understand what that remark was supposed to mean. Did it mean that she was silly thinking that it could be anything otherwise than getting a ride home? Or did it mean that it was silly to think that she would get a ride home? She wanted clarification but she was too afraid to say anything more to the crusty old man.

"We'll see you at home Thora," her mother said. "Don't get into any trouble." She climbed into the front seat. "What the hell happened!" she squawked at her husband. "Can't you do anything without getting into a fight? Look at your clothes! They are ruined! They are beyond repair! If you think that I am going to mend them, you are wrong, Mister! I'm not going to be your seamstress if you keep acting like a common street brawler!"

"Oh, shut up Cora!" Langley shouted just as loudly back. "I don't need an old nag telling me what to do!"

"Apparently, you do! I have never been more ashamed to carry the Meadowford name as tonight! You acted reprehensibly this evening, my husband!"

"Will the two of you just shut your mouths and get me the hell home!" Thaddeus exploded from the rear seat.

"Yes, sir," Langley said. He put the car into gear and they drove away leaving Thora alone in front of the restaurant.

Chapter 12

Two Chauffeurs

    State Street was the main business artery for Grappling Haven. It possessed most of the town's shops and service outlets. It was a haven for the young who gathered here trying to find something to keep themselves occupied on the long summer evenings when there was little else for them to do elsewhere. Thora and Rebecca came here on occasion to meet with friends and to attend the nickelodeon to ostensibly watch flicks from the silver screen and newsreels. They seldom paid attention to what was being shown as the true show was in the audience where the boys and girls would intermingle and cavort with each other and get tangled in the webs of hormones and emotions that would invariably be created when adolescent boys and girls meet. When her parents discovered the true antics that occurred during outings to the cinema they quickly put an end to the girls' matinees out on the town much to Thora and Rebecca's chagrin as they were developing growing and consuming interests in members of the opposite sex.
    As she stood in front of Cristo Pando's she could see down the street where the kids were lining up for a talkie presentation from Hollywood. She saw some of her girlfriends from school there. These were the very girls that Rebecca used to call when her sister was at home. Rebecca was the more popular of the twins but Thora had believed that she stood her own with the

circle of friends as well. To see them there in line laughing and gossiping with one another, Thora felt a pang of hurt that she was not included with them. She wanted to watch a movie too rather than stand here on the street as a distraught child waiting for a stranger to appear in her great uncle's Bentley.

She had been here thirty minutes already and there was no sign of the chauffeur at all. Every time that a car would drive by she would lift her head in the hope to see the black luxury vehicle. These hopes would sink as fast as her head when it invariably turned out to be somebody else's car. There were a few jalopies with rumble seats that would cruise by. They would be filled to the brim with older kids cruising by searching for some action in a town that was infertile for creating any activity that could be construed as constructive.

On one of these occasions some of the older adolescent males took note of her on the street. One of the boys began whistling at her and making catcalls. Thora found this exhilarating and flattering until others in the same car cried out, "jailbait!" Then the catcaller was ridiculed by his rabble-rousing cronies and the boy to salvage his status within the group made some disparaging remark to her about playing with dolls. The car would drive by and Thora would feel grotesquely inadequate. She did not know how to react. She wanted to yell back some rude comments of her own but no rude comments would come to her.

Art Rozelle and his party stepped out of the restaurant. They had their meal and looked quite sate. The union lawyer chomped off the end of a long cigar and then lit it. His wife and two children, teenaged girls older than Thora, waited on the sidewalk only feet away from where she stood. "Damn," Mrs. Rozelle said. "I don't think that there are any taxis in this forsaken place." She was looking up and down State Street.

"There has to be Rita! One brought us here, remember!" Art responded.

Before Thora knew it she started offering the Rozelles some information that they appeared not to know. "The taxi service stops at seven at night," she said.

"What kind of nonsense is that!" Art exclaimed. "It stops at seven? In most towns that's when the business commences!"

"Well, it stops here at seven," Thora said in defiance and in defense of her little town.

"Ain't that just great!" Art groaned. "How are we going to get back to the motel now?"

"Where are you staying?" Thora did not know of any motels in Grappling Haven.

"We are staying in Forestville," Mrs. Rozelle answered.

"Forestville is twenty miles away!" Thora cried. "That is too far to walk."

"Tell me about it!" Art griped. "This is a fine god damn mess we've gotten ourselves into!" He was shaking his head and trying to relight his cigar. It had gone out.

"The taxi driver from Forestville should have told us that there is no service here!" wife Rita offered.

"How is he supposed to know that we were intending to go back?" Art volleyed at his wife. "Really Rita you have got to learn that the world does not center around us!"

"He might have taken a cue that we were at a motel and that we were not carrying any bags!" Rita retorted.

"But he might not know a damned thing about this town. You're a Meadowford kid, aren't you?" Art suddenly said to Thora. "I recognize you from inside."

Thora nodded. She was not sure if that was a wise thing to do. Maybe the man was going to start yelling at her the way that he yelled at her father.

"That was your dad that got all worked up over his steak, wasn't it?" Art said. His eye seemed to be sizing her up for a potential sparring partner.

"He likes his food just so," Thora answered. "If it isn't that way he can get upset."

"That's an understatement if I ever heard one," the man laughed. "Tell me would he get very upset if we were to ask him for a ride back to the motel?"

Thora knew if her dad was to be asked that question he would go through the roof. Art Rozelle was from now on a lifelong enemy to her father after that incident in the restaurant. There would be no way that he would ever agree to give this man a ride back to Forestville. "I don't know," she answered in an ameliorating way, not wishing to offend the feelings of this man who had predicted that the family business would go tits up.

"What are you doing out here? Waiting for him to pick you up?" Rita Rozelle asked.

"No, my parents have gone home. I'm waiting for my uncle's limousine to show up to take me home," Thora responded.

"Still living the high life, eh kid?" Art smiled through his cigar. "These days are going to end for you soon enough once Dearborn Cable crashes."

"Don't be smart with the child Art!" Rita chastised her husband.

Thora did not like being called a child especially in front of the Rozelles' two daughters. Both girls were several years older than she was and they seemed more adult than her. She did not want them thinking of her as a little kid.

"Maybe the limousine driver will be courteous enough to give us a ride back," Rozelle suggested. "Do you think that it would be okay? What is your name anyway?"

"It's Thora."

"Thora, that's a pretty name. Do you think that it would be okay?"

"The child does not have the authority to say one way or another if it is permissible, Art!" Rita pointed out. "You should know that."

The comment stirred up Thora's anger. She did not want to be treated as a minor. She wanted to show the Rozelles that she was very much a grown up and that she could make decisions on her own. "Of course, it is okay to give you a ride back to your motel," she said with as much finality as she could muster.

"Are you sure?" Rita tested her commitment.

That commitment was not sure at all but she had already given her go ahead to the plan and she was not going to back down. In the rear of her mind she saw the faces of Uncle Thaddeus and her father contorted with rage upon discovery of what she had just done. She tried to shut out these faces. "Of course it is okay, Mrs. Rozelle. I wouldn't say so if it wasn't."

"Where is this limousine?" Art asked, scanning State Street for Uncle Thaddeus' Bentley.

"It should be coming soon," Thora said. She was wondering how she was going to convince the chauffeur to make the long drive to Forestville. She was also recalling that James Whattam had said that the car was running low on gasoline. Hopefully that would not be an issue. She had no money to purchase gas. Maybe the driver did and if not then surely the Rozelles did.

Ten minutes slowly drifted by with the party waiting in front of Cristo Pando's with no sign of the Bentley. Art Rozelle was growing more impatient by the minute. His wife tried to keep him subdued. Their daughters did not say anything. They bore long faces that hardly disguised their disapproval of their current situation.

And then Thora spotted Rory McQuoid come walking down the sidewalk in their direction. He walked with a pompous gait that declared that he was a fertile bull patrolling his pasture. When he saw Thora his eyes suddenly lit up. For a moment there seemed to be a bit of fear etched in them. He knew that his war with Langley Meadowford had only just begun and that he should be soon expecting an enemy counter-offensive. When he saw that she was not with her parents, the fear dissipated and a cocky attitude took its place. This mindset magnified when he caught sight of the two Rozelle girls.

"Good evening Thora!" he said in a phony ingratiating way. "Who are your friends?" He nodded courteously to Mr. and Mrs. Rozelle but he then quickly focused on the teenagers.

Thora did not answer Rory. After what he had done to her parents' car she could no longer look at him with any kind of admiration. She remembered what Rebecca said about him—that in ten years' time he would be in jail. There was no future in Rory McQuoid.

He didn't seem interested in what she would have to say any way. "It's a fine night in town tonight, eh ladies?" he said with a twinkle in his eye to the Rozelle girls.

"It was until you showed up," the older of the two girls said, her voice reeling in sarcasm.

"Get away from my daughters, punk!" Art Rozelle growled through his cigar. "They know riffraff when they see it!"

"Don't call me riffraff, sir. This is my turf, not yours. I'm the one who rules here," Rory showed that he was not afraid of Mr. Rozelle. He was taller than the man but Art Rozelle was stout and square. Underneath his tourist clothes there was undoubtedly a powerful physique that could shred apart the wiry street hoodlum.

"What is it about this town? Everybody wants to be the tough guy here!" Art cried out. "You are nothing, boy! If I take you back to Detroit you would not survive one hour on the streets before you would be sprawled on the pavement with your brains bashed out!"

"You are not in Detroit now, buddy!" Rory snapped back. He was lifting his fists indicating that he was ready to brawl.

"Why don't you go away!" the older daughter said. "You are never going to impress me."

"Leave my dad alone!" the other girl said and sprang in between Rory and Mr. Rozelle. "If you want to hit someone, hit me!"

Before Thora knew it this younger girl's leg shot out and landed squarely in Rory's chest. The force of the impact sent him rearing and stumbling. He looked up in surprise at the girl.

"My daughters are students of karate. They know how to defend themselves," Art Rozelle laughed.

"Growing up in Detroit a girl needs every defense that she can get," Mrs. Rozelle added.

Thora found herself laughing as well. The street bully got what he deserved.

When Rory saw her doing this, he said, "What are you smiling about, kid? After these tourists are gone you won't have anybody to stand behind!"

"I'll have my father! He isn't afraid of you and he will see you ruined, Rory McQuoid!" Thora retorted with brazen fortitude.

"Do you think that I'm scared of your dad?" Rory smirked. "I took pity on him. I could have had him sprawled on the pavement with his brains bashed out!"

"You must be pretty dumb, kid," Rozelle said. "You can't think up your own threats! Now get out of here before I sick my daughters onto you!" He took a step forward toward the hoodlum.

"Thora, I'm not going to forget this!" Rory glowered. "I don't care how much your sister begs for you, you are going to get it some day!"

"Rebecca?" Thora gasped. "You know where Rebecca is?" This was the second time that the punk mentioned her sister this evening. Was she still in town? She didn't board a train out west afterall?

"If I do, I'm not telling you!" Rory said as he pushed his way through the Rozelles to continue his stroll down State Street.

Thora ran after him. "No wait, Rory! Where's Rebecca?"

"I said go away, kid!" Rory hissed, pushing her against the shoulder.

Thora came to an abrupt halt. She felt tears start to well in her eyes. "Come on, Rory, please! You have got to let me know? Where is Rebecca? Is she safe?"

Rory smirked. "Safer than you are!" He tucked himself into a door.

When Thora looked up she saw that it was a pool hall. In the window was a sign that read, 'Gentlemen Only'. She could not go in after him. She and the rest of her gender were excluded from gaining entrance. "You can't stay in there forever Rory. I'm going to wait until you come out!" she hollered through the door. She had no intention of actually waiting for the punk.

She was so angry that she could feel the hairs bristle on her neck. What did that creep know about her sister? What was he not telling her? She could not imagine that Rebecca would take up with him. It would be so unlike her. Rory McQuoid was the antithesis to all of the values that Rebecca held dearly. He was probably just having some fun at her expense, Thora rationalized. He probably became aware through the gossip of the street that Becky had flown the coop and that her parents were frantic in trying to find her.

The problem was that her parents did not seem to be frantic in finding their estranged daughter. They seemed to be coping pretty well without her. They had not changed their routines and rituals in the wake of her absence. Her name was rarely uttered. It made Thora question how much Langley and Cora Meadowford really cared for their daughters. If she were to disappear and never return home how much anxiety would that create in the two of them?

"Is that the car?" Art Rozelle called out to her. Thora turned and saw the man pointing towards the street. Down the road a ways a shining black Bentley was starting to work its way up State Street. It looked like it was Uncle Thaddeus' limousine.

"I think that it is," Thora said, taking one last look through the doorway of the pool hall. She could not see too far in due to the layout of the joint. It had an elbow that veered to the right that blocked any vantage of the billiard tables and the seedy characters leaning over them lining up their shots. She walked away and joined the Rozelles.

When the limousine was within twenty feet of Cristo Pando's, Thora lost her certainty that it was the correct car. This one looked newer and shinier than the one that belonged to her great uncle. Still she did not rule out that it could be Thaddeus' car. She stepped out onto the pavement and waved her hands at the driver of the car.

The vehicle came to an abrupt stop. "You can get killed pulling stunts like that?" a man's voice said from inside.

Thora leaned through the window from the passenger side of the car and looked at the driver. She did not recognize the fellow who was looking elsewhere and not showing his face but she was not truly expecting to identify the man. Her Uncle Thaddeus rarely retained a chauffeur or any other servant for that matter for more than a month. He was always finding fault with the drivers and dismissing them. In fact this one was not even aware that he lost his job as of yet. He will discover that when he returns the limousine to Thaddeus' house. Yet, when she looked upon the fellow he did not seem to fit the description of the chauffeur that Thaddeus had unintentionally provided earlier. This man looked a little too old to be the kind to be cruising the streets trying to impress women that he was the owner of an expensive car.

"Are you looking for Thaddeus Meadowford?" Thora asked the driver. She could not see the man's face as it was turned to the road looking at the oncoming traffic.

"Who?" the man said with some consternation. He was not wearing the typical uniform of a chauffeur. This man was clad in expensive rags that could only have come from the big city.

"This is not Thaddeus Meadowford's limousine?" Thora asked although she was now certain that it was not.

"Sorry, girl. This car is mine!" the driver responded, turning and giving Thora a smile.

Then Thora recognized him. She was surprised that she had not recognized him earlier. It was her guardian angel. It was Samuel Angus Meadowford the First. "It's you!" she gasped.

"What can I do for you?" the man asked, taking only a quick glimpse at her before turning his attention back to the rearview mirror. He seemed to be distant and not wishing to engage in any familiar conversation. He did not reveal any traces that he was here to protect her, as she may have believed.

Thora could feel this attitude at once. She even began to entertain the notion that the driver may have been a complete stranger that bore a similarity in appearance to her guardian angel. She was about to admit to the man her mistake when the rear door to the Bentley opened and the Rozelle family began to pour into the car.

"This is awfully kind of you," Art Rozelle said. "Not many people would take it upon themselves to drive strangers twenty miles away. There will be a handsome tip for you when you drop us off."

Thora was sure that the driver was going to throw the presumptuous

Rozelles out. Nobody is as courteous as to go that far out of the way to help people that they did not even know, especially well-to-do people such as the Rozelles so obviously were.

"This sure beats a taxi," Rita Rozelle said as she seated herself on the posh leather seat.

The driver said nothing. He waited for the last of the Rozelle daughters to climb in. Once she had positioned herself comfortably, he turned to Thora who was still standing on the pavement leaning against the passenger window and asked, "Aren't you coming in?"

At that moment Thora knew that this was not a case of mistaken identity. The driver was indeed who she thought he was. It was so odd that he would be looking out for the Rozelles as well. Maybe this guardian angel had more to care for than just her.

"No, I have to wait for another car," she said. The Bentley that belonged to Uncle Thaddeus would sooner or later show up and she knew that there would be hell to pay if she did not abide by his wishes and direct that car back to the old man's house.

"It should be coming soon," the driver smiled.

Somehow Thora knew that the driver knew. "Drive carefully," she said to the man.

"Thanks kid, for all of your help," Art Rozelle said loudly from the back seat as the car pulled into gear and out onto State Street.

For an instant Thora thought that she saw blood all over Art's face but she quickly realized that it was nothing more than the play of the evening's shadows.

True to the driver's words, two minutes later another Bentley came driving up State Street. This one Thora was certain belonged to her Uncle Thaddeus.

Once again she waved down the car. It stopped and the chauffeur rolled down the window. "Can I help you?" he said.

Thora looked inside and saw that this was indeed the driver that she was looking for. He was a young fellow, hardly more than twenty years old. He wore the uniform that Uncle Thaddeus insisted all his help had to wear. "You're here for Thaddeus Meadowford, right?"

"Indeed I am, young lady!" the man grinned underneath his chauffeur's cap. His smile revealed a rather exaggerated look that Thora at once recognized as being induced by the consumption of alcohol. The guy had been drinking to pass his time while waiting for the Meadowford party to dine.

"He's already gone home," she said, choosing to ignore the driver's rather intoxicated condition. The smell of booze emanating from the car was very present even though it had been intermingled with a strong dosage of cologne that Thora guessed the driver chose to use to mask the smell. "He's asked me to tell you to take me home first and then for you to get the car back to his place as soon as possible." She did not want to elaborate further to let the fellow know that he had just joined the ranks of the unemployed. That was Uncle Thaddeus' job. Not hers.

"They've gone already?" the chauffeur said with some surprise. "I didn't think that I was that long."

"Our meal was shortened due to some unforeseen difficulties," Thora said. She started to open the door to the rear seat.

"Not so fast, my little beauty," the chauffeur said. "If I'm late already what difference does it make if I am even more late." He shut off the motor and started to climb out of the limo.

"What are you doing?" Thora cried.

"I'll just be a few minutes," the driver said. "There's somebody in there that I need to talk to." He indicated the pool hall. He didn't wait for Thora to express her objections. He jogged into the premises and disappeared, leaving the thirteen year-old girl sitting waiting on the sidewalk.

She was stewing with anger. She was tired of people making her cater to their whims and not paying any reciprocal courtesy to hers. Her dad and Uncle Thaddeus had forced her to remain behind and wait for the driver against her wishes. And now this careless cad in chauffeur cap was doing the same. It made her feel irate and she began to grumble.

Passersby must have heard her mumbling to herself but they paid her no never mind. They must have envisioned her as just another aimless youth waiting to go nowhere in life.

The few minutes that the chauffeur asked for turned into almost forty-five minutes. The skies overtop of the downtown core of Grappling Haven were beginning to darken and the streetlights had come on. Several jalopies with drunken robust teenage boys had driven by and had made their catcalls at her. She was beginning to grow afraid that one of these cars would actually stop and that some galoot would climb out and try making a pass at her.

This fear forced her to take some action. The only action that she could think of doing was to break the bylaws of the town and enter the pool hall and demand that the driver take her home at once. She started for the door when Rory McQuoid suddenly stepped out.

He seemed very animated and enraged. He turned around and yelled some obscenities back into the pool hall. He was holding his hand to his nose. Thora could see some blood trickle through his fingers.

Someone inside hollered back at him with an equal skill at colorful language. The final words were "You stay the hell out of here forever!"

This infuriated Rory and he took his rage out on a nearby garbage can. He kicked the aluminum object so hard that it sustained a dent before it toppled over and spread its medley of refuse upon the sidewalk.

Thora wanted to ask the punk if he was okay but she thought better of it. She did not wish for him to turn his hostilities upon her. It was best to try and remain unseen for there was no knowing what Rory would do.

Unluckily for her though, the brash street hoodlum saw her. "What are you still doing here?" he shouted at her. "I'm not going to tell you anything about your sister! Now get the hell away from me!" He went to shove her aside.

Thora stepped out of his way before he could make contact. This served to provoke the kid even more. "I tell you to get away from me!" he gnashed out viciously like a rabid dog.

"I'm not asking you anything!" Thora protested. "I'm just here waiting for my driver! He's inside there!"

Rory started to laugh. "Do you mean that moron with the chauffeur's cap?" His laugh that at first seemed put on took on a genuine aspect. "You're going to be waiting a long time! Your driver is passed out at a booth in there. It'll take a parade of trombone players to wake that fellow up!"

"You're kidding!" Thora gasped.

"The guy is as drunk as a skunk!"

"Well isn't this the shits!" Thora sighed. "How am I to get home now?"

"Not my problem," Rory was still chuckling. He had taken his hand away from his nose. The bleeding had stopped but his upper lip bore a red stain that required some good soap to remove.

"Are you hurt?" Thora asked.

"I can take it," Rory said. "I've had worse."

"I don't understand you, Rory. Why do you choose such a life? It's going to get you nowhere." She did not know why she said it. It just came out. It was like she felt sorry for the guy and that she wanted better for him.

"You don't look like you are going anywhere yourself kid," Rory responded. "You rich bitches expect the world on a silver platter. When that platter is removed then you are more lost than the rest of us. At least I know how to land on my own two feet."

Thora started wondering if his comment had something to do with her sister. Was Rebecca in some kind of turmoil now that her silver platter had been removed? But she chose not to address his remark in that manner. Instead she said, "Oh yeah? I'll show you what we rich bitches can do!"

She had not had any preconception of the action that she was going to take. It just came to her naturally. She walked down the sidewalk to the parked Bentley. She climbed into the driver's seat and saw that the keys were still in the ignition. She was hoping for this. She turned on the engine, took a peek into the rearview mirror for any oncoming traffic. When she saw the way was clear, she turned her eyes back to the sidewalk where a stunned Rory McQuoid was still staring in disbelief. "This is what we can do!" She stomped her foot onto the gas pedal and screeched her way onto State Street.

Chapter 13

The Streets of Grappling Haven

She had never driven a car in her life before. Not once had her father offered to teach her or her sister. Langley Meadowford was of the impression that women should not drive. They did not have the constitution to be able to make all the snap judgments that were required when driving an automobile in traffic. Cora, his wife, never tested his decree. She did not show any interest or inclination towards helming the Motorized Egg or any of the previous vehicles owned by her husband.

Thora was so unlike her mother in this regard. Almost every time that she was an occupant in any car she watched the driver go through the myriad of routines that were required to make a stationary object suddenly attain the dynamics of motion and to direct that motion so that it not only avoided other objects but arrived at a predetermined destination. One time she asked her dad if it was okay for her to drive the car in a parking lot. Her dogmatic father instantaneously rebuked her.

His ban on female driving also was extended to boats. Back on Pioneer Lake she and her sister were never allowed to take the Grappler out on their own. At first this was alright with the twin girls until last summer when they watched their younger cousin Jack take the boat out under the supervision of his father, Tom. Jack performed marvelously. The girls were proud of him but at the same time envious that he was given an opportunity that their father adamantly denied them. They pleaded with him for a chance to helm the boat on their own but Langley stuck firmly to his guns and would not give in even when Uncle Tom went up to bat for them. It almost ended up in fisticuffs between the two men and probably would have hadn't Rebecca withdrawn the request.

Now, here she was finally driving. The feeling was exhilarating and a little unnerving. Uncle Thaddeus' Bentley was much larger than the Motorized Egg. It possessed a more powerful engine and was far more responsive to the press of her leg or the nudge of her hand. Added to this was the fact that it was nighttime and her vision was restricted by the limitations of the dark. Thus far she had figured out everything in the handling of the vehicle except for the lights. She could not figure what instrument on the dash was responsible for turning on the headlights. She had pulled one knob and that turned on the windshield wipers. There were other knobs there as well but she found that she did not have the luxury in time to try them out. All of her attention had to be fixated on the road.

She was driving in a stream of traffic both with her and coming at her. The lights of the oncoming traffic had a mesmerizing effect upon her. She almost felt an unconscious drive to steer into them. She had to actively fight this strange motivation and stay true to her side of the road.

Luckily Uncle Thaddeus did not live that far away. It was only two miles as the crow flies and maybe three miles as the road lies. The whole route was lit up with electric streetlights so she never lost her mental map of the way to go. She was growing more comfortable with her driving skills as she moved along. She was now just settling into a groove where she felt that she had all the car's systems save the headlights under control.

She had moved out of the downtown core and was entering into the residential part of Grappling Haven. The traffic was less heavy here. There were fewer oncoming vehicles with their hypnotic headlights. She was coming up to her first turn from State Street. She slowed down and stuck her arm out to make the appropriate hand signal to indicate her turn. As she did so, a flashing caught her eye in the rearview mirror. This was soon accompanied by the wail of a siren.

Her first reaction was that the police had spotted her driving without headlights and were now coming after her. She felt jitters run through her as she began imagining all of the repercussions that were going to come her way for driving illegally.

Then she saw that there was another set of flashing lights and sirens following the first set. She must have been in real big trouble to have two police cars coming after her. Her dad was going to shred her alive when he finds out and she sensed that her vision was becoming blurry because of the tears that developed.

Resigning herself to her forlorn fate, Thora brought the Bentley to a full stop and waited for the police cars to arrive. She was too afraid to imagine the scene that was going to play itself out when the police discover that the driver of the dark car was just a thirteen-year old girl.

The oncoming police cars did not seem to be slowing down. They were rushing at her at a reckless speed and she started to get really scared that they did not see her and that they were going to plow right into her. She felt an urge to flee from the car before it was smashed. But her legs were hesitant to move.

The flashing vehicles were now within feet of her and she braced herself for the impact. But then at the last moment the first vehicle swerved to the right to avoid her. The second vehicle did the same. The two emergency vehicles continued racing down State Street and out into the country where it became a rural road. Thora noted that the second vehicle was not a police car but an ambulance. Something very bad must have happened on the road up ahead.

Catching her breath and her composure, Thora placed the Bentley into gear and negotiated her turn. She followed a labyrinth of streets and boulevards until she came up to Apple Grove Court, the street where her Uncle Thaddeus lived. As she approached his house she saw that the lights were still on. This was unlike her uncle. At the lake he was always early to retire, often going to bed immediately after supper. This had the effect of putting a real blanket over any evening entertainments that the Meadowford family may have planned. When Thaddeus was in bed the girls were forbidden to play at the piano. This peeved their mother more than it did them. Cora always thought of her girls as trained monkeys at the keyboard and would force them to go through an assortment of old standards and some difficult pieces written by Chopin and Brahms. But when Thaddeus was in his chamber there would be no standards, no Chopin. Everything had to be kept on an even keel and relatively silent.

To see that the old codger was still awake surprised her. It was after ten o'clock. She guessed that he was waiting for his limousine to return. He would be especially cranky tonight.

When she pulled into the driveway she saw the lights in front of the house come on. As she brought the car to a stop, she saw the old man wrapped in a housecoat step out of the door and stomp down the sidewalk to the driveway.

Thora did not even get a chance to open the door when Uncle Thaddeus began smashing his fist against the window. Even though his words were muddled by the glass that separated it from the interior of the automobile, Thora could hear him clearly.

"What in dickens have you been up to!" he railed. "I have half a mind to call the police and charge you with theft! Get out of my car at once!"

The girl meekly opened the door to the car. She had to literally push it against the thin frail body of her great uncle to get out. "It's me, Uncle Thaddeus! Thora!"

"Thora?" Thaddeus screeched. "Where's my driver?"

"He's not here," she said, stepping out of the car and onto the driveway.

"Then who drove the car?"

"I did." She felt like a lop-eared puppy ready to be viciously scolded by its master.

Uncle Thaddeus did not say anything for a moment. His eyes were searching the interior of the Bentley looking for his driver. He obviously did not believe her. He came from the same school of thought as his nephew regarding female drivers. "You drove the car?" he finally said once he was satisfied that his chauffeur was not skulking in the backseat.

"I had to get it home to you," Thora answered. She was feeling very nervous and vulnerable in the presence of the old man.

"Then where is the driver?"

"He's back at the pool hall sleeping it off."

"Sleeping what off?"

"The booze, Uncle Thaddeus. He was quite drunk!" Thora teetered on her feet to give accent to her explanation.

"Where would he get booze? This is Prohibition. There is no booze!" the old man snapped. It was a line that was often used by the adults to make it seem to their children that everybody in the land was law-abiding.

"I don't know where he got it but he was drunk," Thora said. It almost felt that her Uncle Thaddeus was blaming her for his driver's condition.

"So you took the car and drove it home? You could have gotten into an accident! Where are your senses, girl?" Thaddeus no longer seemed to be interested in conversing about his chauffeur.

"You wanted your car home, didn't you? Your driver whom you were going to fire anyway was tanked to the gills with alcohol. I saw no choice but to drive the car home. I got it here safely, didn't I? I didn't get in any accidents!" Thora could not believe that she was actually shouting back at her Uncle Thaddeus. She had never done this before in her life even though many were the time that she wanted to.

Uncle Thaddeus started walking around the car and inspecting the body and tires to see if the car had sustained any damage. He was once again calling her a liar. "Drat!" he said. "I can't see anything in this light."

"Look, Uncle Thaddeus, I told you! I didn't get in any accidents!"

She saw her uncle stoop over. He was examining something on the rear bumper. "What's this here?" he said. He started running his finger over the area. "It's a scratch!"

At once Thora went on the defensive. "I didn't do anything Uncle Thaddeus! Honest!"

The old man did not answer her. He stormed into the house. A few moments later he reappeared with a flashlight. He at once went to the bumper and turned the light onto it. "There's a scratch six inches long here! Where did that come from?"

"I don't know!" Thora cried. "I didn't do it!"

"Well somebody had to do it! It wasn't there before!" he practically shouted.

Uncle Thaddeus was a fastidious and meticulous man and took a very keen obsessive interest in his possessions. If he said that that scratch was not there before Thora could be sure that it wasn't. "It didn't happen when I drove the car. It must have happened when your chauffeur was driving! He was really drunk!"

"I don't believe you! You are just a girl. Girls have as much ability to operate a motor vehicle as a chimpanzee!"

She was now crying. She knew that the man would not believe her and that there was nothing that she could do to convince him of her innocence.

"Stop your crying kid! You are not going to get any sympathy from me!"

Before Thora could put a block on her words she rang, "Why are you such a mean man, Uncle Thaddeus? Why do you want everybody to be scared of you?"

"Oh hush, child!" Thaddeus gritted his teeth. "I'm not a mean man! But I am not very tolerant of people that do not show me and my property any respect!"

"I could have left your car in town and walked home, you know," Thora sniffled. "Then you would have really seen what kind of respect your property would have received. You saw what they did to my dad's car! Is that what you wanted me to do, Uncle Thaddeus? Leave the car in town? That scratch on the bumper would be nothing compared to what would have happened to it there!"

"Then you are admitting that you caused the scratch?" Uncle Thaddeus focused on the one sentence that Thora should not have said.

"No, I didn't do it!" She said as calmly as she could. She really had felt like screaming it.

Uncle Thaddeus looked at her. His hair was all on end and in disarray. His face was as haggard as Thora had ever seen it. The man was very old and looked every bit his age and then some. "I'm tired and I have had enough of this for one day. I'm going off to bed. I will be calling your father in the morning and telling him about your little escapade." He started to walk toward the house.

Thora suddenly realized that he was just going to leave her standing here. "Hey!" she called out to him. "How am I going to get home?"

The old man froze in his steps. He turned around to face his grandniece. Even though it was draped in shadow Thora knew that there was a very bitter scowl upon his mien.

"I can't walk home from here in the dark! It is too far!"

"And what do you want me to do about it? Drive you home?" he answered. "Girl, you should know that I no longer drive!"

"Then how am I going to get home?" She thought of the Rozelle family predicament earlier this evening when they discovered that there was no taxi service in Grappling Haven after 7:00 p.m. She was now in the same boat as them.

"It's none of my concern," Thaddeus said dismissively.

"Well, it should be! You are the one that made me stay in town waiting for that drunken sot! I could have gone home with my mom and Dad!"

"Then you should have waited for that drunken sot to sober up and drive you home. That was the arrangement I made and you agreed to. I carried out my end of the agreement. It is not my fault that you were negligent on your responsibilities in the bargain." He started walking away once again.

"Uncle Thaddeus!" her voice resounded. "You are going to do something about this and you are going to do something about it now!"

Thaddeus threw his hands up in the air. "Very well! Very well! Come inside. We will call your father and have him come pick you up!" He went on grumbling and mumbling unintelligible utterances afterwards.

"Thank you!" Thora said. "I am glad that you have come to your senses!" She started to follow him into his house.

The home of Thaddeus Meadowford was large and ungainly in its lack of gardens and other outdoor accoutrements that would break up and beautify the bland yellow brick walls. The building was apropos to the character of its owner. Uncle Thaddeus was an unimaginative sort that was more concerned with bottom lines than sprucing up the contours of his life with lively decoration. Thora recalled that Aunt Faye once described him as a soulless creature bent only on continuing to build barriers around himself that would shield him from the rest of the feeling world. Although the house was huge it possessed no substance. It made no statement. It was just there.

As Thaddeus opened the door and allowed her inside, she felt the continuance of this empty entity. The furnishings and fixtures of the house were as charming as a businessman's office. There was the slight nod to opulence but the styling was cold and unapproachable. This very much summed up the man. The world would pay as much attention to Thaddeus Meadowford after he died as it would to the stock market figures of seventeen years ago. It would know that the figures were there but that these figures amounted to nothing as far as the present day was concerned.

He was a mean and boring man to Thora. She knew of not a single person that liked him. Her grandfather tolerated him but did not seem to love him. Aunt Faye abhorred him. Langley, her father, only approached him out of a parasite's need to get at the resources he possessed. Other than that Langley would have nothing to do with the man. Even her cousin Jack would flee the room at the lake once Uncle Thaddeus would lanker in, huffing his jowls in disapproval at anything that came within his line of sight. Uncle Thaddeus may be a rich man but he was a dreg in the social order.

Thaddeus went to the telephone, an archaic model, and began spinning the handle to get the operator. He was not one to remember something as unimportant as a telephone number. He preferred that people cater to him. "Give me Langley Meadowford," he snorted into the mouthpiece once he had an operator on the line.

"I don't care what his number is! Just patch me through!" His telephone sat on a blank cream wall that was devoid of any personality. The old man faced the wall, holding his shoulders in such a way that Thora could not see his face.

A few moments later he said, "Cora? Thaddeus Meadowford here. Get me Langley." He did not exchange any pleasantries with her not that Cora would desire such a thing. She hated the man with a passion. She only thinly disguised her spite for him out of courtesy to her husband's bloodsucking needs.

Thora did not understand why Thaddeus could not have just simply provided Cora with the message to come pick up their daughter. Perhaps it was that 'women are incapable of performing complicated tasks' mentality of his showing through once more.

"Langley, come pick up your daughter. She is at my place," Thaddeus commanded once the nephew came on the line. He looked like he was ready to hang up the phone when Langley must have said something.

"Not her. The other one!" Thaddeus grumbled. Thora guessed that her father must have thought that Rebecca had showed up at Uncle Thaddeus' place. That was as likely to happen as a snowball fight in Venezuela. Rebecca hated Thaddeus the most.

"What? Your car's tires are all flat?" Thaddeus said. There was a rage building up in him.

"Well, if you had not provoked the imbecile, none of this would have happened! You have got to learn to ignore these lesser lights. They will go away on their own if you don't torment them!"

"What about your daughter? How are you going to pick her up?"

Thaddeus slammed his fist against the bland wall as Langley spoke. It was obvious that he was asking his uncle if the girl could stay overnight.

"Can't you drive that thing on flat tires?"

Her great-uncle must have been very desperate to get rid of her, Thora surmised. The thought of her staying over was very uncomfortable for the old man.

It was not a very pleasant prospect to Thora either. She had never stayed over in this house. It always seemed that it was a funeral parlor in disguise. The place was rank with age and the atmosphere associated with death's door. She found herself wishing that her dad would find a way to come get her. She did not want to stay here at all.

"I'm not going to provide any breakfast," Thaddeus said. "As soon as the girl wakes up I will be sending her home. She can walk in the light."

Thaddeus hung up the phone and stared at the blank wall for a moment. He was probably trying to incorporate the new exigencies of the night into his scheme of things. Thora was doing the same. She had no desire to stay for breakfast either. As soon as the sun is up she told herself that she would start walking home. Hopefully she would be able to do it before her great-uncle got up. She recalled that at the lake the old man was an extremely early-riser. He was often milling about in the kitchen and living areas of the Black Island cottage at about the same time as the myriad of songbirds began piping in the nearby pine trees. Even if he were up she would simply just scoot out the door with nothing more than a quick 'thank you' to him.

"I don't have any pajamas for you," Thaddeus said as he turned around to face her. "You are going to have to make do with the clothes on your back."

"That's okay, Uncle," Thora responded, making sure that there was no accidental eye contact between the two of them. She did not want to look into his gray eyes. She did not want to get to know this man at all.

"You can have the room that is opposite my study. If you have to go to the washroom there is the one down the hall from it."

Thora nodded. She was glad that he was offering her the main floor bedroom and not one on the second floor where he slept. This maximized the distance between the two of them. She realized that he held the same motives as her. He did not want to get any closer to her either. There was an unspoken pact between the two of them that they did not want to get to know each other any better. Things were quite satisfactory when they remained strangers.

"I am off to bed now," he sighed. "Be sure to turn out the lights. I do not want to squander money on needless expenses."

"I'll do that Uncle Thaddeus."

"Very well," the old man said. "Have a good night."

"You too."

Chapter 14

Gods and Ghosts

Thora did not know her Uncle Thaddeus' home at all. When he mentioned his study, the main floor bedroom, and the washroom, she pretended that she knew where he meant but after the old man disappeared up the steps to his bedroom, Thora realized that she was lost. She did not know the layout of the house whatsoever. It was an imposingly large edifice that had a series of cloistered rooms that seemed to be arranged haphazardly on the floor with no rhyme or reason to any grand design.

She began to roam down a corridor that seemed to be the most likely candidate where the set of rooms that Thaddeus mentioned could be found. Yet as she peeked through the doors, she found that these rooms were pint-sized compartments where Thaddeus' domestic help would sleep. None of these rooms were currently occupied. She guessed that these servants were temporarily dismissed while Thaddeus had been away to Canada and then Michigan. Evidence for this conjecture was revealed by furnishings that were covered with sheets to shield off the summertime dust. He would be recalling the help soon enough.

When she peered through the final door along this corridor and saw that it also was a tiny room barely large enough to fit a cot and a chair, she was startled to hear someone snoring in the bed. She quickly shut the door.

Someone was here with them. She was not entirely alone in this house with her Uncle Thaddeus.

She quickly and quietly left this corridor of the house, making sure that she did not do anything to wake up the person. Maybe Uncle Thaddeus retained one servant for the summer to look after the place and to make sure that its daily maintenance was kept up and that it would not get run down.

Coming into the main foyer, she paused for a moment to catch her bearings. She must have just come out of the servants' quarters. There was another hall that led to the west wing of the house. That must be where Thaddeus' study and the bedroom allocated to her must sit. Just before she started into it she heard the old man call out from upstairs, "Turn out that dratted light, for crying out loud! I am not made of money!"

Thora found the switch to the overhead chandelier and flicked it off. It left the room lit only by the moonbeams that came in through the large bay window. It seemed to be enough illumination for her to navigate into the west wing. As she entered the hall the light from the lunar orb was unable to penetrate to its end. She was in a grope and feel situation. She cautiously took small steps forward with her hands running along the wall trying to make sense out of the physical aspects of the foyer. She eventually felt the ribbed presence of wooden trim that snuggled to a doorway. Her fingers made contact with a glossy lacquered door that was shut. She found the doorknob and turned it.

The door creaked open. She was sure that Uncle Thaddeus heard it—it was so loud. At the opposite end of the room was a tall rectangular window where the soft light from the moon was able to creep in and give some definition as to what was in front of her. There was a massive grotesque desk that dominated one wall. Upon it were literally hundreds of documents strewn about in such a messy and unstable fashion that the girl was sure that the pile must have fallen from the desktop many a time and that each time it did it was brought back up in one more degree of randomness. This room had to be her great uncle's study. The bedroom that was given to her must be the next room. As she started to shut the door the change in air pressure caused the pile of paper on the desk to once more lose its balance. It slid to the floor like a crumbling layer of earth.

Thora groaned. She could not leave the papers scattered on the floor. Uncle Thaddeus would see them in the morning and accuse her of snooping.

She had no choice but to place the pile back on the desk. She entered the study and at once had to stifle a cry of agony. She had stubbed her toe on a paperweight that sat on the floor. In the dim light she saw that there were objects everywhere on the hardwood surface. She would have to turn on the light to negotiate her way safely. She made sure that the door was closed before she flicked on the light. She did not want Uncle Thaddeus to become aware that she was trespassing in the heart of his empire.

When the light came on she was astonished at the state of disarray of this room. Uncle Thaddeus was in dire need of his servants' return. The study made up for the sparse furnishings elsewhere in the mansion. This room was as cluttered as a backroom at a public library. Books and papers were everywhere. There were tables resting against tables with boxes piled up beneath them and above them. One would have to possess a key or legend to try to finagle any sense out of it.

How could Uncle Thaddeus live this way? It was dreadfully obvious that this was the room that he most frequented in his home. It was indeed his den and lair.

As Thora lifted her eyes she at once felt a shiver run through her. There on the wall partially obscured by some of the boxes was a portrait of Thaddeus' father, Samuel Angus Meadowford the First. It was one taken of him at an earlier age than the portrait in Margaret Whattam's cellar. The first Sam was only in his early twenties when this picture was taken. Thora was struck about how much he appeared like her father Langley when Langley sported his moustache. She had not noticed the resemblance before but now it was striking. The two could have been twins just as much as she and Rebecca were. Of course Langley was a little pudgier than his grandfather and overall had a softer appearance but that was due to the hard and dedicated work Sam the First had done during his lifetime. He had built a dynasty that ensured that his progeny would not have to undergo the excessive demands of life.

She started to gaze at the other pictures and artifacts that hung on the wall. There was a photograph that had to be of Black Island prior to the erection of the cottage. She would recognize that bald rock anywhere. Where the building now sat there was some juniper shrubbery splayed across the surface. Those bushes had to be removed in order to construct the cottage. She started to turn her attention to another picture when something crept into her mind. It was triggered by the motion of her eyes as they drifted through the picture's shrubbery. For the briefest of instances, she thought that she saw the sleeping face of an Indian boy within the bramble of the juniper. It made her feel uncomfortable. It made her feel some trepidation. She became aware that she had been dawdling and that the longer she remained in this room the more likely Uncle Thaddeus would catch her here.

She started to pick up the pieces of paper that had fallen to the floor and returned them to the desk. She was making certain that she recreated the pile as similar as possible to the stack that had been there when she first entered the room. Uncle Thaddeus was a stickler for detail and he would notice if his papers had been tampered with.

The last piece of paper in her hand was on IRS letterhead. Emblazoned in thick bold capital letters were the words, "NOTICE OF ARREARS". She really did not know what the phrase meant but as her eyes quickly scanned the contents of the document she was astounded to discover that Dearborn Cable was in debt for its taxes for over $600,000. That was a lot of money. The memo was dated June 30, 1929. That was just over two weeks ago. She wondered if Uncle Thaddeus paid the bill and then she reasoned that he probably did not because he had only arrived home just today. He had been gone from Grappling Haven since the start of June.

No wonder he looked so tired and distracted today. No wonder he was meaner than his usual self. Oh well, Thora thought, that this was his problem and not hers. She was satisfied with the pile she created. She shut off the light, left the study and quickly found the bedroom assigned to her.

It was a cozy room, bigger than her bedroom at home. The bed was sprawling and bore a canopy over it. It was quite luxurious, actually. It was nice for her uncle to give her this room rather than one of those cramped rooms in the east wing allotted to the help.

She crawled under the sheets and was ready to fall asleep. It had been a long and crazy day. Her disastrous attempt at supper seemed like days ago but that was only six hours ago. That was hard to believe. The evening had been filled with so much action that she should have been exhausted but now that she was finally in bed she found that she was having a hard time falling asleep. There were too many uncompleted thoughts from the day that were vying with each other in her mind. They all wanted closure when all that she wanted to do was close her mind and drift into the serenity of sleep.

For some reason that tax bill kept demanding the most attention to her thoughts. The family's company owed a lot of money to the government. When she coupled this item with the secretive dialogue between Uncle Thaddeus and James Whattam concerning some sort of arrangement that they were looking to complete with her dad, Langley, she was starting to sniff out something rotten. Was Uncle Thaddeus looking to unload his financial problems onto his nephew? Was he planning to leave Langley with a company that was ready to fall apart? Didn't Art Rozelle say something to the effect that Dearborn Cable was going to go tits up because it would not permit its employees to become unionized?

Thora did not have much in the way of business know-how but she got the real sense that her father was going to be played for a dupe by the conniving old man. As much as her dad was the bane to her life she knew that she would be remiss if she did not warn him about this conspiracy. But she knew how he would react. All of his life he wanted control of Dearborn Cable and now when it would finally be dangled in front of his face he would grab at it no matter how much it would drag him down into the depths of despair and financial ruin. No, he would not listen to any warning given to him by his foolish little girl. He would allow his greed and lust for power to get the better of him and he would then be stuck with a ship that would sink faster than the Titanic.

Somewhere in the mix of darkness and anxious thought, she had fallen asleep. She had not realized that she had done so but when she heard the creep of footsteps emanating from the hall outside of her room she rose up in her bed with the kind of overwhelming start that could only come when someone is yanked from the depths of slumber.

Someone was outside of her room. Her sensitive ears were picking up the faint sounds of a breath being held in check.

She wanted to call out her great uncle's name but her voice would not be produced. Perhaps if she had done so and it was Thaddeus out there then he would go into a gruffy tirade that this was his house and he was permitted to go where he pleased without having to concern himself over the effect that it would have upon others. She kept quiet, lying back down and pulling the covers up to her eyes.

Her line of sight gave her a glimpse of the crack beneath the door. There was a slight shift in the amount of light there as compared to the blackness of her room. The moon had found a way to create a weak glow in the hallway. The only method that it could do so in her mind was if the door to the study was open and the light filtered through from that room's large window.

In that faint light she could see something moving. She could not tell what it was. She was not even sure if a human was making it. It seemed to be intent on just remaining outside of her doorway as if it were listening in on any sounds that she was making. It remained there for long moments just lingering in the hallway. It was as silent as the night. It did not seem to be in any hurry to move away.

Thora was terrified. She quietly crept deeper into her blankets. She recalled that sleeping servant at the end of the east wing. She suspected that it must have been him but she had no idea who he may have been. Uncle Thaddeus went through servants at a prodigious rate. None ever seemed to stay under his employ more than a month or two before they could no longer tolerate his tyranny or he would find fault in their work and summarily dismiss them. In effect whoever it may be outside of her room was a stranger. She had been strongly impressed during her life not to trust strangers and in particular male strangers.

What was he doing out there?

Just when she was at the point to cry out to the person to go away, she heard the footsteps resume. They were going in the opposite direction towards the heart of the house and away from her room.

Thora sprang out of bed and silently slipped across the room and very cautiously opened the door far enough so that her eye could sneak a glimpse of the prowler. She immediately saw that the door to the study was open, as she had suspected. Peering further down the hall she could see the outline of a lanky matronly figure clad in flowing robes move surreptitiously away from her. There was something extremely eerie about the woman. She possessed an almost vapor-like quality that made her seem to be not bound to this earth.

The figure suddenly stopped. Thora's heart did the same. The figure turned its head back to peer down the hallway towards Thora's room. Thora could not see the face of this stranger but she was sure that she was able to see hers. At once, Thora raced back to her bed. She was scared out of her mind. She was sure that the woman was a ghost.

She could hear the sound of footsteps coming back towards her room.

The air felt suddenly cold and she sensed a malignancy in the atmosphere that was growing more tangible by the moment. She was convinced that this nocturnal visitor was a spirit sent by the netherworld to summon her to her final fate.

The doorknob to her room began to turn. Thora could no longer contain herself. She let loose a scream that came from her very life fluids.

The night visitor in turn screamed. It was a deep yowl that spoke of a being being brought to the very edges of destruction.

"What in blazes are you trying to do? Scare me to death!"

The voice was very familiar.

The light was flicked on flooding the room with a sharp, painful luminescence that pierced through the sheets that covered the girl's head.

"Uncle Thaddeus?" Thora peeped. The voice was definitely that of the old man. She pulled herself out of the sheets and saw her great uncle standing at the doorway. He was dressed in a floor-length nightshirt complete with sleeping cap. His hand was holding his heart as if it were producing some aftereffect from the scare that he must have received when she scorched her lungs with her cry. "Was that you out there creeping outside of my room?"

Uncle Thaddeus was trying to catch his breath. "Why were you in my study?" he asked. His eyes were accusatory as if she had committed some very wrongful act.

"I went in there by mistake," she answered. "It was dark and I couldn't see where I was going."

"You went through my papers, didn't you? You are as doggerel as that mother of yours!" he retorted, still huffing to get control of himself and gain composure.

"The stack of papers accidentally toppled over with the draft created in the room when I opened the door. I just merely put them back on the desk," Thora explained, knowing full well that this would not satisfy the man.

"Did you see something that you were not supposed to?" he asked. He was shrewdly watching her, ready to detect any sign that would indicate that she was fabricating her response.

"Nothing," she said, trying to steel herself to keep any messages that her body might produce held within her and not exposing them to his discriminating eye.

His eyes were penetrating and would not leave her face. He finally said,

"It would make no difference if you saw anything. You are incapable of understanding the complications of adulthood. You are nothing but a witless passenger in life meant only to procreate and further denigrate the pedigree of our once proud bloodline."

He was an insulting old man and she could not believe his audacity in breaking into her bedroom during the night just to throw hurtful accusations at her for actions she did not commit. Her back up was up. She was not going to let him get away with this. His remaining time on the planet was limited. He would be gone and she would live on. It was time to let him know that posterity was not going to be kind to his memory—that he would be thought of as only a dusty old artifact not worthy of being remembered.

"Who in the hell do you think you are?" she shouted at him, as he was about to leave the room. "I'm tired of having to act frightened of you because I am suddenly realizing that there is nothing scary about you at all. You are just a pathetic old man with a toothless bite!"

She did not hold back. She wanted this old tyrant to know how much his fellow human beings despised him. She wanted him to realize that he possessed a grim future and that he would burn in the fires of hell for eternity because of his selfish, cruel ways.

When she finished her spiel, she saw that her remarks had no effect upon the old man. At least his face did not portray that he had been hurt in any manner. "Child, you are not scaring me for I do not live by that fantasy," he smirked. "I am soon to die but there is no great arbitrator in the sky that will mete out punishment upon me for the way that I have treated others in life. We are only given one life and when that life comes to an end it is all over. There is no heaven. There is no hell. There is simply the quietude of death and in that quietude there is no mind that will lament the errors that were committed in life."

Thora took a deep breath for she could not believe what her uncle was implying. "You are an atheist?" she gasped.

"If you so wish to label me thus go right ahead. The concept of God does not even creep over my horizon. The word 'atheist' still implies that the concept of a deity is part of life. I am not even willing to allow it to go that far!" He seemed to take pride in speaking his beliefs.

The girl was astounded by what he said. She had never known an atheist before and to discover that one lived in her extended family overwhelmed her. Of late she had been questioning her own spirituality but she would never have gone as far as Uncle Thaddeus has gone. She may have even gone on to question if there was life after death had not a certain spirit revealed himself into her life of late.

"I don't know if there is a God or not but I can tell you this Uncle Thaddeus and that is that we do go on after death! I have firsthand proof of it!"

The old man smirked once more. "Are you about to tell me about your misinterpreted superstitions regarding strange occurrences that do not readily lend themselves to practical explanations? If so, don't. I don't want to be bored by the trite perceptions of ill-informed minds that cannot grasp the underlying truth that exists in such phenomena. Just remember that we as a people are still learning about the world that surrounds us and that in time all things will become explainable without having to resort to any supernatural devices such as gods and ghosts."

He seemed so haughty and so full of himself. She wanted to strike him down. "Then what would you say if I were to tell you that your father has been visiting me of late? He has entered my life and he has taken the role of my guardian angel."

Uncle Thaddeus produced a phlegm-based cackle in his throat. "What would I say to that? I would say that you are resorting to a defense mechanism to help you cope with all of the recent events that have unfolded in your life that you so readily would call traumatic because of your weak constitution. There is no one out there that is protecting you, my girl. You will learn this soon enough."

It didn't even faze him. He quickly dismissed the idea that the ghost of his father was visiting her. He did not give it one iota of credence. He did this so swiftly that Thora made an acute observation. "Maybe you are using a defense mechanism, Uncle Thaddeus!" she said. "Maybe you are so fast in denying things so that you can live with yourself for all of the mean things that you have done onto others! Maybe the world would be a better place for you if there were no gods and ghosts?"

This comment had taken the old man off guard. His bushy eyebrows lifted. "Touché!" he said. "There is some hope for you afterall!"

"I wish that I could say the same for you," Thora said. "But there will not be any unless you change your ways. Don't you want people to like you?"

"At my age that does not matter much," he said. "I am self-sufficient. I don't need others. Others may need me and that is why they pander about me, such as that sycophant father of yours. I know that he sees only money and opportunity in me and that he would cast me to the dogs once that need was satisfied."

Thora could not help but giggle at the remark. Uncle Thaddeus was seeing through her father, afterall. "He is that obvious, isn't he?"

"He's plainer than the nose on my face and you have to admit that I have a pretty prominent honker!" Uncle Thaddeus smiled.

Immediately Thora noted that it was one of the first times that she had ever seen a pleasant expression on the old man's face. It definitely was the first time that she was the source of his smile. All of a sudden he did not seem to be that bad of a man. All of a sudden there seemed to be a soul residing within that frail old body. She could feel that she was beaming herself. But that light spirit lasted only a few brief moments when she thought of her father. "Why does he have to be that way Uncle Thaddeus?" she asked. "Why does my dad have to be the embodiment of all things disgusting about our people?"

"You'll be surprised Thora," he said. "You will some day learn that your father only appears to be a bad sort and that underneath his hard exterior there is a little boy that only wants to please others but does not know how to do so. He thinks that the only method that one can make another happy is if that one holds all the cards. Once your dad holds all the cards I think that you are going to discover that he is a very generous man."

"But I don't think that he will ever hold all the cards or recognize it when he does," Thora said. "He will always be wanting more, more and more."

"That is very astute of you to perceive that, girl. I am afraid that you are right on that account, not only for your father, but for most of us, including myself," Uncle Thaddeus said. "I wanted nothing but the best for my family but what I failed to realize was that the accumulation of material objects is a poor replacement for the love and dedication that any man already possesses and has available to give. I lost my family because of this and I fear that Langley will have the same fate fall upon him."

Thora could not believe the admissions that her great uncle was offering to her. She would not have ever suspected that such thoughts resided in him. He no longer seemed to be that miserable old throwback to the great capitalists at the dawn of the industrial age. But there was one thing that was disturbing her and she thought that this was the best time to address it. The old man may soon return to that crabby iconoclast and forever hold his tongue on his motivations. "If this is the way that you feel," she began cautiously. "Then why tell me are you planning to play my father for a dupe and unload the sinking Dearborn Cable onto him."

Almost at once the furrow on Uncle Thaddeus' brow grew sharp as the smile fell from his face and into an abyss where it could never come out. "You have been snooping afterall!" he charged.

"I just noticed the tax bill in your study," she admitted. She forced herself not to get scared by his tactics. She knew now for certain that he possessed no real bite. "And earlier I sort of overheard some of the stuff that you and Mr. Whattam were saying and I put two and two together and came to realize that you want my dad to take the company off your hands."

Uncle Thaddeus seemed to be able to control himself as well. He kept his temper in check and said, "Your father has often said that if he were in charge of the company that he would do things differently. All that I am doing is going to give him the opportunity to ply his ideas and to see if they will work. If they do then your father may have everything that he ever wanted and his generous spirit will come out much to your satisfaction."

"But you know that that is not going to happen," she said. "I heard what Mr. Rozelle said. Our company is ruined and my father will never be able to rescue it."

"Have faith in your father, girl!" Thaddeus responded. "He has a very strong business acumen. The challenges that Dearborn Cable face can be surmounted by a man who has the know-how and has his family behind him!"

Thora was not buying his pitch. "It really doesn't matter what you say, Uncle Thaddeus. The fact of the matter is that my dad does not have the money to buy the company."

Thaddeus once more smiled like a man that knew he possessed the trump card. "But you are forgetting that your father stands to inherit your grandfather's share of the company. Using that as collateral he can easily buy me out."

"Aren't you forgetting about Aunt Faye?" Thora pointed out. "She will be receiving a large share of the company herself."

"Tut tut, child," Thaddeus clucked. "Your Aunt Faye told your grandfather that she is not interested in the company. All that she wants from him is his share of the cottage on Pioneer Lake. She doesn't want anything to do with Dearborn Cable or Sambo's possessions elsewhere."

"And how do you know this?" Thora asked.

"Sambo told me!" Thaddeus grinned. "In fact he showed me a draft of his will that he has filed with William King. It shows that your father is to inherit one hundred percent of Sambo's shares in Dearborn Cable and the house here in Grappling Haven. Your Aunt Faye is to receive his share of Black Island as well as all the capital that Sambo had invested elsewhere. This is a nice tidy nest egg for her that I would value at almost $3 million. I am going to offer her the opportunity of buying me out of Black Island for perhaps $50,000. I'm not interested in going there any more and I know how she adores that place."

Thora could not quite grasp what the man was talking about but she felt a sudden emptiness in coming to intuit that Black Island will no longer belong to her branch of the family. It was all going to belong to Aunt Faye. She sensed that her frivolous days of lark and adventure upon the waters and shores of Pioneer Lake were now forever gone. Her parents would never want to go there even in the unlikely event that Aunt Faye would invite them.

"When did you see this will?" she asked.

"Sambo showed it to me last winter after he had that mild heart attack. That had scared him and he wanted to get his estate in order," Thaddeus said. "He had to show it to me as I had to provide my consent to his proposed dispositions seeing that I was a very interested party."

"But that was last winter, Uncle Thaddeus," Thora piped. She saw a ray of hope that might preclude the directions in the testament. "My parents had a big fight with Grandfather on the morning of the day that he died. I would not be surprised that Sambo wrote my parents right out of the will that morning."

Thaddeus nodded his head. Thora could see that this was news to him. "I had noticed the deteriorating condition of the relationship between father and son for some time," he admitted. "But I saw the will and my brother was going to concede one hundred percent transfer of the Dearborn Cable shares to Langley. And you say that that fight between Sambo and Langley took place on the day that Sambo died. I would daresay that even if Sambo had a change of heart he did not have sufficient time to change his will."

"But who knows what happened between Aunt Faye and Grandfather after my family left the island on the Madoqua Empress? She may have convinced Grandfather to take Langley out of the will." Thora knew that she was grasping at straws. She truly wished that Sambo had done so. If Langley did not inherit his share of the company then he would not have anything to be able to buy out Uncle Thaddeus. He would have no ticket for the sinking ship.

"Even if that happened any such document that was produced could be easily challenged in court," Thaddeus said. "Right off hand I can think of several ways of having any revised will thrown out of court. Your grandfather's mental capacity could be brought in question. I would even testify that I had seen him talking to himself on the island. No, I don't think that there is anything to worry about on that account. Your father is going to get the company."

Thora felt her heart sink. Her family was going to lose it all. She just knew it. She did not have faith in the financial prowess of her dad. She had heard the accusations cast against him about how he squandered personal fortune on needless luxury that was beyond the family's means. She knew that these accusations were well founded. "I guess we will find out what happens when the will is read," she sighed.

"That will be soon," Uncle Thaddeus said with a twinkle in his eye. "My advisor Mr. Whattam informed me that he received a telephone call from Mr. King and that Mr. King will be back here in Grappling Haven next Monday and that my brother's will can be read publicly as early as that evening."

"Uncle Thaddeus, why do you want to do this to us?" Thora cried out. "You know that my dad is never going to be able to carry the company. You know that Dearborn Cable is going to go belly up soon. You are an old man soon to die. You won't have to live long in a destitute state. I have the rest of my life and I don't want to be poor."

"Child, have faith in your father!" Uncle Thaddeus answered. "He can do it. He can save the company. I know it!"

"You are just saying that so that you don't go broke. You will come out of this well and fine. But not my dad and mom and me and my sister. We are going to go to the poor house because of your greed."

"I see there is no convincing you," Thaddeus shrugged. "You are as lacking in the venturesome spirit as my ex-wife. To strike it big girl you have got to take chances. Now tell me what future will there be for your father if we allow events to follow your cautious guidelines?"

"I already told you. We would not go to the poorhouse!"

"But yes you will Thora. If Langley does not take advantage of this opportunity I am afraid that I am going to have to put my shares out on the open market and I know precisely who will gobble them up. They will be agents for our competition who will force Dearborn Cable to undergo liquidation. Then what will your father have? He would have some capital gain but that won't last for long. Without a proven track record in management your father will find that he would join the ranks of the unemployed. From there destitution can only follow."

Thora did not understand a lick of what her great uncle was trying to say but she sensed that whatever it was that he said was so full of holes that its ominous picture could not be taken as a viable let alone a certain depiction of the future. Yet she chose to keep these sentiments to herself. She did not want to get caught in an argument where she had insufficient tools to say anything sensible.

"Girl, opportunity is sitting at your family's door! You should be excited by what it has to offer!" Uncle Thaddeus tried to sound enthusiastic but all that Thora could hear was a man trying to pull a fast one.

"I'm too tired to be excited," she said through a feigned yawn.

"When the morning comes and you recall these words I assure you that you will be in a hurry to get home and impress upon your father, your dad, what a glorious vista is set ahead for him and the rest of your family."

"If you say so," she yawned again. This one was one that came out naturally.

"We will see you in the morning," Uncle Thaddeus said.

"Good night Uncle Thaddeus," Thora's mouth once more gaped open.

The light to her room was shut off and shortly thereafter Thora's mind was turned off as well.

Chapter 15

Radio Station Personalities

The tinny sound of a radio coming from beyond her door pulled the tendrils of sleep from her mind. She slowly opened her eyes and at first did not know her whereabouts. It took her a few moments to realize that she was under her Uncle Thaddeus' roof.

The room was awash with a gentle sunlight that came in through the window. There were many pictures on the wall that she had not noticed the night before. These were photographs of earlier times here in Grappling Haven. They were taken of a house that Thora knew did not stand any longer. It was the house and yard of Samuel Angus Meadowford I before the money started pouring into the family.

Back then the family had lived on a farmhouse that sat at the eastern perimeter of the town along State Street. From what Thora knew Sam Senior was a poultry man selling both eggs and his chickens to market. On the side he tinkered in mechanics and for some reason seemed to be engrossed by pulleys and cables. He had outfitted the farm with these devices and created a conveyor system that routed feed to his birds as well as another system that moved freshly laid eggs from the nest to a gathering bucket inside the barn. Others became interested in his techniques and he soon found himself busy setting up farms and then industries with his cables and pulleys. When the auto industry in Michigan started to look toward streamlining their manufacturing process they came to Sam Senior and shortly thereafter Dearborn Cable was founded.

Sam loved the mountainous country of western Pennsylvania and had no desire to relocate to Michigan. He built up his empire in the Midwest State but kept his roots in Grappling Haven. He sold the farm and built his large mansion in the town. Where the farm had been a plaza was erected and the town crept out towards it and engulfed it within its borders.

The pictures that hung on the wall of that farmhouse showed another way of life that Sam Senior must have missed as he became more and more involved with his company. It was perhaps this longing for a close relationship to Nature that was the impetus behind the man taking fishing trips up into Canada and discovering the serene and charming beauty of Pioneer Lake.

Sam Senior inherited the farm from his parents at a very young age. They had died of a nasty flu that had torn through Grappling Haven taking almost thirty victims with it. The death toll not only included Sam's parents but his three sisters as well. Sam was left on his own at the age of fourteen and he had shown the ingenuity to survive and prosper. Thora always admired the man. She knew these stories about him through her grandfather. Sambo lionized the memory of his father, Sam Senior.

It was sad to think that the two Sams' times on this good Earth had come and gone and now the planet was left in the hands of newcomers that just did not seem to possess the strength of character and the wherewithal that these two men had. There were no longer any strong characters in the Meadowford family, Thora thought. It was the weak that inherited the Earth. The strong had died.

She included her cousin Jack Thurston in this grouping. Even though he never attained manhood there was something about Jack that spoke of a very promising future. He was smart and he was not easily discouraged. He tackled challenges with an enthusiasm unequalled by his peers. He was not afraid of hard work. He possessed the qualities of a winner. It was a very sad day when that future was stripped from him when the lake that he loved so dearly claimed him for itself. That was almost a year ago.

And now with the death of Sambo only the lesser figures in the Meadowford clan remained. Thaddeus paled to Sambo. He did not possess the air of greatness that surrounded his brother. Langley was a far cry from his dad. He could never fill his shoes. As for the female figures in the family, Thora had no doubt that Aunt Faye could have been every bit as formidable as her father yet Aunt Faye did not seem to possess the right kind of drive that made achievement a priority. She had been derailed along the way and did not seek to find the way again.

Thora's sister Rebecca seemed like she was following Faye's path. Becky was brilliant at school and she was popular with her friends. Yet due to her parents' severe shortcomings in providing nurturance in their home, Rebecca answered the summoning of the wild spirit and she left. Thora prayed that she was all right. The secretive insinuations made by Rory McQuoid disturbed her. She hated to think that her sister had taken up with the hoodlum's crowd and was wasting away her future hanging out in the seedy sections of town living moment by moment and not thinking of what sat past them.

As for herself, she possessed no delusions of grandeur. She did not have her sister's wits or her charm. She believed that the only way that she could sustain the quality of life that she was accustomed to was through marrying some rich boy. Being part of a well to do family had earmarked her for this kind of future. Yet if the family was to go broke no son of any wealthy family was going to give her a second look. She might be doomed to an existence that was barely above subsistence.

This thought made her very uncomfortable. She at once climbed out of bed so that she did not have to entertain this stream of consciousness any longer. She walked out into the hall and at once was nearly floored by Uncle Thaddeus' blaring radio. The old man must have been hard of hearing. No one with good hearing would play anything so loud. It was practically deafening.

There was only one radio station in the Grappling Haven area. In the evening the station was okay as it played all the serial dramas and comedies that came out of the studios of New York and California. But during the day the airwaves were devoted to personalities of extremely bucolic and rural sensibilities. These men would ramble on for hours regarding hog futures and innovations in livestock feed. Periodically they would intermingle their chatter with music that was recorded in the Ozarks. Thora admired these antiquated dirges but she despised the radio station by day nonetheless because of the bumpkins that commandeered the radio signal.

She was surprised that Uncle Thaddeus would listen to this station. He did not seem like the kind of man that would be interested in listening to yokels blab inanely about the price of sheep in Pittsburgh or whether it was better to let a field sit fallow or to go ahead and fertilize and plant. Yet, he had the radio station on. And he was playing it loud.

She put her hands to her ears and ambled her way through the hall toward the main foyer. She had promised herself that she would leave the house as soon as she got up. But with the new morning she discovered that she was not quite up to taking on the long hike to Pine Street and her home as of yet. She needed a bit of time to gather herself.

When she stepped into the dining room of the house she caught the shadow of someone who was standing just inside of the adjoining kitchen. She assumed that it was her Uncle Thaddeus and called out a 'Good Morning' to him. She had to do so loudly to make herself heard over the radio.

The person in the kitchen jumped with a start. He was apparently not expecting to hear any voices other than the rural radio personalities.

Immediately Thora saw that this person was not her Uncle Thaddeus. This was some stout, balding character dressed in the light green servant uniform that her great-uncle demanded his help to wear.

"Who are you?" the man said. His eyes were wide and there was worry imprinted on his fleshy cheeks

"I'm Thora," she answered. This must have been the man that she saw snoring in bed last night when she went down the wrong hallway.

"Are you a guest in this house?" he inquired.

"Why, yes!" Thora responded. The servant probably was not made aware that she had stayed overnight here. He was still looking at her suspiciously as if she were an intruder with malice in her heart. "Is Uncle Thaddeus around?"

"Mr. Meadowford? He is your uncle?"

"My great-uncle," Thora clarified. "I'm the granddaughter of his dearly departed brother, Sambo."

The servant nodded. He seemed that he no longer looked upon Thora as a threat, if a young girl could be looked upon in that manner anyhow.

"Mr. Meadowford left earlier this morning on an urgent call. He did not tell me that there were any guests here."

"I assure you that I am a guest. Go check the bedroom in the west wing. You will see that the bed is unmade. That is where I slept. How come Uncle Thaddeus had to leave so early? What time is it anyway?"

"It is half past seven in the morning," the servant answered. "Mr. Meadowford left approximately an hour ago."

"How did he leave?" Thora at once asked. She remembered that Thaddeus said that he did not drive any longer and he did not have a chauffeur.

"He took a taxi, if that is any of your business."

"What would make him hit the road at such an ungodly hour? He never mentioned any early appointments last night."

"Mr. Meadowford is not answerable to me," the servant responded in a snooty fashion. "He does not tell me his affairs. But," the expression on the man's face suddenly changed. It took on the look of someone who enjoyed a good conspiracy. "If you ask me it had something to do with that terrible accident last night."

"What accident?" Thora's mind was conjuring images of the police car and ambulance that sped past her when she was driving the Bentley home.

"It was all over the radio this morning," the man said. "A family of four from Michigan was killed just outside of town."

Thora gasped and at once knew that the victims had to be the Rozelles.

"There was a deer involved in it too," the servant continued. "There were deer tracks found near the wreck. The people on the radio conjectured that the deer must have stepped out in front of the car causing it to swerve and lose control."

The girl was not really listening to what the man had to say. She thought of that family. It was similar to hers—a husband, a wife and two daughters. All of them were dead now. It was so hard to believe. They were fully alive in the evening when she last saw them enter the Bentley driven by…

Thora could not complete the thought. It was too unimaginable to conceive. The ghost of Samuel Angus Meadowford the First, her guardian angel, drove the limousine. Could it be? Could it be that the ghost was once more trying to protect her? But how could the ghost interpret the Rozelles as a threat? Sure, Art Rozelle represented a faction that was behind the financial crisis at Dearborn Cable but he was more just a messenger of the bad news and not the cause of it. Why would he have to die? And moreover why would the rest of his family have to die?

She was starting to feel very sick. Even though it did not make sense to her she knew that she was extremely implicated in the death of the family. Why would the ghost go to such extremes?

"The strange thing about the accident is that all four members of the family were found in the backseat of the wreck. This led the police to wonder who exactly was driving the car," the servant continued. "They assume that it had to be the man but how would the man end up in the back seat? If anything he should have been thrown forward through the windshield yet his twisted carcass was in the rear seat with the mangled remains of his family."

Thora had an answer to the mystery. But she was not going to tell the servant this. She did not know if she could tell anybody this. Who would believe her anyway? All that she knew was that she had to somehow contact the spirit of her great grandfather and demand an explanation.

"You look very pale, my dear," the servant said. He was polishing a silver tea service at the entrance to the kitchen. "Are you all right?"

"I don't feel well," Thora admitted. "I think that I might know the victims in the tragedy."

"That was precisely Mr. Meadowford's reaction when we first heard the news on the radio earlier this morning," the servant said. "He at once called his business associate, Mr. Whattam, and arranged to meet him at Mr. Whattam's office at 7:00 a.m."

Thora could not understand her great uncle's reaction. Outside of the normal human response of grief at this sad news, there should not have been any reason for him to require counsel from his legal advisor. How did Art Rozelle's death change things for the old man? She could not figure it out.

Then almost as an answer to her question the two radio personalities started talking about the accident over the airwaves. "We have learned a little bit more detail regarding that crash last night that killed four out-of-towners," the announcer named Smitty said. "It appears that the car was owned by Grappling Haven's own Thaddeus Meadowford."

"He owns that big black 1928 Bentley that I am sure you folks around town must have seen cruising State Street from time to time," Smitty's partner Earl interjected.

"That's the car!" Smitty concurred. "Not many of us here in the old G.H. can afford to drive one of those babies!"

"As far as I know Meadowford has the only one in not only the town but the whole county!" Earl said.

"Anyway, Earl, it now appears that the car involved in the accident was a 1928 Bentley," Smitty spoke over his partner.

"That'll be bad news for old Thad, wouldn't it? If news was not bad enough for him already. I heard that things are not going well for his company in Michigan. There is a lot of labor unrest there."

"It is interesting that you point out that Michigan connection, Earl. The victims, whose names have not been released yet, were all from Detroit."

"Do you think that Mr. Meadowford was the driver of the car? Oops, I should have not said that. I could get us in a libelous situation, couldn't I?

"I think that you are alright to make that conjecture. I highly doubt that Mr. Thaddeus Meadowford or any of the cronies that he associates with would be listening in to this station, anyhow. It would be beneath them," Smitty chuckled.

"We are a station for the people Smitty and we will always champion them first before we act gingerly for those that think that they are better than us."

"Such as Thaddeus Meadowford and the whole Meadowford clan. I heard that Langley Meadowford was up to his old antics last night. A caller told me that Langley got involved in an altercation with a tourist yesterday evening at Cristo Pando's. The shouting match got so unruly that Mr. Pando was forced to throw Langley and his party out."

"Good for Cristo!" Earl declared. "It is high time that these Meadowfords realize that they are not Grappling Haven royalty."

"Well, the way things are going for them, I would not be surprised that one day that they become panhandlers in this town."

Thora grimaced at the remark. She could not believe that these two buffoons were ridiculing her family in public. She promised herself that she would let James Whattam know exactly what the two announcers were saying over the public airwaves about the Meadowford family. James would see that the bumpkins would get their just desserts.

"And now this accident on top of everything else," Smitty said. "Thaddeus Meadowford is a frail man. I don't think that he is going to be able to take this. He would be still mourning the loss of his brother, Sambo."

"Sambo, now there was an elegant chap," Earl cut in. "He almost made us like his family."

"Too bad the rest of them were not like him," Smitty agreed. "Anyway, we have another caller on the line. I believe that the caller is Cristo Pando himself. Hi there, Cristo, another beautiful summer morning here in Grappling Haven, isn't it?"

A crackly voice came over the radio. The phone connection between the station and Cristo's house was not very clear. "I can't tell yet. I still have my curtains closed," the caller said. Thora could clearly hear the Macedonian accent. It definitely was Cristo Pando.

"So there was an altercation at your establishment last night, I am given to understand," Smitty asked.

"First of all I want you to know that I run a fine business," Pando said. "I want my patrons to enjoy a wonderful evening when they visit my restaurant. I do not permit hooliganism. Last night Mr. Langley Meadowford went out of his way to pick a fight with a guest and his family. This guest was from out of town and may very well have been one of the victims in that terrible accident."

"Oh my gosh!" Earl cried out. "There were four of them! A married couple in their early forties and two teenaged daughters."

"That's them!" Cristo rasped.

"I was just thinking Earl," Smitty said. "You never see Thaddeus Meadowford driving his Bentley."

"That's right Smitty! He usually has a chauffeur."

"Thaddeus Meadowford was at my place last night," Cristo said. "I had him thrown out as well!" The man said it with big, boisterous pride.

"You threw out old Thad!" Earl let out a hearty laugh.

Chuckling as well Smitty added, "I have heard that there is no one in town as tough as you Cristo. I know that I sure wouldn't be wanting to mess with you!"

"Yes, I threw out that snooty old codger. I sent him to the streets along with Langley and his ugly wife and their miserable little brat girl," Cristo boasted. When Thora heard the restaurant man call her a brat she wanted to reach into the radio and strangle him. She wanted to groan but she was afraid she would miss some of the stuff being said.

"They just had the one girl with them last night?" Smitty asked.

"It is interesting that you point that out Smitty," Earl cut in. "I have heard rumors that one of the twin Meadowford girls has run away."

Thora's ears perked up at the comment. These radio personalities were asinine. She wanted James Whattam to do what he could to see to it that they were fired.

"I've heard that rumor too," Smitty said. "Things in the Meadowford world are caving in, aren't they?"

"I just wanted to say that when the party of four from Michigan finished their meal, I saw them standing on the sidewalk," Cristo interrupted. "They were waiting there along with the young Meadowford girl. I saw a black limousine appear. It fits the description given for Thaddeus Meadowford's car. I could not quite see the driver but from what I could see I held the impression that it might have been Langley Meadowford himself that was the chauffeur."

"Are you sure Cristo?" Smitty asked. "You could get us in big trouble if you are wrong on this matter."

"I'm positive, Smitty! It was him! The family all got in the car. Only the brat Meadowford kid was left behind."

Thora recalled the pictures of the younger Samuel Angus Meadowford the First. She remembered how she thought that he did bear a striking resemblance to his father. She also vaguely recalled that Cristo Pando and his maitre d', Harvey, were periodically peeking out of the entrance to the restaurant. It seemed to her at the time that they wanted to be sure that the Meadowfords did not try to get back in.

"Have you gone to the police with this information?" Earl enquired.

"Not yet, I just got out of bed, for crying out loud!" Cristo moaned in a thick Macedonian accent.

"Well, I think that you should," Earl implored. "This is a very serious matter. If Langley was the driver of that car and he did not remain at the scene of the accident he has broached the law."

"What I don't understand is if Langley Meadowford was involved in a scuffle with the victims in your restaurant why in heaven's name would he be offering the family a ride home? It just doesn't make sense." Smitty said.

"Unless he had some nasty intention," Earl quipped ominously.

"I saw what I saw," Cristo said. "I'm not making this up. Why would I want to make up such a story? What would I have to gain by it?

"We're not calling you a liar, Mr. Pando!" Smitty clarified. "All that I am saying is that it seems very odd that Mr. Rozelle would accept a ride from a man that he was practically in fisticuffs with only moments earlier."

"Smitty, you said the name. You are not supposed to do that yet," Earl cautioned his partner.

"What difference does it make? The Rozelles are from Michigan. They won't know anybody here!"

"But they might have some kin here in the Grappling Haven area that are unaware of the fatal accident," Earl responded.

"If they had family ties here then they would have been getting a ride with them rather than Langley Meadowford, now wouldn't they?"

"Still we have to follow the rules, my friend. We were not to announce the names of the victims until we got the go ahead from the authorities," Earl sounded somewhat angry. Smitty and Earl were noted for their periodic blowups on the airwaves. It was these occasional spats that kept their listenership so high.

"I think that they might go to blows," the servant in the kitchen said. Thora had practically forgotten about him, she had become so engrossed by the dialogue between the two bumpkins and Cristo Pando.

"I was there," she said to him. "I saw the family get into the car. It was not Uncle Thaddeus' car and it was not driven by my father!"

The servant smiled at her. "A daughter is expected to defend her father. You will say anything to keep his nose clean."

"Oh yeah? Want me to prove to you that that wasn't Uncle Thaddeus car?" she snapped. Her back was up. "Go look in the driveway. You will see his car sitting there!"

"Madam, I escorted Mr. Meadowford to his taxi this morning. There was no vehicle in the driveway. Have a look yourself!" The servant pointed to a window that overlooked the sparse front gardens of the house.

Between the azaleas and shrubbery Thora could see the entire loop of her great uncle's driveway. There was no Bentley parked upon it. She ran outside to ascertain that she had a view of everything and that the car was not being obscured by any object. There was no vehicle there. The Bentley was gone.

She went to the garage to see if it was parked inside there. The garage was empty. Where did the car go? She knew as an absolute fact that she had driven it home last night. Uncle Thaddeus would know the same. He had pounded his fists upon it when it came home so late. She went back inside.

"Where did it go?" she demanded of the servant. "It was there last night! That is an absolute fact!" Her voice sounded histrionic. She felt histrionic. She did not like her mind being fooled with.

"It never came home last night," the servant responded, keeping his cool. "It was in an accident on the county road."

"That was another car!" Thora cried. "Uncle Thaddeus saw the Bentley here last night! He should have noted that it was missing this morning!"

"Mr. Meadowford was in a rush this morning trying to get ready before the cab arrived. I doubt he would have even known if his fly was done up he had become so preoccupied once he learnt of the car crash," the servant said with a smile. He seemed like he was enjoying this. It seemed he wanted her to be confused and hurt. "And ask yourself this, Miss Meadowford, if your great uncle did not realize that the vehicle in the accident was his why would he have gone into such a frenzy and rush off?"

Thora did not have an answer to that question. If events unfolded the way that she believed then it truly was inexplicable why Thaddeus would behave in such a panic. The death of Art Rozelle truly did not change anything concerning Dearborn Cable and its suffering relationship with its employees. It did not change anything concerning his desire to unload the struggling company onto his nephew.

Yet she knew that what she experienced was true. One cannot fabricate in one's mind the sensation of driving a car for the first time in one's life.

"We have a visitor at the studio," Smitty said over the radio.

"It's Officer Bombino from the police," Earl said.

"I have police at my door too!" Cristo Pando crackled over the airwaves.

"Good morning Officer Bombino," Smitty chimed.

"Put some music on for a while, boys," a man with a deep but distant voice said from the radio station. It was apparent that the microphone was not enhancing it.

"I've got to go now," Cristo announced. The line that he was on suddenly became dead.

"What's this all about?" Earl asked the policeman.

"Put some music on. Entertain your listeners," the policeman demanded.

Thora knew Officer Bombino. He was a no nonsense type of man that possessed not an iota of friendliness. Most of the children at school were afraid of him. He spoke to them harshly and was intolerant of any rowdy behavior. Officer Bombino once slapped Rory McQuoid across the face in the schoolyard for some brash comments that the hoodlum made. When Rory protested the tough Bombino swatted him once more.

Fiddle music started to fill the tinny speakers of the radio. Apparently the two radio personalities complied with the policeman. Thora could not recognize the particular piece but she knew that it came from the mountains of West Virginia and that the player was Jim Spence, a man gaining tremendous popularity in the communities that looked to country music rather than jazz as its source of inspiration and medium of celebration.

"I think that the jig is up for you father," the servant said with that irritating smile of his. "Leave it to Smitty and Earl rather than the police to uncover the crime that was committed!"

"Oh you shut up!" Thora hissed. She despised the man even though she did not know his name. But she knew that he was right about how it took the two bumpkins to hatch the insane idea that her father was responsible for the accident that killed the Rozelle family. She stormed over to the radio and turned the knob and shut it off.

"Uncle Thaddeus would fire you if he knew that you played the radio so loud!"

"He can't do that," the man said. "He already fired me. He said that my snoring disturbed his sleep."

"Then what are you still doing here?" Thora demanded. In the rear of her thoughts she noted that her great-uncle was at least still true to form in this respect. He never retained his employees for very long.

"Just cleaning up after myself and gathering my things," the servant was still smiling. "And then I will be on my way."

"He trusts you to be alone in his house after he fired you!" Thora found this aspect to be unbelievable. Uncle Thaddeus was not a trusting man. And he was certainly smart enough to know if you do someone an unpleasant turn you can fully expect to receive an unpleasant turn back.

"He was in a rush. He had no time to watch me like a hawk!"

Thora groaned. She could feel the appearance of responsibility come crawling up her spine. She could not leave the house until this man was gone.

"Then you go gather up your things," she said. "I will tidy up the kitchen."

"No need to do that young lady, I have just finished!" The man snapped the drying towel in the air with a magician's flourish and placed it neatly on a rack. "Now if you excuse me I will pack up my things." He walked past her. There was a bit of the imp in his eyes and Thora at once knew that he could not be trusted and that he had tricks up his sleeve.

As he disappeared into the east wing where his tiny room sat, Thora heard the low rumble of tires on asphalt and saw a reflection of light move across the room. Someone was here.

Chapter 16

Langley Is Taken Away

Shortly thereafter there was a loud rap at the door. It was not a friendly knock. It was the kind of thump that openly declared that trouble was coming.

The girl wondered if she should open the door. She wanted to run and hide. But she sensed that it would be of no avail. Whoever was at the door would come in and find her.

She looked over to the east wing to see if the servant had it in him to perform one more task for his former employer. But she saw no one coming. The servant was not responding.

The knock came again. This time it was more forceful. This time it was joined by a loud, firm voice. "Open up. It is the police."

A forest of butterflies was suddenly released from her stomach. She was frightened silly. She knew what this would be all about. Yet as much as she wanted to take flight, she knew that she had to address her fright and answer the door.

She put her hand on the knob and could feel that there was another hand on the opposite knob. The policeman was working it to see if it would open on its own.

As the door swung open Thora could feel the man fall forward somewhat. He was taken off guard by a door he expected that would not open.

When the girl saw the face of the policeman, she immediately felt some relief. It was Sergeant John Herman. She should have recognized his voice. Sergeant Herman often came to the school to give talks on safety to the children. All the kids liked him. He did not have any of that mean façade that Officer Bombino possessed.

"Sergeant Herman!" she said with dismay. "What are you doing here?"

"Miss Meadowford," the sergeant responded. "I was about to ask you the same question."

"I stayed here at my uncle's last night," she answered.

"Who's that?" the sergeant asked. He was looking past her at something behind her.

Thora turned around and saw the servant. He had changed his shirt. He no longer was wearing the green tunic that was supplied to him by Uncle Thaddeus. He was now wearing a raggedy shirt that only hoboes would wear.

"That's Uncle Thaddeus' servant," she said.

"Where is your Uncle Thaddeus? Is he up?" The policeman was looking suspiciously at the servant. Thora could see that he was trying to compare the face to faces in his memory of known criminals.

"He's not here," she answered. "He has gone to have a meeting with Mr. Whattam."

"Did he take his car?" Sergeant Herman asked. His eyes never left the servant.

Before Thora could answer the servant responded despondently, "What kind of question is that? You know that his car was wrecked in that accident last night?"

"And how would you know something like that?" the policeman retorted.

"I heard it on the radio!" the servant said. He had his characteristic smile once more. There was something about that smile that said that it was cloaking some underlying sinister spirit.

"That wasn't his car!" Thora said loudly.

"And who exactly are you?" Sergeant Herman asked. He did not possess any of that pleasant personality that shone through during his visits to the school.

"I am, or rather, I was in the employ of Mr. Thaddeus Meadowford," the servant smugly replied.

"Was?"

The servant cleared his throat, "Mr. Meadowford was not charmed by my sleeping habits."

"He snores a lot!" Thora chimed in.

Sergeant Herman nodded. He was still casting a shrewd eye on the man. "You still haven't identified yourself. What is your name and where are you from?"

"I'm Bewdley Beacon," the servant answered. "I come from Buffalo, New York."

"You come all the way from Buffalo just to be a manservant to Mr. Meadowford?"

"In a roundabout way, yes."

"And are you returning to Buffalo now that your services are no longer required?"

The servant, Mr. Beacon, paused for a moment and then his smile grew larger. "That hardly seems likely. I have nothing to go back there for. I will probably just move on to the next town and see if my fortune fares better there."

"Why is it that you seem so familiar to me?" Sergeant Herman said. "I know that I have seen you somewhere before."

"I would hardly know where you would have for I am certain that I have not seen you before," Mr. Beacon responded. "Now, if you have no further questions to ask, I would like to get back to my packing. I want to catch the first bus to Forestville this morning."

"What do you know of this man?" the policeman almost snapped at Thora. "Is he who he says he is?"

Thora shrugged. "I just met him this morning," she answered honestly. "I do not know who he is. All that I know is that he likes to play his radio almost as loud as he snores."

"How do you know that he snores?" Sergeant Herman's eyes narrowed.

"I was in his room last night and I heard him," Thora said.

"You were in his room?"

Before Thora could confirm that she was, Sergeant Herman barked, "Okay, that's it!" He drew out his revolver and pointed it squarely at the servant. "Put your hands up! You are under arrest!"

Bewdley Beacon gawked at the policeman in disbelief. "Under arrest?" he cried. "For what?"

"Get your hands up!"

The servant slowly started to raise his hands. "What kind of madness is this? I don't know why you are arresting me? I have done nothing wrong!"

Thora was shocked as well. She did not know why Sergeant Herman was behaving so absurdly.

The policeman strode past her, undoing the handcuffs from his belt. He started reading the servant his rights.

"You got to tell me what I did wrong!" Bewdley cried out.

"You know what you did wrong. You had a minor in your room last night, you pervert!" Sergeant Herman blasted at him while roughly yanking Bewdley's arms down behind his back and cuffing him.

"I did no so thing!" the servant vehemently protested.

Thora said nothing. She did not understand any of this.

Once Bewdley Beacon was restrained, the policeman returned his attention to her. "I am going to have to have a statement from you later today," he said. "Come by the station and we will take it down."

"Yes, Sergeant Herman," Thora said, not knowing what she was agreeing to.

"Now, before I go, I just want to confirm one thing with you, young lady. Are you absolutely certain that your uncle went to Mr. Whattam's house this morning?"

"That is what Mr. Beacon told me. I don't know for certain as I was asleep this morning when my great uncle left," she responded.

"You had better not be lying about this," Sergeant Herman said to the servant, while digging his knuckles into the man's rib cage. They started out of the door.

"But that wasn't my uncle's car in the accident last night," Thora said out loud to the policeman.

Either Sergeant Herman did not hear her or he chose to ignore her. He shoved Bewdley Beacon into the rear seat of the police car. The vehicle still had its flashing lights on. Then the policeman got into the driver's seat and sped out of the driveway.

She was alone in her great uncle's house. She looked about it and felt very small and out of place. She felt very small and out of place in the whole world. It had gone strange on her. Nothing was normal any longer. Nothing went according to the design she created for her summer a month ago back when she sat daydreaming in her classroom. Back then her summer was to be spent basking upon Pioneer Lake. When that changed, she was to go to Manhattan with her sister and parents. But that plan now was highly unlikely. Things have gotten real bad in her life. She hated her existence nowadays. She saw no hope in the future. For the first time in her life she contemplated whether it would not be better that she just simply cease to exist. In the realm of the afterlife she would be reunited with her grandfather Sambo and her cousin Jack. They were two figures that could be relied upon. It seemed that nobody living possessed that quality any longer.

For some reason she thought suddenly of Margaret Whattam. That woman appeared to be reliable. That woman appeared to have a genuine concern for her. Maybe she should call her and have a visit with her and allow her to ease her tensions.

But she could not do that right away. She had to get home first. She had to let her parents know that she was okay. She had a sneaking suspicion that her Pine Street house had already been visited upon by the police.

She took one last look at the house of her great uncle. Her original estimation yesterday was that it was a soulless place. She pretty much still clung to that opinion. She didn't care if she ever saw it again.

As she stepped out of the door and into the warm morning sun she found herself wishing that the warmth were genuine and that there would be a beautiful day ahead of her. Somehow she highly doubted that it would be. Beauty had gone out of her life.

When she was about two blocks away from the house she realized that she did not lock the door to the mansion. She made a face of disappointment in herself. She should have remembered to do that. But she was now too far away. She was not about to turn back and correct her mistake. In all likelihood Uncle Thaddeus would be back soon anyway. There might be an irate phone call to her house but that would be the extent of the damage.

It was a one-hour walk from Uncle Thaddeus' house to the Meadowford abode on Pine Street. By the time Thora rounded the corner that brought the house into view she saw that there was a police cruiser in the driveway. Its flashing lights were on. She stopped in her tracks. She had supposed that the police would show up to her house. They would be conducting a roundup of all the significant figures in the Rozelle affair. Cristo Pando had said in no uncertain terms that Langley Meadowford played a very important role in the fiasco at his restaurant and that he, Langley, was the driver of the car that later got into an accident that killed the entire Rozelle family. Yet even though she knew that the police would come to the house she still was surprised to see them there. It made her heart sink further into the abyss.

She saw the front door of the house open and she witnessed her father, in handcuffs, being escorted to the cruiser. He was still in his pajamas and appeared as unkempt as a dusty mongrel.

They had arrested her father! Why? She couldn't understand any of this. Her dad had nothing to do with the accident. She had to do something about it right away. She ran at a full sprint towards her house.

The police car was pulling out of the driveway just as she was coming up to it. "Stop!" she screamed as loud as she could. "He had nothing to do with it!"

The policeman in the car looked at her as he backed up onto the street. His stare was empty. She had as much significance to him as the sidewalk his cruiser rolled over.

Her dad did see her however! He was in the backseat and he was crying out her name. "Thora! Thora! Do something about this!" The metal skin of the cruiser muffled his voice.

"Dad!" she cried. "What are they doing to you?" Tears were streaming down her face. Her hands were reaching for the door handle. It was locked and would not give no matter how much she jerked at it.

The police car was placed in forward and sped away. It left Thora running after it. After a while until she saw that her dogged attempt to rescue her father was desperately futile. She stopped and stooped forward in order to catch her breath. They had taken her dad away. They were accusing him of the deaths of Art Rozelle, his wife and his two girls. He played no role in it. She knew that for certain. It was the ghost of her great grandfather, Samuel Angus Meadowford the First, that was responsible and not Langley. Why was this ghost doing this? He had led her to believe that he was her guardian angel. Thora could see no protection in having her father arrested and possibly charged for manslaughter if not murder.

As she gained a semblance of composure she walked back to the house. She walked by the parked Motorized Egg. She saw the ugly scratches Rory McQuoid had inflicted upon its paint job and she noted that all the tires seemed to be inflated. Either Langley fixed them this morning or he had lied to Uncle Thaddeus last night. At the moment she did not care either way.

The door to the house was still open. She stepped through it and called out, "Mom! Mom! Are you here? Why did they take Dad away?"

She heard some sobbing from the living room. It was her mother. When she entered the room she saw her mother sitting on her favorite seat at the end of the couch. She was still in her nighty and her hair was set in rollers. She was leaned over resting her head on her palm. She was crying. She was drinking as well. Thora noted the freshly poured glass of scotch sitting on the end table. "Mom! What is going on!"

"Go away!" her mother hissed, not budging from her posture of misery. "I don't want to deal with you right now!"

Thora was not going to heed her words. "Mother! They arrested Dad! Tell me why!" she demanded.

"I said go away, you little tramp! This is all your fault!"

"My fault?" The words fell like a sledgehammer onto her. She somehow expected this even though she knew that there was no way in the world that she should be blamed for anything that happened.

"If you knew how to cook like the way I taught you we would not have been on the town last night!" Cora spat. She lifted her head. Her eyes were red and venomous.

"But Dad was not involved in the accident! I know that for certain!" she responded, choosing not to let her mother's accusations get the better of her.

"What do you know? You can't even cook a meal!" Her mother took a long haul from her glass.

"You know that Dad was not in that accident! You were with him here at home last night when the accident happened."

Her mother chuckled cynically. "Was I? Your dad went out in the car last night after we got home. He was out looking for you just when the accident happened."

This bit of information took Thora by surprise. She had not realized that her father had done this. Yet it still didn't matter. Her dad could not have been in the accident. He was in the Motorized Egg not the Bentley. "But the accident involved a limousine. Dad was driving our car!"

"That is not the way the police see it," Cora said. Her eyes narrowed and were looking deeply and penetratingly into hers. "They saw the condition our yellow car was in. It looked like it was involved in an accident." Thora remembered how Rory McQuoid had vandalized the car. "They said that your father could have chased the car that family was in and smashed into it, killing all the occupants inside and then he left the scene of the accident and returned home here."

"What?" Thora could not believe her ears. "What about the driver of the Bentley? What happened to him? The Rozelles were all in the backseat."

Cora looked at her with her mouth dropped open. It was like she had never thought of this aspect before. "How do you know this?"

"I heard it on the radio," Thora explained.

The woman looked at her with blank eyes that indicated that there was very slow movement in the brain that sat behind them. "Where were you last night?" her mother at last said.

"You know where I was. I was at Uncle Thaddeus' house. Remember he called here to ask Dad to come pick me up!"

By the lost expression in her mother's eyes, Thora could see that she possessed no recollection of this at all. She probably was too drunk.

"And that was when your father got into the accident?" her mother guessed.

"No!" Thora rasped. "The accident happened before that!"

"And how do you know this?" her mother seemed that she was already so diluted with alcohol that her faculties for reasoning had been shut down.

The daughter rolled her eyes in exasperation. She sensed that she would not be able to communicate at all with her mother. "Because I saw the emergency response team going out to the accident before I even got to Uncle Thaddeus' place. Dad was still home then. It wasn't until I got inside the house that Uncle Thaddeus made the phone call asking Dad to come pick me up."

Her mother's eyes were blinking at an almost continual rate. It was clear to Thora that she did not understand anything that she was saying. How many drinks did she have already this morning? Thora decided to continue and not wait for any acknowledgement of what she previously said. "And Dad said that he couldn't come get me because the car had flat tires. And then Dad asked Uncle Thaddeus if I could spend the night there. Don't you remember any of this?"

Her mother's drinking was getting worse and worse. She seemed bent on self-destruction through the bottle. She had never been much of a drinker in the past but ever since they returned home from Pioneer Lake it appeared that she was on a non-stop binge. Cora Meadowford was trying to escape the world and its plethora of problems that were presenting themselves to her these past few weeks.

"What are we going to do about this mom?" Thora asked. "Are we just going to leave Dad in jail? Shouldn't we be doing something to get him out?" She was beginning to realize that her mother's plan of action seemed to be to just wallow in her booze and allow its effects to magnify her already great sense of self pity.

"Go away girl, I am trying to think this one out," Cora finally said through her blinking.

"Mom, you are just getting more and more drunk," Thora said. "That's not going to get you anywhere. We got to do something for Dad right now."

Without any hesitation she left the living room and her wallowing mother and went to the hallway to where the phone sat on the wall. She had decided then and there that she was going to call Margaret Whattam for help.

But before she picked up the mouthpiece the phone rang. It gave her a start. She automatically answered the ring. "Hello."

"Hello, is this the Meadowford residence?" a male adult voice that she recognized but could not immediately place said on the other end.

After Thora affirmed that it was, the man continued, "This is Barkley Smith, Smitty, from the radio station in town. To whom am I speaking?"

Thora's first reaction was to hang up the phone but she couldn't do that. "This is Thora," she said through vocal chords that felt suddenly seized.

"Thora, you are one of the twins, aren't you?" Smitty asked. "You are such pretty girls, real flowers in our community. May I speak to your father?"

"My dad is not here," she answered. Why was this man calling? Immediately, she realized that she might be on the radio station live. "Am I on the air?"

"Yes you are girl! You are speaking to all of Grappling Haven. Can you tell us if you have had any visitors in blue uniforms at your place this morning?"

Even though she felt petrified that she was on the radio, she still could feel anger rise in her from the man's snooping question. He was looking to belittle the family and make a mockery of them in front of the entire community. "I think that you already know the answer to that Mr. Smith," she said sharply.

"Please call me Smitty! There's no reason to get formal about this," the man kept a lively bright tone to his voice. It sounded phony to her.

"And you can call me Earl," another voice suddenly popped through the speaker of her phone. "So the police have already come to your place, have they? Did they charge your father?"

"I don't know. Why don't you ask them? They are there with you right now, aren't they?" Thora felt righteously enraged by these two bumpkins. She could not believe the audacity of the two men to call her house on live radio to ask such embarrassing questions.

"Is your mother there?" Smitty said in a tone that showed that he did not want some smart aleck kid on the phone with him.

Thora was afraid that this question was going to be asked. There was no way that she wanted her mother to go on the phone given her condition and mood. She would permanently cement the family as the town's laughing stocks for years to come if she were to say anything at all.

"She's not here," Thora said.

"Who's that on the phone?" Cora could not have picked a more inopportune time to blurt out her question from the living room. The girl was sure that her mother's voice carried to all of the households in the community and surrounding countryside.

"Who is that in the house with you?" Smitty asked on the phone.

Yes, the beauty had left her life. Damned if you do and damned if you don't. Thora did not know what to do. She wanted to throw her hands up into the air and just give up. "It's my mother," she said into the phone's mouthpiece. "She just stepped in from the outside. Mom, it is for you!"

"Who is it?" Cora stumbled out of the living room and appeared in the hall.

"It's Mr. Smith," the girl simply replied handing the phone over to her mother.

"Mr. Smith? I don't know any Mr. Smiths," Cora mumbled. There was a detectable slur in her voice. "Hello, Mrs. Cora Meadowford here," she said. Her eyes were looking directly at Thora. These eyes were saying that the girl had better not have placed her into any trap.

"Smitty from the radio station? Yes I have heard of you!" Cora responded. Her face held an expression of surprise and disdain simultaneously. "You are one of the two jokers that make our community appear like we are all backwoods inbreeds to the rest of the nation."

Thora could not make out Smitty's reply to her mother's insulting comment. She, herself, cringed when her mother made the remark.

"I don't care if you believe that you are an ambassador for the common folk because that is an honor that I am not going to take away from you. You go right ahead and be their spokesman Mr. Smith. I don't give a cuss. I just don't want you to have the audacity to think that you are speaking for all of us here in Grappling Haven. There are some of us in this town that still have dignity and pride in our character and in the manner that we were brought up."

"Yes, I was at Cristo Pando's last night," the cadence in Cora's voice changed.

Thora knew what was being said on the other end of the line without actually hearing it. Smitty was going to illustrate to her mother that there was no dignity in anybody that starts up a fight in a posh and fine restaurant.

"My husband was only airing a legitimate gripe about the quality of the meat that he was being served!" Cora said quite animatedly.

"It was that other man that actually started the shouting match! Had he just allowed Langley to say his piece then none of this would have happened."

"No."

"No," her mother mumbled. Thora did not know what was being said here but she sensed that Smitty was trying to take over the conversation and was working towards a series of logical manipulations that would make Cora fall to her feet in front of his listening audience.

"No, that is not right!" Cora said. "That is not the way that it happened. Anybody that was there would tell you that it was Cristo Pando that escalated everything. Had that seedy little Greek stayed out of it, none of this would have happened!"

Thora was starting to lose track of the conversation. She was finding that her postulations on what Smitty might be saying were not quite making sense given her mother's responses. She thought of the radio up in her parent's room. She would listen to it on the air and get both sides of the conversation. She raced up the stairs and turned on the wireless. It took a few seconds for the huge comely beast to warm up. Surprisingly, the radio was dialed to the Grappling Haven station.

"Had that seedy little Greek stayed out of it, none of this would have happened!" It was her mother's voice. She either just repeated herself or there was some sort of time delay on the live conversation.

"We spoke to Cristo Pando earlier today," Smitty's voice came softly out of the speaker. Thora had the volume turned very low so that her mother would not know that she was listening in. "He told us his side of the story. Other listeners that called in saying that they were there at the restaurant corroborated this. All of them are in accord in saying that it was your husband, Mr. Langley Meadowford, that was the instigator of this brouhaha."

"They say that because they are the little people that have it in for we Meadowfords and the other members of the noble social circle that we travel," Cora replied.

Thora was lying on her parent's bed listening. When she heard what her mother said she felt that she could almost vomit. Friends at school would forever alienate themselves from her given the very snobbish remark made by Cora.

"Now, how can you say that Mrs. Meadowford? Most of our listeners cannot afford a meal at Pando's. The callers this morning are the very people that you would deem as your peers. It was these peers that pointed the finger at your husband and proclaimed him as the man who started the fight."

"Well, they are liars then!" Cora snapped.

"That is enough about what happened at the restaurant," Earl cut in.

"What? Who is that?" Cora yelped. Thora could imagine that her mother was given a start when she heard a second voice on the line. The woman probably did not realize that she was on the air and that everybody that she had accused of being a liar heard her say that. She would not be able to deny any of this the next time that her path crossed theirs.

"It is Earl, Mrs. Meadowford. Am I detecting the presence of some bewitching agent making your words a little hard to pronounce this morning?"

He was referring to Cora's slur. Thora wondered when the radio station personalities would pick up on that. They would not openly state that she was drinking for the consumption of alcohol was illegal not only here in Grappling Haven but across the land.

"I don't know what you are talking about, bewitching agents? I think that this conversation is over and I will bid my good day to you two gentlemen."

"No wait!" Smitty cried. "You haven't told us what has happened to your husband this morning. On what grounds did the police take him away?"

"My, word spreads fast in this hovel community of near-sighted hedgehogs, doesn't it?" Cora laughed sarcastically.

"They arrested your husband, didn't they?" Earl asked.

"As a matter of fact they asked Langley to go along with them back to the police station for some questions!" Cora said with a huff. "There were no charges being laid. Langley, being very community-minded, went with them on his own accord."

"Well, what kind of questions would they be asking your husband?" Smitty asked.

"Maybe they are going to ask him to be the fundraiser for this year's charity!" Earl quipped.

This produced a chuckle from Smitty. "No, I think that they want to reserve that honor for Mrs. Meadowford. She is an icon for the Christian spirit of giving and a strong upholder of the American value that all men are equal!"

Both men laughed heartily at the jokes.

"Now, seriously Mrs. Meadowford, why do you think that the police are interested in questioning your husband?" Smitty broke away from the giddy spirit that temporarily had overtaken him.

For a moment Thora thought she heard her mother yelling downstairs. The sharp screams were not heard on the radio's speaker. Not yet, at least.

"They wanted to know his whereabouts last evening after we left the restaurant," Cora Meadowford answered. It was clear that she did not find any of the preceding humorous. It more than likely went over her head. Had she understood the nasty jabs at her character she would have went into a tirade or just simply slammed down the phone.

"Why would they want to take him to the station just to ask those simple questions?" Earl was trying to goad her into saying something incriminating.

"Oh, I don't know!" Cora shouted loudly. It was the shout that Thora heard moments earlier. It attested that there was a time delay on the live broadcast. "They seem to think that my husband was involved in that accident last night."

Cora had taken the bait.

Smitty and Earl may have the personalities of bumpkins but they knew what they were doing. They were professionals at getting their victims to say things that should not have been said.

"And why do you suppose that is?" Earl asked the open-ended leading question.

"Because of the fight in the restaurant, I suppose," Cora admitted. "The people that got killed were the very people that my husband had the tussle with."

"People get killed in motor vehicle accidents all the time, Mrs. Meadowford. Most of these never involve any malicious intent. Why do you suppose the police believed that there was malicious intent in this one?" Smitty asked.

"Who says anything about malicious intent?" Cora growled.

"What kind of mood was your husband in after he was thrown out of the restaurant?" Earl quickly asked.

"What kind of mood is any man in when he is so unceremoniously treated?" Cora responded. And then she added, "Langley was very angry. He had been wrongfully treated and he was humiliated in front of his friends."

"How long did he stay angry?"

"He still is angry, if you want to know the truth! My husband has suffered many major setbacks of late including the death of his father. Then he was dealt a concussion at his father's funeral by that ingrate Tom Thurston. And to top it all off he learned last night that the company that he stands to inherit is being boycotted by the major auto manufacturers in Detroit."

"Hold on a second!" Smitty rasped in an incredulous tone. "Are you telling us that Dearborn Cable is in trouble?"

"This is major news for our community!" Earl added at once. "There are many people here in Grappling Haven that have invested quite substantially in the Meadowford company. Are you saying that the company is being boycotted? Why?"

"I don't know the answer to that. It has something to do with Dearborn Cable refusing to be unionized or something silly like that," Cora responded.

"Why would the company not go unionized?" Earl asked. "Any major manufacturing corporation nowadays must have unionized labor in order to compete on the market. Why would the company do something so inane as to guarantee its failure?"

"Having unionized labor means that the company would have to pay more in salaries and benefits," Cora said. "That would only drive the cost of the product up. I can't understand why Detroit doesn't see this. We are offering them top rate cable at bargain rate prices and they balk at it! There's something fishy about this."

"Indeed there is something fishy!" Smitty retorted. "And I would say that the smell emanates from Dearborn Cable. Its management is trying to maximize profit by minimizing cost. It is not allowing its labor force to share in the bonanza it reaps."

"Dearborn Cable will soon have new management, gentlemen, and then you will see that the people here in Grappling Haven will not have to worry about their investments. There will be a sound leader heading up the company."

"Is Thaddeus Meadowford finally giving up the helm?" Earl asked.

Simultaneously Smitty had a question of his own. "And who might this new leader be?"

"Why, my husband Samuel Angus Meadowford the Third, or Langley as you know him!" Cora said with gushing pride.

"Langley is going to be in charge? Oh my Lord!" Earl cried.

"I hate to burst your bubble Mrs. Meadowford but how can Langley run a company when he is going to be locked up in jail?" Smitty commented.

"Who says Langley is going to be locked up in jail?" Cora crowed.

Thora heard a scream come from the floor below her where her mother was talking live to the radio personalities.

"The writing is on the wall Mrs. Meadowford. There is a very strong case that your husband committed vehicular manslaughter last night. It is going to take a miracle for him to walk away from this one scot-free."

"Have you made any arrangements to get Langley out on bail?" Earl asked.

"I doubt that they have set the bail amount as of yet, Earl," Smitty said. "But you can bet that the Meadowfords are going to have to dig deep into their pockets to spring their black sheep out."

"Am I on the radio?" Cora suddenly asked.

"Why, yes, Mrs. Meadowford, indeed you are on the radio. You didn't know?"

A scream filled the airwaves. It was the one that Thora heard earlier. "You didn't tell me that I was on the radio! I am going to sue you people and your bosses!" Cora sounded like she was on the edge of hysterics—drunken hysterics at that.

"Smitty, we got another caller," Earl said. "I think that we have heard enough from Mrs. Meadowford for the moment."

"Good grappling morning to you!" Smitty said with boisterous glee.

"Hi. Smitty?" It was another woman on the other end of the line.

"Yes, this is Smitty. To whom have I the pleasure to be speaking?"

"It's Mrs. Margaret Whattam. I just want to tell you that what you and your partner are trying to pull here is crass and beneath even the low standards that the two of you have already set for yourselves. You are circumventing the legal system. You are declaring Langley Meadowford guilty before he even had a chance for his day in court. Every man is innocent until declared guilty. What you and your partner have done here is ensure that Mr. Meadowford will not get a fair trial here in Grappling Haven as you have tainted the jury pool. You…"

"Now, now Mrs. Whattam, hold your horses, honey!" Smitty cut in on Mrs. Whattam's spiel. "We have done no such thing. We have merely asked Mrs. Meadowford a few questions to answer our listeners' curiosity. We have not once intimated that Langley Meadowford is guilty."

"But yes you have Smitty!" Mrs. Whattam said. "You said that there is a strong case that Mr. Meadowford committed vehicular manslaughter last night!"

"Saying that there is a strong case for vehicular manslaughter is a far cry from saying that the man committed the crime!" Earl spoke up, defending his partner.

"We are just community servants keeping our town apprised of what is going on on the streets, Mrs. Whattam," Smitty said.

At that moment the bedroom door opened. Thora had been lying on top of the unmade bed listening with an addict's drive to the narcotic talk coming over the radio. She jumped with a start.

It was her mother.

Cora waddled over to the radio and abruptly shut it off. "Get out of my bed," she said. Her angry face was crumbling into a pathetic expression of hurt and sadness.

Thora instinctively left the bed and started heading towards the door. She did not know what to say to her mother. Smitty and Earl had treated her harshly and made a mockery out of her.

As she closed the door behind her she heard her mother start sobbing.

Chapter 17

View from the Top

"You should have phoned us," Margaret Whattam said as she was driving the family vehicle down State Street. Thora was sitting in the passenger seat beside her. She marveled at the way that the woman handled the car. She could not recall if she had ever been in a vehicle that was driven by a woman before. She found the experience to be uplifting and promising. Margaret was proving her father and Uncle Langley wrong concerning female drivers. They had all the same skills as men when handling a car.

"I would have but I did not have any change," the girl answered. They were talking about when Thora was stranded outside of Cristo Pando's yesterday evening.

"We would have seen to it that you were taken home last night. Maybe that would have prevented your father from going out onto the town and getting into this mess that he has found himself in," Margaret suggested. She did not do it in any condemning mean-spirited fashion. She was simply presenting an alternate scenario that may have lead to less troublesome circumstances.

"The thing is Margaret that my dad was not involved in that accident as far as I know," Thora replied. "In fact it wasn't even Uncle Thaddeus' car. It was another Bentley that was identical to his."

"Now how likely is that Thora?" Mrs. Whattam asked in a tone that conveyed that she might have been an excellent schoolteacher. "Your uncle's limousine is quite unique for this part of the state. Had this been Pittsburgh or Philadelphia there may be other Bentleys. But not here in Grappling Haven."

"I know what I saw and I tell you that it wasn't his," Thora responded without getting righteously angry over the question. "The one that picked up the Rozelles was driven by a man that looked almost exactly like my great grandfather, the one that you have a portrait of in your basement."

"How could it have been that man Thora?" Margaret said as she stuck out her arm to signal a left hand turn. They were pulling into the office building where her husband had set up his practice. "That man is long dead."

Thora did not know if she wanted to mention to the woman that she had seen the ghost of Samuel Angus Meadowford the First quite often of late. She was not quite sure how Mrs. Whattam would take it.

"Maybe it was a case of mistaken identity," Margaret said as she found a parking spot. "I have noted that your father and your great grandfather do have similarities in appearance."

"I would know my own father if I saw him!" Thora almost cried. She managed to hold it back and have it come out as a muted gasp of excitement. "It wasn't Dad. And besides even if it was Dad that would fail to explain how he could have been driving two vehicles at once."

Mrs. Whattam geared down before shutting off the motor. "Two vehicles at once? I don't know what you mean."

"The police think that our yellow car was involved in the accident. But Cristo Pando has said that my father was behind the wheel of the other car, the limousine. How could my dad be driving both at once?"

Mrs. Whattam lifted her eyebrows. "Interesting," she said. "I never thought of that." She placed the keys to the car in her purse.

"And another thing," Thora said eagerly. She wanted to say as much as possible before they left the car. "The limo that did belong to my Uncle Thaddeus showed up later on in front of the restaurant. The chauffeur was drunk and fell asleep inside of the pool hall. I ended up driving it home last night."

"You what?" Mrs. Whattam was startled by what the girl said.

"I drove the Bentley back to Uncle Thaddeus' place last night," Thora repeated.

"Well if that is the case where is the car now?" the woman responded. "Your Uncle Thaddeus had to take a taxi to get here this morning."

"He doesn't drive you know!" Thora retorted. Even though she knew that her answer was correct, there was a nagging realization in the back of her mind that the Bentley was not there in the driveway this morning when she left Uncle Thaddeus' house. She had no idea what became of the car.

"He says he doesn't drive but he will if he is forced to," Mrs. Whattam said, placing her hand on the door. She nudged it with her shoulder so that it would open. "And believe me, knowing the miser that he is, he would have taken the car this morning had it been there rather than forking out money to a taxi driver."

Thora quickly looked around the parking lot in front of the office building. There was no Bentley parked there. "Is he still here?" she asked her friend as they stretched their legs outside of the Whattams' car.

"As far as I know he is," Margaret said. "He had better be here or else this trip of ours is all for naught."

The reason Thora and Margaret were visiting James' office was to rendezvous with Uncle Thaddeus. They were going to inform him about Langley's incarceration and try to persuade him to post the bail of $10,000 that the judge had set at Langley's hearing earlier this morning. After hearing Margaret mention how miserly Thaddeus was, Thora held her concerns that the man was not going to be compliant.

Margaret was certainly being a great help today. After Cora had thrown Thora out of her room, the girl did not know what to do. She could hear her mother wailing in her bedroom. Cora was crying herself to sleep. Soon the wails turned into snores and the girl realized that her mother was not going to do anything about her husband in jail.

Thora saw no other choice but to enlist the help of Margaret Whattam. Even though her parents did not like this woman and her husband, Thora knew that the woman would come to her aid. She realized that when she heard Mrs. Whattam staunchly defending Langley's rights on the radio.

She phoned the woman and told her about her father's predicament and her mother's condition. Instead of making any condemning remarks about Cora, Mrs. Whattam told the girl that she would call the police department and get some information.

About ten minutes later while her mother continued to snore up in the bedroom the phone rang and it was Mrs. Whattam on the line. She had learned about the bail posting and asked if Cora would be able to raise it. When Thora said that her mother was still sleeping it off, Mrs. Whattam immediately suggested that they should recruit Uncle Thaddeus to post the bail. Margaret got off the phone once more to call her husband and determine if the old man was still with him in his office. A minute later she called again and said that Uncle Thaddeus was there and that they should meet him at James' office. The woman said that she would be over to pick up Thora in five minutes.

Those five minutes were very torturous minutes for the thirteen-year-old girl. She feared that her mother would wake up and demand to know what was going on and once she learned she would do something to throw the plans askew. At first the girl could hear her mother snoring. It gave her comfort as she desperately watched the road from the front room window for Mrs. Whattam's car. But when the snoring ceased, Thora felt her heart stop. Her ears were propped to listen for anything emanating from the upstairs bedroom. There was not a sound. The girl told herself that she could breathe again.

But then she heard the unmistakable sounds of footsteps upstairs. Her mother was up! The bedroom door opened and then the washroom door closed. Thora's eyes were glued to Pine Street. She was hopelessly wishing that they would conjure up the Whattam car. It didn't show up.

The toilet flushed.

Using the distracting sound of the whooshing water in the porcelain bowl Thora slipped outside of the house as quietly as she could. She would wait for Mrs. Whattam there and pray that her mother does not spot her standing at the end of the driveway.

Finally she saw the red vehicle appear in the distance down her street. Mrs. Whattam owned the only red car in town. It had to be her. She was starting to feel some relief when she suddenly heard the front door open.

"Thora, what are you doing out there?"

"Oh nothing, Mom. Just checking to see if there are any dandelions sprouting in the driveway." It was a chore that was often delegated to her by her father. It was a chore that she did not like. It hurt her fingers trying to pinch the tiny chute of a newly formed dandelion bud. She hoped that the answer would satisfy her mother and that the woman would go back inside of the house before Mrs. Whattam arrived.

"You don't have to worry about that now," Cora answered. "There is plenty more to do in the house that should be done before we start worrying about dandelions." She remained standing at the door. It seemed to Thora that her mother knew that something was up.

At that moment Mrs. Whattam's car arrived.

Thora turned around to her mother and said, "See you Mom!" She had prayed that her mother would go back in the house before Mrs. Whattam's car appeared. But it was now too late. All that she could hope for was that Mrs. Whattam would speed away before Cora could do something to stop it.

The girl opened the door to the car just as Cora cried out, "Who is that?"

"Quick!" Thora said to the woman. "Let's get out of here before she does something!"

But Cora was already doing something. She ran down to the end of the driveway in her pajamas and curlers and grabbed hold of the door before Thora could close it. "What's going on here?" Cora said, stooping her head low to get a view of the driver. "Margaret Whattam!" she almost spat as her hand clutched onto Thora's shoulder.

"Hello Cora," Margaret responded.

"What are you trying to do? Kidnap my child?" Cora's face was crimson with fury.

"Mom, please! We're trying to get Dad out of jail!" Thora pleaded while taking hold of her mother's fingers and trying to break them away from the shoulder that they were painfully digging into.

"You will do no such thing!" Cora rasped, now using her freed hand to grab onto Thora's hair.

"Someone has got to do something for your husband," Margaret said. "It is obvious that you are not doing anything." She reached across Thora and tore Cora's arms away.

Thora took advantage of the motion and shoved her mother. The woman was still under the influence of alcohol. Her sense of balance was not very stable. She fell back onto her hind side. The girl quickly slammed the door shut and begged Margaret to get going.

Mrs. Whattam at first was reluctant to do as instructed. She was concerned about Cora.

"She'll be all right," Thora said. "She falls all the time. She won't even remember this."

The driver stepped onto the gas and the red vehicle drove away leaving Cora Meadowford unceremoniously lying on her rump screaming her head off.

As Thora started to follow Mrs. Whattam to the front entranceway of the office complex where her husband conducted his practice, she wondered what kind of retaliatory action her mother might have invoked since they left her lying at the end of the driveway. She would have no idea that Mrs. Whattam had taken her daughter to rendezvous with Uncle Thaddeus at James Whattam's office.

The office building was thoroughly modern. As soon as they moved through the front revolving door Thora could hear the whirr of a machine that significantly cooled the air from the oppressive summertime heat outside. In fact this air conditioner made it almost frigid inside of the building. Her summer dress was not adequate to deal with the chilly air.

Margaret walked to a device that Thora rarely experienced in her life, an elevator. This office building possessed the only elevator in town. A man dressed in a red waistcoat with gold-fringed epaulets greeted them there and asked what floor they required.

"Fourth floor," Mrs. Whattam cheerfully responded stepping by the man and walking into the car.

"To the top it is!" the elevator man returned the pleasant demeanor and smiled at Thora as she strolled past him.

This building was also the tallest in Grappling Haven. Thora had never been to this building before and it pleased her to realize that she was going to its uppermost level. She was looking forward to the view that this height would afford her. She was hoping to see her house from this lofty vantage.

When the elevator door opened Thora was given her wish for a spectacular view. There was a huge window directly in front of the elevator and Thora could see her town spread out before her. She was not disappointed. She had not expected her town to appear so big. She started searching for recognizable landmarks and there was one readily available. The tall spires of St. Andrew's Church dominated the skyline of Grappling Haven. The steeple almost climbed as high as the office building. It looked so pretty to her.

Below the church were hundreds of roofs that seemed to be cascading upon each other like a plate of scalloped potatoes. It was hard to see the lawns and streets that separated them. Yet she knew that those lawns and streets were there. She had seen them many times from ground level. There was one disappointment however for the girl. The vista from the window was in the wrong direction. Her house was on the opposite side. She started pacing down the hall. Hopefully there was a window on the other end that would give such a view of the southeast where Pine Street was set.

"Where are you going Thora?" Margaret Whattam called out. "James' office is this way."

Thora knew that if she explained what her purpose was that Mrs. Whattam would have no problem with that but she felt compelled nonetheless to acquiesce with the woman and go to the office immediately. Maybe after their little meeting with Uncle Thaddeus she would duck down this way to see if she could glimpse her house.

The only sign that James Whattam had on his office door was a brass plate with his name embossed upon it. It did not even indicate what kind of business Mr. Whattam ran.

Mrs. Whattam rapped on the door and stepped inside. Thora followed her into a large room with whitewashed walls. On one of the walls was that painting that Margaret had created—the one that Uncle Thaddeus had said would put into question James' credibility as a professional legal advisor. When Thora looked at it she found that she had to agree with her great uncle. It was one of Margaret's earlier works. It was a portrait of James' father. The work almost looked juvenile. Margaret had come a long way in developing her talents as an artist since she produced this work.

"Margaret? What are you doing here?" James Whattam said. He was sitting at his desk with a pen in hand. He was writing some notes on some sort of legal document. He was the only one in the room as far as Thora could see. Uncle Thaddeus was not here. Where did he go?

"Good morning to you too, dear!" Margaret responded to her husband. She said it in a manner to vilify him for not giving her a cheerful salutation upon her arrival.

"I'm sorry, honey," James said, rising out of his chair and spreading his arms to give his beloved wife a large hug. "Good morning to you too!" he said. "I've been so busy trying to get the final draft to this thing done that I temporarily lost my sensibilities."

"Oh, I know how it is, my baby," Margaret cooed inside of his arms, patting him on his back. "You have way too much work."

At that moment James noticed Thora standing in the room. He saw the expression on her face. "Some day you will fall in love, my child, and you will be doing things that you would never believe yourself capable of doing!"

Thora realized that she must have held some disapproving look on her face that displayed her awkwardness when she was forced to look upon the affection of others. Her tongue was tied to give any kind of response to the man.

"Is Thaddeus gone?" Margaret said, as she broke the embrace much to Thora's relief.

"No, he is here," James responded. "He has gone to fetch finalized versions of the agreement from the typing pool on the second floor. He should be back shortly. Is he the reason that you are here?" His eyes fell upon Thora. He was looking to her to give the answer to his question.

"Yes," Mrs. Whattam said. "We need to see him concerning Thora's Daddy."

"Langley?" James piped with surprise.

"He's in trouble," Thora broke through her silence. "He's in jail!" She could see that her remark was news to the legal and financial advisor.

"In jail? Pray tell why?" he gasped. He was looking at Margaret for the answer to this question.

"The police seem to think that he caused that terrible accident last night," Margaret responded.

"What accident?" James said.

Now it was Thora that was taken aback by the response. She had assumed that the accident was the reason that James and Thaddeus had met so early this morning. Afterall didn't the servant say that as soon as Thaddeus heard the news on the radio that he at once called his advisor to set up the appointment. And didn't this servant also make mention to the police that Thaddeus Meadowford could be found here at James' office? Shouldn't the police have already been here?

As Margaret started to tell James about the tragic crash that claimed the lives of the Rozelle family, Thora could not hold her question back any longer. She cut in on Mrs. Whattam's description to say, "How come you don't know this? I would have thought that the police would have been here by now!"

"No, there has been nobody here this morning," James said. "Just Thaddeus and me. Now, wait a second!" He paused to look at the girl. Thora could see that behind the eyes the man was thinking deeply. "I did step out to get breakfast for Thaddeus and myself about two hours ago. I was gone for maybe half an hour. When I came back with our bacon and egg sandwiches, I did note that there was a marked change in the old man's demeanor. He seemed to be more preoccupied and less interested in the wording of the clauses."

"I bet that the police were here while you were out!" Margaret said. "They have visited all of the people involved. They even went to Cristo Pando's house."

James nodded. "I seem to remember seeing a police cruiser drive by while I was waiting at Potato Pete's for my sandwiches. It didn't faze me at the time. But when I come to think about it, you hardly ever see the police at that time of the morning."

At that moment the door to the office opened and Uncle Thaddeus came striding in. His head was facing downward into the documents that he held in his hands. "These papers appear to be in order," he said. He had not noticed that there were others in the room besides his financial advisor. When he did, he jumped. "Margaret? Thora? What are you doing here?"

Thora at once could see that Uncle Thaddeus knew the reason for their presence. Nonetheless she blurted, "Oh Uncle Thaddeus you have to help my daddy! He is in jail!"

Margaret Whattam picked up where Thora left off and told the old man about the $10,000 bail.

"$10,000! That is a huge sum of money!" Uncle Thaddeus responded. "I don't think Langley and Cora have that kind of money kicking about!"

"No, they don't!" Thora cried. "That's why we need your help!"

Uncle Thaddeus appeared flabbergasted that such a request would be made of him. "You want me to put up the money, do you? Do you think that I have $10,000 set aside that I can dole out every time someone in the family gets in trouble?"

"He's your nephew Langley!" Mrs. Whattam said. "He has no one else to turn to!"

"He should have thought about that before he got himself into trouble!"

"But he didn't do anything wrong, Uncle Thaddeus!" Thora spoke up. "The police say that he caused the accident that killed the Rozelles. But…"

"Yes, yes. I know what the police think. They were here earlier to talk to me," Thaddeus grumbled, confirming James' hypothesis. There was a slight smile of pride on the lips of the advisor.

"Well, what did you tell them?" Thora demanded. "You told them that he was innocent, right? You told them that it was not your car that was in the accident, right?"

"All that I told them was that the last time I saw Langley last night was when he dropped me off home after that disaster of an evening at the restaurant," Thaddeus said impatiently. He then added, "I said that I did not know about his whereabouts or actions afterwards."

"But what about your car? They think that it was your Bentley that got wrecked!" Thora was thoroughly disappointed in her great uncle's reaction. She was disappointed yet she was not surprised. He was acting in typical Uncle Thaddeus fashion.

"They never mentioned anything about my car," he responded as he placed the papers onto James' desk. "I think that we can go ahead with our plans. I am satisfied with the wording and the figures," he said to his financial advisor.

"But the police think that it was your car!" Thora reiterated. "You know that it could not possibly be your car. You saw me drive it home last night!"

Thaddeus nodded. "Yes, yes, I saw you drive it home last night," he agreed without lifting his head in her direction. It was as if he were trying to force his will to deny her presence and her purpose here. "Where should I sign these pages? Over here?" he pointed to a blank line.

"So you know that it could not have been your car!" Thora was not about to give up.

"I know no such thing!" Thaddeus snapped. "My car was not there this morning when I got up! It is highly likely that your father could have come during the night and taken it!"

"What about the bail?" Margaret Whattam asked while Thora looked up in disbelief at her great uncle. How could he think such a thing?

"How would my dad get the car in the middle of the night?" Thora demanded to know. "You phoned him at ten o'clock when I got to your place, remember? The accident had already happened by then. I saw the ambulance and the police car going out to the scene!"

"What about the bail?" Margaret asked again. She was not going to permit Thaddeus to answer Thora's question. "Regardless if Langley is guilty or not it is up to family to do whatever they can to help prove his innocence."

"Margaret, please, this is not our affair," James spoke in a loud whisper. His eyes flared somewhat to add emphasis to what he said.

The woman snatched up the papers from her husband's desk. "A bill of sale between Thaddeus Lloyd Meadowford and Samuel Angus Meadowford III," she read the title of the document. "I would like to remind you two gentlemen that under the law an incarcerated man can not conduct any business."

Thora thought that she detected a wink in the woman's eyes that was directed at her husband. Then she thought she saw a reciprocal gesture return from the man to the woman.

"That is right, by Jove!" James said out loud. "Margaret has a point there. A man convicted of an indictable offence cannot engage in legally binding contracts since he is considered to be a ward of the state. As long as Langley is in jail he will not be allowed to enter this agreement with you."

Thaddeus' mouth dropped. His eyes narrowed and he gave Mrs. Whattam a sinister glance. "Well this is a very disturbing turn of events!" he coughed.

"There is a way around this Thaddeus," James at once said. "We can add an additional $10,000 to the asking price. We can add a proviso to the document that this $10,000 will be refunded pending settlement of any legal action that the buyer may be involved with."

Thaddeus was stooped over James' desk. "No, no. No refunds! The asking price has just gone up $10,000. It will be the penalty Langley pays for his foolhardiness."

"Then you will do it?" Thora cried out. She did not fully understand what had transpired but she got the sense that her great uncle was now amenable to the idea of bailing her father out.

"Regrettably, I will do it," Uncle Thaddeus sighed.

Thora almost felt like embracing the old man and giving him the biggest thank you kiss that she had ever given anybody. But somehow she realized that the thank you kiss belonged to Mr. and Mrs. Whattam. She did not know what they did but they did pull some fast one on the old man.

"This document will need some rewriting now," James said. "We have to change the selling price and have the typing pool redo it all. It should take about half an hour."

"And then we go to the police station to get Dad out?" Thora was beside herself with glee. For once something was turning out all right.

"I'm afraid so," Uncle Thaddeus mumbled.

"What if Thora and I wait for you at Potato Pete's?" Margaret suggested. "All this excitement this morning has left me with a rather large appetite."

"That sounds fine to me, my dear," James said. He stood up and gave his wife a loving peck on her cheek much to the chagrin of Uncle Thaddeus. Thora however this time thought it was a most beautiful thing.

As they left James Whattam's office and Thora saw the huge window overlooking Grappling Haven she remembered that she wanted to see if there was a similar view offered on the other side. When she explained to Margaret her desire the woman enthusiastically endorsed it.

When Thora rounded the corner she saw that there was such a window on the south side of the office complex. She followed the rooftops of the businesses along State Street for about a mile or so before she spotted the recognizable synagogue at the corner of State and Fourth Avenue. She could not actually see the street but she saw the attics and the roofs of the houses here. She could only go down about two blocks before the giant elm trees of the street obscured the homes and she lost all sense of where she was. Pine Street was about two miles south of State Street. The juncture of Fourth and Pine was out there somewhere in that wash of trees and shingled housetops but Thora was not able to pick out the street let alone the house. It somewhat disappointed her. She had hoped to see home. She realized that she was not able to see this tall office building from her yard. Why should she expect that the opposite were true?

She was about to walk back to where Mrs. Whattam was waiting for her by the elevator when something caught her eye. A small white cloud had suddenly appeared over the horizon. It was the only one in an otherwise perfectly clear sky. This cloud had an odd shape. It was long on the bottom but narrow except for its center. There it piled up on itself to give an outline that was almost human. She all of a sudden realized that she had seen this very shape before on that day that they buried her grandfather. It was of an Indian paddling a canoe. This cloud that she saw out there above the roofs of Grappling Haven was identical to that one.

It raced across the sky and was seemingly coming directly to the office building. As it drew nearer facial features appeared to form in the cloud's head. These were stern features of an angry Indian that may have been wronged one too many times by white men. The eyes in this wispy head were peering to something in the distance as the canoe coursed across the skies of the town. Then suddenly and unexpectedly these eyes turned and looked directly into those of the girl that was watching them.

Thora jumped back with fear. She felt that she had been penetrated by something alien and frightening. She almost screamed but she was able to check that reaction. She was breathing heavy. She tried to gain control of her breath before she hyperventilated. She blew out of her mouth, calming herself.

Margaret Whattam must have seen her odd behavior. She came racing over. "Thora, what is it?"

The girl caught her breath and pointed out of the window. She was not able to articulate what she saw. "Look out the window," was all that she was able to muster.

As the woman stepped to the tall opening in the building, she said, "That is quite the spectacular view, isn't it? You could almost see your house from here."

Thora realized that whatever she saw out there must have been gone or else Margaret would not be talking about spectacular views. The girl wandered to stand beside her friend. And she gazed out onto the sky over Grappling Haven.

There was nothing there—just a perfectly clear morning sky that was announcing that the weather today at least was going to be wonderful.

She took a deep breath and tried to eradicate the image of the Indian from her mind. "I tried to spot my house but I just can't figure it out."

"The view from the top is a different perspective, my dear," Mrs. Whattam said. "It is one that we are not used to. We keep thinking of ourselves as being creatures of the ground but we are far from being such. This is the view that is meant for our souls. Take it in Thora! You are where you belong."

Chapter 18

The Message Board

It took James Whattam and Uncle Thaddeus more than an hour before they finally showed up at Potato Pete's. Margaret and Thora by that time had finished a sumptuous breakfast of ham and eggs with home fries, strawberry jam, and orange juice. The two females were very sate from the hardy repast. Margaret was sipping at a cup of coffee and smoking her third cigarette since finishing the meal. Thora just sat and watched the people come and go out of this very popular diner.

Potato Pete's was Cristo Pando's main competition. Unlike the more refined restaurant this one was not named after its owner. There was no Potato Pete. He was just a fictionalized character concocted by the restaurant's real owners. Potato Pete was depicted as a cartoon-like wagon train cook from the Old West. The emphasis here was on large meals that could be quickly made to satisfy large appetites that needed almost instantaneous relief. The food was greasy and salty. This was what the public wanted. For every customer that Cristo Pando received Potato Pete got at least five.

Thora recognized some of the customers that came into the diner. Some of them were there at her grandfather's funeral and heard the sermon that Reverend Barton had made. One old lady walked up to the booth and said to Thora while patting her hand, "I haven't forgotten you, child. We are going on a motor vacation to the Carolinas next week. When we return I will invite you over for dinner."

The girl looked down at the liver-spotted hand and felt ill at ease. She did not want to have any meal with this rheumy-eyed woman and her family. Yet she could not find it in herself to openly reject the woman. She told the lady that she was looking forward to it. She hoped that this engagement would be one of those that were so open-ended that it would never come to fruition.

"I heard about your father," the woman said, still holding Thora's hand. "That is sad news indeed. It is more important than ever that the community shows to you that the sins of the father need not be draped over the daughter. We do not hold you to blame for the despicable actions of that man."

"Now Mrs. Rodham there is no need to say such a thing!" Margaret Whattam spoke up. "Mr. Meadowford is an innocent man until he is proven guilty."

"Mrs. Whattam will you ever outgrow your naiveté?" Mrs. Rodham answered. Her wrinkled face was askew. "Innocence is lost at the commission of the act and not when a tribunal decrees it so. Those poor people are dead now. They won't die when the court determines that Langley Meadowford was guilty of manslaughter."

"My dad is innocent!" Thora said harshly to the woman, drawing her hand away. "I won't go to any house that thinks otherwise!"

Mrs. Rodham looked aghast at her. It appeared that the woman could not believe that a youth could talk so disrespectfully to a senior citizen. "Oh, you are still green my child. You have much to learn. Luckily life has much to teach you."

"Haven't you heard the expression, 'Out of the mouth of babes'?" Margaret Whattam said to rebuke the older woman. "Enjoy your vacation in the Carolinas, Mrs. Rodham. Drive carefully for by the time that you get home Langley Meadowford will be driving the streets of town once again!"

The old woman walked away from the table without saying anything more.

"I wonder if they all think like her?" Thora asked her companion. She was scanning the faces of the patrons of Potato Pete's. Every one of these was staring in her direction.

"It doesn't matter what they think Thora. It is up to the courts to make the decision whether your father was guilty of the crime," Margaret said.

Thora noted that her friend did not look her in the eye. "And what do you think?" she asked Margaret.

"It doesn't matter what I think either, Thora. It is up to the courts to decide."

To the girl that was as clear an indication that Margaret Whattam did not believe Langley was innocent either. Moreover it was an indication that the woman did not accept what Thora had said in demonstrating Langley's innocence. The girl suddenly felt that something was lost between her and Mrs. Whattam. Maybe it wasn't lost. Maybe it was never there in the first place.

When Uncle Thaddeus and James Whattam showed up in James' automobile in the paved parking lot of Potato Pete's, Thora sighed with relief. She could not stand to be in this restaurant a moment longer. She could not stand to be in the exclusive company of Mrs. Margaret Whattam any more. She felt betrayed and she felt more lost than ever. Nobody was truly on her side. She was discovering that she was the only one that walked her path in life.

James honked the horn of his car. He did not really have to for his wife had seen him as soon as his immaculately clean and shiny vehicle crossed the curb to enter the parking lot. But the melodious sound of the horn must have been irresistible to him.

As Thora walked out of the restaurant, she heard one of the patrons say, "Look at those ostentatious Meadowfords! They still act like they own the town!"

Margaret stuck her head down through the car's window and gave her husband a kiss. "We will meet you at the police station," James said.

"I'll be right behind you!" Margaret answered and gave him a second kiss.

"For God's sakes!" Uncle Thaddeus squawked. "Do the two of you have to always act like monkeys in heat!"

Thora reluctantly rode with Mrs. Whattam the mile down State Street to the Grappling Haven Police Station. The two women did not say a word. Mrs. Whattam had the radio on. Even though it was set to the local station Smitty and Earl were not on. Music played instead. It was a jig by Jim Spence that had a real toe-tapping rhythm to it. "Got to love Jim Spence!" Margaret hooted as she cruised down State Street.

Jim Spence's music did not do anything to make Thora hoot. She could only think of her dad behind bars. She could only think how ashamed he would feel when he found out that it was Thaddeus' money that would spring him.

The police station did not offer much in the way of parking space. Mrs. Whattam had to be satisfied with a spot nearly a block away from the station. When she and Thora reached the front of the police building they found James and Thaddeus waiting on the steps. Uncle Thaddeus seemed somewhat winded from climbing them. They waited a few moments for him to catch his breath and then as a group they entered the building.

Thora never had been in the police station before. She had a mental picture of it. This picture displayed a couple of desks in front of a wall of barred jail cells where the most terrible men of society sat staring out with malice in their eyes and vicious intent in their hearts. The real Grappling Haven police station was not anything like this. The front room was like a hotel's lobby with a long desk that divided the space between where the public could go and where they could not go. There were no jail cells in sight. At the desk were two uniformed policemen. Thora recognized one of the men although she did not know his name. She had seen him patrolling the streets of the town. The other policeman had his head looking into some log. He did not bother to lift it when the Meadowford and Whattam group came in.

Standing in front of the desk was a juvenile that Thora had seen before as well. The boy went to her school and was maybe three or four grades behind her. She did not know his name either. She was rather surprised to see him in here, as he did not seem to be a troublemaker. One of the officers was attending to this boy. Thora could catch some of the conversation. "These are the papers that you have to fill out," the policeman said to the boy. "Once you have completed them return them here and we will send them off to Washington."

The boy took the documents handed to him and turned around and saw Thora. A rather sheepish smile came to his face. Thora returned the smile. "I'm going to be a G-man!" the boy said enthusiastically, "I want to arrest all of the mobsters!"

Thora did not know what a G-man was but she pretended that she did.

"That's very good," she said. Then she added, "As long as you stay out of trouble with the police, you can be whatever you want to be."

"All the boys want to be G-men nowadays," James said with a pleasant smile. He rubbed the boys' hair. "They will find ways of nailing those gangsters even if they have no other recourse but to look at the mobster's financial records!"

For some reason Uncle Thaddeus' face reddened at the remark. "Can we get moving on this James? I haven't got all day."

"Can I help you?" the policeman behind the desk asked.

The party of four stepped up to the desk. James Whattam acted as the spokesman for the group. "We are here to post bail for Langley Meadowford," he said.

The policeman looked up at Thaddeus. "Mr. Meadowford, I should have recognized you," he said.

Uncle Thaddeus appeared disturbed for some reason. He looked at the policeman and said, "Yes, yes. Can we get on with it?"

"There are some forms that are going to have to be completed first," the policeman said. His warmth had left him and he became more abrupt and more bureaucratic. He reached below the desk and produced a wad of paperwork. "We need these filled in triplicate."

"Good God!" Thaddeus groaned. "This can take all day!"

"Oh, it's not that bad!" the policeman smiled. This smile was not warm. It was wicked. "Just take these forms over there to that booth and fill them out."

And it was bad for Thora. Time crept down to a standstill as James and Uncle Thaddeus worked together providing answers to the dozens of questions asked on the record. Margaret had found a waiting bench that had some magazines spread out on an end table beside it. She picked one up. It was a woman's magazine that was strewn with recipes, fashion and short stories. She invited Thora to get a magazine of her own but when Thora looked through the available choices none caught her fancy. A good comic book would have suited her but there were none available.

She sat down beside Mrs. Whattam and began contemplating the necessity of her presence here. She wasn't really needed. She was not coughing up the money to get her dad out. Uncle Thaddeus and Mr. Whattam did not require her help in filling out the forms. There really was no utilitarian purpose for her to be here. She had already done what she had set out to do and that was to recruit Uncle Thaddeus. And now that that was done she could just saunter off through the front door and meander her way back home. But she did not really want to return to that house to sit alone with her mother. Cora would be as venomous as any Egyptian snake right now. It was best not to enter that house until she was in the company of her newly liberated father.

Also she could not leave because she wanted to be here when the police let her father go. She wanted to show him that he had her full support. He had not been the greatest of fathers but he was the only father that she had and she loved him dearly. She wanted him to know that. Life had not been good to him of late. He lost his father. His wife no longer trusted him and she had taken up the bottle. He was attacked by his ex-brother-in-law and suffered a concussion and a detached retina as a consequence of it. One of his daughters had run away. And now he was in jail for a crime that he had nothing to do with. The poor man needed some family support and she wanted to be that support.

There was a clock on the wall behind the counter. It was one of those twenty-four-hour military clocks that did not stop at twelve. Thora's eyes kept returning to it periodically. The longest that she could keep her eyes away from it was three minutes. It was moving with the lethargy of a turtle on a sunny afternoon. All told it had moved maybe twenty-five minutes since she first took the seat beside Margaret. The waiting was becoming unbearable to the girl. Her glances over to the two men working at the papers on the table showed her that they were not making swift progress with their task. Margaret Whattam seemed to be deeply enthralled with a short story in the magazine. The two policemen that were behind the counter did not seem to have much to do at all either. Not a single new customer or whatever you would call someone seeking police services had come through the door in the twenty-five minutes. One of the policemen was working at some paperwork of his own while the other man sat upon a stool and was fighting his eyes to stay awake.

Thora felt like she could scream. The boredom was eating her alive. Her mind started working on possible excuses that she could give Uncle Thaddeus and the Whattams for why she had to leave. She knew that no matter what she told the Whattams it would be sufficient enough to them.

But Uncle Thaddeus was likely not to let her go. Her clothes could be on fire and he would demand that she stay.

She could not take it any longer though. She had to do something. She got up from the bench and started wandering around the room. Once she stood up she saw a cork bulletin board that she had not noticed before. This board was covered with a host of things. She wished that she had seen this earlier. It would have given her something to do.

The first thing that she noticed on the board was a section called "Missing". Here was a list of people that had strayed from their usual haunts. There were items on missing senior citizens that had walked away in their pajamas from nursing homes. There were wives looking for estranged husbands. There were husbands looking for estranged wives. There was a name or two under each of these headings. But the list that contained the most items was for runaway children. Thora could not believe that that many children had fled their homes. At once she started to go through the list. She was hunting for her sister's name. But Rebecca's name was not on the list.

She turned around to the policemen. "How come my sister's name is not on here?" she asked. Her question broke the silence in the room. The Whattams and Uncle Thaddeus lifted their heads and gazed at her.

The policeman that had been working on some form looked up at her with a disturbed expression on his face. "Pardon?" he said.

"My sister has been missing for over a week now. How come her name is not on this list?"

"Did someone fill out a missing person report for her?" the policeman asked.

"I don't know," Thora answered truthfully. She would have thought that her parents would have done so. Most parents would have. But her parents were Langley and Cora Meadowford. They were too conscious of their position in society and what a missing person report would mean to that position.

"You can't get on that list without a missing person report being filed," the policeman answered, returning his face to the paperwork that he had.

Thora looked dumbfounded at the man. Wasn't he interested in Rebecca's disappearance? She looked over at Margaret Whattam to see what she thought. But Margaret was not giving her any attention either. The story that she was reading must have been too captivating.

The only sound in the room came from the two fans that were blowing constantly. She had to break that silence again. "I want to file a missing person report," she announced.

The policeman grumbled and put down his pencil. "Are you sixteen years old?"

"No."

"You have to be at least sixteen to file a report," he said, summarily dismissing her.

"Mrs. Whattam will file the report," she said, volunteering the services of her friend.

Margaret looked up at Thora with a puzzling look. "Pardon me, my dear?" she said. "Did you mention my name?"

"I did!" Thora said. "Can I get you to fill out a report for Becky?"

"Fill out a report for Becky for what?" It was clear that Mrs. Whattam had no idea what she was talking about. She must have not been paying attention to anything that had been said earlier. That would explain her prior unwillingness to help. The story must have been terrific.

"Is the lady related to the missing person?" the policeman asked.

"No," Thora responded.

"Then she can't fill out the form. The only people that can fill out that form is the missing person's immediate family, provided that they are of the age of majority," the policeman said.

Thora felt exasperated. "But my dad is in jail! How can he fill out the form?"

"Once we get your father out we will see to it that he completes a form for your sister," Margaret said. She returned her attention back to her magazine.

"As if he would," a disappointed Thora sighed. If a missing person report was as complicated as the bail form, they could be in this police station all day.

She turned her attention back to the bulletin board. At first her mind was not taking in anything that was posted there. It was too busy buzzing with her state of helplessness. But as these feelings began to abate she took note of another section on the board. Here was a showcase of all the people that the police were searching for in relation to crimes. It was a 'Wanted' list. There were many names here. So many names that Thora could not believe that there was one policeman sleeping on a stool while all these suspected criminals were at large.

Some of the names on the list had mug shots attached to them. She scrutinized the faces and at first could not find one that she recognized. When she read about these individuals and their crimes she realized that the policeman sleeping on the stool was probably occupying his time in the best way. Most of these criminals lived in far away places. Most of these crimes were committed in far away places. It was highly unlikely that there would be a Grappling Haven connection.

She found it interesting to read about these murderers, thieves and robbers. They were such vile men. The pictures of them showed uncomplimentary portraits of mean, vulgar brutes. These men looked like criminals. She thought of her poor father behind bars. He did not look like a criminal. It made her feel so good to know that he would soon be ousted from here.

As she continued studying the faces she finally came across one that she recognized. It was Uncle Thaddeus' chauffeur, the man that was too drunk to drive the Bentley home, and the man that fell asleep in the pool hall. "It's him!" she cried out loud.

"It's who?" Mrs. Whattam said in a manner that told Thora that she was repressing an urge to tell her to shut up.

"It's…" Thora realized that she did not know the man's name. She had to read it from the notice. "It's Delaney Wesley Mandrake a.k.a. Del the Duck!"

"It's who?" Margaret answered, closing the magazine onto her fingers. They were marking the spot where she had left off in her engrossing story.

"It's Uncle Thaddeus' chauffeur!" Thora cried out, looking over to her great uncle. She had his attention. His old eyes were slightly rolled back to the top right corner of his head as if he were searching for an identifier for the latest new hire that filled that position. He went through so many employees that it must have been hard for him to keep track.

"Del the Duck!" Thora repeated. "He was the chauffeur that I had to wait for last night. He showed up drunk and fell asleep in the pool hall."

"And why is he listed on that board Thora?" Mrs. Whattam asked.

Thora looked at the list of crimes allegedly commissioned by Del the Duck. There were about nine of them. All of them were categorized as grand theft auto. When she relayed this information to the others James Whattam was the first to comment. "Really Thaddeus you must research the backgrounds of potential employees. Hiring a car thief as a chauffeur! My God, man, you are inviting your car to be stolen!"

"I bet that it was Del the Duck that took your Bentley!" Thora said. "After he woke up in the pool hall he must have wandered to your place and driven the car away!" In the back of her mind Thora was starting to get a good feeling about this theory. Del's past record in addition to her testimony would make a strong case that her dad could not have possibly taken the car and gotten into that accident.

"Are you talking about Delaney Mandrake?" the policeman behind the counter asked. He seemed to have grown interested in the conversation.

"Yes!" Thora piped. "We think that he stole my Uncle Thaddeus' car last night."

"I hardly would think so," the policeman answered. "As far as I know the dead don't steal cars."

"What do you mean?" Thora said in shock. She had not expected such a response.

"We picked up the body of Del the Duck from Clancy's Billiards at around midnight last night. As far as we can determine he died of alcohol poisoning."

Thora's mind clouded over for a moment or two. It was like she was trying to shield this news from entering her consciousness. If Del the Duck was dead in the pool hall then who would have taken her great uncle's car from his driveway? He had been her most likely candidate but now it seemed that that it could not have been him. If it wasn't Del that took it then who did?

"Did I overhear you say that Mr. Mandrake was in your employ?" the policeman asked Uncle Thaddeus.

"I fired him last night," Uncle Thaddeus said. "The man failed to pick me up at the restaurant when we were finished dining."

"But didn't you say that you went home with your nephew last night?" the policeman asked. Thora knew that he could not have possibly heard her great uncle say such a thing. He must have picked up that information from listening to the local gossipers Smitty and Earl.

Regardless of how the information was conveyed, Uncle Thaddeus did confirm it.

"Then Mr. Mandrake would not have been formally given his dismissal papers, I can presume," the policeman concluded. He walked over to the message board and began pulling out the tacks that held the card with Delaney Mandrake's name.

"Yes you can presume that," Uncle Thaddeus grumbled. "It is one of the many things that I have on my itinerary today. I don't know where you are going with this."

"Since Mr. Mandrake was not given his dismissal papers then by law he could still be considered in your employ at the time of his death," the policeman was showing that he had a keen understanding of the laws that were his duty to uphold. "And since Mr. Mandrake does not have any known next of kin the onus falls on you as his employer to take care of the interment arrangements." He tore up the card in his hands.

"What!" Uncle Thaddeus gasped, looking to James Whattam to come to his rescue.

"State law clearly states that when there are no next of kin for a body that the employer of that body is deemed to be next of kin and that the said body would be released to the employer to make satisfactory final arrangements for the disposal of said body."

"Is that true?" Uncle Thaddeus asked James.

"I will have to look that one up," James answered.

"What in the dickens am I going to do with the body of a car thief!" Uncle Thaddeus cried.

"Wait a moment!" James said out loud. "We don't have any formal record of hiring this man, do we? And if we don't have such formal record then we are not legally responsible for the man."

"But you already admitted that he was your chauffeur," the policeman said shrewdly. "I would be very careful where you go with this. Something tells me that giving a pauper's funeral would be far less costly than anything that might involve the IRS."

"What's he talking about?" Thaddeus whispered loud enough to James that the whole room could hear him.

"He's saying that we have circumvented the laws regarding hiring practices by taking on Del under the table. There is a whole slew of income tax issues involved here that we neatly avoided by just paying Mr. Mandrake straight cash without recording it on our books. He might be right that it would be better for us just to bury Del and accept the losses."

"I don't like any of this," Uncle Thaddeus mumbled. He was looking over to Thora. His eyes were saying that he blamed her for all of today's troubles.

The girl had enough presence of mind to turn her head in another direction to avoid the contact. She did not understand what the issue was. She did not want to understand it.

The policeman pulled out another stack of forms. "You are going to have to complete these today as well and pay a $1,000 processing fee," he said with a sinister smile.

"One thousand dollars!" Thaddeus seemed like he was going to have a coronary. "Since when does it cost so much to bury a man?"

James tugged on Thaddeus's shoulder and whispered something. The only phrases and words that Thora could pick up were something about 'buying his silence' and 'IRS'. She did not have the foggiest notion though what James meant.

She still kept her eyes away from her great uncle. She was unconsciously looking at the public message board once more. All of a sudden a picture that she had not noticed there before jumped up at her. He wore his hair differently nowadays but the face was undeniable. It was the picture of Bewdley Beacon—the servant that was hauled away earlier this morning from Uncle Thaddeus' place. She kept her mouth quiet as she read about Mr. Beacon. It seemed like he had a history of swindling people out of their money and that on occasion he was prone to act violently. He was wanted for the murder of an elderly man in Western New York State.

The policeman delivered the release papers for the body of Delaney Mandrake to the table where Uncle Thaddeus and James Whattam worked at the bail papers for her father. On his way back the policeman noted that Thora had taken interest in the blurb about Bewdley Beacon. "We have him in the back room too," he said out loud. "You are lucky Mr. Meadowford that this one did not have more time or else someone would have to be filling out the papers for the release of your body."

"What are you talking about?" Thaddeus said through his trembling jowls.

"Bewdley Beacon. He was your butler, wasn't he?" the policeman answered.

"I don't remember precisely what his name was but it was something like that. Why are you bringing him up? I fired him this morning. Do I need to show you his employment record as well?" Uncle Thaddeus was disturbed and he was showing it. His life was falling apart and the wolves were now circling him ready to take him painfully down.

"We have him here behind bars," the policeman said. "Really Mr. Meadowford you have to be more careful with who you hire. Did you know that Mr. Beacon has stolen more than $50,000 from his previous employers, all doddering rich old men like you, and that he slit the throat of the last one in Tonawanda, New York?"

"Bewdley did that?" Uncle Thaddeus turned white.

"If I were you when you get home I would carefully check all your valuables to see if they are still there. Maybe also make an enquiry at the bank to determine if your bank balance is where it should be."

"Who else is working for you nowadays Thaddeus?" James asked.

"It almost seems like you come to our wanted board for your recruitments," the policeman laughed, not giving Thaddeus a chance to answer his financial and legal advisor. "How a fool like you ever got rich is beyond me! Here, I am slaving to make an honest buck and I am forced to witness silly old men like you with money to burn wasting it all on bums like Mandrake and Beacon! Why don't you hire me as your personal security advisor? I will steer you straight on who to hire and I will see to it that your belongings are kept safe."

"And charge such an exorbitant fee that Mr. Meadowford would be better off just allowing the thieves to rob him blind!" Mr. Whattam said.

The policeman smirked. "It was just a thought."

Thora was not really paying attention to the conversation. She was thinking of Bewdley Beacon. If this man were such a scoundrel then would it be unthinkable to think that he had some sort of involvement in the accident last night? Afterall he was in the house and he had access to Uncle Thaddeus' car. Could he have not stolen the car and hid it somewhere and in that way prevent the primary evidence from being available to show that the Meadowfords were not connected with the accident? But why would he do such a thing? There was only one obvious answer. Money. He may have planned to somehow blackmail Thaddeus and Langley and make them pay a large fee for the return of the Bentley that would exonerate Langley in court.

Suddenly a plan of her own was hatched in her mind.

"Is it possible that I can visit my dad while we wait for the papers to be signed?" she asked the policeman.

Chapter 19

Loyalty

"We don't allow visitors," was the immediate response from the policeman.

"Since when!" James Whattam immediately jumped on the officer.

"We don't allow visitors under the age of sixteen unless they are accompanied by an adult," the policeman clarified.

"Then I wish to visit Langley Meadowford," Margaret Whattam volunteered. "I would like to have Thora with me."

There was anger printed on the policeman's face. He did not like this at all. "How close are you to finishing those papers?" he asked James.

Mr. Whattam smiled wickedly. "I would say that there is still at least an hour's work here."

"Can't you wait an hour? Then you can have all the time in the world with your dad?" the policeman offered the girl.

"Mr. Langley Meadowford has the right to receive visitors as long as he is considered to be under detention," Mr. Whattam said. "At present he is still considered to be under detention and is thus entitled to have visitors."

"Oh very well," the policeman grunted. "You can have five minutes. Once that time is up you are to leave at once." He held up his watch to show that he would be carefully keeping track of the time.

Thora was all set to go into the backroom as the policeman had called it and visit with her dad. She started walking towards the door.

"Not so fast young lady!" the policeman snapped. "You and the woman have to first complete a questionnaire before you are permitted to go back there."

"Damned bureaucracy!" Margaret winced when she saw the simple questionnaire. It was five pages long. "I swear that you are going to drown in paper one day!"

"Look, no one is asking you to go back there!" the policeman responded. "I'm not forcing you to fill out this stuff. But if you want to have your visit the two of you are going to have to each fill one of these out. Rules are rules."

Thora took the questionnaire from the policeman. Like Margaret said it was five pages long—five foolscap pages that were neatly stapled in the upper left corner. A quick glance at the first page revealed that the form should not be that difficult to complete. The girl's only problem was that she did not have a pen or pencil to work with. When she asked the policeman for one he told her that all the pencils were currently in use. He pointed to Uncle Thaddeus, then to James, and then to Margaret. All had police station pencils in their hands. "You'll just have to wait."

"Or I could go buy one from the corner store," Thora said, reaching into her pocket to see if she had any change. She could feel a pair of nickels there.

"The nearest corner store is about five blocks away, young girl. If you want to walk that far go ahead but I would think that you would be better off just waiting for one to come available," the policeman said.

At that moment Thora noticed that the other policeman, the one that had been sleeping on a stool behind the counter, possessed at least two pencils in his upper pocket. "Can't I get a pencil from him?" she asked.

"From who?"

"From him!"

"Here, Thora, use my pencil," Margaret insisted, extending her pencil to the girl. "I will complete the questionnaire in my head first and then I can quickly jot down the answers."

"Are you sure?" Thora asked. "He's got a couple of pencils sticking out of his pocket."

"I'm sure."

Thora took one last look at the sleeping policeman. His cap was pulled down and leaned on his nose, obscuring his face. Yet there was something vaguely familiar about the chin of the man.

"Go on, Thora. If you want to visit your dad you had better get cracking on those questions," Margaret said with some exasperation. Thora sensed that the woman wanted nothing more than to return to her magazine story.

The first page of the questionnaire was very simple to complete as Thora had guessed earlier. All that it asked was personal details such as name and address and occupation. However Page 2 of the form became considerably more difficult. It enquired about the visitor's relationship with the incarcerated and if the visitor possessed any knowledge concerning the accused that should be addressed in a court of law. Thora thought about these questions for a moment before jotting down her answers. She indicated here that she believed that the accused was innocent and that if she were to testify she would bring irrefutable proof of this innocence.

Page 3 dealt with the visitor's criminal record. Thora had none so all that she had to say here was 'Not Applicable' to these questions.

Page 4 asked for names and phone numbers of character references that would support the veracity of the visitor's claims. Thora had to think for a while about who to use here. She did not think that using her father would be appropriate since he was the man behind bars. She opted for the Whattams and her mother in that order.

The final page of the questionnaire required the girl to read a paragraph that outlined a plot where somebody perpetrated a crime. There were all sorts of extenuating circumstances that led the protagonist to resort to the commissioning of the wrongful act. Thora was asked in the end to determine if the protagonist was guilty and to give support for her decision. If she found the protagonist guilty she was also to determine what the sentence should be.

She looked up at the policeman and asked, "Do I really have to complete this?"

"You have to complete every question," the policeman said.

"But what does this got to do with visiting my dad?" she complained.

"It gives us an idea on what kind of person we are letting into our restricted areas," the policeman responded. "We don't want criminally inclined people wandering around in our secured premises."

"Just say that he is guilty and give him the maximum penalty," Margaret said. "That is what they want to hear."

"But I really don't think that he is guilty!" Thora exclaimed. "All those things that went wrong in his life gave him no resort but to do what he did."

"Look Thora, do you want to visit your dad or not?" Margaret snapped. "What does it matter what you say here? There is no real living person here that is going to suffer because of your decision."

Mrs. Whattam made sense to the girl and she quickly wrote down her replies even though in her heart she could hear the protestations of the protagonist crying out for mercy and compassion.

When she was done she handed the form to the policeman and gave Margaret the pencil. Her hard pressing had dulled the point on the writing instrument. Margaret looked at the pencil and grimaced. She took it nonetheless and began scribbling down her answers as quickly as she could.

The policeman was glossing through Thora's responses. "You are a very cruel-hearted person for a girl," he commented as he examined Page 5. "You would throw the man behind bars for life? I sure hope that I never get you as a judge."

"Don't worry," she answered. "I don't think that I will ever be a judge anyway. Besides by the time that I ever become a judge you would be so old that the only crime that you could do is wet your bed!"

"Thora!" Margaret cried. She placed her hand over her mouth trying to suppress a giggle.

The policeman turned red in the face. "And what sentence would you give a geriatric bed wetter?" he asked.

"Three hours washing his clothes and linens," Thora quipped.

"That's not that bad of a sentence," the policeman smiled. "Perhaps you are not that bad of a judge at all."

"Oh yes, I am. You'll have to hang your clothes to dry. That would make me a hanging judge!"

The policeman groaned at the joke. Thora felt pleased that she had finally been able to crack the man's crusty official exterior and find a fellow human being inside.

"I'm done now," Margaret announced, handing the completed questionnaire to the policeman. He quickly scanned the final question. "You would acquit the man?"

"There are all manner of arguments based on legal precedents that have been set that would clearly establish the man's innocence. To hold him behind bars would be criminal," Margaret said with some authority.

"My wife at one time helped me through law school," James said from his table. "I don't think that I could have passed without Maggie's help."

"Can we go see my dad now?" Thora tugged on the policeman's arms.

"Very well," the policeman answered. "But remember you have only five minutes, starting now." He took out a set of keys and escorted the woman and the girl to the thick steel door behind the counter.

As soon as he opened it the musty stench of unclean bodies and old tobacco spilled through the door and into Thora's nostrils. It was almost enough to make her gag. Her eyes fell upon a series of cream-colored bars. Some of these bars had the paint worn away at about three to four feet above the dark grey floor. She guessed that this was where the inmates must have frequently grabbed onto the bars to have a look at what was beyond the cells. She could hear people talking. She recognized one of the voices as that of her dad.

The policeman led them down the corridor of the elongated room that was divided between the corridor and the jail cells. Thora at first could not see how many people were behind them but when she reached a certain point about a third of the way down the corridor the bars no longer obscured her view of the cells. There were only two people in here—her dad and Bewdley Beacon. The fact that all the people incarcerated by the town of Grappling Haven were connected to the Meadowfords did not escape her. What did this say about her family?

"Thora?" Langley Meadowford called out when he saw her. "What are you doing here?" He was still in the pajamas that he wore at home when he was arrested. He looked to be in complete disarray. Not a hair on his head was set in place. His cheeks and chin were covered in an ashy shadow. His beard must have become very fertile since entering this jail.

"You have five minutes," the policeman reminded her before leaving her and Mrs. Whattam alone in the corridor. He locked the door to the backroom behind him.

"Oh Dad!" Thora could feel the tears well up in her eyes. "We are going to get you out!"

"Your mom is posting the bail? Where would she get the money?" he said in dismay. Then he looked at Mrs. Whattam. His eyes grew a little sinister. "What is she doing here?"

"The policeman would not let me visit you alone," Thora answered. "You have to be sixteen to do that."

"So why isn't it Mom that is escorting you?" Langley demanded to know.

"Mom's not here. She is at home. You know how it is," Thora said. She mimed the action of someone taking a sip from a drink.

Langley sighed out loud. "I know how it is." He looked at Mrs. Whattam and took a defensive posture. "This is none of your business," he said to her.

"If Mrs. Whattam did not volunteer to accompany me I would not have been allowed to visit you," Thora pointed out.

"I wish that you would have not come to visit. This is not a place for a girl your age to see." Langley became suddenly parental. Perhaps he did this to show Mrs. Whattam that he was a good father despite the fact that he was behind bars.

"I had to see you Dad! I had to let you know that we are getting you out!"

"Who's getting me out? You said that your mom is not here."

"Uncle Thaddeus is, Dad!" Thora piped.

"Thaddeus? That old miser? He is paying for this?" Langley held his mouth open in surprise.

"He'll be expecting the money back," Margaret clarified.

"What about me? Will that old codger spring me too?" Bewdley Beacon asked from the cell beside Langley's.

Thora gave the man a dismissive look. "I would hardly think so. You are nothing to him."

"Don't talk to strangers, honey," Langley said while glaring at the man in the adjacent cell. "You never know where they came from and what is on their minds."

"Your daughter and I are acquainted, Mr. Meadowford," Bewdley said. "She was in my room last night, you know!" He said it in a manner that was meant to stir up rage in Langley.

It worked.

"You were in his room?" Langley was aghast. He gawked at his daughter.

"I went in there by mistake trying to find the room Uncle Thaddeus gave me," Thora admitted. She assumed that the two inmates had established that they had Thaddeus Meadowford in common, one as an uncle and the other as an employer. "I heard him snoring and I quickly left." She remembered that when this fact was told to the police they immediately arrested Mr. Beacon. "It was all very innocent," she added to try and convince her father that no harm had been done.

"If it was innocent then why am I in here?" Bewdley responded. "I wish that you would have told the police that!"

"I am glad that I didn't," Thora replied. "I saw the posting for you on the board here. You are a very wicked man!"

"What did he do?" Langley asked.

"He has been making a career out of swindling old men like Uncle Thaddeus out of their money. But more than that he killed the last man that he worked for!" Thora had no problem uttering her charges. She was on this side of the bars. Bewdley Beacon was on that side. "I don't know what he had planned for Uncle Thaddeus but I think that he is the one that stole the car."

"What car?"

"Uncle Thaddeus' Bentley. The car that will prove you innocent of the charges against you, Father!" Thora felt a moment of triumph as she declared her thoughts.

"Is that true?" Langley snapped to his uncle's one-time servant.

"The girl suffers from hallucinations and a flighty mind!" Bewdley retorted. "I did no such thing. She heard me sleeping in my quarters. How could I have taken the car? I don't suffer from bouts of sleepwalking."

Langley studied the man for a moment. "And what excuse do you have regarding the man that you allegedly killed?"

Margaret Whattam chose this moment to cut in. "Don't answer that!" she said in a loud voice to Bewdley.

Both Langley and Thora turned to the woman in surprise. What was she up to?

"Do you have legal representation?" she asked Mr. Beacon.

Before Bewdley Beacon could say anything, Langley sniped, "Chasing down business for that husband of yours, are we Mrs. Whattam?"

"My husband is a practicing attorney in the State of Pennsylvania," she addressed Bewdley directly, ignoring Langley's jab at her.

"Lady, I know who your husband is," Bewdley responded. "He works for Mr. Meadowford. I could hardly afford his services."

"You'll be surprised," Langley said. "Word has it that Mr. Whattam will soon have nothing to keep him occupied. It's my conjecture that he will work dirt cheap."

Thora felt betrayed my Mrs. Whattam's offer. "Why do you want to defend him?" she cried. "Can't you see that he is the enemy!"

"Thora, weren't you the one that told me that every man is innocent until proven guilty?" Margaret answered. "Mr. Beacon is entitled to legal representation in order to defend himself against the charges laid upon him. Surely you don't want justice to be miscarried?"

Margaret Whattam was proving to be a complex woman to Thora. She was not that devotedly loyal friend like the girl had once thought. There were things ticking inside of the woman that Thora just could not understand.

"But let somebody else defend him!" Thora answered. "Show some loyalty!"

"I will inform my husband about you," the woman said to the inmate. "He is in the front room completing the bail papers to get Mr. Meadowford out. I will see to it that he comes in to see you."

"Margaret," Thora cried out. "Everything that I have told you is true and I firmly believe that this man did something last night that caused the accident that killed the Rozelles. I think that he has framed my father somehow."

"Girl, you have nothing to support your allegations! As soon as you start mentioning ghosts, any self-respecting jury member will be throwing out your testimony! Even your Uncle Thaddeus is convinced that your father took the car."

"Pardon me?" Langley cried out loud. "Uncle Thaddeus thinks that I stole his car?"

"He said that," Margaret answered. "He would…"

"If he thinks that then why is he posting my bail?" Langley railed.

"He doesn't know what to think," Thora spoke up. "I'm sure that I can convince him to see things the other way."

"It doesn't work that way Thora. In court your great uncle would only be asked questions of fact and not on conjecture. Thaddeus will support the fact that he witnessed a dispute between your father and Mr. Rozelle last night. He will confirm that he made a phone call to your father last night and that his car was missing this morning. He won't be asked any further questions because those are all the facts that he knows. He doesn't have firsthand knowledge about anything else," Margaret Whattam explained.

"Then he can't say that I took his car," Langley pointed out.

"He can't say that in a court of law but that is what he believes."

"If he is against me then why is he trying to get me out?" Langley crowed, pulling his fingers through his hair. The grease from his scalp made the individual strands stand on end. He looked like he held no dignity whatsoever.

"He is getting you out so that he can conduct some unfinished business with you," Margaret responded.

"What unfinished business is that?"

"He intends to sell you his share of Dearborn Cable. He cannot do that while you are locked up behind bars," Margaret spoke frankly.

Langley's eyes opened a little wider. Thora sensed that the greedy little boy was waking up in him. But then the rationalizing adult in him spurred him to see reality. "How can I do that? I don't have any money."

"My husband and Thaddeus have all the arrangements worked out. It is their conviction that your father has left you all his shares in the company. You will use these shares as collateral to buy out Thaddeus."

"I will be mortgaged to the hilts!" Langley cried.

"Yes but you will be the majority shareholder of Dearborn Cable." Margaret answered.

The greedy little boy was wide-awake now. "The company will be mine?"

"The company will be yours provided of course that your father's will has not changed."

"The reading of the will is coming up soon. Dad's attorney, William King, should be back in town any day now," Langley was rubbing his hands in anticipation.

"So you are going to go through with it?" Thora asked her father in dismay. "Didn't you say that the company is in big trouble? Didn't you say that the car companies in Detroit were no longer going to do business with our company? Why would you want to buy a company that is going to go tits up?"

"Thora, watch your tongue!" Langley snapped. "Where did you pick up language like that?"

"I will use language like that if it will make you come to your senses Dad!" Thora cried out of exasperation. "We will go broke if we buy the company!"

"You didn't hear me clearly girl. Dearborn Cable will go belly up if they continue with the vision of their present fossilized management. But once I am in charge I will make such changes that will enable the company to accept and then overcome the challenges it has before it. Under my vision Dearborn Cable will become an industry leader once again."

Thora listened to the dreamer in her father and she sunk to lower levels of despair. She had a gut instinct that everything that he said would ultimately be wrong and that the company would be bankrupt before the year is out. Her only hope was that her dad would not get the financing he needed to buy the company. She prayed that her Aunt Faye had somehow managed to convince Sambo to rewrite his will and that the name of Samuel Angus Meadowford the Third was stricken from the document.

And if that failed then that her father would be prevented from carrying out business because he had been found guilty of a capital offense. She would rather see him in jail than bankrupt.

"Isn't it convenient that the man that spearheaded the automakers' boycott of your company is now out of the way," Bewdley Beacon remarked. This comment sent shivers up Thora for if it was true then her father would have motivation to murder Art Rozelle.

"I'm going to make sure that I get to see you hang!" Langley viciously retorted.

"Not if I see you hang first!" Beacon replied. "If called upon I will testify that I saw you steal your uncle's car in the middle of the night."

"That's a lie!" Thora gasped.

"Is it, young lady? You were asleep. How would you know?" Bewdley grinned wickedly towards her. "After you left my room and went to yours I was roused from my sleep when Thaddeus visited you. I got up for a drink of water when I noticed someone walking in the driveway. I went up to the window and saw a man that would fit your father's physical description go into the car and drive it away."

At once Thora thought of her great grandfather, Samuel the First. He had a striking similarity to her father. Could he in his trickster way have been the culprit? But then she quickly eradicated this hypothesis. Bewdley Beacon was making it up. Had someone stolen the car at that time both she and Uncle Thaddeus would have heard the engine start.

"You are lying!" she said. "If you had seen this happen you would have told Uncle Thaddeus about it in the morning."

"Now, why would I? What would I gain in helping that old fart out! He had done nothing but treat me like dirt since I first met him. I owe him no favors!"

Sadly, Thora realized that in this point the former servant was telling the truth. He felt no loyalty towards Uncle Thaddeus and honestly she could not blame him. Uncle Thaddeus was a true cad to anybody that worked for him. The servants at Black Island were treated very badly. Even Capers the cat was given more respect than anybody under Thaddeus' employ.

At that moment she heard the metal clanging of a bolt being worked in the locked door at the end of the corridor. The policeman reappeared, "Okay, time is up! You have had your visit."

"We'll have you out soon Dad!" Thora promised her father.

"I'll have my husband come in and see you," Margaret said to Bewdley Beacon. The woman still intended to help the very person that in Thora's eyes was truly culpable in last night's tragedy. She gave Margaret a dirty look. Margaret averted her eyes as if she pretended that she did not see it.

When they returned to the front room Thora saw Uncle Thaddeus and James Whattam still going over the papers they needed to complete in order to bail her dad out. What kind of information was being asked on those forms that would make it take so long to fill out, she wondered.

She then noticed that the other policeman, the one that was sleeping behind the counter was gone. "Where did your friend go?" she asked the policeman.

"What friend?" There was an aspect in the officer's eyes that said that he thought her question was very peculiar.

"Your partner? The one that was sleeping over there?"

"Girl, let me smell your breath to see if you have been drinking!" the policeman said. "I have no partner here. I am running the shop by myself like I have been doing the last fifteen years!"

"Are you alright?" Mrs. Whattam asked her.

Thora said nothing. She would have said nothing even if she still considered Mrs. Whattam her friend. She knew that she saw that policeman sleeping upon the stool. He was as obviously there as anything else was there.

She quietly started walking to the chair where she had sat earlier. As she did so she noticed something on the stool where the phantom policeman had sat. It was a tiny chit of paper. She at once went to fetch it.

"Where do you think that you are going?" the policeman shouted. "That is a restricted zone."

Thora snatched up the piece of paper and she looked at it. Upon it was written, "Do not let this happen." She felt herself go frigid. She instinctively knew that the message was meant for her and that it came from him. She thought that she had recognized the chin under the policeman's cap.

"Give me that!" the policeman grabbed the paper from her hands. When he saw the message, he crumbled the chit in his palm. "You are lucky that that was not a confidential official record, young lady!" he said to her.

"That message was meant for me!" Thora cried.

"That message was not meant for you! It was from the little boy that you saw here when you first came in. His parents want him to become a G-Man. The boy doesn't want such a future. He secretly passed that message to me so that I could do something to stop it from happening."

Even though she had no way of ascertaining it she knew that the policeman was lying. An earlier thought that she had came back again. She was the only one that was traveling this road through life. Nobody else would be with her along that path. It was a thought that would repeat itself in all the days that she had left.

Chapter 20

Preparing for a Family Get-Together

It was the evening of the day that Langley Meadowford had been released on bail thanks to the forced generosity of Uncle Thaddeus. As soon as he got home from the police station he went to the washroom and took a very long shower. Thora could imagine that he was trying to scrub away all the germs that feasted upon him in that unsavory cell of his. He was also probably trying to wash away the memory of Bewdley Beacon.

Uncle Thaddeus and James Whattam had handed him a document for his signature. It was the agreement to buy out the older Meadowford of all his holdings in Dearborn Cable. Langley had placed this contract on the dining room table.

While he was in the shower, Cora Meadowford stumbled upon it. She had been drinking all day long and was in a very ugly state of mind. She had not forgotten how her daughter had raced away from her this morning in Margaret Whattam's red car. As soon as Thora and Langley had come through the door she unleashed a very nasty scolding upon the girl. She had not even welcomed her estranged husband home. He walked around her without a word and went straight up to the washroom for his shower after placing the unsigned contract on the table. Thora withstood the tirade and let her mother's hostility spill out. When Cora went to strike her she neatly stepped out of the way so that the slaps fell upon thin air. Eventually Cora had burned herself out and swaggered away where she stumbled upon the contract.

She looked at it but was probably too drunk to make out what it said. She threw it on the floor and said something before disappearing back to the family room where her highball was waiting for her.

Thora saw the paper that Thaddeus and Mr. Whattam had so meticulously worked on. It was strewn on the floor bent over upon itself as if it were waiting for some more punishment. The girl thought of another piece of paper she saw today. That one had said, "Do something about it." She saw her opportunity to comply with the message from the ghost. She picked up the contract from the floor and shredded it with her fingers leaving its pieces wherever they fell.

When her father came downstairs after his shower, he went directly to the dining room and saw the remnants of his contract tattered on the floor. He cried out his wife's name in a bellow. Thora watched her mother stagger from the sitting room, her eyes heavy with drink. She might have been roused from the opening stages of an alcohol coma.

"Did you do this?" Langley demanded to know. "Did you tear up this contract?"

"I saw her do it Dad!" Thora immediately said before her mother could say anything. A devil had been born in her this day. She did not know what had made her say this. It had not been her intention to incriminate her mother. Cora's inebriated state would most certainly have difficulty recalling what effects she had upon the environment of late. Indeed, Cora's droopy eyes and bloated cheeks conveyed that she had no recollection whatsoever of the document at all let alone what she had done with it.

"Why did you do it!" Langley railed. "That paper represented our dreams come true!"

Cora had not said anything. She just stared out of a face that was far more asleep than aware. "What did you say that I did again?" she finally mumbled. She was rank with booze and the smell of her sickened Thora.

"Look at her dad! She is so drunk that she doesn't remember a thing!" Thora cried. "But I saw her tear it up!"

The telephone had chosen that moment to ring. Cora instinctively went to answer it. Langley pushed her aside, "You are not going to answer it!" he commanded. "I don't want it publicized that we have an afternoon lush residing under our roof." He grabbed hold of the phone and immediately changed his tone to a receptive and courteous voice. "Good afternoon, Langley Meadowford here."

Thora watched him on the phone. His expression that had been so close to unadulterated rage moments before metamorphosized into one that stood at the very edge of elation.

"Yes, Mr. King, we will be there!" he said. "Seven p.m. at your office! Got it! See you there!"

He set down the telephone and at once cried out an uncharacteristic 'Whoopee!"

"What is it Dad?" Thora asked.

"That was Bill King, your grandfather's attorney. They are going to read Granddad's will at his office tonight!" He was as giddy as a schoolboy. He was a far cry from the man that had been dragged in his pajamas to jail this morning.

Thora could not feel the joy. Her stomach had flipped with the news. She was shuddering with apprehension. Tonight her father might inherit nearly fifty percent of the shares to Dearborn Cable. The thought sickened her. She looked at the shredded paper on the floor and realized that that was her life that was shredded down there and not the contract between her father and Uncle Thaddeus. The contract could be replaced. Her life could not.

Her mother did not react at all. She was still rubbing her arm where Langley had pushed her. "That hurt Langley!" she moaned through a face that was breaking up into tears.

"Didn't you hear me Cora?" Langley said. "They are reading the will tonight. You have got to be there too so for God's sake sober up at once! Thora, take your mother to the washroom and see to it that she gets under a cold shower!"

"She'll never be sober in time, Dad," Thora replied. "Maybe we should try to reschedule the reading." She saw her mother's condition as a possible stay of execution for the inevitable. Any stay might be long enough for her to find a means from stopping this from happening.

"Are you mad? I can hardly bear the anticipation right now. We are not going to request a postponement! Get her up to the shower!"

Thora had no choice but to comply. She took her mother by her arm. "Come on Mother, we are going to have a shower," she said. She absolutely abhorred the idea of what her father was asking her to do. But she felt cowed into doing it.

"I don't want a shower, Rebecca!" her mother groaned, her eyes almost entirely shut. "All I want is my bed."

"It's not Rebecca, Mom. It's Thora. Rebecca ran away to get as far as she can from this repressive household," she said softly so that her father could not hear her. "We're going to first have a shower." She turned to her father. "I don't have to take her clothes off, do I?" The notion was entirely repugnant to her.

"That's the customary way civilized people take showers," Langley responded. "But by the looks of her just toss her in with what she has on. We can deal with the mess later. Don't take too long. And use only cold water because I want to have a shower afterwards."

"But you just had a shower Dad!"

"This is going to be the most important moment in my life, girl. I want to look my very best! Now get her to the shower."

It was a monumental task testing the very limits of her patience to get the besotted Cora Meadowford up the stairs and into the bathtub. The woman kept on trying to break free. She had no conception about where she was being led. She just wanted her bed and if she could not have her bed she would just fall asleep where she was. The smell of alcohol seeped from her very pores. She was so pungent that a few times Thora began gagging.

When she finally got her in the bathtub, she allowed the woman to sit down. There was no use trying to make her stand. The water would reach her down at the bottom as well. Thora closed the shower curtains as much as she could before reaching over and turning the cold water faucet on. Her mother screamed. The cold water from the faucet was running directly onto her back. She started to get up to get away from it. Thora had to push her down and with her shaky hand pull out the knob for the shower.

At once an icy spray came from the showerhead. The freezing water was dousing Thora's arms and shoulders. She was forcibly trying to keep her mother in the tub. Her mother was struggling and screeching like a baby with mumps. Although she was drunk to the hilts Cora Meadowford possessed a lot of power in her diminutive body and she was using all of her strength to get out. Her survival instincts had kicked into gear and it was a terrible battle for the girl to overpower her. The girl was forced to climb into the bathtub herself.

Thora was now soaked to the skin in the cold water. Her hair was sopping wet. Her mother was fighting back with reckless abandon, slapping her, biting her, and scratching her. "Are you trying to kill me!" Cora howled.

"Just trying to sober you up Mom!" Thora answered, doing her best to see that the water was hitting her mother. Most of it was pouring on her instead and she felt frozen.

After a minute or so of enduring this numbing torture Thora could not take it any more. She shut off the showerhead and started to climb out of the tub while the icy water from the tap still poured onto her frantic mother's spine. As the girl tried to get out of the bathtub she felt a hand grab the back of her top and drag her back. Her foot slipped from underneath of her and her head crashed hard against the porcelain. At once her head felt spinny and her stomach woozy.

Then she felt a hand around her throat. She opened her eyes and saw her mother on top of her. The woman had somehow swung Thora's upper body around so now that the cold water from the faucet was mercilessly cascading upon her face. Her mother was holding her pinned there.

The girl began to buck and toss trying to knock her maddened mother from her. She wanted to cry out, "What are you doing!" but she was unable to do so as the water poured relentlessly upon her face, filling her nostrils and mouth with chilling eddies that mercilessly strangled her ability to breathe. She could barely keep her eyes open. She was only able to snatch glimpses of the world beyond her oppressed body. But one of these glimpses provided a snapshot that absolutely sent terror into the girl's heart. She thought that she saw the face of a ghost underneath the wet hair of her mother's. It was that face that had been rearing itself when she least expected it of late.

Thora began screaming. She sensed that her mother was not going to let her go. She sensed that her mother was actually trying to kill her. Everything became blurry to the girl as she tried to free herself from the woman that had given her birth and now was taking it back.

She thought she heard a loud bang and a ferocious holler. Then she felt the weight being taken from her and the water finally come to a stop. She lie there freezing and gasping for air, her eyes tightly shut lest she see that ghost again.

In the background she could hear something terrible happening. It came with thumps and screams and vibrations that trembled through the bathtub's molded porcelain. When she finally opened her eyes she could see the silhouette through the shower curtain of her father viciously beating her mother.

"Dad, stop!" she cried as she painfully lifted herself from the bathtub and flung open the shower curtain.

There she saw her mother with her nose bloodied, crying frantically while staring into the mirror. Her father had left the washroom. From the other side of the door, her father bellowed, "Now get yourself ready! And make it fast! I have to take a shower!"

"Mom, are you okay?" Thora sobbed. Her loyalties had flipped when she saw her tiny vulnerable mother in such a terrible state of despair. She selectively forgot that only moments ago this little vulnerable mother had tried to drown her. How could that beast of a man do this to the woman that he married?

Wiping the blood from her nose, Cora looked at her through the mirror and said, "Girl, you are soaking wet! You had better dry yourself and get ready. Father has an appointment, you know."

Thora should not have been surprised by her mother's reaction. The woman would get dragged by her hair through Hell itself by the man she married and come out of it with nothing but admiration for him. Yet, it still bothered the girl until she realized that she was displaying the same characteristic. Wasn't this the woman that held her tight while the freezing water spread its icy smothering tentacles over her face? Why was she suddenly defending this woman? "Who said I was going?" she answered, taking a towel to wipe her face.

"Of course, you are going. This is a family event and you have to be there!" Cora responded. She seemed coherent. The cold shower must have worked. She seemed sober. There was only a remnant scent of alcohol upon her. Thora wished that she had stayed drunk. Then, there might have been a way of postponing the reading of the final will and testament of Samuel Angus Meadowford the Second.

Two hours later the Meadowford clan from Pine Street was in the waiting room of William King, Attorney At Law, in downtown Grappling Haven. Mr. King's office was on the opposite side of the street from Cristo Pando's.

The large window from the waiting room looked out onto the busy restaurant that only last night was the first scene in a terrible cavalcade of events that brought such misery and ridicule upon the family that were looking out at it from across the street a night later. As the evening before, Thora saw the ruffian Rory McQuoid strutting like a peacock down the sidewalk on the restaurant's side of the street. He was walking his turf, king of his domain. She wondered what he knew of her estranged sister. She wondered what he knew of the accident that killed the Rozelles. She was convinced that this self-absorbed cock was a key to unraveling a lot of the turmoil that plagued her family. McQuoid disappeared into Clancy's Billiards, the pool hall where Del the Duck died.

A few minutes later Uncle Thaddeus arrived in the waiting room. James Whattam accompanied him. Mrs. Whattam did not tag along. When the two men entered the waiting room, Uncle Thaddeus pointed to the art that hung on the wood-paneled walls. "See how the paintings act like an undercurrent to the professionalism of this room," he said. "One walks in here and one knows that one is going to get first class service. You should really do something about that portrait in your office, James. It could only drum up some more business for you if you had something more suitable and apropos to the world of business and finance."

Thaddeus did not at first acknowledge the presence of his nephew and his family. He walked past them as if they were little more than pieces of furniture. He seated himself along a couch that sat under the window that Thora had been looking out. His legal advisor took his lead and also chose to ignore the Meadowfords of Pine Street. This was probably a wise thing to do for the feelings of animosity had not diminished between James and Langley.

The reading was scheduled to commence at 7:00 p.m. It was now 7:10. Thora could hear Mr. King in his office talking on the telephone with some client. His deep voice did not appear to be in any hurry to wrap up the conversation. He still had plenty of time because not everybody was present in the waiting room as of yet. Faye Thurston had yet to arrive. It was so like this woman to always be late.

"So," Thaddeus said to Langley, finally acknowledging that he was there. "Have you had a chance to go over the contract?"

Langley cleared his throat and his face turned rouge. "I gave it a glossing over," he lied. "I haven't signed anything yet because I don't want to count my chickens before they hatch."

"Tut tut Langley!" Thaddeus groaned. "This meeting tonight is nothing but a formality. You know that your father has given you all of his shares."

"I can't say that with certainty, Uncle," Langley responded. "You never know what antics my sister may have been up to in those final moments of dear Dad's life."

"Even if she twisted his arm and had him make her the sole benefactor to all of his estates, that will would be thrown from court as it will be easily shown that Sambo was not of firm mind and that he acted under duress brought on by his greedy, conniving daughter."

"Oh, you must be talking about me," Faye Thurston said as she entered the room and caught the last words from her uncle's mouth.

Thora looked up at her aunt and was taken by surprise. She would have believed that the woman would have been dressed to the nines in the latest fashion from Paris. Instead, her aunt wore a simple cotton dress that was not even properly ironed. The collar and the pleats were wrinkled. Even Aunt Faye's face which was normally done up so pretty was plain, drab and washed out. The woman appeared like she had been enduring a long bout of depression and grief. Perhaps she was. Or perhaps she made herself appear so pathetic as to gain sympathy from the others that were present. Thora knew that her parents would read Faye's looks as the latter.

"The world does not revolve around you, my niece, as much as you may be convinced that it does," Thaddeus grumbled. It was a poor attempt to cover up being caught in the act of gossiping.

"And I know for certain that it does not revolve around you either, my uncle," Faye retorted. She had come by herself. Nobody was here to defend her. She would have to do that for herself. And Thora knew that she was fully capable of doing so.

For the first time since that night before Sambo died, all the major living Meadowford family members were together save for Rebecca. But she was considered a child and would have had only minor status like her twin sister, Thora. Thora appreciated this status for the moment. They were sitting on a volatile powder keg and anything whatsoever could set off a calamity the likes of which Grappling Haven had never seen before.

Faye nodded to Langley and Cora but did not address them. There were no more seats available in the waiting room where she could sit. She had to stand by the desk of Mr. King's secretary. The elderly woman only worked daytime hours and was not there for this reading. Her chair was occupied by James Whattam.

When the legal advisor saw that Faye had no seat, he offered his to her. She declined saying that she preferred to be standing that way she could run if she had to. It was a joke that the rest of the clan did not find amusing.

A very foreboding and uncomfortable silence filled the room as no one dared say anything. All that could be heard was the traffic down on State Street and the occasional comment made by Bill King to whomever he was speaking to on the telephone in the other room.

Finally James Whattam broke the silence. "At least I have the courtesy to start my meetings on time," he said in almost a whisper to Thaddeus across the room. William King would be considered a professional adversary to Mr. Whattam and would have to compete in the same small market for the limited business that this town had to offer.

"I agree with you," Thaddeus concurred, looking at his timepiece that he kept in his waistcoat pocket. "Quarter past seven! This is intolerable. Thora, go knock on the door and tell Mr. King that we are all here and waiting!"

Thora looked up at her great uncle in surprise. She had not expected to be called upon to perform such a task. She turned to her mother and father to see if she really had to do this.

"Go, girl! We can't wait forever!" her father encouraged her.

"You seem awfully anxious to get disappointed," Faye said to him. "And I would have thought that you would have been accustomed to waiting seeing that you were detained behind bars by the police. Really Langley, doesn't the name Meadowford mean anything to you? When I heard the news this morning I was in shock! Father must have rolled over in his grave!"

The woman held back no punches. Thora was sure that her father would do likewise but instead Langley surprised her for he addressed her instead of his sister. "Thora, do as Uncle Thaddeus says, and knock on the door."

The girl knew that there was no getting out of this. She looked around at the faces of her family and saw that all of them, save Aunt Faye, were pushing their eyebrows forward as a signal for her to get moving. Aunt Faye was smiling at the rest of them as if she possessed some secret knowledge that made her superior to them. "You are not going to like this," the woman seemed to be saying to them.

Thora knocked on the door. She heard the conversation that the lawyer was having with whomever abruptly stop at her rap. "Yes?" William King said through the door.

"We are all here!" Thora said in a voice that did not quite match the volume that she wished to convey.

"Come in," Bill King said. "I can't hear you." He then said something to the person he was on the line with.

Thora turned the knob and one end of William King's plush office came into view. It was like a museum with fancy pieces of art sitting upon shelves in front of a library of color-coordinated legal texts. Her very first impression was that this man was a well-organized patron of the arts. As she pushed the door further open Mr. King's giant and domineering desk took over the picture. This colossal piece of dark oak had upon its surface a scene from the Great War done in miniature replicas complete with inch tall wooden soldiers from both the German and Ally armies. Her cousin Jack would have loved this desk.

Finally when the door was all the way open Mr. King came into view. His back was turned to the girl. With telephone in hand he was looking out of his window onto State Street. Thora had never met her grandfather's advisor before but she was immediately taken by his familiarity, even from his backside. When he turned around to see who had come into his office, Thora nearly fainted. The man sitting at the desk was the ghost of Samuel Angus Meadowford the First. She had no doubt of it whatsoever. It was not just a case of a similar resemblance. It was him. "What are you doing here?" she gasped.

"This is my office," the ghost said. "The more appropriate question is what are you doing here?"

"This is not your office!" the girl responded. "This is the office of Mr. King!"

Aunt Faye must have heard the strange conversation and decided to intervene. She stepped past the disbelieving Thora and announced, "We are all here Bill," she said indicating that she was of the acquaintance of the lawyer. She did not react as if there was an imposter sitting in the thick leather chair of her dad's advisor.

The ghost smiled at Thora with a twinkle in his eye as if he were telling her that his guise was working and that he would succeed in fooling everybody else that he was William King. "Very well," he said to Aunt Faye. "Tell the others that they can come in."

As Aunt Faye complied leaving Thora alone in the room with the imposter, the girl heard the man wrap up his conversation with the person on the other end of the line. "Sambo," he said. "It's time now to start the fun and games. I will call you later to let you know how it went."

Did he say Sambo? Was he talking to her grandfather? Thora was aghast. But before she could ask any question the rest of her family filed into the room. The reading of Samuel Angus Meadowford's final will and testament was about to begin.

Chapter 21

Reckoning (Part One)

The lawyer assigned Langley the duty of finding enough chairs to seat the family. The office that looked so spacious at first now had taken on a very cramped atmosphere as six chairs were positioned in front of the large oak desk. As soon as Langley scrounged up a chair it was taken. Uncle Thaddeus of course scooped up the first one, the one that sat closest to the window and nearest to William King's desk.

Thora had remained standing by the door. She could not believe that no one had noticed that the man who was going to conduct the reading was not William King, the legal and financial advisor to her grandfather. This man sitting at the desk was the ghost of her great grandfather, Samuel Angus Meadowford the First. How come nobody could see it? He surely must have been resorting to some magic that only ghosts possess, a magic that can deceive the living into seeing things not as they really are but as they assume that they are. She did not want to entertain the notion that perhaps she was the one that was being deluded.

Once all the chairs were set in place and the Meadowford clan along with James Whattam was seated, the host and executor of the will, the supposed William King reached into his great oak desk and pulled out a legal-sized manila envelope. The shape of this envelope revealed that it had been opened and closed numerous times. Thora had not taken note of this but her father did.

"By the shape of that envelope it looks like there have been some last minute rewrites made to that document," he declared. He was watching his sister Faye out of the corner of his eye.

Mr. King lifted his eyes upward from the envelope. "Mr. Meadowford was a careful man. He was meticulous about the allocation of every item that belonged to his estate. This necessitated frequent revisions whenever there was a change to his portfolio."

"Are you sure that some of these revisions were not written after his death?" Langley commented suspiciously.

"Mr. Meadowford are you calling into question my credibility as an honest man?" the lawyer acted like he was quite disturbed about the remark made by her father. The ghost was performing just the way that a real executor would behave when the authenticity of his documentation was alleged to be dubitable.

Langley would not be browbeaten. "Listen, we are talking about my future here and I am not about to have it hoodwinked by two characters trying to pull a fast one over me." The comment was pointed at both the executor and Faye. He looked over to James Whattam. "Is there any way to see if that will is genuine?"

Mr. Whattam groaned. "I am not your counsel, Mr. Meadowford. I represent your uncle Thaddeus Meadowford. What I suggest to you is either find your own representation or just to listen to the reading of the testament and then determine if you have been hoodwinked or not."

Cora was sitting directly beside Thora in the room. The girl heard her mother whisper to her father not to trust anybody here. Thora looked up at the executor and caught him smiling like a Cheshire cat to her. What was he up to? She was cautious about exposing him since she was sure that the others gathered here would believe that she was quite insane. They were not seeing Sam the First. They were seeing William King. But she promised herself that if the will that was presented here proved to be a great divergence from what was expected she would cry out that it was a fraud.

"Can you just get on with reading the will?" Thaddeus grumbled. "My nephew suffers from a paranoid personality. I am quite sure that once we hear what my brother has said Langley will quit his childish whining."

Cora was not about to have her husband so summarily dismissed as a bratty juvenile. "Why are you here any way, you old coot? Sambo hated your guts. He isn't going to be giving you anything."

One thing Thora had to give her mother credit for was that she was not intimidated by the old man's domineering ways. She would stand up to him. She would call him on his bark and reveal that there usually wasn't any bite.

Thaddeus' jowls dropped as his saggy eyes widened. He lifted his large hand in the air and summarily waved the woman off as having the significance of a housefly.

"As Mr. Meadowford's representative, I can assure you that his interests are just as much at stake here as anybody else," Mr. Whattam said to the group and not choosing to give Cora any eye contact.

"Never mind her, Jim. We will see to it that she falls out of the picture very soon," Thaddeus said.

"And what does that supposed to mean?" Cora cried out.

"Your days with your husband are numbered, my dear!" Thaddeus retorted. "You might not see it but the rest of us do!"

Cora turned to Langley in shock. "Langley, say something! Defend me! Tell them that it isn't true!"

"He isn't saying anything because he knows that it is true!" Thaddeus laughed. "You are no Meadowford you crass bargain basement commoner! You will soon be returning to the fly smitten trash that spawned you!"

Langley sat quiet through the exchange. His eyes rolled up on several occasions but he did nothing to defend his wife.

"Langley, say something!" Cora demanded. "If it is true what the old goat says then I will let you know that I will take you to the cleaners! You won't have one red cent to your name after I am through with you!"

Thora wanted to add that he would not have one red cent anyway if Thaddeus and Mr. Whattam have their way and unleash their scheme of dumping their bankrupt business onto him.

"Cora, can't you just be quiet and let it rest!" Langley finally said. "Let's hear what Mr. King has got to read to us! Never mind anything else for now!" He turned to his sister Faye. "But if I hear anything fishy I tell you right now dear sister that I will fight it in court!"

Aunt Faye adjusted herself on her seat and was pretending that she did not hear what her vindictive brother said. "Can we just get on with it?" she said to the executor. "I have other appointments to which I must attend later this evening," she added.

"Yeah, probably with either travel agents or foreign investors!" Langley sniped. "You already know what that will says and you already know that you are getting it all! I know what you did when you were left all alone with Dad after we left the island!"

Faye smirked. "You have never changed an iota in your life, big brother! Even as a boy you were always jealous and suspicious about my relationship with Mom and Dad. You just could never accept that I was their child too!"

"There is a difference between suspicion and observation, Faye! Mom and Dad always doted over their little princess while they just left me to fend for myself!" Langley complained.

"For God's sake!" Thaddeus thundered. "They were trying to make a man out of you Langley! They were trying to instill some independence and self-reliance in you. Their efforts were wasted! You have to this day remained an inept, capricious brat that has had everything handed to him on a silver platter!"

"Well, you are hoping to capitalize on this silver platter now, aren't you?" Langley shot back. "I could take my shares in Dearborn and sell them to somebody else and then invest that money elsewhere! I don't have to follow through with your plan, Uncle Thaddeus! Then we will see who relies on whom when your albatross takes you to the bottom because you never properly fed it and taught it how to fly!"

Thora found herself pleased with her dad's response. He was talking the way that she hoped he would and describing a course of action that just might keep her family from sinking to the bottom. For some reason she chose that moment to look up at the executor. Not surprisingly, she found that he was looking at her. He was shaking his head slightly back and forth as if to say that her thoughts would never happen.

Langley's sharp comments had the effect of taking the wind out of Thaddeus' sail. The old man grumbled to himself something that was inaudible to the rest and then asked the executor to please proceed and stop allowing the remains of his family to implode.

Everybody else in the room had grown silent as well. All of the attention was focused upon the man behind the big oak desk who had been fumbling with the edges of the manila envelope.

It was time for the will to be read. Thora could feel herself starting to hold her breath. She knew that whatever would be read to the Meadowford family would not be the final will and testament of Samuel Angus Meadowford the Second, the beloved Sambo. Whatever Sambo truly wished would not be revealed here. She wondered if it would ever be aired anywhere.

The alleged William King pulled out a neat bundle of paper from the envelope. Each of the score or more of pages were tidily squared and fastidiously stapled together. If there were any last minute revisions to the document it was not evident in the package. There were no loose pages with the scrawl of an old man's shaky hand in the set of leaves. Thora knew that her father would be looking for such an addition. If he saw one he would immediately cry out that the will had been tampered with. It was not going to be that easy for him with the tidy package that came into display before the gathered Meadowford eyes.

On the front page was a cherry wax seal that gave the package an air of authenticity that made it hard to dismiss as a fraud. From her spot Thora could see three signatures. From her lessons at school she knew that one signature would belong to the individual making the will, one would belong to a witness, and the third would be that of a notary public—presumably Mr. King in this instance.

Mr. King donned a pair of spectacles. As he put them on Thora could detect that he was smiling ever so slightly and impishly towards her. She now knew for certain that the ghost was about to have some fun and games with the Meadowfords.

The executor cleared his throat. "If everybody is ready, I will begin," he said.

Thora looked around at her family seated in the six chairs. All were looking on with anticipation in their eyes. They were ready to hear the testament.

William King began to read. "I, Samuel Angus Meadowford, the son of the man with the same name, hereby do declare that this is my final will and testament. It is a document that will disperse the items that became tagged to me during my long and fortunate life. These items of some worth are worthless in comparison to the knowledge and wisdom that I accumulated over my many years of walking this Good Earth. It is this knowledge and wisdom that I would rather disperse for it seems to me that they are far more priceless than any of these estates and articles that you now sit here and wait to be doled upon you like it was Christmas morn.

"Life has been good to me. It was the luck of my soul to be born into a prosperous and caring family that..."

"Is there much of this fluffy stuff?" Langley interrupted. "Can't we get to the meat and potatoes?"

"Oh Langley, you are such a boor!" Aunt Faye complained. There were tears in her eyes. Thora imagined that these tears must have been conjured by hearing the voice of her father from beyond the grave. Thus far the text of Sambo's final will and testament was written in a style very reminiscent of the way that her grandfather spoke. The girl could almost hear him speak as well.

Mr. King lifted his head and looked at Langley overtop of his spectacles. The executor, the ghost, was not amused with the interruption. "Sir, I kindly remind you that what I am reading to you is what your father wanted to represent his last words in this life. He was a dignified man. Show him the respect that he deserves."

"Sambo could be a windbag at times," Thaddeus cut in. "When he got older he could go on for hours in endless rhetorical verbiage that could quickly be surmised in a sentence or two. Must we be exposed to one more of these longwinded extracts from an enfeebled mind?"

"Are you calling into question the mental state of the dearly departed?" Mr. King asked. "If so, challenge it elsewhere. This is a formal meeting where Mr. Meadowford's testament is to be read in its entirety. If you have no desire to listen to it then I will ask you to kindly leave."

"Yes, go, Uncle Thaddeus!" Faye piped. "I find it reprehensible that you sit here like a vulture waiting to grab up some spoils when you did not even have the common decency to attend your own brother's funeral! Dad always looked up to you and defended you when the rest of the world was ready to tie an anchor around your neck and throw you into the lake. And this is the way that you treat him? You are a cad, Thaddeus Lloyd Meadowford. Sometimes I wonder who is worse—you or that vile brother of mine!"

"May I have some order here!" William King spoke loudly to have himself heard above the cackling Meadowford family. They were all at each other's throats. This family was divisive and dysfunctional. It was surprising that they had managed to spend all those summers together at Pioneer Lake without tearing the island apart.

One by one the feuding Meadowfords fell into line and returned their attention to the executor. Cora was the last one to cease and desist from her carping. She was busy defending the fine and noble character of her husband—the man that only a few hours ago was punching her in the face in a crowded bathroom. The makeup that she wore was starting to grow thin and her black eye was beginning to reveal itself.

Once Cora finished what she had to say, Mr. King returned to the text of the will. "Life has been good to me. It was the luck of my soul to be born into a prosperous and caring family that fostered in me the desire to not only increase that fortune but to look into ways of dispersing my gains so that others may prosper as well."

"He's going to give away everything to charity!" Langley cried out, once more interrupting the reading.

"It doesn't say that!" Faye responded.

"It doesn't say that now but it will!" Langley dropped his head into his hands out of anxiety that his prediction may come true.

Thora had to wonder if the ghost had already started editing the testament's text to suit his trickster needs. He was up to something and it could only be no good.

"Yet," Mr. King began reading Sambo's words from the will once more, "As the years have gone by I have learned that the best way to help those less fortunate is to teach them how to help themselves. By operating a smooth ship everybody gains. A captain does not hand over control of his vessel to the crew and allow them to run the ship. That would be courting disaster. A captain holds onto power in his boat and steers it for harbors where the treasure is aplenty and there he shares this booty with those that loyally serve him. The crew is satisfied and the crew feels security in knowing that they are in capable hands.

"A good captain knows his crew. It is akin to what the Lord says about the relationship between a shepherd and his sheep."

"My God! Is he going anywhere with this?" Thaddeus cried. "If I wanted to be near metaphors I could read a novel instead of listening to this drivel!"

"Oh, will you not stop Uncle Thaddeus!" Aunt Faye growled. "We could have been done listening to the will if you were not interrupting its reading at the end of every sentence!"

"A good captain knows his crew," Mr. King read louder, carrying the weight of his voice above the bickering audience. "It is akin to what the Lord says about the relationship between a shepherd and his sheep. The shepherd will protect the weak ones and ally himself with the dominant ones. He keeps control of the goal of the flock. I will not presume that keeping control of those to whom I shall bestow and bequeath my estate is my agenda. I have no desire to rule from beyond the grave. Yet I do wish that those that receive some benefice from me take into consideration the advice that I give them now as they enter a phase in life where I will no longer be present.

"To my dear brother Thaddeus who has been a partner in life with me and who I value as a worthy businessman I say simply this. Do not be so recalcitrant in the way that you venture into your twilight years. Be open to new suggestions and new ideas. Our ways worked when we were younger when we took bold steps and tasted the fruits of our keen and astute minds. But the world has caught up to us now and some have even strode past us. We must try to match these steps and perhaps rely on the judgment of others if we wish to succeed. Our minds are not as sharp as they used to be."

"Yours might not be as sharp dear Sambo," Thaddeus said. He had been sitting on the edge of his seat when Sambo had centered attention upon him. The words that his dead brother provided seemed to be anti-climatic to the old man and it appeared that he was immediately dismissing them. Perhaps it was anti-climatic, Thora thought. If Thaddeus dumps Dearborn Cable onto Langley, the old man would most likely go into retirement and no longer make ventures into the world of business.

"To my son, Samuel Angus Meadowford, the third to be named thus," William King read. At once Langley sat up. His eyes darted back and forth at the other faces in the room. Thora could sense that her father was expecting to be publicly ridiculed by his dead father. Mr. King read, "No father could have as much pride in his son as I do you." He paused.

The words startled everybody present and none more so than Langley. Langley's relationship with Sambo had always been poor and paltry. To hear such words made Thora immediately think that the ghost was pulling an antic here.

And then after allowing the statement the chance to sink in William King continued. "For I have absolutely no pride in you at all."

Langley groaned out loud while sinking deep in his seat and covering his head with his hands so that others may not see. Thora had to believe that the ghost was not rephrasing what her grandfather had said. These were indeed the words of Sambo.

The words of Samuel Angus Meadowford the Second continued. "I do not know where precisely I failed you son. I brought you up using the same principles that my father used in rearing me. Yet somewhere something went wrong. Whether it be that our success in finance gave you the insight to realize that you were able to obtain anything you want without having to earn it through the sweat upon your brow or whether your constitution came upon you from factors present before birth, I could never manage to overcome these deficiencies and I am afraid that I have raised a parasite upon society."

"He's not going to give me anything!" Langley crowed.

"Stop your bellyaching boy!" Thaddeus stewed. "Sambo is merely taking this opportunity to pour out some character assassination that he held inside for years. He did not have the guts to say these things in life for fear of reprisal. He is using the sanctuary of the grave to say his piece. His words will never leave this room. We will see to it that the acid in my brother is forgotten. His voice will not be heard any more once this meeting is over." The old man sat up in his chair and looked about the room. He was using his presumed position as head of the family to ordain a commandment to those of his lineage. His eyes stopped at Aunt Faye. These words were particularly addressed to her.

Aunt Faye rolled her eyes back defiantly. She would not live by his dictums, her face said. She would do as she willed.

"I prayed that when you married someone from a lower socioeconomic strata," the executor read from Sambo's final will and testament, "that the stronger work ethic background characteristic of the laboring classes would become adopted by you but instead you chose someone with the temperament of a usurer and common thief."

Sambo was talking about her mother. Thora always held the impression that her grandfather never liked his daughter-in-law much although he always tried to hide it in front of the twins. Now it seemed that he felt compelled to give his negativity expression. The girl had to wonder if the ghost was playing his tricks. Or were these the actual words of her grandfather? She gazed over at her mother and saw that she held a stoic yet challenging expression. It was like she were defying the dead man and saying that she could take his worst punch and still survive.

It wasn't until the next sentence was read that all commotion broke loose.

William King read, "I had hoped that your unfaithfulness would be enough to shake this woman loose yet…"

"Foul!" Langley cried out loud. "This will has been tampered with! Father only learned of my affair the morning of the day that he died!"

Everybody save Thora missed the fact that he openly admitted to cheating on his wife. Perhaps later when the family cooled down they would reflect on this admission but at the moment they hotly fought over the issue of whether Aunt Faye had taken advantage over her father's grave disappointment in Langley's conduct and had him rewrite the will striking Langley's name from the list of benefactors.

"Father knew of your indiscretions for quite some time," Faye immediately retorted when Langley made his charge that she behaved in a duplicitous fashion. "We all did! Only your wife seemed not to know but I believe that she had selective blinders on. She wanted to cling onto you and your fortune no matter what you did!"

"You had this will rewritten!" Langley shouted. "These words being read to us sound like they came from your tongue and not Dad's! He would never say such things to Uncle Thaddeus!"

Aunt Faye stared at her brother for a moment, sizing him up while finding the right words to deal with him. "You did not know your father Langley! Did you ever spend some time with him just talking and listening to what he had to say? He loved you despite the fact that you time and again broke his heart. You and your wife knew no end in finding ways to hurt him. Dad could have lived many years longer had you not injected him with ceaseless stress by your behavior and deeds!"

"It was you and that troublesome charlatan husband of yours that caused Father grief!" Langley hissed. "Your open and frankly libertine and reckless lifestyles caused much fret to him and weakened his heart and made him susceptible to the coronary that finally did him in."

"Reckless? How were we reckless?" Faye's composure was beginning to deteriorate.

"I will tell you how!" Langley said, holding his head up high so that it seemed that he was looking down his nose at her. "You could not keep your children safe! You lost two boys due to your neglect! My girls lost two cousins because you and Tom were so wrapped up in yourselves that you failed to watch over them. Don't you think that Dad's heart was torn apart over these incidents? He lost the only guarantees that the Meadowford name would be carried on!"

Faye's composure was now entirely gone. She charged at her brother with her nails outstretched like a cornered leopard. "My boys were Thurstons not Meadowfords! It was you Langley that was responsible for Jack's death!" she screamed.

"Me? How?" Langley gasped, as he was busy thwarting his sister's lunges at him.

"You were the one that had those spikes in your pocket when you went swimming! Had you have removed them like any normal man then no nail would have entered the waters and lodged itself in the rocks!"

"Oh, give me a break!" Langley cried. "That is the most feeble excuse I have ever heard!"

Faye was bawling now. Her face had degenerated into a horrific contusion of raw emotions. "How else would that nail end up there if it did not fall from your pocket? Dad and I spent our lives cleaning up after you. And as for Percy it was you that picked that fight with Tom that day causing us to draw our attention away from the boy. Had you not done so Percy would have been a strapping teenager now and would have been something that Father could place his pride even though he did not carry the Meadowford name. I somehow sensed all my life that you would take away from me anything that I truly cherished. My premonitions were true! You took both my boys from me Langley Meadowford and for this I damn you to Hell and wish that there will be no end to your suffering for there will never be an end to mine!" She pushed at his shoulders and made him unstable.

Langley fell over the chair that was behind him and unceremoniously crashed onto the floor. Before he could get up Aunt Faye had stormed out of the room.

Chapter 22

Common Ground

For some reason Thora felt impelled to follow her aunt out of William King's office. She was expecting to see Aunt Faye race out of the waiting room but instead found the woman standing in front of the window with her hands buried in her face.

From inside the executor's office she could hear Thaddeus raising thunder over the unexpected incident that disrupted the reading of his brother's will. He was placing the brunt of the blame onto Langley. Langley tried to defend himself by pointing out the fragile nature of his sister's constitution but Thaddeus would hear none of it.

Thora saw her aunt pull her face from her hands. She was listening to what was being said in the other room. And then Faye noticed her standing there. "Get away from me," she said softly.

"I just want to make sure that you are okay," Thora answered. There was such a tangle of emotion and divided loyalties running rampant within her that she did not know where to begin to piece things together again.

"I'll be alright," Faye sighed. "I just need a private moment to gather myself up."

Thora understood where her aunt was coming from. She was feeling the same way too.

"Listen to them in there," Faye said. "They are my family. Have you ever seen a more misguided lot than them? I tell you that after this reading tonight I will have nothing to do with any of them for the rest of my life."

"I wish that I could say the same," Thora admitted. "But I am still a girl and I am afraid that I am stuck with them for a few more years at least."

"My intuition tells me that you should do what your sister has done and fly the coop. It might be the best thing that you could do. You would be able to rescue yourself from the vermin's venom that pours out of them. But my heart tells me otherwise. You must stay with them, it says. You may find the key that unlocks their true dispositions and save them from what the future holds for them if they continue down Perdition's path as they are now doing."

"I thought that you don't care for them," Thora said.

"Of course I care for them. They are my family. I would not get so hot under the collar if I did not care," Faye admitted. "I do not truly blame Langley for the loss of my boys. Both deaths were just unfortunate incidents that are beyond the responsibility of anybody. I do not place any credence in the postulation that Percy and Jack's death are part and parcel of the curse that some believe has been placed on the Meadowford family."

"What curse is that?" Thora had never heard of this notion before. It sent a chill up her spine in discovering that there might be some black cause behind all the tragedy that fell upon her family.

"Oh, I shouldn't have brought it up," Faye said. "You don't need to be made witness to what is ultimately nothing but nonsense."

"Tell me, Aunt Faye!" Thora beseeched the woman.

"No, never mind Thora. It will only upset you," Aunt Faye said. She was pulling out a compact from her purse to redo her face.

"I am already upset!" Thora cried. "Please tell me. If there is a curse on my family I want to know!"

Aunt Faye took a deep breath. "Very well. I will remind you though that this is nothing but some post hoc explanation for why our family seems to be singled out to have more than its fair share of heartache."

"Just tell me about it. I will not subscribe to it, I assure you. I like to think that my head is put on right," Thora said. She knew that deep inside that she would take the curse for reality and that it would forever change her way of thinking about everything.

"It all is tied to that parcel of land that our family possesses upon Pioneer Lake," Aunt Faye began.

"Black Island?"

"Yes, Black Island," Aunt Faye nodded. "Before your great grandfather purchased it from the Canadian government this island was rumored to be a sacred ground for the local Indians. They held a belief that some holy boy was buried there long ago and that one day this boy would awake and return the land to his ancient forefathers. When Samuel the First bought the land a woman approached him from the tribe demanding that he hand back the land to the Indians. When he refused this woman leveled a curse upon the family. Afterwards our family has had a string of bad luck. Many of us died there—your grandmother, your grandfather and your two cousins."

"All because of the curse?" Thora asked. She found the story chilling yet very fascinating.

"Some would think so. I don't, myself," Aunt Faye said.

"Who thought so?"

"Your grandfather, my father, for one. When his father told him about the incident Sambo wanted to return the land to the Indians. But Sam the First weighed in against the idea, saying that it was nothing but superstition. And when Sam the First died it was Uncle Thaddeus who demanded that we keep hold of the island despite my father's urging that we do otherwise."

"So why did Sambo continue to go to the lake every summer when he felt this way?" Thora had to ask.

"He did so for his wife and his children. My mother loved it up there and she would not entertain any idea of us giving it up. And then when the lake took her, it was your father and I that made sure that our family would not run and hide from this curse. I lost two boys to the lake and still I felt compelled to continue venturing up there. I can't describe why I felt this way. It was a compulsion that resided so deeply in me that I was powerless to resist it. But for some reason that compulsion is gone now. After my father's death I suddenly feel liberated from that overpowering desire to go there."

"Why would that be I wonder?" Thora asked. She was trying to assimilate this new information in her mind and she wanted to present the best questions that would illuminate this new take on things.

"I really don't know," Aunt Faye began applying the rouge to her washed out cheeks. "It just sort of feels that I have accomplished whatever I needed to accomplish there. Don't ask me what this accomplishment is because I don't know but I do know that whatever it is it is done."

For some inexplicable reason Thora understood what her Aunt was saying although she too had no idea what the woman had accomplished. She returned her thoughts to the curse. "Do you think that the curse is over now that Grandfather has died?"

"I really don't know, child," Aunt Faye was beginning to appear that she was feeling exasperated by the subject. "It very well may be for I will let you in on a secret. If it turns out that I inherit your grandfather's entire share of the cottage I intend to stop going there. The memories I have there are too painful now. I can no longer step upon the rock without images of all those that died being conjured up in my mind. There were many happy times on the lake but they are far outweighed by all the sadness that happened and I fear that there will be nothing but sadness on Black Island from now on. It is time for me to move on and enter a new phase of my life."

Thora took a moment to digest what her aunt said. She had heard that Uncle Thaddeus believed that Aunt Faye would get all of Sambo's interests upon Pioneer Lake and that her nuclear family would be shut out from it. "If you do get the cottage does this mean that my family will no longer have the privilege of going there?"

Aunt Faye looked up at her. There was an aura of spite in her newly made up gaze. "If I do not intend to go there then it goes without saying that your family will not be going there as well, child! Your days on Black Island have come to an end. Cherish the memories that you have there for you are never going to get to relive them again."

"Why?" Thora cried. "Just because you have grown tired of it doesn't mean that the rest of us have to give up on it!" Images of the island were springing up in her mind. She was viewing every vista from the top of the turtle-shaped rock. She was seeing her family frolicking upon the water in the Grappler. She was seeing the Madoqua Empress landing upon the great dock. She was seeing her grandfather dressed in his whites sitting upon the bench by the waterside smoking his pipe and staring out into the deep blue water. She was seeing her mother cooking in the kitchen. She was seeing her Uncle Thaddeus walking to the outhouse with a newspaper in hand. She was seeing her cat Capers sitting in ambush waiting for a chipmunk to come by.

She was seeing her Uncle Tom and cousin Jack playing siege engine just off shore. She saw Jack looking up to her. She saw in his eyes an unimaginable sadness that would not go away. It was those eyes that were the last thing that she saw.

"Thora, open your eyes!" Aunt Faye said sharply. "The rift between your parents and myself can never be narrowed. We are mortal enemies. We can never share the same space again. And since you are the spawn of my enemy these feelings have to be extended to you as well."

"That is highly unfair of you Aunt Faye!" Thora spat. "The lake is part of my birthright as well! I am born a Meadowford. My great grandfather bought the island for future generations. You have no right to take it away from us."

"No one rules from the grave, my child!" Aunt Faye spat. "Sam the First is long dead. His dream that there would be Meadowfords upon Black Island at the dawn of the new millennium is long dead as well. We tried to keep it alive but we are a family consisting of vastly different individuals, none of whom can get along for even a short meeting like this let alone an entire summer. You saw the fireworks in the next-door office. You know that there is no way that the tensions between us can be eased. It is time we went our separate ways. We share no common ground—the common ground that we do have, Black Island, is only illusory and the faster that we get rid of it then the better it will be for all of us!"

Thora did not say anything. She saw the adamancy in her aunt's face. She was bound and determined that the era of the lake has come to an end for the family. In the background she could hear the muffled voice of Uncle Thaddeus from the next room. She could not make out what the man was saying. But hearing his voice reminded her of something. The grumpy old man still owned fifty percent of the island and the grumpy old man was still family.

"You can't force us to stay away!" she said to her aunt. "Uncle Thaddeus will still let us go up there!"

Aunt Faye laughed. "I'm afraid that you are not up to date on the latest developments in the family, child. Uncle Thaddeus has sold me his interests in Pioneer Lake. He doesn't want any more part of it. He hates it there because he feels that it can no longer offer him the peace and solace that it once did before the arrival of the newer generation."

"Are you referring to my generation?" Thora was aghast at this news. She felt the finality of everything. The beautiful vistas of Pioneer Lake would never imprint themselves upon her eyes again.

"No, my generation," Aunt Faye said. "Thaddeus has very little tolerance for me or Langley. I think that he feels this way because his own children had abandoned him. He has come to realize that modern people only have disdain for his arcane ways. He doesn't want to be viewed as some cumbersome relic from the past but he is still unwilling to change."

"I don't care what Uncle Thaddeus thinks!" Thora retorted strongly. "It is highly unfair that he sold you his share to the cottage without first consulting my father. He could have sold his half to the both of you!"

"Your dad is not interested in Pioneer Lake Thora! He has more than on one occasion suggested that the family rids itself of the place and that we invest the money elsewhere. Even if Thaddeus had offered Langley his share I am positive your dad would have turned around and sold it quickly."

Thora could hear her father in the other room. He was complaining about something. And then the door opened and Langley stepped out into the waiting room. He was mumbling something to himself until he realized that there were others in the room with him.

"You are still here!" he said in shock.

Aunt Faye just looked up to him with menace in her eyes. She didn't say anything to him.

"If you are still here then maybe we can get this thing over with," he said.

"I thought that you said that the will was bogus," Aunt Faye broke her silence.

"The others convinced me to at least give the will a listen before I condemn it," Langley responded. "But I will tell you that if I feel that one sentence rings untrue I will appeal it in court. I am not going to be hoodwinked out of anything that rightfully belongs to me! Come on, sister of mine, let's go back in the room and listen to what our father who art in heaven has decreed for our futures."

Chapter 23

Reckoning (Part Two)

When they reentered Bill King's office, Thaddeus looked up at them in shock. "Look what the cat dragged in!" he declared. "Maybe we don't have to reschedule this dreadful event afterall."

Langley reiterated what he said in the sitting room about his willingness to listen with a careful ear to what the final will and testament of his father had to say. He repeated his intention of taking the will to court if anything sounded circumspect, unscrupulous and suspicious to him.

The executor, William King, asked everybody to be seated and then he requested them to hold back on their comments and opinions until the testament was read in its entirety. He was looking directly at Langley. Thora's father nodded to show that he would acquiesce to this arrangement even though the girl knew that he would not do so. And she had a strong feeling that things were going to be read to this group tonight that none of them would expect. They did not realize that the man presiding over this reading was not William King, the attorney that represented Sambo's interests during life. The overseer of this somber event was the meddlesome ghost of Samuel Angus Meadowford the First. Nobody else could see it but she could.

The man behind the desk started reading from the alleged text of the testament. In a deep and resonant voice he read the purported words of

Samuel Angus Meadowford the Second. "I have one more bit of personal advice to give out before I play jolly St. Nick and hand out my belongings to those I have the honor to deem as my heirs. This advice goes to my daughter, Faye Meadowford Thurston. You have suffered deeply in life, my girl. You have experienced loss that is far beyond any loss that has ever come my way. Know this my darling princess that I empathize with your grief as much as any father can empathize with a child that has been forced to endure such overwhelming tragedy. There is nothing that I can do to undo the pain that you have suffered but I promise you that if there is a Heaven after life I will search out Percival and Jack and we will build you a home in Paradise that will be ready for you upon your arrival in the hopefully distant future."

Thora stole a glimpse of Aunt Faye. She expected to see the woman in tears after that beautiful promise made to her by her departed father. Instead she saw a steely gaze on the woman's freshly made-up face. The gaze was not focused anywhere but there was something about the expression that said that her Aunt Faye did not put any stock in what was said.

In the background Thora heard her father whisper to her mother, "Listen to those buttery words! He is going to give her everything!" The whisper was on the verge of being a clarion.

"Now, it is time for me to enter the phase of this document that I am sure my son Langley and his eager wife Cora are waiting for," William King read. "It is time for me to bestow my earthly possessions upon those that I deem worthy of them. But before I start divvying out everything, I would like to request that a moratorium be placed on these possessions. I want the benefactor to promise to hold onto whatever is given to him or her for a period of at least 365 days from the date of the reading of this will. If they do not agree to such a term then the transfer of goods becomes null and void and the item will become the property of the Samuel Angus Meadowford Junior Foundation, a charity that I wish to create that will give assistance to the retired workers of Dearborn Cable Limited. As chairperson to this foundation I would like to appoint my oldest living grandchild and that would be Thora Meadowford as she was born before her sister Rebecca."

"What kind of crap is that!" Langley crowed. He could not contain himself.

Thora felt herself shiver. She had not expected to hear her name be mentioned in any of this. She at once strongly suspected that this clause was the prank that the ghost held up his sleeve and that the real Sambo had not actually made such a decree. She could not imagine chairing a charity foundation. She honestly did not even know what the term meant.

"I said what kind of crap is that!" Langley said even more forcibly.

Uncle Thaddeus was beside himself in rage. A moratorium meant that his nephew would not be able to mortgage his new holdings in Dearborn Cable to buy out the old man's shares for at least one year.

"You tampered with the will!" Langley railed at his sister. "This is not the legal final will and testament of our father! I am going to fight this thing to the bitter end!"

James Whattam spoke up. "I like to remind you Langley that any civil action that you take will in all likelihood take more than a year to complete. It is rather futile for you to fight it. If you contest the will then all of your father's assets would be frozen until the courts make their decision. This means that you do not even get access to whatever you are bequeathed until a verdict is established. If you don't contest it you will have immediate access to your inheritance and reap any benefit that this windfall creates."

"We'll see what I get," Langley muttered. "If the bitch gets everything then you can bet your ass that I am going to appeal."

"Ladies and gentlemen, remember your promise to remain silent until the final and will testament has been read in its entirety. Please refrain from making comments until I have finished." William King scolded the Meadowford throng.

Gradually the room fell into a silence. Nobody appeared satisfied with what had been said thus far. Thora could almost sense that this dissatisfaction would only intensify before Mr. King was finished reading.

"To my brother Thaddeus, a partner throughout my life, I bestow upon you the portrait of our mother that currently hangs in the drawing room in my home. I know that you have always cherished this painting and that you were upset when our father gave it to me when he died. It is now yours my brother. Hang it in such a spot where you can draw inspiration from her as you enter your twilight years."

Thaddeus smirked. Thora heard him comment to Mr. Whattam that he never cared for that picture and that it was a running joke between the brothers about how much Thaddeus treasured it.

"Please, Mr. Meadowford, I asked for silence!" the executor snapped.

The picture was all that Thaddeus was to receive from his brother. Either Sambo felt that his brother did not require anything more to add to his vast holdings or there was genuine animosity between the siblings and Sambo held no desire to bestow anything more than a token to Thaddeus.

"To my daughter Faye Thurston," William King began the next clause of the testament.

"Here we go!" Langley blurted. Thora could tell that her father could not contain himself. She saw his hands grip the armrests of his chair. His knuckles were turning white.

"To my daughter Faye Thurston," the executor repeated. "I bequeath upon you one hundred percent of the share of the property on Pioneer Lake in the Province of Ontario, the Dominion of Canada bestowed upon me by my father."

Thora shot a glance at her father to see his reaction. His face was in a state of suspended animation. He had been told previously that it was likely that Faye would get the cottage and that he would get the business. Thus far the will rang true to his expectations. Even though Langley did not react, his daughter reacted internally. The bottom of her stomach fell out because with those words she had been stripped of ever hoping to return to the fun and frolic of Black Island. Those days were now forever gone especially after what Aunt Faye had said to her in the other room about her intentions with the island.

"As well as this property I leave my daughter, Faye Thurston, ten percent of my net holdings in Dearborn Cable. An audited description of these holdings can be found in Appendix A of this testament. And fifty percent share of the profits from the sale of my house at 10 Cherokee Hills in the Town of Grappling Haven one year hence from the reading of this will. The other fifty percent shall go to my son Langley."

This was an unexpected turn of events. According to the preconceived notion of what was on the will Faye was not to receive any of the shares in the company and none of the house. Her ten percent in the company would confound all of the figures that Thaddeus and James Whattam had so meticulously worked on these past few days. Thora's father was flabbergasted. He roared his objection and his intention to declare the will null and void. But oddly Uncle Thaddeus did not react in any vitriolic display. Thora thought she saw the old man steal a nodding glimpse to his financial advisor and then to his niece, Faye. It almost seemed like he was aware of this unexpected clause. Thora got to thinking. Hadn't Aunt Faye said that she bought Thaddeus out of the cottage? Where would she get the money? Unless of course she swapped her ten percent share in the company for his fifty percent in the island property? But with the moratorium did this not mean that that trade could not come into effect until one year from today? Until that time Thaddeus would still own half of the island and that meant that there was still hope that she could once again taste the gentle breezes upon the rock and gaze upon the sanguine beauty of Pioneer Lake.

"To my granddaughter Thora Meadowford," William King read out loud. He was ignoring all the commotion in the room and was choosing to barrel through the reading whether its words were heard or not.

Thora heard her name mentioned and she gulped. She had not expected to be willed anything. This was twice the ghost mentioned her. She knew that this was his prank and that her grandfather Sambo had not actually named her in his final will and testament at all.

"Thora again?" her father cried out loud. His head swung over to her. Upon his face was the strangest expression. It was a face that the apostles must have held when they learned that Judas had betrayed Jesus. He somehow believed that she had conspired with her aunt to create this bastardization of a will that thus far was practically shutting him out of any of his father's estate.

"To my granddaughter Thora I hereby entrust her to be the first chairperson of the Samuel Angus Meadowford Junior Foundation. The outline of the mission, goals and organization of this charity foundation can be found in Appendix B. To this foundation meant to provide for retired workers of Dearborn Cable I hereby bequeath sixty percent of my shares in the corporation and all of my liquid assets including my bank accounts as outlined in Appendix C."

Upon hearing the award being made to the newly established charity, Langley threw his hands in the hair and cried out, "I don't believe this! I don't believe this!"

Cora stood up beside her husband. She threw her arms around him and looked venomously at Aunt Faye. "You are not going to get away with this!" she warned menacingly. "This will will be thrown out of court!"

Aunt Faye lifted her shoulders and said innocently, "I assure you that I have nothing to do with this! These are the arrangements that Father made long before his death."

"In the event that Thora Meadowford is still a minor at the time of the reading of this testament," William King read. "Then I appoint Faye Meadowford, my daughter, to act in her proxy until Thora attains her majority."

This clause drove home to Langley that his sister had Sambo rewrite the will. Faye was in control of seventy percent of Sambo's holdings in the company. This translated to thirty-five percent of the actual stock in Dearborn Cable. It would be eight years before Thora would come of age at twenty-one and legally attain her majority.

"I don't want to listen to this fiction any longer!" Langley rasped. "I am filing my appeal at once with an attorney!"

"I would like to remind you Langley that you are presently out on bail pending charges of manslaughter. Your rights as a citizen at the moment have been curtailed. One of these rights that have been suspended is your right to initiate any legal action," James Whattam said to the man. "You cannot invoke any appeal on this until after your innocence has been determined or in the event that you have been found guilty of the charges until the date that you have paid your penalty in full to the government. By then it will be too late—the window for initiating an appeal to a legal document such as this will and final testament is 180 days from the date of its first reading."

Langley stared at his uncle's advisor through wide-open eyes that were trying to find a means to deny what was being said. Thora knew that her father detested the attorney and that his mind was working feverishly trying to find a weakness in the legal jargon that Mr. Whattam had spouted to him. Finally his eyes softened somewhat. "You are telling me that I have to accept this garbage to be what my father actually wanted?"

"You should have thought about this yesterday before you went off the handle and created that accident," Mr. Whattam responded.

"But I did not do anything!" Langley protested. The evening sunlight was beginning to glisten in the tears that had formed in his eyes.

"There seems to be substantial evidence accumulated by the State to show that you did do something," Mr. Whattam said coldly.

Thora did not know what to think. She was able to follow most of what was being said although some areas seemed fuzzy. One thing that was evidently clear to her was that like it or not her father now seemed to be clear from having to go down with Dearborn Cable. Any conniving that Uncle Thaddeus had cooked to dump the sinking ship onto his nephew was now all for naught. If he wanted to unload his holdings in the corporation he would have to work on Aunt Faye rather than her brother.

Langley did not like it.

"And finally to my son Samuel Angus Meadowford the Third," William King took advantage in the lull in the uproar. "Along with the fifty percent share of the sale of my house at 10 Cherokee Hills in the Town of Grappling Haven one year hence, I hereby bequeath the remaining thirty percent of my holdings in Dearborn Cable. I know that you will be upset with this arrangement, son, but you have upset me time and again. If you choose to divest yourself of these newly gained holdings one year after the reading of this will you are to give the Samuel Angus Meadowford Foundation first option to purchase these holdings at a price no more than the lesser of the value of the stock as of the day of this reading or its value one year hence."

"Talk about a slap across the face!" Langley said through clenched teeth. "This is all poppycock and will not stand in court. If I am legally not permitted to enter an appeal then I want you Uncle Thaddeus to launch the action!"

Uncle Thaddeus had been sitting strangely silent through the reading of the final paragraphs of his brother's will. It was as if he were trying to come up with a new strategy that would save his neck before Dearborn Cable went bankrupt. Thora could tell that he was not very pleased with what his advisor had been saying. If James Whattam knew that Langley was essentially powerless in orchestrating a more affable will then why did he have Thaddeus go through all the tedious work of drafting an offer of sale of his financial interests in the company?

Upon seeing Thaddeus' lack of response Cora Meadowford announced that she would launch the appeal.

"You are unable to do so Mrs. Meadowford," William King said. "You are not listed as a benefactor."

"But I am his wife!" she shouted, pointing at Langley.

"As the spouse of a benefactor you are still not permitted since your husband has pending criminal action," James Whattam responded.

"Then it is up to you Uncle Thaddeus to do something!" Langley cried. "You are not going to stand just for a measly picture, are you?"

The old man lifted his head up. The bags under his eyes were immense. It was like there were living caterpillars underneath his skin that twitched and wiggled. Never before had Thora seen the man look so tired and defeated. "There is no point in protesting the will," he said. "By giving me that offensive piece of art my brother has acted in accord with the spirit of the law and has given me something. When a man has children and grandchildren then it is these generations that are to be the primary benefactors in an estate settlement. Brothers and sisters are to receive only the miscellaneous and sundry."

"But you got to do it on my behalf!" Langley grew vehement.

"Son, no court is going to strip away capital from a charity just to appease a spoiled brat with a criminal record!" Thaddeus spoke frankly. "Perhaps I too should transfer my assets in the company to this trust fund." He turned his gaze to his financial advisor. "Maybe we should look into this possibility, James? Maybe I can have the trust fund buy me out?"

James shook his head. "Bad idea, Mr. Meadowford. The assets in this trust fund are frozen for a year as well. Even if you could convince Mrs. Thurston to purchase your shares she would not be able to do anything until a year from now."

"It's all freaking hopeless for me then!" Langley spoke loudly and unabashedly. He was not ashamed to let his plea for compassion show itself to the members of his family.

To Thora he appeared pathetic. He was very much a little boy not being allowed a second piece of cake. His ministrations were not going to get him anywhere. All that they did was show that he was an immature brat and that he would be incapable of running a large corporation like he desired.

She found no sympathy for him. She was inwardly pleased with the way that the evening played itself out. Her darkest fear that her immediate family was going to go bankrupt now seemed to be abated. It was all thanks to that man sitting behind the big oak desk. When she stole a glimpse in that direction, she saw the ghost of her great grandfather secretly smiling at her. He had said that she should do something about it. In the end it was he that had done something about it. He prevented Langley from getting the inheritance and then entering into that scheme to buy out Uncle Thaddeus. She mouthed the words, "Thank you" to the ghost.

The ghost pretended that he did not notice. Instead he tidied up the pages of Sambo's will and was about to place them back inside the envelope.

"Hold on a minute," Langley demanded. "Before you put that away let me have a look at that document! I want to see if there has been some last-minute editing done to it!"

Before the executor could approve or deny the man's request the final will and testament of Samuel Angus Meadowford the Second was snatched from his hands and brought up to the scrutinizing eyes of Langley Meadowford. Langley raced through the pages and his face showed his disappointment as he failed to find any examples of erased or altered text upon the document. But then he came across something. His eyes lit up. "What's this?" he demanded to know. His finger was pointing to something on one of the latter pages of the text. He held it up for all to see. "This will has been tampered with!" he bellowed. "Have a look at this."

James Whattam stepped forward and examined the page that Langley held. After a moment or two he looked up at the younger Meadowford and stated that he could not see anything wrong.

"Are you blind? Can't you see it?" Langley roared. "Look at that there!" His index finger rammed into the page so hard where he allegedly saw a mistake that it poked a hole right through the document, forever obliterating whatever he saw.

"If there is no other legitimate business to be conducted I move that we close this reading," Mr. King said, reaching out to take the page away from Langley.

"Not so fast Charley!" Langley snapped. "You are not going to pull one over our eyes. This will has been altered and cannot be the true testament of my father!"

"It looked fine to me," James Whattam said to his fellow attorney. "Mr. Meadowford must have spots in front of his eyes."

"Spots in front of my eyes? Horseshit!" Langley blurted. "I will tell you what I saw. I saw that figure of thirty percent supposedly going to me was altered. It looked more like it originally read eighty percent." He began leafing his way back to see the figures used for the others. "Ah ha!" he cried like a cheap detective. "Have a look at this! This is the section where my dad purportedly gave sixty percent to that trust fund. What I see is some doctoring here. The amount my dad intended for the Samuel Angus Meadowford Junior Foundation or whatever the hell that it was called was ten percent not sixty percent. The one in the ten was made to look like a six!"

"Let me have a look!" James Whattam demanded. He tried to take the page from Langley. But Langley would not let him have it.

"I'm not going to let you ruin this!" Thora's Dad rasped. He clutched onto the page so hard that it began to crumple in his hand.

"Sir, you are trying to ruin this will!" William King declared. "The breakdown of the figures that I read to you is correct. You can rest assured on that!"

"Horseshit!" Langley reiterated his earlier crass remark. "My vision is good. I have never had a problem seeing."

"May I remind you Mr. Meadowford that you only recently suffered from a head injury and it has been clinically proven that these kind of injuries can produce faulty eyesight!" Mr. Whattam said.

"You are not going to get away with this!" Langley hissed. "I know what I saw! I was supposed to get eighty percent of the corporation!"

"Not eighty percent of the corporation!" Uncle Thaddeus spoke up. "You do not have control of my fifty percent!"

"Eighty percent of Dad's holdings in the corporation. I stand corrected," Langley averred to his uncle.

"I have your father's handwritten notes Mr. Meadowford," William King said. "There you can see that your dad did play with the figures before finalizing the breakdown. I have them in my filing cabinet in the adjacent office."

"So you admit it! You admit that the will has been altered." Langley sounded triumphant.

"Yes, I admit it! Your father did make changes to his final will and testament. He made changes in your favor. He initially had you down for only ten percent of the company. Then he had a change of heart and decided to give you a little bit more!"

Langley's face sunk somewhat. "Give me his handwritten notes! I want to see it for myself!"

"Very well," Sambo's attorney grudgingly muttered and started to leave the room.

"Hold on, Sir!" Uncle Thaddeus called out. "Can you vouch in front of another attorney that what you said is the truth?"

"Indeed I can," Mr. King responded.

"Then I see no need for you to go fumbling through the reams of paperwork that you must have in your filing cabinets," Uncle Thaddeus said. "I hold no desire to sit here all night just to appease a bad little boy's whim. I do have better things to do."

"As do I!" Aunt Faye concurred. "Langley, you have behaved atrociously all of your life. You have been a thorn in Father's side for years. What makes you think that he would act favorably to you when you have never acted favorably to him?"

"Because Langley is Sambo's eldest son and it is only right that the eldest son gets the lion's share of the estate!" Cora spoke up.

"Are we to go through another round of bitter sibling bickering?" James Whattam protested. "As an attorney I am fully satisfied that what business that has been conducted here tonight was legitimate and above board. There has been no tampering or fudging. The interested parties received what they were supposed to receive. I second Mr. King's motion to close this meeting!"

"You have no say here at all Whattam!" Langley shouted. "It is beyond me why you are even here. You are not an interested party! It is not up to you to close this meeting."

Cora turned to Uncle Thaddeus. "And that goes for you too!" she said with venom. "You don't have to stick around to verify whether this shyster is telling the truth or not! Go home, go away and good riddance to you!"

Mr. King did not take too kindly to being referred to as a shyster. "I was willing to comply with your wishes," he said to Langley. "But now after enduring the abuse from you and your vindictive wife it is going to take a court order for me to reveal to you the notes made by your father! This meeting is closed and out of my office, every one!"

Langley was not satisfied with the summary dismissal. He lunged with his fingers hooked towards the attorney. It seemed that he had the intent to strangle Mr. King. Thora watched in dismay as her father's hands closed in on themselves right through the neck of the executor as if there were no neck there at all. This gave her definitive proof that Mr. King was the ghost that she believed that he was.

Yet at the same time that Langley tried to choke Mr. King, Mr. Whattam came out of nowhere and grabbed Langley by his jacket and hauled him backwards. Through gritted teeth he said, "I remind you Mr. Meadowford that you are currently out on bail. Any behavior that can be deemed anti-social will see to it that you are immediately incarcerated again without any hope of release until you have had your day in court!" It seemed to Thora that Uncle Thaddeus' attorney took a quick jab to her father's lower ribs before releasing him.

Her father began to pant excessively. "I will have you charged with assault Mr. Whattam," he said through his wheezes. "You hit me in front of witnesses."

"I didn't see anything," Uncle Thaddeus said.

"I didn't either," Aunt Faye concurred.

Thora knew full well that her two relatives saw everything that she did. They were directly lying to him.

"You saw it, didn't you Cora?" Langley asked his wife.

"I wish I did Langley!" his wife answered. "But Thora blocked my view."

"Then what about you, little girl? You saw what this man did to me, didn't you?"

Her father looked so pathetic. He was having the worst day of his life where absolutely everything and everyone went against him. She saw James Whattam punch him and she knew that everybody else outside of her mother saw it as well.

It was William King that saved her from having to decide what to admit. The executor chose this moment to start dialing his phone.

"Who are you calling?" Langley abruptly asked.

"I'm calling the police. I will not stand to be manhandled by riffraff like you!" the attorney said as his fingers worked their way through the four digits of the telephone number.

"Just forget it! Just forget it!" her father retorted. "You win for now but I am telling you that someday I will get a court order and then expose you and my corrupt sister as frauds trying to swindle me out of what is rightfully mine!"

"That day is a long time coming," Mr. King said.

"If ever it happens," Mr. Whattam added. "There are only 180 days open for you to appeal Meadowford. Given your current legal status I find it highly unlikely that you will ever have the chance to lobby your grievances."

For a brief moment Thora felt compelled to come to her father's defense. She was about to announce that it would be her intentions to grieve the will's authenticity. She reasoned that this would open up her father's chances to have the terms of the document revisited and perhaps he would receive a more satisfying settlement. As she opened her mouth to say her piece she saw Mr. King slowly rock his head side to side as if he knew her intentions and that he was advising against them.

"I will mail all interested parties copies of this will within the week," the executor said, not allowing Thora a chance to say anything.

The Meadowfords filed out of the office led by Faye. She had come out of this reckoning far better than what was thought beforehand. She got Black Island, half the mansion and she personally got five percent of Dearborn Cable and control of another thirty percent for the next eight years. This would guarantee that she would have a major say in the future of the corporation.

Thaddeus followed her out. He got a portrait of his mother that he did not much like. He still held fifty percent of the company but he no longer had someone who would buy him out. He was stuck with his ship and barring finding another purchaser he would have to go down with it as the corporation fails.

The Pine Street Meadowfords were the last to walk out. Langley did not even come close to receiving his expectations here tonight. He was now in an uncertain future. He possessed fifteen percent of the company but that would not meet his requirements to continue life as he had been accustomed even if Dearborn Cable pulled off a miracle and proved to be prosperous. He was going to have to redesign his ambitions and pray that he could somehow be absolved of the manslaughter charges pinned on him.

Thora was the last to leave William King's office. The executor of the will smiled graciously at her as she walked past him as he held the door. Just as she was about to enter the waiting room he stooped over and whispered in her ears, "Remember your dreams, Thora Thunder"

Before Thora could say anything the door was shut leaving her to ponder what he meant by the remark.

Chapter 24

July Turns to August

Three weeks had passed since the reading of the will. July had become August and the days grew to be hotter and lazier. The remainder of the seventh month of 1929 had been relatively quiet as compared to its stormy beginning for the Meadowfords of Pine Street.

The family still had not heard anything regarding their missing daughter Rebecca. Thora had managed to convince Mrs. Whattam to file the reams of paperwork involved in producing a missing person report. Rebecca's picture now hung at the police station and the post office but nothing came of it outside of a few cases of mistaken identity when strangers came up to Thora convinced that she was her sister. Whatever knowledge the punk Rory McQuoid had about Rebecca still was not revealed to Thora or anybody else. She began to suspect that he had been just making it up in order to aggravate her and her parents.

The family also had not heard a word from Aunt Faye either, outside of through the mail as she forwarded legal and government documents to Thora in care of her parents. These documents pertained to the setting up of the Samuel Angus Meadowford Junior Foundation. Thora was the official chairperson for this pension fund but since she was a minor Aunt Faye took care of all of the administrative issues. Faye, through the mail, was only keeping Thora apprised of the development of this fund set up to help retired workers from Dearborn Cable. Thora did not understand any of it. She didn't care either. The way that she saw it was that the company and the trust fund would be long bankrupt before she attained her age of majority. She would never have to get involved.

The family did hear from Uncle Thaddeus occasionally through the latter part of July. The old man really did not have much to say. He called only to find out the status of Langley's pending court case. Thaddeus had put up $10,000 bail for his nephew. He was probably more interested in making sure that Langley was not skipping out of the state and the country rather than expressing any genuine concern for his nephew's well being.

Her father had no intention of skipping the country as far as Thora knew. If he did have such designs he was keeping it a secret from her. She rather doubted that he did. Most of July had been very hot and humid and Langley started experiencing severe headaches that were brought on, no doubt, from the head trauma that he received at the hands of Tom Thurston at Sambo's funeral. There were many days that Langley would not climb out of bed until noon, disheveled and unshaven. He seemed not to care any more about what happened to him or his family. He would come downstairs and take a handful of pills and then return to his room for the rest of the afternoon. In the evening Thora heard him snoring from his room until around midnight or so. Then she heard him get up and go downstairs. What he did down there she did not know. He would not return to bed until four in the morning or so.

This had the effect of exasperating his wife, Cora. The woman was searching more and more for solace out of the bottle but instead of solace she found more bitterness. She had grown nearly impossible to be around. She was cantankerous, bullying, vile and uncaring. Thora started to truly hate her and avoided her as much as possible.

As part of staying clear of her mother Thora tried calling her network of friends that she had shared with Becky. Most of these girls were away on summer vacation and the few that were still around tended to not be very interested in rendezvousing with her. They did not have to say it but it was obvious that they preferred Rebecca's company to hers. This bothered the girl somewhat but not to the degree that she felt hurt by it. She always was a bit of a loner. Perhaps this group of friends saw this and never warmed up to her. In the end Thora was left to her own wiles to find entertainment and stay out of her mother's hair.

She took to reading. Grappling Haven had a fine library along State Street. It was a bit of a jaunt to get there but when she arrived she was able to treat herself to a large assortment of literature in a multitude of genres. The books that seemed to entice her most concerned the supernatural and in particular those dealing with ghosts and other paranormal phenomena. She was sure that this stemmed from her encounters with the spirit of her great grandfather. She took out as many books as she was permitted and carried them home to read in the backyard, her bedroom, or any place that she was sure that Cora would not frequent.

At first she started with ghost fiction but found that these tales were not actually educating her on the subject. They were amusing stories, some even quite chilling in their telling but they were not satisfying her need for understanding. She started venturing into nonfiction dealings of the paranormal. These books approached the subject matter from a variety of directions some of which were so farfetched that she had to shut them and wonder about the sanity of the writers. But there were some that captivated her, even enthralled her. There was one writer in particular that captured her. This woman, Myra Stanley, wrote about her experiences with the appearance of long dead relatives in her home. She had inherited a house that at one time belonged to these dead relatives, her father's great grandfather and great grandmother. Not soon afterward strange things began happening in the century and a half-old building. Items would go missing and then reappear in places that they should never have logically been found. The walls had a way of creaking that sounded more like bickering human voices than just the groans of a building settling on its foundation. After about a year in the house Myra Stanley, who was a spinster and lived alone, was wakened by laughter emanating in the kitchen downstairs. She nervously ventured down the steps and saw an old man and old woman sitting at the table, he smoking a pipe and she mending a doily. They did not seem to be aware of Myra's presence. They were talking in a foreign language that Myra believed to be Dutch since her ancestry came from the Netherlands. Myra did not understand a word of it but she noted that the pair seemed quite jovial. They spotted her on the stairs and motioned for her to come down and join them. Myra cautiously did so and soon lost all her fear as the pair's genuine bonhomie drew her in and made her feel welcome (even though this was her home). This was the start of a relationship that lasted years. The old pair taught her Dutch and she gradually got to know them. They were her ancestors Jakob and Truus Nells. They had married in Holland in 1777 and had come to America shortly after the Revolutionary War came to an end. They built the house that Myra lived in and raised a large family of twelve here. Their children and their grandchildren came and went and Jakob and Truus remained in the house. Then when the first of the great grandchildren appeared the Nells decided that they had earned a vacation and they returned to their home country for an extended visit that turned out to last decades. When they finally came back to the house they built in America they discovered that a stranger had taken up residence in their home, this stranger being Myra Stanley. According to the book that Miss Stanley wrote she still lives with Jakob and Truus.

What captured Thora about this book was that Myra Stanley lives in Hawkins Corners, Pennsylvania. Hawkins Corners is only about a forty-five-minute drive away from Grappling Haven.

Upon learning this little tidbit of information Thora became preoccupied with the notion of trying to contact the woman and compare notes with her. Not knowing whether Hawkins Corners would have telephone lines, the girl decided that she would write Miss Stanley. So one afternoon she sat in the backyard and began composing her letter to the woman. In the missive she told Miss Stanley about the strange occurrences that had happened in her life of late. She told her about Samuel Angus Meadowford the First and how he always seemed to be around in her time of need and that he always came to her rescue. She admitted to the woman that she did not entirely trust the ghost. She sensed a true mischief-maker in him. Before closing the letter she also made mention of those few other occasions when she believed she saw another ghost, this one an Indian paddling a canoe through the skies.

Thora mailed the letter and soon had forgotten about it because events in her family were beginning to heat up again. A policeman came to the door and gave her father a summons for a court date for the manslaughter charges. This court date was August 5. To this point Langley had not done anything about hiring himself an attorney to defend him. Cora persecuted him to no end that the family was not comprised of paupers needing a court-appointed lawyer. She told him that he had to stop procrastinating and do something about getting some representation. The problem was not going to go away. She suggested that he should use William King, his father's attorney. Langley quickly pointed out that Mr. King would have nothing to do with him after he had nearly strangled the attorney on the night of the reading of the will.

Cora began naming some other possible attorneys and Langley always had some reason why that choice would not work. Cora never mentioned James Whattam. She knew that the enmity between Langley and Mr. Whattam ran too deep for them to ever enter into a relationship. It surprised Thora that Langley named Uncle Thaddeus' legal advisor as a possible candidate. He reasoned that it was in Thaddeus' best interest that his nephew beat the charges. Once Langley's name was cleared then he could go about making arrangements to buy out the old man of his holdings in Dearborn Cable.

"Have you gone mad?" Cora had cried. "James Whattam is a fraud! Look what his advice has done to the Meadowford estate? We are going broke because we listened to him! You don't want that charlatan Langley!"

Cora had chosen the wrong reason in Thora's eyes to harangue Langley. Her father should have been scolded for still entertaining the idea of buying Dearborn Cable. His fifty percent share in the sale of Sambo's house would not give him near enough money to buy Thaddeus out. The sale of that large estate was still a year off. He had no financing and even if he did buying Dearborn would be such a catastrophic mistake.

Not heeding the advice of his wife Langley telephoned the office of James Whattam and arranged for an appointment. The day of the appointment Langley was spruced up and shaven. He looked dapper and the kind of man that would be above suspicion. He went to his appointment and two hours later returned with a large smile on his face. James Whattam had accepted him as a client and promised that he would do everything that he could to beat the charges. When Cora asked him how much this would cost him, he would not elaborate outside of saying, "Who can put a price tag on the cost of freedom?"

James Whattam had called Thora a few days later to give her account of that fateful night. He conducted his interview over the telephone. Thora recounted to him how there had been two Bentleys, one belonging to Uncle Thaddeus and one driven by a ghost that looked something like her dad. She told him that the Rozelles were passengers in the other limo and not Uncle Thaddeus' automobile. She told him how later Del, the chauffeur for Uncle Thaddeus, showed up drunk and went into the pool hall where later he died. She told him about taking the onus upon herself to drive the car home and seeing the two emergency vehicles race by her as she did so. She recounted to him her night at Uncle Thaddeus and her encounters both were Uncle Thaddeus and his servant Bewdley Beacon and her discoveries that the Bentley was missing and that there had been the tragic accident.

Thora was still thoroughly convinced that her father was innocent of the charges. She knew for certain that it was the ghost that was behind the killing of the Rozelles. Yet when she explained the events of that terrible night to Mr. Whattam she sensed that he was not buying it. He said that her memories of that evening were not considered reliable as she was a minor and moreover her description of the events was way out of accord with the descriptions made by others. Moreover than this, Mr. Whattam suggested that the girl should perhaps seek some psychoanalysis. He felt that all of the emotional trauma that Thora experienced this summer had an undue effect upon her capacity to function as a healthy adolescent. He relayed this message through a compassionate and caring manner that did not seek to belittle the girl yet when Thora was finished with the phone call she felt suddenly tense and frightened. She held the premonition that her world was going to cave in around her.

This feeling was confirmed the next day when Thora received a telephone call from Margaret Whattam. Even though there was no reason to feel on edge, Thora was right away in a defensive mode when she heard the voice of the woman that she at one time believed to be her friend. Margaret was far too complicated of a woman to the girl to place her wholesale fealty and trust upon. There were aspects to Mrs. Whattam that the girl had no problem to befriend but there were other aspects that felt very cold and distant to her. She could hear in the tone of Margaret's voice that morning that she was dealing with the distant and calculating aspect of the woman. Thora decided that she would remain very cautious and not say anything that might have deleterious aftereffects. She assumed that the purpose of the phone call had to do with what the girl had told Margaret's husband the day previously.

"Good morning Thora," Margaret began on the telephone.

Thora was standing in the hall. She was facing in a direction that placed her mother in her line of sight. Cora was in her favorite spot, on the sofa of the living room. She had beside her her first soldier of the day—a highball mixed with a cola. Thora could see that her mother was trying to listen in.

"Good morning Mrs. Whattam," Thora whispered, turning around so that her back would be to her mother.

"It is yet again another wonderful day gracing us," Mrs. Whattam said in a false singsong tone that told Thora that there was some ulterior motive behind the telephone call.

"Another day without rain!" Thora responded. "We are enjoying a perfect summer."

"I'm not sure if the farmers will think so," Margaret laughed. "And maybe we will be sorry about it ourselves come the winter when we have to pay exorbitant prices for our fruits and vegetables. But who can think of winter on such a glorious day as today!"

"Yes, you are right," Thora answered, wishing the woman would get to the point before Cora's attention would be stirred.

"What are you doing today?" Margaret asked. "If you have no plans I was wondering if you would like to join me in a visit to an old friend who lives in the countryside. She has the most marvelous garden filled with azaleas and rhododendrons."

Immediately Thora's guard went up. Why would Margaret want her to come along on such a visit? Even though Thora had no plans for the day she certainly was not persuaded to spend her time in some garden out in the middle of nowhere with Mrs. Whattam and a stranger. But the girl had no time to devise an excuse. She heard a creak emanate from the living room. Her mother had rearranged herself on the couch—perhaps to seat herself in a better eavesdropping position. "I love gardens," the girl said.

"Good!" Mrs. Whattam said. "I shall pick you up in an hour's time. It is going to be humid out so I suggest that you were something breezy."

After getting off the telephone Thora looked over her shoulder and saw her mother staring at her. "Who was that?" Cora asked in a despondent way.

"That was Mrs. Whattam," Thora replied. She saw no purpose in lying about it.

"What did she want?"

"She has invited me to come along on a trip to the countryside to visit an old friend of hers."

"What friend is that?" There was a sour expression on her mother's face. But this was nothing unusual. There always was a sour expression on her mother's face.

"She didn't say."

"I trust that you turned her down. You have many chores to do around here."

"They are all done," Thora answered honestly as she completed her daily regimen of tasks earlier before her mother even got up of bed.

"That woman is up to something," Cora said. "And I don't like it."

Thora held the same sentiments but she was not about to tell her mother so. "I see no harm in going. It'll keep me out of your hair." She quickly went upstairs in order to avoid a confrontation. She was hoping that the booze would kick in early this day and that Cora would soon forget Thora's plans as she drifted off into the oblivion of alcohol.

But her mother at times was like a bloodhound. Once she was given a scent she would not give up on it. A moment after Thora had shut her bedroom door it opened and in walked her mother. "You aren't going anywhere today, young lady!" she said in a forceful manner. "Especially with that meddlesome woman!"

"It's just a visit to a friend of hers!" Thora responded.

"What friend? Ask yourself this, girl. Why would Margaret Whattam want you to tag along to visit a friend of hers? She hasn't called you in the past for such visits. There is a purpose behind everything that that woman does and I tell you that she is up to something."

"Up to what?" Thora asked.

"You tell me! Isn't it odd that she calls you shortly after her husband interviewed you? What did you say to him? You had to have said something in order for her to take this sudden interest in you?"

Thora had to admit to herself that her mother's thinking was not flawed by alcohol at this moment. The two phone calls definitely must have a connection of some sort. But she could not make the connection at this moment. "I just told him about what happened the night of the accident, that's all," she said.

"Goodness me, you didn't bring up that nonsense of a second car again, did you?" Cora remarked.

"Well there was a second car!" Thora cried. "I know that for a fact! I was there. You were not!"

Cora's face took on an angry demeanor. "How come nobody else saw this second car?"

"Because nobody else was there! Mother, don't you want Dad to be proven innocent? I have the proof that he was not involved in that accident but nobody is listening to me!" Thora could feel the tears begin to form. She was tired of having to defend herself and it hurt her that nobody believed her.

"Don't take that tone with me, young lady!" Cora hissed. "Of course I want your father to put this terrible nightmare behind him but I don't think that we have to grab at straws in order to do so."

"Then how do you propose for Father to prove his innocence? Outside of what I witnessed, everything else points its finger at him!"

This comment drew a stinging slap across the face but nothing else. Cora was rubbing her smarting hand but she was at a loss for words on how her husband could be shown to be innocent of the charges.

"Why did Dad have to act that way that night!" Thora cried, wiping her palm across her cheek to alleviate some of the pain from the slap. "If he would have acted normal like everybody else's Dad then suspicion would never have been cast his way."

"Your father was merely pointing out that his steak was not done to his satisfaction," Cora answered. "It was that pugilistic Michigan fellow that escalated the matter. Had he kept his trap shut then none of this would have happened!"

"Your words sound like you think Dad is guilty!" Thora said.

"I have faith that your father is innocent."

"You only have faith because you were too drunk to know!" Thora charged. "You are always drunk! Why are you always drinking? Don't you know that it is against the law?" Prohibition was still in effect as far as the girl knew.

"It is none of your business how I decide to conduct my life! I have no other amusements. I have no girls that care for me and take an interest in me. It is all about them and it never is about me!" Cora was beginning to cry.

"You have never taken an interest in us! You only look upon us as something that shows your status in society. You want two perfect little daughters, demure debutantes that you can show off to your friends. Well, Mother, I have news for you. You are down now to just one daughter and she does not want to be a demure debutante. She wants to grow up to be anything other than you! And you have no friends any more! No one comes calling on you and you would much rather call on the bottle than to call them! You are losing it all because of your drinking! Is that what you want? I can have Dad drive me down to his bootlegger and he can swap me for a case of gin if you like, Mother. Is that what you want?"

Thora did not know where the words were coming from that were pouring out like poison out of her mouth. Her mother thus far had not reacted to what she said. She just looked at her with her face askew and aghast. Finally the woman said something. "You will never be like your sister!" she hissed. "Rebecca got all of the smarts while you have become nothing but a bumbling dreamer that cannot tell the difference between reality and fantasy."

"Yes Becky got all the smarts!" Thora concurred. "She was smart enough to get out of here! But I am learning Mother! I just might get smart enough some day to follow her example!"

"You know where the door is," Cora responded. "I'm not stopping you!" She paused for a moment. "But if you take one step out of that door then don't expect it to be open when you come back with your tail between your legs!"

"Are you talking about right now? Are you saying that if I go with Mrs. Whattam that I should consider myself no longer part of this family?" Thora cried. In her mind she was wondering how this present crisis arose. How was it that an ultimatum was thrown at her? Everything had begun innocently enough. It was just a phone call.

"You're damned right it starts right now!" Cora said sternly.

"But Mother, this has nothing to do with what we were fighting about. This is something entirely separate from that issue!" Thora begged. She was not ready to take such life-altering steps at the moment. She did not really want to go to the country with Mrs. Whattam. She did not care to make this the bone of contention into a matter of principles. But her mother was pushing for that.

"If you take one step out of that door this morning I will consider it your good bye!" Cora made herself perfectly clear.

"Then I will not go!" Thora said. She backed down and conceded the argument to her mother.

"Call that meddler and tell her not to come here!" Cora said. Her face had not changed an iota with her victory over her daughter.

"Cora!" Langley's voice called through the bedroom wall. "Let her go if she wishes!"

"What did you say, dear?" Cora shouted so that she could be heard in the adjacent bedroom.

"I said let her go! It will give me peace and quiet!" Langley answered. "I can't get any sleep the way you two carry on!"

Thora's mother smirked. "You have had enough sleep for five lifetimes!" she mumbled softly. Her eyes lifted to look directly into those of her daughter. "See what you have done!" she growled. "You have disturbed your father! I should throw you out of the house for this!" The volume of her voice started to rise.

"You are doing it again Cora!" Langley rasped. "Let Thora go with that woman. It will get her out of our hair for a while!"

Thora smiled at her mother. It was a condescending smile that laughed at her. It said to Cora that in reality her father would much rather prefer that Cora left the house permanently than for Thora to leave. The girl did not win the argument on her own. Her father was the one that won it for her. She walked past her mother to go to the washroom and freshen up. As she did so she could see into her parents' bedroom. There to her dismay she saw that Langley was softly snoring on the bed. He was sound asleep and appeared to have been so for quite some time.

Someone else had come to her rescue and she had a good idea who it was. He always came to her rescue.

Chapter 25

Tale of Two Women

Mrs. Whattam turned down a gravel lane that Thora had never noticed before. Even though she had been in this vicinity northeast of Grappling Haven dozens of times in her life she had never noticed this old road before let alone go down it. When she mentioned this fact to her driver, Margaret smiled for the first time since she picked the girl up at the Pine Street house. "Eventually we go down all roads in life and every road that we go down gives us a better picture of where we are."

It was as stupid an answer as Thora could have ever imagined. Margaret Whattam had a reputation of being flighty amongst the women in town. Thora's Aunt Myra, Cora's older sister, had said that Margaret should have been born a duck rather than a human being. She had the curiosity of the waterfowl and the same knack of looking dumb.

"Who exactly are we going to visit?" she asked Margaret as they started driving beside a long cedar fence that reminded her of another fence on the road to Silent Hills Cemetery where a herd of grumpy cows had tried to impale her upon their horns. "Do I know her?"

"I don't think that you do Thora. She never goes into town for anything. She is totally self-sufficient on her property. Her name is Josephine Bianco. She is a childless widow. Her husband died about fifty years ago," Margaret explained. "Ever since then she has been on her own."

"How do you know her?" Thora was curious. The Whattams lived in Grappling Haven for only around five years. That meant that they were still newcomers to most residents' eyes. How could this newcomer know of this road and this old woman that Thora had never heard of before?

"I know of her through her books," Margaret said. "Mrs. Bianco is an authority in the world of Psychology. I discovered her in the library and then learned that she lived just outside of our community."

"Isn't that coincidental!" Thora cried. "I have had a similar experience." She related to Mrs. Whattam how she had taken up reading and had come across the work of Myra Stanley and how Myra lived in the area as well.

"You didn't write a letter to that old quack, did you?" Margaret laughed. "You should have consulted with me before doing anything like that. Myra Stanley is a fruitcake. She has been exposed as a fraud even though she would never admit it! She had visitors come to her supposed haunted house. They watched her indulge in lavish conversations with the thin air. They did not see anybody. It is the opinion of the professional community that Myra Stanley is a paranoid schizophrenic with the talent to pen her hallucinations into a compelling tale."

Thora felt somewhat disconcerted about what Mrs. Whattam had to say about Miss Stanley. She felt that it was her duty to defend the old writer. "Just because others don't see them doesn't mean that they are not there!" she responded.

"I have read Miss Stanley's book as well," Margaret said.

"And you don't believe a word of it?"

Mrs. Whattam took her eyes from the road for a moment and looked Thora in the face. The girl could see that something troubling had descended upon the woman. "We all have our own worlds that we live in, Thora," Margaret said. "This is our own personal reality but there is something larger than personal reality, it is the reality of the group. If the consensus of the group is that the personal reality of a single individual varies significantly from the group consensus then there might be something seriously wrong with the individual. Such is the case with Myra Stanley. Her ghosts, Jakob and Truus Nells, do not conform to the generally accepted construct regarding paranormal phenomena and as such it makes their reality somewhat dubious. They…"

"You are talking in such big words Margaret!" Thora cut in. "I am afraid that you have lost me." She had drawn her eyes away from the driver and was gazing outside. There was a steady incline to the land. The pastoral farm country had given way to wooded land with a feral aspect to it that reminded the girl of the terrain around Pioneer Lake. She half-expected to see a deer come running out onto the gravel lane that they were driving.

"It is a simple as this," Margaret said. "Suppose every ghost that people have seen over the eons was an apple then when someone comes around and tells of a ghost that is an orange you would have to believe that that person did not see a ghost for all ghosts are apples."

"But the person that saw the orange still has seen something. Just because it does not fit in nicely with what everybody else sees does not mean that it does not exist!" Thora countered. She was starting to suspect that this conversation was now more about her than Myra Stanley.

"You are very right in that Thora! The orange does exist and we have to ask ourselves why does nobody else see the orange other than the person that sees it. One of the first explanations that we would have to explore is the reliability of that person's perceptions. If we discover that that person has some faulty wiring then we can rest assured that this orange does not actually exist in the world beyond that person."

"In other words that person needs psychological help. Is that what you are saying?" Thora commented bluntly.

"So to speak, yes!" Margaret answered. She had returned her visual attention to the road. It was now beginning to wind as it climbed higher into the escarpment.

"Well, I read Myra Stanley's book too. She did not come across as a loony to me!" Thora retorted. "Her ghosts were very real. Nobody could describe such things without actually seeing them!"

"I'm not saying that the woman did not see her ghosts. What I am saying is that those ghosts are only real to her. Nobody else can see them!" Margaret had lost a bit of her composure in responding to the girl. "If you know anything about psychology Thora you would know that people that suffer from dementia praecox are subject to very vivid and elaborate hallucinations. Scientists believe that this is caused by some imbalance in the brain. Myra Stanley seems to be experiencing most of the symptoms associated with this mental illness. This to me gives proof that Jakob and Truus Nells are just phantoms of her mind. They do not have an existence outside of her."

"Well, they do now. I believe in them!" Thora said, crossing her arms over her chest in a display of refusing to accept what Mrs. Whattam said. "And what about this woman that you are taking me to now? She has many parallels to Miss Stanley. She lives alone far away from anybody else. She writes books. What makes you think that she is not crazy?"

"Josephine Bianco does not write about ghosts and has them do bizarre things. If anything her writings try to address the problem and find solutions for it. Never compare the two women."

"Why? Because it would be like comparing apples to oranges?" Thora could not resist the comment.

It served to break the tension that had been building between the two occupants of the car as it approached a series of hairpin turns along some very elevated country. From her side of the window Thora was treated to a spectacular view of the valley where her home community of Grappling Haven sat. She could see the grid pattern of the streets and houses at the center of the valley. The town's limits were clearly perceptible where the built-up land suddenly gave way to farms. On the opposite side of the valley she could see the southern hills climb upward into the sky. Along that upcountry sat Silent Hills. She could barely make out its groomed lawns upon the slope. She saw the road that she walked after Grandfather's funeral. She followed it with her eyes back down into town. From where she was now that road did not seem that long but it had taken her many hours to walk it on that fateful day. The cows that meant to hurt her were somewhere along that road.

"I am taking you to Mrs. Bianco's place for a purpose, as you may have guessed," Margaret Whattam said, breaking Thora's enchantment with the land.

She felt her guts quiver at the statement. "I had a feeling that you were," she muttered.

"I care for you Thora, that is why I am doing this!" Margaret responded. "You have gone through so much trauma of late and what I want to show you is that there is still promise for you and that your future can be bright once more."

"What's this woman going to do to me?" Thora demanded to know. She was starting to feel scared. Although she had heard of psychology and psychologists, she really did not know what they did. She knew the names of

Freud, Adler and Jung but that was the extent of it. They were all German fellows that seemed to belong to a different world than the one that she belonged. They did not seem to have a place here in the beautiful landscapes of Western Pennsylvania.

"She is just going to talk to you, that's all!" Margaret said, taking her hand away from the steering wheel to place it on Thora's hand.

The girl could feel the sincerity and reassurance in the warmth of Margaret's fingers but before she could delve too deeply into it the car made a sharp turn along a cliff side that fell hundreds of feet. Once it rounded the bend there was a white-tailed deer standing directly in their path.

Margaret tore her hand away from Thora and slammed on the brakes. The back end of the car swayed grotesquely as the vehicle almost spun around. Thora felt her neck snap as the car came to a stop. In front of her the deer looked at her for a moment before casually leaving the road and taking to a rocky path on the hillside. The girl turned to the woman and said, "Did you see that!" She knew that these hills that surrounded Grappling Haven were home to many deer. She had seen them occasionally but that did not take away from the sublime pleasure whenever her eyes were lucky enough to spot one. Each time was like the first time. She moved to the door to climb out of the car to see if she could still spot the creature. As she did so the automobile bucked as if it were on a teeter-totter.

"Don't move!" Margaret cried. Her face was white and her eyes were so wide-open that they looked like they could fall out.

Thora froze instantly. She immediately grasped the situation that they were in. The backend of their car was hanging over the cliff. Any sudden displacement of the distribution of weight in the vehicle could send it falling down the rocky precipice.

"We are in big trouble," Margaret said.

Thora sensed that she was trying to be brave but the stark realization of their predicament was overpowering her sense of control. "What are we going to do?" the girl cried, her head cocked over her shoulder to peer at the back of the car. Through the rear window she could see that they were high in the air overlooking the distant town of Grappling Haven.

"I don't know," Margaret admitted. "But we have to do something soon before a car comes around the corner and knocks us down the hill!"

The girl glanced at the road in both directions. They were on a bend.

A driver would have little warning that there was something on the road ahead of him. Even if the driver were able to brake in time to avoid a destructive collision his car in all likelihood would still nudge the vehicle that she was in and that would be all that it would take to send her and Mrs. Whattam to their deaths. For some reason the girl saw the image of her mother in her mind. Cora would be yelling at her and saying that she got what she deserved for putting her trust in the irresponsible Mrs. Whattam.

"We've got to go through the windshield," Margaret said. "It is our only way out."

"How are we going to break it?" Thora responded. There was nothing immediately available in the car that would smash through the thick glass.

"I wish that I would have consented to buying the convertible like James had suggested!" Margaret sighed out loud. "Then we would not have had to contend with this dilemma!"

"A convertible would have been lighter and not have been able to hold the road. We may have been dead already had you given in to your husband," Thora said. She was starting to feel remarkably calm given her situation. In the back of her mind she knew that they were going to get out of this and who would be the one responsible for their rescue.

"That doesn't make me feel any better," the woman responded. She too was looking for something to break the windshield. When she couldn't find anything she started pounding at it with the ball of her fist. The glass sustained the blows without any sign of weakening from them. The motion of Mrs. Whattam's attempts caused the car to veer and pitch. It started to roll backwards. Thora and Mrs. Whattam stared at each other in wide-eyed terror. But then its momentum stopped before the car plunged over the precipice. The vehicle was now in an even more desperate and precarious situation, teetering on the brink.

Thora had held her breath through the slide. When it ended she said, "That is not going to work. What if we both exit out of the doors at the exact same time? Would that work?" As far as she could tell she would be able to make purchase to the roadside in such an effort.

"That won't work Thora!" Margaret groaned. "My door is hanging over the open air. If I step out I would fall to my death!" The woman was openly bawling now. "Oh Thora! I am so sorry for dragging you out into this! I should have left well enough alone instead of poking my nose into business that is not really my affair!"

Thora did not know what to say. A visit to a widow psychologist in the country did not seem so bad now compared to this. "It's not your fault that that deer was there!" she answered, reaching across to wipe the tears from Margaret's eyes.

She should not have done this. The motion caused the car to make a deep sway and it seemed like it was going to fall. But miraculously it held its ground when Thora swiftly pulled her arm back.

"Let's start praying Thora!" Margaret said. "Let's pray for a miracle!"

The financial advisor's wife began reciting the Lord's Prayer. Thora joined in but she could not get caught up in the fervency of the message to the divine. It just did not ring true to her and she could not see how an "Our Father" would convey to God that they wanted his help. Another quote from the Bible seemed to be the better advice for action and that was 'the Lord helps those that help themselves'. Praying was not going to get them anywhere. They had to do something.

Before Mrs. Whattam could finish the final stanza of the prayer, Thora said, "What if we both climb out my side?"

"For thine is the power and the glory forever and ever. Amen. I don't think that that would work Thora! If I go to your side I would upset the balance in the car and it could send us to our deaths," Mrs. Whattam responded. She did not appear to be offended that the girl had interrupted her prayer.

"But maybe instead of sending us down, it will make the car's hold on the ground stronger," Thora said. "I noticed that when I put my arm on your side of the car that we just about toppled. Maybe if you had your weight on my side then the car will be all the more sturdy?" It seemed like common sense to the girl. She was starting to grow frightened about putting her common sense to experiment.

"You might be right," Margaret concurred. "Is it worth a try?"

Thora shuddered. The woman was placing the onus of the experiment on her. If things went wrong then it was her fault, not that there would be any final adjudicator doling out marks for responsibility. "Well we can just sit here and hope that somebody comes by to get us out of this jam!"

"And run the risk that they would plow right in to us?" Margaret quickly retorted.

Thora thought that then it would be at least their fault for the accident and not hers.

"I say we go with your idea, Thora."

Slowly Margaret Whattam began shuffling her weight with ever so slight movements towards Thora's side of the car. Her motion set a rocking motion in the vehicle as its center of gravity was being shifted. It was going through a pendulum effect trying to achieve a new stasis point. Upon feeling this motion Margaret suddenly stopped. "I'm scared Thora!" she cried. "I don't think that it is going to work."

Thora was scared too. She was glad the woman stopped. Her fingers clutched at the upholstery of the seat as the aftereffects of the shift in weight worked its way through the car. The cycle of rocking seemed to ease and the threat of tumbling was growing less severe. When it came to a resting point, the two females sighed a collective groan of relief.

"I think that we are more stable than we were earlier," Margaret said. "Maybe it is going to work. All that we have to do is a little bit at a time." The woman had moved maybe two inches closer to Thora's side of the car during her first attempt. At this rate it was going to take a long long time before they were in a position to bail out of the car.

"I don't know," Thora replied. Her eyes were fixed looking out the back window. Upon the horizon of the opposite hills of the valley she thought she saw a small cloud forming. It seemed to have emanated directly above Silent Hills Cemetery.

"I'm going to move again," Margaret warned. "I want you to get as close as possible to the door as you can to give us both room on your side."

"Maybe we should move separately," Thora answered. "If both of us shift our weight at the same time it might be too much for the car."

"That's a good idea Thora," Margaret agreed. "Don't make too sudden or too dramatic of a move. Keep your attention on the motion of the car. As soon as you feel that it is starting to go freeze whatever you are doing, okay?"

Thora started to do as instructed. Her eyes were still looking out the rear window. She could see that cloud start moving across the valley overtop of the town of Grappling Haven. She paid it no attention. All of her mind was focused on the movement of her body as she gingerly lifted her derriere from the seat and swayed her hip very delicately in the direction of her door. The backend of the car started to go down. Thora froze. For a moment it appeared that this momentum would not abate but then it came to a stop and started to lift upwards once more. It went through several permutations of this motion before it gradually came to an end. Thora's left flank was flush against the door. Her hand was on the door handle.

It was now Margaret's turn. The woman waited for the trembles in the car to come to a complete stop. When they did she started to slide towards Thora. The vibration in the vehicle began anew. Its back end dipped. To Thora it did not seem like it had gone down as far as it did before. It seemed like they were winning this battle. She was about to announce her observation to Margaret when she took note of that cloud that had been slowly drifting their way.

It was not a normal cloud. It was the feathery image of a ghostly Indian paddling his canoe of ether across the heavens. It was the same man and vessel that she had seen at her Grandfather's funeral and from the office building in Grappling Haven. The canoe and its occupant were only a hundred feet behind the car.

"Holy smoke!" Thora suddenly cried out.

The shrillness of her shriek startled Mrs. Whattam. The woman jumped in fright. The suddenness of her motion rattled the frame of the car. Whatever purchase it had on the gravel was now lost and it slipped backwards and became free from any contact that would hold it back.

It started downward. Both occupants screamed as the front end of the car came overtop of them like a Ferris wheel at a carnival. Thora was certain that her life was now over.

But then the unexpected happened. The wraith-like apparition of the Indian and his canoe came underneath of the falling car and caught it in its bow. The vehicle landed upside down in the vessel. Both Thora and Mrs. Whattam crashed into the ceiling of the cab. From her upside down position the girl could see the stoic mien of the Indian ghost through the back window. Determination was etched on the man's strong jaw as he began paddling in earnest to work against the unseen current he was up against.

He stroked his paddle of gossamer against the air. The muscles in his bare arms were rippling as he pushed deeply into the currents of gravity that had a hold of him. Upward the canoe began to go.

Her neck was sore but Thora managed to espy the cliff that she and Mrs.

Whattam had fallen over. The Indian was climbing up the air currents in front of the sheer face of granite.

And then where the road was etched upon the cliff's face, the ethereal vessel slid over the edge of the drop-off and onto solid ground. The Indian put down his paddle and rubbed his hands together. He stood up. It was then that Thora realized the dimension of the man. He was a giant. He must have been at least twelve feet tall. Spitting on his hands he bended his knees and shoved his fingers underneath of the roof of the car.

He hoisted the vehicle up, rolling it over the gunwale of the canoe. Inside Thora and Margaret fell back into their seats as a result of the Indian's endeavors. The car fell from the side of the vessel and back onto the gravel road. It rocked back and forth on its four wheels, tossing the two occupants about inside.

When it came to a rest, the Indian sat down once more in his vessel and began to backstroke. The canoe slid from the road and back out into the air. With a neat carve into its unseen medium, the front end of the vessel swung around and started working back in the direction from where it came.

Thora watched in utter amazement as the canoe slowly vaporized and disappeared from view. She had no words to explain what had just happened. It was so far beyond belief that it had to have been a dream. If she were alone when this happened she knew that nobody would believe what she experienced. But luckily she had Mrs. Whattam with her. The woman would be able to validate everything that had happened.

When she turned to see the woman's reaction, she saw that Margaret Whattam was out cold. There was a nasty contusion over her brow. The woman was hurt in the accident but was she alive?

Chapter 26

The Other Side of the Mountain

Thora at once looked for signs of life in the unconscious Mrs. Whattam. She saw that the woman was breathing. She began shaking Margaret by the shoulders trying to revive her.

A few moments later Margaret's eyes opened. There was a very lost expression in them attesting to the condition of her mind. Thora knew that Margaret was disorientated and probably did not know where she was.

"It's me, Mrs. Whattam, Thora," the girl said, placing her face in full view of Margaret's field of vision. "We've had a bad accident but we are out of it now."

Mrs. Whattam mildly shoved Thora aside to look out the window of the car. As she did so she rubbed her hand over her temple and felt the contusion there. It seemed like she was slowly piecing things together to help explain where she was.

"We fell over the cliff Margaret," Thora said, feeling her eyes well up in tears as she realized how close to death they had actually come. "If it had not been for that ghost we would have been dead!"

At once Margaret jerked her head around to look at the little girl. There was such an expression of denial in her face that Thora at once knew that the woman did not remember any of it. "What are you talking about?" she said. Her words were slow and obviously painful.

Thora reiterated what had happened to them. Margaret's behavior clearly expressed that she did not remember a word of it. The wife of Uncle Thaddeus' advisor placed her hands on Thora's face. Her fingers were feeling for bumps. She pulled Thora's eyes wide open and probed for signs of brain injury in them. It didn't seem like she saw anything there.

"What's the last thing that you remember?" Thora decided to play another angle and maybe rebuild Margaret's memory from this tactic.

"I remember going around the corner and seeing the deer. After that I can't recall a thing!" Margaret answered.

"You don't remember hanging over the cliff's edge and feeling the car start to slide over it?" Thora was aghast that Margaret would have no memory of this. At the time she was very lucid. She had fully participated in everything. She had no head injury then.

"We were hanging over the edge?" Margaret responded in dismay.

"Yes!" Thora exclaimed. "Here, come out of the car and I will show you the tire tracks!" She knew that those markings in the gravel would be her proof that what she said happened really did happen.

Margaret scanned the adjacent land from the seat of her car. From where she sat behind the steering wheel Thora knew that the woman would not be able to see the tracks. But Margaret saw something. "We have got to get out of here," she said. "We are sitting ducks out here for anybody coming up or down the road!"

She started the ignition of the car and to Thora's surprise the engine started as if it were brand new—which it was. Margaret was driving this year's model. She put the car into gear and drove it around the bend and past the scene of the accident.

"Aren't you going to stop?" Thora asked. "Don't you want to see where we fell over?"

Mrs. Whattam's face tensed as if she were wincing from a sheering pain in her head. "We can't stop here Thora! It is too dangerous. This blasted road is far too winding!"

"You don't believe me, do you?" Thora asked. It was either that or the woman was unwilling to accept the near tragic circumstances of her recent past.

Margaret never commented. She just continued driving. "This is a dangerous road. I could not imagine what it would be like in the winter. You would not find me driving it on a snowy or icy day," was all that she said.

The car reached as close to the summit of the hill as the road permitted. Deep woodlands covered the peak of the mountain. They were as wild today as they must have been back in the days when it was only Indians that wandered this country. Thora had never been up here although she was able to see this mountaintop from home every day of her life. She had always wanted to come up here on a family drive but her father would not have any of it. He said that this was hunting country and was only made for men with guns and bows. It was not meant for girls and tourists.

The girl kept her eyes open to see if she could espy another deer or any other woodland creature between the majestic evergreen trees that grew thickly upon the upper echelons of this mountain. Not an animal was to be seen. She was still upset that Margaret would not believe her about what happened. She wondered how the woman would describe the chain of events that occurred down there when they just about died. She put the question to Mrs. Whattam.

"If you ask me we just spun around on the road," Margaret answered, keeping her eyes fixed on the road as it veered around to the other side of the mountain. "As we spun we must have knocked our heads against the steering wheel and dash, in your case, and rendered ourselves unconscious. We were damned lucky that nobody ran into us or else we might have fallen over the cliff like you imagined. And if that happened we would not be here talking about it right now."

Thora had to admit that it was a solid reasonable answer and had she not experienced the cliffhanging terror she might have believed her. But Thora knew for a certainty that the car did hang over the cliff and that it did eventually fall and was scooped up by the Indian ghost's canoe. That moment was as real to her as any moment in her life. There was nothing vague about it. There was nothing ethereal or otherworldly about it. It happened as sure as her name was Thora Meadowford.

"You must have imagined your ghost as a result of the head trauma you received," Margaret added.

"You felt my head. There are no injuries!"

"There might not be any surface signs of injury but believe me girl for you to come up with a story like that only ascertains the proof that you did get hurt," Margaret asserted.

The car was on the other side of the mountain. From up here a whole new vista was given to Thora that she had never seen before. There were more mountains on the horizon, some even taller than the one that they had just climbed. There did not seem to be any signs of human settlement in the broad expanse of terrain ahead of them. The road was sharply slanted downward. It headed into a narrow and dark valley. The land down there must get very little sunshine.

"Your friend lives down there?" the girl asked. She could only imagine what kind of gloomy persona Josephine Bianco would have if she dwelt in such a light-starved locale.

Margaret nodded. "Yes. She has lived there for many years."

"No wonder she never comes into town," Thora said. "That would be one hell of a drive for an old woman, especially in winter!"

"Mind your tongue, Thora Meadowford!" Margaret chastised her for using the phrase 'hell of a'.

"Sorry."

"We are friends Thora but I still want you to respect me as an elder," Margaret said. Her hands were tightly clenched on the steering wheel as the road started to repeat the breathtaking winds and curves that it possessed on the other side. The woman's foot was constantly tapping the brakes to offset the acceleration from going downhill.

"It just slipped. I won't say it again."

"And as your friend Thora I am taking you to Mrs. Bianco's place so that you can meet the woman and enjoy her company and perhaps learn a thing or two from her about how we women are not as helpless as our men think we are."

"That's not the real reason, is it?" Thora immediately responded. "You said Mrs. Bianco is a psychologist. You are taking me there so that she can test to see if I am crazy like you seem to think that I am."

"Now where would you get an idea like that from?" Margaret acted like what Thora said shocked her.

"Don't pretend that it isn't so," Thora said. "I have gotten to know you this summer and I have learned how you like to stick your nose into other people's business!" Thora could not believe that she could have said such a thing. It almost sounded like her father or mother was speaking out of her mouth.

"Girl, if you really did not trust me then why did you decide to come along with me? No one said that you had to!" Margaret's face looked hurt but Thora was not sure if it was genuine pain.

"I didn't know that you were taking me to a psychologist back then when you asked! Had I known I would have surely declined your generous offer!"

"I am doing this because I am concerned for you, my friend. That is all! I have heard some very strange words come out of your head this summer and I must admit that it frightens me." She reached her hand across the car to take hold of Thora's. The girl noted that the woman had affirmed the real reason why they were driving this dangerous road.

Thora immediately drew her hand away. "Remember last time you tried to take my hand. A deer came out of nowhere and we ended up falling over a cliff."

"That is precisely what I am talking about!" Margaret cried. "People don't fall over cliffs and get rescued by cloudy Indians in gigantic canoes. People who think such things are disturbed!"

Thora laughed. "It does sound ridiculous, I know!" she admitted. "But I tell you that it happened and if you really cared for me you would have stopped the car and had a look at the tire tracks showing where we slid off the cliff!"

"I said it then and I will say it now. If we would have parked the car to go check out your alleged tracks chances are that we could have been run over by another vehicle coming up or down the road!" Mrs. Whattam retorted.

"There has not been one car on this road since we got on it!" Thora retaliated. "I don't think that we would have been taking too big of a risk to just take a moment and see whether I am delusional or not!"

"Enough said Thora! We did not stop and that is that!" Margaret growled.

Thora could see Margaret's hands grip the steering wheel all the tighter. The woman was as autocratic and arbitrary as Langley and Cora. As her legal guardians and protectors Langley and Cora had a right to act that way. But not Margaret! She had no rights in the overseeing of Thora's development into adulthood. A rash decision came to the girl. She knew that it would be wrong to act upon it but she acted upon it nonetheless. No one but Langley and Cora could boss her around.

"Stop the car!" the girl said firmly.

"What?"

"I said stop the car right now! I am getting out!"

Margaret turned to the girl with shock written upon her face. "Get out here? In the middle of nowhere? Are you mad?"

"You think I am already so what difference does it make! Stop the car Margaret. I want out!"

The woman laughed nervously. "And what will you do when you get out? Walk home? Have adventures with killer cows and mysterious ghosts? I am not going to stop the car Thora. I am trying to help you. You have got to understand that! You have to let me help you. Believe me you will be thankful later!"

"Who says that I need help anyway? There is nothing wrong in my life! Things are going well. Mom and Dad are great to me. They give me everything that I need." Thora hated being put in the position to defend herself.

"Girl, I have seen the way that your mom and Dad treat you! I know friends that treat their dogs and cats better than the way Cora and Langley treat you! They should be thrown in jail for what they have done to you. I think that they are the real reason why you invent this ghost that comes to your rescue all of the time."

Thora bit down on her lip and stared forward. Margaret was not going to stop and let her out. She was going to continue to drive and carry out her agenda.

The road began to flatten out as the car made it to the bottom of the valley without falling over any cliffs. Its two occupants had been silent for several moments as Margaret concentrated on her steering. Once the gravel lane straightened out she said to the girl, "Maybe Mrs. Bianco will see that your parents are the root of the problem as well. If she does she could recommend your case to Children's Aid who will pull you out of that house and place you in a more caring household."

"Become a foster child? Are you crazy!" Thora blurted. There were several foster children at school. They seemed to be the most maladjusted and destitute students there. They dressed the most poorly. They smelled vile and their bodies often bore bruises and scrapes of unknown origin.

"Not a foster child Thora but an adopted child," Margaret answered.

"Who is going to adopt me? I am thirteen! I am practically grown-up! People want to adopt babies not teenagers!"

"I know of someone who might want to adopt you," the woman said.

"Who?"

"Me."

"You?" The woman's answer startled Thora and set her aback. She had no idea that Margaret Whattam would think this way about her. "But who says that I want to be adopted by you? I don't trust you! You try to do sneaky things behind my back!" More words of denial poured from the girl's lips. She was not sure that she meant any of them but she allowed them to flow from her unguarded and unchecked. The thought of being the adopted child of Margaret and James Whattam was a complicated one for her. They possessed personality traits that Thora was sure would be more amenable to her peace of mind. They were loving and caring and they would take a genuine interest in her life. Such traits were not present in Langley and Cora Meadowford. Her real parents were selfish and self-centered and squabbled all of the time. They created a home that was filled with angst and commotion. Yet this was the only home that Thora knew. She could not imagine a home any different. There were real emotions in this house. There was something very artificial and removed about the domestic domain of the Whattams. It would never feel right living there. She would feel awkward and would inwardly long to be reunited with the socially maladroit Meadowfords.

Thora took a moment from her mental comparison of the two households to look upon the driver of the car. Margaret's lower lip appeared to be in a struggle to keep from trembling. The girl realized that her words must have really struck the mark and inflicted some serious pain. "I'm sorry," she said right away. "I didn't mean to hurt you." She reached across the car and put her arm over Margaret's shoulder. "You just surprised me with what you said."

"My timing was poor I must admit," Margaret quivered. Her foot left the gas pedal to slow the vehicle down to a stop. "I should have not made such a remark especially after we had an argument. I just want you to have a better life Thora!" she cried, throwing her arms around the girl. "I anguish over you every night when I go to bed. I think of how wonderful my life is living with

James and then I think of you living in that war zone under the dictatorship of those two awful people. I just want to pull you out of there and let you enter my house where you will be treated with courtesy and dignity and given all the love a girl like you deserves."

Thora could feel that she was crying herself. "I didn't mean all those awful things that I said to you. It's just that I don't know what to think any more. My whole life has gone upside down in the last year. All the people that I really cared for in my life are gone—Rebecca, Grandfather and Jack, my cousin. I'm all alone now and I am forced to watch everything fall apart. My mother has become an alcoholic. My father is constantly getting into trouble and is sliding downhill so fast that I can't really see him being anything other than a transient in the not too distant future. On top of all of this I am being made witness to very strange things that my mind tells me cannot really be happening yet at the same time everything in me tells me that they are happening. I am not inventing these things. I truly am seeing them!"

Margaret drew her in tighter. "And that is why I want you to visit with Mrs. Bianco. She is going to help you get over these things. She is a remarkable woman. You will like her. She is not a Sigmund Freud in drag displaced to a country setting. She is a genuine lady and she sees the world from a woman's perspective. She will help you see things in a better light and guide you into a life of promise rather than regret."

Thora pulled back somewhat. "But I don't know if I am ready for any of this. You sprung this onto me out of nowhere and it has scared me. It is out of fright that I reacted the way that I reacted. It was fright that made me say things that I do not necessarily mean."

"Mrs. Bianco is not going to ask you to make any commitments that you do not want to make. She will just simply listen to you today. If you never want to come back she will understand."

"It's nothing more than that?" Thora looked for reassurance in Margaret's eyes.

"It is nothing more than that!" Margaret smiled and leaned forward and kissed the girl on the cheek.

Thora did not jump although there was an instinctive reaction in her to do so. She could not remember the last time that she had been kissed by anybody. Langley and Cora had probably not kissed her since she was in her swaddling clothes. The feel of warm moist human lips upon her cheek felt so tender and endearing. She wanted to languish in them for as long as she could. Yet her Meadowford upbringing started to climb to the surface. "Why did you do that?" she asked.

"I did that because I love you Thora like a mother loves her child," Margaret said through tears in her eyes. "I want you to know happiness Thora and I truly believe that Jim and I can give you that."

The girl took a moment to think of the other member in the Whattam tandem, Jim. She hardly knew the fellow at all. He had never done anything with her to create an atmosphere where friendship could blossom. In fact he seemed rather distant to her and he seemed like he was comfortable in that role. He certainly could not have instigated this offer of adoption. It all had to come from Margaret. Thora wondered if the woman had even spoken to her husband about this. "And Jim is behind you on this?" Thora had to ask.

Margaret straightened herself up behind the steering wheel. "I haven't really talked to Jim about this but I know the man. He is full of compassion and he would do anything that would make me happy. He knows how I long for children and it hurts him that we are unable to conceive."

"But would he want somebody like me?" Thora piped. "Wouldn't he prefer to adopt a baby? Why would he want me? He doesn't like my parents. Wouldn't he think that whatever it is in my parents that he doesn't like would be present in me as well?"

Mrs. Whattam sighed. "I often talk to Jim about you and how you possess something noble in your heart that is not there in the hearts of your parents. I tell him who I am profoundly troubled about what those two are doing to you. He firmly believes that the best thing for you is to get out of that house as well."

"But that does not necessarily mean for me to move into your house, Margaret," Thora said realistically. "If you were to talk Jim into adopting me and providing that my parents do let me go without a fight, what if things do not work out? What if those things that your husband despises in the Meadowfords reveal themselves in me? Wouldn't that cause undue strain upon your marriage and perhaps cause it to deteriorate? I would not want to be responsible for a marriage breakup."

"You speak remarkably mature for a girl your age, Thora," Margaret said. "It is this maturity in you that I think will cause the scenario you describe to never happen. Jim would see this aspect in you and he will come to respect it and even cherish it."

"If you think that I am so mature and stable why are you taking me to a psychoanalyst?" Thora could not resist the question.

The question caused Margaret to momentarily smile as if she were conceding that Thora had won the argument. But then the woman answered. "Maturity and mental illness do not necessarily have to be diametrically opposed. It is possible for these two qualities to be resident in the same person. Your parents have damaged you Thora and I want to see you fixed. To me the best possible solution is for you to become our daughter but in the interim and in the event that that does not happen then I want you to have the best help available."

"And Mrs. Bianco is the best help available?"

"In my eyes she is. And like I said earlier this visit does not have to be anything more than what you want out of it. It can be just a one-time thing and even if it is such I do believe that you are going to have fun today."

"Then what are we waiting for?" Thora responded with feigned enthusiasm. "Let's get this car going and go have some fun!" Inside her mind, Thora was thoroughly convinced that fun was the last thing that she was going to have today.

Chapter 27

By the Brook

Five minutes later the car being driven by Mrs. Whattam came to a stop in front of a copse of weeping willow trees along the roadside. There was a rusted aluminum mailbox sitting on a leaning dried-out cedar post at the edge of the gravel road.

"We are here!" Margaret announced.

Thora looked about her and besides the mailbox she could not see any evidence of human presence anywhere. There was no dwelling in view. There were no gardens. There were no electricity poles. There was not even a driveway. All that there was was a path between the trees that led into the forest. "Are you sure that we are here?" the girl asked. It just did not seem like anybody could possibly live here.

"It is rather rustic, I must admit," Margaret laughed.

"It is beyond rustic! It is absolutely primitive!" Thora grinned. Not even the cottage upon Black Island was as wild as this place. "Where does she live? I don't even see a house!"

"Mrs. Bianco lives in a ravine that you can't see from the road," Margaret answered. "It is only a few hundred yards in from here!"

Thora could not imagine anybody living in such a place as this—let alone somebody that has been deemed to be an authority in the science of human nature. If she was such an expert on the psychology of the species why did she choose to live so far away from them and any of their amenities? What did this say of her impression of those she chose to study? What did this say about her so-called 'expertise'?

"Come on Thora!" Mrs. Whattam said in a singsong tone that was more in keeping with the breezy personality others associated with her. "It is such a beautiful day for a walk in the bush!"

Thora stepped out of the car and was at once engulfed by the flood of scents that a verdant terrain generously pours into the air. Everything smelled so pure. It harkened memories of Pioneer Lake in the early summer. How she wished that she could be there right now sitting on the rock of Black Island and overlooking the serenity of that Madoqua lake.

Margaret started to walk towards the path.

"Is it safe to leave the car here unattended?" Thora asked. "You didn't lock the doors!"

The woman chuckled. "Thora there might not be another car or person down this road for a week! We have nothing to worry about! The squirrels are not interested in taking leisurely drives!"

Something inside Thora told her that Mrs. Whattam had just jinxed herself and that something wrong was going to happen to her brand new vehicle. But the girl chose not to act upon the premonition. It was Margaret's car and not hers. If she chooses to be reckless with it then that was her affair.

They entered the forest and walked upon a curving and winding path. The ground was dark and moist. Thora could not remember the last time that it rained so to see the damp condition of the turf surprised her somewhat. The roots from all the trees regularly crossed over the path making the hike rather cumbersome. The girl had to keep her head tilted downward lest she tripped over one of these gnarly obstructions.

Mrs. Whattam was ahead of her and moving with the grace of a gazelle along the path. "Isn't it wonderful out here Thora? Don't you feel an absolute delight from being surrounded by all of these trees? It is like they are telling us that we belong in their company and that we should not be wasting our time living in towns and cities where the forest has been hacked down."

For the most part Thora had to agree with the woman. She only wished that they would put sidewalks inside of these forests so that people would not have to worry about tripping. Her neck was getting sore from having to look downward continually.

After a few minutes Mrs. Whattam announced that she was at the edge of the ravine. "Mrs. Bianco's house is just down there! I can almost make out her roof!"

On the tails of Margaret's words Thora became aware of another smell in the air. This one did not have the pleasant aroma that the rest of the forest seemed to possess. This one was almost rank and foul like there was something rotting in the bush. "What's that smell!" she cried out to her companion.

"I smell it too!" Margaret said. "I think that it is coming from over there!" she pointed to a location to her left. She leaned forward in that direction and then she suddenly slipped and fell. She disappeared from Thora's sight.

The girl ran as fast as she could to catch up to the woman. When she reached the edge of the ravine, she saw Margaret at its bottom. She was wrapped around the thickly barked trunk of a huge tree. It did not look like she was conscious.

"Are you okay?" Thora cried out to her friend. Her stomach was twisted, as she feared Margaret was dead. She carefully maneuvered herself down the ravine's slope. It was layered with a tangle of roots and loose sedimentary deposits that gave way to the weight of her feet. It was small wonder that Margaret had slipped.

Thus far Margaret had not answered any of Thora's cries. Slowly and carefully the girl descended down the slope until she was upon Margaret. She immediately saw that Mrs. Whattam appeared to have severely twisted her left ankle. It was swollen already to twice the size of its counterpart. Margaret's head was propped up against the tree's trunk. Thora could see that she was alive from the rise and fall of her chest. But the woman was unconscious. She must have rendered herself thus when her skull collided with the tree. There was no sign of blood anywhere.

Immediately Thora began crying out help towards the rustic log cabin that she could see to her right. She knew that she had to get Mrs. Whattam in there and put her on a bed. She also knew that for her to physically to do so would be a tall task. It would be better to have someone help her. Margaret had said that Mrs. Bianco was self-sufficient. The old woman would know what to do. Thora had no idea what to do.

She began calling out Mrs. Bianco by name. There was no answer.

"Go to the house," Margaret whispered. She had come around. Thora could see the marked pain in the woman. Through gritted teeth Margaret added, "Mrs. Bianco is hard of hearing." Her head rolled onto her shoulder. "I'll be alright until then," she said, for the first time opening her eyes. "Just go!" The woman's eyes shut once more.

"I'll be back as fast as possible!" Thora promised. She started towards the cabin. As she drew closer to it she at once was taken in by the increased foulness in the air. Whatever that rank smell was seemed to be coming from around the house.

The cabin that the old woman lived in seemed to come right out of an eerie and grim European fairytale. It was made of old logs that did not fit tightly together. There were many spaces between them that practically gave the girl a view inside of the structure. The roof was covered by cedar shakes. Most of them were curling at the edges and quite a few of them were gone. Bleached moss grew here and there upon the roof. The building had more spider webs, beehives and wasp nests than Thora had ever seen in her life. Even the outhouse at Pioneer Lake was in better shape than this cabin. Surrounding the cabin was a deck. Thora estimated that nearly half the boards making up this deck were either rotted, snapped in half or missing altogether. She was not entirely keen upon placing a foot upon it for fear of falling through or having a tetanus laden rusty nail pierce her foot.

She had been calling Mrs. Bianco's name throughout her entire approach yet she never received an answer. The awful smell seemed to be strongest here right at the cabin. It was so foul that Thora covered her nose with the sleeve of her sweater. She still called for the woman but she was getting the impression that nobody was home. How anybody could call this place home was beyond her. Mrs. Whattam had said that Mrs. Bianco was self-sufficient. Thora could see no signs of self-sufficiency at all. This place was falling apart. The forest was taking it over as far as she was concerned.

"Mrs. Bianco!" she cried out one last time from just beyond the deck of the cabin. She was debating about going inside of the building. Her better judgment told her not to do so for there would be something inside of it that would scare the hell out of her. Yet her friend, Mrs. Whattam, was in dire need of help. The woman was out there by herself in the forest. She was barely conscious and would not be able to fend for herself if some creature of the woods took an interest in her.

She could not dither any longer. She had to go inside of the building. Mrs.

Bianco might be there. Mrs. Whattam said that the woman was hard of hearing. She might be stone-deaf Thora began to realize. She forced herself onto the planks of the wrap-around deck and heard it creak and felt it give. Her foot broke through on her second step. The snapping sound startled a mouse that squeaked and dashed right over Thora's toes as it ran for escape. This gave Thora a fright. Even though Pioneer Lake was rampant with mice the girl never quite got used to them. Capers had lots of work to do there and was often fighting a losing battle. She wished that she had the cat with her now.

She made it to the doorway of the cabin. A huge spider web covered most of its frame. A black and yellow arachnid with a body as big as a quarter sat at the center of the web daring the girl to try to go through. After a few moments of mustering her courage the girl lifted her leg and kicked the door open. The spider scurried to some concealed corner where it could skulk and contemplate how it was going to jump the girl and suck her life juices from her.

"Mrs. Bianco!" Thora shouted as loud as she could as she saw the dark interior of the house from the doorway. There was no doubt in her mind at all. The terrible smell was coming from inside. She could not see anything within the cabin. The only light that entered it came from the door. There were no windows. How anybody could live here was way beyond the girl. Even the caves that cavemen dwelt in were more amenable than this place.

Thora's back grew rigid as she realized that she had to go inside of this hellhole to find the woman. The thought itself of doing this was unimaginably terrifying. How could Margaret Whattam think that anybody who would choose to live in such awful conditions would be able to help her with her psychological problems was laughable. Anybody choosing to live in such squalor as in this cabin would be the more likely candidate to need psychological treatment.

"Anybody in there?" she called from the doorway. Her voice sounded very nasal as she had plugged her nose between pinched fingers to avoid the pungent smell coming from inside. Even with her nostrils sealed the girl could still detect the terrible odor. There was only one thing that could smell that bad and although the girl had never had first-hand experience with it she instinctively recognized it. It was the smell of death. Was Mrs. Bianco lying dead inside of her creepy cabin? Margaret said that Mrs. Bianco was an old woman. Old people are more likely to die. And given that the woman lived the life of a reclusive hermit it was highly likely when that her time came nobody would be there to administer to her corpse's needs. It would just lie wherever it dropped and stay there until someone finally came around for a visit.

The idea that there might be a dead body inside scared the willies out of the girl. There was no way that she was going to go inside of that place and find a half-rotted cadaver lying sprawled out upon a bed.

Thora turned and started off the dilapidated deck. She was going back to Mrs. Whattam and tell her about her friend's demise. She did not concern herself with how she was going to deal with Margaret's condition. That problem will work itself out later.

Just as she rounded the corner of the cabin, her toe caught on one of the deck's loose boards. She went falling forward onto the soggy forest floor. A partially unburied root tore at the skin upon her knee. It smarted badly. She started to hoist herself from the ground and saw the mud and blood on her leg from the fall.

"Are you all right, Miss?"

Thora turned around. Coming from the forest at the backside of the cabin was a gray-haired lady. She was neatly attired in a crimson skirt and a powder blue sweater. Her hair was neatly bound up in a bun upon her head. In her hands she was carrying a bouquet of forest flowers, trilliums Thora believed they were. The old woman possessed a gentle smile.

All at once all of the foreboding that Thora had felt earlier disappeared, as she took visual hold of this grandmotherly character coming out into the clearing.

"Mrs. Bianco?" Thora asked.

"That is my name, child," the old woman said as she stepped closer. "Let me have a look at that knee of yours." Mrs. Bianco set down her flowers and began gingerly rubbing the mud away from Thora's leg with her liver-spotted hands. "It does not appear to be too bad. Just a scrape. I have had worse!"

"Mrs. Bianco, I'm Thora Meadowford. I am a friend of Margaret Whattam. She is just over there. She has banged her head and I think that she has twisted her…"

"Now, now, my dear! I am an old woman! I can only do one thing at a time. Let's get you cleaned up first!" Mrs. Bianco said in a pleasant matronly fashion.

"But it is just a scrape! You said so yourself! I do not need any help. It is Margaret that needs the help!" Thora implored.

"Meadowford, you said your name was?" the old woman commented. "Why does that name sound so familiar to me?"

"You must have heard the name from your visits to Grappling Haven. We are considered to be one of the more prominent families there," Thora answered. "But we got to do something about Mrs. Whattam!"

"I don't think that I know it from there. My visits to town are so infrequent that I have hardly gotten to familiarize myself with anybody from there." The woman had taken Thora's hand and was leading her to a stream on the opposite side of the cabin. Thora had not noticed this brook earlier.

"But you know Mrs. Whattam from there. She has come to visit you here in the past. She slipped down the ravine and fell against a tree. She really really needs our help at once!"

"One thing at a time, my dear," Mrs. Bianco replied. She was obviously shutting out Thora's impeachments for help for her friend. "Meadowford. Meadowford. Where have I heard that name before?" she said as she took a wooden bucket that sat at the stream's edge and scooped up some of its water. She set the pail down on the ground beside Thora and began wiping some of its icy contents on the girl's knee.

Thora at once winced from the pain as the frigid water strove to soak itself in the small yet tender flesh wound on her knee. "Well, if you don't know of our name from town then I am afraid that I don't know where you would have heard it before. Unless," Thora had a sudden thought. "Unless Margaret told you about me." Of course that would be the answer. Mrs. Whattam must have already conferred with the old woman prior to taking the girl out here.

"I haven't spoken to Margaret for months now," Mrs. Bianco said. "She has not been here since the spring when the first of the wild flowers began to bloom in the glades. And I have not been to town since last summer. Whatever Margaret may have told me about anybody I'm afraid I have long forgotten. Memory does begin to fail you with age, you know. But the name Meadowford sticks in my craw like an unidentified shadow. Tell me about yourself and your family and maybe you can draw out this nagging shred of a memory that torments me now."

"Can't we do this after we get Margaret?" Thora exclaimed. "She is just over there!" She pointed in the direction where her friend was lying bent around the old tree.

"Margaret will be just as fine there as she would be here," Mrs. Bianco smiled. "If you saw my home you would know that I do not possess anything that will comfort the injured. From the description you provided me of her condition I believe that what Margaret needs now most is just rest and comfort and believe me the forest ground can hardly be matched by anything we humans can create." Mrs. Bianco patted Thora's hand and repeated in reassurance, "She will be fine."

Thora was not so certain but she had to concede that Margaret had described the old woman as a healer of sorts thus making the elder wiser regarding the treatment of those that are hurt. Who was she to refute the wisdom of an old woman? Yet Thora still could not help but say, "Are you sure?"

"Positive, my child. Margaret will be fine. I predict that within the hour you will see her walk here to the house. She will seem somewhat shaken but you will sense that underneath that she is strong and hale." The way Mrs. Bianco spoke was very uplifting. Thora felt it in her heart that the woman could not be wrong in this matter. "In the meantime until Margaret recuperates why don't you and I just sit here by this brook and talk? We can have a very lovely time, you and I, getting to know each other."

Thora grinned for she agreed with the proposal. Outside of the disturbing smell that emanated from the cabin this was just about the most serene place that she had ever been—even more serene than the front rock of Black Island.

"Now tell me about yourself Miss Meadowford. How is it that I know your name?" Mrs. Bianco had seated herself on the ground beside the stream. Her long crimson skirt looked like a large red flower that grew out of the earth.

"I don't know how you would know my name," Thora admitted as she sat down beside the woman, careful not to touch the large red skirt. "The only way that I can guess is that Margaret must have told you about me but you would have a memory of such a thing if it were to have happened, right."

"Like I said, memory starts to fail you as you get older," Mrs. Bianco answered. "But I am certain that Margaret did not tell me. I have not seen her since the spring. I've not seen anybody since the spring."

"You have been all alone for all these months without any human company?" Thora found the notion disturbing and outstanding.

"I suppose that I have. Time drifts differently when you are alone. It may seem to you at the time that it has come to a halt, as each moment is long and languorous. But before you know it a week has gone by. And then a month. And then a season has passed and you wonder where the time went." Mrs. Bianco paused. She was perhaps reflecting upon the significance of what she had just said. Then she continued, "But through it all I have never felt alone or lonely. The forest provides so much in the way of company that you begin to cherish the small creatures as much as you would cherish the presence of another of your kind. I have made the squirrels and birds my friends. They do not fear me. They look upon me as part of the natural order."

"But what of the frightening animals that live in the forest? What of the bears and wolves?" Thora knew that if she lived out here in the forest by herself she would be in a constant state of terror wondering about every snap of a twig on the forest floor.

"There are no wolves in Pennsylvania," Mrs. Bianco said. "They have been long ago extirpated from this area. There may be none in our country at all. The wolves are to be found only in Canada nowadays, I am afraid."

"In Canada?" Thora remarked. "My family travels to Canada every summer. We have a retreat in the wilderness there on Pioneer Lake. I have never seen a wolf in all the seasons that I have spent upon the island we have there."

"Canada, you say?" The expression on Mrs. Bianco's face revealed that a memory might have been jogged by the name of that country. "Pioneer Lake?" she then added.

"Yes, Pioneer Lake in Canada! It is in the Province of Ontario. We Meadowfords have had a summer retreat there since the 1880's or so. My great grandfather built..."

"Your great grandfather is Sam Meadowford, isn't he?" Mrs. Bianco suddenly said.

Thora felt her jaw drop in amazement. "Yes he is! How did you know that?"

Mrs. Bianco flipped her hands over in the air. "I don't know," she said in a playful cherubic fashion. "I just did!"

"But I don't know how you would know that!" Thora exclaimed. "Margaret must have told you and now you suddenly remembered!" It seemed to be the only logical explanation. Yet why Margaret Whattam would tell this forest hermit about Samuel Angus Meadowford the First did not make any sense to the girl. Unless Mrs. Bianco had visited the Whattam house and seen the portrait that Margaret did of the founding father of the Meadowford dynasty and enquired about him.

"I don't know how I know it but I just know it," Mrs. Bianco repeated herself. The sprite was gone out of her. It now seemed to be replaced with something very devoid of passion and emotion. "Sam Meadowford died in 1907. He had two sons Sam Junior and Thaddeus." The old woman's tone was deadpan and her delivery was slow and deliberate. "The two boys took over Sam's enterprises and his estates. This included the cottage on Pioneer Lake. That lake has been nothing but a curse on your clan ever since."

"How do you know all this?" Thora was starting to get frightened.

Instead of answering her question, Mrs. Bianco continued reciting Meadowford family history. "Sam Junior's wife June drowned in that lake in around 1917. Within the year Sam's grandson Percy was also taken by the lake. And then in 1928 Percy's younger brother Jack was killed in the waters just off of Black Island."

"Stop!" Thora cried out loud. She felt like she was sitting with a demon. Nobody should know that much about a stranger on the first time that his or her paths crossed.

"Know this Thora Meadowford. Your family does not rest after they die," Mrs. Bianco said. She was staring the girl directly in the eyes. What Thora saw in Mrs. Bianco's eyes was something that she felt could only be evil. There was a blackness and an emptiness in them as if they were the mirrors of a great cold void that enveloped everything and was now closing in on itself.

"They still walk the Earth because of that sleeping Indian boy," Mrs. Bianco said. "Most of them are still in Canada but some of them are here in the natal cradle of the Meadowford line."

"What sleeping Indian boy?" Thora gasped. She recalled that picture that she saw at Uncle Thaddeus' place of Black Island before any structures were erected upon it. She recalled that juniper bush that sat spread out over the rock. Inside that bush the girl had thought she had seen a pair of Indian eyes.

"His name cannot be said for once uttered the world will cease to exist as it now does," Mrs. Bianco said enigmatically. "But even as I speak to you there are opposing forces on Pioneer Lake that battle over the soul of this sleeping Indian boy. Young Jack stands alone against those that seek to destroy the slumbering child."

"Jack my cousin?" Thora cried. "What on earth are you talking about! Jack is dead!"

"He does not know that he is dead," Mrs. Bianco responded in her trance-like state. "He feels abandoned and does not know why his family has left him. He is frightened as he must endure the torments and terror inflicted upon him by those that the lake had taken before him."

"That's crazy!" Thora screeched. "Jack is dead! Jack's spirit is not there at Pioneer Lake! Spirits leave the Earth upon death!"

"If they do then why are you visited upon by the ghost of Sam Meadowford? Should not his spirit have moved beyond the veil of mortality and entered the new kingdoms of the dead? Yet you see him. He visits you sometimes as a friend and sometimes for inexplicable reasons that serve to profoundly disturb you. Yet you do not deny his reality and his presence."

"How do you know this?" the girl trembled. "Who are you?" She was beginning to believe that she was having an encounter with a devil sent from Hell that wanted to drive her mad.

"Do not deny that young Jack Thurston perseveres and continues," the woman said, not answering Thora's question. "And do not think that he will fight the battle alone for he is but a child and the forces that seek to destroy him are ancient and strong. You must fight for him too Thora Meadowford. You must wrest the spirits of Grappling Haven and cast them to the new kingdoms of the dead. Not until they are mollified and eased shall those that can help Jack Thurston be able to lift their swords in his defense."

Thora listened to the words of the woman. They seemed mad and beyond any contextual relevance to the girl's life. The notion that Jack was still alive in some sense was something that she had prayed for but the idea that he was still up there on Pioneer Lake by himself fighting against evil forces was just too stretched. She did not know how Mrs. Bianco could have so many of the names and places in the Meadowford world correct but what she was proposing could never be correct. Jack was dead. She had seen his stiff body with the hole gouged into his brain from through his eye. She had wished that she had never seen that. It was an image that stuck to her ever since. It was an image that she was sure that she would never forget. What Mrs. Bianco blurted was something that she wanted to forget as well. The forest had gotten to the woman. She was as wild and insane as some of the birdcalls that echoed in the coniferous canopy above her. How could Margaret Whattam believe that this woman could help her with her problems? The woman was nuts. Thora had to get away from her.

"I'm going to go help Margaret now," Thora said to the woman. She lifted herself from the ground and saw her reflection in the stream before her. There was something odd about that reflection. It showed her and only her. It should have produced an image of Mrs. Bianco as well.

"Wait! Do not go as of yet!" Mrs. Bianco uttered. "There is more to tell!"

"I don't want to hear any more of this cockamamie! Your mind has taken a wrong turn!" Thora said in as calm and rational a tone as she could muster.

"Look to the lynx!" the old woman said. "When the lynx appears then you will know that Sam Meadowford has gone to the new kingdom."

"You have lost your links! Your links to reality!" Thora practically shouted at the woman and raced off into the forest. She did not dare to look behind her. She did not know what kind of being she just encountered but she was sure that whoever or whatever that was it was not the Mrs. Bianco that Margaret recalled and looked up to. She ran with haste and did not heed the roots and rocks that stuck their heads out onto the path. One found a way of snagging her toe as she raced by. Thora lost her footing. As she wavered in the air before hitting the ground her head had spun back to that what was behind her. For a moment she thought that she glimpsed the form of Mrs. Bianco. It no longer held anything human in shape. Instead it was something hideous and indescribable. And then Thora's head hit the ground and her world went black.

Chapter 28

The Fungal Citadel

"Thora. Thora."

The girl heard a familiar voice calling her name. She opened her eyes. She felt like she had been sleeping for hours and that she had dreamed many dreams. But when the world came into view she could see the dark terrain covered by pine needles sprawl out before her to the stand of trees that demarcated the clearing. She quickly surmised that she was still on Mrs. Bianco's property and that perhaps only a few moments had passed since she tripped. It was a strange sensation. She had felt that she had stepped out of time and now was returned to it with only a few seconds having gone by. The damp ground was cold and seeping into her stomach. She was sprawled on it. She started to climb up to her arms, lifting her head upward and seeing Margaret Whattam hobbling in her direction.

"Margaret," she said. The act of talking made her feel woozy.

"What happened to you girl?" Margaret responded. She was favoring the one leg over the other.

Even through her dizziness Thora could clearly see that Mrs. Whattam's one ankle was swollen to three times the size of the other one. "I must have fallen," Thora said.

"And banged your head! You have an awful bruise on your forehead!"

Margaret exclaimed as she finally reached Thora. "How long were you unconscious?"

"I don't know," Thora admitted. "I don't think that it was very long."

"I looked at my watch when you left to get Mrs. Bianco. It was then 12:30. It is now 2:00 o'clock. You were gone an hour and a half. Where's Mrs. Bianco?" Margaret's nose wrinkled. "It is very rank here, isn't it?"

Thora spun her head back around to the brook and it all came back to her—her conversation with what she thought was the old woman. She remembered every word of that strange dialogue but most of all she remembered that image she witnessed as she was stumbling—that horrible thing that sat at the stream's side. It had to have been a demon from Hell itself. Whatever it was it was not there now.

"Mrs. Bianco is not here," Thora answered. She had decided that if she reported what she saw and heard to Mrs. Whattam then the woman would have it firmly fixed in her mind that she was absolutely mad. Margaret would never accept any talk about the Meadowford dead wandering the Earth and she would never believe that the girl had a little visit with something insidious and diabolical.

"Did you look for her or call for her?" Margaret asked. Her eyes were widening. Thora guessed that she was making the connection between Mrs. Bianco's absence and the gut-wrenching stench emanating from inside of the cabin.

"I did," Thora said. "But there was no answer."

"Did you look inside?" Margaret indicated the dilapidated structure sitting in the clearing.

"I didn't dare," the girl replied. "I got frightened. It is dark in there and it stinks worse than any septic tank!"

Margaret took a deep breath. "I can't say that I blame you. I'm terrified myself right now and I am an adult."

Thora believed that the woman could not be half as terrified as she was. She had seen what actually resides here. She had heard the dark things that that spirit had said. "She's dead in there, isn't she?" she peeped.

"We don't know that yet," Margaret practically whispered.

"Do we have to go in there to find out?"

"If we don't then who will? We can't leave her remains to rot here or be torn apart by wild animals." Margaret was obviously building up the courage to make that awful investigation of discovery.

"There are only squirrels and birds here. They won't tear her apart." Thora was having equal difficulty in marshaling her resolve to enter the cabin.

"There are far more ferocious denizens in this forest than just squirrels and birds and even they are not as innocent as what we like to believe. Just think of the crows and ravens. They are birds. They would eat your eyes out and then peck at your brain."

"Margaret, please!" Thora exclaimed. "If you talk like that then I will never go inside the cabin!"

Mrs. Whattam started to giggle. "I guess I was a little graphic there, wasn't I? But like it or not we have to go inside and make sure of what is in there. It might not even be Mrs. Bianco. It could be just a dead animal in there. They can stink to high heaven themselves!"

"And if it were a dead animal in there then where do you suppose Mrs. Bianco would be?" Thora responded. "She is not here and I would gather that she would not have been here for quite some time. Nobody of sound mind would allow a dead animal to just lie and rot inside of her house without doing something about it! It has got to be the body of Mrs. Bianco. And I say that we let the police go inside instead of us!"

"That is an out for us, isn't it?" Margaret reconsidered.

"It's not like we are going to be able to do anything about it if there is a body in there! You have a swollen ankle and I'm just a girl. We can't be carrying a stinking corpse all the way up that hill and then to your car!" Thora added.

"You have a point there," Margaret nodded. "But shouldn't we at first make sure that it is a body in there before we have the police come out all this way just to find a half-decomposed squirrel?"

"Believe me, there is a body in there!" Thora retorted.

"How can you be so sure?" Margaret's eyes narrowed. "Do you know something that I don't know? What were you doing for an hour and a half while I sat helpless at the bottom of the ravine? You said that you were only unconscious for a few moments."

"How would I know how long I was out? I was out! I didn't have any way of tracking time!" Thora trumpeted defensively. She did not want to be put in the position of having to reveal to the woman that she had been talking to Mrs. Bianco's ghost and that that ghost said some things that Mrs. Whattam would construe as evidence that the girl was quite mad.

"But what were you doing before you tripped and fell? Something must have frightened you for you to become so clumsy. You carefully navigated the path with its myriad of stumbling obstructions without falling. Why is it that you fell here where there is hardly anything to make you lose your footing?" Margaret asked some astute questions.

"I told you what scared me!" Thora rasped. "It was that smell and the woman's absence! I was quickly able to add up the evidence and determine what took place here!"

"So you don't have any firsthand knowledge that can allow you to unequivocally say that Mrs. Bianco's body is inside of the cabin!" The woman was demonstrating how she was able to get her husband through law school. "We must have that firsthand knowledge before we send the police on a wild goose chase!"

Margaret was not going to let them just simply walk away from this horrid place without investigating the interior of that fetid building. Thora had to use another tactic. "I'm not going in there!" she said bluntly. "If you want to see a decomposed body then go ahead and be my guest! I'm staying put."

Margaret's face did not know whether to turn blanche or rouge. It was obvious that the thought of going into that cabin alone scared her. And she must have felt some sort of rage for the girl's stance regarding entering the creepy cabin. "Very well. If that is the way that you want to be then I will go in there alone." She took a deep breath and started to hobble and hop her way toward the cabin. When she reached the deck that surrounded the building she stopped and seemed to be studying the boarding there. A moment or two lapsed. Then she finally said, "I can't go any further in my condition. I would surely break my neck if I tried to cross that verandah!"

"Maybe if you get a walking stick that would help!" Thora offered. There was plenty of bramble in the vicinity and there should be something that would give Margaret the support that she needed to negotiate the boards.

"I would still hurt myself," Margaret retorted. "You're going to have to go in instead of me."

The girl felt a charge surge through her veins at her companion's proposal. "I already told you that under no circumstances that I am going to go in there!"

"One of us has got to go in!" Margaret cried. "There is nothing inside of there that is going to harm you even if there is a dead body. If I try to go in then I am going to trip and injure myself and if that happens, then you are going to have to come inside anyway to fetch me. So no matter which way you look at it Thora Meadowford you are going to have to go in!"

"Not if you take a walking stick! Then you won't slip and fall!"

"What if I use you as my walking stick?" Margaret posed a question. "The two of us will go in together and that way neither of us will be alone. What say you?"

Thora was afraid that the woman would use this tactic. It was a sensible plan from Margaret's stance. But Margaret did not know that the girl had all the proof in the world that Mrs. Bianco's body was inside of the cabin. Thora had encountered the old woman's ghost. Maybe she should tell Mrs. Whattam what actually happened during the hour and a half that they were parted? Margaret would think that she was crazy but didn't Margaret already think that she was crazy? Wasn't that the reason why they were out here in this God-forsaken forest in the first place—to have the wise Mrs. Bianco help the girl overcome her madness? The urge to tell Margaret was becoming overbearing. What she experienced was too stress-laden to keep cooped up inside.

She was about to open up when Margaret said, "Very well. I can see by your hesitation that you are not even willing to go inside with me. I will go in alone. Fetch me something that I can use to keep me propped up."

"Are you sure?" Thora asked. She felt like a worm. She could well imagine what loathsome creature Mrs. Whattam would call her for her cowardly behavior. Yet, the woman had offered her a reprieve from going inside or relating her tale. And the girl decided to accept the offer. She went to find a walking stick for her companion. As she did so she thought about how much she had proved herself to be her father's daughter. Langley would do something like this. Cora would too. And here she was emulating her parents' weak dispositions by taking the easy way out. She quickly found a stick and started back toward Mrs. Whattam. Her mind was in a conundrum. She did not want to be like her parents. She was trying to convince herself that she would not act the way that they would. She was building resolve to go into the cabin with Margaret or even by herself. She thought that she had mustered all the courage she needed to do this by the time she handed the walking stick over to the woman. But as the stick passed hands Thora did not say anything. She remained quiet and she remained in her spot as Margaret took the stick and tested it for strength.

"This will do," the woman said. "You stay here and be ready to come inside if I call you. This should not take too long." Thora saw the woman swallow something. It was her fear.

Margaret started onto the verandah. She had to hop onto the boards. The force of her weight made them creak but they held. The woman made frequent use of the walking stick, testing every step before she took it. It was a slow process and in Thora's mind an overly cautious process. Maybe the woman was trying to ply for sympathy through her actions? Maybe she was using her nonverbal motions as a plea for Thora to come and help her? Whatever it was, Thora did not take the bait. She stood at the edge of the verandah and watched the disabled woman hobble inside the cabin.

"Can you see anything?" Thora almost immediately called out to her.

"It is very dark in here and it stinks so much that I think that I might faint!" Margaret's voice came through the open portal.

"Is there anything there that you can use for a light?" Thora responded. She was vicariously traveling inside of the cabin along with her companion. She wished that there would be illumination and that the matter could be resolved.

"Not a thing!" Margaret called out. She seemed to be deeper inside of the morose shack. "Oh Thora! This is terrible! I feel like I am wandering in Hell!" Fear accented her call and Thora could feel the desperation drip from the woman's vocal resonance.

"Then get out of there, Margaret!" Thora piped. "You have nothing to prove by being inside. Let the police come and investigate!"

Suddenly there was a thump and a scream bursting through the doorway. It made Thora's hair stand on end. The ensuing silence was worse.

"Margaret, are you okay?" the girl peeped at the cabin's dark gate.

Her friend did not answer.

"Margaret, are you okay?" Thora said again. She had an instinctive intuition that everything was not okay and that something awful had happened to her friend.

"Margaret!" she cried with a frenetic edge to her voice.

"Margaret! Margaret! Margaret!"

The woman was not replying.

Thora could only imagine that the woman must have stumbled and knocked herself unconscious again. "Come on Margaret! Stop fooling around! I am getting very scared!"

Something moved in her periphery's deepest corner. Thora's head jerked in that direction. All she saw was the corner of the building. There did not seem to be anything there. Her mind must have been playing tricks with her she decided when there was no further motion in that direction. She was about to resume calling out to her friend when she thought that she heard a rustle in some leaves that the wind had piled up along the side of the cabin. And then she thought she saw an irregular shadow break up the cabin's contoured shade made by the afternoon sun. There seemed to be something catlike about that shadow. And then it disappeared. Perhaps it was one of the visiting squirrels that Mrs. Bianco mentioned that she befriended. But that was not Mrs. Bianco that told her about it. It was some nefarious denizen from the netherworld that spoke of a relationship of camaraderie between the former occupant of this abode and the creatures that make their livelihood on this land. Perhaps the real Mrs. Bianco had no such friendship with the little furry animals here?

Thora waited several moments to see if there would be any further evidence of something there with her but none came. All was still—outside of the cabin and inside of it. Margaret had made no sound whatsoever after the thump and scream. Thora could only postulate that the woman had hurt herself or had done something even worse. She was slowly coming to the realization that she was going to have to do something about it. It was one thing to leave a body that may have been dead for months alone in the cabin but it was quite another matter to desert someone that may be still alive and injured in there. Like it or not she was going to have to go inside.

Why was life giving her such horrific options all of the time? Why could not her life sail along smoothly like the Grappler on a sunny summer afternoon? She was sure that the friends she shared with her sister Rebecca were never getting into predicaments like this. It was only her family that was getting into trouble. It must have something to do with that curse that Aunt Faye had mentioned. It was the curse that fell upon the family because Sam the First had taken sacred land away from the Indians on Pioneer Lake. The ghost of Mrs. Bianco fortified the reality of that stigma by saying that the Meadowford dead never rest. Her cousin Jack was brooding on Black Island. Sam the First was getting into mysterious mischief here in Grappling Haven. Was he behind all the mystery in this remote valley glade? She hadn't seen any evidence of him as of yet but she would not be surprised if he suddenly showed up. Afterall it was the ghost that tricked her mother to giving her consent to this visit in the countryside in the first place. Had he not pretended to be Langley then Thora would have been forced to stay at home. She wished that the ghost had minded his own business. She would not be caught in this frightening position she was in now had he kept his nose out of it.

She realized that she was tarrying. Margaret was inside of that cabin and in all likelihood in desperate need of help. What was the girl doing about it? Just feeling sorry for herself like a typical Pine Street Meadowford. She told herself to get moving. She closed her eyes for a moment and to her great surprise said a little prayer asking for safety. This was so unlike her. She never resorted to beseeching what to her was a dubious Almighty to come to her side.

Once her eyes were open she started toward the doorway. The withered planks on the verandah sagged at her weight. She could feel the sponginess inside of them squeeze and drip out water that may have been trapped in them for decades. The rot was set in on these boards. As her eyes lifted to take in the cobweb-laden exterior walls of the cabin she saw that the rot had been set in them as well. This was a fungal citadel ripe with germ and disease. It oozed with dirtiness. How anybody could live here was beyond her. Only a maddened mind would consider such a place home.

She was upon the doorway. She had been here earlier and saw how dark the cabin's interior was. This time however it was not quite as dark. The angle of the sun had changed and some of its light was able to shine through the doorway. It lit up a debris-strewn floor that attested that animals had gotten inside. The stores of Mrs. Bianco had been raided and pilfered and the non-edible remains were left scattered everywhere overtop of the less than pristine hardwood floors. There was a small table sitting opposite to the door. Upon it the animals had not only laid waste to the items that sat upon it they also left their black greasy feces strewn all over it. It was a disgusting sight that almost made the girl vomit. There were cupboards hanging on the wall behind the table. Some of the doors were left open revealing dark recesses that would be ideal for the scurrying creatures to brood and reside. She didn't doubt that there would be a creature in there right now but she sure as hell was not going to investigate.

Margaret was not in this room. Thora could not see anything human-sized sprawled on the floor. Her companion had gone deeper into the cabin. This kitchen area seemed to be the center of the house. There were walls and open doors on each side of it. It seemed that the room to the right was smaller and although she could not see inside of it Thora guessed that it would be a pantry and storage area for Mrs. Bianco. She doubted that Margaret went that way.

This meant that the woman would have gone to her left to what probably was Mrs. Bianco's bedroom. The godforsaken smell seemed to grow in intensity in that direction. This would be if any place the location where the decomposing body of the old woman would be found. And this would be where Margaret went.

Thora held her breath and proceeded inside of the cabin. Her eyes flitted about in every direction lest something came out to greet her. She highly suspected that bats would make their abode in this cabin. She had lived with bats for years upon Pioneer Lake and in all of that time never grew accustomed to them. They still scared the dickens out of her. But as she stepped deeper into the gruesome cabin no bats suddenly darted out at her. If they were in here they were keeping quiet and to themselves.

As she moved in the direction towards the bedroom she noticed a woodcutting hatchet leaning against the wall. Something inside of her told her that she should arm herself with it. She took hold of the weapon and as its head passed through the sunlight Thora could see that its end was reddened. Blood? She threw the instrument down in fear. She would have no part of it even though she rationalized that Mrs. Bianco in all likelihood used the small axe to behead chickens and the blood was theirs. The girl used to have awful nightmares of headless poultry running about after her dad had decapitated them up at the lake. Killing supper was something else that she never got used to even though she had been exposed to it for most of her life.

All of her dark remembrances from the past seemed to well themselves up as she slowly ambled inside of Mrs. Bianco's cabin. This was an excursion into the abyss promised to those that had not lived by God's accord. Once again she found that she was saying a prayer for safety.

The door that led into the bedroom was only partially opened. Its planked body obscured what was past it. All that could be detected in there was a wall with some hanging garments upon it. One of the long robes almost looked like it was filled by a body. Thora took a gulp and then forced herself to continue.

At that moment a sudden gust swept in through the front portal of the house and swooshed through the kitchen disturbing everything that was not pinned down. The vacuum created in the wind's aftermath sucked the bedroom door shut with a slam.

Thora looked about to see if anybody or anything came into the cabin with the gust. Nothing caught her eye but she sensed a deeper foreboding lurking within the walls of the shack. Although she could not see it she was sure that something had entered the place and that it may have slipped past her and into the bedroom.

The weather outside had become breezy. The walls of the cabin began to rattle in a rhythmic way that sounded almost akin to the vibrations made by someone breathing. Her eyes darted about the room trying to detect the presence but she was not able to focus on anything. Things had changed but she was not sure what things had changed. Everything inside of her told her to take flight and scurry out of the front door and get out of this unholy place but she could not abandon her companion here. She had to do something for Margaret. She once again picked up the axe.

Holding it firmly in her grip she started to the bedroom door. Inside that room past the door she could hear all manner of wheezes and eerie howls. Her common sense told her that these noises were being produced by the wind and not by a gaggle of banshees that had descended upon the dying body of her companion with the aim of tearing her soul from it.

With her right leg she solidly kicked the bedroom door opened. It swung on its hinges to reveal in the twilight dark sinister shadows hovering over top of someone lying on the floor. At once and without time for reflection Thora lifted her axe and started swinging downward upon the shadows.

Before the hatchet came down and struck into the meat of the attackers the body on the floor had rolled over. The axe crashed into the flooring of the room embedding itself in the hardwood.

"Have you gone crazy!" someone shrieked.

The next thing Thora knew she was being manhandled and wrestled to the floor. In the half-light that spilled from the kitchen the girl was able to see that it was Mrs. Whattam that had been her assailant. The woman was struggling to peg down Thora's scrambling arms and legs.

"What has gotten into you?" Margaret cried.

Thora felt tears fill her eyes as she relaxed her limbs and no longer put up a fight to stop her companion.

"I thought something was attacking you!" she whimpered, starting to realize that Mrs. Whattam might interpret her actions as an attempted murder.

"There was nothing attacking me!" Margaret harped. "I had banged my head on the pillar and it must have knocked me out. Luckily I came to or else I would have had that axe buried in my skull!"

Thora postulated that it must have been the wind that had woken up the woman. She was glad that it did but she still could feel that there was something inside of the room with the two of them. "I could have sworn I saw a host of spirits herding upon you and that they were trying to drag you away to Hell!"

"I can assure you that no such thing happened, my girl," Margaret sighed. In that sigh Thora heard the woman's uncertainty finally click over to the position that she now fully believed that the girl was psychotic.

"I know what I see," Thora answered. She felt that her world would never be the same anymore. Margaret would see to that. "And I know what I feel! There is something inside here with us and it wants to harm us!"

"It is your mind that wants to harm us Thora!" Margaret spurted. "You are growing more and more delusional. Soon you will not be able to make the distinction between what is real and what is not. And when that time comes you will have to be removed from society lest you do truly bring harm upon yourself or someone else!" The emphasis was on the 'someone else'. Margaret was rising to her feet, freeing Thora from her hold.

"Oh my God!"

Chapter 29

Peter Down to Nothing

"Oh my God!" Margaret cried. Her extended fingers covered her mouth while her eyes were exploding from her head.

"What is it?" Thora beseeched from the floor. Was the woman finally seeing those terrible things that she had been seeing all along? Thora's eyes fell upon the axe wedged into the floor beside her. Her hands reached out to take hold of its hasp.

"My dear Josephine! My dear Josephine!" Mrs. Whattam moaned. "What has become of you!" She was stooped over the small cot in the center of the room.

Thora climbed up to her feet. She held the axe in her hand. Her eyes took hold of the cot and the hideous foul thing that lied upon it. A blackened grotesque face with features that were bloated in some places and rotted in others protruded out of the top of the white blanket. Long matted gray hair flowed from the head onto the comforter. The eyelids were open but the sockets were empty. The crows and ravens must have had a feed.

This was the thing that was stinking up the whole valley. This was no doubt the body of Josephine Bianco, the preeminent and reclusive psychologist that Margaret Whattam so admired and had befriended. She must have been dead for months judging by the state of her decomposition and the horrendously offensive odor that exuded from her.

"Oh Josephine!" Margaret lamented over the corpse. "Had I known that you were in trouble I would have been here long ago!" She sat down on the side of the bed and began stroking the corpse's gray hair. It seemed that her love for her friend was greater than her instincts to keep clean.

This prompted Thora to say something. "I wouldn't do that if I were you. You don't know what she died of. There could be some terrible disease all over her. It could be creeping into your skin right now because you touched it!"

"Don't you say a thing like that!" Margaret shouted, turning her head towards the girl. The woman's eyes fell upon what Thora held in her hands. "And for God's sake put down that axe!"

Thora set the hatchet onto the bed. "Sorry," she said. "But I really think that we should not stay here any longer. We don't know what killed her and we sure don't want to be exposed to any of these germs in here."

"My friend died a peaceful death, I know it," Margaret answered. Her hands were more than running through Mrs. Bianco's hair now. They were actually patting the scalp and skull of the rotting cadaver. Thora began to wonder who was calling the kettle black? At this moment Mrs. Whattam seemed to be the insane one.

Yet the girl decided not to address this issue. Rather she chose to confute what the woman said. "I don't think that she died a peaceful death!" she said. "Look at the expression on her face. That is not one that you would associate with a quiet drift into death while sleeping!" Thora pointed to the cadaver's face. Mrs. Bianco's lower jaw was extended. It left her with the gaping mouth of someone suffering from extreme agony or fear.

Without saying anything Margaret reached down to Mrs. Bianco's face and closed the mouth. She started to adjust the blankets. She was going to pull them over the body's head in the respectful gesture that the living give privacy to the dead. As she did so Thora saw her hand expose something that was earlier covered by the sheets. It was a rope. It was tied tightly around Mrs. Bianco's neck.

"Holy Christ!" Thora rang. "She's been murdered!"

Mrs. Whattam saw the rope too and she started to try to undo it as if this act would rescue the old woman from a strangulation that took place months earlier.

"Stop!" Thora cried. "You have to leave everything the way that it is. You are getting fingerprints all over the rope!"

The woman was in a state of shock and did not heed the girl's words. She continued to try and undo the rope from the body's neck.

"I said stop!" Thora reiterated. "The police have to see the evidence the way that it is!"

As she tried to coax her companion out of her ritualistic behavior Thora wondered who could have done such a thing to this elderly recluse. She could only believe that mortal hands did not do it. There was an evil resident here and that evil possessed legions of netherworld denizens that were eager to do its work. She had seen one of these demons earlier in the form of Mrs. Bianco. The spirit had her fooled at first by the guise but the actions that the spirit took gave away its true purpose. If it were a spirit that had killed this poor woman on the bed then there would be no fingerprints.

Margaret Whattam pulled her hands away as she seemed to understand what Thora said. "Who could have done this to her?" she expressed to the girl through a face that was crumbling up into raw emotion. "Who could have done this to her? She was a beautiful being that loved all of life and would never have harmed any one!"

Her hands fell onto the rope again. The deteriorating quality of her face went into a state of abeyance. "There is something strange here," she mumbled. "This rope seems fresh. It doesn't have any discoloration or markings on it as you would expect when the flesh that it is tied to is rotting and spewing upon it." She looked back up at Thora again. The girl immediately recognized the suspicion in Margaret's eyes. "What were you doing for that hour and a half?"

"What do you mean?" Thora responded. She could half-guess what thought had entered her companion's mind.

"You were in here earlier, weren't you?" the woman said. "You were the one that tied this rope around Josephine's neck!"

Thora was shocked by the accusation. It was what she suspected Margaret to say but at the time that she had the premonition she had thought it ridiculous. Margaret would not think such a thing. But now the accusation had been baldly and boldly uttered. How could the woman think that she would do such a thing? It gave revealing testimony to what Margaret really thought of her—that she was so totally psychotic that she would inflict an indignity upon the dead.

"I didn't do any such thing!" the girl bellowed.

Margaret pulled loose the rope and held it in front of Thora in display. "Look at the condition of this!" She pulled back the blankets from Mrs. Bianco's body. "Look! Look!" the woman screamed. "See the stains on her clothing? See the stains on her blankets? They were caused by the process of decay!"

Thora could see the dark brownish areas where the blankets and pajamas had soaked up the fluids produced by the decomposing body.

"Now look at this!" Once more Margaret held the rope before Thora's eyes. "It is in pristine condition. There is not a drop of rot upon it! It could not have possibly been used to kill Josephine! It could not have possibly been tied around her neck for more than a day or so!" The woman's eyes narrowed. "What kind of devil are you?" her voice sounded very bitter. "Defiling a body is a terrible criminal offense Thora Meadowford if one did it out of a sound mind! Defiling a body is the act of a lunatic!"

The girl looked upon the woman in dismay. "You could not possibly think that I did this!" she exclaimed even though she realized that that was precisely what Mrs. Whattam thought.

"Now I understand why you were so reluctant for us to come inside of here! You didn't want your dastardly deed to be revealed! Oh you are sick Thora, sicker than I thought! We are going to have to get you institutionalized so that you can get the help that you so desperately need!"

"I didn't do this!" Thora spat. "I would never do such a thing!"

"But then who did? There has been absolutely nobody here in months. You were missing for an hour and a half and you never provided me with a satisfactory explanation about why you were gone so long!"

"I did tell you! I told you that I was knocked out because of my fall!"

"You said that you were only out for a few seconds! Where did all of the rest of the time go?"

Thora started to wonder if she should tell Margaret what really happened during that period that they were separated—about the visit she had with a demon in the guise of Mrs. Bianco. Should she tell her about how that demon at first was as friendly as apple pie but then mysteriously began rhyming off Meadowford family history and then ending her spiel with enigmatic advice telling Thora that she had to get rid of the ghosts that haunt her and to look to the lynx? Margaret would find such a claim extremely outlandish but at least it would not have the despicable connotations that defiling a body possessed.

"Well, where were you?"

The girl still did not respond.

"I will tell you where you were," Margaret said, still sitting on the side of the bed. "You were exploring in this cabin and you found my friend lying dead here. You carried on a conversation with her. I know that because I was able to hear your voice from where I sat under the tree. And then you discovered that the body was no longer rigid from rigor mortis. You placed the ghastly expression on its face and you found the cord and you tied it tightly around its neck."

"You heard me?" Thora asked.

"I could hear you but I could not make out what you were saying because of the distance," Margaret answered.

"Did you hear someone else talking to me?"

Margaret laughed. "Only the insane can hear their hallucinations. I did not hear any other voice other than yours!"

"But you must have!" Thora beseeched the woman. She realized that Margaret must have heard the conversation she had with the spirit by the brook. "I was talking to Mrs. Bianco or at least what I thought was Mrs. Bianco!" the girl cried. The secret that she was not going to reveal was out. It was now time to see how Mrs. Whattam would react to what really happened.

"You have got that right when you say what you thought was Mrs. Bianco. You were experiencing a hallucination Thora. I am glad that you recognize it."

"No, no. That is not what I was trying to say!" Thora rang. "I was not in here when I talked to her. I was out there by the brook. She was not in this ugly form that you see her now. She looked alive and healthy and she was cheerful and dressed in gay colors and she wanted to help me because I had scraped my knee. Have a look for yourself!" Thora lifted her skirt to reveal the scrapes upon her joints. "See the wounds are cleansed! Mrs. Bianco had done it!"

Margaret glanced at her knees and shook her head. "Put down your skirt Thora. It is not very ladylike. I didn't see any scrapes there!"

"You didn't because they were cleansed by the ghost!"

The woman closed her eyes tightly. "Your hallucinations are even worse than I thought. If you are actually experiencing phantom senses of touch then you are in deep trouble," she sighed, opening her eyes. "We have got to get you to help today! Your hallucinations are starting to become dangerous. Who knows what kind of harm you are capable of inflicting upon yourself or others?"

"You are not listening to me and you do not believe anything that I say!" Thora felt besmirched. Even if Margaret were acting out of a caring heart she should still give Thora the chance to explain herself.

"I am listening very carefully to what you are saying Thora and that is why I propose to you that we get out of this place at once and once we get back to civilization I will take you to a hospital so that we can start your treatment!"

"You mean that you are going to commit me to a mental hospital, right? That is your plan!" Thora could feel her world tail spinning. If she did not do anything to stop the woman she might just find herself locked up in a padded room this evening.

"I didn't say that," Margaret replied. "I said that we are going to get you help and we will do whatever it takes to get you healthy again."

Thora saw her companion eyeing the axe that sat on the bed on the other side of the cadaver. She got the sense that Margaret believed that she was going to reach for it and use it upon her and that the woman was going to snatch up the weapon before Thora had a chance to do so. At once, the girl's hand dashed for the wood-chopping utensil but before she could claim it as her own Margaret hands were upon its hasp as well.

The two living occupants of the room began a struggle of possession overtop of the rank body of Mrs. Bianco. "Let go of it Thora!" Margaret said through clenched teeth as she was using all the weight of her body to win the tug of war.

"No, I won't let go of it!" the girl rasped back. "I am not going to let you lock me up in a mental hospital! You have gone far too overboard Mrs. Whattam! You have no right or authority to do so! You are not my guardian! Only my parents can do such a thing to me." Thora was pulling back on the blade and sensed that even though Mrs. Whattam was an adult she had more strength than the woman and that it would only be a matter of time when the hatchet would be hers.

"Believe me I can do this!" Margaret spat back. "After what I have witnessed today the authorities would not give a damn about what your parents have to say about this issue! I am a fine upstanding citizen in the community! I am not a man charged with killing four people! I am not an alcoholic whose memories are so blurry that she cannot recall what happened five minutes ago!"

"You don't say those things about my parents!" Thora growled. She was feeling righteously angry towards this meddlesome woman that was trying to tear her world apart. "You are nothing but a flighty dreamer that all of Grappling Haven laughs at! How dare you think that you are superior to us! I would not have you as a parent even if you were the last woman alive!"

"And I wouldn't want you for a daughter if you were the last child alive!" the woman retaliated. She grew fiercer in her tugging and Thora's fingers started to lose the grip that they had upon the hatchet. But she was not finished fighting. With her free hand she reached across the cadaver and grabbed Margaret by the hair and began yanking at it with everything that she could muster.

Margaret screamed from the pain as her hair was being torn from her scalp. She still clung to the hatchet. Thora had not let go of it either. Margaret lunged at Thora and wrapped one arm around her and pulled the child into the rotting body beneath her. Thora could feel foul stuff ooze into her pores. It absolutely disgusted her and she lost her head in rage. With the ferociousness of a cornered bobcat she pushed upward against the weight of the woman and she managed to make Margaret lose her balance. Mrs. Whattam fell over to her side. She groaned and then she collapsed.

At that moment something began to move in the bed. It was not Thora and it was not Margaret. Out of the corner of her eye Thora could see Mrs. Bianco's decomposed body start to rise. All at once Thora was filled with the most unimaginable terror. She leapt from the bed before the cadaver could grab her. Her leap was clumsy and she fell hard onto the floor. She swiftly scrambled up and as she did so she saw what looked like the hatchet wedged into Margaret's side. She did not know for sure. She did not know if Margaret had fell upon it when she was tossed or whether the hideous thing had planted it there. She could not tell if Margaret was alive or dead. She did not want to afford the time to find out.

The cadaver was sitting straight up in bed. Its eyeless head was pointed towards the girl. It was black and it was ghastly. "Run little girl of the forest run," it said. "But you will not get far. We know who you are and we know where you can be found and we will visit you and torment you until the end of your days!"

Thora wished that she could be defiant but she was terrified. All that she could do was run. And run she did. She scrambled out of the cabin and out into the yard. She did not dare to look behind her lest she were being followed by that harbinger of death. She knew full well that she was leaving Mrs. Whattam behind and that there were going to be severe repercussions to be paid. She knew that no one would believe her when she said that a body had come back to life and that it was an accident how Margaret got hurt or killed. Her life had hit absolute bottom. Nothing was ever going to be the same.

She fled up the ravine and along the path that led back to the road. She miraculously was able to avoid all the snags and roots that sought to trip her up. When she finally reached the country road she saw that the car was not there. She remembered how Margaret had failed to lock the car and how she had the premonition that it was not going to be there when they got back. The vehicle was gone. It was not up or down the gravel road. Even if she had taken a wrong path she should have been able to see the car for the stretch of road was flat and straight for well over a mile in either direction. There was no car to be seen.

She looked behind her to the path to see if anyone or anything had followed her. As best as she could make out nothing bothered to chase her. She was on her own and even though she knew full well where she was she felt entirely lost. She did not know what to do. What were her options? She felt forsaken. She hated her life. She hated the people in her life. She hated being afraid. But she knew that she had to continue. She had to carry on even though she did not know how.

How was she going to resume her life after all of this? It was impossible. As soon as she got back to Grappling Haven there would be questions regarding Margaret's whereabouts. How would she answer those questions? Where would she even start? Her mother was aware that she had gone on this trip with Margaret. She felt reasonably certain that James Whattam was told about his wife's plans for the day. It would not be long before the girl would be sought out for some answers.

Maybe she should go back to the cabin and get Margaret out of there? Even if the woman were dead she would be able to explain the death as an accident. That path seemed to be the least troublesome for her to travel. Yet there was something far more frightening than a life locked up in an asylum down there. Whatever that monster was that resided in the cabin its foul heart was the epitome of evil to the girl. There was no way that she could even entertain the notion of rescuing Margaret. She had to make as much distance as she possibly could from that cabin.

But in what direction would she make that distance? Back to Grappling Haven and what surely would be an institutionalized life, whether it be jail or the mental hospital? Or should she strike out in the opposite direction and begin the life of a fugitive? For some reason the voice that her Aunt Faye had heard within her grandfather's coffin came to mind. It had said, "If birds do not migrate north and south then you shall nest in the west." Maybe it was time to take that advice and venture out to California.

Her only problem was that she did not know which way was west. She did not even know whether the road she stood upon had a north-south or an east-west orientation. Yet it was the only road that she had and she had to follow it one way or the other. She was reasonably certain that if she turned to her right it would take her back to town. She had no idea what would happen if she should take it to her left. Did the road just peter away to wilderness or did it have an ultimate destination?

It was then that she noticed the car tracks on the gravel surface. She saw where Margaret's red vehicle was parked along the side of the road and she saw that it pulled out from that stationary spot and that it drove off in the opposite way from Grappling Haven. Whoever took the car had not come back this way for there were no tracks coming back. The road must not peter down to nothing. It had to go on.

And Thora decided then and there that she had to go on as well. Returning to where she came from would mean a halt to her life. If she wanted to live and she did, she had to take this road to wherever it may lead and hopefully she would find a way to live and a way to overcome the dark shadows that had come into her life and roosted upon her. She was going to break free from their shackles. She was going to liberate herself. She was not going to adhere to the path that they had set down for her. She had her own path and she was going to follow it.

Chapter 30

The Other Face of Summer

That day when she had to walk from Silent Hills back to Grappling Haven had been torturous and testing of all her mettle. She had to contend with ghosts and brazen bovines while walking seven miles back into town. Yet it had proved to be nothing compared to the girl's hike down this nameless road where at one time Josephine Bianco had marked out her address. Here there were phantoms and there were the beasts of the wild and the distance that she had to travel was endless and she was heading in the opposite direction of home.

Hours had passed since she had escaped from the demons and the horror of that cabin set in the woods. She had been walking down the gravel road ever since. It had carved out a path through the wilderness. There was no sign of humanity upon it anywhere. No one else sought to make a life out here. This was the refuge for the birds and the animals.

The treetops were alive with bird song from all manner of plumage. There were many familiar trills such as those from redwing blackbirds and orioles but there were also many calls that Thora could at best only vaguely recognize such as the screech of what she believed to be owls hidden in the canopy that towered above her. Owls had always made her nervous ever since she witnessed a friend's kitten get taken by one right out of the friend's backyard. To hear the little cat's feeble mews was heart rending to the girl as she watched the huge grey bird carry the creature away. She recalled how helpless she and her friend felt. They were not able to do anything for the kitten. They never saw it again and they never allowed their minds to dwell on the matter because the experience was too raw and tore at the very framework of their sense of security.

As she walked down the road she knew that no owl would be able to clutch at the back of her head and carry her off to a treetop and start ripping the flesh from her body. She was far too big. Yet even with this knowledge she still did not feel safe from them. She did not feel safe from anything at the moment. Everything was against her. Everything was out to get her. She was that helpless kitten in the owl's talons. She was waiting for the world to unleash its wrath and its hunger upon her.

She tried to keep it out of her mind. Yet that was hard to do. Her fear was tantamount and it would find recesses and cracks within her mental framework where it would wash into her thoughts and so overwhelm her that she would wish that she were dead. Why was she created if all that she were meant to do was to suffer these crushing fears and be placed into situations where her actions had such deleterious effects upon those around her? Why had Margaret Whattam taken it upon herself to be the girl's champion? If Margaret had left well enough alone then she would not be lying dead or dying in that forsaken bedroom and Thora would not be running away from her life. But Margaret had to meddle. She had to take her out here into the forest. Even when the powers that be twice warned her to stay clear from the cabin Margaret persisted. She had fallen over a cliff but she continued her quest to visit Mrs. Bianco. She had fell down a ravine and severely twisted her ankle but she still managed to get inside of the cabin. It was like Margaret was hell bent to deliver Thora to those that resided in that den of terror. It was as if Thora was meant to hear the message delivered to her by the spirit and that it was Margaret's sole mission to see that she received it.

If everything else in her life was so misconstrued and laden with latent meaning why not Margaret Whattam as well? What made the woman so interested in her? Surely it could not have been that lame sermon given by Reverend Barton at Silent Hills? Reverend Barton was always trying to stir up more interest in his church and he would employ different schemes that sought to keep the church front and central in the lives of those in the community. The notion of church as family was a theme that he resorted to periodically in his sermons. The idea of making someone an ambassador of that good will was somewhat novel but it really did not break any new ground. Why did Mrs. Whattam bite on this one? Perhaps it was because she was a relative newcomer in the congregation. She and her husband were rarely in attendance at Sunday services. Was she really that gregarious that she wanted to participate in Reverend Barton's family and adopt a troubled girl to be her surrogate daughter for the girl that she could never have? Or was she a servant to something altogether different?

The Meadowfords had been doing well in their business before Uncle Thaddeus took on James Whattam to be his financial and legal advisor. Ever since Mr. Whattam was hired the business had begun to sour. Thora had never thought before that things started to go wrong for Dearborn Cable as a result of James' poor counsel but as she walked down the road she started to realize that maybe it was James Whattam that was at fault for the financial wreckage that the company had become. Was it James' purpose to see the ruin of the Meadowfords? Was he sent by the same nefarious master that had sent his wife Margaret? If things were not like they seemed then why couldn't James and Margaret Whattam have ulterior identities, identities associated with dark malignant forces that were seeking to destroy the once proud and noble Meadowford family?

The more Thora thought about it the more she saw that she could not rule out such an ostentatious hypothesis as the thinking of a paranoid mind. James and Margaret were out to ruin her. The girl could no longer feel any sympathy or regret for the lady with the hatchet in her side. Yet she also knew that nobody would believe her if she made such assertions about the socially acceptable Whattams. They would think that it was more proof of the insipient madness that had come to reside in her. Grappling Haven would never think of her as an innocent again once it discovered what happened at the cabin in the woods. She would be branded a murderous lunatic and she would be locked away until the breath in her ceased.

She had to get away from there. She had to find a new life. She was not altogether too sure about nesting in the west. The thought of traveling across the great expanse of the nation was daunting to her. For all of her time at Black Island the wilderness still did frighten her. Sleeping under the stars was a very scary proposition. She needed the security of walls around her.

Then trepidation crept into her heart as she realized that her present actions would most assuredly guarantee that she would be sleeping under the stars this evening. There was nothing down this road but forest and wetlands. There were no homes and hearths down there where she could nestle in front of a fireplace and peacefully slip into slumber. All that this road promised was mosquitoes by the thousands, strange and haunting birdcall, terrifying and mysterious rustling in the offing, wet uneven ground that would never conform to the contours of her body, and a loneliness where there would be nobody to confide and confer with. What in the hell was she doing? She would surely die of privation if she were to continue down this path. How would she feed herself in the wild? How would she feed herself if she did happen to stumble into a community? She had no money. She would be defenseless against any predatory male that would look upon her flesh with ravenous eyes and not be held back because of her minority or what was popularly branded as her 'jailbait' status.

She stopped in her tracks. She had to reevaluate everything. Going forward was no longer an option. Going back was her only alternative. But going back was not really going back. She could never resume her life where she had left it off. She had closed that chapter in her life when she chose to abandon Mrs. Whattam in the cabin. Once the woman creeps and crawls and drags herself back to civilization word would get out of the Meadowford twin's questionable deeds. The community would act fast upon it and see to it that young Thora Meadowford would be placed in a sanitarium to vegetate and sink into a morass of perpetual sadness and gloom.

Was there nothing happy in the world any more? Wasn't childhood supposed to be the period in life where one could frolic and be fancy-free? Wasn't it the place that when one is older one could reflect back upon with warmth and cheer? Her childhood certainly was no longer such a place. It had become a living nightmare. Yet when she was younger she did have such a place—Black Island upon Pioneer Lake. Those summers that she had up there were magical in every way. They were days filled with enchantment and serenity. Even though there was always the presence of those that found ways to sour the glory they still were no match to what the island and the lake could evoke in their primordial splendor. When she was there she had believed that there was no way that those days would ever end. They held the aspect of eternity within their aura. The rest of the world did not exist. The rest of the world was only a gritty shade that could easily be subdued and subliminated and not have to be dealt with. Even at the end of the season the promise of the endurance of the island's magic made her believe that while she slipped back to the Pennsylvania winter it would not be long and soon the spring would beckon and like a migratory bird she would fly north and into the embrace of the lake country once more.

It was there now. It was the height of summer. The regattas would be flourishing. Sailboats of every kind would be ripping seams into the waters of Upper Pioneer Lake. Mount Horeb would be bustling with tourists. People would be dressed in bright clothing and even brighter smiles as they flocked to the shores to splash in the lake. The water would be very warm this time of year. Nothing God created in Heaven could compare to what he made on Pioneer Lake. Yes, it was all there now. There. Not here. She was hundreds of miles away. She was living upon the other face of summer—the face of unbearable heat, annoying insects, impossibly long days and overwhelming hopelessness.

How she pined that she could be there now! Why did they have to come home this summer? Her parents had torn their two unwilling girls from paradise and dragged them back to this tired little town. They had done this even before Sambo died. Maybe if they had not done so, her grandfather could have been still alive. Things may have turned out different.

But what happened happened and there was no way that she could undo it. Or was there? Thora stopped on the road and thought about it. Right now she was free. She was not answerable to anybody. If she wanted to she could do what she pleased. Nothing more would please her than to return to Pioneer Lake. And outside of a few small logistical problems nothing was stopping her. Why could she not go up to Black Island? Nobody was around to prevent her. Not even her lack of money prevented her. All she needed to do was stick out her thumb and hitchhike. She could catch rides all the way into Canada and right up to the lake and it would not cost her a penny. If she were really lucky she could even get there before the day is out. There were always plenty of Pennsylvania license plates to be seen in the hinterland of Ontario. People from her state quite frequently traveled into Canada's playpen. It was not really that ridiculous to pray for that stroke of luck that would place her into a car that was bound for Laketown or areas further north.

She suddenly felt giddy. She felt renewed and invigorated. The world could not be that nasty if it had such places as Pioneer Lake upon it. And she was now resolved that she was going there. It felt like it was the last day of school and that she had the whole summer ahead of her—a whole summer to be spent on those tranquil rocks that comprised Black Island. She couldn't believe how simple this was going to be. She couldn't believe that she had not thought of it before. She could have done this weeks ago and not had to endure the tyranny of her parents and the treachery of Margaret Whattam.

But that didn't matter now for she was going to make up for it. She would make haste for the lake, go across Robinson Bay and climb out upon the great dock and look up at the summer home built by her forefathers. There would be no grouchy Uncle Thaddeus up there looking surly and despondent that his peace had been broken. There would be no conniving Langley Meadowford moping about the tedium and making plans for the day that he ruled the roost. There would be no Cora Meadowford endlessly orchestrating the events of the day while casting disparaging remarks about everybody else there. There would be no Grandfather and no Jack. That was somewhat a drawback but Thora knew that she could cope with it for their spirits would be there and she would relish in them while taking in the endless sunshine. There would be no Rebecca. Or maybe there would be a Rebecca? Her twin was a lot like her and maybe Becky had made her way directly to Pioneer Lake when she ran away a month ago. Maybe Becky was there!

There was one friend that was definitely there and she hoped that she would get there before it was too late for him. Capers was there. Her cat was still upon the island. Hopefully he had been able to fend for himself all of this time. Hopefully he would have been able to keep himself alive on the chipmunks and mice that abounded on the island. The girl started imagining her magical reunion with her dear Capers. She could almost feel him rubbing his bony furry body against her shins. She could almost hear that motor inside of his chest purring away out of sheer happiness that his Thora had come back to him.

"I'm coming Capers!" she said out loud. She was convinced that she finally had a plan of action. She was going to the lake and nothing was going to stop her.

But her conviction took a minor setback as she took in her surroundings.

She was still out here on this ghost road. The only car that had driven down this road all day was that of Margaret Whattam's and it was stolen. She could still see the tire tracks that were carved into the gravel. It headed off in the opposite direction from Grappling Haven. It had never come back. That told Thora that the road could not have been a dead end like she was afraid that it might have been. It told Thora that she need not backtrack. She could go forward and not have to show her face in the Grappling Haven vicinity again. This to her was a good omen.

She started walking again. Her steps had a revitalized vigor. The soles of her feet had a direction once more. They didn't care how many times they had to slap themselves against the gravel for they knew that with each slap they were one step closer to Pioneer Lake. She was going to the lake! She couldn't believe that it was true! But it was! Her life had meaning once more!

Chapter 31

Wander the Earth

Her feet ached. Her soles cried out in agony. They did not want to endure any more contact with the never-ending gravel. Yet when she lifted her head all that Thora could see was the road stretched out before her for miles upon miles. She had been walking many hours and she guessed that she would be walking many more.

The enthusiasm that had taken hold of her when she finally had given herself a destination was starting to lift. Some doubt had crept into her mind. She had expected such and had built up defense mechanisms not to allow that doubt to take control of her actions. She was determined to carry through with her plan.

Yet the daylight hours were beginning to wane. It was still light outside but the sun's intensity had diminished and the shadows were growing longer. The sun was behind her now. It had found a divot in the elevated topography to the northwest and was spilling what it had left inside of itself through this dip in the western mountains and onto the gravel road that Thora walked upon. This informed the girl that she was heading in a southeasterly direction. She was walking into her shadow. It was immense and well defined. It was as if she were a giant strutting her domain.

Yet she did not feel like a giant. She felt small and insignificant. The sun was still with her but for how long? Soon it would sink past that divot and then the valley would be immersed in darkness. She tried not to think about it or the growing hunger emanating from her stomach. She had not eaten anything since she left Pine Street early this morning. That seemed so long ago that it almost felt like that had been part of another life. So much had changed since breakfast. She had thought her life miserable then but the problems of the morning paled terribly to the problems that this new day had sent her way.

She was committed now to a night on the road. Even if she suddenly had a change of heart and decided to go back there would be no way that she would reach shelter before the night was upon her. All the fears and doubts that she had as a child regarding the dark were emerging and beginning to make their presence felt in her mind. She tried to force some rationality into her thoughts and told herself that there was no point in being scared, that being scared would not help her situation. She was smart enough not to try to delude herself into thinking that there was nothing to be scared of, for there was plenty to be scared of. She started to list all of her sources of fright but quickly ceased the mental exercise for all that it was doing was heightening her fear. It was not even dark yet. Why work herself into a fright? Besides there could be the off chance that she might find a house down the road or there may yet be someone driving a car along it in either direction. There would not be a road if nobody used it, she reminded herself. The road had to have some purpose.

But not a car had come down it in all of this time. Not even any horse-drawn wagons. The only tires that rolled over the gravel this day were those of Margaret's stolen car. She could still see the tracks etched into the gray rubble that composed the route. Who would have taken that car? Whoever that did must have been walking this forlorn road prior to coming upon the red vehicle parked along it. What a lucky stroke for that person! Why couldn't she have been so fortunate? If she had the providence to find a car she would have danced with joy! But as far as her eye could see there were no abandoned vehicles sitting along the side of the road up ahead. Whoever had stolen Margaret's car was not parked out here in the middle of nowhere waiting for her.

She started to recall the stories that abounded in Grappling Haven about dangerous highwaymen who lurked along the network of roads outside of town. These men were touted to be extremely hostile especially towards young women. Could it have been one of these highwaymen that had taken Mrs. Whattam's car? Thora began to shiver at the thought. Could one of those monsters have traveled the very route that she was taking? She turned around and looked behind her. She saw nothing except for the road that she had traversed. It stretched as far back as she could see. She had walked every inch of it. Turning around and looking ahead of her she saw the same road stretching as far as she could see. She would have to walk every inch of it.

More time went by and the girl continued her arduous hike. The sun was now long below that divot and the darkness of the valley continued to grow. She remembered her first impression of this valley when she and Margaret first saw it from their lofty perch in the mountain. Back then she noted that it was a dark place. She had wondered how anybody could live down there. Now she was in that valley's throat, wandering down an endless road between the two sets of highlands to the north and the south. Maybe it would have been a good idea to have forsaken the road and made her way into the upcountry? Maybe she would have found another road, a well-used road with plenty of traffic and kindhearted drivers that would be willing to stop and pick up a tired girl weary of all her exertion? It was too late to explore that alternative. There was no way that she was going to head into the hills at this time of day. She would stay to the road.

Her hunger and her thirst had grown more than her fear. She had been keeping her eyes open these last few hours for berry bushes. It was funny. She had always believed that there would be plenty of these bushes out here in the wild but now that she had a very intense desire for one of these bushes there were none to be had. Perhaps that was a good thing. Berry bushes attract bears. She certainly did not want to encounter one of these beasts out here. She was not sure if they were out here or not. Some in the community would testify that the mountain country around Grappling Haven abounded with bears while others said that there was not a black bear to be found within a hundred miles of town. It was funny but the people that said that there were bears were the same people who talked about these desperate highwaymen out here. The people that denied the existence of the bears also attested that there were no highwaymen lurking outside of town. Thora had to believe that the truth must have rested somewhere between these two extremes. This meant that there were some highwaymen out here and that there were some bears as well.

Her grandfather had told her up at Pioneer Lake that bears come out only at night. She wished that he had never said that to her. She wished that she never remembered him telling her. The last thing that she wanted to encounter out here was a hungry old bear. She was sure that just the sight of one would cause her to die on the spot. Her ears were acute and she listened for the sounds of the forest that surrounded her on both sides of the road. Now and then she heard a snapping of a twig, or the echo of something running through the trees. When this happened she froze on the spot and dared not move. But thus far nothing ever came of it and she would soon continue her nervous trek.

The muscles in her legs ached. Her back was sore. Her stomach was raging. Her throat was raw, her fear was mercurial and darkness was all around her. She had arrived into the night. She had no shelter. She had no food. All that she saw was what was above her head. This was a swath of the Milky Way galaxy that was framed by the outline of the trees at the road's edge. The stars were as brilliant here as they were up in Canada. It almost looked the same as it did at Black Island. It possessed that clarity and that sharpness that could only come when the skies were not dampened by the extraneous light produced by human civilization. This sky could never be as clear from her Grappling Haven backyard. There most of the stars would have been drowned out by the street and house lights. Instead of being in awe of the millions of stars above her Thora found herself longing for that tame Grappling Haven sky. There she would be in the protective bosom of her species. Out here there was no such protection offered. Out here she was just as much a prey item as any deer or squirrel.

And what was preying on her was not a bear or a wolf or some other fierce hairy creature. What were preying on her were mosquitoes—mosquitoes by the thousands. They somehow had found her and had descended upon her in a merciless, buzzing onslaught that would drive the sanest man mad in a matter of moments. Her hands were continuously waving in a frenzied attempt to keep the obsessive bloodthirsty critters at bay. Despite her frenetic efforts the insect horde found plenty of cracks in her defenses and they poured in, lighting upon her and drinking their fill before scurrying off to allow others of their kind the chance to feast. What would these little fiends have fed upon if she had not happened on the road tonight? Why couldn't they have gone off to torment the other beasts of the forest and leave her alone? Let them bother the bears and the wolves. Let them so overwhelm these predators that they would not have the opportunity to plan an ambush of a little girl of the forest.

If there was one saving grace about the ceaseless insects it was that they served to keep Thora's mind away from her fear. She did not have the chance to be scared because she was so preoccupied in keeping her exposed flesh free from the sucking mosquitoes. Any thought of trying to find cover was superceded by the necessity of fighting these relentless creatures. She continued walking along the road through air that was literally thickened by the countless busy bodies composed of chitin.

In the darkness she found that she was having difficulty seeing and staying to the road. More than once she inadvertently ventured off the gravel and onto the wet soil that sat upon the road's shoulders. More than once her face was slapped by unseen boughs that hung over the road ready to take down its victims.

It was a night of hell. It was an endless night. Tired, aching, hungry, thirsty, frightened, itchy, and driven insane by the constant throng of mosquitoes, Thora persevered and continued walking, sticking to the road as best she could. She had no time for thoughts. She was not given a chance to think because of the predatory insects. She moved along the road with the instinctual guidance of a beast mentality and she did not give in to any of the primal needs that coursed through her body.

After what seemed an eternity she saw the early glimmers of dawn. She had survived the night. The mosquitoes had abated somewhat with the new light of day and she was able to relax her defensive patrol of her body. As the sun's luminescence gradually began to fill the valley she saw that the terrain that she occupied was in essence no different than it had been the day before. It was still that same gravel road stretching straight as far into the distance as she could see, its perimeters outlined on each side by tall trees. The sight of this depressed her terribly. It was like she had gone absolutely nowhere.

A strange thought came to her mind. What if she had died and she was now in some afterlife? Could this be her Hell, she wondered—to wander forever along an old gravel road that stretched for eternity. Or was it Purgatory? Definitely it was not Heaven. Heaven could not be so miserable as this place that she found herself in. Regardless if it were Hell or Purgatory, if it was the afterlife then that would have meant that she would have had to have died somewhere along the line. She tried to figure out precisely where that could have happened. Perhaps that fell creature that took on the shape of Mrs. Bianco had pounced upon her and instantly killed her before she even left the old woman's property? Or maybe a bear snuck up on her from behind and killed her without her ever being aware of it?

The demon had said that the Meadowford dead were meant to wander the Earth because of the Indian's curse. If this were so then this was not Hell or Purgatory. It was the same world that she spent her entire life. She was meant then to continue to roam it until a lynx would appear to usher in a new age. But as Thora's exhausted body continued to walk more of the road she began to realize that she could not be a ghost walking the Earth because the mosquitoes of the night before would not be interested in a lifeless body. They craved the juices of life. The juices of life were not present in the dead.

Or were they?

What would those mosquitoes have fed upon last night if she had not been there? They obviously had to feed upon something for there were so many of them. If there were nothing for them to eat then they would have surely died out. Maybe the mosquitoes fed upon the spirits of the forest? And if this were so then she could very well be a cursed Meadowford dead endlessly wandering the Earth.

The road ahead of her and behind her had not changed. How could a road be so endless in the middle of Pennsylvania? It just did not seem right. Yet there was no doubt that the road was here and that it never changed a degree in all the time that she walked upon it.

And there still were those tire tracks upon it. They seemed as fresh now almost a day later as what they appeared like yesterday. Where did that car go? Why did it never come back? Was its driver another hapless soul condemned to drive for eternity down such a monotonous road?

Once again Thora's thoughts turned to the driver. Who could it have been? What man or woman would be walking down Mrs. Bianco's road? The only logical answer was that it had to be one of those depraved highwaymen. She was glad that he found the car and was now maybe hundreds of miles away from her. She dreaded the notion that such a person could be lurking in the vicinity and ready to spring upon her. Somehow such a real person was more frightening than the ghostly images that the girl had already seen since leaving home yesterday morning.

By the time the sun had reached its zenith, Thora was still upon this road and absolutely nothing had changed. The distant horizon was the same as it ever was. It was unceasing. It was reinforcing more and more her growing conviction that she had died and that she was now in some overwhelming afterlife that held no mercy for her. Her body complained in every way that a body could imagine. She was hungry. She was thirsty. She was aching. She was exhausted. She was all these things simultaneously yet not one of them was strong enough to take her down. She continued. She persevered. It was like she was impervious to death. If she had already died then it would make sense that she was impervious to death. She only wished that she were impervious to suffering for the suffering was relentless and taxing.

Yet she continued to walk. She not once entertained the notion of turning around and heading back the way that she came. She had invested too much into this road. She could not turn around and make it all for naught. She had to go on. She had to believe that there was an end to this road and that from there she would be able to find her way up to Pioneer Lake.

She wondered about Margaret Whattam. Did the woman survive the wound? Did she manage to get back to Grappling Haven? Thora prayed that she did but knew deep down in her stomach that Margaret was still there in that cursed cabin. Whether alive or dead Thora did not know. And no one had discovered her as of yet. Had someone come upon her then most assuredly they would have spotted the single set of human tracks on the road and the person would have alerted the police and they would have come following. They would have caught up to her by now.

She took a glance back behind her at the road she traveled. She could see the pronounced signature of her tracks steadily leading up to where she stood. There was no vehicle in the distance. But sooner or later there would be. James Whattam knew where his wife went yesterday and by now he would be fully aware that something had gone wrong. He would have gone to Mrs. Bianco's place and found Margaret there. Surely, that should have happened by now. How come there was nobody following? In the world of the living Thora should have already been apprehended. They would have seen her trail and they would have been onto her so fast that she should have been already locked up in jail or the asylum. More and more the girl was beginning to realize that she was no longer in the world that she knew. More and more it seemed to be a certainty that she had already died. In the real world, the world that she knew, she would have been captured by now.

A chill rushed over her body with this realization. When she first hypothesized that she was dead she was not really convinced of its veracity. But now it seemed far more likely that it was true. She had left the coils of mortality and was now in some purgatorial afterlife where she was forced to eternally walk a tired old road. It was such a stark and terrible realization that she began to cry. She sat down on the road and immediately felt the relief in her legs. She had been walking for too long. How did she merit this awful fate? She had not been a bad person. She may have made mistakes along the way but she never acted out of malice. Why was this road her ultimate destiny?

She sat for a long period of time on the road immersing herself into the deepest pool of self-pity. She hated everything that life had given her. She hated the people in it. She hated herself. She cried and she cried. She continued crying until she realized that it was not getting her anywhere. Maybe there was a reason why she was put on this road? Maybe the road itself was a clue that told her that she had to keep on going? Roads lead from one place to another. Roads do not exist just for their own accord. Roads were the maps of time. Roads through time transport people from one location to another. Roads were the essence of change. Perhaps this road was meant to change her and once she had changed then she would be at the end of the road.

She looked at the road she sat upon once more. It had not changed. It possessed the same physical attributes that it had once she had started down it. The trees that lined its sides were ultimately the same. They may go through permutations in species and height but they kept repeating themselves. She had to get past these permutations. She had to reach her journey's end.

Getting up to her feet she once again began to walk. She no longer felt as scared as she did before. Somehow the conviction that you are dead makes you tend to worry less about your safety. And Thora was now convinced that she was dead. She was a Meadowford dead. She was meant to wander the Earth.

Chapter 32

Porcupines of the Night

Night was once more approaching. Not a single car had come down the road. Not a single animal had left its tracks upon the gravel. She had not expected either. She was dead and she was in the afterlife and this was her private universe, as miserable as it was. She long ago had given up on the notion that she was that same little Thora Meadowford, plagued by ghosts and mountainous problems that were forever escalating. None of that mattered any more.

It did not matter that her sister Rebecca was missing. Becky was a smart girl with a good head on her shoulders. She would not fall victim to the snares that life would set along her path. She would maneuver around them and come out smelling of roses. Her sister would one day overcome all obstacles and set her own course and that course would most assuredly give Rebecca success. Thora had no worries over Rebecca any longer.

It did not matter about her father's upcoming court case. Whether he was found guilty or not was none of her concern. She knew that her dad had nothing to do with the murder of the Rozelle family. They died at the hands of Samuel Angus Meadowford the First. But no mortal court of law would ever tag the crime on a ghost. It was best to leave the arrogant heir as the scapegoat and let him take the fall.

It did not matter about her family's finances. If Langley wanted to throw it all away it made no difference to Thora. He was no longer supporting his daughters. The only one that he was looking after was his alcoholic wife. Let the money run out. Let the booze run out. It would be good for the both of them. They needed some humbling.

It did not matter that she would be held accountable for the fate of Mrs. Whattam. She knew that she was innocent and that was all that mattered. If they wanted to go ahead and think that she was a grizzly axe murderer then let them go ahead and think so. She was dead already. They could do her no harm. As for Mrs. Whattam she brought it onto herself. If you play with fire you are going to get burned. Thora felt no remorse over what happened to the woman. Margaret was the one that brought their lives into danger, not Thora. Even when they hung over the cliff it was Thora that had behaved rationally not the woman. As the girl pondered that moment she began to wonder if that was not the time of their deaths. Maybe no Indian in an ethereal canoe had rescued them. Maybe they had fallen to the rocks below and died battered and gory upon them. After that episode her life had become increasingly bizarre and separated from the normal laws of reality. Whether she died then or later it did not matter. She was dead now and she was wandering the Earth. She was intent on going to Pioneer Lake and to Black Island to keep her cousin Jack company. She would go there if she ever got off of this infernal road.

It still had not changed in the day and a half that she walked it. She had learned in school that the average speed of someone walking was about three miles an hour. If she were going at that rate then it was altogether feasible that she had walked one hundred miles. She doubted she traveled so fast and so far. Most of her trek had been slow, guarded and trepid. Maybe she only moved at one mile per hour. That would mean that she had gone perhaps thirty miles altogether. Thirty miles in reality was not that far for a country road. Given the even terrain of a valley floor it was not altogether unfeasible that such a road would be as straight as any milled board. She was beginning to realize that this road she was upon was not entirely dismissed from the laws that govern nature and that it was not prima facie evidence that she had entered the afterlife. Perhaps she was still alive. With that supposition came a host of worries. All those elements of the life of the girl known as Thora Meadowford could not be simply written off. They could all still be very real. Becky's future was something to worry about as was her father's verdict and the family's impending financial doom. She was still answerable to what had happened to Margaret Whattam. If this were a real road in the real world then it will come to an end eventually and it will join up to other roads that will join roads that lead to Pioneer Lake. Either alive or dead Thora was determined to go to the lake, to her sanctuary from all the madness that had encircled her.

Then as the night was just about to fall the girl witnessed something that she would have never believed she would see again. In the distance with some moonlight glinting off its hood was a car. It was not any car. Its hue was not black like every other car in the county. This car was red. It was Margaret Whattam's car! It was not parked at the side of the road. It sat right dead center of it. Its driver did not show any concern for it. He or she just left it there.

All at once the fantasies that the girl had concocted about her universe disappeared in a flash. She no longer believed that she was dead for she had never felt so alive. Excitement coursed through her veins that all her misery in the last thirty-six hours had come to an end. Apprehension was making every bit of her brain work. Was the driver still there? What kind of person was he or she? Was she in danger? Why had the driver decided to stop the car? Was he or she aware that there was a thirteen-year old girl approaching? If the driver was aware what recourse was he or she going to take?

Thora almost instantaneously knew that she had to leave the road at once even though she wanted to shout out with glee that her stay in Purgatory had been reprieved and staved. Being alive meant that there was a survival instinct in her. That instinct had appeared to be gone when she believed that she was dead. But it was here now and making its presence felt in an undeniable fashion. She had not traveled all of that distance for naught. She had to do something to ensure that she stayed alive.

Slipping off the road and into the tangle of bushes at its side, Thora moved stealthily forward. Her eyes had acclimated to the growing darkness and she was able to see most of the roots and branches that would give her presence away if she were to step upon them. She had not dipped too far into the forest—just far enough so that she felt relatively safe that any occupant in the car would not see her yet she would still be able to see the vehicle.

Nothing moved in it as she continued moving forward. The mosquitoes of the evening had spotted her and were beginning their assault upon her in unending waves. She could not afford herself the luxury to swat them away. To do so might blow her cover. She had to shut her mind from them and ignore their paltry existences. Like a predator of the forest she moved onward, oblivious to everything but her prey—the car.

The darkness was a hindrance. It made it hard to see through the windows. There were a few moments where she thought that she detected something moving inside but each time it turned out that all she saw were tricks of her eyes as they tried to accustom themselves to the difficult luminescence of the moonlit night. She had mistaken the top of the steering wheel a couple of times as the pate of someone's head. She wished that if there was someone in the car that they would make their presence felt with certainty. She did not relish coming up to the side of the vehicle to discover someone hidden inside. She thought of calling out to the car and letting its occupant know that there was somebody approaching but she did not know what kind of person would be in there. It was more than likely that the person would not be somebody trustworthy. Afterall, the person had stolen the car. That was as good as any sign of the moral scruples of the individual.

She continued onward until she was directly adjacent to the red car. She was hidden in the roadside vegetation. The car looked undamaged. It did not seem to have been involved in any accident or experience any major mechanical breakdowns. From where she skulked she could not see anybody in it. That did not however rule out that the vehicle was vacant. A person could be sleeping upon the seats. Taking a deep breath, she built the courage to venture towards the car. All her senses were attenuated, particularly her hearing. The hum of the mosquitoes and the peeping of frogs from within the forest made it difficult to isolate other sounds but as far as she knew her ears could not pick up on anything else.

She was beside the car now. She had crept across the road as low as she could get to avoid having her body seen by lurking eyes within the cab. She listened intently. Her breathing was so loud that she was sure that it could be heard by anyone inside of the car. She slowly started to rise, when there was a snap in the forest behind her. The sound startled her. Her elbow bumped against the car door causing a low thud that would certainly vibrate inside the automobile. Her eyes dashed back to the trees to see what produced the unexpected sound. They could see nothing.

She could hear nothing from inside of the car either. If someone were in there they would have known of her presence by now. She stood up. It was no use trying to use the element of surprise any longer. She peered through the window of the car. Seeing the neat trimmings of the upholstery and the careful manufacturing of the dash and steering wheel produced an aura of comfort in the girl. It made her feel warm inside. It brought out sensations of being in a welcoming home. It made her think of Margaret Whattam and the good intentions that the girl had believed the woman possessed. It was so far removed from the uncontrollable wilds of the forest. Her eyes slowly moved to the backseat of the vehicle, almost afraid to look. There was nobody there.

The car was abandoned. She placed her hand on the hood. It possessed the same temperature as the air. It had been abandoned some time ago. She went around to the driver side and saw footprints in the gravel. They were a man's footprints. The shoe size was broad but not overwhelmingly long. The imprint of the sole showed that the shoe was in relatively good shape—not the tattered footwear that one would associate with vagabonds of the road.

Her eyes followed the path of the tracks. She had expected to see them make a course straight down the road. But the actual trail did not follow expectations. It almost immediately veered off to her right and into the dark forest, into the very area where she had heard the snap before.

Was he out there right now watching her? A very creepy sensation came over the girl as she lifted her eyes into the undergrowth beneath the trees. Was there someone lurking in there, ready to pounce upon her? A chill went through her body. She was feeling frozen. She did not know what to do. Her eyes slid back down to the interior of the car. She was desperately trying to see if there was something inside of it that she could use as a weapon. She could detect nothing usable.

There was another snap in the trees. Thora jumped and then she bolted down the road as fast as she could. She did not dare look behind her in fear that she would see some crazed lunatic with some hideous knife racing after her. She ran until her lungs demanded that she stop and then she ran some more. Finally her legs would not take another step. She had to stop. As she did so, she snuck a peek behind her. At first there was nothing there just the car sitting in the moonlight. She was surprised at how little distance she had made. She had expected that she had gone quite a bit further. Then as she sat catching her breath she saw something move out of the forest. It was the size of a large loaf of bread. Judging by the shape of its body, Thora realized that it was just a porcupine. Was it this creature that made the snapping that sent her off in near raving terror?

The lumbering creature headed directly for the car. It did not seem very cautious. It acted like it was walking upon safe ground. It had been here before and it had grown accustomed to the presence of the metal and rubber human artifact. Thora watched from her relative safe distance as the porcupine began chewing upon the front tire of the vehicle. They had porcupines occasionally on Black Island and they did present a problem. They seemed to like gnawing upon anything coated with a resin. Uncle Thaddeus despised the creatures and once charged at one with axe in hand to hack the animal to death. Its quills were no match to the heavy head of the old man's woodcutter. The girl had never seen the grizzly act itself but she saw the mutilated carcass that Uncle Thaddeus tossed into the water for the sunfish, perch and crayfish to eat. Ever since then she had a soft spot in her heart for the porkies as the family called them.

She was beginning to feel somewhat better. Her breath had been caught and she was starting to have her doubts that the man who drove the car was still in the vicinity. This car could have been abandoned a day ago already, she reasoned. It would have traveled far faster than she could ever walk. Whoever was in it would be long gone. As she watched the porcupine peaceably chew at the tire, she believed that she could almost hear it masticating. What a tasty find for the little animal! Despite their formidable arsenal that they carried on their backs, Thora found the creatures to be cute. They had the sweetest teddy bear eyes.

Suddenly something roared. Its sound echoed through the narrow of the road and caused the girl to jump. Looking down the road toward the car she saw that it had come alive. Its headlights were turned on and she could see the startled porcupine petrified before them. The car screeched forward and mercilessly ran over the animal's head and it was now coming straight at her.

She knew that if she did not move that she would share the same fate as the hapless porcupine. She started dashing to the roadside as Margaret Whattam's car was targeting her in its blinding beams.

Thora had to leap to get out of the way. She crashed into the bramble just as the car raced by her. She kept low and crawled further into the protective cover. Her heart was pounding and her hands were shaking so much that they could not give her balance as she slipped deeper towards the trees.

She heard the car slam on its brakes. Their eerie cry was like a banshee screaming its fury. The vehicle was going to come around back for her. She could not afford to just simply lie and wait in the hope that she would not be seen. She had to get out of here. She had to get to a place where a car could not go. She had to go into the forest. She stood up and looked towards the road. The first thing she saw in the car's headlights was the squirming body of the porcupine. It was in its death rattle. The car itself was roaring back towards it and the girl. There was no more time left to just watch. Thora raced into the trees and began scrambling through them. It almost seemed like they had designs to catch her and hold her for the crazed driver in the car. Their branches and their roots seemed to come alive and try to trip her up. She did her best to avoid them.

Behind her she could hear the brakes once more. The car had come to a stop at the place where she had left the road. The driver was definitely aware of her and it appeared that the driver was going to come after her. Thora was not going to give him a chance.

She continued racing through the trees. She could feel the soggy earth beneath her feet begin to slowly rise in elevation. She did not care how much noise she was making. It was no time to be careful. She ran wildly and furiously through the thick underbrush, its bramble catching hold of her clothing and ripping it and shredding it. She was sure that the driver was now running after her. Who was he? What malicious intent did he have? She did not want to find out. She ran a long time without looking behind her. When she finally did dare to look back she was able to see the stationary headlights of the car on the road way down below her. But these were not the lights that had drawn her attention. What drew her eyes was the lone light that was moving swiftly through the forest between the parked car and her. He had a flashlight! He had an advantage over her!

There was no time to be a deer caught in the headlights of a car. She had to continue moving and to try and carve an untraceable route through the trees. This would be hard to do given that the wet ground was perfectly inscribing her footprints. How she wished that she were still on the road and in her Purgatory! There was a kind of safety there. When you are dead nobody can kill you.

The land was climbing upward at an accelerated angle. It was growing more difficult purchasing sound footing. Several times her feet began to slide on the slimy forest surface. The person with the flashlight was gaining on her and seemingly not having any trouble with the slick ground. It made Thora begin to wonder if this man were indeed a living human being. She had too many encounters with the dead to rule them out. A ghost would not have difficulty navigating the ground but then again a ghost would not need a flashlight.

She continued scrambling upward. The land was doing all that it could to hamper her progress. She was slipping and sliding and found that quite often she was using all four limbs in her wild race to safety. Her breath had become pants, a searing pain was issuing from her chest. She was growing exhausted.

Yet her pursuer kept on coming. It was like he was driven with a madness to catch and kill her. She could not understand why he would want her dead but she was not going to question him on his motivations. She ignored her pains and her shortness of breath and continued pushing herself until she could not push herself any longer.

She had no idea about the terrain that she found herself. It was littered with trees both standing and fallen. It had so many rocks poke out of the ground that nothing could run at a full gallop upon them. She feared that one of them would eventually catch her toe and send her crashing to the ground. It almost seemed inevitable.

And then the inevitable happened. Her shoe did not clear the point of a particularly sharp rock. She lost her balance and went chest-first against the ground. She knew that she had to get up but her energy had been spent. She had nothing left. She was now preparing herself to become the driver's victim.

The light was only fifty feet away from her. The man that held the flashlight could not be seen as he was hidden behind the beam's blinding glare. He had done an amazing bit of tracking to follow her through the tangles and weaves of this gnarly night forest.

"Okay, I give up!" she called out to him. She had armed herself with a large rock that her fingers had the good fortune of discovering just below the surface. It was a solid stone with many sharp edges that could inflict damage. It was her intention not to go down without a fight.

"Miss Meadowford? Is that you?"

Chapter 33

Encounter in the Darkness

The masculine voice was immediately familiar to Thora. She had heard it before. She had heard it relatively recently. But she did not know to whom it belonged. She did not accept it as the voice of a friend. She did not let go of the stone that she clutched in her hand.

"It's me," she said out loud.

"What in God blazes are you doing out here?" the man cried.

Thora could see the flashlight working its way up to her. He had still yet to place her in its beams.

"You tell me what you are doing out here!" she said defiantly to the man. She still could not place him but his identity was at the very cusp of recognition. "At least I am not here trying to kill anybody!" she added.

"And neither am I!" the man responded.

"Then why did you try to run me down and then chase after me like a mental maniac!" she blurted.

"Who said that I tried to run you down!" the man said. His flashlight was moving to the left and then to the right as it tried to hone in on the girl.

"I said that you tried to run me down!" Thora railed. She discovered that she was now more angry than scared. "You started that car and pushed the gas pedal right to the floor! I was right in the middle of your headlights!"

"Was that you? I thought that it was a deer!" the man responded.

"Do I look like a deer?" Thora demanded as the man's flashlight finally fell upon her.

"Thora Meadowford!" the man said. He kept the flashlight firmly fixed on Thora's face. "So we meet again!"

She still did not know who he was. His identity just kept itself in the offing, just slightly outside of her ability to recall.

"Do you always try to run over deer?" she asked.

"I'm a hungry man! I have not had anything to eat in nearly two days. Not since I left town in rather a hurry." The man was now only feet away from her. She moved her arm and the rock behind her so that the flashlight could not pick it up.

"Why did you leave town in a hurry?" the girl responded.

"Come on Thora, you are a smart girl. I think that you could figure that one out."

All at once the man's identity came into focus. "Bewdley Beacon!" she cried out. It was Bewdley Beacon, the man that had been Uncle Thaddeus' servant, the man that got fired for his noisy sleeping habits, the man that the police had taken away, and the man that was wanted for murder near his Buffalo home.

"At your service!" Bewdley said coyly, shining the flashlight under his chin to display his oversized, thick features and a smile that Thora at once labeled as hideous.

"You are supposed to be in jail!" the girl said, as she straightened her knees and stood up. Bewdley Beacon was one of the last people that she would have expected to see out here. Bewdley Beacon was one of the last people that she would have wanted to meet out here. There was something fundamentally untrustworthy about the fellow, something shady and something evil about him. She kept her stone behind her back. She was not going to let go of it yet.

"I'm not any longer!" Bewdley grinned. "I didn't like my prospects in there. I think that they were fixing to have me take a seat on a chair that would not treat my bottom too well! So I broke out!"

"But how? They had you locked up behind two sets of doors!"

"Doors have keys, Miss. I just borrowed the keys from the man who held them."

Thora thought for a moment of the bureaucratic policeman that looked after the Grappling Haven jail. She had eventually befriended him. He had called the Pine Street house several times since her initial visit to the police station when her father received his bail. His calls were ostensibly just to find out if Rebecca had returned home so that he could pull down her missing person notice. He liked to keep his public message board current. Quite often the missing would come back home but nobody would bother to notify the police, he said. After Thora told him that her sister was still on the lam, the policeman turned the conversation around and asked how she was doing. She learned that the policeman's name was Sergeant Peter Kyle. She wondered if Sergeant Kyle's message board now contained a notice about her.

"Do you mean Sergeant Kyle?" she asked the man behind the flashlight. "You didn't hurt him, did you?" Peter Kyle was the father of four teenaged sons whom he cared for dearly. Thora did not personally know any of the sons as they were older than her but they had attended the same school that she did and all four of them had been lionized for their athletic prowess in track and field.

"Let's just say that I had to do what I had to do. Sergeant Kyle was not very willing to give me the keys!" Bewdley snidely retorted. "I daresay that my lawyer will be a busy man if they ever catch me!"

Thora remembered that James Whattam had agreed to accept Bewdley as a client much to her chagrin and the chagrin of the family. Mr. Whattam was going to defend this despicable drifter that had left a trail of crime and victims along his path. She did not know much more of the details regarding the defense and how that story was developing. Margaret Whattam never talked about the Beacon case with her. "I think that you might have lost your lawyer, Mr. Beacon. That is his wife's car that you have stolen!" she sarcastically laughed.

"I gathered that when I scoured through it looking for a bite to eat. There was not so much as a candy bar in there but there were plenty of notes in the glove box with the Whattam name on it. What in the devil was her car doing out here on this forsaken road? And where is she? I have a suspicion that she is at home just wondering what happened to her car and I have a suspicion that I was not the first thief to get behind that steering wheel."

"Are you insinuating that I stole the car?" Thora cried out. Inside she was thankful that Bewdley seemed to be unaware that Mrs. Whattam was out here in the wilderness as well and not comfortably at home filling out paperwork regarding a stolen vehicle.

"By your very words to me on the morning that we met you are an accomplished driver. And I only see you out here. I don't see Mrs. Whattam. That tells me that you engaged in some joyriding, Miss Meadowford."

The girl was about to deny the man's conjectures when it occurred to her that it would be prudent for her to let him think such. She did not want him to know that the last she saw of Margaret Whattam, the woman had a hatchet in her side and was dying next to a bed where a corpse lay in a dark room of a remote cabin along this very road.

"So we are both fugitives from the law," Bewdley said, stepping closer to the girl.

Thora rotated the stone in her hand behind her back. She was working it so that the most damaging surface would be available to her when she needed it. As far as she could see Bewdley Beacon was unarmed save for the flashlight. It appeared that it could be all the weapon that the man needed to inflict some skull-crushing punishment upon her. She could not determine what exactly Bewdley's intentions were. She highly doubted that they could be friendly. "I'm not a fugitive!" she spat, her voice clearly betraying the anxiety that she was feeling.

"Stealing a car is an offence, young lady! They will put you into reform school when they catch you!" Bewdley retorted. He was still narrowing the gap between them.

"You stay where you are!" Thora demanded, pulling the stone out from behind her back and holding it threateningly at the man.

Bewdley suddenly laughed. "What are you going to do with that?" he scoffed. "If you beat my brains in with it then it is certain that you will be incarcerated, young lady. Is that what you want?"

"You just stay back!" she glowered. "Toss the flashlight onto the ground or I will wing this stone right at your ugly face!" She did not know if her threat packed any wallop. By the smirk on Bewdley's lips it did not appear to scare him at all. Yet, despite the smirk, Bewdley flicked the flashlight ahead of him. It landed at Thora's feet. The light was pointing directly at her. She could not see past it. Bewdley was lost in the shadows. She was sure that he was going to jump her when she reached down to pick up the lantern. "If you try anything I will smash this rock right through your lousy teeth!" she warned as she slowly bent her knees to reach the flashlight. She swiftly scooped it up and turned its beam in the direction of the man.

He was there. He had not moved. She could not understand why he was still there and why he did not move. It would have been his perfect opportunity to turn around the advantage in this standoff.

He was still smirking. "Now that you have the upper hand, Miss Meadowford, what do you propose to do? Take me back to Grappling Haven and get whatever paltry reward they have on my head?"

Thora had not thought past this moment. Going back to Grappling Haven and returning an escaped criminal to behind bars would go a long way toward clearing her name in town. She could inform the police about Mrs. Whattam and Mrs. Bianco. Perhaps Margaret's life could be saved if she were still alive. The incident that took place at the cabin was an accident as far as Thora was concerned. She was not the hand that thrust the hatchet into the woman's side. When the dubiousness of those events were coupled with the girl's heroic deed in capturing a dangerous murderer the townspeople would not want to condemn her to a life in an asylum. She would have their sympathy. She would be invited to more dinners around the community.

But the town would still remember that she was the daughter of Langley Meadowford and they would hold their prejudices against the arrogant family that believed that they were above the law. They believed that Langley was responsible for the deaths of the Rozelle family. They would believe that she was behind all the mayhem at the cabin and they would not rest easy until she was safely locked away.

"You did it, didn't you?" she addressed Bewdley Beacon.

"I did what?"

"You were the one that killed the Rozelles!" she charged. "You took Thaddeus' Bentley out after I went to bed. You hunted down the Rozelles with that car and used it to slay them!" This was not the way that Thora had seen the events of that night but when she saw how nobody else would listen to her version she was trying to discover another plausible explanation for the missing limousine.

"Girl, I had nothing to do with that unfortunate incident," Bewdley responded.

"Then what happened to Thaddeus' car?" she demanded to know. "It was not there in the driveway the next morning. I know for a fact that I had driven it to his place that night!"

"You already know my account for that evening," the man said. "I'm telling you this as God's truth! I woke up that night shortly after you had left my bedroom. I came out for a drink of water when I heard something outside. Taking a peak out the window I saw a man climb into the car and drive it away."

"How come you did nothing to stop the man? How come you didn't let Uncle Thaddeus know?"

"I was very groggy at that moment, child. I was barely awake. For all I knew it could have been Del the chauffeur just moving the vehicle into the garage. I saw no reason for upsetting the whole house for a case of mistaken identity. It wasn't until I met your father in jail did I realize with certainty that he was the man that had taken the car that night."

The way that Bewdley spoke seemed to be entirely above board to Thora. Either he was a good actor or he was speaking the God's truth as he described it. Yet there was something that disturbed the girl about the account. She had seen the ambulance and the police car racing out of town while she drove Uncle Thaddeus' Bentley home. This had to mean that the accident had already taken place. And she knew that there was a second Bentley. She had seen the Rozelles climb into it. She had seen the ghost of her great grandfather behind the wheel. The events of that night were still dizzy to her. She still could not come up with a rational explanation for what had happened.

"Are we going to just sit out here in this forest all night long and be the fodder to the mosquitoes?" Bewdley Beacon asked, snapping her out of her thoughts.

Thora looked at the man standing fully illuminated in the beam of the flashlight. She had a feeling that she was going to be spending some time with this dangerous man.

"We have a car down there available to us," Bewdley went on. "Wouldn't it be wise to get inside of it and away from these infernal creatures?"

The girl saw the wisdom in the suggestion and gave her consent to the plan. She followed behind Bewdley as they worked their way down the forest-covered slope to Mrs. Whattam's car. Thora held onto the flashlight and the rock and she was prepared to use either upon the man's cranium if he pulled any stunts.

But Bewdley Beacon did not pull any stunts. He made as direct a passage to the car as possible through the undergrowth in the darkness. When they reached the road he turned around to Thora and asked, "Who drives? Me or you?"

Thora had no intention of getting behind the wheel. She would lose control of the situation if she were the driver. She told Bewdley to drive. Once they were settled in the car Bewdley turned to Thora. "Where to, Ma'am?" the man said in a parody of a highly sophisticated British chauffeur.

She had been thinking all during their descent down the hill about where they were going to go. Although she knew that returning to Grappling Haven held its attractions and may have been the most prudent route to take but by the time Bewdley's question was put to her she had decided to rule that alternative out. Grappling Haven spelled trouble to her, immediate trouble with very quick consequences. She held no desire for quick consequences. She needed time. "We go that away!" she said, pointing the still-lit flashlight straight ahead down the road in the opposite direction from town.

"I don't think that there is any need for the light any longer," Bewdley said. "We are probably going to want to conserve our batteries." As Thora turned out the light, Bewdley placed the car into gear and began driving down the road into the darkness.

Chapter 34

The Fugitives

The first thing Thora noticed as the car started down the road was the fuel gauge. It was reading less than a quarter of a tank. She did not know how far that would get them. She hoped that it would get them far enough to reach the next gas station. And even if there was enough gas to get them that far she wondered if they had enough money to pay for it. She didn't have a penny on her. If Bewdley had escaped from jail he very well could not have much in the way of coinage in his pockets as well.

"Have you got any money?" she asked him, pointing the flashlight toward the fuel gauge.

"We're not going to be wasting any money on filling the tank," the man said. "We can't be entering any settlements with this car. It will most certainly have been reported as stolen by now and people will have their eyes open for it, especially with its flamboyant red color. It is a flag to anybody that may be aware that it has been stolen."

Even though the man was right, Thora could not help but grunt her disappointment. She had believed that she had been through with walking and that they would have driven this vehicle all the way up to Pioneer Lake. It was still her intention to go there. She did not particularly relish the idea of taking Mr. Beacon along with her but she hoped by the time that they started getting near to her beloved lake country that she would be able to ditch the man.

"How far will this gas get us?" she asked.

"Maybe another twenty miles or so," Bewdley answered. "But we will be abandoning the car long before the gas runs out."

"Why's that?"

"The engine is overheating. If it hadn't overheated already then I would have been long gone and you would still be out here walking in the middle of nowhere. But you must have been aware of that," he said, turning his head towards her and looking at her suspiciously. "Why else did you stop where you stopped, where I found the car."

Thora was not about to tell the man that the car was where he found it because someone lived there. If she were to do so Bewdley might get it into his head that Mrs. Bianco's place might make the ideal place to wait and hide while the heat to capture him cooled down. She did not want him turning around and going back. She did not want him to know that Mrs. Whattam, either dead or alive, was back there. "So what did you do after the car overheated?" she asked him, trying to deflect the attention from her. "That had to have happened almost a day ago already!"

"I did what my nature told me to do," Bewdley replied. "I slept."

"You slept?" Thora started to laugh. "You have the police after you and you decide to go to sleep in the middle of the road in a stolen car? You don't sound like a very smart man, Mr. Beacon."

"What else was there for me to do, young lady?" Bewdley grinned. "I had a very exhausting day yesterday. Escaping from jail is not exactly a sedentary activity, I will have you know! I daresay that I have not run so much since I was a child. Maybe I ran more yesterday than I did in all of my boyhood. Had I not found the car I do believe that I would have dropped dead from all of the exertion!"

"That is quite the distance between here and the town," Thora commented. "You could not have possibly run all that way. You must have had help along the way. How else would you be able to go that far without being captured?"

Bewdley chuckled. "The police car parked in front of the building did lend a helping hand!" he admitted. "Sergeant Kyle kept the keys to it in his jacket pocket. I drove the cruiser as far as the ridges." He reached for something on the dash. A moment later the top of his head sported a policeman's cap. "I borrowed this from the police station as well lest anybody got suspicious why a civilian was driving around in a copper's car."

The police cap was several sizes too small for Bewdley's head. "It looks ridiculous on you!" Thora remarked. She could feel a trace of laughter at the back of her throat as she found it amusing. She did all that she could to suppress it.

"So why did you give the police car up?" she asked. "Surely it was a better car than this one?"

"It was the damnedest thing!" Bewdley said. "I was going up that long hill with all of the curves when suddenly there was a deer in front of me."

"So you swerved to miss the deer and drove the car over the cliff!" Thora finished the man's story, wondering whether it was the same deer that had nearly cost Mrs. Whattam and her their lives. Was the deer some sort of ghostly sentinel watching over the mountain and keeping people away from Mrs. Bianco's place? Was the deer meant to keep watch on approaching vehicles and keep them off this road? Was that the reason why this road was so deserted?

"That isn't exactly right," Bewdley responded. "I'm not going to endanger my life so that a forest creature can survive. I hit the deer with the car but the animal got caught in my wheel well and caused me to start spinning. Luckily I had the presence of mind to jump from the car just before it and the deer flew over the cliff."

At once Thora felt sympathy for the creature and anger towards this cruel man who showed such disdain for the sanctity of life. She recalled the spasming porcupine from earlier in the evening. That had been done willfully by Bewdley. She found nothing charming about the man. She wished that it had been him that was caught in the wheel well rather than the deer.

"I hiked down the other side of the mountain and when near collapse from exhaustion I discovered the car," Bewdley continued.

"That's not very far from the top of the mountain to…" Thora stopped. She was about to say Mrs. Bianco's place, but she checked herself before she blurted it. She looked to the man to see if he picked up on her mistake. If he did, he was not showing it. She continued, using a new phrase that would not lead her down to the same error again. "You must not be a very healthy man if that little trek exhausted you and caused you to sleep almost a day afterwards. I believe that you must be a lazy man, Mr. Beacon." She could not hide her disgust for the man that sat beside her. His flabby gut hung over his belt and everything about the man spoke of someone that spent a lifetime of slovenliness.

"Like I said the car overheated so what else could I do? I had noticed that not one car had driven down the road in all of that time that I walked and drove upon it. I felt relatively safe to take a quick nap."

"And that nap turned into a day of sleep! You could have gotten out of the car and started walking!" Thora said.

"I did get out of the car when I saw you approaching," Bewdley answered. "I snuck into the bramble and hid and watched you investigate the car. When you walked away I crept back inside of the car. I could not handle sitting outside with the mosquitoes any longer. I was going to bide my time and let you disappear on the road up ahead. But that was when you turned around and looked back."

"And that is when you started the engine and tried to run me down!" Thora cried. "I thought that you said that you thought I was a deer!"

"This is the forest primeval my dear! The law of the jungle prevails here. It is the survival of the fittest and I had to ensure that I survived!"

"With the help of a car! Without it you would have been dead long ago for you are not fit!" the girl spat. Any burgeoning trust that she may have developed in the man was gone. She knew that Bewdley would kill her the first chance that he got.

"I did not know that it was you Miss Meadowford," Bewdley responded. "Had I known it was you I would have not gone to such extremes!"

"Baloney!" Thora snapped. "It was because you knew that it was me that you tried to run me down! You knew that I could identify you. Had I been a stranger you would have just sat quietly in the car and let me disappear." She felt the flashlight in her hand. It felt so inadequate as a means for defending herself. Bewdley Beacon was an extremely dangerous man. She wished that she had something more lethal to protect herself.

"Let's stop all of these accusations, shall we?" the driver said. "Whatever is past is past. We are together now, two criminals on the lam. It is time that we forge a fellowship to see to it that we retain our liberty and not have justice descend upon us."

The girl agreed but told herself not to get lulled into complacency. The man was not to be trusted. She would have to keep her guard up at all times.

The headlights of the car illuminated the stretch of road ahead of it. It was more of this dreary straightaway through the valley floor. How could a road be so ceaselessly droll? The distance that they went in the car in the few short minutes that they drove would have taken her hours on foot. The monotony of driving through a tunnel in the trees was having an effect upon her. She was beginning to feel very drowsy. It had been so long since she last slept. Her body no longer craved sleep. It demanded it. Yet Thora fought back against the urges within her. She had to remain alert lest the well-rested Mr. Beacon would take advantage of her.

"Do you sometimes wonder if you and I have not wandered past Perdition's gate?" Bewdley said to her, snapping her out of a near somnambulistic state.

"What do you mean?" she said through a yawn.

"This road is nothing like any road that I have encountered before," Bewdley said. "I never have witnessed anything so featureless. It just seems to continue and continue mile after mile without any significant changes whatsoever. It almost makes me feel like I am on the highway to Hell."

In the back of her mind Thora was pleased to hear such a comment come from somebody else. She had the same feeling about the road. Yet she was not going to admit this to Mr. Beacon. She did not want this commonality of experience become something that would create a bond between the two of them. He was a loathsome, despicable man and she was not going to befriend him. "To go to Hell means that you have had to die. I don't remember dying. Do you?"

"No, I don't either," Bewdley said. "But this engine of ours may soon die. It is beginning to knock just like it did yesterday before it overheated. Drat, I had hoped that we would have found some semblance of civilization before it gave up the ghost."

There was no semblance of civilization to be seen in the distance ahead of them. It was just the same trees adding definition to the parallel contours of the road. "How long before it dies?" Thora asked. She had hoped for the same thing as him.

"I got maybe five more miles on it yesterday when it first began to sputter. Maybe we will get the same out of it today."

"What if you pee into the rad?" the girl suggested.

"I beg your pardon?"

"One time on the way to Pioneer Lake our car was starting to overheat just like this one. My dad stopped the car and seeing that we had no other available liquids he had all of us pee into a bottle. He poured this bottle into the radiator and it bought us enough time to get to a gas station where we got properly serviced."

"I am not going to do anything so boorish as that!" Bewdley squawked. "Besides I don't need a pee. I had relieved myself in the forest when you first approached the car. Do you need a pee?"

As strange as it seemed for she had not gone in all of the time that she was on this road, Thora did not need a pee.

"Well then," Bewdley said when he saw that there was no answer coming from the girl, "It seems like your idea is all for naught."

About two miles later steam was starting to slip out from the edges of the car's hood. The sequence of overheating was beginning. It would not be long now before the radiator would overflow and the engine becomes so hot that it could no longer function. Thora glanced past the steam and onto the road that was being illuminated by the headlights. It was more of the same. Their hopes were dashed. They were not going to be getting off the road any time soon. "So what do you propose to do now?" she asked her partner who was drawing the overheating vehicle to a halt. "Go to sleep?" She said it sarcastically but in truth there was nothing more that she would rather do. She had been taxed to her very limits and could not endure much more.

"Sleep is a luxury that we cannot afford," Bewdley responded. His eyes were looking up into the rearview mirror.

At that moment whatever he was looking at caught her eye as well. There was some light far in the distance behind them. "What is it?" she gasped, suddenly feeling a surge in her veins.

"It's another car!" the man answered.

"Another car?" She had grown so accustomed to the virtual emptiness of this road that the likelihood of seeing someone else driving it seemed as impossible as winning the jackpot in the Irish Derby.

"Quick! Get out of the car and make for the woods!" Bewdley commanded. "We don't want to be discovered." He was already crawling out of his door.

The two fugitives slipped into the underbrush and traveled several hundred feet in the dense tangle. Then they ran parallel to the road for several hundred feet before cutting across the road and onto its other side. They went through the brush until they found a spot that gave them sufficient concealment yet offered them an unobstructed view of the road.

"He is going to stop, you know that," Thora whispered. "He'll see our tracks and he will find us."

"He will be looking for us on the other side of the road, he won't discover that we have crossed over for some time yet," Bewdley said in a low voice. "I have a plan!" He outlined his strategy to Thora as they watched the approaching vehicle draw nearer. As it did so more definition was added to it and they saw that it was not just any car driving up but a police car.

As soon as the police car's headlights shone on the stranded red car in the middle of the road it turned on its flashers. Its siren was nearly deafening in the forest, the acoustics of the valley served to amplify the scream and added additional harmonics to it. It was one of the most frightening moments Thora had to ever endure. Its wail sounded as though all of the minions of Hell were suddenly descending upon her. Yet she and Bewdley Beacon did not scramble away. They remained in their hiding spot. They had a plan to carry out.

The police car came to a full stop and carefully the officer inside of it stepped out, leaving the door open and the headlights on. He held a revolver pointed at the abandoned car. "Come out with your hands up!" a deep voice said in resonant tones. Thora immediately recognized the voice. It was Officer Bombino, the policeman that had interrupted the Smitty and Earl radio show the morning that her father was arrested. She knew that Officer Bombino was a very stern, deliberate man and would take no nonsense. He would shoot if he had to. Suddenly Bewdley's plan seemed so inadequate when it had to deal with Bombino as an adversary.

Bombino moved cautiously forward to the car. His pistol was sure in his hand. When he finally reached the car he sprang into a position to have his gun aim straight at the driver seat. He discovered that it was empty. He then stepped closer and began peering inside looking for hidden occupants. Upon realizing that there was nobody inside, he gazed down at the road and almost immediately spotted the pair of tracks leading into the forest. He lifted his head. As he did so he placed his hand on the hood of the car. He pulled it immediately away and started shaking it. He just learned that the engine was still hot, that would tell him that whoever was in the car could not be that far away.

Thora knew that Bombino knew precisely whom he was dealing with. He would know that it was Bewdley Beacon and Thora Meadowford out there somewhere. He may have not known previously that the two were connected but the pair of tracks, one a man's and one a girl's, were undeniable proof that Grappling Haven's two fugitives had joined up.

"I know that you are out there!" Officer Bombino called out. "And I know what you are trying to do." Much to Thora's chagrin, the policeman spun around and was facing the side of the road where she and Beacon were hiding. It almost seemed like he was looking directly at them for a moment. "Your trick might work on a green horn but not on a seasoned cop like me!" Bombino said out loud, almost as if he knew exactly where they were.

Thora wished that Bombino could get her out of this but she knew that there was nothing that the Officer could do that could help her. Her tangle of troubles in Grappling Haven was too thick for anybody to hack through and release her from its deadly strangle hold it had upon her. She remained quiet and sat perfectly still.

Bewdley Beacon also was silent and frozen in motion. He was not fool enough to give their presence away.

Bombino was still looking in their direction. Thora could almost see his ears moving as they tried to pick up on any ambient sound in the forest.

Several long moments lapsed before finally the policeman returned his gaze to the other side of the road. With his gun pointing in the direction that he was facing he slowly began following the tracks.

It was at this moment Bewdley tapped Thora on the shoulder. It was time to enact the plan. The two fugitives began creeping toward the police car. It was difficult to make their passage through the underbrush silent. Every inch of space seemed to have some branch or tangle that was all too willing to produce a snapping sound.

Bombino had not left the side of the road as of yet. Periodically his head would suddenly fling back behind him. He probably did not hear anything but Thora was sure that he was like many of the men of the area, a hunter. He would have an understanding of the tactics of the forest—including one of its oldest tricks, doubling back.

Each time that the officer did turn around, she and Bewdley would instantly freeze and not move a muscle until the other side of the road took up Bombino's attention once more. The two fugitives had made it now to a point almost adjacent to the car. Thora believed that as soon as the policeman moved into the bramble on the opposite side of the road they would make their dash.

Then finally Officer Bombino stepped into the underbrush. Thora was all ready to run like she never ran before when Bewdley's hand grabbed her by the bicep and held her back. She did not understand and was about to whisper to the man that he was blowing their opportunity, when she saw movement on the other side of the street.

Bombino suddenly reappeared in view. He had been expecting a wild dash. Somehow Bewdley Beacon had expected the policeman's expectations. The policeman boldly strode across the gravel to the fugitives' side of the road. He stood there not more than fifty feet away from them. His gun was pointing in their direction. Thora held her breath while slinking lower into the brush.

The policeman's eyes scoured the area. If it had been any lighter out the girl was sure that he would be able to see them. But then finally the policeman walked away and returned to the tracks on the other side of the road. After a moment or two of hesitation he ducked into the forest.

"Wait until he gets a little deeper in there," Bewdley whispered directly into her ear. The man's breath was hot and moist and had an unpleasant odor to it. What was she doing aligning herself with him? She should be doing all that she could to reveal their presence to Officer Bombino.

A few moments lapsed. They heard a snap in the opposite forest. It seemed to come from several hundred feet in. Once again Thora was ready to run but Bewdley held her back.

Once again Officer Bombino suddenly emerged from the forest and came to investigate on their side. Thora understood now that the policeman must have thrown a stick in the forest to produce the sound. He was trying to flush them out.

Once again Bewdley seemed to know the man's games. He and Thora remained motionless until Bombino returned to the tracks and committed himself to the opposite forest. This time Bewdley instinctively knew that the policeman was not going to be coming back. They waited a few moments until Bombino was deeper in the tangle on the other side.

And then he and Thora ran as fast as they could towards the police car. They did not run with reckless abandon although Thora's heart demanded that they should. They still had to be careful to keep as quiet as possible. Bombino had a gun and he would shoot if he had to. Thora grabbed hold of the passenger door and slipped inside while Bewdley ran around the back of the car to reach the driver's side. The girl shut the door. It made a thick thud that echoed into the forest.

Bewdley was now in the driver seat; his eyes were quickly taking a synopsis of the dash and the gear stick. As his foot plummeted down on the clutch pedal, his hand was working the gears into forward.

At that moment Officer Bombino emerged from the forest. He was running with fury imprinted on his brow. His gun was held out ahead of him and his finger was on the trigger.

The police car lunged forward so swiftly that Bewdley did not have time to steer around Margaret Whattam's car. The cruiser clipped the red vehicle and sent it into a clockwise rotation. Fortune was on the side of the fugitives for the red car fell directly into the path of the bullet released from the policeman's gun. Over the roar of the engine Thora heard Bombino swear with rage as he had to scramble past the obstructing vehicle to get a clear shot at his escaping cruiser.

They were flying down the road at breakneck speed. They were making some distance on the policeman. Bombino's second shot hit the rear window, shattering it in an explosion of broken glass. Thora felt several pieces wedge themselves into the back of her seat. But she was untouched. A quick glance over to Bewdley showed that he came out of it unscathed as well.

Bewdley Beacon was laughing with manic delight. "We've done it! We've done it!" he cried.

Thora risked looking behind her and saw Officer Bombino far back there on the road beside Mrs. Whattam's battered car. She was not feeling as elated as her partner. She still had her fears. "He's not going to be able to drive that car and come after us, is he?" she asked Bewdley anxiously.

"The engine's overheated and the front end of the car sustained considerable damage in the collision. It would take Jesus Christ himself to raise that car from the dead!" Bewdley laughed.

They were driving faster than Thora had ever gone before. She watched the speedometer eclipse one hundred miles an hour. The road was still a straightaway but ten minutes later the road did something that it had not done yet. It turned.

Bewdley slowed down to negotiate the bend in the road. As he did so a voice came on the car's radio. "Officer Bombino," a man's voice said. "Come in please."

Chapter 35

Hawkins Corners

Bewdley slowed down to negotiate the bend in the road. As he did so a voice came on the car's radio. "Officer Bombino," a man's voice called in a droll monotone. "Come in please."

Thora looked down in shock at the radio equipment sitting beneath the dash. She had not expected to hear anything. It felt like someone had suddenly joined them inside of the car.

"Ignore it," Bewdley said. He was working the car around the deep curve. The car's center of gravity had shifted and Thora found herself leaning into the man.

"Officer Bombino, report please!" the radio voice filled the car.

"Find a way to shut that damned thing off," Bewdley ordered. "That guy will continue squawking until he hears Bombino answer."

"But Bombino is not going to answer. He is stuck way back there on the road!" Thora said. She was feeling a bit giddy about the whole thing. She felt like a child taking part in a practical joke.

"It will be a long time before he sees any civilization!" the man agreed. They had made it past the bend in the road. The car was heading north now and Thora saw the first signs of dawn as the skies were lightening up.

She was still trying to find the control knobs to the radio. "I can't find the on off switch," she said to Bewdley.

"Start flicking anything or everything. Sooner or later you will hit the right button."

Thora did as she was told, clicking this and pushing that but thus far she did not get the right button for three more times the police dispatcher came over the speakers requesting for Officer Bombino to call in.

"I just can't find it," she complained to Bewdley.

"Who is this?" the police dispatcher suddenly said sending a chilling twinge into the girl's heart.

"Holy shit! You have gone and done it now!" Bewdley gasped and then bit on his lip.

"I said who is this?" the police dispatcher demanded. "Where is Officer Bombino?"

Bewdley signaled to Thora to keep quiet and not say a word. He was reaching down and trying to shut the radio off himself.

"Where is Officer Bombino?" the dispatcher repeated.

The two occupants did not reply. Then on the dispatcher's third iteration of the same question he was finally cut off mid-sentence. Bewdley had found the knob to silence the radio.

"This is no good," he growled. "They know that someone's got Bombino's car and they are going to be coming out after us. We're going to have to ditch this car soon!"

Up ahead on the road the car's headlights were beginning to illuminate a street sign. It was the first indication that they were at last coming out of the wilderness and back into domesticated lands. Thora squinted her eyes and read, 'Hawkins Corners—10 miles'.

"Hawkins Corners," she said out loud. "That name sounds familiar."

"Well, it should, shouldn't it?" Bewdley continued his growling. "It is part of your neck of the woods. All these hamlets and villages should sound familiar to you!"

"I've never been to Hawkins Corners in my life," Thora responded.

"Well, let's hope that you do get there!" the driver retorted. "Hopefully that clown on the blower has not spread word about us to whatever law they have in Hawkins Corners. You can bet that they are looking for a stolen police car. I wish that I did not tell you to play with that confounded radio!"

Thora wished that Bewdley did not as well. Yet, her mind was not overly concerned about their peril. It was busily working on a trifling detail about why the name of the village ahead was so familiar to her. Where had she heard it before? She knew that she came across it only recently.

They were speeding past more forests and they were working their way uphill into higher country. They were finally leaving that eternal infernal valley behind. Back there was a fuming policeman named Bombino. He had miles to go by foot before he would ever reach the town with the name that was driving Thora mad trying to recall its significance. Sooner or later another patrol car from Grappling Haven would pick up the policeman and they would be following after them. And probably sooner than that another patrol car from Hawkins Corners would be heading down the road to Grappling Haven on the look out for a police car.

Dawn had officially arrived. From their height on the hill Thora could see the glowing red orb of the sun lift above the horizon and send its rays over a deeply rich green terrain that carpeted everything. These were all trees. She was surprised at the immensity of the Pennsylvania wilderness. She would never have believed that it existed.

"We should be reaching town any minute now," Bewdley said. "I wonder why nobody has come out for us yet?"

"Maybe it is because it is so early in the morning?" Thora suggested. "I doubt a place as small as Hawkins Corners would have a round the clock police service."

"By God, I think you are right!" the driver exclaimed. The expression on his face took on a wholesale change. Gone were the dour brows of impending doom. They were replaced with hope. "I think that we have time to find ourselves something else to drive!"

The unending trees came to a sudden halt as they drove past the first piece of land where the conifers were cleared to make way for a homestead with cedar rail fencing and several cows chewing at the browned chutes of vegetation that broke through the rocky ground. Even though the house on the property left much to be desired it appeared almost palatial after seeing nothing but forests for so long.

They continued driving. Bewdley had not let up on the gas pedal whatsoever. They flew past the farm and then others. "Hawkins Corners," Bewdley said almost to himself. "The name suggests that two roads must meet there. I wonder where the other one leads."

"Maybe it will go to Canada," Thora replied. She had not disclosed to her companion her desire to return to the Madoqua Lakes and find refuge upon Black Island.

"Why would you want to go to Canada?" Bewdley piped, his eyebrow lifted to display his curiosity and his consideration of the suggestion. The eyebrow lowered. "No! We're not going to Canada!" he asserted. "Going to Canada means crossing the border. They would never let a pair of fugitives across!"

"All I said was that maybe the road goes to Canada! I did not say that I wanted to go there!" Thora stormed.

"Before we go anywhere we have got to get ourselves another car! Start watching the farms to see if there are any vehicles available to us."

"They all have got cars!" Thora replied. "Are we looking for something in particular?"

"All the cars I have seen so far are beat-up old wrecks that could not even get out of the driveways that they are parked in. Look for something that is late-modeled. And find one fast. Police cars draw attention. I don't want to drive into town with one."

A minute later they could see the built-up area of Hawkins Corners ahead of them. It was nothing more than a general store, a bank, a church, a school, an inn, and about five old houses that must have been built before the Civil War. Nothing resembling a police station could be seen. Bewdley noted its absence and seemed to relax some more. "Thank God for hick towns!" he sang. "They are the backbone of America!" He felt safe about driving into downtown Hawkins Corners.

There were corners in Hawkins Corners. The general store, the bank, the inn, and the church sat upon them. There was also a highway sign at the intersection. As the stolen police car came upon it, Bewdley looked over to Thora. "Which way shall we go? Left or right?" he asked.

Thora did not answer him for her eyes fell upon something that they had not realized was there before. The church had obscured it from them. There, next to the bank along the highway was a police station. More than that, there was a policeman standing outside of it, smoking a cigarette and drinking a coffee. The policeman lifted his head when he heard the approaching vehicle. The girl got the distinct impression that every passing car was something notable in such a small town.

"Holy cow!" Bewdley gasped. "We are in for it now." He chose to turn in the opposite direction of the police station.

Thora kept her eye on the policeman. He was lifting his cigarette to his mouth and seemed to be taking only a pedestrian interest in the police car from another jurisdiction. His hand came up to a wave. Behind him, the girl noted that the sign in the window of the police station said 'Closed.' She realized that the man was only arriving at work and would not have been aware of any all points bulletin warning him to be on the lookout for a stolen Grappling Haven police car. It still seemed odd that the policeman did not react to the presence of another officer in his territory. It almost seemed that the policeman was not even surprised to see the Grappling Haven car. It was like it was an everyday occurrence to him.

Bewdley and Thora drove casually onto the highway, she keeping her eye on the policeman. The cop continued to drink slowly from his coffee and actually lit up another cigarette. He seemed to be in no hurry to start another day of work.

"That was too close for my liking," Bewdley said. "We have got to change cars soon."

It was then that Thora noticed a used car lot. There had to be about thirty cars ranging from practically brand new models all the way back to the invention of the automobile. "Want to try in there?" she asked, looking behind her. The highway had curved and they no longer were in a direct line of view with the policeman.

Bewdley's eyes lit up when he saw the myriad of cars. "Let's pick one from near the back, that way it would be some time before anybody notices that it is gone." They pulled into the car lot. There was nobody there. It would be hours before whoever runs this place would show up to commence business on another lazy day.

Behind the parking lot was a ravine. Bewdley instructed Thora to climb out of the car and start checking the cars for keys. As she did so he drove the police car into the ravine and quickly hid it down there so that it would not be easily seen. By the time that he climbed out of the gully, Thora was standing beside a fairly new automobile.

"Does it have keys?" he asked.

"They all do!" Thora smiled. Hawkins Corners was a very trusting community. Any car dealer in Grappling Haven would never be so lax about security. Hoodlums like Rory McQuoid would be joyriding every night if the keys were left in the ignition.

They hopped into a black car that would not draw attention to itself; it was so run of the mill. There were five other cars alone in the parking lot that were identical to it. They pulled out of the car lot and onto the highway. Although Thora did not have her bearings she felt that they were driving in a northeasterly direction given where the low-lying sun sat in the sky. She felt more at ease now that they were not in a police vehicle. Nobody would be looking for them in this car.

The town of Hawkins Corners was drawing to an end. There were only a few more houses left before the land opened up into large tracts of soil dedicated to mixed agriculture. She was still somewhat bothered by why the town was so familiar to her. It was just at the edge of recognition for her yet it would not make that last hurdle and enter the domain of identification. Her eyes were casually reading the names on the mailboxes of the farms as they passed. People were making livelihoods out here in the middle of nowhere. Their worlds may know no other horizons than what was presented to them along this mountain road. Their realities could vastly differ from those who lived elsewhere.

Then upon a farm that was maybe five miles northeast of Hawkins Corners Thora read the name 'Myra Stanley' on a mailbox that appeared not to have been emptied in weeks. It all came to her at once. This was why Hawkins Corners was so familiar to her. This was the home of the author Myra Stanley, the woman who wrote a detailed book of the ghosts that had come to live with her.

"Stop!" Thora cried out to Bewdley.

Bewdley Beacon spun his head around to gawk at the girl. "Stop for what!" he cried, his eyes flying everywhere trying to see what would make Thora bark out the command. He was clearly panicked that there may have been approaching danger.

"That's Myra Stanley's place! We have got to visit her!" Thora squawked.

"That is whose place?" Even though Bewdley knew nothing about Myra Stanley, he had drawn the car to a halt on the shoulder of the road.

Thora explained to him who Myra was and how it would mean so very much to her if they could have a visit with the old woman. When she finished Bewdley looked at her and said, "We are not going to pay any social calls, Miss Meadowford. We are not going to advertise our presence to anybody!"

His foot stepped onto the gas and the car started moving down the highway once more.

The girl never issued a complaint. The man's reasoning was perfectly correct. Staying in the vicinity in a stolen car was an open invitation to get arrested. It was a smart move to keep moving. Besides two ghosts now occupied the back seat of the car. She was sure Bewdley did not see them and in a way she was thankful for it. She did not have to put up with his protestations and his interruptions. She could have a nice conversation with their two guests, Jakob and Truus Nells. She did not know why this could be so but she just knew that it was. She felt at peace in their company. It was the first time that she felt peace the entire summer.

Jakob and Truus had climbed into the car when Bewdley had drawn it to a rest. They simply slipped through the doors and seated themselves behind the pair of fugitives.

"Thank you for stopping," Jakob said in a thick European accent. "Usually Frau Nells and I have to jump into the moving automobiles. They go faster and faster all of the time and it gets harder for us to hop a ride. We are not spring chickens any more."

"Ya ya, Jakob, you say that as if we are ready for the grave. We worked hard all of our lives and that has made us strong," Truus chuckled. "I am Frau Nells and this is my jackass husband Herr Nells." The old woman bent forward to reach Thora's hand and give it a shake. "Jakob and I like to go for rides now and then. Being cooped up in a house can make us go crazy."

These were the ghosts that Myra Stanley wrote about in her book. These were the ghosts that Mrs. Whattam had said could not possibly exist. In fact Margaret had gone so far as to say that Myra Stanley was a fraud. Thora could see that the old spinster living outside of Hawkins Corners was the furthest thing from a fraud. The pair of ghosts in the rear seat was the proof of that. The girl stole a glance at Bewdley to see if he was aware of anything strange happening. His eyes were on the road ahead of him and he seemed to be preoccupied with whatever thoughts a man like him could possess.

"He is not a nice man," Truus said of Bewdley. "He has done bad things. I can see it in his face."

"Mama, mama. You are always saying things like that!" Jakob retorted. "You know nothing of the man. He can be a saint for all you know."

"Be quiet Jakob!" Truus glowered. "I can see it in the space of his eyes. They are narrow. Bad men always have narrow eyes!"

"I have narrow eyes! Does that mean that I am a bad man?"

"No, just a stupid man!" the old female ghost laughed. "You have a big nose. If you have narrow eyes and a big nose you are just a stupid man. But if you have narrow eyes and a pointy nose like this man then you are a bad man. Haven't you learned anything in all the years that you have been alive Jakob?"

"Maybe it is because I have narrow eyes and a big nose that I have never learned this thing!" Jakob answered. He looked toward Thora. "Never mind us, little girl. We always carry on like this. After a lifetime together we can get on each others nerves by just simply breathing!"

"I am Thora Meadowford," she introduced herself to the spiritual passengers. As she did so she looked over to Bewdley.

"I know who you are," the driver groaned. "You must be as starved as I am to start talking so silly! We've got to find ourselves some food soon."

"How can that man say he is starved?" Truus Nells crowed. "He is as fat as a pig. He can stand to fast for a season or two!"

"Come on Mama! Leave the gentleman alone. He was kind enough to stop and give us a ride, wasn't he?" Jakob retorted in defense of Bewdley. "Tell the man that there is a restaurant up the road from here. It has the most delicious sausages in the state."

Thora relayed this information to Bewdley.

"How do you know that? I thought that you said that you had never been here before," Bewdley answered.

"I'm just guessing," Thora replied. "Every highway must have a restaurant along it and don't these roadhouses usually have the most tasty food around!" she scrambled her retort. She knew that he did not see or hear the ghosts behind him and if she were to admit their presence to him he would think her crazy. Maybe she was crazy? What made her right and him wrong? Maybe Jakob and Truus Nells were figments of her imagination that she created in her fragmented mind? But regardless if they were actually there or not in the real world they were there in her world and it was to her world that she was consigned and it is in her world that she had to live with whatever came to enter it.

"I don't think that we can risk stopping at a restaurant so close to the town we got this car. We are going to have to go farther," Bewdley sighed.

"What kind of reason is that?" Truus said crossly. "I have never heard being too close to where you buy a car as a reason why you cannot stop at a nice nearby restaurant!" Thora saw the woman with her arms folded over her chest glaring at Bewdley Beacon. Truus had swiftly determined that there was something underhanded about the man.

"If you can't stop at a restaurant then might I suggest some juicy apples," Jakob spoke up. "We will be coming to a grove shortly. The apples are just coming into season. You will see the orchard in maybe a mile or two on your right hand side."

"How do you know these things, girl?" Bewdley squawked when Thora passed on the information.

"I just do," was all that Thora could say.

Just as Jakob had said they saw some land given over to apple trees on the right. The car came to a stop and all of the occupants poured out to investigate the trees. The apples were small and green but to Thora and Bewdley's emaciated eyes they looked magnificently ripe and ready to devour. They began plucking and toting their caches to the car. They wanted a goodly supply of them for their trip.

As Bewdley and Thora picked apples, the girl saw Jakob and Truus sit upon an old fence and hold their faces upward into the sun. There seemed to be sublime pleasure etched upon their expressions. They loved the land. They loved the Earth. Maybe it was this love for the world that they were born into that kept them here. They chose this place over Heaven.

These were such pleasant ghosts. They were so unlike the spirits that resided at Josephine Bianco's cabin. They were nasty entities with gruesome dispositions. Thora felt a shiver run through her as she reflected back to that clearing in the forest. She had been shielding the memory from her consciousness for quite some time. She did not understand what happened there and how Mrs. Whattam fared. She was sure that her interpretations of the events would differ vastly from what others would conclude had happened. They would say that there were no supernatural evils lurking about the premises. They would say that she was responsible for whatever befell Margaret. They would say that she defiled the body of Mrs. Bianco. They would demand that she be locked up in an asylum for the criminally insane for the rest of her life.

When the events at Mrs. Bianco's were coupled with the night that the

Rozelles were killed Thora realized that she alone knew the truth behind it all and those who labeled themselves as sane would never accept that truth. She looked once more at the Nells ghosts as they leaned peacefully upon the fence. She doubted that anybody outside of maybe Myra Stanley would see them. People had already labeled the ghostwriter as insane. They soon would be labeling young Thora Meadowford insane as well.

Chapter 36

The Old Dutch Couple

Not a single vehicle had passed while they collected their apples and Thora recollected on incidents that she wished that never happened. In the distance the girl could see a barn. Slightly hidden behind it was a farmhouse. She doubted that there were any prying eyes watching them.

When they returned to the car Bewdley was voraciously jawing his third apple. Its juices were running down his chin. "It isn't exactly what I was looking for but I guess it has to suffice," he said in between bites.

Thora was chewing on her first apple. Its acids were tingling her tongue and gums. It was not a very tasty piece of fruit but like Bewdley said it would have to suffice.

They were driving down the road again. The Nells couple had taken their places upon the backseat. "That was very nice," Jakob said.

"It was nice but it was too short!" Truus added. "It is a beautiful morning. What is the rush? We could have sat there for another hour or so and feel the sun on our faces. Why are we in such a hurry?"

"Meadowford you said your name is," Jakob interrupted his wife.

Thora nodded.

"You are not related to Wilbur Meadowford are you?"

"I never heard of him," Thora answered out loud.

"Never heard of who?" Bewdley cut in.

Before Thora could answer, Jakob Nells went on to explain. "Wilbur Meadowford lived in a town not too far away from here, Grappling Haven. Have you heard of it?"

Once again Thora nodded and said, "I am from there." She could feel Bewdley looking at her curiously, wondering what was getting into her.

"Then you must be related to him. Wilbur died in 1812. He was killed in a skirmish with the British not very far from here. He and his wife had only one son, Dinsmore was his name. Maybe you have heard of him?"

"Sorry," Thora said. "I haven't heard of him either!"

"Who have you not heard of?" Bewdley barked. "I don't know what has gotten into you but you are babbling away like a lunatic!"

Thora could feel her face crunch up. She was growing angry with the man and his constant interruptions. "Just drive Bewdley!" she spat. "Let me live in my own fantasy world!"

At the same time Truus was haranguing her husband. "The girl is not even fifteen years old. How is she to know people that lived a hundred years ago!"

"Because Dinsmore is a distant relative of hers! I see it in her face. She has some of his features! She has the same forehead and the same square chin!" Jakob retorted in defense.

"Dinsmore Meadowford," Thora said out loud. She didn't care what Bewdley thought. "There is something vaguely familiar about that name. Did he have a son named Samuel Angus?"

"No," Jakob answered overtop of Bewdley's grunt. "Dinsmore had three sons—Martin, Zachariah and Dinsmore Junior. They all had sons of their own and I do believe that one of them was named Samuel Angus."

"Which one?" Thora was finding this conversation not only educational but also exhilarating. She knew that this was information that her father would not know.

"I can be wrong on this because Frau Nells and I had returned to the old country for several years and lost touch with our old friends but I think that it was Dinsmore Junior that had the boy named Sam."

"It was him!" Truus put in. "Martin and Zachariah were killed in the Civil War. Only Dinsmore Junior survived and he carried on the family farm in Grappling Haven until the flu killed him and most of his family."

"Killed everybody except for Samuel Angus!" Thora cried out. She remembered this part of her family history. The disease that struck the rest of his family did not cut down Samuel Angus the First. Samuel continued farming and had developed a sideline business in supplying cables to other farms in the area. Truus and Jakob had given her independent verification of the authenticity of her family background.

"Listen, if you are going to live in your fantasy world can you at least have the decency to keep it quiet!" Bewdley growled. "You scared the dickens out of me just there!" The car was only starting to settle down now after the wild swerve it endured when the man jumped at the girl's sudden cry.

"Be quiet you!" Truus growled at the man. "You are our chauffeur and not permitted to interrupt our conversations!" She swatted her hand against the back of Bewdley's neck.

The man reached back and began rubbing where he had been hit. "My neck is getting tingly," he said. "I think that we have been sitting too long."

"Yes, you are right young fraulien. Only one survived the epidemic and it was young Sam," Jakob said.

"Samuel Angus Meadowford is my great grandfather," Thora asserted proudly.

"Then you are related to Wilbur," Jakob seemed pleased.

"Yes, he is my great great great…" Thora was trying to count back the generations but was growing confused and had to start all over again.

"Just say that he is an ancestor of yours," Jakob laughed. "It is easier that way."

"Have you seen him of late?" Truus asked. She was leaning forward looking into Thora's eyes.

"Seen who?" Thora readily understood whom the old woman was talking about yet she did not want to openly confirm it until she received more input from the ghost.

"Of course she has, Mama! If she can see us then she can see others," Jakob said.

"Have you seen Samuel Angus?" Truus asked the girl directly.

"Yes I have. Several times," Thora responded. In her heart she felt a certain joy that there was someone else finally acknowledging the presence of her great grandfather. It didn't matter to her that this confirmation came from other ghosts.

"When is the last time?" Jakob asked. He seemed rather anxious.

Thora had to think back. It seemed to her that it was when her father told her mother that it was okay for her to go along with Mrs. Meadowford on the trip into the country. She did not actually see the ghost that time. She just heard him. The last time that she believed that she actually saw the ghost was the night that the Rozelles were killed. He was the driver behind the wheel of the other Bentley. She relayed this information to the Nells.

"How long ago was that?"

"Several weeks ago," Thora said. "But I have seen other spirits since. I keep seeing an Indian in a canoe. He almost seems like he is my protector."

Very grave expressions settled upon both of the ghosts. "Tell us more about the night that you last saw Samuel Angus," Jakob asked. "Was there anything different about him that night?"

"No," Thora said. "At least I did not think so at the time but when I learned later what happened I could not really understand how it could have happened. Up to that point my great grandfather always did good things for me. But that night he allowed four people to get killed and have my father blamed for it. That, I just could not understand."

Truus studied her for a moment and said, "That wasn't him."

"It was him! I saw him!" Thora protested. She did not want the ghosts to begin to deny her account as well.

"Listen my little one," Jakob said. "There are things happening that you are not aware of. All is not well in the land of the wanderers. A dark force has suddenly shown itself in the last month and it is casting its mischievous tricks both upon the world of the mortals and on those of our kind."

"This force often takes the guise of an Indian. When he paddles his canoe into your life you can expect nothing but turmoil afterwards," Truus said. Her words had a haunting echo in Thora's mind.

"I have seen this Indian several times," the girl said. "All the happiness that I have had in my life has disappeared since seeing the canoe in the sky."

"Listen," Jakob said, leaning forward to be as close to Thora as possible. "We used to have regular visits at our farmhouse from Wilbur Meadowford. I am not talking a hundred years ago but only last month. He came everyday for years. One day near the end of June he came to our house. The policeman from Grappling Haven was visiting at the same time with our descendent Myra. They were in the bedroom when Wilbur entered the house. Wilbur was wild with excitement. He told us that he had just seen the Indian in the clouds and that that Indian told him that there would be no rest for any wanderers until a great northern spirit awakes and says his name. Wilbur said that the wanderers would be divided and that terrible battles will take place between them and that those that perish would never walk the land again. He also said that those wanderers that descended from him would be the first to go as the Indian said that it was the Meadowfords that were to blame for this schism in the spiritual world. It was the last time that we ever saw Wilbur." Jakob sat back in his chair.

"The Meadowford curse!" Thora said out loud, recalling the words that her Aunt Faye had said. She had said that the dead in the family were doomed to walk the earth after they died. It now seemed from what Jakob had said that even in death her family was in danger.

"It might not have been Samuel Angus that was responsible for the deaths of that family," Truus said. "If you have not seen him since then maybe the mortals were not the only ones to have their lives taken that night."

Thora thought about it. She was thinking of what she saw at Mrs. Bianco's cabin. Had she witnessed an actual transformation? Before her mind could delve deeply into that memory she saw Truus burst into tears. "Josephine is gone!" she gasped.

"You read my mind!" the girl said. She was sure that she did not utter any of these thoughts.

"It is easier to do that than to wait for a person to find the right words to express themselves. Putting a thought into the right words quite often changes that thought," Truus said. "I have also learned from your thoughts that the night of the accident was not the last time that you came across someone that you believed to be your great grandfather. The next day you met someone at the police station whom afterwards you suspected of being Samuel Angus and that was the quiet policeman. He had left a note that you thought was meant for you. The note said, 'Do not let this happen'."

Thora recalled the occasion and explained to the Nells that the note was actually from the little boy that was being forced by his parents to go after a career in government.

"No, that is wrong," Truus said. "The note was meant for you. It came from the real Samuel Angus. I think that he is in big trouble and that he is being hunted by the Indian in the canoe." There was great fear in the old ghost's voice. "You have not seen him since? Maybe it is too late for him."

"And you have seen terrible things since then, haven't you little girl?" Jakob stated. There was concern in his eyes. "You have seen the demons take Josephine Bianco."

Thora could feel the terror growing inside of her. She had shut out most of her memories from the cabin while she journeyed on the lonesome road. She wanted to think of them as nothing but a bad nightmare that should be forgotten. She had seen the spirit of Mrs. Bianco come out of the forest. The woman had exuded nothing but charm and comfort. She had been what everybody pictures the ideal grandmother to be. But then while they chatted alongside the brook there was a change in this spirit. It grew hideous and ominous and it began spouting such awful things about the Meadowford clan. And then there was the monster in the bedroom. These were very dark beings that frightened her so immensely that the only way that she could defend herself against them was to deny their existence in her mind.

"Don't deny them their existence!" Truus warned. "You must keep your eyes open for them all of the time. If you are blind to them they will enter your life and then you will see horror on such a scale that you will be instantly corrupted and tainted and cease to exist as who you are."

"And you will become one of them!" Jakob added.

"Why me?" Thora cried out.

The car did a sudden veer and then corrected itself. Bewdley Beacon looked at her angrily. "You are scaring the shit out of me, kid!" he shouted. "You are babbling away like a lunatic. I have half a mind to toss you from the car!"

Truus glared at the man. "Tell him if he does that then you would let the police know where he is. He won't get rid of you, child. He needs you."

Thora passed on the information to Bewdley. The man smirked, "You are right, presuming that I let you live!"

A coldness enveloped the girl. Up to this point, she had not realized the capacity within the man. Bewdley Beacon was already wanted for murder and he had likely killed a policeman back in Grappling Haven. This man was not going to let her simply walk away when the time came for them to part company. She knew too much. All this talk about ghosts and demons was frightening but it still seemed one step removed from reality. Bewdley Beacon was reality in the raw.

"He's the one that strangled Josephine!" Truus Nells gasped. "I read it in his mind. He did it two months ago just before he came to work for your uncle."

"But she wasn't strangled!" Thora whispered so softly that she may have not even said it. "The rope was put around her neck long after she died."

"The stains on the bed and clothing came from the decaying stomach," Jakob explained. "There are no such acids in the neck vicinity. The rope would stay in tact."

"We have to get you away from this man," Truus said. "He is evil and he is dangerous. It is too bad that Officer Bombino was not around."

"How do you know Officer Bombino?" Thora asked. The question was meant to get the conversation sidetracked so that they would not have to dwell on all of the gloom that had appeared in the car.

Truus laughed lightly. "Officer Bombino and our descendent Myra have had a special friendship for over a year now. He comes several times a week and spends a few hours with her. I shall give you no more detail than that for you are just a little girl."

"That will explain why the Hawkins Corners policeman did not act like anything unusual happened when he saw the Grappling Haven police car," Thora said. "He was used to seeing it drive by."

"The policeman is like clockwork my child," Truus grinned. "Every Monday, Wednesday and Friday he arrives at the house at six o'clock and he stays until ten and then he leaves."

"He won't be arriving on time this morning," Thora said. "He is in the middle of nowhere without anything to drive. It will take a day before he crosses any civilization."

"I wouldn't count on that," Bewdley answered her. It told her that he heard what she was saying. "You're forgetting that the dispatcher in Grappling Haven heard our voices on his radio. They will be sending out a car to him immediately."

"But they would not know where he is," Thora said. "They don't know that he is on the road to Hawkins Corners. He could be anywhere."

"They would have sent out an all points bulletin by now to all surrounding police stations to be on the look out for a stolen police car. That cop back in town should have heard that bulletin by now," Bewdley retorted.

"He still would not act on it because as far as he is concerned he had not seen anything unusual this morning. He saw Bombino's car arrive on time on its way to Miss Stanley's house," Thora answered.

"And how do you know something like this?" Bewdley demanded. "You know nothing of anything little girl! And will you please keep your trap shut! Your babbling is driving me crazy! I can't think straight. I am trying to figure out a place for us to run but I can't think of anything because of all of your yammering!"

"Tell the man to relax!" Truus said. "There is nobody following you! No one knows anything about the two of you!"

"You are not even in a police car any more!" Jakob added. "If anybody sees you drive by they will think that you are nothing more than a father and a daughter out for a drive. There is nothing unusual about that."

Thora tried to convey this information to Bewdley but the man would have none of it. As far as he was concerned half the state troopers in Pennsylvania were on their tail.

They were driving a well-used highway now. There were cars behind them and there was oncoming traffic. They were coming up to the city of Pittsburgh. The forests and farms were giving way to residential areas. The air lost its pristine quality. It appeared discolored and tainted as they were entering the metropolis.

Jakob Nells turned to his wife, "Mama, maybe we should be thinking about going back home now?"

When Thora heard the old man ask the question a sudden fright overtook her. She did not want to be left alone with Bewdley. She felt very comfortable in the company of the ghosts and felt a certain sense of immunity from harm in their presence.

Truus Nells must have seen the desperation on Thora's face. "And why do we want to go home now? What do we have to do there? Let us spend some time with our new friend. We can always go home later."

Thora thought that Jakob would merrily accept his wife's proposal. But the old man was anything but cordial about it. "You know that they are following her and if they see us with her then the same fate that befell Wilbur and Samuel Angus could come our way."

Truus bit on her lip and tried to hide any anxiety that she may have been feeling from Thora. "We have lived a long time Jakob. Aren't you getting a little tired of it? It is the same thing every day. We get up. We go for a ride. We come back. We sit with Myra and then we go to bed. There has got to be more to life than this."

"But we will have no life if we stay with the girl," Jakob whispered, trying to keep his words hidden from Thora. But the girl heard them clearly and she realized that the Nells would have to pay a great price if they decided to stay with her. She did not really understand any of the rationale behind it but it was very evident that whatever it was it represented the gravest danger to the old Dutch couple.

"You don't have to stay with me," she said to Truus and Jakob. "I'm a big girl. I can look after myself."

"Stop babbling!" Bewdley roared. He flung a backhand towards Thora's mouth. The girl turned her head just in time to deflect the blow with her shoulder.

"He grows more dangerous all of the time!" Truus cried. "We are decent folk, Papa. Decent folk do not leave little girls in the company of murderers!"

Jakob sighed. "Yes, you are right Mama. We must get the girl away from this man as soon as possible."

"And take her home with us!" Truus added.

"I never said that," Jakob retorted. "You know and I know that that can't be possible. Sooner or later the girl is going to be found and then it would be all over for us."

"I don't want to go to your house," Thora said. "I want to go to Canada!"

"I am taking you to Canada!" Bewdley answered. "I think we will be safe from the law there." They were driving by the highway sign declaring the city limits of Pittsburgh, Pennsylvania.

Thora sat back in her chair and saw the distance fires of the steel mills. The great tufts of flame licked up into the sky. It seemed to be a vista of Hell. She realized that they would have to go through Hell to get to the paradise on the other side.

Chapter 37

Pittsburgh Pickpocket

"I think that we can let our guards down a little," Bewdley said. "There's anonymity in the big city. People don't look at each other with as careful an eye here as they do in those cloistered backwoods settlements where you come from."

"What are you trying to say Bewdley?" Thora asked. Her eyes were watching the endless stores along the busy road. There were businesses catering to everybody, to every culture that existed on the planet. The faces that walked the sidewalks were not the same kind of faces that she saw back in Grappling Haven. These were faces that came from every corner of the Earth. It was so far removed from what she had been accustomed to back in Grappling Haven.

What struck Thora the most were the flapper fashions that had permeated society. The short hairstyles accompanied by the short skirts were everywhere. It was part of the new feminine expression that came as a result of the suffragette movement. Women were liberated nowadays. They were free to pursue any kind of career that they desired. The days of the housewife were numbered. Her mother's kind was growing extinct. Even the fashionable Margaret Whattam seemed conservative compared to the ladies that strolled this busy thoroughfare.

"They look like courtesans!" Truus Nells squawked. "Where is their decency? A woman should never show her knees in public!"

"Ah, Mama, it is no different here than in Amsterdam!" Jakob laughed. "The women there are showing far more than just a pair of knobby knees!"

"You keep your eyes in your head Papa!" Truus said with disgust. "These girls would have nothing to do with an old fart like you!"

Thora chuckled. Yet when she looked out of the car's window she felt out of place. She would be a fish out of water if she went out onto the street. She hoped that Bewdley held no plans of actually getting out of the car and milling about. Pittsburgh scared her. It was not her world and she held no desire of making it her own. Yet in the rear of her mind, she possessed a frightening feeling that one day this city would be her home.

"I'm saying that we can maybe stop here and have a bite to eat and maybe even spend the night," the driver said.

"But I thought that we are going to Canada!" Thora protested.

"We are, girl! But what is the rush! We will be in your precious Canada before the week is out!" Bewdley was starting to look for a spot to park the car.

"Don't be so glum!" Jakob said to the girl. "This is what you want! The city is going to give you the chance to get away from him!"

Thora looked back at the old ghost. She wanted to tell him that even though Bewdley was an evil man he still represented her only way of getting up to Pioneer Lake. How would she get up to the island if she suddenly were to become a vagrant on the streets of Pittsburgh? She would much more likely end up like one of the flapper harlots that seemed to flood these streets than find another way to reach the wilds of the Canadian interior.

"You go to the bus station and buy a ticket for Toronto!" Truus told her. The old ghost woman had read her thoughts once again.

"But I have no money!" Thora cried out.

"Neither do I! But that is not going to stop us!" Bewdley chimed, settling the car into a diagonal parking spot.

He stepped out of the vehicle and stretched and began rubbing out the creases in his clothing. "The first thing I have to do is get me some new duds," he said. "I don't want people thinking that I am a hobo."

Thora remained seated inside of the car. She did not want to climb out. The ghosts were still behind her. "If I get a bus to Toronto will you come with me?" she asked them quietly.

Truus smiled at her. "Of course we will, little one."

"I just hope that the bus is not crowded. I would hate to have to stand all that way," Jakob put in.

"You can sit on the knobby knee of one of these street women!" Truus retorted. "That should make you happy."

"Are you going to sit in there all day?" Bewdley rapped on the window. "Come on out and stretch your legs and then we can find some real food."

Reluctantly Thora complied with his wishes. She could feel building apprehension within her as she realized that she was going to have to make a desperate move in the upcoming hours and she was not sure that she would be able to carry it off.

The mid-August heat was appalling on the Pittsburgh street. The air was rank and heavy with the odor of industry. It was difficult to breathe. She felt that she had just entered through the gate of Hell. She saw the two ghosts move through the car's door as if it were not there. Jakob and Truus Nells still dressed in the garb from their bygone era. They looked like farmers with their heavy rags draped over them.

"I smell garbage!" Truus immediately protested, her nose trying to wrinkle up into her brow.

"It's not that bad Mama. It smells much better here than fertilizing season in the spring when we have to spread the pig manure onto the land!" Jakob responded. His eyes were fixed on a pair of women dressed in the flapper uniform as they passed by. "Besides the land never has such delightful creatures crossing over it!"

"Jakob Cornelius Nells! My father warned me about you!" Truus responded, taking hold of the man's chin and averting his head so that he would look in another direction.

By now Bewdley was already walking down the sidewalk with his head held backwards telling Thora to hurry up. He would not take his eyes off her. He seemed to sense that she would bolt the minute he was not looking. Thora did what she could to hasten her gait. Her legs were somewhat stiff from all that sitting in the car. They still were not quite recuperated from her long walk down that endless country road.

There were a series of restaurants along this stretch of the block. The fare was Asian and European. The exotic aromas from their kitchens wafted into the street even at this early hour. It could not have been any later than nine in the morning yet these restaurants were already cooking up dinner. For some reason Thora recalled something that her grandfather had said about Cristo Pando's. He said that the reason he liked the place so much was because they never pre-cooked their meals. It meant a little longer wait to dine but the waiting was well worth it. These city restaurants would not compare to Cristo's. The fiery Macedonian would be a millionaire if he opened up a place in the city rather than in such a remote bumpkin town as Grappling Haven. Thora wondered why he didn't.

"All these joints are closed!" Bewdley spat as he vigorously strolled past the restaurants. "Where can a man get a bite to eat at this time of day?"

Thora was finding it difficult to keep up to the man, he moved so briskly.

"Let him get ahead of you!" Jakob said to her. He and his wife were walking beside her. They did not bother to dodge any people coming down the sidewalk in the opposite direction. They simply went right through them as if they were not there. It had stunned Thora to see this but after she saw the expressions on the faces of the passersby she realized that she was not near as stunned as they were. Their mouths would invariably drop as if they were trying to hold back a sudden rush of bile up their throats. Their eyes would become distant as they wondered where this unexpected nausea had come from.

"Yes, let him get ahead of you!" Truus urged. "As soon as he is not looking, step into a store and find a hiding place."

The girl still had mixed feelings about such a plan. She knew that Bewdley Beacon was a killer and that he held schemes for her demise. Yet she still saw him as her only viable means to getting to Canada. A bus was not an option to her since she did not have any money for the fare.

"Hurry up girl!" Bewdley called back to her. He was maybe twenty feet ahead of her and he was standing in front of a diner that was open. He did not take his eyes from her as she approached. As she stepped into listening distance he said, "I can taste the ham and eggs already!"

"How are we going to pay for this?" Thora asked him. "We don't have a penny between us."

"You are a newcomer to the road, milady!" Bewdley smiled. "There are ways and means for everything. Come on inside!" He put his hand on her back and gently nudged her through the door.

As Thora stepped into the narrow diner she was overwhelmed with the sweet aromas of breakfasts by the dozen being served to the crowded and noisy clientele. There were two stools side by side available at the counter. Bewdley pointed to them and led her there. Thora looked behind her and saw Jakob and Truus Nells standing at the entrance. They were inside but seemed somewhat hesitant to step any further in.

"What's wrong?" she called out to them. She was no longer concerned what Bewdley thought of her inexplicable behavior.

"All these people here make Mama nervous," Jakob answered.

"It is that and the smell of the bacon!" Truus added. "It makes me feel like I am going to be sick."

"Why don't you just wait outside of the door?" Thora suggested. "We'll be out as soon as we can." She turned her head back to the counter and almost jumped when she saw a redheaded waitress leaning forward toward her. The woman was looking toward the empty entrance and was wondering whom the girl was talking to.

"The child has an active imagination," Bewdley explained to the waitress. "She gets this way whenever she is famished."

"Well then we had better see to it that we give the young lady a good hearty breakfast!" the waitress grinned, revealing a mouth with some missing teeth. "What will it be, Miss?"

Thora looked over at Bewdley. Her eyes were demanding some form of answer from him to the question on how this breakfast was going to be paid.

"Go ahead and order anything you like," he said. "But make it snappy. I want to get at this food as soon as possible. I'm even hungrier than she is, you see," he smiled to the waitress.

Thora looked up at the menu sign above the waitress's shoulder and spotted the breakfast section. Pancakes jumped out at her immediately. "Can I have pancakes?" she asked and watched the waitress scribble down her order. "And if it is possible could I have blueberries in them?"

The waitress's eyes lifted above her spectacles. "I will see if we have some, if not, how about strawberries?"

Strawberries sounded wonderful to Thora. "Can I have both strawberries and blueberries if possible? And can I have some orange juice and toast as well? And jam on the toast?"

"Is that everything? No coffee?"

"I had better not drink too much. We have a long drive ahead of us today," Thora explained to the waitress. "We're going to Canada."

She felt her foot be suddenly kicked underneath of the stool. She looked over at Bewdley who signed to her that she had better not say too much.

"Canada, that is such a lovely country!" the waitress said. "I have a cousin who lives there, I think in Montreal. She says that they all speak French up there. Can you speak French?"

"Not a word of it," Thora answered. She was watching Bewdley out of the corner of her eyes to make sure that she was not revealing too much.

"Maybe you better look up my cousin if you want to get around. She'll help you with the language."

"I'll have the three eggs and ham combo," Bewdley announced cutting the woman off. The waitress's face suddenly became sharp as if someone had pinched her. "And a coffee. And a newspaper if you got one."

The waitress went to place the order. As she did so Bewdley leaned toward Thora and said, "Why did you go and tell her we are going to Canada for? The less people know about us the better."

"Canada is a big country, Mr. Beacon. It…"

"It has only so many entrances to it," Bewdley cut Thora off. "If they know that we are going to Canada they will be watching the borders."

At that moment the waitress returned with the newspaper. She placed it face down in front of Bewdley. The back page of the paper was an advertisement for a new department store opening up in Pittsburgh. "I'll be right back with your coffee," the waitress said. "How do you take it?"

"Black with two cubes of sugar," Bewdley responded coldly.

"I still don't know how you are going to pay for this?" Thora whispered to the man. "Dining and dashing would draw more attention to us than any comments made about our destination."

"No worry about that, my child," Bewdley smiled. He held up a twenty-dollar bill between his two hands. He kissed the money.

"Where did you get that?" Thora asked, noticing the man that sat beside Bewdley. This man had a fairly large hip pocket in his sports coat and she could see the top of his wallet peaking out. Bewdley had lifted the money from him and the man was none the wiser.

Her companion placed his fingers to his lips in a conspiring manner telling Thora to remain hush.

The waitress soon returned with their breakfast. "It is your lucky day, young lady!" the woman declared. "We have both strawberries and blueberries!" She set the plate in front of her.

Thora ate voraciously. She was so hungry that she could not concern herself with manners. Yet as boorishly as she ate she was not near as uncivilized and barbaric as Bewdley Beacon. The man ate with the decorum of a medieval pauper. He tore into his ham and eggs like a lion at a kill. His mouth was covered with eggs. He smacked while he chewed. If Uncle Thaddeus ever witnessed his servant eat he would have fired him long ago. There was no way that Thaddeus would put up with such ill-begotten table manners.

They were just about finished their breakfast when the man beside them suddenly blurted out, "For crying out loud! Where did it go?" He was directing the question to his dining mate, another gentleman. "I could have sworn that I had a twenty on me!"

The other man groaned, "Looks like I am paying for breakfast yet again." He was reaching into his breast pocket for his wallet. "I really wish that one day you will pay Bob. I can't afford springing for these meals all of the time."

"But I swear that I had the money on me! I saw it in my wallet this morning when I left the house."

"Yeah, likely story!" the other man said, opening up his wallet. "You are going to pay me back at work!"

From where Thora sat she could see a silver badge flash inside of this wallet. The man was a detective. Bewdley had pickpocketed a cop!

Bob looked at the floor to see if his money had fallen there but it was not to be seen. The two men left the diner. Bob's eyes were following the floor, still hoping that his missing money would appear. He walked right through Jakob Nells at the doorway. He flinched and then he disappeared.

The two ghosts had stood at that entrance patiently all the while that the girl and the man ate. Thora could see that the couple was talking to each other but she could not hear what they were saying. By the expressions they held she judged that it could not have been friendly banter. Without knowing for certain, she guessed that they must have been discussing their present circumstances. Jakob believed that it would be dangerous for he and his wife to chaperone Thora to Canada. He was convinced that some malignant force was chasing after the girl and that that force would either kill he and Truus or it would somehow transform them into something evil. Truus, on the other hand, believed it their duty to make sure that the girl was safe and that they should be there for her to protect her from not only this malignant force but from Bewdley Beacon as well. Thora was sure that the couple was continuing that argument.

"How was breakfast?" the waitress broke into Thora's thoughts. "Would you like anything else?" She pulled the empty plate away from the girl.

"No, I'm fine," Thora mumbled, wiping her mouth with her napkin. "It was a very tasty breakfast! The blueberries and strawberries were perfect!"

The waitress smiled. "I will let the chef know. And how was your breakfast, sir?" she asked Bewdley. Thora noted that the woman's face had immediately fallen upon sight of the unkempt man.

"The eggs were a bit too runny for my liking," Bewdley said. He still had remnants of them at the corners of his lips and a piece on his chin.

"We can't satisfy everybody but we certainly make it our aim to try!" the woman's eyes averted back to Thora. "Your dad always this grumbling?"

Almost immediately Thora answered, "He is not my dad."

There was a rumble underneath of the stool. The girl sensed that Bewdley had tried to kick her but missed. "He's my uncle," she quickly added, guessing that Bewdley did not want anybody to think that there was no connection between the two of them.

"How much?" Bewdley asked, taking the napkin and finally wiping the egg from his face.

"Three dollars should cover it," the waitress responded.

"Three dollars! That's highway robbery!" Bewdley complained, handing the woman the twenty-dollar bill.

The woman took the money and began making change. Her hands were pulling out quarters from the till.

"I don't need any coins, just the bills!" Bewdley said, denying the waitress any gratuity.

As they started to leave the diner, the woman called out to them, "Sir, you are forgetting your newspaper!" She had lifted the paper out to him.

Thora could see the front page for the first time. She at once blanched. On its cover was a large black and white mug shot of Bewdley. Beside the picture in big, bold letters was the words 'WANTED FOR SLAYING A COP".

Bewdley must have seen the picture himself. He snatched the paper from the woman and briskly headed out of the door. He walked right through Truus Nells. As soon as he was outside he began running towards the parked car. "Come on! Hurry up!" he cried out to Thora.

Without thinking, Thora was about to start chasing after the man when Truus grabbed her by the arm. "What are you doing? Don't go after him!"

"Go back in the restaurant and ask them to protect you," Jakob urged.

"Come on girl! We got to get out of here!" Bewdley called out frantically. His face was white with fear. People on the street were staring at him. "What are you looking at!" he squawked at them.

"Don't listen to him. This is your chance to get away!" Truus cried.

Yet as much as Thora wanted to comply with what the ghosts were telling her to do, she found that her legs were instinctively moving towards Bewdley and the parked car. She knew that it was a mistake and that the man was very dangerous but he represented a known commodity. To return to the diner would mean opening up a brand new page to her future with entirely unknown consequences. She felt as perilous as Bewdley Beacon was she was still able to handle the man. She might not be able to handle anything that came her way if she went back inside.

Chapter 38

Leaving the City Behind

"Are you crazy?" Truus Nells cried out as her body went through the car's door. "This was your best chance to get away from this monster!" She slid herself into the seat behind Bewdley. Bewdley was already backing up the vehicle into the busy Pittsburgh thoroughfare. "Opportunity like this is not going to knock twice!"

Jakob Nells had to scramble to get into the car before it sped away. He had to hop onto the hood and come through the window and crawl his way through Thora to get to the backseat. As his essence slipped through Thora, she experienced a dizzy sensation that momentarily blacked out her consciousness. When it returned, Bewdley had the car in forward and was moving through the traffic at a speed that was approaching reckless in manner. The man wanted to get away from the diner as fast as possible.

Thora never answered Truus. She did not know how to answer the ghost. There was no rational explanation why she would have gone with Bewdley Beacon. She had her freedom back there at the diner and she knew it. Now, that she was sitting in the front seat beside the murderer she had to wonder why she had chosen to do so as well.

"You surprised me, girl," Bewdley said. "I didn't think that you would choose to come with me. I would have given up on you and left you there if you did not come after me."

"I surprised myself too!" Thora admitted. "But I want to go to Canada and you are going to take me there, right?"

"If there was a way to get into Canada without going through a border station I would," Bewdley said. "But things have changed!" He lifted the newspaper up and showed Thora the front page. "They will be looking for me there!"

"See! I told you that it was crazy for you to follow this man!" Truus rasped from the rear seat. "He is not even going to take you where you want to go! We are in big trouble now, Fraulein!"

Thora's eyes fell upon the mug shot. The picture had been taken somewhere else other than Grappling Haven. The man in the photograph appeared much younger and leaner than what Bewdley looked like nowadays. "You don't look like that any more!" she pointed out to the driver. "They might not recognize you at the border!" Even though she uttered these words she realized that she had immediately recognized the man in the picture even though he was younger and thinner. Trained men would have no problem picking out Bewdley.

"They'll have other pictures of me available to them! This puss of mine was shot at the jail in your miserable little town. They'll be wiring that one out long before we reach Fort Erie or Niagara Falls."

"Then where are we going to go?" Thora asked. "We can't stay here either."

Bewdley started giggling. "Man, oh man!" he said. "I got lucky there at the diner. I was sitting right beside a cop and I didn't even know it. I even got some of his money!" He obviously did not hear Thora's question.

Thora winced at the memory. "That was a little too close for comfort." She sighed. "It goes to show you that you don't look anything like the picture."

"Stop cheering for the man!" Truus groaned. "You are making me think that you are on his side. He is not your friend. He is your enemy and he means to kill you!"

"Cops don't memorize the most wanted lists. They are given only one mug at a time to go after and they will go after that mug with the tenacity of a hound. But at the same time they are oblivious to all other mugs. I'm just lucky that those two guys were not reading the newspaper at the time."

"You didn't answer my question. Where are we going?" Thora said. The car was in some heavy morning rush hour traffic as people were making their journeys to work. They were on a four-lane street. Bewdley was weaving his way through the cars as best as he could. They came to a stoplight. Sitting next to them waiting for the light were the two detectives that they had seen at the diner.

"Keep your eyes forward," Bewdley demanded. "Don't look at them."

"It's you that is going to draw attention to us with the way that you are driving!" Thora answered. "You are driving like a lunatic!"

It took forever for the light to change. Periodically, Thora would steal glimpses of the two detectives. They appeared to be not interested in who was sitting beside them. They seemed to be engrossed in their own conversation.

"Open the window and cry out for help!" Truus urged.

"Do it!" Jakob repeated.

But it was at that moment that the light changed and the vehicle carrying the two plain-clothed policemen turned down another street. Thora never acted.

"Girl, you keep on surprising me," Bewdley commented as he resumed his reckless weaving through traffic. "You had a golden opportunity there and you let it slip by."

"You are taking me to Canada and that is that!" Thora responded, crossing her arms over her chest in a display of frustration. She felt so mixed up inside, not knowing what was the right thing to do.

"Don't hold your breath on that one," Bewdley answered. "Maybe in a few days we can make an attempt to cross the border when the heat has abated but we are not going there today when my face is on every newspaper across the state." His finger jabbed at the picture that sat between the two of them. "Why don't you read me what it has got to say?"

"I don't want to," Thora smirked. All that she wanted to do was cry.

"Read me the damned thing!" Bewdley barked. "Make yourself useful!"

The girl took a deep breath and sighed. She realized that the man would not let up on his demand until it was satisfied. She might as well get it over with and then she could go back into her own little world. She picked up the newspaper and unfolded it so that the entire front page was displayed to her eyes.

She read, "Wanted for slaying a cop. Two days ago, what once was a sleepy town of Grappling Haven woke up to find out that yet another murder had taken place within the vicinity. Peter Kyle, forty-four, one of Grappling Haven's beloved sons, was mercilessly shot to death as a result of a bold escape from the community's jail. Bewdley Beacon of no fixed address wanted for a murder in Tonawanda, New York, overpowered Sgt. Kyle and shot the jail supervisor from point blank range, instantly killing the father of three teenaged boys.

"Beacon, forty-seven, fled the town by means of a police vehicle and was last seen heading north. An all points bulletin has been issued across the state and into neighboring states. Beacon is described as armed and dangerous. He stands 5 foot 8 inches and is portly built. His hair is dark and he possesses no distinguishing features.

"One month ago Grappling Haven was the site of what police called a vehicular homicide when a family of four were killed when the car they were riding in was purposefully struck by another vehicle allegedly driven by Samuel Angus Meadowford, thirty-seven, from Grappling Haven. Meadowford is currently out on bail.

"Funeral arrangements have been made for Sgt. Kyle at St. Andrew's Church in Grappling Haven for Saturday. It is expected to be a large service as policemen from around the state and across the country come to pay homage to one of their fallen." Thora looked up to Bewdley and said, "That's all that it says."

Bewdley groaned. "Armed and dangerous? I ditched the gun right there on the spot. It had almost backfired on me when I shot Kyle. I think that if I were to have taken another shot it could have blown up right there in my hand."

"Listen to that beast!" Truus seethed. "He shows no remorse at all for what he has done. He took a father away from three good boys and all that he could talk about is the gun. I wish that it would have blown up in his face!" She reached forward and grabbed at Bewdley's eyes. The car swerved wildly as the man screamed in pain. Thora was tossed against the door. She still clutched at the newspaper, tearing away half the front page.

"My eyes are burning!" Bewdley cried. "I can't see!"

"Mama let go of the man before we get into an accident!" Jakob crowed.

"Maybe we want an accident so that we can get away from this monster!" Truus retorted.

"The little girl can get killed if you don't let go!" the male ghost pleaded.

Truus drew back her hands. Bewdley's eyes were red and wet with tears. He was opening and closing them, trying to regain his vision. He had slowed the vehicle down to a crawl. Behind him frustrated drivers were honking their horns for the car to get moving along the busy thoroughfare.

"I don't know what happened there!" Bewdley squawked. "All of a sudden my eyes felt like they were in the coals of a campfire! I have no idea what brought that on but it hurt like hell and I was blind for a few moments."

Thora knew the reason why but she was not going to tell him. "Can you see now?" she asked.

"Yeah, I think so," the man said as his foot came onto the gas pedal and got the car moving again much to the delight of the drivers behind him.

Thora was about to say something when her eyes spotted an article on the exposed third page of the newspaper. Its headline read, 'Meadowford Arraigned'. "Oh my God!" the girl blurted.

"What is it?" Bewdley asked.

"There's an article here about my dad," the girl answered. "It says that Meadowford is arraigned. What does that mean?"

"Read the article and see what it tells you," Bewdley said.

Thora cleared her throat and began to read from the paper once more. "A grand jury has found that there is sufficient evidence to proceed with a criminal trial in the case of Samuel Angus Meadowford, a.k.a. Langley Meadowford. Meadowford has been charged with four counts of vehicular homicide when the car that he was driving slammed into another vehicle and killed Arthur Rozelle, his wife Rita, and their two adolescent daughters Gloria and Millicent, all from Detroit, Michigan. It is alleged that Meadowford, thirty-seven, was enraged with Rozelle, forty-one, due to business differences between Meadowford's company, Dearborn Cable, and the autoworkers of Michigan. Rozelle is an attorney for the union. If convicted Meadowford could receive the death sentence."

The paper fell from Thora's hands. She felt entirely destabilized. "The death sentence," she muttered. It was her worst fear realized.

"You are as white as a ghost!" Truus Nells cried.

"They can't kill my dad because of this," Thora whimpered. "Can they?"

"Homicide is homicide, my girl," Bewdley commented. "It doesn't matter what you use as your weapon, if you purposefully kill someone and you get caught, you are going to face the chair."

"But my dad is innocent! I know he is!" Thora's voice rose. "I can testify that I saw the ghost of my great grandfather drive the car that the Rozelles were in. We've got to go back to Grappling Haven to protect my dad!" Thora could imagine the anguish that her parents were experiencing right now. Not only were both their daughters missing but also now they have to deal with a possible conviction that could end her father's life. Her troubles seemed very minute when compared to theirs.

"That is the last place that I will go back to!" Bewdley sniggered. "I'm facing the same kind of sentence as your dad and there is a lot more evidence to support my conviction than there is against your father."

"What do you mean?" Thora looked at the driver and saw him in a different light. He no longer was a monster to her. He was just a man trying to cope with the problems dealt to him in life.

"There is no direct evidence that your father actually killed that family. All of the evidence is circumstantial. There are no firsthand witnesses to the actual crime. The State won't have my testimony where I can tell them that I saw your father steal the car from Thaddeus' driveway. The only evidence that they have is that they saw the fight between Langley and Rozelle at the restaurant and that some people believed that they saw Langley driving the Rozelles out of town. This might be enough to get the State a conviction of manslaughter but it is not enough to have your dad fry."

Somehow Bewdley's words managed to comfort Thora. She listened to him through hoping ears that his assessment of the situation was correct. "If they do convict him of manslaughter how much time will he get?"

"At most only two to five years, that's all," Bewdley said.

"Still that is a lot of time for someone who did not do anything wrong," Thora answered.

"Girl, if your father gets two to five years then he will be the happiest man in the world because he got away with murder!" Bewdley responded as their car started leaving Pittsburgh city limits and enter into open country once more.

"He didn't murder anybody," Thora said.

"Oh yes he did! I have firsthand knowledge that he did!" Bewdley bore an enigmatic smile on his face.

"All that you saw him do is steal the car and you were not even sure that it was him," the girl retorted. Gone was the different light that shone on Bewdley. The man had once again returned to his monster status.

"You don't know all that I know, girl!" Bewdley grinned wickedly.

"What more could you know?" she looked him plainly in the eye, trying to read past the smile.

"Don't forget that I spent several hours alone with your father in that jail before he got his bail."

"Did he tell you something?" Thora just could not get a handle on the signals that the man was sending or hiding.

"You don't want to hear what he had to say."

"Yes, I do! Tell me!" her voice was almost shrieking.

"Your dad confessed to him that he killed that family!"

The voice was not that of Bewdley Beacon. It came from Truus Nells.

"You don't want to hear what he had to say," Bewdley repeated.

Thora swung her head back to the ghosts in the backseat. Truus had read her mind earlier. It stood to reason that she could read the man's as well. "My dad told you that he killed the family, didn't he?" she pointed the question to Bewdley.

"You are very shrewd, Miss Meadowford!" Bewdley answered.

"Tell me what he said!" Thora demanded.

"There's not much to be said," Truus said. "Your father simply said to this monster that he was glad that he taught Mr. Rozelle a lesson and that Rozelle would never make the same mistake again."

"That's not confessing to a murder!" Thora protested.

"To the monster it is!" Truus said. "And there is more to it. The monster recalls a wink that your father made when he made this comment. That to the monster is proof enough that your father confessed to the murders."

Thora thought about it for a moment. She could envision her father making such a statement and winking at the same time. It was very characteristic of Langley. It seemed to her that had her father said the same thing to her with the same gesture she too would have believed that he had admitted to the crimes.

But if Langley did kill the Rozelles how would that explain her experiences of that night? She saw the police car and the ambulance. They had sped by her while she was driving Uncle Thaddeus' car home—the very car that was in the accident. Something was fundamentally wrong with the facts of the evening.

"It can be confusing when one sees into our realm," Jakob said to her.

"Do you read thoughts too?" Thora thought more than said.

"We all do," Truus supported her husband's statement.

"It is highly likely that your father did commit that heinous act with the car that you were driving," Jakob Nells continued. "And that you saw the rescue vehicles go out to the scene of the accident."

"But how?" Thora complained. "There was a big difference in time between when I saw the ambulance and the time my father would have gotten out there."

"You saw into the future my dear, that is all," Jakob said in a comforting voice. "You saw portends of what came to pass hours before it happened."

"Such is the way in our realm. It takes some time to get used to it and you never really do get a full comprehension of it but it is the way that things work once you slip past the mortal coil."

"So I saw what happened before it happened?" the girl mused on the thought for a moment. It made the facts feel somewhat more cohesive than before. It did make her father a much more likely candidate to be the commissioner of the crime. Yet there were holes in the story. It did not explain why there were two identical cars and that the Rozelles were killed inside of Thaddeus' car.

"Consider the possibility that you did not drive your relative's vehicle home but instead you drove the mystery car and it was this mystery car that your father used instead," Truus offered. "That would mean that the family was in your relative's car. It clears up the picture, doesn't it?"

Thora pondered the idea. It fitted the facts better. But how did Delaney Mandrake, Thaddeus' chauffeur, end up driving the mystery car rather than the vehicle that he was supposed to be driving?

"Think about it, girl," Jakob said. "Delaney was drunk. The odds were that he had to have left the car some time or other to relieve himself or to purchase his bottle. While he was out of the car, the vehicles were switched. It is not a very complicated thing to do!"

The girl sat for a moment and tried to put everything into order. While Del the Duck was buying a bottle, a ghost drove up in the mystery vehicle. He took Thaddeus' car and left Delaney with the other one. The ghost picked up the Rozelles in Uncle Thaddeus' car. Later, Delaney appeared with the mystery car and Thora was forced to drive it herself when the man went into the pool hall. As she was driving it she had a vision of the ambulance and the police car. When she got to Uncle Thaddeus' place, her father came and stole the car and drove out to find and kill the Rozelles, leaving them dead in Uncle Thaddeus' car. It was a bizarre tale but it did tie in all of the facts. But why would her father resort to homicide? He was not a good man but he was not a cold-blooded murderer either. It just did not seem right.

"The orchestrators of the events of that evening could very well have manipulated your father into doing what he did," Truus said. "They could have driven him the way that the monster drives the car."

"And if that is the case then my father is innocent!" Thora declared out loud. "He did not do it of his own accord!"

"No one is going to believe the truth," Jakob said. "A mortal court would say that your father was insane if he were to testify these facts that ghosts made him do it. They would lock him away in an asylum for the rest of his life. I think that our driver here is correct when he says that your father would maybe get the lesser charge of manslaughter as long as your father keeps his mouth shut regarding his motives in the accident."

"Maybe you are right," Thora sighed. It was a complicated story that seemed to have more the substance of ghosts than anything mortal. But four mortals died because of it and a fifth's life would never be the same. She wondered why the ghost would be so hostile towards her father. Her only answer seemed to be that it was that Meadowford Curse. Indian spirits were behind it all.

"Five people died that night, Fraulien," Jakob said. "Don't forget the one called Del the Duck. Isn't it rather peculiar that he should die of alcohol poisoning that very night? I don't know this as a fact but I would highly suspect that there was more poison in the man's system than just alcohol."

"Of course I am right!" Bewdley declared with a broad smile.

CHAPTER 39

The Gas Station

"Now, I am willing to bet that you no longer want to go back to Grappling Haven. You don't want me telling the judge what I heard, do you? If I did, your father would be sitting on the electric chair!" Bewdley's smile grew even wider.

They were coming up to a turnpike. The highway joining up to theirs was one that led to Philadelphia. If they remained on the one that they were following they would be heading towards Western New York State. Thora sensed that Bewdley wanted to head east and not north. She needed him to remain on this highway and not make the turn to Philadelphia. The only way that she knew how was to recruit the help of the ghosts once more. "Grab his eyes," she said to Truus.

"What did you say?" Bewdley turned to her.

"That's no surprise," she said. "I said that that is no surprise."

"What is no surprise? That your father would sit on the electric chair?"

At that moment Truus' hands covered Bewdley's eyes while Thora seized the steering wheel and made sure that the car did not take the turnpike. Bewdley was howling in agony while the car successfully drove past the Philadelphia turn off. Once the turnpike was behind them Truus let go of the man's eyes while Thora continued to steer.

"It happened again," Bewdley said through streaming tears. "My eyes feel withered. I don't know what is going on. I never had this kind of problem before."

"Is there a history of blindness in your family?" the girl asked.

"I don't know," Bewdley said, while wiping away the tears from his eyes and cheeks. "I was an orphan. I was raised in a foundry in Buffalo, New York. I can take the wheel now." His hand took the steering wheel and he started looking around at his surroundings. "Damn! We missed the cutoff!"

"Cutoff to where?" Thora said innocently.

"I wanted to go to New Jersey," Bewdley said. "The state is relatively poor. They don't pour much money into their law enforcement budget. We wouldn't have felt the heat there as much as in the richer states."

"There'll be other turns for New Jersey later, won't there?"

"Not for a hundred miles or so and none like that highway. It will take us straight there. All the other routes involve lots of turns."

"Maybe we just take the next exit and backtrack like we did back on that road last night," Thora suggested, hoping that Bewdley would not take her up on it.

"It's too damned bad that this highway is divided here. I could have made a U-turn but with that dumb wall sitting there, I can't do that," Bewdley groaned. "I don't think that there is another exit for at least ten miles. Damn! That seizure could not have picked a worse time to happen!"

Thora sat quietly for a few moments and then she said, "What do you suppose is causing these seizures?"

"Damned if I know!" Bewdley retorted. "I've never experienced anything like it before."

Behind him Truus Nells was sniggering. "And you will continue to have these seizures whenever you step out of line, you monster!"

Thus far Bewdley did not seem to be suspicious that unseen forces were manipulating him. He appeared to believe that his burning eyes came on from something internal rather than external. The girl thought that maybe this was the way that her father had been manipulated into murdering the Rozelles. It wasn't that hard to do. It was almost like steering a car.

"Thank you for having the wherewithal of taking the steering wheel when that happened," the man said to the girl. "If you had not done so we could have ended up in a very nasty accident."

"You're welcome," Thora answered, she was trying to suppress a giggle.

"I just wish that you would have taken that turn back there."

"I didn't know that you wanted to take the turn. You didn't tell me."

Bewdley sighed. "I guess I didn't," he said. "But isn't it rather coincidental that I get that seizure right when I needed to turn? And that we are still now on the road that will take us to Canada, the place where you want to go?"

"What are you trying to say, Mr. Beacon? That I caused your eyes to burn?" Thora said in feigned dismay. "How could I do that?"

Bewdley shrugged his shoulders. "It beats me but either the gods are on your side or there is something happening here that I just don't understand."

"Believe me, the gods are not on my side!" Thora responded. "If the gods were on my side do you think that I would be sitting in this car with a known murderer?"

The man smirked. "Just be quiet for awhile while I figure out where we're going. And keep your eyes on the traffic and let me know if you spot anything suspicious."

"Suspicious, like what?"

"Cops!" Bewdley spat. "I don't want any of them sneaking up on me."

"They wouldn't be looking for this car, Bewdley. There are almost as many of this model and color out here as there are electricity poles along the highway," Thora answered. She looked along the side of the road and did not see one pole. They were in the wilderness once more. Nobody needed electricity out here.

"I just don't trust that waitress back there at the diner. I think that she is going to make the connection between us and the face in the newspaper and she'll tell the police."

"She still doesn't know what car we are in and which way we were going," Thora answered.

"She could have watched us climb in the car and she knows about our Canadian connection because someone here opened her yap and spilled the beans!" Bewdley glared at her. "Now, do you see why I don't want to go to Canada?"

Thora's skin went cold. Bewdley's paranoia made sense. He presented a plausible storyline that could easily happen. Maybe they would have to find another way into Ontario rather than through Niagara Falls. Were there other ways? She did not know. She sat quietly and pondered their options while Bewdley drove.

Behind her she could hear the snoring of Jakob and Truus Nells. They had fallen asleep. She did not know that ghosts slept. She would have thought that they didn't, given that they did not have bodies that needed to recuperate from the energy expended from their waking lives. But the pair of them was fast asleep, probably lulled into it by the monotonous highway and its ceaseless vistas of bland pastoral landscapes.

Miles of this land slowly unfolded before her. Periodically they would go through built-up areas but as soon as they reached the hubs of these villages and hamlets they would be exiting them. She had been quiet like Bewdley requested and she was on the lookout for police vehicles. She had not seen any. She wondered if Bewdley had worked out any alternate plans for their destination. If he had, he did not let on to her. Maybe he was growing complacent. It had been well over two hours since they left the diner and there had not been any sign that they were being followed. Perhaps, he realized that his fears were unfounded and that they were safe on this road.

It was around noon hour judging by the position of the sun in the sky when Bewdley broke the silence. "We're going to have to get gas soon. Keep your eyes open for a service station."

About five miles further from this point they came into yet another slumbering hamlet. It had a gas station that also served as a general store. Bewdley brought the car to a halt in front of the gas pump. He handed Thora a dollar bill. "Go inside and buy as much candy as this will get you while I fill up."

At that moment there were a pair of gaping yawns issuing from the rear seat as the Nells woke up from their nap. "Where are we?" Truus asked as she looked around. "Where are you going?"

"Inside to get some candy," Thora replied. "Want to come with me and stretch your legs?"

"That sounds like a good idea," the old woman said through another yawn. "Papa, you come with us too."

"No, I think that I will just stay here," Jakob answered. "I'm not quite awake yet."

"Papa, you come with us!" Truus said sternly. "Unless you want to stay with this monster."

At once Thora got the idea that Truus meant for her to make her escape from Bewdley at this gas station. The girl looked around at the beat-up old store and the small community that surrounded it. It did not seem like a very practical place to stage such an escapade. How could she get away from Bewdley here? There was no place to run to. There were no people to offer her protection. She did not voice her opinion to Truus and allowed the old couple to accompany her inside. Behind her a gray-haired man wearing a Pittsburgh Pirates baseball cap rose up from a wooden stool and attended to Bewdley.

She stepped inside of the store and heard the tinkles of bells overhead. As she looked upward she saw an elderly lady behind the counter. Thora guessed that it must have been the gas attendant's wife that operated the store. The old lady had dyed brown hair and she sat upon a wooden stool behind the counter. Her gray roots were visible from yards away. The woman was surrounded by a treasure trove of merchandise that hung from every conceivable place. There were stands of postcards, magazines and comics, and newspapers cluttering the space in front of the counter. Thora immediately spotted the picture of Bewdley's face on the newspapers. If nothing else traveled fast in this community the news certainly did. She hoped that the man serving Bewdley would not recognize him. The store's dusty hardwood floors were covered with a cornucopia of shelves that presented baked goods, canned goods, boxed goods and everything else that was good. And it had candies galore.

"They will rot your teeth out!" Truus warned as she watched Thora stockpile a cache of jellybeans and jawbreakers into the fold of her arm.

"They are little bursts of energy," Thora responded.

"Grab as many as you can get!" the old ghost smiled. "You are going to need a lot of energy in the next few minutes."

"I don't know if it is a good idea to do it here," Thora said, looking around in the store and out of the window to the sparse little community. "There is no place that we can go." She sensed the old woman behind the counter was watching her very closely. She probably suspected Thora as a potential shoplifter.

"Pardon me?" the old woman called out. "Did you say something?"

Thora realized that the old woman heard her speaking to Truus and believed that the little girl was talking to herself. "Oh no, I was just singing!"

Thora answered. "A beautiful day like today just makes one want to sing out with joy."

The old woman smiled. "I know what you mean. I can sing the whole daylong but my husband will tell me to shut up. He doesn't like my voice. He says that I sound like a parrot with laryngitis. But when the sun is out and it is summertime where can a girl's heart go to but to song!" The woman's last line was in a scratchy falsetto voice that quickly grated the nerves.

"She's a wacky old bird!" Truus commented. "And she does sound like a parrot with laryngitis."

"Oh my, Mama!" Jakob trilled. "If only you could sound so good as that lady!"

"And what is that supposed to mean, Mister?" Truus looked crossly at her husband. He was standing by the window watching Bewdley and the gas attendant.

"I have never seen you before," the old woman behind the counter said to Thora. "Are you just passing through?" She, too, was looking out of the window. "Is that your father?"

Immediately Thora affirmed that he was.

"He looks familiar to me," the woman said. "Although I can't place him."

Bewdley's picture was staring the woman in the eye from a nearby newspaper.

"She's going to recognize him," Truus said. "Tell her who you are and who he is and ask her if there is any place where she can hide you."

"I can't do that," Thora responded. "Bewdley would know that she helped and he would do something terrible to her."

"Then just tell her to call the police once we are gone. Tell her to get the license plate number of the car and give it to them," Jakob said. "That way nobody gets hurt here and we can get rescued from the monster as Mama calls the man."

"That is a good idea, Papa. Do it Fraulien!" Truus urged.

At first Thora was resistant to the idea. She selected some candy cigarettes and licorice pipes while she struggled with the suggestion.

"He will kill you sooner or later if you do nothing," Jakob added.

Thora knew that this was true. It was enough for her to commit to the scheme. "The reason that that man looks familiar to you is because his face is all over the newspapers," she said to the old woman as she dropped her stash of candy onto the counter. As soon as her hands were free she pointed to the picture in the newspaper. "That's him."

The old woman looked at the newspaper and then turned her head and looked outside. "That is your father?"

"That isn't my father. I was lying then," the girl explained. "He has kidnapped me and he means to take me to New Jersey or someplace."

The old woman once more gawked out of the window. "It doesn't quite look like him." Her skin had blanched and her hands were trembling.

"Look, what I want you to do is as soon as we are gone call the police and tell them about us. Give them our license plate number and tell them where we are and where we are going."

"But I don't know where you are going?" the woman complained in a jittery voice. She seemed very weak. She seemed that she was on the verge of losing consciousness. She had lifted her hand to her forehead and her body was swaying upon the stool that she sat upon.

"What's wrong?" Thora asked. "Are you okay?"

The woman turned her eyes towards Thora. They seemed wild with fright. "I have a heart condition," the woman confessed. "I have just come out of the hospital last month after two weeks there recuperating from my third heart attack. I'm afraid that I can't handle excitement very well. He's not going to harm George, is he?"

Thora assumed that George was the name of her husband, the man that was serving Bewdley. "No, he wouldn't do that," she answered. "Bewdley doesn't want to leave a trail behind him. You and George will be safe."

"George is not in much better shape than me," the woman said. "He's had liver problems and his stomach can hardly hold down a thing. If he gets nervous he is liable to spill all that he is got in there in a jiffy." She was peering out of the window at the gas pump.

"It would look good on the monster to wear someone's stomach all over him!" Truus cackled.

"Tell the lady that if she does not want to help she does not have to," Jakob said. "We can get out of this mess on our own. We don't need her help. I don't want these two to die from fright."

Thora thought that that was a good idea. She relayed the message to the old woman. At the end she asked, "How much for the candy?"

"You take it all for nothing!" the woman sighed. The relief in her face was very evident.

"No, I will pay for it," Thora insisted. "He would get suspicious if I come back to the car with the dollar bill still in my hand."

"I wish that I could help you," the woman said. "It is not my way to leave a girl in trouble but given my heart condition if I get involved I am afraid that I will die from worry that that man would come back here and get his revenge on us for snitching." She took the money from Thora. "That will be ninety-three cents."

"I wonder how her heart would take it when she reads about your murder in her papers a week from now," Truus commented, shaking her head. "I don't like weakness in people."

"Now, now Mama. How can the old woman help anyhow?" Jakob responded. "Even if she lets the police know about us being here I think that we will be long gone and likely in another car by the time that they respond."

The woman gave Thora her seven cents in change. As she did so, she said softly to the girl. "Don't you worry, young lady. You will get out of this, I swear," she winked. "I don't like weakness in people either!" There was resolve and commitment in her eyes.

"You see them?" Thora was astounded.

"I've been seeing them for a month now. I'm soon going to be one of them so I don't know what I am so worried about. They've got it good. They don't have to cook or eat or worry about dying. I will call the police as soon as you are gone." The woman raised her head and looked directly at Truus Nells. "I don't want to read about the child's murder either. There is enough killing on this Earth."

"You are a good woman, Mrs...."

"Hartman. Mrs. Lilly Hartman," the woman answered. "Now, you better get going or else he will get suspicious."

As they walked back to the car, they saw that George the attendant had returned to his stool. Bewdley was sitting in the vehicle. Its engine was running.

"I'm surprised that she saw you," Thora said to her ghostly companions.

"The dying often see us," Truus answered.

"And we can see the dying," Jakob added. "We know who will soon be joining us."

Thora turned to him. "Am I joining you soon? Is that why I am seeing you?" An unearthly chill swept over her as the fragility of her mortality came to her mind.

"You are healthy, my child. It is the sick that see us. Someone that is fated to die from unnatural causes does not have the gift to see the world that they will be entering," Jakob replied. "I don't know why you see us or the other spirits that you have seen. Something tells me that there is something very special about you and that is why you see things that others do not see."

"I don't know if I would call it a gift," Thora sighed, just before she entered the car. "I think that it is more of a curse."

Chapter 40

Dreams of the Dead

"What took you so long?" Bewdley said as Thora stepped into the car. He was eying her very suspiciously.

Thora expected such a reaction from the man and had a prepared answer for him. "They have a huge selection of candy in there and I couldn't make up my mind." She displayed the bag of her goodies to him.

"You didn't talk to anyone in there, did you? I saw the old woman look out at me several times." They pulled out of the gas station and once again were driving down the highway.

"She was just being friendly and curious. You know how small town folk are. She wanted to know where we were from and where we were going."

Bewdley's face lit up. "What did you tell her?"

"Don't worry. I did not tell her the truth. I said that we were from Pittsburgh and that we were going to visit my grandparents in New York State, that's all." Thora was not sure that her lie was very convincing. She could almost feel her face discoloring as she spoke.

Bewdley shook his head back and forth. "That's not any good," he said. "She knows the direction that we are going. We're going to have to alter our plans. Was there any newspapers in there with my picture on them?"

"I never noticed any papers," Thora said.

"That's a lie!" Bewdley blared. "I saw a paper on the old man's stool. It looked like the same paper as back at the diner."

"I said that I did not notice any papers. I did not say that there were no papers!" Thora snapped back. She looked back at the Nells in the backseat. She was entertaining the idea of the ghosts inflicting some punishment on the man.

"The way that old woman looked at me I could swear that she recognized me!" Bewdley said.

"Well, that is a danger that you are going to have to face almost anywhere that you go, Bewdley. Your face is everywhere. Sooner or later someone is going to figure out who you are and finger you."

"They won't recognize me in Canada," Bewdley said. "They don't carry American news stories up there."

Thora almost felt thrilled when she heard Bewdley mention Canada. She knew that she had to hide this excitement. "And how are we going to get into Canada?" she asked. "I thought that you said that they would be looking for us at the borders."

"There are more ways of getting into Canada than by road," Bewdley said.

Thora could almost see the man's mind scheming. She sensed that Bewdley already had a plan worked out. When Bewdley did not say anything, she decided that she had to prompt him for it. "Well, what other ways are there of getting into Canada? Are you going to tell me?"

"Hush, girl, I'm not telling you anything. If something happens to us and we have to part company I don't want you carrying around my plans in your little noggin," the man responded.

Thora decided that she would not pursue the matter further. She knew that sooner or later he would reveal his plan to her. She pulled out a candy cigarette and began nibbling at it as the Pennsylvania countryside whistled by her. She could not believe that they were going to Canada. She wished that she had not told Lilly Hartman to call the police. The police now would ruin everything. Periodically she took a look behind them to see if there were any police cars trailing them.

"Don't do that or he will get suspicious," Truus cautioned her. "If Papa and I see anybody coming we will let you know."

Thora nodded. She did not dare voice an answer to break up the silence in the car.

A sign on the road announced that the New York State border was seven miles away. They would soon be leaving Pennsylvania and entering into another state. She wondered if Pennsylvania police would have any jurisdiction in New York.

There were several vehicles in front of them and several more behind them. The car had slowed down considerably. "Some old jackass up ahead does not know that we are allowed to go fifty miles an hour on this highway," Bewdley said to her. He seemed to be impatient as if he wanted to get out of the state as well. He stuck his hand out of the window and signaled a right hand turn.

"Where are you going?" Thora asked.

"I'm not staying on any road that allow turtles to crawl upon it," he responded and he turned down an old gravel road. It almost reminded Thora of the road that Mrs. Bianco had lived on.

"Does this road go anywhere?"

"It is going to take us exactly where I want to be going," Bewdley answered. "I know this territory inside out. We won't be followed on this road. Very few people know about it and even fewer take it."

"You had better tell the monster that someone else knows about the road," Jakob said. Thora turned around and saw the old ghost pointing to a dust cloud behind them. Another vehicle had turned down the road.

"Holy shit!" Bewdley exclaimed when Thora told him. "Are you sure that you did not tell anybody about us?" His foot pushed the accelerator down as far as it would go.

"I didn't say a word! I swear!" Thora lied. She could not tell if the car following them was a police car or just someone else who happened to know about this road. She prayed that it would be the latter. She did not want her passage to Canada to come to an abrupt end because of police intervention.

The car behind them also began to speed up. And through all the dust she thought that she could see flashing lights. There was no doubt to her now that it was the police. Mrs. Hartman had come through with her word and she had called them.

"It will soon all be over," Truus said to her.

"I don't want it to be over!" Thora responded in a sob.

"Neither do I, my girl!" Bewdley said. "And I don't think that it is yet. I have a few tricks up my sleeve."

He swung the steering wheel hard left and the car nearly tipped over as it barely negotiated a turn and onto another road that was in even a worse state of condition than the one that they just left. It was strewn with axle-breaking potholes. The car bounced and pounded on the road. Thora had to hold onto the door to keep herself from being thrown about.

"They've made the turn too," Jakob announced. He and his wife were not being tossed about. They had no corporeal matter and were not subject to the whims of gravity.

Bewdley spun the car once again onto another road. This gravel lane headed into some hilly, forested country. The police car behind them made the turn as well. Thus far they had not gained on them but these cops were doggedly determined to hang onto their trail.

They just went over a crest of a hill. There immediately came into sight another hill. They were in a small valley between the two lumps on the earth. The car behind them could not see them. Bewdley sharply turned the wheel once more and pulled into a driveway. Thora stared out the back window and saw the police car race by. They did not see the wanted vehicle in the driveway. They must have assumed that Bewdley had continued down the road.

"Thank God for hilly country!" Bewdley cried out loud. "This land here is more wavy than Lake Erie on a windy day. It would be miles before the cops will realize that we are no longer ahead of them." He placed the car into reverse and pulled out back onto the road and began backtracking.

All the while Thora stared out the rear window expecting to see the police car to suddenly appear. Thus far it did not show. And thus far no other police cars were in the vicinity. When they came upon the first country road that they had turned onto from the main highway Bewdley resumed his way down it in an easterly direction. "They'll be looking for us somewhere to the north. They won't think of looking here."

"There's not a chance that they can suddenly appear ahead of us, is there?" Thora asked nervously. She still did not feel safe.

"No, the only way to get back onto this road from up there is to come the way that we did. They won't realize that for some time yet. The roads that they are on will take them all the way up to Lake Ontario. They won't even suspect that we are down here." Bewdley seemed to be relatively assured in his statement. This attitude went a long way toward making the girl feel safe.

"I don't know why you are feeling so good," Truus said. "We just blew our only chance of rescue. You are a very mixed up child. You cannot stay with a decision very long at all."

Thora felt like telling the old ghost to shut up. She never said it but Truus heard it. The ghost folded her arms over her chest and crumpled her face into an expression of disappointment. "Papa," she said after several moments of uncomfortable silence, "I think that we should think about going home. We are not wanted here any longer."

Thora cringed. She feared this reaction but somehow she expected it. More than anything else she wanted the Nells to stay with her. She knew that they offered her protection that she could not get elsewhere. Yet every time that they did something to assure her security she would somehow or other veto it or find a way to undo it. She could understand how this would frustrate the ghosts, Truus in particular. Yet, if she were to follow their advice it would send her back to a life that she no longer desired to resume. The old life of Thora Meadowford was besot with problems compounding upon each other. She did not want to go back to that life. And although staying with Bewdley meant a very uncertain future with grim, hopeless prospects it was still an existence that had not entirely foiled her designs of capturing that essence of hope and happiness that had completely gone out of her life in Grappling Haven.

Jakob had read these thoughts in her. He almost seemed like he understood her position. "I have walked the Earth a very long time," he said to her. "And in this time I have witnessed that eventually the problems of the day do go away. Going back home is not a bad idea, little one. There is a price to pay but once that price is paid you can carry on. Staying with this man here will not allow you to carry on. He will bring your life to an end and then all is over."

"If he does that then I just carry on like you," Thora said. She was unconcerned if Bewdley heard her. "You don't seem to have it that bad. You get to go on little adventures every day. You don't have to worry about dying."

"You don't know what it is like being one of us," Truus said through tight lips. "You have never dreamed the dreams of the dead. Believe me I would rather have my worst nightmare in life than one of these dreams."

"Our dreams are unlike yours, girl. In your dreams there is a part of you that ultimately knows that it is a fantasy and that your real life exists elsewhere in some place safe," Jakob continued. "In the dreams of the dead we do not have that safety. Wherever our dreams lead us we are ultimately in that place."

"And most often these dreams take us to a place where there is such suffering that it is unimaginable. We find ourselves in the lands of demons who are so full of hate that if they look upon you you can feel your essence burning in a fire so hot that the sun would seem like a cool place," Truus said and shivered.

"Don't you dream of good places though too?" Thora asked. She envisioned that the Nells must visit Hell in their dreams.

"By staying to the Earth we are unable to have our minds wander these good places as you call them," Jakob said.

"Didn't you say that your love of the Earth was the reason that you have not moved on?" Thora protested. She was not quite following the logic of what was being said.

"We love this world," Truus admitted. "And on a good day there is no place better anywhere than this world. On a good day the grandeur of this world is well worth the horrors that we must endure in our dreams. But the good days are less frequent now while our dreams become longer and deeper and more terrible."

"Then why don't you just give up on the world and go to the good places?" Thora cried.

"Girl, your babbling is driving me nuts!" Bewdley said, tapping Thora in her shoulder. "Can't you just be quiet? I don't want to be forced to put a gag on you."

"We can't do that," Jakob said. "Something binds us here. We do not know what it is but it keeps us tied here like a dog in a yard. We have had long conversations, Mama and I, about what it is and we have yet to discover it."

Thora wondered if maybe it was her that kept the Nells bound to the Earth, that it was their ultimate mission here to protect her.

"You seem to have a large sense of self-importance," Jakob laughed.

"As silly as it sounds Jakob and I have talked about this possibility," Truus said overtop of her husband's chuckle. "But it just does not seem so. We are not ancestors to you. These ties to the mortal are usually reserved for kin and not for strangers."

"We share no blood," Jakob added. "The ghosts of your ancestors are bound to the Earth because of you or someone else that is alive in your family."

"Then you are here because of Myra," Thora asserted. "She is your descendant."

"She is our descendant but there is nothing in Myra's life that requires intervention from her ancestors. She has matters under control and she is not destined to do great things," said Jakob.

"Or have great problems," Truus added. "Myra is quite ordinary."

"Not in the eyes of many people who read her book," Thora smiled. "Many of them think that she should be put into the insane asylum."

"As many think the same about you," Truus said. "And you know that you are not crazy!"

"I think that I have learned that it is others who determine if someone is crazy and not the person himself or herself," Thora responded.

"Believe me, I have long ago determined that you are certifiably nuts!" Bewdley crowed. "I thought I told you to be quiet. Stop talking to your imaginary friends! They are not here!"

"Want me to give him a bout of blindness?" Truus asked.

"No, not blindness Mama, deafness!" Jakob leaned forward and put his hands over Bewdley's ears.

The man cried out in pain. He took his hands from the steering wheel and began rubbing his oversized ears. Jakob removed his fingers from the inside of Bewdley's ears and said to Thora that the man would have to contend with a very loud ringing in them for at least the next ten minutes and that his hearing would never be the same again.

"I don't know what's happening to me!" Bewdley rasped. "I've never had a health problem in my life until I met you."

"How did I do it?" Thora asked him. She saw Bewdley's eyes read her lips but could see in them that he did not hear what she had to say.

"I can't hear you!" Bewdley complained. He continued rubbing at his ears, trying to adjust the mechanisms inside of them so that they could properly interpret sonic vibrations once more.

Thora reached across to the steering wheel and righted the direction of the car. It had been veering towards the opposite side of the road. Bewdley brought one hand back to the wheel and concentrated on driving.

Periodically, he would switch hands so that he could alleviate the itch or burning sensation or whatever it was from the other ear.

"Well, that seems to have solved our problem with interruptions from him," Truus smiled.

"We should have thought about it a long time ago," Jakob agreed.

"So if it is not Myra that keeps you bound here, then what does?" Thora returned the conversation to its original topic.

"We don't know," Truus admitted.

"I think that is one of the reasons Mama and I go out for drives every day. We are trying to find our purpose."

"We even went back to the Old Country to see if we could find it there, but the only thing we learned there was that life has changed so much there that we could hardly recognize it," Truus said.

"We did learn that we did make the right decision when we were young and decided to leave Holland for a new life in the New World," Jakob said. "Before that we often wondered if we did. But we learned in Holland that our roots were no longer there and that where we truly planted ourselves was here in the United States of America. We love this land. It is in our blood."

"Then maybe you are here because of the land itself," Thora speculated. "It is your…what's the word for it, it is your legacy to your descendants."

Truus and Jakob simultaneously lifted their eyebrows as if Thora had hit upon something. But then Truus negated the notion. "The land has no soul. How could it be the land?"

"How do you know that the land has no soul? The Indians seem to think so," Thora spurted.

"Sometimes I wonder if the savages themselves possess souls," Truus said. "Sometimes I think that they are nothing but the Devil's mockery of God's greatest creation."

Thora was astounded to hear such words come from the old woman. They could have been right out of the history texts from school. Truus spoke very much as a product of her times when white settlers came into country that belonged to the red man and threw out its former occupants, and then ascribed onto these people terrible traits when they tried to regain what was rightfully theirs. Didn't the same scenario play itself out a hundred years later on Black Island when her great grandfather declared the rock as Meadowford domain? Weren't there Indians that challenged this declaration but were unable to put teeth into their challenge? When were the white people going to accept that they wronged the red people? "Maybe you have to open your hearts to the Indians and then you could be set free?" she suggested.

"You have no right to judge us, Fraulien!" Jakob said. "You don't know how it was then. We came to this land because of religious persecution back in the old country. Holland had fallen under the control of the Spanish and they brought their Catholic ways to our Protestant country. We came here because of the freedom of religion that is valued here. We did not come here to be the targets of the heathens' arrows and hatchets. But all around us not a year would go by without some family being massacred by these soulless savages."

Truus took up her husband's argument. "We tried to be tolerant but when these devils raid your neighbor's farm and strip away the scalps of the adults and take the younger children into captivity, you just find that this tolerance quickly erodes."

"Did you ever try to look at it from their point of view?" Thora said. "The lands that you occupied was theirs since the beginning of time. Then you come into that land and force them to move out without even giving them any proper recompense. How would you react if that happened to you? Wouldn't you do everything that you could to get it back?"

"We would take it to a court of law and have the judge set matters straight," Jakob said.

"Okay, imagine that court of law was made up of nothing but Indians and the laws that they upheld were nothing but Indian laws? And that every time someone like you went up to this court the judge ruled against you? Would you still place your hope in that court? That's what the Indians had to contend with, white judges and white laws. Do you think that they received fair treatment in these courts?"

The Nells were silent for a moment before Jakob once more spoke. "We still would not have carried out such horrendous acts of terror on their people the way that they did upon us."

"Oh, Mr. Nells, you might not have done such despicable acts yourself but your white government did," Thora protested. "They were on a course to exterminate the Indians, their men, their women and their children. The real savages came from the Old World and not the New World. The Indians were a noble people, a people who knew how to live with Nature and to love the land. Look around you," Thora pointed out to the countryside that they were driving through, "This is what the Indians were trying to protect. Think back at what you saw in Pittsburgh. Remember the dirty air and the filth everywhere, that is what the white man brings."

"Oh, you don't know, little girl!" Truus groaned. "You did not have to live in a time when your life was in constant peril because of these folk. By the time that you were born the savages were no longer a problem because we were finally able to put them into their place."

"You would think differently if you came from our time," Jakob added.

"Your time is over now, Mr. Nells, and my time has come. People don't think about the Indians the way that you do any more. Nowadays we recognize that we made big mistakes in the way that we treated this country's first citizens," Thora pointed out. She was reciting lessons that she had learned in school just this past semester.

"Those are just words, Thora. Mama and I have seen some reservations on our travels and from what we witnessed of the squalor we can see no love of the red man in the government," Jakob said.

"This conversation is not getting anywhere," Thora sighed. "I just sense that your shackles to this world is related to your prejudices against the Indians and I think that once you learn to overcome these feelings that you will no longer be tied to this Earth and the terrible dreams that you dream."

Jakob leaned forward and patted the girl on the hand. "Little one, I know that you mean well but you can no more change us than we can change you. We are who we are."

"I just hope that you will stay with me and not leave yet," Thora said to the man.

"I think I heard that!" Bewdley declared. "I still have that blasted ringing in my ear but I think that I heard you say something."

Thora ignored the driver's comment. She needed to see the affirmation in Jakob's eyes that he and his wife were not going to leave her.

"We promised you that we would stay with you until you got out of this mess," the old ghost said. "Such promises are not bandied about lightly. We gave you our word and by that word we will stay with you." He turned around to his wife.

At first there was disappointment etched in Truus' brow but it slowly gave way to a smile of commitment. "We will stay with you but it would be nice that now and then you might listen to what we have got to say," she said.

"We want nothing but the best for you, Fraulien. When we offer our opinion or advice we would appreciate it that if you accept it that you remain committed to it and not throw it out once something else comes up that at the moment may seem to be a better option. Do you promise us that?" Jakob asked.

Thora thought about it for a moment. She wanted to agree but she knew herself too well and knew that such a promise would be very difficult to keep. "I can't promise you that," she said softly. "All that I can promise is that I will try."

"Trying is good enough for me," Jakob responded. He looked to his wife.

"It is good enough for me too," the old woman reluctantly said.

Chapter 41

Empire State Crossroads

"We don't have to worry about those Pennsylvanian cops anymore," Bewdley said. "They have no jurisdiction over us here."

"Why?" Thora asked. She spoke loudly so that the man behind the wheel could hear her. Outside of her car window she saw absolutely nothing that would tell her that something had fundamentally changed. They were still passing through rural country that was dominated by dairy farms and tracts of land given over to corn. The corn was starting to grow tall. Even from the road she could see a multitude of the green ears of the crop weighing down upon the stalks. The sight of it made her mouth water. She had grown extremely tired of the candies that she had in her bag. They were no longer cutting it. Her body craved real nourishment.

"We are in the Empire State now," Bewdley answered.

"How do you know?" There was nothing to indicate that they crossed state lines. There were no highway signs.

"See that farm back there," Bewdley said. "It had the New York flag hanging from its verandah. The farm just to the south of it had the Pennsylvanian flag. These farmers have a way of telling you where you are without you having to consult any roadmaps or highway signs."

"So now we only have to worry about the New York police instead, right?" Thora smiled. She knew that nothing fundamentally had changed.

They were still in the state of trouble no matter where they were on any roadmap.

"Yup. But they don't know that we are here," Bewdley responded. He looked down at the gas gauge. Thora's eyes followed his gaze and she saw that they had just about used up all the fuel that they purchased at the gas station run by Lilly and George Hartman. "And they won't know what car we are in. It is time for us to do some shopping again," he said to her. "Keep your eyes open for an unattended inconspicuous vehicle."

About three miles up the road from where Bewdley made the request Thora was able to provide him with another popular late-model sedan that sat at the entrance to a lakeside resort. The car was parked along the road and was obscured from the beach by the stand of white birch trees. Fortuitously the keys were in the ignition. Bewdley turned the engine over and noted that it had a full tank of gas. "We have our new car!" he beamed to the girl.

Thora was cautiously watching down the lane to see if anybody was aware of them. It didn't appear so. She started to open the passenger door of the car when Bewdley told her to go back to the first car and drive it. He didn't want that car left in the vicinity where the new car was taken. It made sense to Thora and she went back to the car where the ghosts were still sitting in the backseat. Both had fallen asleep and were dreaming. If they were in the nightmares that they professed that they experienced their bodies did not reveal it. Both Jakob and Truus slept peacefully. She started the car while Bewdley pulled up alongside of her in the new sedan. "Follow me," he instructed. "As soon as I see a good spot to dump your car I will pull over."

She pulled onto the road behind him. She had trouble shifting the gears and the car jerked and lunged. The awkward motion woke up her passengers. Both at first just stared forward as they were making the adjustment from wherever they came to where they were now. It took nearly a minute before Truus said, "Where's the monster?"

"He's in the car ahead of us," Thora replied. She was concentrating on her driving. Another company than the company that made her dad's Motorized Egg or her Uncle's Bentley made this car. The gears were set up differently and the clutch didn't behave the same.

"And what are we following him for?" Jakob asked.

Thora explained Bewdley's plan to the ghosts.

"I repeat, 'and what are we following him for?'" Jakob said with dismay.

"Fraulein, this is your golden opportunity to make your escape!" Truus declared. "We have our own means of locomotion and he is in a separate vehicle! Stop the car Thora and turn around! We can drive to the nearest town and report everything to the police there!"

Thora kept driving. She had no intent of complying with the ghosts' wishes. She had hoped that they would have stayed asleep and not become aware of what was transpiring.

"Girl, if you don't do what we say you are signing your own death warrant!" Jakob protested. "This is your chance to escape!"

"We can't get anywhere with this car," she finally said to the ghosts. "It is almost out of gas!"

"But it still has gas now and we should use every drop of it to try and reach a town!" Truus said.

"Maybe there is a town ahead of us," Thora offered, trying to find justification for continuing to follow the path of Bewdley Beacon.

"Thora, you promised that you would listen to us!" Jakob said. He was keeping his voice rational although Thora was fully aware that there was fire burning behind his sedate eyes.

"You people just don't understand!" she cried. "Can't you see that he is not going to harm me and that he is taking me to where I want to go!"

"Well, if he is not going to harm you then there is no point for Papa and I to stay with you any more, is there!" Truus glowered.

"No!" Thora blared. "I don't want you to go! I want you to stay with me!"

"What for Thora? You just said that you are not in any danger and that you trust that man!" Truus responded.

"Well, what is it?" Jakob demanded. "Is he dangerous or is he not?"

"I wish that you guys would be quiet! You are making it hard for me to drive this car!" Thora protested.

Bewdley's sedan was slowly increasing the distance between them. They were coming up to a crossroads where on the other side of the intersection the road climbed upward and veered to the right. Bewdley would be out of sight by the time she came up to the crossroads.

"Is he dangerous or not?" Jakob repeated.

"Yes! He is dangerous!" Thora finally agreed. "But I need him right now. Can't you understand that?"

"I can understand that the man driving the car in front of us is a known murderer that will kill you soon and that you right now are in a vehicle that can garner your escape from him yet you do nothing to help yourself!" Jakob said. "You are a troubled young lady Thora and in my estimation in desperate need of help that Mama and I cannot give you."

"You have to get to a town Thora and find a doctor there to help you," Truus spoke as persuasively as she could. "You have gone crazy and you can no longer think rationally."

Bewdley stopped at the crossroads and then pulled through. Thora came up to the stop sign and she geared down for it. The car jerked and tossed as she was having difficulty negotiating the sweet spots in the transmission. The car finally came to a stop.

"Where did you learn to drive?" Jakob almost growled.

Bewdley's car disappeared behind the hill's landscape.

"Turn here!" Truus said.

Thora placed her foot onto the gas pedal and started driving through the intersection when suddenly a ghostly hand reached over her shoulder and swung the steering wheel around to the right and the car made the turn onto the other road. At once Thora slammed on the brakes. "I don't want to go down this road!" she wailed at the ghosts, pulling at the steering wheel and trying to win over the direction of the car.

The vehicle slid off the road and slowly descended into a deep ditch where it came to a rest at its bottom. Thora had been jostled about but had not been hurt. The ghosts had not even shuffled an iota through the mishap.

"Thora, be reasonable!" Jakob implored. "You have got to take this road! It is your only chance!" He was looking over his shoulder towards the hill. Sooner or later Bewdley would reappear and the ghost's gambit would come to an end.

"I want to go to Canada!" Thora began bawling. "I don't want to go down this road!"

"Girl, you are acting like a baby!" Truus growled. "If you were my child I would give you such a spanking!"

"But I am not your child and you have no say over what I do!" Thora protested through her tears.

Truus moved her hands forward towards Thora's face. "You are forcing me to do something that I do not want to do!"

Thora implicitly understood the threat. The old woman was going to inflict pain onto her to coerce her to start driving. Truus' fingers were a hair's breadth from Thora's cheeks. Soon she would experience an unbearable burning sensation. "Drive the car, child!" Truus warned.

"It's too late!" Jakob moaned just as his wife's fingertips lit on Thora's skin. "He's coming back for us!"

A wild tingly spasm ran through Thora's cheeks. She instinctively clamped her jaw shut. Her teeth gnashed against each other so hard that it felt like her chin was going to buckle. Her need to scream hysterically caused her mouth to open up again.

When Truus released her fingers from Thora's face the girl thought that she now had a second mouth. The residual pain lingered in her jaw and it felt like her lower eyelid had gone numb. The tears had clouded her eyes so much that all she got for a sense of her surroundings was a murky configuration that provided very little detail.

"We are through with you!" Truus hissed. "We wanted to help you but you are beyond help!"

Slowly Thora's vision returned. She could see the angry faces of the Nells in the backseat. Behind them she saw the black sedan pulling up to the side of the road where her car had slid off. "I don't want your help!" Thora rasped at the ghosts. "I don't need you any more!" She was extremely angry that the ghosts had resorted to such extreme measures in trying to make her do their whim. She no longer considered them allies and wanted to get away from them as quickly as possible. She flung the door open and threw herself inside of Bewdley's car. Behind her the ghosts stared at her in shock at her sudden actions. They still sat in the other car. Its engine was still running.

"What's going on?" Bewdley said with surprise. "I thought that you were trying to give me the slip!"

"The car was practically out of gas," Thora said trying to catch her breath and wiping the tears from her eyes. "I thought that this crossroad would be as good a spot as any to get rid of the car."

"It's a good spot. You can barely see it from the road," Bewdley admitted. "It would be better if we threw some branches onto it so that you can't see it at all."

"I don't think that we have time for that," Thora said. "We want to get out of here as fast as possible." Her eyes were fixed upon those of Jakob Nells. There was such disappointment in them that she felt like she was the scum of the Earth to leave him and his wife in such a remote and desolate spot. If only they could have seen things her way. If only they could understand.

"You're right," Bewdley agreed. "You never know what can happen out here." He began turning the car around and heading back to the intersection. When they reached the crossroads Bewdley stopped and looked at her. "What happened to your face?" he asked. "There is a big red spot on your cheek."

"It must have happened when I slid in the ditch," Thora improvised. "I think that my head went into the steering wheel." She looked back to where her car went off the road. From this spot the vehicle could not be seen at all. She began to realize that she could not have chosen a better spot. When the car is eventually found and reported, the police would be led to believe that the two fugitives went down the other road rather than this one.

Bewdley pulled the new vehicle onto the road and began climbing up the hill that veered to the left. As he did so Thora was still looking back to the intersection. She knew that she was making a big mistake. Truus and Jakob Nells were her allies and they had nothing but the best intentions for her. They were old and they had accrued a lot of wisdom over their years. It was very foolish for her to so simply cast this invaluable source of assistance away just so that she could get to Canada. What was up there at Pioneer Lake for her anyway? Nobody in her family was there. The place would be lonely and frightening. It would not be able to provide for her. She might have a nice day there when she first arrives but after that it would be bleak and desolate. Why did she so desperately want to go there? Why would she abandon the help of the Nells for it? She felt like she was going crazy. Things were under her control but yet they were not. Life was traveling with reckless abandon and she was only just clinging on hardly able to appreciate the ride that she was experiencing. Maybe an insane asylum was the best thing for her.

The car reached the top of the hill. In a moment it would start descending into new land for her and she would not see Truus and Jakob Nells again. But just before the swaying grasses of the hilltop obscured the remaining fragments of the crossroads, Thora for a fleeting moment thought that she saw two wisps of wind climb from the ditch and start moving in her direction.

Chapter 42

The Five O'clock News

The afternoon was long. Its length was perhaps extended because she had fallen in and out of sleep countless times as the sedan drove through backcountry and was beginning to penetrate into the heart of New York State. Each time that she woke she saw that nothing substantially had changed. It was the same dreary agrarian landscape under the same glaring sun. The day seemed endless and it seemed like they were getting nowhere. The only thing that indicated that time was passing was the reading of the fuel gauge. It was moving steadily downward. It was tracking time through the expenditure of gas. They had less than half a tank now.

"Where are we?" she said through a yawn to the driver, Bewdley.

"We are getting there," he said, remaining aloof in providing her with details about their destination. He had not disclosed to her his plans about how he was going to get across the border.

She looked up at the position of the sun in the sky. From what she could connote it seemed like they were still going in a general northerly direction. Sooner or later Lake Ontario would come into view and when it did that would be when Bewdley's scheme should become evident. For now the lake was nowhere to be seen and the girl contented herself with milking this lackadaisical time with her periodic bouts of sleep. She was extremely tired. She hardly had any sleep at all since she left her house and she had been through so much in all of that time. Her episode at Mrs. Bianco's place seemed like ancient history to her now yet that was only a couple of days ago. She wondered about the fate of Margaret Whattam. Surely by now she had been either rescued or her body discovered. Her loving doting husband would not have left her stranded there forever. Thora sighed. She wished that she had somebody like that that would care for her so deeply and intensely. She saw how her parents reacted when her twin sister Rebecca had run away. Langley and Cora hardly batted an eye. They just carried on with their lives as if nothing had happened. Of course, things were mitigated because of all of the upheaval in the Meadowford household—the death of Sambo, the reading of the will, the accident and the murder charges. Losing Becky was just only one more headache for them to endure. She was afraid that her own disappearance would be just as traumatic for them as Becky's. She came from a family that ostensibly just did not care when one of its members fell.

It still bothered her about Mrs. Whattam. Margaret in her own way was a friend much like the Nells. The woman had taken an interest in the girl and tried to make her life better. And how did the girl repay the woman? By leaving her battered and injured in a room with a demon. The girl shuddered at the thought.

"Why are you shaking?" Bewdley asked her. "You're not cold, are you? I can roll up the windows."

"No," Thora sighed. "I'm not cold. Leave the window open. I need the fresh air to wake up." She answered him automatically; her mind was still in the process of persecuting herself for the way that she had been treating others. She still felt very bad for the way that she had disappointed the Nells ghosts. They were her salvation yet she walked away from them. She wondered about that fleeting image that she saw of two winds upon the crossroads. Had the pair gone back home to Hawkins Corners to be in their house with Myra Stanley or were they still committed to her and were following her? She almost prayed that they were, yet, she had not seen anything since that could make her believe so. But did not the pair of them vow to her that they would see her through to Canada? She knew that people like Truus and Jakob placed an enduring value on their word. They would not give up on her as easily as she had given up on them.

"I can stand for some sleep too," Bewdley said. "It has been an exhausting day. All this driving is very demanding on the mind and body."

"And I know how much you like sleeping!" Thora quipped, recalling how Bewdley had almost slept a whole day after Mrs. Whattam's car had overheated on that desolate road where Mrs. Bianco lived.

"I didn't quite hear you," Bewdley answered. "I still have that incessant ringing in my ears. It is almost like someone poked a finger into them and pierced the eardrums." His eyes narrowed as he spoke.

Thora realized that the man was suspicious about that incident but there was no logical way for him to conclude that she had been responsible for it. "I asked you what time is it," she spoke loudly and clearly.

Bewdley looked at his watch. "It is just about five o'clock," he said. "I don't think that we will reach where I want to go today. I don't really want to drive in the dark with this car. I am not sure if the headlights work."

"Where do we want to go?" Thora asked.

"You are a tenacious one, aren't you?" Bewdley smiled. "I'm not going to tell you but I will leave you with this clue and that is that you will be pleasantly surprised."

Thora felt her eyebrows lift at the comment. It was expressed in such an amicable way that she felt very at ease in the car. In many ways, traveling with this murderer had been the most relaxing time that she had spent this summer. She really did not feel any stress with Bewdley Beacon despite the ominous warnings from Jakob and Truus Nells. He just did not seem to be the kind of man that would hold dark murder in his heart. "If you are not going to tell me that then at least you can tell me where we are going to spend the evening," she said.

"Don't worry, we will find a place," he responded. "We won't be staying in any fancy hotel or even a bed and breakfast. We are fugitives and we will have to just content ourselves with sleeping under the stars in a place where no man can see us."

The girl smirked at the thought of another night in the wilderness. But then this night would be different because she would not be alone like that first night when she fled from Mrs. Bianco's place. This night would be one that she could actually get some sleep unlike the night before when after joining up with Bewdley they spent the rest of the night driving.

Bewdley reached down to the dash on the car. Thora had not noticed it before but this new sedan that they were driving came equipped with a radio. The Motorized Egg did not have one and as far as she knew Uncle Thaddeus' Bentley did not have one either. "I wonder if I can catch some news on this contraption." Bewdley said as he turned the knob.

All at once the car was filled with a grating hissing sound as the radio was capturing dead air space between stations. Even Bewdley appeared to have heard it judging by the way that he jumped. "Try and find a station," he said to her. His finger pointed to the radio's dial.

Thora began slowly moving the chrome controller. She had not moved it very far when the hissing started to break up and there seemed to be a small semblance of organized signal coming through. It almost sounded like music was struggling to overcome the static, but as the girl tried to fine-tune it in she could not capture it. She continued adventuring with the dial. A semicircle away she honed in on a station that was coming in relatively clearly. This station was playing music as well. It was a piano piece by Chopin that she immediately recognized. She and Rebecca used to play this one together. She momentarily got lost in memories of her sister and the wonderful times that they spent side by side upon the piano stool. Even though they were forced to tap the keys by their taskmaster mother, there still was something beautiful about the way that their two souls joined in creating the pastoral harmonies.

"Keep going," Bewdley said. "That music will put me to sleep."

Thora held onto the station for a few moments longer, reveling in the sound and the memory. Then her finger twisted the dial and she moved through another thick band of static until she came upon a radio station that came in as clear as if it were airing from the backseat of the car. The station had to originate from somewhere nearby. It was bellowing out a stomping fiddle refrain that Thora knew could only come from that king of Shenandoah, Jim Spence.

"See if you can turn it up," Bewdley said.

Thora tried to do so but at first accidentally took the station off signal.

"No, no, no!" the driver groaned. "That is wrong!" His hand came down and found the volume knob once Thora returned to the radio station. He turned the volume up full. Even though the tinny speakers could not do the music justice it still sounded great to her. She found that her hands were clapping together to the beat of the music. Jim Spence's music made the dreary landscape come alive. Suddenly the land appeared to have a soul. She wished that the Nells were there at that moment so that they could witness this proof to what they had refused to believe. The West Virginian violinist had tapped into the essence of the land and brought it out in stirring and sweeping joyous cadences that seemed timeless and enduring.

Out of the corner of her eye Thora saw Bewdley smiling. The man was enjoying the music himself. He could not be all that bad if he liked music like this. Once again the girl wished that the ghosts were here to see this. They would not be so dead set on her getting away from him if they could see that this monster was not really a monster.

When the piece came to an end an announcer began to speak. His voice was blaring and made the speakers rattle. At once Thora turned down the volume to make the man sound intelligible.

"That was West Virginia's own Jim Spence," the man said. "If he does not get your heart pumping then maybe you best look inside your chest to see if there is one beating inside. It's five o'clock in Gallant and time for the news."

"Want me to change the station?" Thora asked while a jingle for a community dry goods store began to play.

"No," Bewdley answered. "It's best that we hear what is new in the world. There might be something on it about us."

"Gallant? I never heard of it," Thora commented as she sat up. Her eyes were looking out onto the countryside. The land was gently sloping. The cornfields had tall poplar trees marking out the fields' perimeters. She could not see any evidence of any nearby town.

"There are a lot of towns that I never heard of either," the man admitted. "I did hear of this one though. Gallant is the town where a miserable jail guard that worked in Rochester lived."

"You were in a jail in Rochester?" Thora piped.

"Girl, I have been in jails all over the Northeast. The stint I did in Rochester was just only two weeks but they were two weeks of hell because of that miserable guard from this town. He took an instant dislike to me and saw to it that I was kept in the hole for the whole time that I was there. He wanted to keep me in there even after my sentence ended. He was plenty pissed off when they let me go and he warned me that if he ever saw me on the outside that he would kill me on sight."

Before Thora could question Bewdley on this incident, the announcer came back on the air and began reading the news. The first few stories concerned themselves with the stock market. Stocks had never been higher but there were some doomsayers that said that all of this growth was spurious and inflated and that a period of adjustment would inevitably have to come and that it was likely that the country would fall into a recession. Thora found the story boring. It was not the stuff that she felt would have an effect on her life.

The next story was about Germany and a popular political figure there by the name of Adolf Hitler. Thora did not listen to what the newscaster had to say. She spoke overtop of the announcer to say to Bewdley, "My Uncle Thaddeus met with that man last winter. He went there to talk to him about opening up a factory there to supply their auto manufacturers with cable. My Uncle was very impressed with him."

"I'm not surprised. Your uncle is a stinking capitalist and he does not care what suffering he inflicts as long as he can make a buck or two," Bewdley responded. "Mark my word, girl, that Hitler chap will bring the world to the brink of war. He's a born trouble-maker."

"Turning to local news, police in the Gallant area have issued a notice to the public to be on the lookout for a Bewdley Beacon," the announcer said.

A knot came into existence in Thora's belly. She saw Bewdley's eyes widened.

"Bewdley Beacon is an escapee from a Pennsylvanian jail where he brutally murdered a guard and made fast his escape. Police believe that he may be in the Gallant vicinity after discovering an abandoned car known to be driven by Beacon on a county road. Beacon may be in the company of a female teenaged runaway from Grappling Haven, Pennsylvania. The pair was spotted together at a gas station in Hackenberry."

Bewdley slammed his fist onto the steering wheel. "You told them!" he roared.

"No, I didn't!" Thora countermanded in an equally voluminous tone. "Now, shut up and listen."

They had missed some of what the newsreader said. But he was still dealing with the same story. "Thora Meadowford, thirteen, is wanted for questioning in an incident that took place in her hometown of Grappling Haven where two women were found in a cabin. One woman, Josephine

Bianco, seventy-seven, was dead and the other woman, Margaret Whattam, thirty-four, was wounded and in a state of shock when rescued by her husband, James Whattam, an attorney in the employ of the Meadowford family. Mrs. Whattam is listed in stable condition in a Pittsburgh hospital. She had suffered a hatchet wound to her kidney. She is expected to survive."

Thora immediately felt relief that Margaret had been found alive and that she would recuperate. As she looked outside of the car window, she felt that she had entered a new world and a new era in her life. Everything was going to come to an end soon. She was now living in the postscript period of her existence.

"Police almost captured the fugitives when Officer Lou Bombino just about nabbed the pair on a deserted Pennsylvania road. Beacon and Meadowford managed to elude the policeman and left him stranded for nearly six hours in the wilderness. They took his car and exchanged it for a used vehicle in Hawkins Corners. The pair next showed up at a Pittsburgh diner. Then their trail was muddied until they reached the Hackenberry General Store. At this store, Miss Meadowford confided to Lilly Hartman that she was Beacon's hostage."

Bewdley's jaw tightened but he did not say anything. He continued driving while the announcer continued with his prolonged story. "Following a short chase where the fugitives once again gave the police the slip they traded vehicles once more. Then just only moments ago it was discovered that they stole a car from a nature preserve and abandoned their Hawkins Corners car at the juncture of County Roads 18 and 44. Police warn the public that the fugitives are extremely dangerous. The public is not to take matters into their own hands. If you spot the fugitives call the police immediately."

The newsreader went on to another news story. "We're going to have to get rid of this car," Thora said to Bewdley.

"Thanks to you," the man said through constrained hostility. "Why did you go and rat us out?"

"I didn't!" Thora said defensively. "The woman recognized you right off the bat. She asked me if you were the person on the newspaper. I told her that it wasn't you but I don't think that she believed me."

"Why didn't you tell me this earlier!" Bewdley stormed. "I would have done things differently had I known."

The girl began scrambling for words. "I thought that I had her convinced that you were somebody else. I didn't want to worry you over something that was not going to amount to anything."

The fist came down hard on the steering wheel once more. "Well, it did amount to something! They are hot on our tail and it won't be long before they have us pinned down."

"In a story related to our top fugitive story, Samuel Angus Meadowford, father of the girl Thora Meadowford, had his first day of court today in Grappling Haven," the radio announcer almost seemed like he purposefully was breaking up the conversation between Thora and Bewdley. "Meadowford is charged with four counts of homicide in the deaths of a Michigan family. Today in trial, witnesses for the state described Meadowford's agitated condition when he got into an altercation with Art Rozelle at a Grappling Haven restaurant early in July. The subject of the fight concerned labor problems at the Meadowford factory in Dearborn, Michigan. As witnesses described their accounts of the altercation, Meadowford sat quietly. But his wife Cora on several occasions disrupted proceedings with outbursts that questioned the witnesses' motives. The judge presiding over the trial was forced to charge Mrs. Meadowford with contempt of court. Mrs. Meadowford now is spending the night in the very jail where Bewdley Beacon had murdered Peter Kyle. The trial will continue tomorrow when it is expected that the State will call upon Thaddeus Meadowford to testify against his nephew."

"Mom's in jail!" Thora laughed. She did not mean to react that way but it just happened. When it rains it pours.

"We'll soon be there too if we don't do something about it!" Bewdley responded. His hand went down to the radio and he turned it off. "I've had just about enough bad news for one day."

"So, we are going to have to get rid of this car," Thora said. She just did not know how to deal with the new order in the world. It was a collapsing existence and one where she could not even begin to guess what her fate would be. She was wanted by the police because of what happened at Mrs. Bianco's place. What was her crime there? She had not inflicted the wound on Mrs. Whattam—that was done by those diabolical spirits that resided in that extension of Hell. She knew that everything depended on how Margaret described events and she knew that there was no way in Hell that Margaret would have seen things the way that she saw them. There was a strong case supporting the girl's limited capacity to function rationally. They would deem her insane and her final plight most likely would be a lifelong commitment to a sanitarium.

"Among other things that we have to do," Bewdley responded.

"What's that mean?"

For the first time since they heard the news report, the man turned to face her as he drove. "That means that our partnership is coming to an end. We are going to have to go our separate ways in order for me to get through this thing."

All at once the Nells' warnings that Bewdley intended to kill her came to Thora's mind. She had picked up on the man's use of the word 'me' rather than 'us'. He was looking at the situation from only his perspective. If they parted company and he allowed her to live then he would have to always contend with the knowledge that she had gained about him. It was far easier for his peace to have her mouth forever silenced. And what was one more killing to him? He had murdered at least three people by her reckoning—the person in Tonawanda, Mrs. Bianco, and Officer Kyle. There may be more for all she knew. He was already facing the chair. Her life did not mean anything to him other than that her death might buy him his freedom if he manages to get out of the country.

"Why are you looking at me like that?" Bewdley cried.

Thora did not want to tell him the reason. She did not want this outcome to be the topic of conversation. "I just don't think that we should separate," she rasped. "I think that we should stay together. We work well as a team!"

"So well that we are the top story all over the news," Bewdley retorted. "If you did not open your yap to that old lady back at the gas station, no one would have been any the wiser about where we are. But you did open your yap and we are in one big mess. We don't work well as a team, girl. It is best that we part company."

Even while he spoke of the end of the partnership Bewdley continued driving along the road. Like all the roads he picked, it was one that was seldom traveled. They had passed only a few cars coming from the opposite direction and as best as Thora could judge there was nobody going the same way as them. It was however farm country and there were farmhouses scattered on both sides of the road. If Bewdley intended to stop the car and drop her off he would not do so here because of these farms. He needed some place where they could not be seen. Then he would kill her and deposit her body or if there were some mercy in his heart he would just simply leave her standing at the side of the road in the middle of nowhere.

The road began a long arcing bend to the right through some very tall pine trees that cut out the day's sun and replaced it with eerie shadows. Somehow Thora knew that this was going to be where the partnership was going to end. Bewdley placed his foot on the brakes.

"No!" Thora cried out. "Please don't!"

"What are you getting so worked up over?" Bewdley said as his foot returned to the gas pedal.

"I thought that you were going to stop and dump me here! You started braking!"

Bewdley laughed. "I was only slowing down to get through this turn. It is a lot sharper than I had imagined. You don't want me rolling the car, do you?"

Thora felt a little silly as her eyes watched the car come out of the bend and onto a straightaway. Right at the end of the bend was a pair of farmhouses on both sides of the road. If Bewdley had intended to kill her here the occupants of these houses might have heard him. Thora guessed that he must have known those houses were there and for that reason did not choose to stop and do what he wanted to do.

"I wish that there was somewhere that we could exit this road," he said. "There are too many eyes here." He continued driving.

Eyes for what, Thora wondered.

Chapter 43

Invisible Roar

Up ahead on the side of the road Thora started to make out someone walking a large dog. Its red fur glistened in the sunshine like it was a coat of stars set against a burgundy ether. As they got closer Bewdley told her to get down. He did not want the pedestrian to see that there was a man and girl in the car. That might tip the stranger off if he had just been listening to the news. Thora did as she was told. She did not want the same thing happening either.

As she sat in the car with her head bent forward and between her knees she saw Bewdley's feet once more move from the gas pedal to the brake. His foot came down hard onto it and the car began to waver wildly. There was a thud and a bounce. When it finally came to a stop she righted her body and looked around. Out of the rearview mirror she saw a man standing over a writhing red coat. Immediately she pieced together what had happened. Bewdley had run over the dog.

The man was crying out in anguish and at that moment turned his head and looked toward the car sitting parked yards away. She could hear his muffled scream of rage. "You killed my dog!" the man roared and started coming at the vehicle. He was reaching for something under his shirt.

Bewdley's foot stomped onto the gas pedal and the car zigzagged along the gravel road trying to carve out a straight path for itself. The grieving dog owner did not reach them in time.

"Damn!" Bewdley said. "I feel terrible! I love dogs! It ran out in front of me and I could not stop in time."

Thora noticed that there were tears at the corners of Bewdley's eyes. Once again she wondered how a man that could be branded a killer could have such soft spots in his personality. She did not believe that he would do anything to harm her.

"I told you to keep your head down," Bewdley's mood instantly changed. "If that guy had spotted you then he could be able to identify us."

At that moment there was an explosion behind them. Shattered glass sprayed everywhere. Thora could feel some of it knick the back of her scalp. She ran her hand upon it and felt something hot and moist in her hair. When she glanced over to her partner she saw that he had been lacerated across his cheek and that several strings of blood were racing down it.

"The bastard took a shot at us!" Bewdley exclaimed as he wiped away the blood. "Are you hurt?" he asked.

Through the corner of her eye she saw that the rear windshield had been blown away. Far in the distance along the road she saw the man still pointing his revolver at them. Instinctively she ducked. When nothing happened, she slowly and cautiously returned to her upright position.

"We're out of his range now," Bewdley said. More blood appeared across his cheek. "Are you okay?" he repeated his earlier question.

"I think that I'm okay," Thora responded. "I might have some minor scratches at the back of my head. Some of the glass got me."

"Let me stop and have a look," Bewdley said. They had rounded a bend and were no longer in sight of the man with the gun. Bewdley brought the car to a halt and he examined Thora's hair. Suddenly Thora winced as she experienced a very sharp pain.

"You have a shard of glass lodged into your scalp," Bewdley said. "I'm going to try and pull it out. It might hurt but we can't keep it stuck in there. Tilt your head my way."

She leaned forward toward Bewdley's chest. She could feel his warm breath flood over her forehead as his fingers fumbled trying to part her hair to get to the glass. If this man intended her death he would not be taking the time to do this, she realized. She also thought that it was rather a risky thing to do given that that dog owner was still back there and might soon be coming into range to shoot again.

"There," Bewdley finally said. "I think that I have got it."

Thora felt something move out of her scalp. It hurt at first but then almost immediately felt soothed.

"This was in the back of your head," Bewdley said, holding a small fragment of glass in front of her eyes. It was about half the size of his fingernail. It did not look like much but she knew that if it had any more velocity or hit her just a few inches lower it might have killed her.

At that moment they heard another gunshot. Thora turned and saw that the dog owner was racing towards them with his gun held out before him. He looked like he was going to fire again.

Bewdley very quickly put his foot on the gas and began driving once more. "That was close," he said as the distance between the car and the pedestrian widened. He looked at the farms that surrounded the road. "I wonder how many of them are calling the police right at this very instance?"

They had driven several miles without any sign of any cops on the road. Thora knew that their luck could not hold out much longer. Sooner or later the police were going to show up and then it would all be over. She could not see how they were going to escape this time. The police knew where they were. They knew what they were driving. It was all just a matter of time.

Both sides of the road were given over to agriculture. Farmhouses and out buildings were strewn everywhere. There were no side roads that could offer them any alternative routes.

They were coming up to yet another farm, a huge one with a stately manse sitting proudly upon a hill. The building almost looked like the White House. It was probably built with that residence as its model. Beside this farm was an immense well-kept barn and beside this barn was an airplane, a crop duster Thora guessed.

Unexpectedly Bewdley pulled into the farm's long, winding driveway. "What are you doing?" she asked.

"I think I have found our ticket to Canada," Bewdley responded. The car drove past the house and onto the field where the airplane sat. As they went by the house Thora looked to see if there was anybody home. If there was they were nowhere to be seen. There were no vehicles parked near it.

Bewdley hid the car behind the barn so that it could not be espied from the road. He scrambled out of the vehicle and went to the airplane and looked at the fuel gauge. "This is our lucky day!" he cried. "It has a full tank."

"You are going to fly this thing?" Thora asked out of amazement. She could not believe that they were going to attempt such a feat.

"Of course. I flew over France during the Great War," he said. "This plane should be a piece of cake to me." It was bi-winged and seemed that it could have been there at Kitty Hawk twenty years ago when Frank and Wilbur were practicing with new designs.

"You were a fighter pilot?" Thora had not expected that Bewdley would have such an accomplishment in his background.

The man nodded. "I was trained by the Army and sent over there to fight the Kaiser and his henchmen and his aces."

"Did you get any kills?" the girl asked. She had read many pieces about dog fighting in school. These aerial duelists seemed like they were harbingers of a bygone era when chivalry meant something, when there was a gentleman courtesy in the derring-do and the rules of engagement were governed by a respect for the dignity of the opponent.

"I really don't like talking about what I did during the war. It brings back bad memories to me," Bewdley said as he inspected the plane to determine its flight-worthiness.

"You did, I just know you did!" Thora harped. She was beginning to admire Bewdley Beacon more and more. There was far more to him than her dad. Langley could never measure up to Bewdley. Her father was not conscripted during the Great War as he was enrolled in a business school in Massachusetts at the time. It did not matter that he was flunking out. He avoided being drafted much to the chagrin of Sambo and Thaddeus. They wanted him to enlist with the Navy and carry out the Meadowford tradition there. But Langley would have none of it. Fighting and defending one's country were for the working class and not the ruling class, he argued and got his way.

"The aerial war over France was not the way that you imagined, girl," Bewdley responded. "It was not a romanticized knight's tale brought forward to the Twentieth Century. It was brutal and it was frightening and death was very real. The carnage created by a crashed airplane is ghastly. A human body should not be so viciously ripped asunder and strewn over the countryside like tomato paste." He was standing by the propeller, his hands feeling the blades looking for any disfigurement there that might affect the performance of the aircraft. "Keep your eyes open while I get this contraption going."

Thora looked back at the farmhouse. There were some open windows facing towards them. There were white curtains fluttering in the breeze. If there were people behind those curtains they were very well concealed.

Suddenly the engine began to spit and then chug. She saw the propellers come into life. Soon they were in an invisible roar.

"Climb in!" Bewdley yelled at the top of his lungs. "We're on our way!"

The girl had never been in an airplane before. She had no idea whatsoever how to board one. Bewdley must have recognized her ignorance and had her place a foot on the bottom wing while grabbing hold of the top wing and lifting herself up. From this height she saw the cockpit. It had two chairs in it, one behind the other. Instinctively she went to the rear seat when she felt a tap on her shoulder from Bewdley. He was standing right below her. He signaled that she was to take the front seat. "But I don't know how to fly!" she complained.

"The pilot sits at the rear," Bewdley bellowed as he hoisted himself into the rear seat.

Thora worked her way into the crammed space allotted to her. It was an awkward feat given her cumbersome skirt that seemed to want to snag itself upon every surface obstruction available. When she nestled down onto the leather seat, she saw that there was a small windshield in front of her. Through that windshield her eyes detected motion coming from the house. Two elderly women were racing out through the door and running towards them. Accompanying them was a pair of snarling, snapping hounds.

All of a sudden the plane lunged forward throwing Thora back against her seat. The path of the airplane was moving directly towards the two women. The approaching plane did not intimidate them. The two women did not scatter out of the way. Thora could no longer see the dogs and imagined that they could have been right under the plane's wings.

The girl wondered if it was Bewdley's plan to run the women and dogs over but then the flying machine started to turn. It was facing a long earth-packed runway.

The engine started to roar tenfold. The two women were only ten yards away. The girl could see the anger in their eyes as they protested loudly against someone taking their private airplane. She could not hear their words because of the plane. They were still coming towards them, their arms were extended forward as if it were their intention to grab the plane and keep it from going down the runway.

But they were not given the opportunity to do so as the airplane began racing down the field at a dizzying speed. Thora felt the draft of wind circle around the windshield and blow at the side of her head. She was terribly frightened by the ordeal. Yet at the same time she was thoroughly exhilarated.

Then suddenly she heard a ferocious growl right next to her. She turned her head and looked right into the exposed teeth of a great hound. The dog must have leapt onto the wing. Its paws were gripping the edge of the cockpit. The creature meant to climb inside.

A hand appeared. It grabbed the hound by the scruff of the neck and then the dog was gone. The animal was flung onto the hard, unforgiving airstrip. Thora did not dare to look behind her. She had seen enough writhing dogs for one day.

The plane started to lift. Thora felt it in her belly. The adjacent treetops that marked out the farm fields were now at eyeball level. She looked over the side of the plane and saw that the land was dropping away from her. A memory of being on the top floor of Jim Whattam's office building came back to her. That had been her previous record in altitude. She sensed that that height would be nothing to what she was going to shortly attain.

Her field of vision encapsulated the manse, its barns, its fields, its runway, its animals and its women. It captured the narrow strip of road that joined this estate to its neighboring lands. It all seemed so small now. It was like looking down onto a space given over to the surface engineering of industrious insects. All of the diligent work could not look beyond what it had declared as its own. Thora now saw that horizons could stretch and that there were no limitations to this process.

Behind her Bewdley began a looping trajectory that brought the airplane once again over the farm, this time at an elevation hundreds of feet above it. The farm appeared to be lost in the immensity of the land that projected outwards in all directions. The two women were nothing more than black disturbances upon a field of green. The road was a thin string that wound its way over the tapestry of the land.

Upon this road Thora spotted racing vehicles to the left and to the right of the farm. She felt a tap on her shoulder. She turned and saw Bewdley's face distorted by the wind. He was pointing to the cars. "We got out of there just in time!" His voice was loud but barely audible in the howling gusts. "Those are cops!"

Thora returned her attention below her and saw the first of the cars pull up to the farm. The others followed it in. If they had not taken to the air they would have been nabbed. There would have been no way for them to escape had they stuck to the more conventional means of travel.

"They can't get us up here!" Bewdley laughed and began arcing the plane to the north.

Thora had not noticed it before but she could see it now. In the distance was a deep blue band that could only be a great lake. It had to be Lake Ontario. On the other side of that lake was Canada!

Chapter 44

Dog Fight

There was still plenty of daylight left. It was no more than six o'clock in the evening Thora guessed. It stayed light until around 9:00 at this time of the year. That would give them three hours to reach the lake and then fly across it.

Yet even though they were traveling well over one hundred miles per hour that stretch of blue that was Lake Ontario was not getting any closer at any impressionable rate.

Below her she could see how her species had altered the terrain. The land seemed to be a quilt work of different patterns, each pattern indicating a particular type of crop that dominated it. The cornfields were a deep green while the wheat fields were golden. Bewdley said that they were cruising at about six hundred feet above the ground.

This was Thora's first time in an airplane and she had to admit to herself that she loved it. Her fear of heights did not seem to be a factor as they soared over the terrain. There was something qualitatively different about sitting in an airplane as compared to being in a tree or standing at a cliff's edge. The land below just did not seem so far away. Perhaps it was because of the way that the ground still overwhelmingly dominated her field of vision that its vertical distance felt to be diminished. If anything there was more land to be seen and that overrode any innate fear of falling response.

She saw the grid displays of several communities as they worked their way northward. It was uncanny how much these villages resembled each other from above. It was in the same way that a robin would build a nest that would look like any other nest that other robins would build that humans built their nests in the same predetermined style as other humans. There was a geometric regularity in the way that the roads would meet each other at right angles and that as the closer you got to the intersection the taller and grander the buildings would stand adjacent to those roads. And then as you drew away from the main intersection the houses would begin to diminish and become smaller and have larger gaps between them. Civilization as viewed from the air appeared to showcase that mankind was nothing more than another species trying to adapt to the ecology presented to it by the land. The land was the dominant force and not the creatures that endeavored to overcome it. Once again Thora thought of how the Indians bestowed a soul upon the land. From the air this soul was very evident. Perhaps Jakob and Truus Nells should see the world from this perspective, and then they would recognize that their ghostly cosmology needed to be broadened.

"I think that we have company," Bewdley shouted into her ear.

She had not expected to hear any voice at all and its sudden appearance made her jump. When she turned her head she saw Bewdley pointing to the southwest. At first she could not make out what he was trying to show her. But then the sun glinted off a surface. It produced a striking momentary flash and then it was gone. And then there was another flash and then another. She was not quite sure what she was looking at.

"They're airplanes," Bewdley said. "Three of them."

As he announced this determination, Thora was now able to make out the tiny shapes of three biplanes flying in a formation in the distance. They seemed to be like a patrol of mosquitoes to her. They seemed to be fixed on a trajectory that would intercept her path.

"Are they coming after us?" she asked her partner, feeling some alarm that she might receive some first-hand experience at dog fighting.

"Not sure," Bewdley responded. "They don't look like they are military planes. But it is better to be cautious than sorry." The plane's motor began to roar at a higher pitch and Thora sensed that their velocity had suddenly increased.

She kept her eyes focused on the trio. They had not altered anything in their flight pattern in reaction to her plane's faster speed. They were probably nothing more than a flying club enjoying an evening flight under the beautiful sunshine. She returned her attention to what was in front of them.

The lake started to take up more of the horizon. She was beginning to make out some cargo ships upon it with long trailing wakes behind them. The crests of the wakes were white and shone in the gloaming glow of the evening. These long steam-powered vessels were moving in identical directions converging at some fixed point on shore.

"They're lakers," Bewdley explained. "It's my guess that they are going to Rochester to either drop off or pick up supplies. Probably both."

As he mentioned the city, Thora could notice a discoloration in the sky to the northeast. It was the fetid contamination that huge groupings of humans produce. The air was being poisoned by industrial waste. For the first time in her life Thora was beginning to understand that the air that enveloped the world was really no different than the waters in the ocean. If you dirty the water the fish soon find it hard to breathe and they begin to die. Those foul emissions coming from the city were doing the same thing to the milieu of life that relies on the air for respiration. She started to yearn for a bygone era when men did not pollute their environment.

They were now almost above Lake Ontario. They were going to be crossing its shoreline somewhere to the west of the city of Rochester. She could see its outlining suburbs lying underneath the discolored tainted air. There were roads leading into it and these strips of asphalt contained a ceaseless flow of vehicles heading in and heading out of the sprawling urban settlement. It was an interesting and busy sight but one that the girl found distasteful.

However when she shifted her focus to what was ahead of her she recaptured the awe and splendor of the pristine Earth as her eyes fell upon the meeting point of water and air. All that she saw was nothing but where sky and lake met and it was spectacular and it took her breath away. There was something very primal and powerful in this vista and it stirred in her a sense of how insignificant she and her fellow humans were in the greater scheme of things. This was where God resided. God did not live in the hearts of humans. He lived on a grander scale and his concerns and interests were at the macrocosmic level rather than the paltry issues of how the smaller creatures that infested the macrocosm interrelated with each other. God did not care about aberrant ants that did not live by their colony's code of ethics. God did not care about aberrant people that stepped outside of the laws set by the dominant classes of the species. God was all about the air, the sea and the land. And if something upset that interrelationship between the three such as the industrial waste that was pouring into all three of them Thora was sure that that would incur God's wrath.

The plane crossed over the dividing line between land and lake. Bewdley tapped her on the shoulder to make sure that she was aware of this fact. She needed no such reminding. She was well aware of it. "We are no longer above U.S. soil," he said to her.

"But we are still in the United States," she answered, showing the man that she was aware that the international border that separated her country and its northern neighbor was somewhere out in the unending water that made up the lower half of her field of vision.

"The flying club is coming out over the lake too," Bewdley responded, pointing to the southwest. Thora saw the three biplanes cutting over the lake's perimeter. Somehow they seemed to be a bit closer than the last time that she looked out at them. They had increased their speed as well and she was beginning to have her doubts that they were a flying club any longer.

"I think that we might have some trouble," Bewdley said. "They are probably under instruction not to engage us until we are over water. They don't want us crashing down on some house below." He pulled back on the controls and the little airplane started to climb higher into the sky. "Let's see if they are just casual pilots having an evening pleasure flight."

Thora watched as two of the three planes matched Bewdley's tactic and began cruising upward to attain the same altitude. The third one stayed below but had altered its vector and was now on an intercepting diagonal with Bewdley's plane.

"They don't know who they are dealing with," the man cried with some bravado. "I flew thousands of miles over enemy territory on reconnaissance missions. The Kaiser's aces could not catch me and neither can these greenhorns!"

The airplane dropped at a vertigo-inducing rate and it veered sharply to the northwest. The force of the gravity pinned Thora to her seat and she watched in terror as the rolling waves of Lake Ontario drew nearer and nearer. She did not quite understand what was going on. Part of her wondered if their plane had been shot down. But then when the plane was no more than a hundred feet above the lake it leveled out and began racing at high speed on a northeast trajectory.

She twisted her neck to see where the other airplanes were. She could not see them anywhere. But then one dropped out of the sky immediately above them. And then there was one directly behind them. She did not know where the third one was. The plane's wings were obscuring her field of vision. As her eyes were trying to look past the wood and fabric design, she saw some of the wing's white canvas begin to tear apart.

"God damn it!" Bewdley roared. "They are shooting at us!" He pulled on the controls and the airplane began to ascend on a very sharp angle. They soared right past the plane that had been above them. As they whistled past it Thora could see its helmeted occupants. The one in front was a gunner while the one in the rear was its pilot. The gunner had no time to react. He had not expected his quarry to make such a maneuver.

Their plane climbed upward and upward. They had not been this high before. From this elevation Thora saw the dark northern shore to the lake start to come into view. It was Canada. It did not seem that far away. But in that vista she saw something flash as the sun caught its metallic body. It was the third airplane and it was coming straight at them. She saw the staccato flashing of gunfire as the plane drew nearer. More of her wing's fabric was being torn apart as the bullets ripped into them.

Bewdley swiftly reacted. He swooped downward and then yawed clockwise to the right and the plane's orientation was now vertical to the lake below them. They were racing sideways and slowly spinning over. It had a dizzying effect on the girl as what was above was now below her and what was below was now above. Her stomach and her mind had great difficulty trying to incorporate this flip flop in her perceptions. The airplane was now upside down and Thora saw the other airplane zip past her. Whether its true position was above her or below her she did not know and did not want to cipher. She saw the other two airplanes coming up to greet her plane. The gunners in them were letting their bullets fly.

Bewdley performed some more aerial gymnastics to scurry away from the line of fire. He was truly proving that he had not fabricated his tale of his wartime exploits. He was a pilot extraordinaire. He was an artist in his flying machine and his canvas was the open sky. He made that plane of theirs dance and perform stunts that defied gravity and common sense. Yet he was in a plane that was equipped with no weaponry and all of his zigzagging and pirouettes were only delaying the inevitable. The other planes were armed and outnumbered him. Eventually they would hit their mark and then hit it repeatedly and savagely and render the airplane inoperable and send it hurling downward to plunge and break apart in the wild moody waves of Lake Ontario.

The man must have realized his position for he suddenly sent his airplane spinning downward towards the lake and straight through the three enemy planes. They had formed a triad below him and were about to launch a flight plan that would have encircled Bewdley. The Great War ace sliced right through the center of the triad coming so close to one plane that Thora may have been able to hop onto its wing. Just before they were upon the lake Bewdley righted the plane and was now flying no more than five feet above the wave tops. Thora saw all three of the other planes begin their descent toward them. From three different mounts came a hail of bullets that were ripping into the water on either side of Bewdley's plane. Sooner or later these bullets would correct their courses and begin burying themselves into the airplane and its occupants.

"We've got to be close to the international border by now!" Bewdley hollered as he kept his plane as snug to the water as possible. There was a danger that they could tunnel themselves right into an unseen slumbering giant wall of water.

"What difference would it make?" Thora cried out.

"They would not have any jurisdiction on the Canadian side of the border. If they shoot us down over Canadian waters then there would be hell to pay for them," Bewdley explained.

"How in the hell would anybody know where the border is out here!" Thora responded. Bewdley was pinning his hopes on something that could easily be overlooked or dismissed. They were wanted fugitives guilty of violent crimes. They were not refugees. The Canadian government would not feel that their dominion had been violated. If they were going to get out of this mess then it would have to take a miracle and that miracle would not be found in any international legislation.

The three pursuing airplanes were now cruising above the waves. They seemed to have an unending supply of ammunition. But for all the bullets that they spent they were not finding their targets. It almost seemed to Thora that something was already protecting them although she could not figure out what it could be.

Then, as Bewdley veered to the right towards the lowering sun, Thora thought for a moment that she saw something very veiled and wispy. It was cloaked over her plane. It stretched from the propeller to the tail. It bore two elongated faces that she had seen before but thought that she would never see again. Jakob and Truus Nells were somehow covering the airplane like a thin but impenetrable transparent surface. Their spiritual hides were absorbing the gunfire and keeping it from reaching its mark. The old Dutch couple had sworn to her that they would protect her and despite her betrayal of them they remained committed to their promise. They were stopping the bullets. They were allowing her and the monster, as they called Bewdley, to live.

A few moments after Thora discovered the real reason that they were still in the air, one by one the three pursuit planes pulled up and away, giving up on the chase. As they lifted away Thora was able to catch a glimpse of the logo painted on their fuselages. They were Coast Guard planes.

"We must be over Canadian waters now," Bewdley said, letting up on the throttle and slowing the airplane down. "Thank God for international borders." He had obviously not seen what had protected him in his wild dash over the American side of Lake Ontario. If the ghosts had not been there then the little airplane that they were in would have been forever lost on the murky bottom of that lake.

"Won't the Canadians send out planes of their own to shoot us down?" Thora asked. "I mean that I highly doubt that we would be welcome guests!" She did not want to tell him about what she saw. He would never believe her. He would rather believe that his flying prowess was able to nullify the expert marksmanship of the U.S. Coast Guard.

"I don't think Canada is equipped with any fighter planes to defend its southern border. It is a poorer country and it also has a different mindset than what we possess in America," Bewdley responded.

Ahead of them they could see the treed shoreline of the Province of Ontario looming ahead.

Chapter 45

Welcome to Canada

But Bewdley was proven wrong. The Canadians did have armed forces stationed in southern Ontario. There was a squadron of fighter planes stationed in Trenton, Ontario. This squadron had been alerted by the U.S. Coast Guard to be on the watch for an airplane carrying two fugitives of the law that were trying to enter Canada over the lake.

No sooner had Bewdley made his comment than Thora spotted six biplanes coming toward them from the northeast. These planes did not appear as sleek and swift as those of the U.S. Coast Guard but they were not all that shoddy. They were deadly killers in their own right. They had lots of fuel, lots of ammunition, and lots of space and they were determined to shoot down their quarry before it came over Canadian soil.

Thora pointed to the formation. She did this more for the benefit of the two ghosts than for the pilot. Truus and Jakob saw the approaching planes and groaned. It could not be easy for them to stretch themselves out and have their essence riddled by incessant gunfire. "The next time you see hitchhikers on the road do them a favor and don't stop!" Truus commented as she fastened her hands to the propeller mount.

When Bewdley saw the planes he as well sighed. "They're not making it easy for us." He pulled back on the controls and once again began a series of evasive maneuvers meant to dodge and elude his pursuers.

The Canadian planes broke formation and splintered off into three separate groups. Thora tried to follow all of them but kept losing them when she switched from one group to another. These planes were using the setting sun to their advantage and were cruising in the blinding glare. Bewdley complained about this fact.

Then without any precursors the six Canadian planes appeared out of nowhere. They had Bewdley's plane entirely surrounded in all directions—front, back, left, right, top and bottom. It must have been a practiced maneuver it was so expertly actioned. There was no space for Bewdley to pull off one of his daring stunts. He had been corralled and forced into a tight box. Not one shot was fired. The Canadians were escorting him.

"Where are they taking us?" Thora asked. She could almost reach up and touch the bottom of the plane that was flying directly above her. Another plane filled up her field of vision to the front.

"My guess is that we are going to their airbase," Bewdley responded. He was looking around trying to find holes in the formation where he could punch out and dash off. Every time he joggled the stick and began a veering motion the Canadians would respond and block the gap.

"What will they do to us there?" Thora's spirits were beginning to sink for she knew the answer. They would send her back to Grappling Haven to face the music. Her spirited romp into freedom was coming to an end. They had been finally captured. The high adventure was over and now it was time for the dreary aftermath where she would be thrown into an asylum for the rest of her days.

Bewdley did not answer her. He somehow knew that she was well aware of what was to become of them.

They were flying towards the northeast. The Canadians managed to ensure that Bewdley stayed to the vector they had selected for him. Thora could see the exasperation in his face as everything he tried was immediately frustrated.

"There's no need for us to be stretched like the skins of balloons any longer," Jakob said. "They are not going to shoot at you." The ghost and his partner let their feet go from the plane's tail. Jakob drew his legs forward until they were overtop of the wing. Then they released their hands from the propellers and drew their bodies back until they both were seated, Jakob on the left wing and Truus on the right one.

"What is happening here?" Truus asked, once she had herself properly squared away on the canvas.

"They are taking us to their base where they will send us home," Thora answered. She was glad that she was reunited with the Nells although their presence did nothing to relieve the sense of hopelessness that was engulfing her.

"Who are they?" Jakob asked. "I don't recognize the insignia."

"They are the Canadians," Thora said.

"The British, you mean," Jakob corrected her.

"No, the Canadians," Thora responded.

"They are their own country now?" the old ghost said with some curiosity.

"They have been for quite some time now!" Thora was surprised that Jakob did not know this.

"Since when?"

"I don't know," the girl replied. "They have been Canada all of my life."

"Did they have a revolution like our nation to throw out those bullheaded Brits?"

"I don't know Mr. Nells!"

One of the planes chose to move ahead at that moment. More of its fuselage came into view.

"That's a Ensign Jack!" Jakob declared. "They are still British! They are still the enemy!"

It dawned on Thora that Jakob Nells was still a product of his times. He had lived through the Revolutionary War when America ceased to be a British colony while Canada remained loyal to the monarch in London. He also had experienced the War of 1812 when hostilities heated up between the British north of the Great Lakes and the new American nation. He would still consider the Brits to be the enemy. He would not know that Britain and America were now close allies and had fought together as partners against the Kaiser and the Germans during the Great War.

"They are our friends now!" Thora retorted. "Canada is our friend and they are their own country too! Don't ask me why they have the English flag on their planes."

"The redcoats can never be my friends!" Jakob protested. "Too many of my brave neighbors fell to the guns of King George. I will not dishonor them by making peace with the sons of the men that butchered them!"

He rose up to his feet and scrambled up to the top wing where Thora could no longer see him. What was he doing? When she turned to ask his wife that question she saw that Truus was straddled on the plane's tail. Then, right before her eyes, the old female ghost leapt back at the Canadian plane that was behind them. She easily hopped over the propeller and windshield and began mauling the pilot. The Canadian planes were single-man craft.

Simultaneously the airplane above them and the airplane to the rear began breaking formation. The one on top yawed to the right and flew right into the wings of the craft that was flying there. The one in the rear picked up speed and crashed into the airplane to the left. Within a few seconds the two ghosts had taken out four Canadian planes. The remaining two, the one below them and the one in front of them, dashed away to avoid being hit by their suddenly disabled partners.

When Bewdley saw the gap that opened up before him he was quick enough in his senses to take advantage of it and he angled to the left and downward where he started skimming the lake top towards the approaching shore.

Somehow both Truus and Jakob managed to get back to the fugitives' plane. They were none the worse for wear after their daring stunts. "Damned redcoats are not going to bully us around anymore!" Jakob huffed as he watched four parachutes slowly descend to the lake. There were some boats in the vicinity that witnessed the spectacle. There was no need to worry about the flyers. They would be rescued.

"What the devil happened there?" Bewdley cried out. He would not have seen the Nells ghosts. The sudden erratic behavior of the Canadian airplanes would mystify him.

"Maybe we have friends in high places," Thora answered. She was in a pure state of glee. They were still free. Their horrible fates had been postponed and they were given a new opportunity to try and eradicate once and for all what destiny had planned for them.

The remaining two Canadian aircraft were nowhere to be seen. Whether they chose to return to base and report the unexplainable accident or whether they were regrouping and about to launch another tactic Thora at the moment did not know.

Bewdley slowly brought the plane upward to an altitude where the craft could clear the sandy cliffs of the northern shores of Lake Ontario. As they climbed upward and Thora was able to glance over the Canadian coast the other two airplanes suddenly came into view. One was approaching from the left while the other was approaching from the right.

Unlike earlier, the pilots this time were making use of their guns. Bullets were zinging at the fugitives' airplane. Jakob and Truus raced to deflect the hailing gunfire before they could inflict any damage. Thora instinctively ducked so that the cockpit could shield her body. She could hear the throbbing of the plane's skin as the bullets pierced the fuselage. When these sharp echoes ended she knew that the Nells had successfully built up their defenses. But before she lifted her head she heard a very nauseating sound. It was the whining cry of a falling airplane. As she dared to look the first thing that she saw was Bewdley. A bullet had found him. Half his neck was torn away in a gory gash. Dark red blood was pumping from it. Yet he was still conscious. "Where did they come from?" he muttered through his bubbling throat. His closing eyes were looking toward Truus and Jakob Nells.

"They have been with us all along," Thora answered. Her eyes were clouding over with tears as she realized that her partner was about to die.

At that moment there was a great explosion above them. The Canadians were not as well practiced, as they should have been. The two airplanes had collided head on. They did not have enough time to make evasive maneuvers once their quarry fell out of the sky and they found that they were on a deadly path. They flew straight into each other and created a massive fireball as they hit.

It was then that Thora realized that she was in very grave danger. Her airplane was racing downward towards the sandy dunes below her. She had maybe just a few seconds left before the plane would pierce into the ground like a giant javelin.

The barely conscious Bewdley seemed to be aware of the dilemma and despite his fleeting grip on life he was still working the stick, doing everything that he could to prevent the crash. He tried to pull back and allow the plane to acquire some lift but he just did not have the strength left in him to match the overpowering grip of gravity. The plane was still heading downward at an unsafe angle.

"Help me!" he gasped.

Jakob Nells responded to the request and placed his ghostly hands alongside those of Bewdley on the controls and the two pulled on it, the dead and the dying. They were desperately trying to yank the plane out of the freefall but they were up against the monumental power of gravity and the nose of the plane was not responding. It seemed inevitable that the airplane was going to pound a deep crater in the sands below them.

"Take my hand!" Truus said to Thora. The old woman had suddenly appeared sitting straddled on the nose of the plane right in front of the girl.

Without any time to think Thora took hold of the old woman's fingers and allowed Truus to lift her from the cockpit. Once enough of her body was out, Truus wrapped her arms around Thora and within a moment's flash had leaped from the falling airplane.

She was out in the open air yet her rate of descent was slower than the airplane. Its upper wing had clipped her and Truus and almost sent the two of them into an uncontrollable tumble. Yet Truus managed to hold onto Thora as the airplane fell past them towards its ultimate fate. Inside that plane Bewdley and Jakob were still working frantically trying to gain control of it.

Suddenly Thora experienced the sensation of swift deceleration. Truus had somehow managed to make her body work as a parachute, slowing down their rate of descent to something manageable and survivable. The girl did not know how the old woman could do it but there was not enough gratitude in the world that she could find to express her thanks.

Below her she watched as the airplane she had been flying in crash into the ground. There was no explosion but there was a loud thud that rose up to her heights several moments after the actual impact. She knew that in that thud Bewdley Beacon had died. She felt a wave of grief take hold of her. He was not a good man. In many ways he was a very bad man. He had done some terrible things to other people in his life and for that he deserved to die. Yet, at the same time, Bewdley had been kind to her, had made sacrifices for her that seemed incongruent to his established character. Maybe she had been some sort of magnet that drew out what goodness was in the man and fostered something in him that would be redeemable when it came time for him to cash in on Judgment Day. She prayed that it would be so. If it had not been for him she would not have been in Canada. She would not have had her freedom. She would not have the liberty to now go forward and make her way up to Pioneer Lake and find the peace that her heart so yearned for. She was glad that she met Bewdley Beacon and she mourned his loss deeply. She had a feeling that she would be the only one in the world to feel that way about the man.

It took several minutes for Truus and Thora to reach the ground. The old woman seemed to have some control over the direction that they sailed downward. She chose a place not too far away from the small crater and debris field that was created in the aftermath of the plane crash.

When they lit upon the ground the sun had settled beyond the horizon and the darkening skies of dusk were deepening all around them. As her feet touched the sand Thora said a small thank you to the masters of fate for getting her through the ordeal. She was now in Canada. She was where she wanted to be.

"Jakob!" Truus called out. "Where could he be?"

The old ghost was nowhere to be seen. They had thought that he would be waiting for them near the crash site but he was not there. Thora did not want to look too closely. She feared that she would see the mangled body or body parts of Bewdley amongst the strewn wood and metal fragments.

"He could not have died, could he?" the girl asked the old woman.

"He's already dead. How could he die?" Truus retorted. "He is around here somewhere." She was crawling through the wreckage looking for her errant husband. Thora could see some desperation in the old woman's eyes. Truus was worried. There was no doubt. She had spent centuries with her mate and would be lost without him. The girl marveled at the depth of love that existed between the Nells. Her parents would never experience such an everlasting bond. Her parents would have been just as happy if they had parted ten years ago.

"Jakob! Where are you!" Truus cried. "Get out and show yourself!"

"You are looking for me Mama?" a voice came from above.

Both Thora and Truus looked upward and saw a figure with its bloated arms and legs stretched outward to capture the air. Jakob had jumped from the airplane before it hit the ground and like his spouse he had made himself into something bilious. When his feet tapped the sand he ran to join his wife. The two briefly embraced but Thora knew that in that tiny moment an eternity of love was expressed to each other.

"The monster is dead," Truus said, as she broke free from Jakob's arms.

"He was not all that bad," Thora replied in defense of the man that had done so much for her.

"He killed people like a predator and he would have done the same to you had circumstances been different," the old woman responded. "You were lucky that he just did not have the chance to carry out his will before he died."

"But he tried to save my life!" the girl protested.

"He was trying to save his own skin!" Truus retorted.

"He was already dying. He did not have to try and stop the plane from crashing. If anything the plane crash would have ended his misery."

"Well, the plane did crash. If I did not haul you out of there your body parts would have been mixed in with his." There was no way that Truus was going to allow Bewdley's deeds to rehabilitate his character. She saw him as a vile man and Thora got the feeling that once the woman pigeonholed someone into something that die would be cast forever and it would be impossible for that person to redeem himself or herself. The girl wondered what pigeonhole Truus had slotted her in.

She chose not to argue the point any further. Let Truus think what she would. Thora knew that Bewdley Beacon was not a devil.

"So this is Canada," Jakob said, looking around him and doing what he could to make sure that the two females did not erupt into any kind of fight over the attributes of the deceased man. "Where is the snow?"

Chapter 46

Pyre

"There is no snow in Canada in August!" Thora scoffed. She had made similar statements countless times in her life when she and Rebecca would tell their circle of friends of their summers at Pioneer Lake. Invariably someone would ask how they could go swimming and sailing in an Arctic tundra. Her countrymen just did not know much about their northern neighbor.

Whether Jakob heard her response or not she was not sure for the old man went over to the crash site and began looking at the debris. "You know," he said. "We could make it look like you have died in this crash as well."

"Why would we want to do that?" Thora responded. She felt a quiver of anxiety race into her bloodstream.

"If they think that you are dead then nobody would come looking for you and you will be free to live out your life without having to look over your shoulder all of the time wondering if someone is about to grab you and throw you in jail," Jakob said.

Thora thought about it for a moment. The old ghost made a good point there. It would guarantee her her freedom. But at the same time it would mean that the ones that she loved would also think that she was dead. Even though her father and mother had done atrocious things to her she did not want to put them into the agony of thinking that they had forever lost a child of theirs. And even though Margaret Whattam wanted to place her in a sanitarium she knew that Margaret loved her almost like a child. The girl had done enough to break the heart of the woman. Making her think that she was dead would only cause Margaret to feel guilt for the rest of her life that she was somehow to blame for the tragedy. She could not do that to her.

"I really don't think that I want to do that," she said in the end to Jakob. "It would create more problems than it would solve."

"They have already given you up as dead!" Truus said. The old woman must have been reading her mind again. "From what I can gather from your memories your parents will not do much to try and get you home even if you did not get into any trouble. But you got into a lot of trouble and they will want to distance themselves as much as possible from you so that your acts will not cast a shadow on them."

The woman hit the characters of Langley and Cora Meadowford squarely on the nose. Her parents would not want to be associated with anybody that was involved in the kind of trouble she was in. Even though Langley was up on murder charges, to them that was not half as stigmatizing as having a delinquent daughter that has the police from two countries, two states and one province after her.

"We should make it look like you died, little Fraulien," Jakob repeated his notion. "It would not be that hard to do."

"How can we do that?" Thora asked. Even though she would not look at the wreckage and the mangled body in it, she was well aware that Bewdley would still be highly recognizable in there. Any investigator would immediately see that there is no body of an adolescent female amongst the debris.

"We set fire to the pile," Jakob said. "And let it burn down to cinders. After the flames go out nobody will know if there was one body in there or two."

"We can leave a bit of your clothing as well," Truus added. "A tattered remnant of your skirt would suggest that you were here and that you perished in the explosion that occurred after the airplane smashed into the ground."

"But there was no explosion," Thora pointed out.

"There are no witnesses that will know that," the old woman replied. "They will think that the fuel burst upon impact."

"They will expect to find you in the pile," Jakob said. "The pilots in the airplanes that survived our skirmish had seen you. They would testify that there was absolutely no way for you to escape."

It made sense to Thora as she thought about it. Nobody in his or her right mind would believe that she got out of the airplane using a ghost as a parachute. Such an idea was insane. Rational thinking would force anybody that came investigating the wreckage to conclude that she had died in the crash.

"Tear a strip away from the bottom of your skirt Fraulien while Papa gets the fire going," Truus ordered. She no longer was allowing the girl to have a say in the matter.

Thora tore a stretch of fabric from her hem. Jakob was leaning over the airplane pieces. He pulled out a lighter from his pocket and proceeded to light the spilt fuel. In an instant flames the height of a man came into existence. Black pungent smoke drifted upward as the fire grew taller and spread over the remaining debris. Jakob walked away from it, his essence almost seeming surreal against the fiery backdrop.

Thora started to walk forward to drop her skirt remnant into the fire but Truus held her back. "You have to wait until the fire is almost out before you throw that in," the old woman said. "If you throw it in now it will burn away and there will be no evidence showing that you were here."

"But won't this fire attract people's attention?" the girl complained. "It is lighting up the sky and probably can be seen from miles around."

"There is nobody for miles around!" Jakob laughed. "I am willing to wager that nobody will discover this spot for at least several days. This Canada is a very deserted country, if you ask me. While I was drifting in the air I did some scouting. I could not see a house, a barn or anything that would suggest human occupation in this vicinity."

"But don't they know that they lost some airplanes around here?" Thora said. "Won't they be on the lookout right around here for those planes?"

"Yes and no. Yes, they will know that there are six missing planes but no, they won't know precisely where these planes went missing," Jakob answered. "Even if the pilots had radios they could not exactly pinpoint their whereabouts to their headquarters. And it is my bet that when the search begins for those planes they will be looking to the water rather than the land for them."

Thora nodded. Jakob was a very practical man and seemed to have a very good head on his shoulder. He appeared to have an answer for everything and had all angles covered. Her eyes drifted to the fire. The flames were licking up everything.

"If they don't know where our plane went down how would they know that our plane went down?" Thora asked a very astute question. "They could still think that Bewdley and I are in the air. They will still be looking for us."

"They will look until they find this wreckage and then they will stop looking," Jakob answered. "We must be careful for a few days until we feel assured that they have found this site."

"Your past is burning away right before your eyes, Fraulien," Truus said, placing her arm around Thora's shoulder. There was some tingling there where the two bodies made contact. "All the problems that you had are now gone and you are being reborn."

"Like a phoenix," Jakob added. "You shall rise from the ashes and begin life anew. Let's hope that you do not make the same mistakes that you have done before."

Thora lifted her eyes towards the ghost's. She knew that he was referring to how she had failed to listen to their advice before and how she had ultimately betrayed them. She wanted to say sorry but feared to do so lest old wounds were opened up in the apology. "I've made plenty," she sighed.

"But that was the old you," Truus said, squeezing the girl a little tighter and causing the sizzling sensation in Thora's shoulder to intensify to almost a painful level. "The new you has learned from the mistakes of the old."

Thora pulled away from the woman somewhat only to alleviate the tingles. "I made a mistake when I left the two of you at the crossroads," she said, although she did not entirely mean it. Had she stayed with the Nells in the other car and driven away from Bewdley it was highly likely that she would still be in America right now and it was highly likely that she would have been captured. At least by sticking with the monster she gained what she wanted and that was to be in Canada.

"We were taken back by what you did," Jakob admitted. "But then as we thought about it we were not surprised. Your heart has never been in to returning home. You have a wayward soul, Fraulien. Mama and I just failed to recognize it at first."

"How did you follow me and keep up to me?" Thora asked the question that was begging for a response. She had been traveling by car and the Nells were left to their own wiles to trace her steps and ultimately rescue her in the air above Lake Ontario.

"It wasn't that hard to do," the old man smiled. "We found an old friend on the road and drove with him as he followed your path."

"Who?" Thora inquired. She had not expected such an answer.

"Officer Bombino," Truus said.

"Officer Lou Bombino from Grappling Haven?" The girl was astounded to hear the man's name.

"Yes, the very man that has been courting the affections of our Myra," Jakob said. "He has been on your trail for quite some time now. When he came upon the intersection where you parted company with us he spotted the car in the ditch and came to investigate. Mama and I were just starting to chase after you when we saw Lou at the crossroads."

Thora recalled seeing ghostly wisps when she and Bewdley had sped away from that locale. That must have been the Nells.

"When we saw that it was him we knew that he would be going after you so we entered his car and thanks to Mama and her mysterious ways we had given him some insight into what he was exactly looking for, namely the new car that the monster had stolen," Jakob grinned at his wife.

"He was almost right behind you when you ran over that poor dog," Truus said. Her face grew heavy with anger while her eyes drifted onto the fire and the burning flesh before her. "I curse a man that can act so cruelly towards animals."

For a moment Thora thought that the woman was going to spit on the fire. The girl wanted to tell Truus about how Bewdley had grieved over that unfortunate incident.

Jakob went on, "Officer Bombino saw the man shooting at you. He stopped the car and warned the man that such retaliation was against the law and that if he had any jurisdiction in that county he would have hauled the man off to jail for his unlawful acts. When the man complained that his dog had just been run over and that the perpetrator of that sorry deed did not even have the decency to stop, Officer Bombino told him exactly who he was dealing with, namely the notorious Bewdley Beacon. He told the man that he was lucky that Beacon had not killed him instead of his dog."

"My heart went out to that poor man," Truus interjected. "That dog meant everything to him. He had been the man's companion ever since he was a boy and the two of them went through a lot together."

"How do you know this?" Thora asked.

"I read his mind," Truus answered with an almost bashful glow.

Thora realized that she should have known better.

"It took us a while to catch up to you after that incident but Officer Bombino made up for the lost time with his aggressive driving prowess. We were rounding the corner at a high speed when Mama saw you and the monster approaching the airplane. Officer Bombino did not see you at first and was about to drive by when Mama touched him on his neck and forced him to look your way," Jakob said.

"Officer Bombino can't see you guys, right?" Thora wanted the point clarified.

"He's not a dying man so he is blind to us," Truus nodded and averted her eyes as if she were hiding something.

"We were racing to the plane in the officer's car just when you took off. Mama and I jumped as high as we could and luckily we caught hold of the tail of the plane and we climbed onboard. I think that you know the rest of the story," Jakob said. He was looking at the fire. Its flames were beginning to ebb as it burned away all that was combustible. "I don't know if we have seen the last of Officer Lou Bombino," he muttered. "The man is doggedly determined."

"He might not even be fooled by this fire," Thora commented. "It will take more than just a burnt skirt to make him think that I died in a crash here. He will be looking for bones."

"That is if he ever comes up here to have a look for himself," Jakob said. "He might just have to be satisfied with what the Canadian authorities tell him in their report. I doubt his police force will have the budget to send him all the way to Canada just to verify what logic dictates had happened here and that is that a Grappling Haven girl died in a plane crash. Your escape from this accident is highly implausible."

Thora nodded. The old ghost had a good head on his shoulders and could grasp outcomes with uncanny surety. Yet, something came to her mind that would nullify Jakob's conjectures. "Wouldn't they be sending my remains back to Pennsylvania for burial?" she asked. "They wouldn't just leave what they thought as me here in the middle of nowhere, would they?"

"And Lou Bombino would want to have a look at these remains just to make sure that they are what they are supposed to be," Truus added, taking up Thora's line of thought.

Jakob hummed a moment or two. "I guess you are right but by the time they do that we would be long gone from here."

"Where is it in Canada that you want to go, child?" Truus asked the question.

"Pioneer Lake," Thora answered. In saying those two words she felt a well of emotion inside of her. Prior to this moment it had seemed like a whimsical dream that she would actually ever get to that lake where her family had created its own legacy. But now that she was actually in Canada and relatively safe from those that would thwart her wish it was becoming very real. She would stand on Black Island again and look out over Robinson Bay and Upper Pioneer Lake once more. She could almost imagine feeling the breezes light upon her face and telling her that everything that had happened this summer was only a nightmare that she could forget and never concern herself with anymore.

"Where is that from here?" Jakob asked.

Thora was given a jolt of reality with the question. She really did not know the answer to it. She only knew the one route to get there and that was from Toronto through to Laketown and from there board the Madoqua Empress to take her to the family stronghold on the island. She did not know any other way of getting there. She did not know Canada all that well. She did not even have the slightest notion of finding Toronto. The only thing that she knew for certain was that Pioneer Lake was north from here and that was her reply to Mr. Nells.

"Is it very far?" was the male ghost's next question.

"Probably far enough, seeing that we have to go there by foot," Thora sighed. It was still going to take a great deal of work to make her dream come a reality.

"And how are you going to feed yourself along the way?" Jakob was being extremely practical.

Thora had not thought of these concerns. "I guess that I will just have to go without until we get there."

"If it is any more than a day's walk from here I am afraid that you will starve," Truus said.

The girl knew that it was much more than a day's walk from where they were. It was a day's drive from Buffalo to Laketown. It was much more likely that it could be as much as a week's walk for her, presuming that she knew the way, which she didn't. "I will survive," she said, determined to not let this factor get her down. "I will live off the land. There are many berries in season right now. And if we come across any towns I will put what Bewdley taught me to use and pilfer myself meals and perhaps even a car."

She knew that she was being unrealistic and she sensed that Jakob and Truus knew this as well. They could read her mind, afterall. Yet, neither said anything. Both appeared willing to go along with her farfetched scheme. Maybe they both were enjoying the adventure of her little escapade as much as she was. After decades being cooped up in that little farmhouse back at Hawkins Corners they were doing something that would alleviate that boredom that they must have experienced back there.

The fire was almost burnt out. There were a few timbers that were still smoldering. Truus instructed the girl that it was now time to put her skirt fragment onto one of these embers.

Thora did so. As she did her eyes caught sight of a charred bone. It had been part of Bewdley. The bones were all that were left of the man that had been her savior. She started to cry thinking of him. She did not care what others thought of him; to her he was a good man.

"We should be getting away from here," Jakob said. "We don't want to be tempting fate."

Thora rose up to her feet. "Which way is north?" she asked.

"I'm guessing that way," the old ghost answered, pointing in the opposite direction from Lake Ontario.

The three started walking. They did not realize it as they walked over the sandy ground that one of them was leaving footprints behind.

CHAPTER 47

Three to the Lake

The terrain was demanding. It went up and down and forced the travelers to make many turns when they suddenly came upon stretches of bog or sharp cliffs that the girl could not cross or climb. Her efforts were made all the more taxing by the fact that she was walking mostly on sand that gave to her step and made the act of walking more strenuous.

They had been hiking for several hours. The sun had long ago set and darkness engulfed them. Jakob knew how to read the stars and from them garner where north sat. Thora's feet were getting very sore and she sensed that she was developing blisters upon them. She wanted nothing more to stop and sleep. Yes, she wanted more. She wanted to eat. She was starving.

"Can't we stop for the night?" she complained to the ghosts. They seemed impervious to the demands of the trek. They had no stomachs that went empty. They had no stinging feet. They could walk all the way through to Pioneer Lake without resting Thora realized.

"Are you sure that you want to stop here for the night?" Jakob asked. "This is Canada. There are still wolves around here that will eat you up as soon as they get wind of you."

"I've never seen a wolf here in all the time that I have been coming here," the girl answered.

"That's because you live on an island, girl. They have not crossed the water to get there, yet. I've heard it said that Canada is brimming with wolves. The people that live in this forsaken country have been not as smart as us in our land of opportunity where we have eradicated all these devil beasts," Jakob said.

"I still don't think that there are any wolves around," Thora responded. She was so tired that she did not care if there were a hundred starving wolves circling her at the moment. She wanted to get some sleep. "I am going to lie myself to sleep right now." She started looking around for something that would provide her a natural bed. She found a rock about twice her size where the wind had carved a depression in the sand before it. This suited her fine and she placed herself in the hole. The sand was deeply cold upon her back. She could feel the frigidity seep into her spine. She told herself that she didn't care. Her need for sleep was far greater than her need to keep warm.

"That is not a very good spot," Truus said to her. "You will get pneumonia lying in such a place. You should have blankets."

"But I don't have blankets," Thora grumbled. "I never had a chance to pack any the morning that I left."

"We should go further. There has got to be a better place for you to sleep than this," Jakob added.

Somehow Thora sensed that her companions did not want to sleep and that they preferred to just keep plodding along. Maybe they were afraid of catching some shuteye because of the terrible nightmares that they experience when they fall asleep. If that was so, it was too bad. She knew her limits and she had long ago surpassed them. If she did not sleep here then she would collapse before they go a half-mile further. "The cold is not going to bother me," she said to them. "You just go to sleep yourselves. If you don't want to go to sleep then you can stay here and stand guard for me from the big bad wolf." She was being very sarcastic and surly to the people that had saved her life. She felt bad for it but she could not help it. She was past the brink and she needed to sleep.

"Suit yourself but don't cry to us in the morning that you feel sick!" Truus answered. "You are already starting to ignore our advice. The new you is fast becoming the old you."

"Be quiet!" Thora mumbled. She was not sure if her words were heard. They were spoken from the region where she was more asleep than awake. The cold had taken control of her back. It felt like it was a sheet of ice. It was as hard as a glacier as well. The sand did little to comfort her. It was almost like it was an agent for the Nells ghosts and their efforts to keep her from sleeping.

But her mind was wholly given over to slumber. It told her to ignore everything else but the sweet waves of sleep in her bloodstream. As she drifted to a deep slumber she thought she heard Jakob say to Truus that he was going to scout ahead to see what was up there.

Her dream was of a snow-covered field where large animal tracks spotted the land. She was working her way across this terrain. The going was very tough and hard as the snow was deep. When she came upon the animal tracks she immediately recognized them as those made by a large stag. She really did not know how she knew this as she would not truly know deer tracks from bear tracks from monkey tracks. She had never studied the footprints of animals before. But in this dream she knew what she saw was those made from a very big deer. She moved further across the field. She was close to exhaustion and even in her dream she felt the need to sleep. Then as she climbed over a small rise in the land she saw a frozen lake ahead of her. Upon this lake was a man equipped with a shotgun. She instinctively knew that this man was her great grandfather, Samuel Angus Meadowford, as a relatively young man in his forties. He was clad in animal hides and almost seemed like he had gone native. He was not aware of her presence. He seemed to be consumed with tracking the stag. Thora did not call for his attention. Rather she just followed him as he stalked his quarry. Then at the other end of the field another man appeared. This one was an Indian, the grandest Indian that the girl had ever laid eyes upon. He was tall and handsome and as feral as the wildcat that stood with him. The cat was a lynx Thora surmised. It had penetrating eyes that peered right into her soul. It so frightened her that she wanted to turn around and bolt away. Yet, she couldn't. She was frozen in its gaze. It was almost like the creature was talking to her. If it was, she did not hear the words. But she did hear the words that transpired between her great grandfather and the Indian. The Indian was warning him that he had to give back the land to the people, that it was very sacred ground and the Meadowfords had no right to it. Her great grandfather would not concede and give in to the Indian. But Thora could no longer listen in to what was being said for at that moment the lynx bolted across the field directly at her. Its hair was raised upon its back and its eyes burned with ferocity. It leapt at her with its sharp long talons outstretched. As it did so Thora screamed. Her scream drowned out what the lynx was saying to her.

"Wake up, child! Wake up!"

Thora felt her body being rattled. At first she thought that it was the lynx mauling her but the way that her shoulders rolled back and forth she realized that it was something else that was jostling her. She opened her eyes and saw Truus Nells standing overtop of her.

"You were having a bad dream," the old woman said in a soft, comforting tone.

The girl was disoriented. It took some time to gather her bearings and realize where she was. The cold in her back was so deep that she could feel it entering her lungs and make her feel extremely congested. She forced a cough to try and clear it.

All the while Truus stood over her. "I told you that you should have looked elsewhere to make your bed. You are starting to get sick."

"My dream was so real!" Thora said to the woman. She still had the image of the lynx going for her throat firmly implanted in my mind. She began to shiver just as much from the image as from the chilly ground that she still sat upon.

"Get to your feet girl and allow me to hug you. It will warm you up," Truus extended an arm out to Thora to help lift her from the sand. Once planted on her legs, Thora allowed the old woman to wrap her arms around her. The tingles started immediately. This interchange of matter between the living and the dead produced its own kind of heat. Thora could feel the cold flee from her body and the phlegm dry up in her chest. They were being replaced by a sensation that was partially painful and partially pleasant. It was an odd feeling.

As Truus held her, she asked her about her dream. Thora told her about it and how there was an element of truth in it, her great grandfather had written down an account of his winter meeting with an Indian and a lynx in the journal kept on Black Island.

"Your dreams are becoming like those that Papa and I experience," Truus commented. "Sometimes it is better to stay awake rather than torment yourself with the horrors that the sleeping mind produce."

"Where is Papa? I mean, where is Mr. Nells?" Thora asked. She could no longer tolerate the zinging and had to pull herself away from the old woman.

"He said that he was going to go out and scout ahead," Truus said, verifying what Thora had thought she heard the ghost say earlier.

"How long ago was that?" she asked. She did not know how long she had been asleep.

"An hour ago, maybe two."

"Shouldn't he be back by now?"

Truus looked out to the land where Jakob must have went. "That is what I think. It is not like him to be gone this long."

"Why don't you go out and try to find him? I will stay here just in case he comes back," Thora offered, reading the worry in the woman.

"And get lost myself? No, it is better that I stay here with you. We can't have wolves or lynxes attacking you, now can we?" She smiled. It was a small lifting of the corner of her lips but it was enough to cause Thora to laugh. From Thora's laugh, Truus' smile became more genuine and then she too was caught up in a chuckle. Before too long both of them were laughing so hard that Thora's sides were beginning to ache.

"What's so funny?"

They turned around and saw Jakob standing in their midst. Unlike the jovial expressions the two females held, the old man's demeanor was very grave. "What's wrong Papa?" his wife immediately asked, breaking free from the contagious laugh that had a grip on her.

"We can't stay here," Jakob responded. He was looking at Thora. "I wandered back to the crash site. There are things there."

The way that the ghost said 'things' Thora knew at once that he was not referring to articles or objects. He meant something living or something that may have been alive at one time.

"What kind of things?" Truus asked.

"Beasts from some horrible place," Jakob said. "They were scouring the wreckage, looking for something. They were like shadows. They moved swiftly and purposefully. They dug like weasels into the pile. I got the sense that not one splinter of charcoal would escape their attention. I also got the sense that they did not find what they were looking for."

"Maybe they were Satan's minions coming to collect the soul of the monster?" Truus offered.

"His soul would have been gathered the moment that he died," Jakob responded. "They were not looking for him. They were looking for somebody living." Once again his eyes landed on Thora.

"They're after me, aren't they?" Thora whispered. The chill in her body had found a new source.

"It's my guess that that is so," Jakob nodded. "These were dark heathen spirits. There were two of them, a large female and a small male. They were talking amongst each other although I could not gather what was being said outside of the fact that the little one referred to the big one as Grandmother and the big one called the little one, Percival. Does that name mean anything to you?"

Thora was horrified and at first could not say anything. The thought that there were dark heathen spirits chasing after her was enough to unbridle any feeling of security that she had. She almost wished that she could return to her dream of the lynx. At least in that dream she had the safety of knowing that it was only her imagination that was running amok.

"Does Percival mean anything to you?" the old ghost repeated.

The girl swallowed the bile that was climbing in her throat. "I had a cousin by that name once. He died about ten years ago. Drowned in the lake."

"And what about your grandmother? Does she still live?" Jakob's hands were holding her by the shoulders.

"Grandmother Wright still lives but Grandmother Meadowford died the year before my cousin did. She drowned in the lake as well." Thora could not understand any of this. Why would the ghosts of her dead relatives be searching for her? She hardly knew either one. She just had vague recollections of them and most of these memories were inspired by the few photographs the family kept of these lost members on Black Island. She was only a tot when Pioneer Lake had taken them. To her they were more strangers than family.

"The lake that took them, is that the same lake where you want to go?"

Thora's head went up and down in the affirmative.

"Why do you want to go there?"

"Because it is my home," the girl responded. "It is the only place in the whole world that will give me sanctuary."

"What makes you think this?" Jakob had still not let go of her arms.

"Because it has always been my home. There, I find peace and serenity.

There, I find wonder and joy. These are things that I cannot find anywhere else."

"But there is nobody up there. It is not the physical place that offers you that peace and serenity. It is the people that are there with you. And there is nobody up there now at all. You will find only desolation, disappointment, loneliness and sorrow there now."

"That's not so!" Thora cried out. "Some of my most beautiful moments on the island are when I am sitting by myself on the rock just looking out onto the water. At times, it is almost like the water is talking to me and trying to comfort me."

"The same water that took the lives of your grandmother and your cousin," Jakob said. "I wonder if they too had beautiful moments sitting by themselves on the rock looking out onto the water?"

"There is another that the lake took as well," Truus spoke up. "The girl lost another cousin to the water just last year, a boy named Jack."

Thora guessed that Truus had read this information from her thoughts.

"That's three to the lake. I believe that this lake thirsts for more!" Jakob said.

"What do you mean?" Thora instinctively knew what the old ghost was going to say.

"I think that it is summoning you to its shores. I think that it will not rest until you too are swallowed by its waters. There are other places that you can go to Thora. You don't have to go to the lake." Jakob finally let go of her. Her arms were still tingling from where the ghost had a hold of her.

"If you ask me, going to the lake is a bad idea if you want to keep your freedom," Truus added. "The police know that you are in Canada and they will learn that your family has property here in this country. They will quickly surmise that this property would be a highly likely destination for you."

"But they think that I am dead!" Thora said. "They won't be looking for me up there if they think that."

"You would wish that they would be looking for you up there if you are to tangle with those two beasts that I witnessed at the crash site," Jakob answered. "We should go back to our country and be far away from this land of Brits and demons."

"No, I am not going back!" Thora declared adamantly. "I'm staying here!"

"Then we can go to other places in Canada rather than that island," Truus responded. "It is a big country and I am sure that there are places that can give you just as much peace and serenity as your summer house."

Thora did not say anything but Jakob must have garnered what her thoughts were. "Can't you see that the lake wants to take you as its own? Look at your family history there! Three deaths! That's..."

"Four of my family died on the lake," the girl corrected him. "My grandfather, the one people called Sambo, died of a heart attack on the lake only a month ago."

"And you will be the fifth, child, if you go! I implore you to stay away from the lake!" Jakob warned. "Those two things that I saw at the crash site meant business. They were driven creatures, riddled with dark purpose. It is my feeling that they seek to harness you and make you a part of their ignomious league."

"It's all connected to that Indian curse upon your family, child," Truus added. "That is how I see it. Your family has crossed these pagan spirits. You all could be doomed to wretched futures walking the Earth in states of constant hunger that can never be satisfied."

The old woman's words were harsh and frightening. Thora could see no hope for herself in them. The glimmer of sunshine in her heart that she felt hours earlier when she first realized that she was in Canada had dissipated into an overbearing gloom. The light-hearted frolic that she had with Bewdley Beacon had been replaced with morose shadows of impending despair.

"Come, we must fly from here before they are upon us!" Jakob said, reaching out to take the girl's hand.

Thora pulled it away. "What's the use in running if they are going to get me anyway?" she said to the Nells. "If my future is to walk the Earth in a constant state of hunger that can never be satisfied, what is the point in putting it off?"

Truus looked at the girl. "I have made you feel hopeless, haven't I?"

"Very," Thora said. She felt tears were on their way.

"There's always hope, Fraulien. Even when things are black, there is always hope. You have Papa and myself with you. We have sworn to protect you and we stand by our words. If those creatures back there want to catch you they will first have to fight us. If that lake wants to take you, it is going to have to wrest you away from us," the old woman said. Thora could see that Truus meant every word that she said.

"I know that we don't look like much," Jakob admitted, "But we are fighters, Mama and I. When the Brits tried to take our farm in 1812, Mama and I stood up to them with our muskets. Three redcoats died on our fields from our volleys. We were relentless like a mother bear in protecting what was our own. Finally, their captain had enough, and decided to take their fight elsewhere, leaving us to bury their dead on our undisputed land. No one has dared to take that land away from us since then. And it is with that same tenacity that I swear that I will not let those heathen spirits take you, young lady. Now, come. We must get out of here. Our fight with them must be elsewhere and not here."

This time Thora took Jakob's hand. She felt a tiny sparkle in her heart. She recognized it as the birth of a new hope. She promised herself that she would nurture this neophyte and allow it to grow hale and strong but realistic at the same time. Jakob and Truus Nells possessed valiant spirits and she knew that they would do everything that they could to make sure that whatever it was that was chasing her would not catch her. Yet, even as powerful as their hearts were, she had to always realize that sometimes that was not enough. She needed a heart that was just as strong and that was where doubt crept in.

They started to dash out into the night, following a path that Jakob had carved out earlier in his explorations. As they ran, they started to hear a low, constant drone humming from the air. They were not alone.

Chapter 48

The Corn and the Rain

"I think that is an airplane," Jakob said. He was looking up in the night air as they cut across a clearing.

Thora lifted her eyes upward. A million stars shone down on her. The broad swath of the Milky Way gave the sky a backbone and made it feel like it was crushing down on the Earth. She was trying to espy movement against this ethereal backdrop. At first everything seemed stationary. Then she saw something moving low along the horizon. She guessed that it was to the south of her. A set of red lights drifted through Cassiopeia. The sound of a single engine working its way through the heavens accompanied those lights. It was indeed an airplane.

"They've found the crash site much sooner than I thought," Jakob said. "It must have been the fire that has drawn their attention. I knew that I should not have lit it."

"But you had to Papa," Truus put in. "If you did not they would have seen that the little girl did not die in the crash. I don't think that we have anything to worry about. We have put in a good distance from there and they won't find us here." She was trying to assuage her husband's anxiety.

Thora knew the real source of the anxiety. It did not reside in that little airplane in the sky. It rested in those 'things' that Jakob called them, those demons that could be relatives of hers. That beast that posed as Mrs. Bianco had told her that her family was cursed to walk the Earth. If that was a truism then it was likely that what Mr. Nells saw digging through the crash site were the spirits of her grandmother and cousin.

"Let's keep moving," Jakob said. They were pushing themselves into some scrubland filled with itchy and stinging nettles. This fierce vegetation did not bother the ghosts. They did not have bodies that could be pricked and scratched and tingled. But the nettles certainly made themselves known to Thora. Yet in a way they helped her keep her mind from the exhaustion that was overwhelming her. She had long ago pushed herself past her level of endurance. Yet she kept on going.

To where? She did not know in this darkness and unknown country. The ghosts had made it abundantly clear that going to Pioneer Lake was a bad idea. In a way, Thora agreed with them. It would be the most likely spot to find her in Canada, presuming that anybody was looking for her. Maybe that airplane would bring to an end any mortal pursuit for the teenaged fugitive from Grappling Haven. But those demons would know better. They would see that she was not amidst the ruins of the crashed airplane. They were the ones that were scaring Jakob Nells and making the group move swiftly through the night.

Still, she felt her heart yearn to return to the lake. It was almost like it was calling to her, summoning her to its waters. She felt compelled to go there the way that the birds feel compelled to fly north in the spring and fly south in the autumn. She was contending with some strong force that she was helpless to resist. She had to go to Pioneer Lake, bad idea or not.

But how was she going to convince the Nells about this? She had been testing their loyalty almost from the moment they gave it over to her. Time and again they spoke of the folly of her decisions and they had to say, "I told you so", on numerous occasions. They would give good sound practical advice and have that advice flaunted back in their faces when she openly acted contrary to the wisdom that they imparted.

On the previous occasions it had mostly been Truus that doled out the warnings and the opinions but this time it was Jakob. Mr. Nells was a good man, Thora held no doubt about this whatsoever. But she got the impression that he was also a very stern man and would be very implacable if his advice were to be shunted. If you crossed him you would never be able to cross back and return to his good side. He still bore enmity to the British for a war that took place over a century ago. He still did not trust the indigenous people of this continent for infractions upon his code of ethics and land husbandry that took place even longer ago. He did not know how to forgive and make peace. Taking him to Pioneer Lake would be a declaration of war upon him.

Yet, she had to go. It had become a primal instinct in her and one that she could not overcome. The Nells would not willingly accept her request to go to the lake. She was going to have to rely upon deception and subterfuge. They did not know where the lake was. For that matter she did not either but sooner or later she would get her bearings and from that moment on she would have to delude her companions and make them believe that they were going elsewhere when in fact she would be taking them right up to Pioneer Lake's shores.

Before dawn the skies that had been clear for so long grew overcast. The stars and planets were disappearing one by one until only a single one shone directly above the horizon. Its solitary light felt like a beacon of hope to the girl as she struggled to keep up with the Nells as they entered a land given over to corn rather than the wild and prickly vegetation that the trio had wandered through most of the night.

"That's Venus, the morning star," Jakob said.

"It does not look like it is harboring in a fair day," Truus responded.

The clouds had just about overtaken the planet leaving only a small sliver of light on the distant horizon where a sun would rise and not be seen by those watching it. Soon that sliver would be gone itself.

"It's going to rain today," Jakob agreed. "And it is going to rain hard."

Already Thora could feel a difference in the temperature. It had fallen dramatically with the appearance of the clouds. It was going to be a cool, rainy summer day—one of those days had she been up at the lake with her family, they would have spent indoors playing boring parlor games and getting onto each other's nerves. Some people enjoy the odd rainy day when on the lake but not Thora. She wanted to be outdoors under the sun. Had the skies never produced another drop of rain that would have been fine by her.

"At least the corn signifies that we are coming upon inhabited land," Jakob said. "Maybe we will soon find a road and from there find direction to some place that will offer us hospice and food for the girl."

They entered the cornfield. Almost from the moment that they stepped within the tall stalks laden with heavy fruit, Thora felt the first drops of rain.

She lifted her head skyward and opened her mouth to allow the soft precipitation to fall upon her thirsty tongue. She did not realize how parched she was. The taste of the rain whetted her craving for more. Her field of vision was limited to the narrow space between the rows of corn. Above her, she saw that somber thick and pregnant gray clouds were dropping their fat dark bellies very low towards the ground. She felt that she could almost reach up and grab them. They were telling her that it was going to be a miserable day ahead of her.

Soon the rain began to fall heavier. The cold drops splatted on her face and she no longer desired to have them enter her mouth. Dropping her head she saw that the Nells were about fifteen feet ahead of her, working their way through the claustrophobic aisle between the rows of corn. They did not appear to be in any particular hurry. It seemed like they rather enjoyed the rain.

The tops of the stalks were starting to bend, a signal that the wind had picked up. In the strange world within these seven-foot giants, the companions were at least sheltered and did not have to endure the chilly breezes. The rain was falling even harder than earlier. Some of it was working its way downward, sliding upon the elongated corn leaves and creating a myriad of miniature waterfalls that were dripping onto the soil and there creating gouges into the earth. Thus far the dirt was dry but it would sooner or later become soaked and muddy if the precipitation continued.

They kept moving. The soil became muddy and Thora found herself slogging along through it. Her clothes were soaked to the skin, her hair hung down on her face like icy fronds. The conditions were altogether miserable and there appeared to be no end in sight. From what she could see past Jakob and Truus the cornfield extended for miles. She saw no hope of soon finding the shelter that she desperately wanted. It started to occur to her that it would be very ironic if they were tromping along a row of corn that ran parallel to a big, old warm farmhouse and that they could not see the presence of such a comfortable abode due to the height of the corn that surrounded them. They could be like mice in a maze, oblivious to the route that could swiftly bring them to sanctuary.

When she mentioned her notion to Jakob the old man cuffed himself on his forehead and said something that sounded like "doom cuff" although Thora knew that that was not what Jakob was saying. He sprang upward to an amazing height. The top of the corn came up to his knees when he made his leap and took his gander. When he landed, his news from his brief reconnaissance was bleak. All that he could see was corn in every direction. "Whoever owns this land must be a millionaire to devote so much of it to just one crop," he said. "I envy the man. This soil is so rich. Just look at the quality of this corn. Astounding! Who would have thought that the land of ice and snow could be so bountiful!"

The ghost certainly did not seem to have his spirits dampened by the dreadful weather conditions. He was a farmer and farmers loved this kind of stuff. His wife did not appear to be down about the gloom either. Her demeanor remained positive. "Smell that rain!" she said to Thora. "It is the aroma of the Lord's breath as He ensures that there will be food on people's tables this winter."

Thora could not share in their mood. She found the conditions that surrounded her to be amongst the most miserable since she left Grappling Haven that what now seemed to be long ago morning.

"Never mind, little girl," Truus said. "We will get you through this and you will be warm and dry soon enough. But don't mope. Moping will just make things worse than they really are."

Thora wanted to say, 'How could things get any worse?' but she kept her tongue in check. She simply nodded to the old woman and kept slugging her way through the mud, every iota of warmth long gone out of her body.

The winds had turned it up a notch. All around her the corn was bending over. The tunnels between the lines of plants had become cacophonous with the wild whistling of the gales that whooshed through them and the low rumble of an approaching thunderstorm. Things were going to get worse, the girl realized, trying to wrap her soaked clothes around her tighter so that she might find some hidden morsel of warmth that may be hidden inside of them.

Periodically Jakob would jump upward to determine if they were approaching any form of shelter. Each time after he came down he would communicate his depressing findings. Even he was beginning to tire from the oppressive weather. The thunderstorm had arrived. The black sky echoed with fierce cracking that made it seem that its very fabric was being torn apart. There were so many flashes of lightning that Thora had to cover her eyes to avoid the glowing afterimages that were blinding her. Then hail started to fall from the heavens, pelting her, the ghosts and the corn with a barrage of stinging, sharp pellets that showed no mercy to those below.

"This crop is going to get ruined if this continues," Jakob called out, his sentence being disrupted by the manic cracks of thunder. Thora saw evidence of the old man's assertions. Holes were being torn into the corn's leaves by the hail.

"We got to get out of here soon!" Truus complained. "I feel like I am being shredded alive!" To Thora's dismay she saw the same holes that she witnessed in the corn displayed on the old woman. She was literally being disintegrated by the unrelenting precipitation.

"I'm no miracle worker Mama!" Jakob retorted. "I can't end the storm and I can't produce a shelter if there is no shelter to be found! All that we can do is keep on going and pray that it all comes to an end!"

The brave man kept pushing himself forward. The wind was coming in directly at him and made his progress very slow. Still he found it in himself to take his lookout leaps now and then. Each time he volleyed himself into the air the wind would catch him and jostle him about like he was a piece of tissue. He had great difficulty in ensuring that he would land upright and on occasion would actually fall to the soaked ground.

The weather was relentless. The thunderstorm seemed to have stalled above the cornfield. Its lightning slashed down to the stalks and smote them with their violent surges of electricity.

"It's almost like this weather has a brain!" Truus bellowed so that she could be heard. "It's like it is purposefully hunting us down and trying to kill us!"

"That's nonsense Mama!" Jakob cried out. "How can weather act with purpose?"

"I don't know," the old woman responded. "It is just a feeling I have." She was looking at Thora. There was suspicion in what remained of her eyes. Some of them had been torn away by the angry hail.

Thora felt diminished by the remark. The old woman could not possibly think that she was to blame for this freak weather. The girl was about to address this unjust allegation when she saw something in Truus' eyes. They had opened up wider.

"There's something following us!" Truus cried out.

Thora turned and saw nothing yet she sensed that there was something there as well. Truus would not respond that way had it been nothing.

Chapter 49

Bellow and Snap

There was nothing there as far as Thora could tell. Yet the way that Truus reacted she was sure that something had to be there. The ghost would not see phantoms.

Jakob, for his part, told his companions to keep moving. Sooner or later they would get out of the corn. Sooner or later the storm would come to an end.

Yet the 'sooner' clause of the proviso did not come to fruition in either case. The cornfield still had not reached an end. The storm lingered on, its bellow and snap still resounding in the turbulent sky.

But whatever Truus had seen or thought that she had seen behind them did not seem to be there any longer. The old woman spent more time with her head flung behind her and watching rather than paying attention to what was in front of her. More than once she stumbled upon a cornstalk, as her head was looking the other way.

"It or they are still there," she periodically whispered. "I can't see them but I sense them."

"Who?" Thora would implore but would not get an answer. The old woman just did not know.

And then after one more bound into the air by Jakob, he finally landed squarely on his feet with some good news. "There is a road ahead," he announced. His statement was punctuated by a particularly loud thunderclap that took some of the hope out of what he said and tempered it with the realization that a road may not be a benign replacement for the cornfield.

Nevertheless, the trio kept moving onward toward the road. If the storm were still savage by the time that they reached it, they would consider biding out the time at the edge of the field until the storm abates.

As they moved, Truus was still worried about what was behind them. The nervousness in her eyes troubled Thora. She too would periodically take a glance behind. Each time she did, she hoped that she would not see anything. She had a strong suspicion that Truus had seen the Meadowford ghosts, her grandmother and cousin. Every time that Thora looked her hopes were satisfied as nothing outside of the cornstalks caught her eyes.

"I can see the end of the field!" Jakob announced.

There, about two hundred yards ahead of them Thora saw an opening at the end of the aisle of sagging, dripping corn. It was almost a portal into darkness for she viewed a strobe-like vista. The sky was pitch black but when the lightning flashed, and it flashed often, the bright light would reveal a wide gravel road whose sides possessed rivulets of water as the rain drained along it. It was not a promising sight but at least it gave her the sense that this long purgatorial trek through the corn was coming to an end.

When they were within fifty yards of the road, Truus cried out that the things were upon them. Thora turned around and saw two figures walking openly down the row. They were no longer trying to hide themselves. One was tall and gray and female and beset with all the degradation in body that comes along with an advanced age. Beside her strode a tiny form about one-third the height of his companion. Seeing the pair, Thora felt an early memory of hers awaken when these two very beings were a part of her life back on Black Island. She had no doubt that she was looking upon her grandmother, June Ritchey, and her cousin, Percy Thurston. Yet both were dead, long dead. So long dead that the girl truly did not have any familiar recollections of them. Her memories of the pair were more conditioned responses to photographs of them rather than actual images of interactions with their flesh and blood.

Grandmother Meadowford and Percy did not appear daunted by the heavy rain. They walked hand in hand. They walked with purpose. And even from her distance away, Thora could feel their eyes solely focused on her as if there was nothing else in the universe to them than her. Rather than feeling any familial congeniality towards the pair, the girl's reaction was that of fright. They scared her terribly. They were dead. They should not be hounding her here in the middle of nowhere just north of Lake Ontario. Why were they hunting her down? She felt hunted. She could not see anything benign coming out of meeting them. They had dark purpose.

With the flash of lightning the girl saw that her grandmother and cousin did not possess pristine faces. Rather, their miens had been degraded with the ravages of death. The skin upon their cheeks had sunk and acted like weights upon their lower eyelids, giving their gaze a ghoulish distinction. Rot must have eaten away most of their lips. What little they had did very little to hide their receding red gums and their very toothsome maws.

Thora's only reaction to the sight of her relatives was flight. She suddenly found new vitality in her sluggish legs. She began running so that she no longer would be at the rear of her group. She fled past Truus Nells and was gaining on Jakob and the road. As she was about to fly out onto the gravel surface, Jakob's hand flung out and grabbed her by the elbow. "Don't go out there yet unless you want to be seen!" the old man warned.

The girl flung her head back. She could no longer see her grandmother and cousin. They were gone. All that was behind her was Truus. The old woman was also looking behind herself.

"Where did they go?" Thora cried out to Mrs. Nells.

Truus did not answer. Rather she walked in cautious measured steps to Thora and her husband. "I don't know," she huffed when she reached her companions. "But I think that they are gone now."

"How do you know?" Thora wanted to hear a strong valid reason from the old woman that would make her think the same way.

"It's just a feeling I have," Truus answered.

That was a strong valid enough reason to Thora. She had learned to place a lot of trust in the old woman's perceptions. If Truus said that they were no longer there then they were no longer there.

But why had they appeared? And then disappear? It was almost like they were shepherding the trio into going a certain direction. Thora could easily guess the direction that her relatives were pushing her. They were going to guide them to Pioneer Lake. They were acting like agents for the water, ensuring that the girl heed its calling and step upon the shores of that once beautiful lake.

All that Jakob had said earlier was coming home to Thora now. He had said that the lake was summoning her. It was taking advantage of all of the girl's fond memories of the island and summer and placing in her an irrepressible drive to go up there. The lake had sent its emissaries to meet up with her to make sure that she did not lose her way. Thora could see that now. Going to Pioneer Lake was no longer a fulfillment of her young desire for sanctuary. Going to Pioneer Lake was now a very frightening prospect and she possessed no desire to make it up there. She would rather face the music in Pennsylvania than to sit upon Black Island's rock and gaze over those brooding dangerous waters. For now she knew the lake's intent. It meant to have her. It meant to keep her. It wanted her dead. It wanted her to become one of its claimed souls that would carry out its evil designs.

Yet, as much as she saw the real nature of Pioneer Lake, she still very much was entwined in her past upon its shores. It still was magical. It still possessed the defining moments of her life and it owned her heart. Recasting her memories and sentiments of the lake was going to be a very tall task. The lake would always be the background of her childhood. When she becomes an old lady sitting in the midst of her brood of grandchildren, she would recount to them her heady and laughing days on Black Island. It was part of who she was. There would never be a way of removing it from her soul.

Jakob started to snore. The noise coming from the old man shook Thora out of her dark thoughts. She had no idea that he had fallen asleep. He was spread out on the muddy ground with his arms and legs outstretched. His mouth was partially opened. It was from there that the snorts and wheezes emanated. She wondered why a dead man would snore. Wasn't snoring a part of the breathing cycle? Dead men don't breathe. Yet Jakob snored. There was no getting around the fact that she heard him do this.

Beside him, sprawled on the drenched land, was his wife, Truus. She too was fast asleep. This was peculiar in itself, as well. A few moments ago the woman was filled with angst and dread, worrying about their two followers. Now, she slept peacefully as if she did not have a care in the world.

Yet, was the sleep peaceful? Both the Nells had told her of their very troublesome and realistic dreams. These reveries were anything but peaceful. They were placed in terrible settings where they had to deal with very meddlesome and dangerous adversaries that sought to destroy them. The girl remembered something that Truus had asked when Jakob first returned from the crash site. The old woman had speculated that the minions of Satan had come to gather Bewdley Beacon's soul and usher him to Hell. Were these very minions chasing after Truus and Jakob Nells in their dreams? Were the Nells ghosts walking the Earth as escapees from the Netherworld? Were they just as much fugitives as she was?

It was a question that she would like to put to them but she knew that she would never ask it. She accepted them for who they are now and not who they might have been in the past. Bewdley Beacon had proven to her that a man can find redemption and overcome his stained past. If he could do it, so could the Nells.

The rain did not seem to trouble the pair. They did not so much as flinch as the water poured over their faces from the overhanging corn fronds. They were sleeping a qualitatively different kind of sleep than that of the living. If she had water dripping all over her forehead and cheeks while sleeping, Thora knew that she would wake up no matter how tired that she was. But these two did not so much as wriggle their noses in an attempt to divert the path of the rain draining from their faces. In fact, the water was pooling over Jakob's eyes and he did not stir. The rhythm and cadence of his sleep did not change.

If they were experiencing troubling dreams at this very moment, they did nothing to betray it. They slept the sleep of the dead.

Thora wished that she could do so. She was overtired. She was beginning to believe that she might never sleep again. She wanted to lie down and shut her eyes and drift into slumber. But there was no place that she could lie down. She would not place herself on the soaked and muddy ground. And even if she could find a place to sleep, she believed that she could not do so. The thoughts of her grandmother and cousin lurking somewhere nearby would keep her awake. Even now, she wondered where they could be. Were they just over in the next aisle of corn, watching her and her sleeping companions through the long, drooping leaves? Were they biding their time before they make their pounce? She hated making such conjectures. She did not like living in curiosity. She wanted things crystal clear.

She decided that she would rid herself of this curiosity by taking a peek into the next row of corn. If her grandmother and Percy were there then at least she did not have to worry about their lurking any longer. She chose a spot between two tall drenched plants, her hands pushing aside the soaked leaves. She felt the cupped rain pour onto her fingers and then down her arms. It did not matter. She could not possibly get any more wet.

As she did so, she thought she caught a fleeting glimpse of something moving in the other aisle. It moved away from her swiftly, as if it were a frightened rabbit dashing towards safety. When her head popped out between the fronds and she glanced into an identical row to the one that she just left, she saw that nothing was there. The result was hardly satisfactory to her. It meant that her curiosity would still linger. Her relatives were not hiding in this aisle. They were nowhere to be seen.

She looked to the mud to see if there was any evidence that someone or something had been here recently. The soil bore no trace of footprints. That did not rule out the possibility that ghosts may have been here recently. Ghosts leave no tracks. The only impressions in the mud down the aisle that she and the Nells journeyed were her own. Jakob and Truus' feet did not produce disturbances in the topography of the aisle. Her grandmother and Percy would do the same.

Her curiosity grew ripe. She was sure that she saw something moving before she entered the new row. Yet as far as she could look down this laneway between the cornstalks she saw nothing. Perhaps they had moved over to the next row. She knew that she should not do it and that she risked the chance of becoming lost but she was kept by her drive to find answers. She moved into the next aisle and then the next and the next. Each new row was a carbon copy of the one that preceded it. Each new row did not give her any new information. If there was somebody nearby she did not see him or her or them.

She lost track of time as she continued with her search. The fear that she felt earlier was being replaced by the rules of the game. It was hide and seek to her now. If there was danger in what she did, she did not give it any recognition. She had strayed from her original bearings in relationship to the gravel road. With each new aisle this road was growing further in the distance. Finally, she reached an aisle where she could no longer see the road. Yet she kept enough of her sense of direction to remember that the road sat to her right. As long as she did not accidentally turn herself around she would know where the road sat.

The weather had settled somewhat. The thunder and lightning were now in the distance. The winds had died down. What was left was only a downpour and it was gradually losing in the volume of rain that it was sending down to the ground.

Thora had been at her little game for several minutes now. She did not know how many rows of corn that she went through since she started. She had lost count. She was beginning to realize that she was wasting her time and that she should return to the Nells. There was quite a distance that separated her from them. If anything decided to attack her she would not have the protection that Jakob and Truus promised. She decided that it was best that she return to them. Her gaming drive was abating and it was being replaced by fear. Why the hell did she allow herself to get carried away and place herself into such a position? She should have stayed with her friends. She started her way back to them. She believed that she was going to be okay because of the tracks that she left behind.

Her trail was there, at first. But it gradually became more washed out with each new aisle. The pouring rain was doing a job erasing and eradicating the path that she had picked. Yet she still had her bearings. The road would be to her left now, seeing that she was going in the opposite direction. Yet, it had not come into sight. It should have by now, she thought. She turned and looked to her right and saw that it was not there either. She began to think that there was the looming possibility that she had lost her bearings and that she might be wandering back into the heart of the cornfield, back to where her grandmother and her cousin might be waiting for her.

She told herself not to allow her mind to play tricks on her. The road will be to her left and that sooner or later she would see it there. She had just not gone far enough yet to see it.

Several minutes later, the road still had not appeared. But the thunderstorm had reappeared. It had turned around on its course and it was now once again lashing out onto the terrain, its furious lightning giving the air a terrifying glow, its resounding thunder making the earth beneath her shake. Yet the earth was not really there at all anymore. Large puddles and even small rivers were beginning to appear in the aisles that separated the rows of corn. Gone was any chance of her espying her former tracks.

She was growing extremely frightened for she now was thoroughly convinced that she was lost. She decided to call out the names of her friends.

Desperately she cried, "Mr. Nells! Mrs. Nells!" Her voice seemed so small against the bellowing thunder. She doubted that she was being heard at all by the old couple. But she started to realize that maybe somebody else was hearing her and that her yells were acting like a beacon for them to hone in on her. She decided that she would have to remain quiet.

In her quiet she began persecuting herself for allowing this to happen. Why could she not have just sat put beside Truus and Jakob? She would not be in trouble then. When Truus and Jakob awake and see that she is not there with them they would once again be disappointed in her. They might even think that she purposefully decided to run away from them. They might declare that it was the last straw and they would turn around and begin their long trek back home to Hawkins Corners, Pennsylvania. She wouldn't blame them if they did. She had not once listened to them. At every stage along their path she was doing something that went against what they deemed as wise.

She also knew that despite their feelings, the Nells would search for her and do everything that they could to keep her protected. She did not merit such devoted friends but she had them. She had to start showing them that she was worthy of them. She promised herself that if she were to be reunited with Jakob and Truus she would listen to everything that they said and would not behave contrary to their caring suggestions.

She wandered through another row of corn. When she came out on the other side, her heart sank for the aisle was no different than the one that she just left. She was hoping that her vows would have made a difference but apparently they didn't. She could not see the road in either direction. She no longer knew if it would be to her left or to her right. With the heavy rains above her there was no way of reading the sky as a compass. She was lost. There was no doubt about it.

Chapter 50

Trampled Plants

She walked into one more aisle. She told herself that if she saw nothing in that one that she would then stay where she was rather than venturing further and possibly getting herself more strayed. If there were nothing, she would return to her previous tactic of calling out the names of her companions and hope that nothing else would be listening.

She cleared the long fronds ahead of her and tucked her head out into the space between the rows of corn. This new aisle had been washed over by the falling rain. The water was at least ankle deep. There would be absolutely no chance that she would see any trail that she may have set down earlier. Looking to the left, she saw no sign of the gravel road.

Then looking to the right and expecting to have the same disappointing result, her heart gave a little leap. About ten yards up from where she stood, some of the cornstalks had been pushed to the ground. She had not seen anything like this yet. She was either in entirely new territory or something was following her. She decided that she had better go and have a look despite all of the fear that such an investigation could entail.

When she reached the fallen corn, she immediately noted that these plants were not knocked down by the rain and wind. They had not been smote by lightning either. Something had trampled these plants down. She could tell so by the way that some of the leaves had been broken. Their ends were bent in half and were pointing upwards. She started to look for tracks but saw none. She was hoping that it was nothing more harmless than a deer foraging in the corn. She had a gut feeling that it was nothing innocuous like that.

From the trampled corn she saw that there was more of the same in the next aisle and then the next. From where she stood she saw that something had cleared a path through the corn, caring not to keep these plants alive. What kind of thing would do that? A bear? A moose? She could see no tracks.

Should she follow? Or should she stay where she was? Following would entail some major risks. Anything that could produce such a slashing through the crop certainly could not be benign. But then again, maybe it could have been the Nells leaving her a trail so that she could find them? Yet, if that were the case, wouldn't they have been calling out to her and wouldn't she have heard them? She believed that she could not have been any more than a quarter of a mile from them where they slept. She would have heard them had they called. For all she knew, Jakob and Truus could still be fast asleep and dealing with desperate trials of their own.

If it weren't the Nells and it wasn't animals that caused these plants to be pushed down, then what was it? Should she follow or should she not? She was in a dilemma and she could not figure out the right answer.

The knocked down corn went as far as her eyes could see. The frequent lightning lit up the trail and she saw that the corn stretched the entire distance of her line of sight. The trail was not a route out of the field. It did not appear to lead to the road.

She started to feel very sorry for herself and she started to cry, as she stood helpless on top of the trampled corn. Why was she always getting into predicaments like this? She remembered feeling exactly the same way when she was stuck in a pond with the huge Holsteins surrounding its perimeters. She thought that she would never get out of that situation but she did, thanks to the help of a friendly ghost.

She felt something touch her shoulder from behind. She froze instantly and did not dare to look around. Her eyes however drifted downward and she saw large male fingers resting on her collarbone. Alarm rushed through her and she pulled herself forward to break free from the hold.

Flinging her head around, she saw the figure of a man standing on top of the broken cornstalks. In the eerie wet light, she could not make out who he was. Her instincts told her to run. What kind of man would be in the middle of a cornfield in such adverse weather? Yet, the girl did not run. She stared in disbelief at the figure that stood there silently with his arm stretched out to hold her gently by the shoulder. There was something about the posture that told the girl that the man was not threatening. If he had been threatening the grip he had on her shoulder would have been tighter and would have induced pain. The touch was anything but aggressive. It was gentle, if it was anything at all.

A flash of nearby lightning produced enough fleeting ambient light to reveal the man's face to Thora. She could not believe it. It was Samuel Angus Meadowford the First, her great grandfather and even more, her guardian angel. He had found her once again lost and desperate.

"Great Grandfather!" the girl gasped and threw her arms around the man. To her dismay her arms collapsed onto themselves as if there was nothing there. Yet she was still seeing him as real as anything. She pulled back. He was a ghost. He shouldn't have substance.

"Great Grandfather, I am lost and I need to find the way back to my friends!" she said to the figure. Even as she spoke the words, she was thinking about how he had found her. She had been lead to believe that the Indian spirit in the phantom canoe had hunted Sam the First down and that she had seen the last of him. That was what Jakob Nells had conjectured when she told the old Dutch ghost about her great grandfather and how it had been some time since she last saw him. Jakob's conjecture had been proven wrong or at least the last part of it had been incorrect. Her great grandfather still survived and still walked the Earth. If there was an Indian spirit on his trail, he had thus far been eluded.

The ghost of Samuel Angus Meadowford the First did not answer her. He stood silent. He was either mute or a figure of very few words. It seemed to Thora that this spirit had never identified himself to her and he may have never said anything at all to her. His actions were his words. He had saved her from the cows. He had cleaned up after her fiasco at attempting dinner for Uncle Thaddeus. He had driven the car that ultimately crashed and killed the Rozelles. His role to her was complicated. He was both guardian angel and an avenging spirit that carried out harsh penalties to those that sought to do her harm.

Despite this confusion in his motivations, Thora trusted the ghost implicitly. He would protect her and he would get her out of this. It pleased her immensely to realize that he was still following her and that she still fell under his aura of influence.

"Oh, Great Grandfather," she sighed, as she gazed upon his form. "I don't know what to do. I just want to go to the cottage and hide there forever and ever." She started to spill out to the spirit all of her anxiety and her conflicts.

The ghost for his part quietly listened. It did not matter that the rain was thrashing through him and tearing away parts of his essence, the way that the hail had previously done to Truus Nells. Truus had reconstituted herself and had become whole again. So it would be with Samuel Angus Meadowford the First.

When Thora felt she had nothing more to say, she asked her great grandfather if he had been the cause of the knocked down corn. He did not reply with words. Instead he pantomimed the motion of a man stroking a paddle. At once, Thora caught the gist of his meaning. He was indicating that the Indian spirit with the canoe had cut down this path through the cornfield.

At once, Thora felt a chill run through her. This was the very spirit that was hunting her great grandfather down. He was nearby and he had not given up on his quarry.

"You must get out of here, Great Grandfather!" she cried. "Save yourself! Don't worry about me! I have friends who will look after me."

The ghost's response was an embrace. He locked the girl in his arms and held her tightly. It was like he was meaning to say that his fate did not matter. He was here for her and nothing else made no never mind. Thora understood this meaning. She did not like it. She did not want to be the cause of her great grandfather's demise. Yet, she instinctively got the impression that there was absolutely nothing that she could do about it. He would stay by her no matter what.

"Do you know the way to Pioneer Lake from here?" she asked, pulling herself out of his arms.

The ghost nodded.

"Will you take me there?" the girl asked. With the words, she almost saw herself taking a dagger and stabbing it into the backs of the Nells ghosts. She was betraying them once again.

Once again the ghost nodded.

Thora felt something akin to a sigh of relief run through her. She had recommitted to her quest of reaching the lake. She now had a viable route there. She need not go back and try to find Jakob and Truus Nells. She was through with them. They may have had her best intentions at heart but they always seemed to run at cross-purposes to what she really wanted. She wanted nothing more than to return to the family stronghold on Black Island. She would not be lonely there, as they had suggested. She would be in the company of her great grandfather, the man that had built the Meadowford estate upon that proud and noble rock on Pioneer Lake, the man that had stated that Black Island would be the family's refuge throughout the ages.

Still, she could not throw all caution to the wind. There were other adversaries besides the Nells that she and her great grandfather would have to contend with. There were the authorities, both Canadian and American, that were looking for her and that might not accept that she had died in the plane crash that had taken the life of Bewdley Beacon. She knew for certain that Officer Lou Bombino would not leave one blade of grass unturned before he was satisfied that the case of Thora Meadowford had come to an end.

There were also those two spirits, the ghosts of her grandmother and her cousin. She had seen them and recognized the foul intent in their eyes. They were not far away and the girl wondered if they were in league with the Indian spirit in the canoe and were acting in concert with him.

And there were the Nells. Yes, she realized, they would impede her as much as they could. Their intentions were good but they were stifling her and forcing her down a road that she preferred not to travel.

Yet, with all these formidable enemies, Thora no longer felt frightened. She was with her guardian angel. With him, she almost felt invincible. The situation was far from grim.

Her great grandfather extended his hand out to her. She did not know if he could read minds the way that Truus and Jakob could but he could not have timed his gesture of solidarity to her at a more perfect moment. She took hold of the thick fingers. She could feel their substance within her petite hands. They felt extremely cold. They felt almost icy. And they felt wet. She had to fight her innate reaction to pull her hands away. She forced herself to hold on, wondering why she was able to feel his hands at all. Only minutes earlier when she wanted to throw her arms around the man and embrace him she had discovered that there was nothing to him. But now there was. It almost seemed like the ghost could will how much of that that composed him would be salient to the mortal.

"Thora! Thora!" a voice called out into the storm. The girl instantly recognized the accent. It was Jakob Nells hollering out her name. He sounded far away. Much farther away than Thora would have expected. It seemed like he was at least a mile's distance from where she was. His call came from her right. It was the opposite direction that she believed that he would have been.

"Fraulien! Fraulien!" Truus' voice joined in on the call. The old woman appeared to be in relatively the same vicinity as her husband.

The girl realized that had she not stumbled upon her great grandfather she would have been hopelessly lost. She had somehow ventured back into the heart of the cornfield and may have inadvertently gone right back to the lands that adjoined Lake Ontario had she not found her guardian angel.

Jakob Nells' voice sounded her name once more. He was still far from where she stood listening but he was narrowing the gap that separated them. If she did not get moving soon he would be upon her. She looked up at her great grandfather and with her eyes she urged him to lead the way out of the corn and to the lake.

Her ancestor produced a small smile that he attached to a nod, conveying to her that he got the message. He proceeded to walk in a direction that to Thora at first seemed all wrong. He was walking towards where Jakob Nells was calling for her.

"It's the wrong way!" she cried. "I don't want to go back to him. I want to get away from him!"

Her great grandfather placed his fingers to his lips, signaling that Thora should keep silent. Thora smirked at herself for her ignorance. She could have betrayed their presence to the Nells with her remark. She bit onto her tongue and held it fast between her teeth less she inadvertently bleated anything else.

Her companion still appeared to be walking in a direction that seemed to be leading directly to Jakob. She could hear the old Dutch ghost calling her name. He was now not more than five hundred feet from her but he was not in any adjacent aisle between the corn. There were many rows still separating them.

"Fraulien!" Truus shouted out. The old woman was still quite a distance from her. She appeared to be searching another sector of the cornfield. The girl could hear in the inflections of Truus' voice that the old ghost was riddled with worry and distraught. She must have been horrified when she woke up from her tormenting dream and discovered that her little ward was gone. A part of Thora's heart went out to Truus. A part of her wanted to call out to let her know that everything was all right and there was nothing to worry about. But if she did that, she knew that the Nells would be onto her in a flash and they would do everything that they could to keep her from following her great grandfather. It was better for Truus to be worried rather than for her to become her keeper again.

She could now start hearing the rustling of the corn produced by Jakob as the distance that separated them had been whittled down to less than ten yards. He might have been in the next row of corn for all that Thora knew. Her great grandfather must have thought the same. He took her by the hand and pulled her into a tiny space between two towering cornstalks. As Thora followed him into this spot, her eyes caught sight of something in the aisle's mud. She was leaving tracks. Jakob would see them at once. She began praying that the old man would not venture into this aisle.

She stood frozen in between the corn. She kept her breath as silent as possible lest it betray her presence. Out of the corner of her eyes, she started to detect motion in the next aisle. It was Jakob. He was moving quietly, like a hunter in the last moments before taking his shot. He was no longer shouting her name. He seemed to know that she was nearby as well.

He was only a few plants down from her. If he walked any further he would see her in her hiding spot. Thora now held her breath. She nestled tighter against the legs of her great grandfather. She could feel him there although he had now become invisible.

At that moment Jakob decided to cross into the aisle that Thora had been walking. He instantly saw her tracks. He moved towards them. All that he had to do was turn his head and he would see her there. Her escapade was over.

But then from somewhere distant, Truus blurted out, "I've found her!"

Jakob stopped dead in his tracks. He was standing directly beside Thora but his head was looking elsewhere.

"I've found her Jakob and she is all right!" Truus cried out once more.

Jakob grumbled something angry to the effect that he wanted to give the girl a good thrashing for her behavior and then he wandered off in the direction that his wife had called.

Thora released a huge sigh of relief. She had miraculously escaped. But she did not understand how this had happened. Who had Truus found? It was not her. She was here with her great grandfather. Was there someone else here in the corn with them? Was there someone impersonating her? She looked up to her great grandfather. He was no longer invisible. He shrugged his shoulders to show that he did not understand any of this either.

As soon as Thora thought that it was safe to speak she said to him, "Are you playing a trick on them?" It was the only possible answer. How else would Truus have thought that she had found her?

The ghost produced an enigmatic smile and then nudged her on the shoulder and gently shoved her back into the aisle. They started walking down this muddy gap between the rows of corn. Soon Thora was able to once more see the gravel road.

Chapter 51

In the Shadow of the Moraine

Her foot stepped onto the narrow gravel road. She had finally left the cornfield behind. Almost in union with this event the rains had come to an end. The thunder and lightning were in the distance and traveling away from her and her companion, her great grandfather Samuel Angus Meadowford the First.

She still felt cautious though. Sooner or later Jakob and Truus Nells would show up on this road as well, either by themselves or in the company of someone who was impersonating her. She did not understand what had happened out there. By rights, Jakob should have found her. He was standing right beside her and if it had not been for Truus distracting him he would have set eyes on her. Her escape from him was as narrow as a hair's breadth. She knew that her great grandfather had orchestrated the maneuver and that he was capable of great trickery and mischief.

They started walking up a hill as the road almost immediately began to climb upward. On both of its shoulders, fallen rain streamed down in fast-moving rivulets. As she reached the higher elevation, Thora paused to look back at the cornfield. Its immensity awed her. It was almost like a deep green sea. It stretched past the horizon. To think that she had traversed every inch of it dazzled her. She saw it as somewhat of an accomplishment. It was like traveling on a different planet inside the narrow aisles of that verdant landscape, a planet with tight narrow skies, a planet with giant flora that dwarfed the visiting human form.

Her great grandfather did not appreciate the stop. He wanted to keep moving. He took her hand and forced her to fall into gait once more. His request was entirely nonverbal. Thora felt that she was dealing with a mute. She did not recall this silent quality in the man earlier. She had memories of him speaking. Wasn't it him that had impersonated her father in order for her mother Cora to give the girl permission to go on the country visit to Mrs. Bianco's place with Margaret Whattam? Why was he not speaking now? It disturbed the girl. There were so many questions that she wanted to ask him but it would be pointless to utter them if there was no voice that would reply.

She did not appreciate being dragged back into step either. She had just finished crossing that giant cornfield and she was at the point of exhaustion. A little rest would be nice to revitalize her. But the ghost of her great grandfather would not have any of it. It was almost like he was rushing to either get away from the Nells in the corn or to get to Pioneer Lake. Thora did not know which reason it was or if it was another reason altogether.

At the top of the road there was a long plateau through more land given over to agriculture. The crop here was cabbage. It produced an unpleasant aroma that hung heavy in the air and served to deepen the girl's sagging, uncomfortable spirits. From what she could see of the panorama before here there were no dwellings or other signs of human habitation outside of the growing vegetables. There were no roads that crossed the gravel lane that they moved through. In the distance she could see another rise in the land as a glacial moraine outlined the horizon and sat as a great divide between her side of it and whatever sat on the other side. Something told her that Pioneer Lake was somewhere on the other side.

At least it was no longer raining and the sun was starting to peak out of gaps in the thinning clouds. Its light caused the moisture on the cabbage leaves to glisten. This shining gave the girl some small measure of cheer despite the long distance that stretched out ahead of her. Pioneer Lake was not just around the corner. It was still far away but with every step that she took she was one step closer to the place to which her heart yearned.

The placement of the sun in the sky told the girl that the early afternoon had arrived. She would have thought that it would have been later in the day than that for it seemed that it had taken forever to get out of the corn and the rain. But the sun does not lie and play tricks. The sun could be relied upon to tell the truth.

An hour later there was nothing but sunshine. The moraine did not seem to be any closer. All the clouds associated with the storm had drifted into the distance. The rain that had produced the glistening on the cabbage had evaporated. All that was left as evidence of the heavy storm was the occasional puddle at the side of the road and even these were beginning to dry up.

But despite the drying sun the air had not warmed up. It remained considerably cool. This fresh temperature was further augmented by a steady breeze that had in its presence a bit of autumn in it. It did not feel like a summer wind. It was the harbinger of an approaching change in season. The summer was coming to an end and the fall was waking up.

This wind disconcerted the girl. She was not one that was enamored with autumn with its changing leaves and its cooler temperatures. Autumn was a busy time of the year and Thora just did not like being busy. Autumn meant school. She did not like school. She wanted an endless summer but she knew that she could not have one living in a part of the world where the seasons were demarcated with definite differences in character.

Periodically her great grandfather would turn around and look behind him. She guessed that he was scanning for the Nells as if they might be following them. They could be following, Thora surmised. If they were they should be able to see her hiking along the road even from quite a distance away. Her great grandfather's display of anxiety told the girl that whatever scheme he had set into place to foil the ghosts from Hawkins Corners was not fool proof. There was a chance that the Nells had not fallen for his trick and were now in pursuit of her.

Yet when she peered backwards she could not see anything moving along the road. If the Nells were there they were either too far back to be seen or they were using invisibility as their modus operandi.

"I don't see anybody back there," she said to him, hoping that she might invoke some form of spoken reply from him. But none was coming. He merely smiled at her and quickened his step, challenging her to match his speed.

When the sun started to slip downward, it chose as its nesting spot the left-hand side of the moraine. This told the girl with certainty that the gravel road was leading northwards. This was an affirmation that they were going in the direction of Pioneer Lake. Thora knew that her precious refuge from the world was some distance considerably north of Lake Ontario but other than that she really did not have a clue about its precise location. She did not have an inkling of where she was now but she knew that the ghost possessed this knowledge. He was the first Meadowford to come upon the lake nearly fifty years ago. She wondered how he had found it. Had he merely just stumbled upon it or did others tell him about it? Family folklore said that Sam the First and some hunting friends used to come up into the wilds of Canada to shoot moose, deer and bear. It was during one of these hunting excursions that Sam discovered Pioneer Lake. It had abundant game and Sam fell in love with the lake and its surrounding territory. Shortly thereafter he purchased an island from the Canadian government and that island became the foundation of the family dynasty.

It marveled Thora that she was in the company of this great man. Her grandfather, Sambo, had nothing but the highest praise and esteem for his father. He was a true pioneer, worthy to have his dwelling upon a lake named for adventurers and those that would homestead in the rugged wilderness. Even Thaddeus saw Sam the First as a stalwart, enterprising individual embodying all the virtues that would make a man a success. Sam the First was an innovator. He was an inventor. His ingenuity allowed the family to climb above its humble farming beginnings and enter into the world of mass manufacturing and lucrative profits.

She wished that the ghost would tell her first-hand accounts of all of his accomplishments. His silence was almost a cruelty to her. Her curiosity craved to hear him speak. On several occasions as they marched toward the moraine on the gravel road she tried to get him to talk but she always came up against a stone wall. He just would not say anything. Was he purposefully being quiet or had he truly become muted? Thora postulated that perhaps the great Indian spirit that chased this man had cast a spell upon him and rendered him speechless. But that was only conjecture. She had no way of knowing until the man actually communicated and thus far he had not.

Maybe Sam was looking over his shoulder to see if that great Indian spirit in his canoe was coming after them? Thora had seen this spirit several times and knew how frightening of a figure he could be. He was a giant in the sky; his canoe easily took up most of the space up there. His brow was grim and his gaze was stern and sober. To have such a man as an enemy would make most bend at the knee and crumble in shameless postures begging for mercy. But not her great grandfather. He appeared to be courageous in the face of this adversity. He ignored the personal danger to himself in order to protect her and to see her through with her mission. Thora loved this man. He was everything that a true man should be. She wished her father Langley could be more like him. Despite the similarity in appearance, there was nothing of Samuel Angus the First in Samuel Angus the Third. Langley was weak and sniveling and given over to behaving arrogantly and shoddy. Sam was strong and silent and allowed his actions to speak nobly about himself.

If only he could allow his mouth to do some of that speaking. That would make her feel more comfortable in his company. She felt that she had done something wrong to him and that he was giving her the silent shoulder as punishment.

As the sun set, Sam the First finally stopped beside a lush green pasture that was very much reminiscent of that cow field where Thora had first met the man. This pasture even had a pond just like the first. He pointed the body of water out to her and indicated that she should go and take a drink.

While she did so, he disappeared from her sight. The water was warm and riddled with green slime. Thora worked her hands through it, spreading the floating minute vegetation away until there was some clear liquid in front of her. She scooped out some of it and put it in her mouth. Its taste was anything but refreshing. It had a warm acidic tang to it and she could feel her tongue getting coated by something or other. But it did not matter. She was thirsty and she needed to drink.

When she had her fill, she turned around and saw that her great grandfather was nowhere to be seen. Sudden anxiety gripped her, as she believed that he had abandoned her here in the middle of nowhere. Her eyes ate up the surrounding landscape trying to root out his form amid all the shades and variations in textures of what sat around her. She could not find him. Either he was invisible or he was gone. She clenched her hands together. What had she done to him to make him give up on her? She went over recent events and saw nothing that could have provoked such a response in him except for her nagging him to speak. Maybe she was pestering him too much? Sam the First was a ghost that was used to being alone. Having a chatterbox as a companion might have eaten at his nerves.

Finally he could not take it any more and he had to get himself clear from this constant source of annoyance. It was the only reason that the girl could reach.

It was growing darker in the shadow of the moraine. Its long stretched tree-covered top glowed in the crimson light of a setting sun on its unseen northern face. The setting gave Thora an eerie almost apocalyptic feeling. She had decided that she would stay by the pond for the night. If her great grandfather came back he would have no trouble finding her.

By the same account, if the Nells happened up the road, they too would have no trouble spotting her. If the Hawkins Corner ghosts were the first to come upon her she would have to make her peace with them yet again and she would join them once more. Something inside of her told her that despite their hard feelings they would take her under their care. They were good people and she was making them suffer with her erratic behavior and her flimsy loyalty.

There were others that might spot her by the pond's side. Thora did her best to shield her thoughts from thinking about them and what they may do. She did not want to linger on images of her grandmother and her cousin or on horrifying visualizations of an enormous canoe silently gliding across the sky.

Despite her mental blocking, her fears were working their way up to the surface and making her feel very vulnerable and exposed out here in the open. When she thought that she could not take it any longer and was ready to take flight, her eyes happened onto a shape coming from the road towards the pond. She knew this form immediately.

It was her great grandfather. He had come back. He was carrying something in his arms that the girl could not make out. When he reached her he dropped his cache onto the ground before her. It was a fat rodent of some sort. It was dead. Its head drooped from its broken neck, its little pink tongue doing the same from its mouth. As she looked at the forlorn creature she tried to determine if it was a beaver, a muskrat or a groundhog. She was leaning toward the latter for the animal's fur was light tan in color.

Her great grandfather started to tear this fur from the animal. His method of doing so seemed more of a demonstration to show her what to do. The girl needed no instruction. She had watched her father skin animals many a time after his return from a hunt. But those were animals that were edible—deer, moose and waterfowl. They were not groundhogs.

She protested that she was not going to eat such a creature but her great grandfather did not listen. He simply proceeded to finish skinning the creature. Once it was done he began gathering sticks and other inflammable materials to build a fire.

"I'm not going to eat that thing!" she cried as he somehow magically produced a flame to ignite the small pile of twigs and leaves.

Still this did not stop her great grandfather. He soon had a good fire going and he devised a stand above the flames where he hung the groundhog's carcass. It was not very long after that that there was a savory aroma wafting in the air and Thora's saliva glands went into production. Not long afterwards, she was ripping cooked flesh from the roasted creature and was enjoying its vibrant flavor in her mouth. However, after several bites she started to think about what she was eating and suddenly she felt a strong aversion being generated by her mouth and stomach. She was eating a groundhog. Groundhogs were not part of the menu for a civilized Twentieth Century human being.

She would eat no more and cast the remaining meat onto the ground. For several moments she thought that her stomach would do the same with the chewed pieces it contained. Somehow she avoided being sick. Perhaps she was so much in need of food that her body clung miserly to whatever little bit it got no matter how repulsive it was.

Her great grandfather was not pleased that she would waste the meat. A good animal had set down its life all for nothing. He would not have it. He picked up the carcass and held it high in the air. Soon crows appeared out of nowhere, cawing with delight that there was something being offered to them. Sam the First threw the meat as far as he could. When it landed, the crows were upon it and eating it up with ravenous abandon.

He then looked at his great granddaughter. There seemed to be disappointment in his eyes, yet at the same time these ghostly orbs spelled out the message that rest period was over and it was time to once again continue the trek.

Chapter 52

Bearings

The gravel road wound its way up the hill, following features etched into it by the great glacier that had created it more than ten thousand years ago. It was not near as tall as the mountains near her home in Pennsylvania but it still held the aura of the spectacular, especially once they started nearing its top. From up there, Thora could make out Lake Ontario in the distance. Its water rippled and shone under an extremely bright moon. It could hardly be separated from the great hanging nighttime sky that sat over it. This was the view from the heavens. This was the view from an earlier age. In all the land that her eyes encapsulated there was nothing that indicated a human presence. This was virgin territory. This was land untouched.

Her great grandfather did not appear to be interested in appreciating the view. He kept slugging his way forward, not once turning around to draw in the overwhelming inspiration that grew out of the landscape.

Thora, on the other hand, would not look ahead of her as of yet. She wanted to behold all that was behind her. She had walked every bit of that stretch between here and the lake's shore. Somewhere back there were the remains of Bewdley Beacon. She wondered if had he lived how different her past day would have been. They might have been still in the airplane, looking for a place to land around Pioneer Lake. But that airplane, like Bewdley, was gone now. She had reunited with the Nells for most of the day. They were back there somewhere as well. Whether they were on her trail or they were being duped to go elsewhere by some manifestation that pretended to be her, the girl did not know.

And somewhere back there were the spirits of her grandmother and her cousin. She did not know what had become of them. They had appeared suddenly and then with the same abruptness they had disappeared. What purpose did they have? What were they up to? She sensed that she had not seen the last of the pair. She wished that she did. There was something very foul about them. They were more demons than angels.

And the greatest demon of them all, the Indian in the canoe was lurking somewhere. She knew it even though she could not see it. Was he up there in that pristine sky, slowly paddling his vessel, waiting for his moment to strike? Out of this concern, she started studying the few cloud formations that had populated the ether. Most of these clouds were over the lake and not the land. Was the Indian hiding in one of these? Then her eyes came upon a great solitary plume on the distant American side of the lake. Its grotesque smoke climbing upward was an affront to the pristine crystal clear nocturnal air. What could be creating such corruption? It was like the flare of smoke rising from a medieval dragon's nostril. Her eyes narrowed and she saw that it was a giant smokestack, so tall that it was visible across the lake. It was vile and contemptible in her eyes and it shamed her that this was the only thing from her nation that could be seen from this part of Canada. What did that say of her country?

She rotated her neck to take in the northern vista. At once, she saw an irregularly shaped series of lights illuminating some spot to the northwest of her. It was a town or a village. It sat at a lower elevation than the top of the moraine. It was not what she expected. She would have believed that she would have seen nothing but what the moon would reveal. There was a community nearby and it was augmenting the light of the lunar orb, sending out an unnatural glow that wiped out whatever stars that were above it.

Elsewhere, the moon lit up forests, lakes and rivers. Ontario was known for its abundance of waterways. From the apex of the moraine, Thora could see why. They were everywhere. These bodies of water sparkled in the moon's radiance like diamonds dispersed haphazardly onto a black carpet. This was what Thora expected to see. Her mind was set to wondering if one of these diamonds could not in fact be Pioneer Lake.

Her great grandfather had chosen a path that was not leading to any of these lakes. He was moving directly towards the village or town or whatever it was. This bothered the girl. She did not want to go to any human settlements. She had enough of them in her life. She wanted to stay true to those lands where her species had not entered and poisoned with their self-serving and Nature-disrespecting ways.

"I don't want to go that way," she called out to the ghost. But Samuel Angus Meadowford the First ignored her demand and continued down the gravel road. He did not even turn around to acknowledge her words.

He was proving to be poor company and he was nothing like what she had expected him to be. The family stories of the man painted him as a laughing, playful character with a hardworking ethic that was tempered with a spirit that everything should not be taken so seriously. What she saw in his ghost was something entirely different. He was a morose, silent figure that seemed driven to humorlessly carry out his grim purposes at whatever cost that they would entail. Thora was discovering that she much preferred the company of the Nells to this man. Truus and Jakob could be overbearing at times but they knew how to keep light hearts. Such was not the case with Sam the First.

Yet, she had chosen to be with him. She believed that he would be her guide to the fulfillment of her dreams. It did not matter what kind of personality the man possessed as long as he brought her wishes to fruition. With a sober, stern heart she continued to follow him through the night. She continued to follow him no matter where he would lead her.

The town grew closer. She could no longer see it as an illuminated geometric design upon a dark backdrop. They had come down the northern face of the moraine and they were now at relatively the same elevation as the community. They soon reached the town's outer fringes. Like every other village that she had come across during her trek, this place followed the same pattern. First were the farms that sat a few miles out from the actual community. Gradually the distance between the farms decreased and the buildings started piling up on each other and taking on non-agricultural purposes. Eventually these warehouses and factories gave over to residential dwellings as the plots of land decreased in size.

They had silently gone past several farms, the only indication of their presence being the dogs barking at them in the darkness of the night. There were no lights on in any of these bucolic homes, the farmers and their wives going to bed so that they could rise up early to greet another day of chores. Soon would be harvest season.

But as they started to enter the built up sector of the community, there were lights on in several of the houses. Thora had no idea what time it was. The gravel road now possessed streetlights on either side of it. It no longer was a gravel road. It had been paved and there were now vehicles parked along it. The houses did not have driveways. They were built at a time before the automobile became a necessary part of life. From the streetlights she could see that these homes were small and humble as compared to those in Grappling Haven but they did have a measure of quaintness to them that made whatever this community was called feel attractive.

Had she been with Bewdley Beacon at this moment, she was sure that he would be checking the parked cars trying to find one that they could heist. Her great grandfather did not have the same mindset. He just walked by them and paid them as much attention as he paid any of the tall trees that elegantly lined both sides of the street. Was it his intention to walk all the way to Pioneer Lake? Did it not even occur to him that driving there would be so much more expedient? She knew that he could drive. She had seen him do so on that fateful night outside of Cristo Pando's.

She came to a stop beside a car that was the same make and model as one of the cars that she and Bewdley had driven while escaping from Pennsylvania. She called out to her great grandfather and suggested to him that maybe they should think of alternative means of transportation. There was nobody around. The adjacent houses were dark. Everybody had gone to sleep in this stretch of town.

Her great grandfather looked at her with an expression that said that she was out of her mind to even think of doing such a thing.

"We're only borrowing it," she responded. "Once we get to the lake the owners can get it back there." She wondered if her great grandfather was admonishing her for entertaining the sinful thought of theft. Yet, it did not seem that way. If she read him right it appeared that it wasn't the concept of theft that made her proposal so outlandish. There was some other reason why he did not think that it was prudent.

"Well, I don't care what you think!" Thora griped. "I know how to drive.

My legs are tired from all of this walking. So if you want to continue marching along, you go ahead. I am going to ride behind you."

She put her hand onto the door handle and saw that it was open. It did not surprise her. People in small towns like this one never lock their cars and houses. They have implicit trust in their neighbors. "Well, I'm not a neighbor!" she said quietly to herself and looked inside at the steering column. Once again she was not surprised to see a set of keys dangling there. These people are going to have to smarten up if they want to be a part of the Twentieth Century. They are going to have to get driveways. They are going to have to lock their cars and houses. Somebody like Rory McQuoid would have a field day here.

She climbed into the car, sat down and shut the door. Almost at once her great grandfather began pounding at the window and gesturing for her to get out of the car. Thora ignored him and turned on the ignition. The car turned on with a roar that would assuredly wake up the residents.

"Are you getting in?" she said through the rolled down window. She was fully impressing upon the man that she was taking the car no matter what.

Her great grandfather just stood there. There was shock upon his face. It seemed that it wasn't that he did not believe that she would have the audacity to actually steal a car. It seemed that he was more surprised that she had the ability to drive.

"Come on, get in, before people start coming out of the houses!" she said as loudly as she dared. She was expecting the ghost to simply glide through the body of the vehicle the way that the Nells did.

Sam the First lifted his arms in the air in a sign that showed that he felt helpless.

"Can't you slide through the door?" Thora remarked. "Well, go over to the other side and climb in."

Her great grandfather walked across the front of the car and came to the other door. He put his hand down towards the handle and then once again he shrugged.

"It's not locked!" Thora said. She was feeling exasperated and she was growing worried that this rather loud vehicle would soon draw the attention of the sleeping people of the neighborhood. So far no lights came on but that did not mean that people were peeking out of their windows.

Sam the First tried once more and got nowhere. He folded his arms across his chest in frustration. Maybe the door was jammed on the outside. The girl leaned over the passenger seat and lifted up the handle. The car door popped open effortlessly. As soon as it was, her great grandfather stepped in and silently took the seat beside her.

She wished that she could draw some explanation from him as to why he could not have gotten into the car himself. But she knew that no words would come out of his mouth. There was no time for explanation anyway. They had to get out of here before they were discovered. She put the car into gear and pulled out onto the deserted road.

Within a couple of minutes, they were at the main intersection of the town. Here were its banks, restaurants and dry goods stores. Thora noted that several of the businesses bore the word 'Welcome' in their trade names. It must be a very friendly place, she thought. There were a few people milling about outside of what looked to be a billiard hall. These were Rory McQuoid types, young and brash and bored out of their skulls. Every town has its Rory McQuoid types. They looked up at the car as it drove by. It offered them a moment's entertainment and then they returned to whatever was occupying them previously. None of them recognized the car much to Thora's relief. If they did they had plenty of vehicles to choose from to make chase.

She started driving out of the town and watched in reverse order as the hierarchy of buildings played itself out, gradually diminishing in size while the land plots grew. They were now in the town's northern residential sector and they would soon be driving into farm country once more.

A road sign was illuminated in the car's headlights. It said that Northmill was thirty-five miles away. Northmill was not that far away from Pioneer Lake! It was the town just south of Osprey Landing. It was the town that Uncle Thaddeus caught the bus bound for Toronto. She could find her lake from Northmill.

Thora could not help but smile. Finally she was getting some geography to this land. She was getting her bearings and it made her feel more than just encouraged. It made her feel great. She knew where she was and she knew where she was going. Even more than that, she knew how to get to where she was going.

She looked over at her silent partner, sitting in the darkness next to her. He was a mysterious man, this Samuel Angus Meadowford the First. She did not know how to read him. There was nothing in his face that she could use as a measure of what thoughts were contained inside the man. There was no smile. There was no scowl. There was only a blank countenance in the eyes. If there were some calculations going on underneath they were not showing. In many ways it was like there was nobody beside her at all. There was something different about the man. He did not seem to be the same person that he was back in Grappling Haven.

And what was it with the car door? Why couldn't he get in? He had been in cars before. She had seen him driving Uncle Thaddeus' car after all. Why was it all of a sudden an impossible thing for him to simply just go through a door? She had seen the Nells climb into cars many times. They went through the door as if it was not there. Didn't all ghosts share this skill?

It was pointless to ask him these questions. He would not answer.

She continued driving. They were out in the country now. The land had grown wild once more with huge pine and spruce trees coming up to the road's edge. This road did not follow a straight course. It tended to wind a lot and she had to keep her mind on it lest she accidentally drive off of it.

The car rounded yet another bend and as it did so, Thora was suddenly blinded. There was an oncoming vehicle with very bright lights that shone into the girl's car. She had to turn her head to avoid the glare. As she did so, she saw the beams illuminate her great grandfather. She had never seen anything so peculiar. In the bright light he did not look like Samuel Angus Meadowford the First. If anything he looked more like his daughter-in-law June Ritchey, the frightening ghost of Thora's grandmother. But then when the oncoming car drove past, the semblance was gone and he once more looked like who he was supposed to be.

The girl decided that her mind must have been playing tricks on her. She was overtired. She knew that she should rest but Northmill was getting closer with every minute. Pioneer Lake was getting closer. She estimated that she was maybe only two hours away from Osprey Landing on the lake. There, she would rest and bide her time for the Madoqua Empress to arrive sometime tomorrow morning.

Tomorrow she would be on that proud steamer and carrier. She was enamored with the Madoqua Empress. She loved the way that its long, sleek form sliced through the waves. There was no better place to be than on its uppermost deck as it did so. To view the myriad of emerald islands sitting upon the rich blue water on a sunny day was like being in Heaven itself.

And there were all those handsome boys that worked on the Empress! She was getting giddy just thinking about it. Maybe they will take notice of her now, seeing that she no longer was in the company of her parents? Maybe they will see her as more mature and begin flirting with her. Wouldn't that be a dream!

She suddenly realized that she had been on the road for several days and had been through everything from thunderstorms to dusty old roads. She never had an opportunity to wash up. Her clothes were filthy, her hands grimy and her fingernails dirty. She must be an awful sight. She had to do something about it before she got on board. There had to be public lavatories in Northmill. There had to be clothiers there as well. How she was going to pay for new clothes, she did not really know. But where there is a will there is a way. Something would work itself out.

What would she like to wear tomorrow as she walked the gangplank to board the Empress? She had noticed many girls and young women in Pittsburgh were garbed in flapper outfits. She kind of liked the style with the short dresses and the straight-cropped hair. Maybe if she had the time and Northmill had a salon she could get herself a new hairdo.

Her mind was pleasantly occupied with creating a new self-image. She was not really paying attention to her driving. It had drifted back to the recesses of her consciousness, its rote mechanics being done automatically. Several times she caught herself going over the median in the road and actually begin driving in the oncoming lane. She had to check herself and return to her side. Not on one of these occasions did her great grandfather do anything to remind her that she was on the wrong side of the road. She saw that he was awake and was fully cognizant of their whereabouts. Yet he had not done anything. It was almost like he did not know any better.

Then on yet another of these careless misadventures, while Thora once more was driving on the wrong side of the road with her mind musing on what color of outfit that she would choose for boarding the Madoqua Empress, another vehicle suddenly appeared, its lights even brighter than the earlier one.

The car sounded its horn repeatedly as the distance that separated the two vehicles diminished. Thora was not paying attention. She was staring in horror at the passenger beside her. The oncoming car's headlights shone brightly and it was fully exposing the weathered and withered face of June Ritchey, her deceased grandmother.

Chapter 53

Big Man with a Big Beard

The approaching car swerved into the lane that was supposed to be Thora's. The two cars narrowly missed crashing into each other as they drove by. Thora dared not look at it as it passed lest her eyes fell upon the enraged driver. She could hear the other car's brakes begin to scream. A moment later its headlights were in Thora's rearview mirror.

She had returned to the lane that was supposed to be hers. The cab of her car was now being illuminated from the rear, leaving her passenger's face in the darkness. This rider now seemed to look more like her great grandfather once again but she no longer knew if it was him.

"Who are you?" she demanded. "You're not my great granddad!"

Once again she was given silence for a response. She had no time to ask further questions. The driver behind her was now upon her and was riding only inches away from her bumper. She must have really pissed the guy off, she realized, for him to act so aggressively.

She started to get scared. How was she going to deal with this fellow? What would she say to him?

Whoever it was was allowing his horn to do his talking. It was constantly blaring at a deafening volume. She wanted to cry out for him to stop and go away. She was sorry what she had done and she would not do it again. No harm was done. Why couldn't this guy just give up and go about his merry way?

And then a huge jolt shook her car. Thora's head lurched forward and almost collided with her steering wheel. The other driver had smashed against her rear bumper. And then he did it again and again.

Thora kept on driving. She knew that the other guy wanted her to stop so that he could harangue her or worse. She was not going to have any of that. She pressed harder on the accelerator, forcing her motor to give her more power and speed.

The other car matched her and smashed her once again. The man was a maniac, Thora realized. What kind of fellow would be so relentless in an attack? She was now more convinced than ever that she would not stop the car if she could avoid it. She would keep on driving.

To add to her problems the road that she was upon began winding this way and then that. With her high speed, it was getting extremely difficult to steer through this serpentine course. More than once she had driven onto the soft shoulder and felt her tires being grabbed by the light gravel. She had to do battle with the steering wheel to get the car back on the road.

Still the other car kept pace and made its periodic lunges and stabs.

"Can't you do anything about it?" she cried out to her passenger. The real Samuel Angus Meadowford the First was her guardian angel. He would have long ago taken action to remedy this situation. But the ghost beside her did nothing. He or she or whatever it was did not even react when the car was heavily throttled by the vehicle behind them. It was like this was nothing out of the ordinary.

But it was out of the ordinary for Thora. She truly did not know how to get out of this mess. She realized though that if she did not stop she was going to end up in an accident and possibly get killed. This realization forced her to ease up on the gas pedal and slow the car down. Maybe the treatment would be less harsh than the medicine.

Her opponent was not expecting her to do this. His car smashed hard against the back of Thora's vehicle. It hit the car at such an angle that it pushed it to its side and caused Thora to be suddenly heading to the ditch on the opposite side of the road. Her foot instinctively pounded on the brake and this sent her car spinning. It whirled around several times before it finally came to a stop in the oncoming lane's soft shoulder. She was pointing in the other direction. Her head was a little woozy from the tailspin but other than that she had come through the collision unscathed.

As she lifted her head to get her bearings she saw that the other car had stopped and that the driver was lunging out of the door. He was a big man with a big beard and a big temper. He had come out of his car with a baseball bat. He was not finished his business.

Thora shrank in her seat. She was scared to death. She began crying and pleading to the ghost beside her to do something to stop what was coming. The ghost just sat there, staring out of the windshield as if nothing had happened at all, as if they were still driving down the road.

"Get out of that car you piece of shit!" the big man bellowed as he approached. He reached down to the door handle and ripped it open. Before Thora could react, she was grabbed by her collar and flung outside and tossed violently onto the pavement. She kept her head down and covered it with her arms, helplessly waiting for the baseball bat to start inflicting its painful pummels.

"Why, you are nothing but a kid!" the big man burst out. "What in God's name are you driving in the middle of the night for?"

Thora took this as her cue that this man was not going to do anything physically harmful to her any longer. Her eye peeked out from the space in the crook of her elbow and she saw the man. He had to be at least six and a half feet tall and weigh over 300 pounds. He was dressed in forest clothes as she called them—a lumber jacket overtop of denim overalls. Had this been Tennessee the man would have been described as a hillbilly.

"You're too young to have a driver's license! And you are a girl, for crying out loud!" the man scoffed. The baseball bat was no longer held out in an offensive position. He had brought it down to his side.

Despite this, Thora said, "Please Mister, don't hurt me!" She was slowly climbing to her feet.

"You have a lot of explaining to do," the man said. "Does your Mama and Papa know that you are out joyriding in the middle of the night? You damned near killed me back there when you were pulling that stunt."

"What stunt?" Thora asked, although she knew full well what he was referring to.

"Driving on the wrong side of the road! You're supposed to stay on the right side of the road. If you don't know that then you will never get your driver's license." Moment by moment the big man was softening his demeanor. The threat of physical violence was gone and Thora sensed that the tongue-lashing was not going to be very vicious.

"You're not from around here, are you? I don't recognize you," he said. His eyes were gazing over at the license plate of Thora's car. It said 'Ontario' on it.

"I'm from Pioneer Lake," the girl offered as she stood up and began dusting herself off.

"Pioneer Lake, that is an hour away! You sure went a long way in the middle of the night."

"I couldn't sleep so I thought that I would practice my driving," Thora lied. "Mom and Dad are going to shoot me when they see what happened to the car."

"It's a little rough for the wear," the man admitted.

Thora realized that it was now her turn to take the offensive. Her car would not have been damaged if this fellow had not flown off the handle. "And that is your fault! What gives you the right to become a human battering ram! I might have accidentally slipped onto the wrong side of the road but what you did you did on purpose! You ought to be thrown in jail for it!"

The look in the big man's face was pained. He was making the realization that he had brutally attacked a young girl. It was shameful what he did and he was beginning to experience the opening throes of remorse. "I didn't know that you were just a kid," he said in defense. "Had I known…"

"So, it is okay to act the way that you did if I was an adult and if I was a man? Is that what you do at night? Rove around the streets and punish anybody that steps outside of the laws of the road?" She knew that she had better be careful in what she said. He was after all a big man with a big beard and a big temper. If she pushed him too far it would not matter if she were a baby suckling at her mother's breast, the man would retaliate. Yet, she could not help herself. The vindictive words just flowed out of her like honey from a tilted jar.

"Look, I'm sorry what happened here! I went a little too far. But so did you! You should not be on the road driving. Maybe if I did not interfere you would have nodded off to sleep and crashed into a tree. The Lord acts in mysterious ways, you know!" The man's statement said that he was not going to be talked down to any more.

"The Lord does act mysteriously but who says that you are an agent of the Lord? I can think of someone else's emissary that would act the way that you did!"

"That's enough said, kid. I'll give you a hundred bucks for your parents. That should pay for the damages. That car was in rough shape in the first place." He was going to settle matters and end this messy affair.

He began reaching into his pocket to dig out his wallet. Thora saw something moving behind him. It was faint and almost transparent but there was something definitely there. All of a sudden the big man's neck was pulled backwards at a speed that no voluntary motion could match. It went so far back towards his spine that a stomach-churning snap echoed in the surrounding trees. The big man fell to the ground. He landed with his back resting on his head. He was dead.

Whoever did this to him had disappeared. Thora stared in horror. She knew who did this even though she never clearly saw the person do it. Her instincts were speaking very loudly to her. They were telling her to get out of there as fast as possible before someone saw her at the scene of the crime.

She raced back to the car. Her companion was sitting in the passenger seat as if he or she had never left it. Thora knew better but for now it did not matter. She had to get moving. The car was stubborn in starting. It took several attempts before the engine kicked in but finally it sputtered into commission. She pushed the gas pedal to the floor and raced off the shoulder of the road and onto the road.

A tap on her shoulder made her turn around to look at her passenger. He looked like her great grandfather once again in the darkness. With his finger making a twirling loop, he passed on the message that Thora was going the wrong way. Northmill and Pioneer Lake were the other direction. The girl nodded and slowed her car down enough to negotiate a U-turn. A minute later she was driving by the scene of the horrible incident. Her headlights lit up the big man with the big beard and the big temper lying unnatural on the pavement. What incredible strength the ghost must have had to do such a thing to such an immense man! She did not know if the spirit beside her was her great grandfather or her grandmother but she had to respect the spirit's power.

She felt another nudge on her shoulder as she drove by the man. The ghost was holding some paper currency in his hands. It must have come from the man's wallet. He moved fast, this ghost. She never noticed the theft.

Her gut reaction was not to accept the money but how else was she going to pay her fare on the Madoqua Empress? They had a strict rule regarding their fees. If you do not pay for your ticket beforehand you are not going to get a ride. And her new outfit from Osprey Landing would not be free either. It would be pressing her luck to try and abscond with it. She was a neophyte to shoplifting and her skills were not that developed as of yet. It was better to just pay for it. She took the money from the ghost without saying a word to him.

She said nothing and kept her eyes forward, concentrating on her driving. She did not even want to venture to guess who was beside her. Maybe in the end it did not matter for whoever it was there was one thing for certain and that was that forces were in play that sought to ensure her arrival upon Pioneer Lake, whether it was from the benign caring of a paternal great grandfather or out of the secretive purpose of a mysterious grandmother.

The road itself now was beginning to act like it too wanted to make sure that the girl got to her destination. It no longer presented challenges and obstacles to her. There was hardly a bend on it any longer. It held long straight-aways that offered her headlights plenty of opportunity to illuminate what was coming. She passed several cars as she was narrowing the gap between herself and Northmill. Each time that a car's headlights suddenly appeared in the distance, Thora steeled her neck and her eyes to make sure that she did not look at her silent companion. She did not want to see a demon riding nonchalantly along with her.

As she drove, she wondered how the Nells were doing. Had they figured out that she was no longer with them and that they were escorting somebody or something else? One hypothesis that occurred to her was that Jakob and Truus were in the company of her cousin, Percival Thurston. If this ghost that she was riding with was her grandmother then it could possibly be that the other Thora was her diminutive cousin in her guise. The grandmother and cousin could have devised this scheme to get her to the lake while at the same time eliminating the opposition from preventing this. The idea made sense to Thora, if this was her grandmother that was beside her and not her great grandfather. She wondered how Percy was going to get away from the Nells ghosts. Jakob and Truus had proven that they were doggerel in sticking to their commitments. She missed the pair. She missed Bewdley Beacon. She missed Margaret Whattam. She even missed her parents. They all seemed to be a part of a past life and that they would no longer figure in her future. Her future was on the lake. She could not believe that she was such a short distance away from it and her new frontiers. She almost felt elation at the idea.

About twenty minutes later she passed a road sign that announced that Northmill was three miles away. She would be there before she knew it. The night was still in full bloom. Dawn was a long way off yet. She would be coming into town in darkness. She would drive its deserted streets unnoticed and then when she got onto its other side she would be less than half an hour away from the shores of Pioneer Lake at Osprey Landing. She was beginning to feel giddy. She was actually going to make it. Her response to this glorious feeling was to depress the gas pedal a little further.

And then when she saw the first farms at the outskirts of Northmill coming into view something else was coming into view behind her. Even in the darkness of night, its black silhouette resonated with overwhelming malignity. It was following the road at above tree level. Its shape was undeniable. It was in the form of a very long canoe. At its center rose a man-shaped thing that harkened to the days before the Europeans came to North America.

It was the Indian spirit.

Chapter 54

The Road to the Landing

The great Indian spirit smoothly slid his vessel through the night air. He moved swiftly and assuredly. His stroke was confident and powerful. He was the hunter and he was upon his game.

Thora was terrified. Her car would not give her the speed that she needed to get away from the menacing apparition. The canoe was gaining on her with every passing second. She did not know what this being wanted from her. He had once saved her from crashing into the rocks below a steep cliff when she and Margaret first started this adventure. But she was not entirely sure if that had truly happened. It may have been a fantasy concocted in her mind when Mrs. Whattam's car spun out of control trying to avoid colliding with a deer. The Nells felt that this giant tribal spirit was some fierce avenger whose sole purpose was to eradicate the white man from the face of the continent. They believed him evil.

And yet there was another interpretation of this entity's mission and that was somehow connected to Pioneer Lake. He was the lake's champion and he sought to ensure that its sacred status was not violated. At the moment Thora could not remember where this interpretation came from. All that she wanted to do was to get away from it.

She looked to her companion, the ghost. Unlike previously when the big man with the big beard had opened attack on the vehicle and the ghost acted nonchalant and aloof, this time around there was genuine concern imprinted on his brow. The Indian spirit frightened the ghost, be that ghost Thora's great grandfather or her grandmother. Maybe it was the ghost that the Indian spirit was looking for and it had nothing at all to do with Thora? Jakob Nells had guessed that this was what was happening.

Yet Thora did not want to put that speculation to the test. She had to do everything that she could to try and avoid being apprehended. Her car was now on the main drag of the town of Northmill. All around her were sleeping houses, their occupants unaware that their nighttime sky was slowing being eclipsed by a canoe that was a city block long and was being manned by a spirit the size of an old oak tree.

She drove with abandon. She heeded not any traffic signs in the community. She flew through stop signs without slowing down and taking the precaution of looking for other traffic. Luckily there was none. She had some sense of where she was going even though she rarely had been to Northmill in the past. If she stuck to the main road it would eventually lead her straight to Osprey Landing.

The great Indian spirit had settled for a speed that matched Thora. He was not gaining on her. He was not dropping back. He kept at the same distance behind her. He was driving her. He was corralling her. He was allowing his prey to wear herself out and once she reached the point of exhaustion where she could no longer find any strength left in her limbs then would be the time that he would pounce upon her and make his kill.

Her great grandfather looked helplessly behind him at the spirit. His mouth was held wide open as if he were horror-stricken. Thora sensed that he was trying to figure out some plan but nothing was coming to him due to his paralyzing fear. She felt sorry for him and wished that she could do something to save him like he had saved her so many times in the past.

The car raced out of the town of Northmill and was now upon the final stretch of Thora's journey to Pioneer Lake. Osprey Landing was less than ten miles away from Northmill. She did not know if she had ten miles left in her. The great Indian spirit was not gaining on her. He was biding his time, satisfied in only keeping pace with her. When was he going to make his strike? When she reached Pioneer Lake's shoreline at Osprey Landing? Or when she set foot upon Black Island? She did not know.

It suddenly occurred to her that she did not have to go to the lake and fulfill the great Indian spirit's plan. She could turn from this road and abort the fruition of the spirit's designs. She kept her eyes open for roads that intersected with the one that she was upon. Thus far none had come into sight. She was well aware that there were other lakes in the vicinity and that these bodies of water would be in the way of any road construction. Yet she prayed for one. It felt like it was her only hope.

And then in the distance she saw what looked like an intersection, a crossroads. Her prayer had been answered and she was determined that she would take the other road. She did not want to signal her intent to the great Indian spirit. She kept to her breakneck speed almost right up until she was upon the crossroad. Then she spun her wheel hard right. Her tires squealed like tortured pigs as her car spun onto the new road. The vehicle was desperately seeking its balance point as it fought the physical forces of gravity and inertia to keep all four tires on the road. Thora's shoulder slammed against the door so hard that it popped the steel structure open and she just about fell out of the car. Yet she clung to the steering wheel and by the strength in her arms she avoided spilling out onto the hard, abrasive gravel. It was a grueling few seconds with an outcome that was not preordained. Anything could have happened. But the girl persevered through it and eventually managed to have her car flying down the new road. The tall pine that lined this route obscured the southern skies and she did not know if the Indian had seen her. She reached out to the open door, took hold of its handle and pulled it shut.

Her companion was still silent and was still staring out of the back window looking for their assailant. But then, unexpectedly, the ghost lunged around and grabbed the steering wheel and tugged at it so hard that the car was beginning to turn.

"What are you doing!" Thora cried out in dismay, fighting for control of the wheel. Her foot jammed onto the brake to stop the car from crashing into the trees. The ghost was still clenching at the steering wheel, trying to turn the car around. It was like the ghost did not want Thora to take this road. It was like the ghost wanted her to return to the main drag to Osprey Landing. She could not understand the motives of her companion.

But then her eyes caught something through the windshield. There, not more than twenty feet away, was the bow of the great Indian spirit's canoe. It hovered only feet above the road. There was no way that a car could get past it. The great Indian spirit, himself, sat in his seat. He had an arrow the size of a sapling fletched and pointed at the car.

Thora stared in terror, waiting for the arrow to be released. There would be no more running. Everything would end in the next few moments. Her short life raced through her head. It was a life of nothing but regrets and hopelessness. Maybe it was a good thing that it would be all over shortly. She just wished that she would not become one of the Meadowford walking dead.

But the arrow remained vibrating in the Indian's tense bow. He was not going to let it go, she slowly realized. He was telling her to turn around and fall back into plan. Her companion was still feebly tugging at the steering wheel. His mouth agog as his bulging eyes peered at the great savage spirit.

Thora took control of the wheel from him. While never allowing her eyes to leave the hunter, she turned the car around and started driving slowly back towards the Osprey Landing road. The giant canoe trailed her, moving silently above the road as if it were a wilderness river. He was being a drover and he was shepherding his flock to his protected pasture, or slaughterhouse.

When she reached the Osprey Landing road, she momentarily thought about turning the other way towards Northmill. But before she could play out this plan, her great grandfather's hand fell upon the steering wheel and stopped it from making the right hand maneuver. Was he a mind reader as well? She never fought him. She complied with his wishes and brought the car onto the road and started driving towards Osprey Landing.

Behind her, she saw the canoe sally the turn and start coming up the road behind her. The canoe climbed to a higher altitude and was once again skimming the air at treetop level. Perhaps this was a concession to the likelihood of higher volumes of traffic on this route as compared to the gravel road that they had just left.

She did not bother to drive fast. There was no point in speeding and trying to elude the canoe. She crawled forward at only twenty miles an hour. She was delaying her arrival on the shore of her once beloved lake. She found now that she was dreading to see Pioneer Lake's moonlit waters. The twinkling waves could only be a bad omen for her now. She felt like a condemned prisoner walking the final yards to the gallows. She could not see anyway out of it. She was destined to die and destined to die horribly. If ever there was a demon from Hell that walked the Earth it was this great Indian spirit. His hard face was chiseled with grim determination. There was not a drop of compassion in the deadly dark pools of his unwavering eyes. He would not have pity on her if she cried desperately to him to reconsider. He would kill her coldly. He would think nothing more of her death than he would of snapping the neck of a squirming squirrel skewered at the end of his growing son's arrow. She was nothing to him.

She was beginning to realize that she was nothing to anybody. Her parents had given up on her. They did not give any evidence that they were staging an all-out manhunt for her. She was as forgotten as her sister. She wondered where Rebecca was. She wondered if she too were not tormented by these visitors from the afterlife the way that she was. Thora doubted it. Rebecca never had ghosts while she had been plagued by them in one form or another all of her life. Despite this Thora missed her sister immensely. Life had become unraveled and fell apart the day that Rebecca declared that she would no longer live under the roof of Langley and Cora Meadowford. Thora had a gut instinct feeling that Becky was faring well and did not have anything tumultuous handicapping her likelihood of survival the way that she had.

An oncoming car suddenly appeared coming from the direction of Osprey Landing. Its twin headlights tore away at the veneer of her great grandfather's face and revealed the haggard expression of her grandmother in its place. The old woman must have realized that her disguise had been eroded. She tried to cover her face with her long, thin spindly fingers. But Thora was seeing through it.

"You're my grandmother, aren't you?" she dared to ask. She was guessing that the ghost had been silent all of this time solely because her feminine voice would give her away.

Still, the ghost did not reply or say anything. She covered her eyes with her hands as if that would be sufficient for Thora not to see who she was.

"You are my grandmother!" Thora asserted, as the oncoming lights grew sharper in definition. "And that was Percy with you back there in the cornfield. He's disguised himself as me in order to fool the Nells. I'm right, aren't I?" The girl's eyes were in the rearview mirror. She noted that where the headlights touched upon the hull of the canoe there was nothing being reflected back. The great Indian spirit had rendered himself invisible to the approaching car.

Her grandmother did not answer. She sat there with her hands over her face and did not move a muscle.

"You are going to tell me that I am right or I am going to steer right into that car!" Thora threatened. "It's probably the right thing for me to do!" She realized that these were not merely words that were coming out of her mouth. She meant it. She would steer into the other car and hopefully die in the aftermath.

The old woman recognized the seriousness in her granddaughter's ultimatum. Her hand came from her face and they locked onto the steering wheel and held it so tightly that Thora could not turn it.

Thora put all her strength in the tug of war against her grandmother. She yanked on the steering wheel with all of her might. And for a moment she had attained a small victory. Her car had pulled out into the oncoming lane. But a moment later, she was once again in her lane. Her grandmother had fought back and had control of the wheel.

At that moment there were new lights added to the oncoming car's ensemble of beams. These new lights were red and blue and they spun around in a repeating series. The wail of a siren accompanied the new lights. The approaching automobile was a police car. The cop or cops inside must have interpreted Thora's wavering driving pattern as evidence that someone was drinking behind the wheel.

Never in her life had Thora been more elated to see the police than at this moment. They would save her from the great Indian spirit and from her grandmother. At once, she put her foot on the brake and brought the car to a halt much to the consternation of the ghost beside her. Her grandmother's hands were grabbing at Thora's leg, trying to lift it from the brake pedal. The muscles in Thora's thighs pushed down all the harder to make sure that the old woman would not get her way.

The police car was now getting closer. To the girl's surprise, it had not slowed down an iota to pull up to the stopped vehicle. If anything, it had increased its speed. It was not interested in Thora's car. It raced past in a symphony of flashing lights and a cacophony of screaming sirens. Thora's heart sank as she tried to decipher what had just happened. Why didn't the cops stop? And then a possible answer popped into her mind. This answer had something to do with her. The grotesquely disfigured body of the big man with the big beard must have been discovered and these cops were going there to investigate.

Once the lights of the police car had vanished, the imposing form of the giant floating canoe reappeared. It had stopped not more than fifteen feet behind her. The great Indian spirit's head was sticking out over its side, looking down at the girl. He made a motion with his neck that signaled that Thora had better start driving once more.

With tears streaming down her face and a sickened stomach, Thora lifted her leg from the brake and the car began up the road once more.

Chapter 55

Klaxons of Threat

They drove through a dense coniferous forest. Huge boughs hung over the pavement from both sides of the road and leaving just a narrow gap where the pavement timidly slipped. It was like driving through the gnarly and twisted throat of a demon. The only saving grace about this stretch of the route was that the trees obscured the giant canoe from her. But she knew that it was still there, still slowly marshalling her to her appointment with the lake.

What did he want of her there? She had repeatedly asked herself this question and never could come up with a satisfying answer. Did he want her to be taken by the lake just like the lake had taken her grandmother and two cousins? If this was his motive then why did her grandmother cower in his presence? The two spirits were not allies, Thora realized. There was some form of enmity at work here yet she could not understand why. Didn't her grandmother also want her to drown in the engulfing waters of Pioneer Lake? If they had the same purpose then why were they not friends?

Asking her grandmother would be pointless. The old woman would not say anything. Thora was starting to believe that there might not be much left to the character of her father's mother. She was just a shell of what she once was. Her grandfather Sambo had idealized the woman and almost worshiped the ground that she stepped upon. Even after she died, he at times would act like she was still there. He would talk to her and consult with her. The hideous thing beside Thora in the car just did not seem to be the kind to engage in friendly banter or to be able to offer well thought out advice. The thing beside her seemed to be one-dimensional, seemed to be driven by just a single purpose, and could not think beyond that framework. She was like a mosquito thirsting for blood, being so consumed by her thirst that she was blind to the danger that getting that blood entailed.

The ghost was sitting in the passenger seat, once again in the guise of Samuel Angus Meadowford the First; once again with eyes stretched wide open scanning the skies in mortal terror for the Indian. What a pathetic creature the afterlife had made this spirit! If this was what was in store for her shortly after her arrival to the lake, Thora did not want any part of it. The Meadowford ghosts were such shallow beings when compared to the depth of character that the Nells ghosts had attained. Jakob and Truus were brimming with personality. They possessed traits good and bad. They were not uni-dimensional like her grandmother. Even her great grandfather, her real one, did not have the articulation and depth of Jakob and Truus. Why would this be so? Thora found herself pondering the question despite her imminent position. Perhaps it was a way of avoiding her eventual fate?

Maybe being a ghost was like being born into life. You are not fully developed as a spirit at the moment of death. You do not have all your full blown ghostly talents when your spirit leaves your body. It takes time to mature. Her grandmother was only a ghost eleven or twelve years. She had not attained all of the skills that she would eventually receive as her spirit continues to walk the Earth. Her great grandfather was dead maybe a quarter of a century or so. He was more developed than Thora's grandmother but he was not as skilled as Jakob or Truus. They had been dead over a hundred years and they were able to do so many things more than either Sam Meadowford or June Ritchey. June Ritchey could not even open a car door as of yet.

These speculations kept Thora's mind away from her peril but she could no longer make hypotheses regarding the maturation cycle of human spirits when she saw a glistening ahead of her. It sparkled with such iridescence that it at once stole all of her thoughts. She knew what it was. She was hoping that she would not have seen it. She was hoping that she would never see it. But she knew that it was coming. This road had only one terminus and this terminus was the point where a shimmering would occur under the moonlight. It was the water of Pioneer Lake as seen from the vantage of the approaching road into Osprey Landing. It was less than a mile away. She had arrived.

How she had longed to be here in her beloved piece of the world again! Had the events of the last day unfolded differently, she knew that she would be in pure bliss if not sheer ecstasy upon seeing those waves twinkle under the stars and the moon. She would have felt that she was at the doorway of her sanctuary that would protect her from all of the poisons that life had hurled at her this disastrous summer. She would have been beyond being happy. She would have felt like she was entering Heaven itself.

But the events had unfolded the way that they unfolded this last day. She had learned that things are not the way that they seem. Pioneer Lake was an enchantress and had lured her to it. Pioneer Lake was a female spider enticing her mate into her web with dances that he could not resist. Bewitched, he comes to the web to have a few moments of unbridled passion before it all comes to a quick end in the mandibles of the female. Bewitched, the Meadowford girl had come to the lake to savor these few moments of sweetness and reliving moments of past idyllic reverie. It was all going to come to an end very shortly from either the ghoul that sat beside her or the giant spirit from a long ago age.

This reality came swashbuckling into her few moments of sweetness with a rapier that slashed violently at all of the wisps of tender emotion that that elusive and tentative sweetness possessed. It came in with its alarming klaxons of threat and Thora became intensely frightened. She was marching to her death. The ghost beside her no longer bothered to veil herself in the attributes of Samuel Angus Meadowford the First. She had become a wicked degenerated mockery of what once was the pretty face of Thora's grandfather's bride. Still, she said nothing. Still, she kept her horrified gaze back behind her to where their shepherd slipped through the sky.

He came out over the treetops. The northern lights spread out from the shape of his canoe like some godly aura proclaiming his mastery and his power. Thora immediately shrank in his audacious presence. How was she going to overcome such a lord of darkness? He was magnificent in his spectral presence. He was the savage prince coming to claim what was his.

She felt hopeless and had an urge to drive her car straight into the lake at the end of the long pier that jutted out from Osprey Landing. But her car under water would not protect her from this pagan god. Going into the lake was precisely what he wanted her to do. It was precisely what her grandmother wanted her to do as well. She could not do it. She would not do it. Her defiance still existed even against such overwhelming odds. But how was she going to be able to defy such an ominous being?

The road was coming to an end in front of her. Osprey Landing was comprised of a stately lodge that overlooked the lake and several rental cottages painted in gay pastel colors. The lodge hosted hundreds of guests during the summer months. There were dozens of cars parked outside of the three-story tall inn made of irregularly shaped flagstone. There were only a few lights on inside. These were the lanterns that lit up the halls between the rooms and the stairwells. Thora doubted that there was anybody up at this ungodly hour of the morning. Her life was at stake and she decided that she blare her horn to wake up the guests inside. But, when her hand when to punch the horn, a bony, spindly hand abruptly stopped her. Her grandmother was not going to permit it. Thora had no choice but to bring her car to a halt. There was no more land left for her. There was only the lake and the water that seemed to be saying to her that she was its.

The great Indian spirit began coming down from treetop level. His massive canoe was now only the height of a man above the pavement. His dark eyes were clearly focused on the occupants of the car. He was not reaching for his longbow. He sat in his vessel, arrogant and proud. In a low voice, he began to utter some words in a tongue that Thora could not comprehend. She could only guess that it must have been in some Indian language, perhaps Hendorun, Algonquian, or Ojibwa. If the words were meant for her, she was at a loss to comprehend them. The timbre of the utterance had the tempo of a command. She believed that he was telling her to get out of the car. His voice was like distant thunder, low and grumbling. It induced immediate fear.

Then, unexpectedly, Thora heard another voice. This one came from inside of the car. This one came from her companion, the ghost of her grandmother. She replied in a wretched, creaky and grating voice in words that sounded hissing and nonsensical to Thora. It seemed like she was speaking in the same language as the Great Spirit.

The great Indian responded to the ghost's reply. It seemed whatever her grandmother said had riled the giant. His words came out this time as a menacing approaching storm.

Her grandmother nudged her suddenly and unexpectedly. The old woman's eyes went to the door. Thora got the message that she wanted out of the car and she needed Thora's help to do so. The girl reached over the ghostly form and opened the door. The ghost of June Ritchey climbed out of the car to stand in front of the spirit that summoned her. Thora remained in the car, shutting the door quickly, as soon as her grandmother was out. She looked at the old woman standing on the pavement. She seemed so small and vulnerable when compared to the enormous spirit that sat in the canoe. Thora felt pity for her. Despite her apparent wickedness that she attained in her death, this woman was still her grandmother. The girl would not exist if it had not been for this woman and now this woman was in grave danger. But there was nothing Thora could do for the woman save to be a witness to her final demise.

There was an exchange in the Indian tongue between the two spirits. Thora could only speculate about what they were talking about. Whatever it was, it was not friendly banter. It came across more like a child being scolded by an adult. Her grandmother seemed to cower in front of the imposing and cold figure. Thora's pity for the woman grew. This was her grandmother. This was the woman that her beloved grandfather, Sambo, had married. And there she was standing in confrontation with the most terrifying of devils that the Earth could spawn. Thora could almost hear her grandfather speaking to her, behooving her to do something to intervene and to save his wife. It was her responsibility to her family to do so.

She realized that the car's engine was still running. Without a second thought, she lifted her foot from the brake and allowed the car to slowly start rolling forward. She turned the wheel so that the vehicle would not drive into the nearby lake. Once that maneuver had been completed, she looked back to the two spirits. Neither seemed to have been aware that she was in motion. The great Indian spirit was still raging upon Thora's grandmother, his imposing form hanging over her like a menacing ogre. Her grandmother seemed to be crying out for mercy. Her hands were clasped together as if in prayer and she appeared to be begging the Indian not to punish her.

It suddenly dawned on Thora that if she wanted to she could make good an escape from this ungodly pair. All that she had to do was follow the lane that was ahead of her that led to the smaller cottages. She knew this land quite well and was aware that the lane intersected with another lane further down that would take her to a country road from which she could go anywhere. It seemed to her that the great Indian spirit was more interested in her grandmother than her. Maybe he was protecting her and he was chiding her grandmother for daring to try and possess her. This was her opportunity to escape and everything inside of the girl was telling her to do so. Just keep going forward and never mind what is happening in behind.

Yet, when her eyes saw the confrontation between the Indian spirit and her grandmother grow more intense, where it actually appeared that the Indian was striking some horrific blows on the pathetic, withered form of June Ritchey, Thora realized that she could not leave the woman in such a desperate situation. Her grandfather's soul would curse her forever if she were to abandon his wife.

Thora's foot pushed down on the gas pedal and she aimed her car directly at the lumbering legs of the savage giant. He and her grandmother looked up at the girl in dismay. The car plowed into the enormous spirit and drove right through him. He was made up of the ether and there was nothing for the car to collide with. A moment later she was on the other side of the great Indian spirit and she was heading at breakneck speed towards the parked cars beside the Osprey Landing lodge. She spun the wheel and hit the brakes. When she finally came to a stop, she had narrowly avoided running into the cars. She had come out of it unscathed except for something that was burning in her mind. In that brief instant that she was actually inside of the great Indian spirit, her eyes were opened to a world that was at once entirely alien to her and yet it was at the same time one that she knew intimately. For the tiniest fragment of time she had an understanding of everything and she had the knowledge of why things were playing out the way that they were. But when that microsecond vanished, so did that knowledge and once again the girl felt oblivious to everything and did not understand what was happening. The burning in her mind was focused on one word, Rautooskee. She did not know what that was except that it was a word of power and that its utterance could have enormous implications on the world.

She did not have the time to recreate what had happened to her in that instance. The Great Indian Spirit had taken notice of her and it was apparent that he was not going to allow her to play like a loose cannon any longer. He charged at the car and tore its roof off as if it were nothing more than a cardboard box. His hand reached down through the open top and he plucked Thora from the driver seat. The girl squirmed and writhed in the painful grip of the hand that was as large as her torso. Before she knew it, she was set down on the ground right at the lake's edge. The Great Spirit said something to her in his language. She did not know what the words meant but she understood their gist. She was to stay still.

In the meantime, while the great Indian Spirit attended to Thora, the ghost of the girl's grandmother took the opportunity to make a dash of her own. The girl watched the old woman race to the lake and dive into the water. She dove with the agility and grace of a creature born to the lake. She was like a humanized form of the great musky Zardo that swam the reefs that surrounded Black Island.

The Great Indian Spirit groaned in frustration as he watched the milky form of June Ritchey disappear into the murky depths. She was gone and this obviously angered the ancient spirit. He was not through with her yet.

Thora was now left alone with this behemoth being. She did not understand him or what his purpose was. She knew that he had been vitally interested in her all along, ever since the day that her grandfather was buried. She was not sure if he was hostile towards her or if he was an ally. He was cold and distant and unfathomable. His eyes, dark and large, would not betray any secrets that he possessed. He stared at her through these heartless orbs as if he were assessing her worth of character and determining that there was not much there. He could kill her in an instant, she realized, and she felt that all things being equal that that would have been his choice. But all things were not equal. There was something about her that made him place his natural instincts aside and permitted her to live—for the time being. He had some role for her to play out. She had not played it out thus far. Once she did, he would be through with her and he might just exterminate her then.

The girl felt helpless in the formidable gaze. Her body tingled with as much squirminess as if his huge hands were still wrapped around her. She was intensely uncomfortable, more uncomfortable than afraid. She could not take it any longer. She had to do something.

"What do you want of me!" she cried out frantically. "Why are you following me? Why can't you just leave me alone?"

DAUGHTER OF THUNDER

The Indian's face did not move an iota. Not one muscle in his face had changed. His pupils remained fixed. They did not expand or contract. He just hulked over her, without a word being uttered, English or savage, from his mouth. Whatever he was planning to do remained a mystery to Thora. He had made sure that he brought her here. He did not allow her to change her course. But now that she was here upon the shores of Pioneer Lake, he would give her no clue.

It was irking the girl. She thought of just simply walking away and leaving him where he stood. She thought of screaming her lungs out to draw the attention of the guests inside of the lodge. Then maybe someone will come running out and set things into motion again. This standoff was just too much for her to bear. "What do you want!" her voice shrieked once more.

She did not expect an answer. She assumed that he would remain silent and stare at her dumbly. But the Great Indian Spirit did speak and he spoke in English. His words were almost silent. They were almost telepathic rather than sonic. "You must free the spirit of the one that shares your blood," he said.

It was a sentence that made absolutely no sense to the girl. Free the spirit of the one that shares her blood. She did not know whom he was referring to. "My great grandfather?" she guessed out loud.

But before the Great Indian Spirit could either confirm or refute her guess, something moved behind the Great Indian Spirit. It was another spirit. He came out of the nearby thicket of aspens. It was Samuel Angus Meadowford the First.

Chapter 56

Life Inside a Novel

Thora at once knew that this was the true spirit of her great grandfather and not her grandmother or anybody else in Samuel Angus Meadowford the First's guise. There was something in the way that his eyes twinkled and the manner in which he held his brow and chin that could not be copied by any imposter. This was her great grandfather and he had come as her guardian angel once again.

He walked boldly and with certainty in his long strides. He marched up to the unaware Great Indian Spirit and kicked him in the ankle. "Leave her alone!" he demanded in a firm and resolved voice.

The Great Indian turned around. He was surprised to see the little man before him. Jakob Nells had speculated that this Great Spirit's mission was to eradicate the soul of the man that took possession of his tribe's sacred lands. If this was his purpose then he now had the opportunity to see it through to fruition. He opened up his arms and swiftly snapped them shut. In his clutches he held Sam Meadowford. He lifted the man into the air so that their two faces looked eye to eye.

Sam Meadowford stared defiantly back at his monstrous adversary. "You don't scare me," he hissed. To Thora his body began to transform into the shape of a vicious snarling black bear. His arms were free and at once he thrashed outward at the Indian with his huge claws. They tore into the flesh of the Indian's nose.

Thora was in shock to see her great grandfather conduct such magic. His ghostly powers had grown since the last she saw him. She doubted that he had this ability to transform himself back in Grappling Haven.

Yet despite his magic, he was nothing more than a puppy in the hands of the Indian. The scratch that the Great Spirit had sustained served nothing other than to stir his anger. He began rattling the bear in his hands. He rattled so hard that the guise of the bear quickly faltered and the ghost was returned back to his true form. The violent shaking had the effect of almost knocking Sam from his senses. He was struggling to keep conscious. The Great Spirit would soon incapacitate his foe and dispatch his soul to wherever it would go once it was freed from its Earthly ties.

Without thinking Thora charged at the Great Indian Spirit. She had to save her guardian angel. She knew that there was absolutely nothing that she could do to harm this massive opponent but it did not matter to her. She acted out of pure instinct. She acted out of pure savagery. She grabbed at the spirit but there was nothing for her to take hold of. Her hands glided through him as if he were not there. This infuriated the girl and made her try all the more. She was proving to be a nuisance to the Indian. He looked down at her from the corner of his eye and with one peremptory motion in his leg, he flung her twenty yards away to land roughly upon the gravel of the parking lot. Her legs stung from the abrasive fall but she was still raring to fight. She quickly sprung up and began racing towards the Indian when she saw two figures come out of nowhere. These figures hurled themselves onto the Great Spirit and began fighting with a savageness that this land had not witnessed in over a century.

These figures were the ghosts of Jakob and Truus Nells. Somehow they had managed to see through Percival Thurston's guise and track her down here to Osprey Landing. They had vowed that they would protect her despite the many times that she had betrayed them. To see them scratching, kicking and biting at the giant stirred Thora's soul. She joined in on the attack.

Her kicks and punches did not amount to much. They made no connection with the Indian's ethereal substance. Yet the mere act of fighting and doing something felt good to Thora. Above her the three spirits were mauling the Great Indian Spirit as if they were a pride of lions upon an elephant. Alone, none of them would have had a chance against the Great

Spirit, but when acting in tandem, they were wearing their adversary down. Jakob had wrapped himself around the Indian's waist and was biting at the spirit's abdomen and jabbing his kidneys with swift knuckles. Above him, Sam, who was still in the Indian's hands, was booting him in the ribs and pounding him in the nose with his balled up fists. And sitting on the Indian's shoulders with squeezing legs wrapped around his neck was Truus Nells. Her hands were gouging into the Great Spirit's eyes. It was a relentless attack and the Great Spirit was having trouble keeping any one of the three ghosts at bay. Whenever his focus fell upon one of them, the other two would increase their efforts to draw his attention away.

Thora saw the Great Spirit's knees begin to buckle as he tired and weakened. He was not going to overcome his enemies. Yet even though he was being beaten, he was still very powerful and dangerous. He crunched his arms in and then let them explode out. The girl's great grandfather was sent flying across the parking lot and landed in the branches of the aspens. But even as Sam was hurling upward, Jakob Nells had scampered up to a new height on the spirit and began gnawing at the spirit's jugular vein. The Indian suddenly started to stagger on his feet as Jakob was inflicting terrible damage upon his neck. He reached upward to try and pull the man away. His hands caught hold of Truus' legs. He grabbed them and whipped her to the ground. As Truus crashed onto the gravel, the Great Indian Spirit stomped on her repeatedly. Her screams sent chills through Thora. The girl tried desperately to pull the old woman away but she was unable to do so. And then the Indian's foot came down one more time. This time it landed squarely on Truus' head. When the foot lifted up there were no more wails of agony. Truus was silent. Truus was gone.

In the meantime Samuel Angus Meadowford the First had returned to the fray. He held in his hand a pointed branch from the aspen tree. He leapt onto the back of the Indian and crawled his way upward until the Indian's head was in reach. Sam took the pointed branch and pierced it into the throat of the Great Spirit. As he did so, he raved madly about how the time of the tribes have come to an end and that there was no room in the Twentieth Century for the Indian.

The Great Indian Spirit was dying. His physical manifestation was growing weak and wispy. Thora was able to see through his form. She could see some lights in the lodge come on through the spirit's torn chest. People were finally awakening to all of the commotion that was taking place outside of their rooms. The Indian was still fighting and had not quite given up. He managed to tear the pointed branch from his throat. He chucked it. It sailed across the parking lot and smashed through the windshield of one of the vehicles.

And then when he was nothing more than a vague veil he reached upward and took hold of the ranting Sam Meadowford. He drew Sam's head towards his mouth and placed it inside. Her great grandfather writhed trying to break free. Just before the Great Spirit disappeared, Thora saw his teeth clamp shut onto Sam's neck. And then both were gone to an unknown place where the living can never go.

Suddenly, Thora felt her hand grabbed. It was Jakob Nells. He was hauling her towards the trees. As she was being dragged, she thought she heard a voice coming from nowhere and everywhere say to her, "Remember what I have told you. Free the spirit of your blood."

Once inside the cover of the aspen trees, Jakob paused for a moment. He was looking back at the parking lot. Several people had come out onto it from the doors of the lodge. They were gawking at the branch pierced through the windshield of one of the cars.

"That must have been a tornado!" one of them said. "Look at what it has done to that car! Hey, isn't that Colefield's car?"

Thora did not hear the response to the comment. Jakob was on the move again. "We can't stay here. You will be found," he said. They traveled several hundred yards until they were at the bottom of a thickly wooded ravine. There were layered sedimentary outcrops everywhere that made their fast pace awkward if not dangerous. Some of them had dark gaps between the shale. They were ideal grottos for raccoons and porcupines. Her companion headed straight for the largest one of these and told her to climb inside.

Complying, Thora felt the air grow suddenly chilled and take on a musty odor. The cave that she was climbing into was surprisingly large. There was room enough for several adults to stand and congregate inside. From the look of the rocky floor, this must have happened in the past. There were cigarette butts everywhere as well as broken beer bottles and potato chip wrappings. People must have come here to carry out clandestine celebrations. Thora knew that the Osprey Landing lodge itself had strict rules regarding alcohol. It observed the laws of prohibition to the tee. Thora was able to see the debris due to several cracks in the ceiling that allowed the dawning light from above to come in.

As Jakob entered the subterranean grotto he said, "This will work for now. Nobody will be coming here to look for us."

Thora doubted that anybody would be looking for them at all for the moment. The people from the lodge believed that it was a tornado that had caused all of that ruckus outside of their rooms. They did not put a human face on the damage. Yet when she looked upon the human face of Jakob Nells, she saw one in great anguish and denial. He had just lost his wife in that battle with the Great Spirit. He had just lost his wife in a battle that was not his or hers in the first place. Truus Nells had died defending the girl from Grappling Haven. And now Jakob who had her company for at least 125 years was alone.

"Oh Jakob, I am so sorry!" she said to him. The words could not even begin to uncover the depth of remorse that Thora felt. She had wronged this man and had him pay an unbearable price. If she had listened to them in the first place they would not have been here beside Pioneer Lake and fighting such a powerful adversary.

"It's not your fault, child," Jakob sighed. "My wife and I solemnly vowed to you that we would protect you. We knew what that promise entailed. We knew that that demon was on your tail and that eventually we would have to fight him and possibly die as a consequence. If that fight did not take place here it would have taken place elsewhere with far worse results. Both Truus and I could have died and the demon lived on. The result that we achieved was a victory over that beast and the price that we paid was only one of our lives. Believe me, my wife would have been pleased with what happened and maybe wherever she is she is feeling content in knowing that we have fulfilled our vow to you."

This was not the response that Thora expected from the ghost. She had believed that he would have been vexatious and condemning in his words to her. It almost seemed that he was celebrating his wife's past existence rather than mourning her loss.

Jakob continued, "Had it not been for you and your great grandfather things may have been different. You fought bravely, child!" he smiled at her. "I saw you fighting with your heart and soul to try and protect us. You could have run and I would not have blamed you for running. You could do nothing to harm that demon while he could have smitten you with just a glance. Yet you charged at that demon and did everything that you could to help bring him down. Truus saw that too and I know that she died knowing that she had made a vow to a person that possessed the moral integrity worth saving."

Thora lowered her eyes to the cave's floor. Her feet were only inches away from some broken glass. She could feel something inside of her tell her to run her toe along the sharp edges of the shards. She had to fight that urge. She was being applauded for something that she really did not feel that she was worthy. When she attacked the Great Spirit, she did so out of instinct. It did not seem like she did it out of any moral decision to act courageous. She just did so because it was the natural thing to do. To accept Jakob's humbling words would be to accept a lie. She did not want to argue the point with him.

"How did you find me?" she asked. "The last that I saw you was in the cornfield all those many miles away."

"I need to sit down. I feel rather tired," Jakob answered. He looked around for a place in the cave that was not littered with debris. Finding one against one of the grotto's wet and icy walls, he seated himself. As he did so, Thora noticed that the flesh of his thighs had been horribly rented.

"You're hurt!" she cried, pointing at the wound.

"I'll live. I have survived worse injuries than this," the ghost grimaced as he struggled to find a comfortable posture. "That demon chomped on my leg when I was not looking."

The sentence served to remind Thora of the last that she saw of her great grandfather. His head was inside of the Great Spirit's mouth. Seeing the damage that those teeth could inflict, the girl shuddered thinking what had become of Samuel Angus Meadowford the First.

"When we got separated from you in that cornfield, my wife and I chose to take a systematic approach to finding you. We went to the road and marked the aisle that we stepped out of with a pile of rocks. We then split up, she going to the left and I going to the right. Our plan was to look down each row of corn one by one to see if we could spot you. When one of us spotted you the other would call out. I had not gone that many rows when I saw some evidence that might have been made by you."

Thora recalled the swath of trampled corn made by the canoe of the

Great Spirit and how Jakob had come to investigate it. He had been only feet away from her yet he was not aware of her presence.

"Then Truus called out telling me that she found you. Before I answered her beckoning, I took one look at the trampled corn and I felt a chill run through me. I knew that something nefarious was out there with us and I knew that we had to get out of there as fast as possible." Jakob began rubbing his wound while he spoke. It must have been painful judging by the way that his face would contort when he touched the bite the wrong way. Something was oozing out of that wound. It was clear and sparkling. It might have been the ectoplasm that served as the lifeblood for the ghost.

"Anyway, when I caught up with my wife, she was standing along the road's edge with whom I assumed was you although there was something about you that just did not feel quite right. When you saw me you almost looked scared as if I were looking right through you. I guessed that was because you had ignored our cautions to you not to wander while we slept.

"You then proposed to us that we go back to the plane crash site because you forgot something important back there. You said that you forgotten your doll."

"I don't play with dolls!" Thora interjected.

"We didn't think you did either. We never saw you carrying one in all of the miles that we traveled together. But you were insistent and you was at the point of tears demanding that we go back," Jakob responded, still running his hand over the wound. If anything, it was starting to look worse as if some rapid infection had taken it.

"I rationalized that it wouldn't hurt going back to the plane. It was going in the opposite direction of the lake and you know how I felt about you coming to this lake." The ghost's eyes narrowed with the comment. "It seems we are here anyway," he sighed. "I need to lie on my back. My head is starting to swim." Jakob lowered his torso until he was lying flat upon the rock. There was some broken glass there but it did not seem to disturb the old man.

"So you went back to the plane with Percy?" Thora tried to get the ghost back on track with his story.

"Who is Percy?" Jakob groaned. His face was betraying the excruciating pain that he must have been experiencing.

"He's my dead cousin, the one that impersonated me," the girl answered.

She wished that she could do something for Jakob but she did not have a clue regarding first aid for ghosts.

"We followed the imposter for a while," Jakob replied through tightly clamped eyes and gritted teeth. "She was babbling away like a child in swaddling clothes and not like somebody who has just attained her adolescence. Truus had taken me to the side and made comment about this odd behavior. We did not know what had become of you. At this point we still had not concluded that we were walking with somebody else other than you. Your imposter was consumed with talking about the joys of swimming and how she wanted to go for a swim in the big lake near the crash. That was all that she wanted to talk about. She would not answer any of our questions about why she had decided to go wandering in the middle of the night. I got to sit up. It hurts way too much on my back. Can you give me a hand?" Jakob extended his hand towards Thora.

When her fingers came in contact with his palm, she felt that familiar tingling that she experienced every time that she touched the Nells ghosts. But this time the tingling was not quite the same. It was distinguishably weaker as if the life force in Jakob was dwindling. It suddenly occurred to her that the ghost might be dying.

Once Jakob was upright, his head began to loll on his neck. He was losing the strength to hold it up. He closed his eyes once more and his jaw was firmly clamped shut. When his facial muscles relaxed, he seemed a little more cognizant of his surroundings once more. "Where was I?" he asked the girl.

"Do you mean with your story?"

"Yes, with my story!" Jakob snapped.

Thora told him where he had left off. She was beginning to wonder if he would live long enough to tell it all.

"When we were almost in sight of the plane crash it started to rain again and that was when we knew we were dealing with an imposter. Even though the rain came down in buckets, your clothes and hair were not getting wet. Your imposter was not very adept at keeping his illusion viable through changing weather conditions. He did not know how to allow his form to adapt to his surroundings. He is still new to the world of spirits. In fact at one point he let his guard down so much that Truus and I actually saw his true form, that of a little boy. As soon as we discovered that we had been fooled, we demanded him to tell us who he was. I guess that we were too forceful and we scared the child away. The last we saw of him he was scampering towards the lake. He still wanted his swim."

Jakob stopped for several moments to catch his breath. His eyes drifted down to his leg. He quietly closed them. When he opened them again, he said, "I do not have much more time."

Thora looked at the wound as well. To her shock it had grown enormously. It was now consuming his abdomen. She could see the ectoplasm dripping from him. "Is there anything that I can do?" she cried. She wanted desperately to save this man.

"There's nothing that you can do, my child. My days of wandering have come to an end. I think I will just finish my story and then be off." There was something akin to a smile on his face.

"You will be with your wife again," she said to him, trying to find something to cheer his spirit.

"Perhaps, you never know! And maybe I will be with your great grandfather Sam as well," he said. "He is a remarkable fellow. Truus and I got to know him well as we walked the land up to this beautiful country."

"You traveled with my great grandfather?" Thora found this astounding.

"How else do you think we found our way up here? We've never been here before. Sam spotted us just after we chased away your imposter. He was investigating the wreckage trying to see if you died in it. When he saw us and determined that we were of his kind, he came up to meet us. He was relieved to learn that you lived through the accident and that you were somewhere in the vicinity lost. He said that you were not lost. He said that he knew precisely where you were going and thus we started our journey together."

Thora had wondered how her great grandfather had appeared out of nowhere on that parking lot and how Jakob and Truus showed up only moments later. Now, she knew. It made her heart feel warm to hear that Jakob and Truus had grown fond of Samuel Angus Meadowford the First and that they got to spend some time together.

"Did you know that most of this land possesses a series of connected lakes and rivers?" Jakob said, after a particularly long period of silence where his eyes were fastened shut and there had not been any movement in his body whatsoever. "I didn't know that. Sam told us. It was by water that we traversed this country. We were on a raft fashioned by Sam out of old logs lying by a river's edge. We moved up the stream with Sam poling the way.

Truus and I felt like we were living inside of a Mark Twain novel. We were enamored with the lifestyle. Around every bend there was something captivating to behold whether it be a blue heron stalking some tiny fish or an old forgotten mill blending into the trees that surrounded it. For the first time in nearly a century we felt like we were living. Of course, all along we could not entirely dive into our idyllic pleasure. We were concerned about you and that always sat within our minds." Jakob paused for a moment and looked down at his body. "I just had to check if it was still there," he said. "I don't feel anything down there at all any more. It has gone numb."

Thora's eyes slipped to look at the man's body. The wound was eating him alive. It had now spread from his neck to his toes. There was no human form left to it. It had become nothing but a pool of ectoplasm that slowly followed the contours of the cave's rock floor and finding cracks in it where it would sink deeper inside of the Earth.

If Jakob saw this, he did not let on to Thora. "We even saw your island in the distance," he said to the girl.

"You saw our island?" the girl had not expected to hear this.

"Yes, Sam pointed it out to us as we moved across Pioneer Lake. We were on the opposite shoreline from it so it was quite far away and we did not have the time to go visit at the moment. Sam promised that we would go there after we were finished our nasty business. We were able to see the great canoe hovering in the sky. We knew that you could not be far away from that heathen that owned it."

"Wait a second! How did you end up in Pioneer Lake in the first place?" Thora cut into Jakob's story.

"Don't ask me, I am new here, remember!" the dying ghost said. "All that I can be certain about was that we came into Pioneer Lake by way of a river, a rapids and a waterfall. Sam said that we were far to the north of where he figured you to be and that we would have to cross most of the lake to get to you. Truus and I were surprised to see how big a body of water your Pioneer Lake actually was."

"It is quite big," Thora agreed. "I have been going there all of my life and I still do not know all of the lake. Maybe this makes up part of its charm and mystery to me. I can be intimate with it yet I can never fully know it." She turned her head. She thought that she heard something just outside of the cave's mouth. But there were no other sounds forthcoming.

When she turned her head back to Jakob, he was gone. All that was left of him was that pool of ectoplasm that was slowly draining itself into the cracks on the floor. Jakob Nells, the ghost, was dead. Thora felt a numbness run through her at the loss of her friend. It was too soon to cry. Crying would come later. For now all that she could think about was that no matter what else she had done to them, she did pave the way for Jakob and his wife to live a richer life than the one that they had cooped up in that farmhouse at Hawkins Corners. The time that they spent with her great grandfather must have been a period of frolic for them, a respite from being old and tired. They got to feel young again and Thora sensed that they would have paid any price at all to have such a feeling once more.

She filled in the rest of the Nells story in her mind. They crossed the rest of the lake from Black Island to Osprey Landing and once there they engaged in the battle with the Great Spirit. Sam's promise to Jakob and Truus to take them for a visit to Black Island had to go unfulfilled. Yet, Thora sensed that the Nells did not feel cheated by this. They had got to live the life inside a Mark Twain novel and that was enough for them.

"Anybody in there?"

CHAPTER 57

A Change of Clothes

"Anybody in there?" the voice repeated itself. It was a small voice, a child's voice. It emanated from outside of the entrance to the grotto. It did not seem to be a menacing voice. Thora felt no sense of threat from it. It was likely a child that belonged to one of the guests at Osprey Landing that had wandered into the ravine to explore its many caves.

Still, she decided not to answer it. What if adults accompanied this child? She did not want to betray her whereabouts to them. She went deeper into the cave and selected to hide behind an abutment in the rock face.

"I can smell you! I know that you are in there!" the little child called out. His head must have been looking through the entrance. There was some echo to his voice bouncing against the walls. "You can't hide from me. I'm good at hide and seek."

Without any reverberation from his footfall against the grotto's stone floor, Thora knew that the child was now inside the cave with her. She tried to push herself deeper into her cranny.

"Come out, come out, wherever you are!" the boy called out as he was roving through the rocky and musty interior. Thora decided to take a peek. All that she saw of him at first was his foot tracks on the floor's wet surface. He was walking over all that remained of Jakob Nells. The girl could not tolerate this. Nobody was going to disrespect her friend this way. She stepped out from her hiding spot.

At once her eyes fell upon her visitor. He was just a small boy, no more than four years old, she guessed. He wore a striped full-bodied swimsuit that had many stains upon it from the rough and tumble lifestyle befitting someone of his age. He was precisely as she remembered him. It was her cousin Percival Thurston, the little boy that had drowned nearly a dozen years ago.

"Percy!" she said in dismay. The boy jumped in surprise.

She had not expected to see him. She thought that he was far away, swimming the big waters of Lake Ontario. At once, she started looking around to see if his companion was nearby. He had been constantly in the company of his and her grandmother, June Ritchey. Had she slinked back from Pioneer Lake now that it was safe for her to do so? Her adversary, the Great Spirit, was gone and she need not worry any longer about the Nells or her father-in-law, Samuel Angus Meadowford the First. Thora could not see her anywhere.

"Are you Thora or are you Rebecca?" Percy asked, once he recovered from the shock of her sudden appearance.

"I'm Thora."

"You are bigger than me now. You're almost grown up!" the boy said as he walked forward towards his cousin. He reached out a hand to touch Thora's arm to see if she were real.

"I'm not that big for my age, really. I'm average in size," Thora retorted, looking into the eyes of the little ghost. There was not much to read in them. They almost possessed that same lifelessness that was present in her grandmother's eyes. Yet beneath them there seemed to be a great sadness that would not have itself concealed.

"You're still pretty big to me," Percy responded. "I have stopped growing. I will always be this size for the rest of my life. Even my brother Jack is bigger than me."

"You know your brother Jack? He was not alive when you..." She was about to say 'died' but something inside of her checked the words before they came out of her mouth. The boy might not know that he is dead and that he had drowned back in 1918.

"Yes, I know Jacky!" Percy said as if he was answering a ridiculous question. "I see him almost every day. He is stuck inside of the cottage and can't come out and swim with me."

Thora remembered the words of the demon back at Mrs. Bianco's place. The demon said that Jack's ghost was on Black Island. Percy's statement was an independent confirmation that Jack indeed still existed. Even though Percy was her cousin as well, she did not know him. He was gone from her life from the age of two. Jack, on the other hand, had been a big part of her summers growing up on Pioneer Lake. Hearing that he was still there gave the girl the spirit of hope once more. She had not given any thought to her plans in the aftermath of the demise of the Nells and her great grandfather. The Great Indian Spirit was now gone and she had nothing to fear from him any longer. The danger about going out onto the lake and going to her island seemed to be over. It could be safe to go to Black Island and be reunited with her dear cousin Jack.

"Why can't Jack come out?" she asked the little ghost.

"He can't open the doors and Grandmother and I can't do it either. I so much want to go swimming with my brother!" Percy said. The little boy was stooped over and running his fingers through the ectoplasm on the stone floor. What he drew appeared to be a pair of staring eyes. To Thora they looked like the chiding orbs of Jakob Nells telling her not to go forth with what she was thinking.

"You shouldn't put your hands into that stuff! It is icky and you will get dirty," the girl growled, smearing her hands over the eyes so that they would not look out at her any more.

Percy stood up and wiped his hands onto his swimsuit. He took the scolding in stride. "I wonder where Grandmother is?" he said to her. "She said that she would meet me here in the morning."

"The morning has only just begun," Thora responded. "But I think that Grandmother has gone on ahead without us. I saw her dive into the water about an hour ago."

"Maybe she is going to meet us at the cottage. Come on Thora, let's get going!" Percy urged.

"I don't think that the Madoqua Empress is here yet," Thora answered.

"Madoqua Empress? Why do we want to take the boat when we can swim!" the little boy shouted. He was very animated and excited.

"I can't swim all the way to Black Island!" Thora laughed. She recalled the family stories concerning Percy. They said that he was a ravenous swimmer. Thora was beginning to see why.

"It's not that far! I swim it all of the time!"

"Well you are part fish!" the girl chimed. "You have gills, I don't!"

"I don't know what you mean."

"Never mind. If you want to swim to the island go ahead. I will meet you there when the Madoqua Empress lands at the great dock."

"And then we go open the door and let Jack out?"

"That will be the first thing that we do when we get there. I promise."

Percy jumped up and down displaying his unabated glee at his cousin's words. He was every bit a little boy. His mind had not aged at all. He was born in 1914, two years before she and her sister arrived in the world. He would have been fifteen years old had he lived. But he died that fateful day in 1918. He remained a four-year old ever since.

"Then let's get going Thora! We can wait for the boat at the pier." Thora guessed that the child had decided that he would accompany her on the Madoqua Empress.

"I can't go out there yet! There might be people looking for me," she said to her cousin. His eyes gawked up at her. There was exasperation written in his pupils. "Why don't you go down to the pier and scout for me and come back and tell me who is out there? It will be fun! You will be like a private eye investigating a case."

"I don't know what you mean," Percy responded in confusion.

Thora was about to elaborate on her statement when she realized that the little boy came from a different time. Tales about private eyes were not popular back in his day as they were in hers. She chose a different tactic. "You can be like a spy in the war. You have crossed No Man's Land and you are surveying the enemy's strength and position."

Percy looked at her blankly. He did not understand what she was talking about.

Thora sighed. "Just go out there and come back and tell me what kind of people you see."

This time the boy understood what she meant. "Aye aye, Captain!" he said, placing his hand in a salute position. Then he dashed out of the cave leaving the girl behind wondering about what kind of information he would have when he returned. She was certain that it would not be very articulate information. It would be the stuff that is conjured up by a four-year old's mind. But she still needed to know. Were the guests at the lodge still under the impression that a tornado had touched down or were they starting to see that there was a human element to the damage created in the parking lot? Did the presence of the stolen car rouse anybody's curiosity?

It was not very long before Percy returned. "There are lots of people there!" he proclaimed. "They are all down by the water putting up their sails on their little boats."

The girl nodded. "I think I know what is going on," she said. "It is around the middle of August, isn't it? That is the time for the Osprey Landing Annual Regatta." She had been to this celebrated regatta several times in the past. The last time that she was here for this event her father had entered the Grappler in the races. The Grappler was the first boat to cross the finishing line but the trophy was not awarded to its skipper. A judge had determined that the boat had missed three buoys along the course. Instead of being a champion that day, her father was disqualified and given a life-long ban on ever competing in this event again. He went back to Black Island disgruntled that day while his daughters returned filled with embarrassment at not only Langley's cheating but his histrionics at the judge's booth. He had gone bananas and acted the way that Percy would have rather than as an adult as his temper got the better of him when he was informed of his disqualification.

"Did you see anybody suspicious?" she asked the little boy.

"I don't know what that word means?" Percy answered.

"Oh, never mind," Thora sighed. Perhaps there would be extra security for her with all the pandemonium associated with the regatta. She could be easily lost in the crowd from any prying eyes. "I think that it will be all right for us to walk out in the open down there." She looked down at her clothes and began to think otherwise. She would stick out like a sore thumb amongst the elite of Pioneer Lake society in these rags. "I wish that I had new clothes," she said. "I've had this outfit on for more than a week through all kinds of weather and adventure."

"I can get you new clothes if you want!" her cousin offered.

"How?"

"There are loads of clothes in the change houses by the waterfront."

The boy was thinking. "Oh Percy, you are a doll!" she laughed. She went on to describe what kind of outfit that she wanted and what size she needed. She knew that Percy was not taking this in, that it was beyond his mental capacity to understand the dynamics of fashionable apparel, but it was fun for her just to describe her desires.

Once again, her little ghostly cousin meandered off into the growing crowds at the Osprey Landing Regatta. Thora waited behind in the cave, wondering what kind of frumpy old woman clothes the boy would have in his hands upon his return.

He worked fast, this cousin of hers. He was back in a jiffy and he had in his hands a beautiful navy blouse and a very pretty pleated white skirt. He even had a pair of glossy black shoes. When Thora lifted the outfit in the air to determine its size, she was very pleased to see that it was almost tailored made for her. Even the shoes were made to order. They didn't pinch her toes or make her feel like she was walking in a pair of boats.

"How did you know what size to get!" she exclaimed.

"That was easy. I just followed a girl that looked almost the same size as you into the change house. As she took off these clothes to get in her bathing suit, I just took what she took off!"

"You were inside a change room with a stripping woman!" Thora was almost in shock.

"What's wrong with that?" the boy retorted. The girl could see that her cousin was not old enough to understand the taboos of his act.

"I don't want you in here while I change. Go stand outside of the cave while I put on these clothes!" she commanded.

The boy did as he was told. Thora took off her old clothing. She could feel her body thanking her to be finally rid of those filthy tattered rags. When she slipped into the skirt and blouse, she could smell the slight aroma of the perfume worn by the original owner. This scent would mask the bad smells that she was sure were emanating from her. The outfit felt silky and divine. Once again her body gave its approval and gratitude.

"I'm ready now," she announced to Percy and worked her way out of the grotto being careful not to smudge her new duds on any of the wet and dank surfaces that made up the cave.

As she stepped out into the ravine, her eyes were almost blinded by the light shimmering down through the trees. A lot of time had elapsed while she was in the cave. It had been dawn when she entered it. She guessed now that it was around ten in the morning on a beautiful summer day. It even felt warmer than it had been the last several days. Everything just seemed like it was going to be a perfect day. It was the kind of day that she pictured it would be on her return to Black Island. She would be there before the day was over. She felt almost giddy.

She took Percy by the hand and the two of them walked up the hill towards the Osprey Landing parking lot.

Chapter 58

The Buffalo Burger Stand

Just as Percy described it and just how she had remembered it from other years, the waterfront before the Osprey Landing Lodge was surging with crowds of people milling about and enjoying the festivities of this annual late summer regatta. The folks were of all ages, from babies in strollers to seniors in wheel chairs. Everywhere they could be seen in this carnival-like atmosphere.

There were many in the water already. Some of the teenagers and young men were horsing around on the logs that had been hauled in for the jousting contests that would be held later on in the day. They laughed and carried on as if they were in a timeless domain where the only thing to worry about were the horseflies and deerflies that would inflict nasty bites when they least expected it. Elsewhere others roved the shoreline in their paddleboats, oblivious to everything except for the relaxing, calming effect of the sun upon their skin. On land, huskers were starting to chime out their calls that they would repeat hundreds of times during the day as they tried to sell their wares to the memorabilia-starved tourists.

But the main focus was on the dozens of sailing craft that had been brought in from all around to take part in the regatta. Just like Percy said, the sailors were hoisting their sails and rigging their lines, preparing for the race that would take place starting at one in the afternoon. Many held up wetted fingers to get a feel for the speed and direction of the wind. There was not much of a breeze as of yet. There was enough though to cause ripples on the surface of the deep blue lake. Thora knew the weather patterns of this vicinity. If there were wavelets on the lake at ten, there would be waves by one. The wind always built up during the course of the day. It was almost like the sun fueled them. These participants in the regatta would not be let down.

The Madoqua Empress had not yet arrived at the landing. When she did she would be loaded with passengers all coming to witness the race and then to dance the evening away to a full orchestra under the moonlight. The Osprey Landing Regatta was always a sublime event. Many came to get engaged or married or to honeymoon at the Regatta. The Toronto papers always were here and afterwards would have full sections in their editions devoted to describing the society news that took place here. Luckily as far as she knew the newspapers chose to ignore writing anything about the antics of her father the year that he was disqualified. They wanted to color the event in cheerful hues and not in the reds and greens of temper and envy.

As Thora looked out upon the water and thought of the steamer, it suddenly occurred to her that the Empress' schedule could be different on the day of the regatta. It seemed to her that the boat spent the day here at Osprey Landing and that it was part of the ambience. This thought served to sink her soul somewhat. She was not one hundred percent sure of this but it seemed to her that in the past that all of her recollections of the Regatta always had the Madoqua Empress somewhere in the background.

She felt a tap on her shoulder. She froze at the touch, fearing that she was about to be apprehended. As she slowly turned, she saw the bright beaming face of Mrs. Alan Wiggins, Lana, as she wanted to be known by everybody. The Wiggins owned a large estate about three miles north of the Meadowford cottage. They were even more well to do than the Meadowfords. They were Canadians from Toronto that made their millions through investment financing.

"Thora Meadowford!" Lana cried out loud in her boisterous fashion. "I am surprised to see you here! I thought that your family went home for the season already. I've not seen any activity on your island in over a month!"

Before Thora could give any explanation or excuse about why Black Island was vacated, Mrs. Wiggins cut in, "Are there any others from your family here?" She was looking about in the crowd to see if she could spot Langley or Cora or Faye or Thaddeus or any other Meadowford.

Once again before Thora could say anything, Mrs. Wiggins said, "I'm sorry to hear about your grandfather. He was such a dear man. He's been sorely missed at Mount Horeb. They are thinking of running a charity on Labor Day Weekend in his honor. The money raised would go to the amputee vets from the Great War. Oh look, there is Marie Deschenes! I must say hello!"

The woman left before Thora had said a single word. The girl sighed in relief but she was aware of a very present danger to her circumstances here. She could not be just another face in the crowd. There were many people that knew her family and perhaps some that were even aware of her fugitive status. She could not run the risk of being recognized. She had to hide herself as much as possible, be as inconspicuous as the houseflies that were beginning to collect around the garbage bins. She would only come out when the Madoqua Empress arrived and just pray that nobody spots her as she boards the boat.

Until it comes, she determined that she and Percy would just bide their time at the fringes of the hoopla, perhaps just sit themselves down in the shade of the trees that bordered the open area. The only problem was that in all of the confusion, she did not know what became of her cousin. She could not see him amongst the hundreds of people that were going in every direction without a care in the world. She just hoped that he would not draw attention upon himself either. It would really stir a commotion if the folks were to realize that the ghost of a boy dead eleven years was amongst them.

And then she saw him. He was down by the water swimming with other children his age. She should have guessed that he would have been there. He loves to swim. He could never get enough of it. The other tots his age were not aware of him. He was swimming circles around them, splashing water in their faces and laughing hard. He was having a wonderful time and Thora decided that he was best left where he was. He seemed to be invisible to everybody else and that was fine even though the other children were getting miffed and confused about the inexplicable sprays suddenly coming out of nowhere and washing them in their faces.

A nearby adult spotted the strange splashes amongst the children. At once alarm went up in him. "Shark!" he cried out loud in a New England accent and began madly dashing towards the lake to rescue the children.

Others that stood near the man looked at him as if he had gone loco. "Stupid American!" one man said to another. "They just don't know anything about this country! There are just as many sharks in this lake as there are ghosts!"

The shark spotter dove into the water and a moment later came out all sopping wet dragging two screaming tots with him. The man looked back anxiously at the lake. There were still other children swimming and there still were the strange sprays coming out of nowhere. "Have you all gone mad!" he cried out loud at a group of picnicking adults. "You sit there and drink your beer while your children are becoming the fodder for a man-eating shark!" The others just laughed at him and left him looking foolish in front of his two children. They tugged at their father's arms trying to break free and return to the water. The frustrated man could no longer contain his anger; he spanked the one child and then the other. He glared at the picnickers and then he stormed away with his crying children, walking right past Thora. She heard him grumble that Canadians just did not know anything about their water systems. "Don't they know that sharks can swim up the St. Lawrence and enter the Great Lakes and swim up the rivers from there? I've heard of bull sharks a thousand miles inland!" Thora wondered who was the recipient of his message. His kids weren't paying any attention. They were too busy bawling their eyes out.

Percy was still in the water and still carrying on with the remaining children. He seemed to never tire of his game although Thora was finding it tiring to watch any longer. There was the strong aroma of barbecued food in the air and it served to remind her about how hungry she really was. She had hardly eaten anything at all during the past week. She spotted a queue forming at a booth that was selling buffalo burgers. There were only about four people in line, none of whom she recognized. The booth sat in a less traveled quarter of the pageant when compared to the dense pockets of people elsewhere. The girl decided that she could afford to risk buying a burger. She should be in and out of there in just a few minutes. Then she could return to this shaded spot and wait for her boat to come in.

She stood up and wiped the grass from her white skirt and walked towards the buffalo burger line. There were just two girls ahead of her in this queue, both in bathing suits. The old Indian woman that ran the counter was serving them. Thora could feel her mouth salivate as the smell of the fried onions and the charring meat washed over her nostrils.

The one girl that stood in front of her was placing her condiments on her burger while the other one waited for her French fries to brown in the deep fryer. Thora watched with eager eyes as the girl took a bite into her juicy buffalo burger. She could imagine that it was her mouth savoring the meat. The girl spotted her looking and smiled.

"It looks good!" Thora said. "I can hardly wait to get mine."

"It is good!" the girl responded. Then her eyes fell upon Thora's clothing. "Hey!" she said. "I have an outfit just like that!" Her eyes began studying the contours of the pleats and the pattern on the navy blouse's buttons. "I wore mine today too!" she said through a swallow.

Thora felt tingles run through her. What luck it would be to run into the true owner of these clothes!

"Wait a second!" the girl exclaimed, reaching forward and taking hold of Thora's blouse to bring the buttons in closer to her examining eyes. "That is my outfit!"

All at once things got confusing to Thora. She could have sworn that she saw her grandmother, June Ritchey, suddenly appear behind the girl and wrap her bony fingers around the girl's necks. The girl started choking and turning blue while the lifeless orbs of Thora's grandmother grew red.

The girl's friend saw what was happening. She at once started slapping the girl on the back trying to dislodge the stuck burger in her throat. The girl tried to hack but she was not removing the food or Thora's grandmother. She was slowly dying in front of everybody. Others had seen the predicament and had rushed to help the girl. Thora saw the wicked grin in her grandmother's eyes, as she would not let go.

"Call a medic!" one of the adults cried out as he pushed aside the girl's friend and started slugging the girl on her back. Thora recognized the man. He at one time was a servant at Black Island but had been let go by Uncle Thaddeus because he refused to be treated like dirt. She could not afford for him to spot her. She slipped out from amongst the growing crowd and returned to her sanctuary in the shade. She had not gotten her buffalo burger and she witnessed her grandmother perpetrating a heinous act.

People started screaming around the buffalo burger stand. Thora caught the gist of what happened. The girl that owned the clothes on Thora's back had died, strangled by the hands of June Ritchey. Where did she come from and why did she do what she did? It was all incomprehensible to Thora.

Those that watched the girl die did not see a wicked old ghost strangling the child. They saw an innocent young lady die, choking on indigestible Indian food. They decided as a throng that it was the fault of the Indians that ran the buffalo burger booth and began railing at the surprised Indians saying all forms of indecent things. One of the men took it upon himself to start tearing the booth apart with his bare hands while another held the cook, a thin Ojibwa man, while another began pummeling him with unforgiving fists.

"The white man will never love the red man," a crackling old voice said to Thora. Thora turned her head and saw her grandmother standing beside her. She held that menacing grin on her face while watching the melee taking place at the booth.

"Why did you do that?" Thora said to the ghost. "Why did you kill that girl?"

"That girl was going to get you into trouble, child," the grandmother said. "She would have gotten you hauled off to jail for stealing her clothes. I could not let that happen. I want to make sure that we go to Black Island today so that we can be with our Jacky."

"But the Empress will not be going that way today," Thora said. "It will be staying here for the night."

"I'll see to it that it doesn't!" the grandmother smiled wickedly. "I have my ways to influence the living." Her eyes drifted back to the rampant destruction taking place at the booth. "As you can see!"

The veneer of civility that the well to do elite of Pioneer Lake cloaked themselves in could no longer disguise itself. What Thora saw was the ugly manifestation of generations of racial prejudice rear its vile head as the white community rose to retaliate for the falling of one its prized daughters. It sickened the girl's heart to know that she was ultimately responsible for everything that happened here. Had she not caved into her desires to vanquish her hunger none of this would have happened. She hated herself for what she had caused and she hated herself even more that she did not do anything to stop it.

"Look!" her grandmother harkened. "The Madoqua Empress!"

Thora turned her eyes and saw the dark sleek shape of the steamer making its way around the corner to enter the bay where Osprey Landing sat. Tufts of white smoke came from her stacks that sat above its two decks. Even from this distance Thora could see the fluttering of hundreds of hands waving and cheering from the vessel to those gathered at the landing. They would be unaware that all Hell had broken loose here at the regatta. They would be expecting to be greeted by a mob of enthusiastic tourists eager to commence all the fanfare that was associated with the Osprey Landing Annual Regatta. The captain of the Madoqua Empress ordered three long blasts from his boat's whistles.

Simultaneously other whistles blew. These came from the policeman that had to keep the order here at the regatta. He was racing his way towards what remained of the buffalo burger stand to try and break up the fight that was taking place. The Indian cook had broken free from the men that held him. He managed to grab a butcher's knife and he was now behaving like a cornered animal slashing out at any that tried to get near him. About ten men formed a semi-circle around him. They were taunting him with insulting jibes, trying to draw his focus elsewhere while others would scramble in behind him and get a hold of him once more. Thus far it was not working.

The Indian woman that worked the counter was raving. Some men had sequestered her so that she would not be able to participate in the fight. Thora saw the way that these upright citizens kept her at bay. Had she not known these fellows to be decent folk, she could have sworn that the woman was being held in such a manner that would not be socially acceptable.

As the policeman came onto the scene, he drew his gun and ordered the cook to drop his knife. The cook would not comply. He knew that as soon as he had disarmed himself the mob would be upon him and would tear him apart limb from limb. The policeman repeated his ultimatum.

"You have no authority here!" the cook responded in a hoarse voice. "This is Jibatigon. This is the sacred lake!"

"Drop the knife, savage, or I will drop you!" the policeman said in a tone of finality.

The Indian man did drop the knife. He dropped it in a manner that it went hurling across the space that divided him from the mob. The knife landed in the throat of the man that had one time worked at Black Island.

While blood poured from his neck, two bullets exploded in the chest of the cook, tearing apart any vital organs that were on their course.

The Madoqua Empress blasted her whistles once more. She was slowing to prepare to dock at the massive mooring pier at Osprey Landing. The cheering people on board were still not aware of what was happening onshore. They believed that they were going to have a day of mirth in the Shangri-La setting. Instead they were entering the crime scene where three people had died violent deaths thanks to a wayward girl that should not have been here.

Thora blamed herself for everything that happened here. Had she not been so doggedly determined to come to Pioneer Lake three people would have had a beautiful day in the warm sunshine of late August. Instead they were now dead upon a lawn where ugly emotions were stilling running high.

"Come, my child. Let's go greet the boat!" her grandmother said, taking Thora by the hand and forcing her towards the pier.

Chapter 59

Black Saturday

The Madoqua Empress slowly maneuvered herself towards the pier. A crew from Osprey Landing was standing upon the cedar boards ready to catch the ropes flung to them from the steamship's crew. Each crew was expert at this and worked with the other crew dozens of times over the summer to make the docking seamless to those paying passengers on board. They would not be aware of the coordination required to bring a huge bulk of floating inertia to a halt only feet away from an unforgiving shoreline that would tear out the bottom of the vessel.

Thora was standing where the pier joined shore amongst many other people who had come to meet the new arrivals. Rather than being enthusiastic and exuberant, the crowd around her was subdued and solemn. They had grim news to relay to whomever they were standing here to meet. Osprey Landing had been the scene of an atrocity today. The Landing and the Regatta would always bear this heinous scar from this day forward.

The steamer came to a stop. The crew on the pier tied down the Madoqua Empress while the crew onboard prepared to lower the gangway to allow the flood of visitors to disembark. Thora watched the crew on the steamer. She remembered how she and her sister only a few months ago drooled watching the muscular bodies of these young men at work. That seemed more than a lifetime ago. Now, she watched them with disinterest in her eyes. She no longer wanted to meet them. She no longer wanted to meet anybody. All that she wanted to do was to go to her island and be left alone. She didn't care if her cousin Jack was there or not. If he were there, she would have him board the steamer and leave the island. She wanted to be by herself. She wanted to be by herself from this day onward. People were only a source of pain to her. She did not need that pain any longer.

The passengers of the Madoqua Empress started to file out. They bore big expressive smiles, as they still believed that they were about to have one of those magical times of their lives. They did not seem to notice that those that were waiting for them could not reciprocate their enthusiasm.

"What's wrong?" one man said to the woman that was there to greet him.

"Oh John, turn around and take me away from this terrible place!" the woman cried. "I don't want to be in a spot where people get murdered!"

"Murdered?" John responded querulously, looking upwards into the crowd. For some reason his eyes fell into the eyes of Thora. The girl had to avert her gaze. She felt that this stranger knew that she was responsible for what had happened here.

Very quickly the news began to spread its way up the gangplank. As it did so, its factual basis grew and became distorted. By the time that it reached the decks of the Madoqua Empress, it was said that twelve people had been shot down in the Pioneer Lake Massacre. The people on board began to become hysterical. They were led to believe that a band of drunken Indians were running amok with their tomahawks and arrows on the Osprey Landing estate. They did not want to be scalped and submitted to horrible pagan tortures. They were going to stay put and they demanded that the steamer return to Riverwood at once.

"See, I told you that you had nothing to worry about," smiled June Ritchey. "The Empress won't be staying here overnight." The old ghost seemed to know that the crowd would react this way. Was that part of her purpose when she strangled the girl at the burger stand?

The flow of people suddenly started to go in the opposite direction. The people wanted away from Osprey Landing. They wanted back to where they came from. The only way back was onboard the Madoqua Empress.

A throng of hysterical tourists that stood behind Thora started pushing her forward toward the steamer's gangway. The girl almost lost her balance, as the mindless crowd plowed onward not caring for what or whom stood ahead of them. There were so many people around her that she began to feel very claustrophobic. She was scared that she was going to be trampled to death.

Her grandmother, possessing no body and no visible incarnation to most eyes, remained stationary as urgent people walked right through her trying to reach the gangplank.

"Aren't you coming onboard?" Thora cried out to her. She was being tussled and tossed like a halfback in a football game.

"I have to wait for young Master Percival," the woman responded. A man had walked through her form. Thora saw a sudden pronounced disorientation in the man's eyes when his body shared the same space as the ghost. When he came out of her, he seemed more panicked than ever. "He is still swimming. You go on ahead, child! We will catch up to you. Be sure to tell the Captain that you want the boat to stop at Black Island." The ghost of June Ritchey turned around and headed back to shore through the worried wave of tourists trying to flee the surprise assault from the crazed and savage Hendorun Nation.

The man that had walked through the ghost was now upon Thora. It seemed that he was going to walk right through her too. She was now on the gangplank and unlike her grandmother she was not able to share a space with anybody. The man would knock her into the narrow gap of water between the Empress' hull and the stone cribs of the pier. She fought hard to keep her footing and managed to stay on the runway. Another girl up ahead of her was not so fortunate. She had been bowled over and fell in between the boat and the dock. With the massive influx of people coming onboard the Madoqua Empress, the steamer was bobbing up and down. This served to make the water where the girl fell very turgid and dangerous. She was screaming for help but nobody would listen. Everybody was too busy saving their own neck.

Thora saw the predicament the girl was in and tried to draw the attention of the crew to rescue her but the crowd was forcing her upward and away. She soon was swallowed into the center of the mob. Any of her cries was drowned by all the pushing and shoving that was taking place.

As she was buried inside the shoulders and chests of fleeing tourists, her ears heard several gun blasts. A moment later a raspy man's voice was shouting out for the crowd to come to order. She could not see him but she guessed that it was a policeman trying to bring the mob into control.

"The Madoqua Empress can not take any more people onboard. She is filled to capacity!" the man said. "Any of you that are not on the gangplank turn around at once. Those of you that are on the gangplank, we will take you as long as you file into the boat in an orderly fashion."

Thora realized that it was not a policeman barking out these commands. It was the captain of the Madoqua Empress. She recognized the voice. She had talked to the man all the years of her life. He was Captain Richard Buck. "Captain," she found herself yelling out at the top of her lungs. "There is a girl that has fallen between the boat and the dock!" She did not know if the girl had been rescued yet or if she were still alive.

"Man overboard!" Captain Buck boomed to his crew.

Although Thora could not see it, she sensed that the crews from the boat and pier were stirring and going into action. She heard the rescue taking place in the gasps of those that were in places that had vantages of the desperate scene. "Grab the lifebuoy!" was cried out by several of those nearby Thora.

"I don't think that she's conscious!" some others lamented out loud.

"No, no, no, no, look! She's moving to the buoy! She's got her wits about her!"

"I think she's dead!"

The commentary was contradicting and Thora did not know what version spoke the truth. All that she did know was that if she had not spoken up nobody would have paid attention to the drowning girl. She felt some satisfaction that she played a role in this. She just hoped that it would have a good ending.

"There! She's got the buoy! Hold on girl! We'll get you out of there!"

The mobs on the deck, the plank and the pier all began to clap. It appeared that it was going to have a good ending afterall. Thora could now get occasional glimpses of the taut line slowly moving upward towards the Empress. At the bottom end of that rope would be the girl.

And then something unspeakable happened, something that shattered the hearts of all those hopeful bystanders. The line went limp and there was a sickening thud that reverberated in the space between the steel hull of the Madoqua Empress and the stone crib of the Osprey Landing pier. Thora knew what that thud was. Another bona fide fatality had taken place on this Black Saturday upon Pioneer Lake.

All her feeling good about herself was for naught. She had patted herself on the back too early. The girl was dead, she knew it.

"She should have held onto the buoy with her hands rather than just be satisfied that her body could do the job," Thora heard one nearby man say to another.

"I saw an old wretch of a ghost yank her down!" a woman could be heard to say. Thora lifted her eyes and tried to spot the woman. Her heart was palpitating and she felt nauseous. Someone else here was able to see ghosts but she could not see this person. She knew from the description the woman gave that the fell deed had to be done by her grandmother. Thora could not see her either but she knew that she was around and that she was the reason that the girl fell to her death.

"Ghosts and Indians! Get me the hell out of here!" cried another on the gangplank. All at once the forward thrust in motion had commenced again as people started pushing upward to climb onboard of the steamer.

"Easy does it!" crewmen were saying. "One at a time or else there will be more that will fall to their deaths."

Thora was now near the top of the gangplank. Through the arms and shoulders of those that surrounded her she could see the lower deck of the Madoqua Empress. The vessel was brimming with passengers, more passengers than the girl had ever seen on this boat or any other boat before. She found herself praying that the Empress was seaworthy enough to sustain all of the extra weight.

At the bottom of the gangplank all form of commotion was stirring as frustrated and disgruntled passengers were being turned back by a crew that had to suddenly become security guards. They had to fight and push back those that would not abide by Captain Buck's decision. It was a very ugly scene and one with an uncertain outcome. This crowd was insane. The only danger here was the danger that they created themselves. There were no Indians here on the warpath. Adults were as skittish as children. And when Thora thought that these adults here were the cream of society, it made her appraisal of the human race sink even lower. She knew that had her father been here he would have been a bull in a china shop roaring up the gangplank and throwing any that was in his way into the lake. In short, he would have acted the way that many of the men did here. Seeing others behave the way that

Langley would showed the girl that maybe he was not as big of a miscreant that she believed him to be.

She finally stepped off the gangway and onto the red planks of the Madoqua Empress' main deck. There was a sea of people before her. She searched for a path through them. She had to get to Captain Buck and ask him to have the steamer make a stop at Black Island. She had a feeling that this was not going to be as easy as it should be.

The Captain would be up on the fly bridge of the Empress where he would have an eagle eye's view of everything taking place below. The girl started to push her way through the throng towards the steps that would take her upwards on the steamer. She kept her eyes fixed on her course and would not look up and identify any of the people that she passed. There would be those that she would recognize and that would recognize her but at the moment with all of the rioting taking place down on the pier nobody was interested on who was onboard.

She reached the stairs and some breathing space. It was less crowded here and the girl was able to pause for a moment to catch her breath. She never imagined that her trip onboard the Empress would happen under such circumstances. She had pictured a peaceful cruise with slow building excitement as the vessel would make its way through the McDougall Narrows and Black Island would come into view. This cruise was going to be anything but that. The boat was as packed as a refugee ship in the Orient. The pandemonium onboard was like that of a warship in the heat of battle. Her nerves were on edge and all that she wanted was for everything to come to an end. This journey of hers from Pennsylvania had been harrowing from the moment it started. It had seen her go through all forms of unbelievable adventure and terror. If she were to tell her story to anybody they would have to conclude that she was insane. All the calamity that she had to endure would be simply unbelievable to most. Yet, she lived through it and experienced it all. Most of the time it felt that she was alone against the world and those that she did befriend along the way invariably tried to thwart her and pay a large price in the end. It seemed that her life was the stage for gods to tinker. But she had endured it all. She survived it all. And now, here she was, finally on the deck of the Madoqua Empress. All hell had broken loose around her but that in no means diminished the fact that she had accomplished what she had set out to do.

Some people were starting to come toward her. They had gotten the idea that they could watch the melee just as well from the less-crowded upper deck. Her time of rest was over. If she did not move she would be trampled. She started up the stairs to the second deck with four men hot on her heels. She could feel herself being pushed along. Her knees were barely able to sustain the shoving.

"Stop pushing!" she yelled out as she neared the top of the stairs. The guardrails were not very high. She knew that she could easily topple over them and plunge into that roiling water between dock and ship and meet a similar fate as that poor girl.

"Hurry up, you little brat!" one man cussed.

The shoes on Thora's feet were not as ideal as she had first believed. She was slipping in them because of her rushed pace. It made climbing these stairs all the more precarious. She had to stop or she would fall. She pulled herself tight against the guardrail and allowed the four hooligans to pass. As she did so, her eyes watched the brawling taking place on the pier. Some of the people had now taken the fight into the water. There was thrashing and splashing and screaming. The scene before her was alive with hatred. It seemed that everybody had lost their minds. And then she noticed something just beyond the bend on the shoreline. It looked like the bow tip of an enormous canoe.

Was he back? She thought that he had died in his battle with the Nells and her great grandfather. More people were coming up the stairs and they would not go around her. They demanded that she go onward. The girl reluctantly complied. By the time that she reached the upper deck and looked back toward that piece of shoreline again, the canoe was no longer there. Maybe her mind was playing tricks with her? She was certain that the Great Spirit had been killed.

Suddenly sirens filled the air. She saw a fleet of police cars racing up the road towards Osprey Landing. They had come to break up the fight. The cars roared right up to the foot of the pier. Policemen armed with billy sticks poured out of the cars and at once began swinging their weapons without prejudice upon the crowd. The girl could not bear to watch. She could not bear to think that she had instigated all of this simply by deciding that she wanted a buffalo burger.

She moved towards the other end of the deck where there was a set of stairs that led up to the fly bridge. That was where Captain Richard Buck would be. She needed him to schedule a stop at Black Island for her. This was something that he might not be willing to do. He had a boatload of frenzied passengers all itching to get to their parked cars in Riverwood.

As she approached the stairs through the growing crowds on this level, a voice came over the Empress' public address system. "Now here this," the highly amplified voice bearing an English accent said. "The Madoqua Empress will not be taking on any other passengers. Any of you that are not on board will have to wait. I have called The Island Enchantress and she is making full steam ahead for here. She should be here in approximately two hours."

The Island Enchantress was another steamer that worked the Madoqua Lakes and was occasionally seen on Pioneer Lake. Although not quite as elegant as the Empress she could carry just about as many people and she was a faster ship.

Thora sensed that the crowd was not going to be satisfied with this proposal. Two hours was a long time to wait in an inferno of terror where even being an innocent bystander could sustain you a rap across the head from a billy club.

The Madoqua Empress' smokestacks began to whistle. There were sounds of chains echoing in the hull of the vessel as the gangplank was being drawn up from the dock.

"Get off the plank you idiots!" one of the Empress' crew yelled at some people who managed to climb onto the gangway before it could be pulled from the pier.

Obscenities were shouted back and forth between boat and pier. As the plank lifted into the air, several men desperately clung onto its end. There they were sitting ducks for the police's billy clubs. These sticks viciously and mercilessly rattled against the men's rib cages. Every one of them was forced to let go. One of them fell into the space between boat and pier. A line from the dock was quickly tossed to him and he was lifted upward into police custody.

Thora started up the stainless steel steps towards the fly bridge. There was a door at its summit that in all likelihood was locked. When she reached it she knocked at it as hard as she could so that it would be heard above the din from the lower decks.

Nobody answered. At least she did not hear anybody answer. She knocked on the door again and this time put her hand on the doorknob. To her surprise she discovered that it was not locked. She opened it and gained a view upon a panel with a myriad of controls upon it. The Madoqua Empress was an old boat but she was modernly equipped.

"Nobody is allowed up here," the distinctive British voice of Captain Richard Buck rasped.

The girl felt the door being pushed shut. Thora buttressed her shoulder and held her ground. "I just need to see you just for a minute, Captain Buck," she called out through the mahogany wood.

"Young lady, I have an emergency on my hand. I have no minute to give to anybody!" the unseen man retorted.

"All I want to do is ask if you can make a stop at Black Island," Thora said.

"I will stop there on my way back from Riverwood tomorrow!" the Captain said, opening the door to gander at the passenger that had the audacity to request such a thing. "I have thousands to evacuate and they take priority. Miss Meadowford!" Captain Buck cried out her name as if he were genuinely astounded. "I didn't expect to see you onboard!" The prim and proper man's bushy white eyebrows lifted.

Thora started to get a feeling that something was going to go wrong for her. She was beginning to suspect that the Captain knew something that she didn't.

As Captain Buck composed himself, he said, "I'm sorry Miss Meadowford I can't take you to your island until tomorrow. I'm afraid that this is going to have to be an express excursion. You see what is happening here. The passengers would rip the Empress apart board by board if they saw that we changed course just to let you off. You can stay onboard and tomorrow morning when we depart from Riverwood I will drop you off at Black Island. Now please, go find yourself a seat." He patted Thora's hand as she left.

The girl did not like the settlement but before she could express her discontent the mahogany door was shut, barring her from bartering with Captain Buck. She started down the stairs to the upper deck trying to work up some contingencies plans in her head. She was not going to ride back and forth between Riverwood and here until tomorrow. That plan was not satisfactory in the least. As she walked down the stairs, she heard Captain Buck's voice over the intercom, "Would the Purser please report to the fly bridge at once."

Thora never paid the comment any attention but as she stepped upon the deck and looked over the side of the vessel she saw that the Madoqua Empress had pulled away from the dock and that the steamer was embarked on its passage to Riverwood. Behind the boat there were some people that were still trying to get onboard. They were swimming after the boat with the hope that the Empress would be forced to rescue them once they were too far from shore to swim back. They were desperate to leave Osprey Landing. Looking back at the pier, Thora could not blame them. The fighting had not ceased with the arrival of the police. If anything, it intensified. What could spur civilized humans to behave so barbarically? It was almost like they had taken leave of their senses or something had taken control of their minds and was forcing them to annihilate one another. The brawling was taking place everywhere upon the Osprey Landing property. It was on the pier, it was in the water, it was on the sumptuous lawns in front of the lodge and dance hall, and it was in the parking lot. It was madness on a scale never seen outside of Hell. All this because she wanted a burger? As her eyes panned across the shoreline they once again came across something that was trying to conceal itself behind a bend. It was the bow of the canoe. This time Thora saw some more of it. This time she saw the Great Spirit sitting in it and staring out at her. He had been disfigured by his fight with the ghosts but he was there and he was alive. Somehow Thora got the distinct impression that he was behind the melee, that he was orchestrating it for some sinister reason.

She could not bear to look at him any longer. She averted her eyes. She no longer felt safe at all. Was he manipulating her like the way that he was manipulating the others? What was she doing that was not the product of her own will? She tried to look at her recent actions analytically but there was just too much confusion around her to allow her the concentration that this exercise required.

Her eyes fell upon the swimmers behind the steamer. They bobbed up and down in the Empress' wake. They were not giving up on their quest to be rescued. Some of them were a fair distance from shore and looked like they were beginning to tire. If they did not turn around soon they would drown. They were screaming out at the Empress, begging her to stop. But the Empress showed no inclination towards saving them. She moved steadily forward over the rolling waves.

Chapter 60

The Captain and the Cop

There was one swimmer, however, that appeared to fair better than the rest in the ordeal. If anything his swimming seemed to get stronger. He cut a swath on the water's surface and created a wake of his own. Thora recognized this swimmer as her cousin Percy. The boy loved to swim and there was small wonder why he did. He was extremely good at it. Had he lived and grown he could very likely have become an Olympian. He swam with the agility of a river otter. He was made for the water. He was actually gaining on the Madoqua Empress and would eventually catch up and climb on board.

As she watched her cousin cutting his path through the water, she recalled a suggestion that he had made. He had said that they could swim to Black Island. Such a notion was ridiculous to her if she was going to start from Osprey Landing. That was almost five miles away from Black Island. But once the Madoqua Empress works her way through the McDougall Narrows the steamer will be less than half a mile away from the Meadowford island estate. Half a mile was longer than she had ever swum before but she did believe that she was able to do it—especially if she were to abet her swimming with one of the Empress' life jackets. A smile came to her face. She had a plan. It was about time to set that plan into motion. She had to find the life jackets.

She believed them to be on the lower deck in a storage room. Hopefully they were not under lock and key. They might be, she realized. She recalled Captain Buck telling her and Rebecca in the past that a lot of tourists liked getting themselves a keepsake in memory of the steamer and a life jacket with the words 'Madoqua Empress' black stenciled onto the orange material was a prized item. Many preservers were pilfered over the years.

The upper deck was densely packed with passengers. There was as much commotion and agitation here as in a gull colony. People were still reliving their horror stories of Black Saturday at Osprey Landing. It surely was a day that not any of them would forget. She winnowed a path through the crowd, trying to work her way to the stairwell that would lead her to the lower deck. As she did so, she kept her face towards the floor to avoid being recognized. There were people here that surely would. When she finally reached the stairwell she discovered that it too was brimming with people upon every step. There did not seem to be a way through them. They had no place to get out of the way. Trying to push her way through would only cause her being noticed and that was the last thing that she wanted to happen.

She began resigning herself to making her dive from the second deck and the swim without the aid of a life jacket. It would not be as easy as a leap from the lower deck equipped with the preserver but she believed that she could still do it. There was no way that she was going to remain on the steamer and wait until tomorrow. In fact, as she thought about it she realized that such an idea could cause her trouble. People would know that she was on the island and if anybody were looking for her they would quickly discover her whereabouts. Swimming was a better idea.

The men standing on the stairwell began grumbling. They were shifting their bodies as if they were making way for someone that was coming through. Something inside of Thora told her to hide. She slid behind some rather tall folk and peeped through the spaces between them at the stairwell.

Pushing his way through the perturbed crowd was Officer Lou Bombino of the Grappling Haven Police Force. He held a surly expression that told the people that he was passing and that they had better keep their comments to themselves or else he would really disturb them.

What the hell was he doing onboard? Thora slipped deeper behind the men that obscured her. She knew what he was doing onboard. He was here looking for her. He had not been fooled by the plane crash. He knew that she did not perish in its fiery remains. He was a dogged cop and very good at what he did. The sight of Lou Bombino frightened Thora more than the Great Spirit and the ghost of her grandmother combined. There was something unreal about the danger that they represented but the menace that Officer Bombino presented was very tangible. It was very real.

She watched the man plow through the crowd on the second deck. He was heading directly to the stairs that went up to the fly bridge. Recalling that the Captain had requested the presence of the purser only moments after she parted company with him, Thora pieced together what was playing out before her. The purser had been summoned by Captain Buck to go find Officer Bombino. This meant that the Empress' captain had already been speaking to the Grappling Haven policeman and had been asked to be on the lookout for the Pennsylvanian fugitive. No wonder Captain Buck looked so surprised when she first came into the control room. Officer Bombino must have come onboard back at Riverwood and rode all the way to Osprey Landing. Maybe this was not his first passage on the steamer? Maybe he had been going back and forth over Pioneer Lake for some time now, knowing that sooner or later his quarry would come onboard.

As Officer Bombino climbed up the stairs to go meet with Captain Buck, Thora knew that she had to get off the second deck and down to the lower one as soon as possible. She had to find herself a hiding place until the Empress cleared the McDougall Narrows and then make her leaping dash over the guardrail and into the water. Hopefully she would be equipped with a life jacket when this happens.

She started towards the stairs once she saw the policeman disappear into the fly bridge. An adolescent girl did not intimidate the men that had cowered in Bombino's presence when he had bullied his way up the stairs. They would not create a partition for her to go through.

"You just stay put, little missy," one man said, pinching her by the shoulder and not allowing her to move. "This isn't a playground."

"Let go of me!" Thora hissed but she was powerless to overcome the man. At that moment her eyes caught the top of the stairwell that led to the fly bridge. Captain Buck and Officer Bombino were standing there looking down at the masses on the second deck. They were not looking her way. That was a saving grace but sooner or later they would spot her. She began to struggle all the more in the man's hands, hoping that she would not cause much of a commotion in breaking free.

"I said stay still!" the man bellowed. He tightened his grip on her shoulder while glaring at her with eyes that said that if she fought back he would escalate the degree of pain that he was inflicting upon her. Thora looked up at the stairs. The man's shout luckily had not drawn the attention of Captain Buck and Officer Bombino. They were still peering elsewhere.

And then out of nowhere the girl's grandmother appeared. She grabbed the man's forearm and drew it to her mouth. She bit deeply and fiercely into it. The man's hold on Thora ended as he yowled in agony and was gawking at a badly bleeding wound just above his wrist. The girl could see that he did not understand how any of this happened. He was not able to see ghosts.

As soon as she was free she began racing down the stairs to the lower level. The other men that were crowded on these steps gave her the room she needed. They must have saw what had happened to the first man and possessed no desire to be wounded themselves by this vicious little girl. Thora sensed that the man's scream caught the Captain and the Officer's attention. She would have to very quickly find some place to hide.

Once she was on the lower deck, she began running towards the storage closets where the life jackets were kept. She looked out onto the lake to check the progress of the Empress. The vessel had yet to even enter the McDougall Narrows. She guessed that it would be at least twenty minutes before the steamer reached the point where she wanted to make her jump.

As she reached the storage closets, she saw two men shoving their way down the steps from the upper level. Captain Buck and Officer Bombino were in pursuit. They were asking those that they passed if they saw where the little girl went. She pulled on the closet's door and just as she feared she saw that it was locked. She was going to be forced to make her swim without the safety of a life preserver. This did not concern her at the moment. She had to find a hiding spot. Her eyes fell upon another closet that did not possess any lock upon it. She grabbed hold of the door and opened it as slightly as she could before crawling inside. Her foot fell into something that clanged and was wet on its bottom. Something wooden and thin toppled against her. It was dark in here but she guessed where she was. She was in the room where the crew kept the boat's mops, pails and cleaning supplies.

As she was catching her breath, she began to realize that this storage closet would be a very obvious place to hide especially when the two men were given directions by those witnesses that saw her running by them. She should have gone elsewhere. But where could she have gone? The Madoqua Empress was not exactly the ideal place for a hide and go seek enthusiast. It did not possess a litany of nooks and crannies where she could tuck herself.

Before she could draw the reigns upon her heightened conditions to calm herself, the closet door opened, drawing in not only the light but also the faces of Captain Richard Buck and Officer Lou Bombino.

"We finally meet, Miss Meadowford!" Bombino smirked. "You, my little child, are in big, big trouble." He reached in to drag her out. But before he took hold of her, he stopped. "Have you got a lock for this door?" he asked Captain Buck.

"I can get you one," the Captain said.

"This room can serve for her holding cell until we reach Riverwood," Bombino said as he looked around at the tight confines of the closet, sizing it up for its potential as a makeshift jail. It was only maybe four feet by six feet. It was cluttered with several pails, mops, brooms and cleaning detergents. "Yes, it could do quite nicely."

"I'll be right back," Captain Buck said.

"We'll be here waiting," the Grappling Haven policeman nodded and smiled to the Madoqua Empress Captain. Turning back to Thora, he said, "I must congratulate you, Miss Meadowford. You have been by far the most challenging suspect I have ever had to apprehend. I went through Hell and high water trying to catch you. You almost had me fooled by the airplane crash by Lake Ontario. You had made it appear like you died there but you forgot about the sand. Your footprints were everywhere near the site. Nobody dead can walk away from an accident and it was highly unlikely that there would have been a witness with the same size foot as yours and wearing an identical shoe that would have trampled the sand around the accident debris."

Thora did not know if she should feel some satisfaction in knowing that she presented Bombino with a challenge. She was still feeling stunned. Everything that she had planned and hoped for had come to a crushing halt. She might as well have died in that plane crash for her future now felt as hopeless as if she had died in that accident.

"We're going to go back home where you will face your charges, young lady. And believe me, I have a book of charges written up on you," Bombino tapped a loose-leaf calendar that he kept in his back pocket. The calendar was fastened by a chain to his belt.

"I am home," Thora heard herself say to the policeman.

Bombino's eyes explored the contours of the closet. "Yes, you are, in a sense. You will see nothing but cells for the rest of your life. I am officially placing you under arrest," he said and he read her rights. The girl could see something sheepish in the way that he went through his spiel. She wondered if he had the authority to arrest her. This was a foreign country and the powers that were invested in him may not extend here. They may only be viable in the State of Pennsylvania, if even there. He might be limited only to the town of Grappling Haven.

"There's no need to handcuff you. You won't be going anywhere," Bombino grinned.

"Officer Bombino, can I ask you a question?" her voice came from her mouth. She felt detached from the sound of her vocal chords. She did not own them. She did not any longer own anything in the physical entity known as Thora Meadowford. She felt that the fate of the body that housed her spirit was no longer her concern. "How come you did not participate in trying to bring peace and order at Osprey Landing? How come you sat like a coward onboard this boat while your experience was desperately needed on shore? People were getting hurt and you did not even try to help them. You would rather bully a little girl than serve the public."

The policeman's face tightened. "I have no jurisdiction here," he said.

Thora smiled. "Exactly!"

"A smart ass, are we?" Bombino groaned. He must have realized that Thora caught him in the act of making a false arrest. "If you think that you are going to be able to avert justice on a few technicalities, you are mistaken, little girl. The Canadian Government is not going to grant you asylum. I have had lots of time to arrange all of this and make it perfectly legal. I have been invested with the power to make this arrest and to take you across the border where you will be tried on many charges."

Thora could not tell if he was making this up or if he had legitimately paved the way to make everything he did above board. Bombino had the reputation back in Grappling Haven for being a stickler for detail and following procedure precisely to the letter. It would have been in character for him to do so here but something did not ring quite true about the way that he was conducting himself. He held the face of a little boy trying to pull the wool over the eyes of wiser adults.

Captain Buck returned with a padlock in his hand. He handed it to Bombino. "It's rather dark in there," he said, eyeing the storage closet and carefully avoiding any contact with Thora. The girl had thought of the man as her friend and it was apparent that the Captain thought likewise. He was betraying this friendship and he knew it and that was why he could not bear to acknowledge her.

"It's dark but it will do. It will only be for a couple of hours," the Officer responded. "I have a feeling that the kid could stand some dark time to catch up on her sleep. She didn't get much this past week."

"Captain Buck, you are not going to let him lock me in here!" Thora cried out directly at the man. "It really smells here to all of the cleaning chemicals! They will make me sick!" The girl was not making this up. The stingy pungent aroma of chlorine had saturated everything inside of the closet.

"Perhaps I can find another spot where you can detain the child," Captain Buck said to Officer Bombino.

"No, this is just fine, Captain," Bombino answered. "Don't get taken in by her histrionics. This girl is the devil in disguise!" He started to place the padlock through the door's hinges, seeing if it would fit.

"I've known Miss Meadowford for most of her life, sir, and I would have to think that I differ on your assessment of the child's character," the Captain said. "She and her sister have always been a pleasure to escort over these waters."

"She's an adolescent now and not a child. Adolescence spoils many promising fruits. I should know. I'm a cop. We're always dealing with the smart-ass pranks of the teenagers of well to do families. They think that just because they have the money that that makes them above the law," Officer Bombino retorted. "This innocent girl that you have had the pleasure to escort over the waters has been involved robberies, car thefts, plane theft, assaults, manslaughter, attempted murder if not murder itself. There are a string of crimes that run all the way back to Grappling Haven that involve this sweet kid. I daresay that you will likely never see this girl again, Captain, lest you have a desire to travel to Pennsylvania and visit her in a penitentiary there."

"I didn't murder anybody!" Thora cried out to the Captain. "It was the ghosts and not me!"

"Ghosts?" the Captain lifted an eyebrow.

"Yes, the ghosts of my great grandfather and the old Dutch couple and…"

"I knew your great grandfather, Miss Meadowford. Sam and I were dear friends. I do not appreciate that you muddy his fine outstanding character by implicating him with murder." The Captain nodded to Bombino. The Officer began to close the doors. As he did so Thora heard the Captain ask the policeman, "Is it possible that the child is suffering from some form of mental disorder?"

"I've seen it before," Bombino admitted as the darkness began to envelope the supply closet. "I tell you though that it irks me when a criminal dodges justice by claiming insanity." His voice started to become muffled as the door was now shut. Whatever he added to his comment was lost in the tinkling sounds of hardware as the padlock was set into place.

Thora was now alone in the darkness. Her dream of sanctuary upon Black Island had been lost. She was doomed to a life behind bars.

Chapter 61

The Supply Closet

There was no way to measure time inside the dark cleaning supply closet. The only light that filtered in came around the door's elongated rectangular perimeter. There was so little coming through that it did not illuminate anything. The door may have shielded the light but it did not obscure the sounds from the other side. It was noisy out there with all of the passengers chattering away like nervous birds in the evening. Yet even though there was a lot of talking taking place Thora could not distinguish the words of any single conversation. All the talk came onto her at once like the cacophonous blare of an orchestra tuning up. Added to the continuous wafting of the chlorine into the air, she was feeling very miserable and thought that she might become sick. There was a small benefit to this nausea. It kept her mind away from her gloomy fate. Her world as Thora Meadowford had ended. She would not attend college and marry a rich man and bear many children. She was doomed to be a rotting hag locked away in a place where society did not have to look upon her craggy face.

The Madoqua Empress' engine provided a steady thrum that vibrated through the storage closet. It was at first unnoticeable but when it suddenly changed pitch Thora became very aware of it. The vessel was slowing down. She guessed that they were entering the McDougall Narrows. Once through this mile-long channel the steamer would speed up again as it comes upon the open waters of Upper Pioneer Lake. It was here that she had planned her daring getaway and swim to Black Island. That plan was not going to see its fruition. It had been forever dashed.

Suddenly Thora thought that she heard something. It was a scratching and it was coming from inside of the linen closet. Turning her head to locate the source of the sound, she pinned it near the top of the supply closet against the steamer's hull. It was probably a mouse. She hated mice. They scared her to no end. She clamped her arms around herself and started to sink to her knees in tears and despair.

The scratching continued. Its sound was too rich and strong to be created by a rodent. Something was out there on the other side of the hull. The girl decided to investigate. She stood up and tried to make out what was there in the darkness. She remembered that there was a series of shelves where some boxes were stacked. She lifted her arms upward and fumbled in the blackness until they caught hold of the rectangular shape of a box. She pulled on the box. As it slid off the shelf, light started to flood into the room. She could not believe it. There was a small window in this closet. It was just a tiny portal but the light that came through it was enough to light up the closet and allow Thora to see what she was doing.

On the other side of the window was her cousin Percy. He was clawing away at the portal trying to open it but he was not getting anywhere. She climbed up the shelves and waved to her cousin. He smiled and waved back. Studying the portal, Thora quickly saw that it opened and that there was enough space for her to crawl out. She could not believe her luck! Someone was smiling upon her and she guessed that it had to be her great grandfather.

At that moment, she heard the sound of someone clearing his throat. It was so near that it almost seemed like it was coming from inside of the cleaning closet. She froze on the spot. There was something about that sound that was very familiar to her. It had to be Officer Bombino. He was sitting or standing just outside of the closet, no doubt keeping guard over his prisoner.

At the same time Percy had intensified his efforts trying to open the window. His inept fumbling was producing loud noises that the policeman could hear. Thora motioned for her cousin to stop before he drew attention upon them. Percy, being a child, did not seem to understand her signals and began clawing all the more at the window.

Thora heard the sound of a chair grating against the wooden deck floor.

"I have to go in there," a young man said.

"What for?" Bombino responded in a manner that said to the young man that he was not going to get in there.

"Someone was sick on the second floor and puked all over the place. I have to get a mop and pail," the young man answered. The young man no doubt was a hand on the Madoqua Empress.

"Better you than me," Bombino groaned.

Thora knew what she had to do. She did not have time to try to get through the window. She had to quickly put the box back in place and make everything look like the way that it was when the door was last opened. As she slid the cardboard crate into spot, she once again tried to tell Percy to stop what he was doing. He was going to give it all away. The boy didn't understand. His little hands continued to scratch at the glass. It created a very tangible sound that was almost saying that the girl might as well give up hope. They would soon be at the spot on Pioneer Lake where she could swim to Black Island. She prayed that it would not take too long for the deckhand to get his mop and pail.

The closet door opened just as Thora seated herself on top of a flipped over wash bucket. "You stay still, kid. You are not getting out yet," Officer Bombino said as the light from the main deck of the steamer lighted up the storage room. "Get your supplies and don't say anything to the prisoner," the policeman barked to the deckhand.

The young man stepped into the doorway. Thora recognized him as one of the youths that she and Rebecca had marveled at. He was thin and muscular and looked like he had all the makings to be her hero. "Is she dangerous?" the youth asked the cop while he looked at her. His eyes did not show any sign that he might have seen her before. His eyes looked at her as if she were an object and that there was no person residing inside of her at all.

"She's a murderer! You're damned right, she is dangerous!" Bombino answered with a sarcastic laugh. "Now get your stuff and get out of here before she tries to escape!"

The youth grabbed a mop that was lying on the floor. It was the thin thing that had fallen on her when she had first scampered into this closet thinking that it would be a good hiding place.

The deckhand started to look around. His eyes fell onto the wash bucket that Thora sat upon. "Excuse me, miss. You are going to have to get off that pail. I need it," the youth said nervously to her. Thora did not move. In the background she could hear Percy scratching at the window. She needed to create a diversion. "She's sitting on my bucket!" the deckhand complained to Officer Bombino.

"Well get her to move!" Bombino said. "You're a big boy and she's just a girl!"

"You said that she is a killer, didn't you?" the youth answered. His eyes were wide with fright. There was perspiration forming on his forehead. It was plain that he was feeling very vulnerable at the moment.

"You take this pail from me and I will force you to eat it bolt by bolt!" the girl glowered at the youth. She was taking delight that she had such an effect on the deckhand. Some hero!

Suddenly a hand reached in through the door and brusquely grabbed her by the arm and yanked her to the floor. "Don't act sassy!" Bombino spat. "Get your bucket and get out of here!" he shouted at the deckhand. "And don't come back here with it full of puke or I'll make you lap all of it up like a kitten, you sissy!"

Officer Bombino was a tough man. He was a compact powerhouse that commanded respect from anyone that crossed his path. The deckhand scooped up the bucket by its handle. It clunked and clanged and made all manner of noise that effectively masked the scratching made by the tireless little ghost outside of the hull. The youth skedaddled away as fast as he could.

"Chickenshit!" Bombino smirked. "They don't make men the way that they used to!"

"And you call yourself a man! You are nothing but a bully!" Thora retorted to him. "I don't see what Myra Stanley sees in you!" She did not know why she mentioned that name. It just came out. The last thing that the girl wanted to do was to start up a conversation with the surly policeman. She needed that closet door shut as soon as possible. She needed to climb out of that window real soon or else her swim would be all the longer.

"Myra is a good woman. You hurt her bad when you took her family away from her," Bombino answered.

"You mean the ghosts?"

"I mean Jakob and Truus Nells, sweet people."

"You knew them?" Thora was astounded. She would have ever expected that big tough Lou Bombino would see ghosts.

"Of course I did! I spent many a night under the same roof with them!"

"You see ghosts?" Thora's mind was on her little cousin outside of the hull. If Officer Bombino were able to see ghosts then he would surely be able to see Percy.

"I don't call them ghosts. I call them spirits and Mr. and Mrs. Nells were nobles amongst their kind. They loved the little day trips that Myra and I used to take them on. Just going into Hawkins Corners or Grappling Haven to look at the shops gave them such enjoyment that they would talk the rest of the night about it. Myra really loved them and I had a great fondness for them as well. And then you came along and ruined everything!" His face contorted and his hands clenched around themselves squeezing each other so hard that his fingertips turned white.

"I never asked them to come along," Thora said. "They just suddenly were there with me, swearing that they would protect me."

"It would be just like Jakob and Truus to take pity on a wayward girl. Myra was heartbroken when she could not find them in her house any longer. I swore to her that I would find them for her. It is a vow that I still mean to keep." His penetrating eyes fell upon Thora's. "Where are they?"

"They're gone," she whispered. "They died trying to protect me."

"What do you mean, 'they died'?" Bombino asked. His neck muscles were strained and his mouth barely moved when he spoke. "They can't be dead. They already are dead."

"They moved on," Thora clarified. "They are no longer tied to the Earth. They fought the Indian spirit that has been chasing me and they were killed. Have you seen that Indian spirit?" The girl was starting to build up hope that maybe Officer Bombino could back up her story and that the courts would come to see that she played no role in all the crimes that took place along her path.

Tears started to form in Bombino's eyes. The man was human afterall. "Myra is going to be devastated. Those spirits were everything in the world to her. Now, they are gone thanks to you!" The anger rising in the man was visible and tangible. Thora sensed that he was going to swat her. She moved her head just in time to avoid a backhand strike across her face. "I'm going to do everything in my power to see that you are destroyed!" he seethed.

He slammed the door on her. He never said anything about the Great Indian Spirit but he had to have been aware of him. He saw ghosts. Thora knew that he would never admit to anybody else that he saw ghosts and that he could verify that she was not mad. The man was obviously hopelessly in love with Myra Stanley, someone else the community had labeled as insane.

Thora had no time to think about the love affair between the police officer and the author of ghost stories. She had to get moving. Climbing back up the shelves and removing the box, she saw her cousin still clawing away at the glass with the total commitment of a puppy digging a backyard hole. She took a moment to look past him to take a reading of where they were on the lake. In the background she could see the Upper Pioneer Lake entrance to the McDougall Narrows. They were now at their closest point that they would be to Black Island. She had to make her escape now. She studied the window to see what she had to do to get it opened. It was just a matter of lifting the latch on the left side and the latch on the right and then the window should lift.

She could not hear anything coming from the other side of the closet door. She did not know if Bombino was there or not. She prayed that the window would not creak as she lifted it. She flipped the latches and began to push upwards. The window moved silently. The lake air rushed into the room giving the girl some much needed fresh wind.

"This is it," she said to herself. It was all or nothing now. She hoisted herself upward and began to crawl through the gap of the open window. It was a snug fit but there was sufficient room for her to get through.

Percy had moved out of her way. He was clinging onto the hull of the steamer. What he was clinging on Thora could not tell. It was like he was a spider sitting on the wall. The hull's surface looked smooth and seamless to her.

"Are you going swimming?" the boy inquired with the enthusiasm of a real four-year old.

"I am!" Thora announced in total giddiness. Seeing the water fifteen feet below her being pushed aside by the steamer's massive hull did not intimidate her. Rather, it invited her. She was being asked to come into her element. She was being asked to go home.

At that moment the closet door once again opened behind her. She could not turn to see who it was. "What are you doing!" Bombino's voice boomed.

She could hear him charge into the cramped room. She started pulling herself further and further out. She was just about clear of the window.

There was a sudden jerk as the policeman grabbed onto her ankles and began tugging at it. He was strong, Officer Bombino. Thora started kicking. All of her body was clear of the window except for her ankles.

"You get back in here, you little vamp!" Bombino rasped.

"Percy, help me!" Thora cried to her little cousin. The tiny ghost sat staring at her, wondering what she was doing. By the sparkle in his eye he must have found it amusing to see Thora dangling out of the side of the boat with her feet kicking and her hands desperately trying to grab onto anything that would give her ballast.

Slowly, the police officer was winning the tug of war. Thora felt herself losing inches as more and more of her body was being hauled back inside of the closet. She never gave up on thrashing her feet. Bombino had her by the knees now and had a better grip on her. The strength of the pull against the girl increased dramatically. He would soon have her back in the boat.

"Let go of me!" she screamed repeatedly. Her head was growing dizzy from being upside down so long. She could see passengers on the upper deck looking down at her. They did not cheer for her. They did not cheer for the policeman. They just stared in awe at the peculiar scene of a girl hanging outside of the boat as if she were one of its rubber fenders. They all must have thought of her as entirely insane.

She stomped her foot and felt it land into Bombino's chest. The man was solid and did not even appear to feel any effect from the kick. There was no weakening in his efforts.

"Granny is coming!" she heard a wispy eerie voice utter just below her. Thora's eyes fell downward and she saw her grandmother's head pop out of the water. The old haggard form slinked out of the lake and crawled up the Madoqua Empress' sleek hull like some creepy long-limbed bog creature. She moved fast and soon she was on Thora. Out of the periphery of her vision Thora saw her grandmother slide through the open window. The ghost's body was occupying the same space as the girl.

A moment later Thora was suddenly plunging into the lake. Before she hit the water she heard a man screaming in agony. And then she was underwater and was descending rapidly. She felt an overpowering force take hold of her and begin dragging her against her will. She knew this to be the vacuum created by the huge steamer. She was being pulled underneath the boat. She would be heading directly to the vessel's enormous propellers. She started swimming as hard as she could but she was no match to the pride of the Madoqua Lakes.

She was deep down. Her eyes were closed and she knew she was heading for disaster. Her ears were stinging from the high-pitched hum from the spinning blades. She did not know how she was going to avoid them. Her death was imminent. She knew that with certainty. The pull on her body was increasing with each moment and there was nothing that she could do to overcome it.

"Daughter of the Usurper remember your promise."

CHAPTER 62

Invitation to the Dance

The voice was as deep and voluminous as the lake. It surrounded her from all sides—top, bottom, left and right. It came from outside of her and inside of her as well. It filled her and it emptied her.

She opened her eyes and beheld a sight that she knew instinctively was impossible. She was still underneath the dark shadowy form of the Madoqua Empress. She could see the vessel's slime-coated bottom only a matter of a few feet above her head. She saw its propellers not much further than that. Yet the propellers were not spinning. They were standing still. A wash of bubbles stood frozen inches away from them. The sound that the boat had been making was silent now. All was silent.

Time was standing still. It had been locked down at this moment, this moment that had to be one of her final moments of her life. Almost immediately, it occurred to her that she must have died, killed in those vicious propellers. But she could feel that her body was intact and that her spirit was still inside of that whole body. Body and soul had not separated. This had to be something different.

Any sense of urgency had dissipated in her. Any sense of wanting was gone as well. Her lungs required no renewal of air. What little was left in them was sufficient for now. The concept of now had taken on an eternal dimension. Somehow she had stepped out of time and entered a timeless dimension where she had all of the time in the world. Yet when she tried to move even a finger she found that she could not do so. Her muscles would not respond. They were locked in the petrified moment.

Something was coming at her from below. She could not move her eyes to see what it was. They, too, were frozen. All that she saw was at the shadowy edges of her periphery where form could not be articulated and defined. But something was there and approaching.

"Daughter of the Usurper, remember your promise," the deep sonorous voice said once more. It filled up everything as if it were the sole entity in all of creation. Even though the resonant timbres came from everywhere, Thora knew instinctively that the shadow at the edge of her vision was the voice's source. She struggled to refine the vague shape and make it something meaningful that her mind could comprehend but such mental tuning was beyond her in this moment of all time. But something inside of her did comprehend and did recognize the locus of the voice. It was the Great Indian Spirit and she was in his domain.

What promise had she given him? Did it have to do with her cousin Jack locked up inside of the structure on Black Island? He had asked her to free him. Or did he ask her to protect him? She could not distinctively recall. Either way she did not know if she were capable of doing so. She was just a helpless child only a moment away from her death, once time is set in motion once more.

The shadow did not come any closer. It remained in the offing, just beyond certain identification, just beyond understanding. Who was this Great Indian Spirit? What was his mission and why did she have to be involved?

"My name is Madoqua," the deep voice spoke as if it were cognizant of the thoughts being generated in her head. "I come from a time long ago and from a land that is no more. I lived in a village with my people, the Hendorun of old. I grew up with my brother Chemung in the house of our father, Blue Sky, the shaman to our people. Even as children, our father instilled in us a reverential respect for everything that Mother Earth bestowed upon us. We were not to take anything for granted. Everything had purpose and if that purpose was to be denied or remain unfulfilled then there would be disorder and the world would pay the price and follow a line that was not meant to be."

Thora could not help but feel that these words were accusatory and that they were directed at her family, that somehow they had thwarted the purposes of the Indians.

"Most of all our father Blue Sky taught us to revere the sacred places above all else," said the spirit Madoqua. "There are many sacred places from the Teaching Rocks to the high cliffs that stand overlooking the northern Mazinaw waters but the place that was most sacred of all were the islands on a lake called Jibatigon. These islands were forbidden to the living. Only spirits were permitted to walk through their forests or stand upon their rocks to communicate with the lake."

Thora wondered why he was telling her this. What did it have to do with her? But she was intrigued. She knew nothing of why the series of connected lakes of which Pioneer was one were named Madoqua. Was this Great Spirit the source of that name?

"So sacred was Jibatigon to our people that only the initiated were permitted to paddle upon its waters and even they, after undergoing intense cleansing and sacrificing, education and meditation, were still not allowed to leave their canoes and light foot upon the land that surrounded Jibatigon and especially not its islands. Our father, Blue Sky, gave my brother and I the holy opportunity to be pilgrims upon the lake, just as we attained our manhood. When our canoe came through the rapids and passed the turtle guard and we began to paddle the sacred waters I felt tremendous humbling and awe for the lands that outlined the edges of the lake. It was the land of spirits. It was the land of my great ancestors. I harkened my ear to see if I could hear them whistle to each other as they hunted the great-antlered stag that roam in the multitudes upon these lands.

"I was in ecstasy but not so my brother Chemung. He could see no difference between these lands and the lands where we were permitted to hunt. He said this unto our father and our father punished him thoroughly for holding such a view.

"Many years later when Chemung and I had attained our manhood, he had not learned his lesson. He was a father himself at this time and he wanted to take his son, Gray Ashes, to the sacred lands. Neither had prepared for such a pilgrimage. Neither had fasted or undergone any of the other purifying rituals that the living must undertake in order to enter Jibatigon. Tragedy soon befell the pair. The righteously angered spirits of the lake took my brother but miraculously his son, Gray Ashes, managed to survive and make it back to the ordinary lands.

"Gray Ashes had learned the lesson that his father never learned. He came to revere Jibatigon and deem it all of the respect that it required. In time he had a son of his own, Rautooskee, he was named."

When Thora heard the name of the son, she recalled that name from before. It was a name that had come to her in a dream. Things were starting to connect for the girl

"Now Rautooskee was an impetuous lad and shared many of the same traits as his grandfather, my brother Chemung. I had taken the child hunting with me on several occasions and witnessed that this boy had a mind of his own and that he would question rather than accept any of our customs. It was a characteristic that I feared would get him into trouble some day.

"My nephew Gray Ashes recognized this in his son yet he believed that with the proper discipline and education that he would be able to harness this streak in the boy and make a fine man out of him. As part of this conditioning, Gray Ashes decided that he would take Rautooskee to the sacred lands where the boy would witness such things that would tame his restless heart.

"It turned out to be a sad lament as the boy and his father never returned. Two months after their disappearance, the council of elders decided that enough time had passed since the pair had left to warrant the Dance of Petition for Gray Ashes and his son. Our people believed that nobody could enter the world of the spirits unless those that he or she leaves behind calls upon the ancestors and harkens them that newcomers are waiting at the lake's edge to step ashore. The Dance of Petition is a beseeching to the ancestors that exalts the deeds of the departed and tells the ancestors why the departed is worthy of joining the eternal tribe."

"What happens if the deceased is not worthy or no Dance of Petition is made by the people?" Thora expressed. She did not know if she had done so verbally or not.

Regardless, Madoqua heard her question and he addressed it. "These spirits wander the Earth until the people dance for them or they become the prey of the Dark Ones that take them away forever. No one knows of their fate for none have ever escaped to tell what happens."

"Has no one ever danced for you?" Thora asked.

The Great Indian Spirit did not answer this question. The girl was certain that he heard it for she heard it herself from her vulnerable and insignificant mind. "Once the council of elders determined that it was time to dance for Gray Ashes and Rautooskee a date for the ritual was set on the night of the next full moon. As the oldest living member of the bloodline of the departed, it was I that would lead the dance. I had to fast until the day of the dance. The only thing that I was permitted to consume was the smoke of burning tobacco and sweet grass. I was not allowed to talk with anyone. I had to shut myself away in my tent and make absolutions to the ancestors. For three weeks I made such abstaining and had grown weak in the body and powerful in my mind.

"On the night before the Dance, I had grown so weak that I could no longer tell if I were awake or in delirium. Upon this night, I had a visitor in my tent. It was the Rabbitman, the great trickster god Chendos. He came to me and warned me that no Dance of Petition should be made for the boy Rautooskee. The child was not dead. He was merely sleeping and that one day a stranger will wake him up and on that day the world would be set right. If a Dance of Petition were to be made for this boy, the ancestors would be angered and would close off the shores to the sacred lands and no one would ever be permitted access to these lands again. And more than that would happen, Chendos promised. He said that if there were a Dance for Rautooskee, newcomers would arrive in the territory of the Hendorun. These newcomers would overrun the people and make them a pale comparison to what they had once been. These newcomers would have no regard for what is sacred and that the very water and land of Jibatigon would become their playground and that the very land where Rautooskee sleeps would be usurped by them and that they would build a house of hatred overtop of the child's bed."

"That's Black Island, isn't it?" Thora said. She knew it in her heart that it was. She remembered how the local Indians were so fervently against her clan taking possession of this island. These Indians were not near as vocal about the other cottages erected on the lake as they were about the Meadowford property.

"I know not that name," Madoqua replied. "When the morning came of the Dance, I at once broke my fast and vow of silence. Being a member of the council of elders, I at once called for a convening of my fellow councilmen. I told them of my visitor and his message while I ate cob after cob of the new corn. They did not accept my story. They believed that I had conjured the tale up out of my known history of bad blood towards my brother, Chemung. When I was younger I fought successfully to prevent the people for dancing for my brother when his son returned with news of his death. I told them that Chemung was not worthy to enter the lands of the ancestors. He had shown disdain to the customs of our people and did not merit being among our honored dead. The council believed that I still held this prejudice against my brother's descendants and that was why I concocted this story to prevent Gray Ashes and Rautooskee to walk the sacred lands. They voted that the dance should go on and if I did not want to participate then the dancer would be my sister's son. He was the next oldest in line.

"On that night I left the village and never returned. I stayed long enough to watch my nephew invoke the dance. Being second in line he too had fasted and undergone the rituals of purification just in case something would have happened to me. When he invoked the names of Gray Ashes and Rautooskee, a dark cloud came over the moon. It had the shape of a pair of long ears. It was Chendos the Trickster. The skies opened up in a deluge and it rained for twelve days and nights. I knew that this rain was the tears of Chendos. He cried for the people had forsaken him. The lands were flooded and the people of my village were scattered. They would never conduct a Dance of Petition again.

"I spent the remainder of my natural days in solitude, traveling everywhere where the rivers would take me. I would not leave my canoe. I wanted to paddle on Chendos' Tears and be constantly reminded of the sorrow he felt at the betrayal of the people. Then years later when I was in my final night of life, the Lord Chendos visited me once more. He told me that after I passed through the gates of death that I would still be a wanderer and a voyager and that I would be so until I found the one that would initiate the Dance of Petition for not only me but for the newly arisen Rautooskee and Gray Ashes."

Madoqua stopped. In that pause, Thora instantly knew that she was the person that the Great Indian Spirit had been seeking. He wanted her to dance. He did not have to ask her. "But I do not know how to dance?" she said in her small voice.

"I do not need to teach you this dance. When the time comes you will know what to do."

"But how will I know when the time comes?" Thora implored. Her eyes struggled to try and see the form of Madoqua in the periphery. She wanted to see his face and read what it was saying to her. But her body was as frozen as all other things around her. She was locked in a moment of time and was powerless to break free.

"You will know the time for I will tell you."

"Why me?" Thora cried.

"You are of the blood of the Liberator, the one that will wake up Rautooskee and you have the gift of seeing. These traits make you the only one that can do this. You will live long enough for the day to come for I have tested your mettle and your heart is strong and you stand valiant against threat and persecution."

"I don't think that I will live past today," the girl said. "As soon as time starts again I will be ripped apart by that propeller."

"Allay your fears. You will live past today, I promise you."

"And what about you? Will you live past today?"

"I will continue to exist until the Dance of Petition is performed for me but you shall only see me one more time and that is when I tell you that you must start the dance. Until that day comes, I will not be a part of your life. You will come to forget me and you will not remember when time stood still for you."

"Then why are you telling me all of this if I am not going to remember a thing about it?"

"There will be a part of you that will remember but that part of you will never see the light of consciousness. It will always be embedded in dream and this dream will guide you through the rest of your days. It is time now for us to part our ways, Daughter of the Usurper. I have given you my message and you have given me your consent."

"Consent? Do you mean that I could have said no to this?"

"You did not refuse to listen to what I had to say. That is your consent. I will see you once again."

Something began moving in Thora's periphery. It was drawing back and receding into the murk.

"No, wait!" Thora cried out.

The shadow paused.

"Is this going to happen soon?"

"I do not know," the voice was more distant. "There are other requirements that must be fulfilled. These requirements do not involve you. Only when these requirements come to pass will things fall into order and you shall commence the dance."

"What are these requirements that you are talking about?"

"They are conditions that you need not know for you are powerless in either hastening them or preventing them."

"But if I am going to forget all of this then why can't you tell me?"

"A part of you will never forget even if it is in dream. It is better that you are not aware of these conditions so that those that tamper with you will not become privy to them."

"Tamper with me? What are you talking about?" Thora did not like the sound of that word 'tamper'?

"You will live past today Thora but you will wish that you had not. The days ahead of you are not going to be happy ones."

Even though her body could not move Thora felt a lump form in her throat. Hearing that she will never be happy again was a devastating blow. She almost wished that time would start again so that she could prevent the sad days ahead of her from happening by being ripped apart by the unforgiving propeller.

"I should have not told you this. I must depart now," Madoqua said. As he disappeared, a sudden current swept towards Thora. She could feel her body being washed away.

Chapter 63

Apotheosis

"Man overboard!"

She heard the cry of alarm as her head broke through the surface. She was right up next to the hull of the Madoqua Empress. She could feel the powerful wash of water being splayed by the steamer's slicing bow. It threatened to dash her upon the steel plating. She looked up and saw several distressed faces gawking down at her from the two decks above. Someone was throwing a life ring at her.

"Thora! Over here!"

It was Percy. He had cut through the surface several yards away from her. His bangs were pressed hard against his eyes. These eyes were filled with boyish élan and playfulness.

"Come on Thora! Let's go swimming!" The boy flipped over and soon all that was left of him were his kicking feet. These slipped under the surface and were gone.

The girl did not proceed to follow. She was disoriented. It felt like something had happened to her and that somehow she was gone from all of this. Now, she was suddenly thrust back into it without the wherewithal to understand the urgency that she needed to quickly act upon.

"Grab the ring!" several people from the boat cried down to her. They seemed desperate that she save herself. Already most of the Empress had gone past her. Soon it would be out of reach as it sped onward to its destination at Riverwood.

Percy resurfaced. "Aren't you coming?" he rang. "Come on Thora, let's swim! Home is just over there! Jacky is waiting for us!"

At the same time there was another splash not that far away from her. A moment later she saw a man thrashing his arms swimming towards her. It was Officer Bombino. He was coming to rescue her. He was coming to take her into custody.

She did not want to be apprehended by the man. Something told her that if he caught her again that she would never be happy for the rest of her life. She started to take in air, inflating herself so that she could endure a prolonged stay under water. As she did so she saw Officer Bombino suddenly be yanked below the surface as if a shark had taken hold of him. He came back up and he was in the middle of a very intense struggle with something that was trying to drown him. Thora saw long bony arms come out of the water. These were wrapping themselves around the policeman's neck and trying to draw him down once again. Thora did not have to guess who the arms belonged to. Her grandmother was on a murderous rampage.

"Come on Thora! Let's go!" Percy pleaded.

In the background Thora saw the Madoqua Empress slow and start to turn around. Captain Buck would not stop for those desperate swimmers back at Osprey Landing but he would do so for her.

She dipped under the water and began swimming as hard as she could. She would not open her eyes. She never grew accustomed to feeling lake water against her optical orbs. She only hoped that she was going in the right direction. She stroked with all of her strength through the water and kicked her feet up and down as fast as she could. When she could not hold her breath any longer, she came back up to the surface. As she did so, the first thing that her eyes fell upon was a distant turtle-shaped island with a lonely building resting on its top. It was Black Island! It was her home. Yet it was so far away. She did not know if she possessed the stamina to swim all of that distance. But seeing the family's estate upon Pioneer Lake once again revitalized her and gave her new strength. It was far away but it was in reach.

She heard splashing and thrashing behind her. She did not turn around to see what it was. The Madoqua Empress was heading back in her direction. She plunged under the water once again and swam with renewed vigor. Her breath held out much longer this time and she felt that she was making good distance. When finally she could not go any further without capturing any new air, she climbed back up to the top of the water. Black Island was once again the first thing that she saw. But much to her chagrin, it did not look to be any closer. It felt like she had gotten nowhere. This time she took a glance behind her. She saw the Madoqua Empress not twenty yards away from her. The vessel was stopped and somebody was pulling someone out of the lake.

"Come on Thora, do not give up! You can do it. You can swim to the island." It was her grandmother who spoke these words. She was not more than a dozen feet from her. There was something wild in her eyes, something that was very dangerous. The girl did not like the look of it.

"Come on cousin!" Percy laughed. "We are going to the cottage to let Jacky out so that he can go swimming too!"

"Is that all you want? To have Jacky swim?" She started to wonder what purpose these two malicious creatures possessed. They did not seem to be interested in saving Jack Thurston. They seemed to be more interested in getting a hold of him.

"Jacky has to become more like us. We need you to open the door so that we can get him into the water," Percy explained.

"What do you mean to become more like us?" Thora asked the little boy.

"Well, you know! He looks at us with scaredy-cat eyes when we stand outside of the window. It is like he thinks that we are monsters," Percy answered, wiping the hair from his face to expose bloodshot eyes that had been open underwater too long.

"Why would he be scared of you? You are his brother and she is his grandmother," the girl said, nodding towards the old hag that was treading nearby. "Have you done something to make him scared?"

"He saw Grandmother kill Grandfather, maybe that is what scared him," the boy replied as if such a statement was an ordinary thing to say.

Thora threw her head around to her grandmother, "You killed Grandfather?" she gasped.

The old woman smiled vaguely and did not answer. She was watching the steamer. The man that was being lifted onboard was wailing in agony.

"She had to," Percy answered for the old ghost. "Grandfather had told her that he did not want her in his life any more and that he was going to do what he could to get rid of her."

"And what could he have done?" Thora listened carefully despite her state of shock at what had happened to Sambo. It never made sense to her that Sambo would die of a heart attack when he was in such good physical shape. The stress that he experienced due to his quarreling offspring should not have been enough to trigger a coronary.

"He was going to get a clergyman to perform an exorcism on Black Island to dispel it of all of its ghosts," June Ritchie responded. "He was going to banish Percival and myself from not only the island but the lake itself. I could not let him do that." The old woman's eyes never left the Madoqua Empress.

"And why would he do that? I heard him talking to you lots of times. They were never threatening words that I heard. They were sweet, gentle words and I got the sense that they were healing words that comforted his lonely soul," Thora said.

"He did not like my plan that I had for Jack," the ghost said, finally turning to look at Thora. If the girl did not know better, she could have sworn that there were tears in her eyes. The drops that glided down June Ritchie's sunken cheeks were lake water dripping from the scraggy gray mop on her head.

"And what plan was that?" Thora was getting a very chilly feeling racing up her spine.

When Grandmother Meadowford did not immediately reply, her vocal grandson responded for her. "We want to have Jacky off of the island and with us all of the time. We don't want him to wake up the sleeping Indian boy."

"What sleeping Indian boy?" the girl asked. There was something strongly familiar about this but she could not pinpoint what it was.

"She doesn't need to know more," the old woman cut in on Percy's answer.

"I sense that you mean Jacky harm," Thora said. "And you need me to fetch him out of the cottage so that you can inflict this harm upon him." Her heart filled with anger. She saw in the horrid face of her grandmother that she hit upon the truth. "He is locked in that cottage for a purpose and that purpose is to be safe from you. I know Jacky very well. He has good senses. I'm not going to endanger him by letting you get inside to get at him."

She started swimming towards the Madoqua Empress. It was time to give up on her childhood and the silly dreams that it inspired. Going back to

Black Island was not going to suddenly make everything wonderful as if she were living in a fairy tale. Going back to Black Island would only place her dear cousin Jack in mortal danger. Going back to Black Island was not going to give her sanctuary. Officer Bombino, if he lived, would know that she was there and he would come and arrest her there. And if it were not Officer Bombino then it would be some other policeman. As her arms stroked through the still warm waters of Pioneer Lake she felt like she was finally waking up. She had done many wrongs while she dreamed. She did not know that she could rectify all of them but she knew that she intended to pay for them.

"You get back here right this minute!" June Ritchey hissed at her. "You are not going to walk out on me."

Thora ignored the threat and kept swimming. The steamer was sitting perhaps fifty feet from her. Through her stroking repetitions she saw a man watching her from the lower deck. She could see that he had a badly mangled arm that dangled unnaturally from his shoulder. This was an injury that he had sustained with his battle with June Ritchey. Officer Bombino had survived the attack. He truly was a tough man for Thora's grandmother was an extremely powerful assailant. The girl had seen her manhandle and slay grown men as if they were newly born kittens in her hands.

"I said get back here now Thora Meadowford!" the old ghost commanded.

The girl continued swimming, choosing to allow a deaf ear to keep her from complying with her grandmother's wishes. The girl questioned herself and she admonished herself. How could she have acted so delusional this past month? How could she allow herself to stray so much from the rational? She allowed her irrational self to rule her actions and look at the trouble this had caused. People had actually died because of her. She thought of all those airplane pilots over Lake Ontario. She thought of the man with the dog on the New York country road. These people were dead because she had allowed her silly notion of Black Island sanctuary sway her from acting responsibly. She thought of Bewdley Beacon. That man was misunderstood and paid the consequences. She did not want to be misunderstood. She wanted the world to know that she was not some displaced dizzy fairy princess living in a delusional world. She wanted to own up to who she was and become viewed as a worthy citizen even if it meant spending the rest of her natural days behind bars. That did not matter if she could somehow regain her dignity. She wanted Margaret Whattam to be proud of her and see in her a noble figure that made the world a little bit better just by her presence in it. She wanted Langley and Cora Meadowford, her parents, to realize that as dysfunctional as they were, they still had created a family and in that family everyone could draw strength from the others rather than just be dragged down by each other's foibles and misfortunes. But most of all she wanted her sister Rebecca to stand tall knowing that she had a sister that was every bit as solid a figure as she was and that she had a lifelong companion that she could confide in and achieve solace. She wanted to rid herself of ghosts once and for all and live amongst the living.

Something cold seized her foot and squeezing it tight pulled on it so hard that her head was dragged under the water. Downward she was dragged, deeper and deeper underneath Pioneer Lake until she was down so far that the sun could no longer penetrate the all-engulfing darkness. She was in a world of blackness, the only thing that she could see were the slightly luminescent bodies of her grandmother and her cousin as they hung suspended in the otherworldly atmosphere under the lake.

"You shall not be seeing the light of day ever again!" the old woman said. Her voice carried just as naturally in the medium of water as it did in the air. "If you don't want to help us get to Jack then you shall die and become one of us!" she threatened. Her hand was still clamped on Thora's foot and as much as the girl tried to break free from the hold she could not.

Percy must have seen the sheer terror in Thora's face. "Don't worry, Thora," he said. "It isn't that bad living here. You get to go swimming a lot and then when you get tired you get to go to the island and watch Jacky through the window. That is if Capers will let you!"

Capers, Thora had forgotten about the cat. She had treasured that pet and it had broken her heart that the family had actually left the poor animal to fend for himself on the island.

"Capers will not be standing guard that much longer," June Ritchey cackled. "His life energy will soon be spent and then he will become nothing but a rotting carcass under the shade of the trees. By then though, you should have spent your last breath."

That last breath was being spent rapidly. Her chest was starting to ache as it struggled to make the remaining bits of oxygen in her lungs try to sustain her life. If she did not get up to the surface real soon she would be dead. She thrashed her foot with all of the wildness that the panic of death could instill trying to shake off the ghost that held it. But her grandmother held on with evil tenacity. "You are not going anywhere," the old woman laughed insidiously. "Unless you agree to open the door for us so that we can fetch Jack."

But Thora would not agree. She clung to her stand. She would not endanger her cousin. She would die here rather than see that her dear Jack was harmed. She would become another Meadowford ghost doomed to walk the Earth before she would let her wicked kin take hold of him.

She felt her head growing light and wispy. Soon that last breath would be gone. Yet she remained defiant and would not give in to her grandmother. Her eyes spotted something coming out of the darkness above her. It was something furry. The long hair rippled up and down as the creature descended rapidly towards her. This distorted its shape and made it look unnatural and unidentifiable.

The creature moved fast like a striking predator. It targeted little Percy first. It opened its mouth to expose two rows of sharp teeth. Through this agape mouth a fierce hiss filled the water. Percy screamed in terror and began desperately swimming to get away from the attacker. The creature followed the little boy, turning its back so that Thora could see it from behind. She recognized the hair pattern at once. It was her Capers!

Grandmother Meadowford shrieked. "That fleabag is possessed!" she cried. She began racing away in mortal terror in the opposite direction that Percy and Capers went, leaving a bewildered Thora on her own, trying to understand where her cat had suddenly come from. Like all felines, Capers never liked the water. But here he was under it acting as if he were as accustomed to it as the fish that lived here. The only answer that she could arrive at was that what she saw was the ghost of her pet. Remembering that her grandmother had just said that Capers would be dead soon, Thora figured that the brave little animal must have died in the last few moments and that once his spirit was released from his emaciated body, he came to his master's rescue, chasing away the demons that haunted her.

But it was all too late, Thora realized. There was nothing left in her lungs and she was far below the surface. She was not even going to try to get up there. Pioneer Lake was about to claim another Meadowford. She prayed that fate would be merciful to her and prevent her from becoming a depraved wretched ghost like her grandmother and her cousin.

A shadow reappeared out of the murk. It was Capers. The cat took hold of the back of the girl's collar and began swimming upwards with the power of a team of horses. Thora barely realized what was happening. Her mind was at the edge of death and she was scanning onto the other side of life. She could not make out any clear images but what she saw did not frighten her. Instead it enticed her. There was an overwhelming aura of peace and contentment emanating from the other side. It was so intense that it made her heart yearn to enter it. She could still feel Capers working to save her life. She wanted the dear cat to give up and just allow her to enter the hereafter so that she did not have to continue into the miserable future that the world had in store for her. She would much rather enter eternity.

Someone was coming at her from the other side of life. It was not very long that she knew it to be Samuel Angus Meadowford the First. He walked up to her through a field with a pond that was very reminiscent of the setting where she had first laid eyes upon him. "I have made my peace," he said unto her. "I have done the job assigned to me and now I can rest. But you child, you still have work to do." He pointed to a lazy elm tree nearby. Underneath it was a sleeping Indian boy. "He has been asleep for a thousand years. When he awakes that is the time for you to get to work."

Thora looked at the little boy so still and at peace lying in the shade. There was something in her that made her know that she knew who he was. She even knew his name. How she knew any of this, she did not know.

"The days ahead of you are going to be hard, child, and it aches my heart that you have to go through with this but there is nothing that I can do for you any more," her great grandfather said. "My days of being your protector are over. You will not see me again until it is all over. Just know in your bosom that as bad as it gets, it will one day get better. Farewell, sweet child." He kissed her on her forehead and then he was gone. As he departed, Thora's glimpse into the hereafter faded.

Her head broke through of the surface of the lake. She could feel life giving air rush into her depleted lungs. Capers had done it. The cat had saved her. She wanted to embrace the little animal and hug it for all time but Capers was gone. There was not a trace of him anywhere to be seen.

But what she did see was someone swimming towards her. It was someone dressed in the uniform of the Madoqua Empress. It was the young man that was nervous around her when she was locked up in the cleaning supply closet. He was coming to rescue her. He was a hero afterall.

CHAPTER 64

Resignation and Retribution

The young man carried her up the rope ladder that hung over the side of the steamer. Thora could feel the strength in the arm that was wrapped around her waist. Her face was only inches away from his face. This was one of the fellows that she and Rebecca ogled on that last day when the family Meadowford was upon Black Island. She wanted to say thank you to him but she was at the point of exhaustion and could not find the energy to muster the words. She was satisfied to merely smile into his face. He kept his eyes averted from hers. There was something about the way that he went about this rescue that told her that it held about just as much meaning to him as having to clean up after a sick passenger. It was just another duty in the line of work that he chose.

When they climbed onto the crowded lower deck of the Madoqua Empress, one of the first people that Thora saw was Officer Bombino. His arm was in a makeshift tourniquet. He had been mauled by Grandmother Meadowford and sustained a dislocated shoulder and some nasty bite wounds in his arm. But he survived the attack. He had to count himself lucky. Not many live to tell about a vicious encounter with the mean old ghost.

Officer Bombino was grinning. "Good job," he said to the youth that had plucked Thora out of the water. "The people of Pennsylvania will thank you for what you have done here today."

The youth merely smirked and turned his attention to Captain Buck who was standing beside the American policeman. "I'll get back to what I was doing now," he said to his superior.

"Get out of those wet clothes, son, and then take a break. You've earned it," the Captain responded.

"Well, Miss Meadowford, we have apprehended you again," Officer Bombino said. "Make no mistake about it, this will be the last time that we will apprehend you. You will not be getting away ever again."

Thora did not say anything. She was too tired. She had been through so much of late that she had worn her body all the way down to the point that all that it wanted to do was collapse. Whether it got up afterwards, it did not matter at this point. She could not see past the moment.

The policeman stepped forward and with his one working hand placed handcuffs on her. "You're sopping wet!" he declared when her clothes brushed against his arm. "Can someone get this girl a towel!"

One of the hands attended to Bombino's request and soon Thora was wrapped in a thick Madoqua Empress towel. It felt so warm around her body. She did not realize how cold she was. The depths from where she came were just barely above freezing in temperature.

The policeman led her to the railing. Then leaning over it, he looked out over Pioneer Lake to the distant island on the opposite side of the body of water. "You really did not think that you could swim that far, did you?" he commented.

Thora kept quiet. As she looked across the lake and saw the hump of land climb out of the lake she realized that nothing could have been so far away as Black Island. Her eyes took in the complex of buildings that sat upon the crest of the isle. Those were the structures that were meant for all time to the people of her bloodline. Meadowfords had built them. Meadowfords knew every stone on that island and had at one time or another picked them up and held them in their hands with the assumption that they would be there as long as the stones were there. That assumption was proved wrong. Somehow she knew that it would be many years, if ever, before any living member of her family would ever set foot upon Black Island again. She could feel the yearning in her to run upon the island awaken once again. Even though the ghost of her cousin Jack dwelled inside those locked buildings and would be in mortal danger if ever those buildings were breeched, she still wanted to go there. It was almost like it was an instinct in her that she was powerless to overcome.

She placed a foot on the railing and started to scale up on it.

"You're not going anywhere," Officer Bombino declared, knocking her foot off the railing with his foot. "You just don't know when to say quit, do you?" he said. "You can forget about your little Shangri-La in the Canadian hinterland. This is the last time that you will ever see it."

The statement angered Thora. She butted her elbow against the man's tourniquet.

Bombino flinched from the pain and his eyes lit up with rage. But he overcame the emotion and summoned the Captain and whispered something to him. Captain Buck looked at the girl with concern in his eyes and then he nodded and went off somewhere.

Returning his attention to Thora, Officer Bombino said, "It doesn't look like much to me, if you ask me. It's just a bare rock with a few trees in the middle of nowhere. Where's the excitement there? If I were to get myself a getaway place it would be in the big city, New York, maybe, where all the action is. There doesn't look like there is anything to do on your island. I would be bored to tears there in the matter of an afternoon, especially if I were a teenager like you. No wonder you have grown so weird. You've spent your summers in isolation away from normal kids."

Thora did not know if the policeman was just taunting her or if he was genuinely expressing his opinion. It did not matter because his words were infuriating her. How dare he belittle her favorite place in the world and make it seem insignificant and unhealthy to the development of fine character. He was just an immigrant's son that held no appreciation for the nobler things in life. He did not have any breeding or refinement. He was a work a day lout that never dreamed in his life.

Captain Buck returned. In his hand he carried a small black leather bag that he handed over to Officer Bombino. As it was passed in front of Thora, she saw that the pouch had the insignia of the Grappling Haven Police Department on it.

Bombino thanked the Captain and said to Thora, "I have something in here that will keep you quiet. I prefer not to use it but I will if you give me reason."

The girl did not know what it could be but the leather bag conjured up ominous feelings in her.

"I would prefer that if you do resort to using it that you do so in a secluded spot. I don't want the other passengers to see it," Captain Buck frowned.

"Finding a secluded spot might be pretty hard to do Captain," Bombino laughed. "This boat is as crowded as a junk in China!"

"Still, try to humor me and take every precaution that you can," the Captain responded. "Now, if you will pardon me. I have business to attend to. Good day to you, Officer Bombino." The Captain nodded at Thora but did not say anything to her. She saw in his eyes that he felt sorry for her and that he knew something that she didn't.

When the Captain disappeared into the throng of passengers, Thora found herself saying, "He's a good man."

"He's all right, I guess," Bombino said. "He's lucky that the boat is filled with obedient Canadians. If this was anywhere else old Captain Buck might have had to contend with a riot. If I were him I would be demanding more order on this boat. I wouldn't be allowing people to mill about and go wherever they choose."

"And then you would probably have instilled that riot by your excessive demands, Officer Bombino," Thora responded.

One of the roaming passengers that irritated the policeman chose that moment to squeeze past them. He bumped into Thora causing her to lose her balance and fall into Bombino's injured arm. Bombino yelped and glared at the passenger with eyes exposing a mind that was all set to tear that bumbling cad apart.

"What happened to your arm?" the girl decided to ask. She wanted to see if the policeman would admit that an aberrant ghost hag did it or if he would create some other more socially acceptable excuse.

Bombino smiled for a moment. He knew what she was up to and he was not going to fall for it. "I got dragged into the propeller," he said, "when you tried to make your foolish escape."

"That's what you told the others but what really happened?" she said.

"You tell me what happened. You were in the water there with me!" Bombino was turning it around. He was not going to admit to seeing ghosts even though Thora knew full well that he was cognizant of what indeed happened to him.

"I know what I saw and you know what you saw and we both know that the boat's propellers had nothing to do with your injuries," Thora responded, successfully answering his question without revealing anything.

"What do you want me to say? That a ghost did this to me?" the policeman answered in a loud voice. Several passengers turned around to look at him.

"You know the truth," Thora said. "And you know that I am not responsible for anything that has happened since I left Grappling Haven. You have no reason to hold me in detention. You have wasted the taxpayers' money on this vacation of yours in Canada! I have committed no crimes. I might have acted stupid but I did not do anything that I should be locked away for!"

"You had better be careful what you say to me, girl," Bombino retorted. "Remember when I read you your rights. Part of it said that anything that you say can be and will be held against you. If you want to get off on an insanity plea you had better talk insanely rather than rationally."

"But you know the truth as well as I do. You know that Bewdley Beacon kidnapped me and that any of the crime that happened during that phase was done by him. He's the one that killed Mrs. Bianco and stole all the cars and the airplane."

"And what about Margaret Whattam? She never saw Beacon at the Bianco place. She only saw you and she can testify that you viciously assaulted her and left her for dead in that remote place."

"That's not the way it happened and you know it!" Thora cried. "The Bianco place was crawling with ghosts and demons and they were the ones responsible for what happened to Margaret and not me. Besides it was an accident. She fell onto the axe."

"If that is what happened then why did you run away and leave her there then?"

Thora took her breath to calm herself. She knew that these questions would be repeatedly asked of her from here on in. She had to find the composure to properly defend herself. "I ran because I was scared. Margaret didn't see the ghosts. She thought that I hurt her when I didn't. I knew that there was no way that I would make her see things differently."

"So you left her in the forest to die!"

"I already said that I did some stupid things. That was one of them,"

Thora admitted. "My world was falling apart. My sister had run away. My dad was being charged with murder. My mother everyday was becoming more an alcoholic. Margaret Whattam was the only friend that I could turn to and she turned her back on me. I did not know what to do."

"You should have called the police and let the courts decide if you hurt the woman or not," Bombino said.

Thora smirked. "The courts would never believe my story and you know that! I had to have time to sort things in my head and that is when I met up with Bewdley Beacon." She laughed. "We made a fool out of you that night on the road, didn't we?" She was recalling the incident on the road to Hawkins Corners where she and Bewdley stole Bombino's police car.

"Theft of an officer's car is a serious offense, young lady," the policeman answered. "From the way that you just talked it appears very clear to me that you were just as responsible in the commissioning of that offense as your partner."

"Beacon stole the car, not me! I just went along for the ride."

"Well, your ride has come to an end, girl. It is now time for you to pay for everything that you did!" Without any warning or indication that it was about to happen, Officer Bombino suddenly stomped very hard onto Thora's foot.

The girl screamed in pain.

"That's for leaving me in the middle of nowhere on a dark night! Nobody makes a fool out of me and gets away with it!" There was a sadistic glow in Bombino's demeanor. It appeared that he actually enjoyed inflicting pain upon his prisoners. It had relieved him of some of the pent up frustration that must have built up in him as he chased the girl across two states and one province.

Thora's yelp caught the attention of several nearby passengers. Their eyes were cast upon the policeman and her. There was something akin to fright and confusion in those assessing eyes. They quickly returned to their previous positions when Bombino barked, "What are you looking at?" at them. They were not going to get involved. They were not going to step in and intervene between a bullying cop and his victim.

When the passengers were facing in the other direction, Bombino once again stomped on the girl's foot. This time, however, he had placed his hand over her mouth so that it would mute her screams. "That's for all the trouble that you have caused me!" he whispered into her ear.

Thora bit into his hand and at the same time swung her elbows into his injured arm. The arm fell out of its tourniquet. Bombino let go of her to mend himself.

As he did so, Thora began to plead with the bystanders. "Please!" she cried. "I'm innocent of everything that they say that I did! Don't let this man hurt me!" She saw it as her only means to ensure that Bombino would act civilly and not as an overzealous brute. These passengers became very uncomfortable at her cries. They peeked at her out of the corners of their eyes but they would not openly turn their heads in her direction.

"What's the matter with all of you!" she demanded. "Can't you see that he is hurting me?"

The bystanders started to walk away from her and the policeman. They were not going to get involved. It was none of their business and they meant to keep it that way.

"You're not getting any sympathy from anybody," Bombino mocked. "You won't get it here and you definitely won't get it at your trial. Nobody loves a spoiled rich brat!" His arm was back in his sling. His other hand was digging into his black leather bag. "I've had just about all that I can take from you," he said.

When his hand came out of the bag, it held a vial of some clear liquid. "This is what I am looking for," he said, holding the vial close to his face so that he could read the tiny printing upon it.

"What is it?" Thora looked at the solution inside of the vial. Even though it had the semblance of water she knew that it was something that would have severe consequences upon her.

"Oh, it is just a little something I carry in the case of an emergency," the policeman smiled wickedly. His hand was once again hunting in his pouch. When it emerged, it held a syringe that was so large that it made Thora's eyes almost pop out of her head.

"What are you going to do that?" her lips mouthed although she knew full well what he was going to do.

Bombino opened the vial and dipped the needle into it. He pulled back on the syringe and all of the liquid was drawn into it. "I studied some pharmacology while I was at police college," the officer said. "I did pretty good at it. I got a C. I would have had an A except I could never quite get the prescribed dosages right. It's been something that I have been working on ever since. You can't be too careful with this stuff. A little too little and it would have no effect on the patient. A little too much and you won't have a patient any longer." He was eying the amount of liquid inside of the syringe. "I think that this is about right," he said.

Thora knew that his spiel was all for show and that he knew exactly what he was doing. Still the sight of the narcotic and the syringe made her head spin with fright. She was never any good at taking needles. Her parents would often have to pin her down at the doctor's office in order for the nurse to give her an inoculation.

Holding the needle upright Bombino managed to draw his prisoner in with his leg wrapped around hers. Once Thora was in range, he jabbed it into her arm. He could have missed the vein altogether and wasted his precious drug but today was Bombino's lucky day. The needle broke through the epidermis and through the wall of Thora's vein. It released its liquid in a gushing explosion that sent a vast quantity of the narcotic into the girl's bloodstream.

Almost at once Thora's senses and mind went very woozy. From her eyes, she saw a world that grew distorted. The outline of Bombino's face was becoming vague while the features upon that face were being washed away. From her ears, all the sound from the world outside of her mended into one blurry hum where not a single noise could be distinguished. She was losing it. She felt her sense of balance dissipate and the last thing that entered her mind was the realization that she was falling.

Chapter 65

The Unconscious Earth

Thora Meadowford had left the world. Thora Meadowford entered no new world. Thora Meadowford temporarily ceased to exist. She was in an oblivious state. There was no pinpoint in that state that housed all that Thora Meadowford ever was or ever would become. There was nothing to Thora Meadowford at all. She stepped beyond time and was as cognizant of herself and the things outside of herself as a stone upon a rocky beach. She had become part of the unconscious Earth and remained as comatose and inert as any bit of stationary flotsam that had washed up on a riverbank after a turbulent ride through the rapids. Like the flotsam she remained still and stalled. The seat in her consciousness was unoccupied and nothing and nobody sought to take it.

But then a slight change in the constitutional makeup of the flotsam came into existence and things were set in place for something to come and claim that seat of consciousness. Thora Meadowford would return to the world. Thora Meadowford would enter time. Thora Meadowford would be set upon the turbulent river again to run whatever that river would present to her. If Thora had the presence of mind to know what was in store for her she would have quickly relinquished that seat of consciousness and remained part of the unconscious Earth.

Chapter 66

Laura and Joe

She did not want to open her eyes. She had been awake for some time now and her ears were picking up a litany of unfamiliar sounds that were not congruent with the last things that she remembered. She wanted to drown out these recent memories for they were horrible to her. All that her mind's eye could see was that shining needle in Officer Bombino's hand. It hung there in isolation from all else around her. It almost held a voice of its own. This voice was telling her that it would be in control of not only her destiny but also everything else in her life. There would be no existence for her beyond the needle. The girl wanted to shunt this image from her mind but she was too afraid to open her eyes to obliterate it because of the sounds that she was hearing.

They were not threatening sounds. They were merely unfamiliar yet in that unfamiliarity they had taken on an ominous aura that told the girl that everything that had comprised her life before was now gone and that these unfamiliar sounds would soon become familiar sounds and the only sounds that she would know. They were the ambassadors for the new stages in her life and that they would occupy every nuance of her existence and that there was nothing that she could do to silence them and eradicate them. She was going to have to accept them and live with them and allow them to be the backdrop to her life from here on in.

They were domestic sounds albeit not the kind of domestic sounds to which she had grown accustomed. They were not the idle chatter and footfall and clinks and clanks of objects being moved here and there inside her Grappling Haven home or inside her Pioneer Lake house. These sounds were more institutionalized. They were the sounds of a host of health care workers setting about their duties. They were the sounds of the patients that permitted their lives to be dominated by these health care workers setting about their duties. Without opening her eyes, Thora knew exactly where she was. She was in a hospital somewhere.

The stiffness in her back and buttocks told her that she was lying in a supine position upon an uncomfortable mattress that refused to conform to her figure despite all of the time that she had lain here. Her wrists felt raw as if something had been gnawing at them for a long, long time. When she tried moving her arms she realized that she was restrained in this bed. Straps held her by the wrists. Soon she recognized that other straps held her by the knees as well. What kind of hospital was this? A mental hospital or was it not a hospital at all? Was it a jail?

Her ears started to pick up on the buzz of a nearby housefly. Before she knew it the filthy little insect had landed on her nose. Its tiny legs were tickling her and she tried swatting at it. But her hands were held back. All that she could do was rock her head to shoo the fly away. Its buzzing wings started anew and a moment later the creature was crawling on her forehead. Once again she shook her head to chase it away.

"I think that she is coming to," a woman's voice said.

"It's about time," a man answered. "The operation is scheduled to start in two hours. That might not be enough time to prep her."

Thora did not recognize either voice to match faces in her catalogue of people that had entered her life. Yet, despite this, these were voices that she realized that she had heard periodically in the periphery of her recent past; that lost past where she did not exist. They had to be employees of this institution and attended to her bedside now and then. As much as her curiosity wanted to see who they were, she kept her eyes closed. She did not want to enter this new phase of her life.

"You know it's a shame, Joe," the woman said. "She's so young. A girl her age should be having the time of her life at this age. But look at her, poor little thing. She's never going to have an existence that goes beyond this hospital."

"This one has already lived more of a life than you or I would ever have Laura," Joe answered. "I read her case record and let me tell you it is a doozey. This gal is a modern day Calamity Jane. Calamity followed her from her home time here in Pennsylvania all the way up to Canada. People died because of this little hellion. I don't feel sorry for her in the least."

"Her eyes aren't opening," Laura answered with some alarm. "Maybe the drugs have not worn out of her system yet."

"She's been drug free for four days now. All the built up medicine in her should be gone by now."

"But don't forget that she was administered high dosages of the psychotropic agent daily ever since August. What is it now? October 29th? That is a hell of a lot of medicine. It could take months for it to wear out of her system," the woman said. "If they ever wear out at all!"

"Don't worry Laura!" Joe tried to allay the woman's fears. "Whatever is left in her now would surely be insignificant and would not endanger her during the operation."

"It is not during the operation that is of worry Joe! It is the interaction of the psychotropic chemicals with the anesthetic. It has been shown clinically that this interaction could lead to coronary arrest."

"That was in patients over sixty years of age, for God's sake. This kid is young and strong. Her heart should be able to endure the interaction," Joe said with a degree of impatience. Then he added, "Besides if she does not survive the anesthesia it should be no loss. She's going to be nothing more than a vegetable after all of this is through anyway. Dying on the operating table might be a blessing for her."

Thora listened with detached interest to the conversation of the two hospital personnel. It was like they were talking about someone else and not her. Given what they said, she ascertained that she was indeed in a psychiatric hospital somewhere in Pennsylvania. There was no mental hospital in Grappling Haven. The nearest one was in Pittsburgh. Officer Bombino must have escorted her all the way back from Pioneer Lake and kept her unconscious with whatever drug that he had.

"Joe, that is a terrible thing to say!" Laura expressed.

"If I were her that is what I would want," Joe answered. "I would rather be dead than a zombie."

"But you don't know Joe, maybe in time they will find a way of curing her and then she could have a normal life. We don't want to rob her of this chance by sending her to the operating room too early and have her die of a heart attack there."

"How are they ever going to cure somebody who has a part of her brain removed? You can't fix something that is not there. She's having a radical lobotomy performed on her. The surgeon is going to cut away a large chunk of her brain. Once that chunk is gone she won't be prone to violent episodes any longer. Then afterwards coupled with electric shock therapy and chemotherapy, she might not be plagued by ghosts any longer. At least that is what they say. I don't believe it. We've got a whole ward of lobotomized patients. All of them are vegetables if you ask me. There's more than a lick of sense in that housefly crawling on that girl in bed there than there is in that entire ward."

Thora heard Laura sigh. "Sometimes I hate the line of work that we are in," Laura admitted. "Sometimes I think that I would have been better off as part of a secretarial pool."

"Don't knock what we are doing. If you were a secretary you might have lost your job today," Joe said.

"What do you mean?"

"You haven't heard the news this morning, did you? I don't know how you could have missed it. The stock market has crashed. People are throwing themselves out of windows all over Wall Street today. Massive fortunes have been lost overnight. It seems like the world is coming to an end, at least the financial world."

"I don't have a radio at home," Laura said. "Never saw the need for one. My family and I prefer to listen to our own conversations rather than what other people have to say."

"We like listening to the music and comedy shows," Joe said. "There is some very outstanding entertainment coming from the radio nowadays. Take for instance, Jim Spence. If it hadn't been for radio he would have still been some unknown hillbilly in the mountains of West Virginia. Now, he is a giant in the industry and he is blessing the world with his violin."

"We like making our own music," Laura replied.

"Then you are not coming of age," Joe grumbled. "So what are we going to do about the patient?"

"I don't think that she is ready yet," the woman responded. "Maybe we should advise that the operation gets postponed."

"They won't listen to us Laura. We're just attendants here. What do we know?"

Thora heard some rustling coming from inside her room. The attendants were up to something. It did not augur well with the girl. She instinctively felt that something unpleasant was about to happen.

"I think that I will shave her anyway," Joe said. "The doctors would get miffed if we did not have her ready on time."

"She's got such beautiful hair. It's such a shame!" Laura sighed.

"Well, if you want we could keep the hair and make you a wig out of it!" Joe quipped.

"I don't think that that is very funny. The hair belongs on her head and not mine."

"Just hold her down and see that she does not move," the man said coldly as an electric buzzing started to hum within the room.

Thora felt a pair of small cool hands take hold of her neck and cheeks and lift her head upright. The feeling annoyed her and she thrashed, knocking the woman's hands from her.

"See, I told you she was coming around," Joe said. "Now, hold her tight."

Laura's hands were once again affixed to Thora's head. Thora heard the shaver come close and then start chewing into her scalp. She yelped in pain and started to put up a fight.

"Not so close Joe! You might have cut her!" Laura complained and then whispered to Thora, "That's all right, honey. Everything is going to be okay." The woman's fingers were gently holding Thora's neck upright.

The girl's neck muscles tightened as she experienced the icy mechanical device mow row upon row along her scalp. Falling hair dropped onto her shoulders and lap. The top of her head grew chilly where the shaver had removed her once full locks. Outside of flinching several times from physical discomfort, Thora still maintained a detached sentiment to what was happening to her. She could no longer conceive that any of this was happening to her.

When the shaver had cut the last of her hair, Thora sensed Laura going about the business of wiping away all the ticklish hair that had fell. She could hear a running faucet in the background.

Several moments later Joe was next to her bed again. "Now for the finishing touches," he said. "Darling, I am going to give you a shave that will be so close that people from all around are going to come up to you just to rub your smooth scalp!"

Something wet and foamy started to layer the girl's head. She could not keep her eyes closed any longer. She had to see what was happening to her. When they opened, they could not distinguish much. The light in the room was hard upon them and forced them to clamp shut once again. A moment later she felt something dangerously sharp scrape along the contours of her skull.

"As smooth as a baby's bottom," she heard Joe whisper as he took a straight razor to her head. He said it in a soothing manner that made the entire procedure rather soothing to the girl. She allowed herself to relax and wallow in the therapeutic massage. The razor slid over her cranium, gently cutting away whatever remaining stubble there was left after the man had mowed down her hair.

When it was done, she felt the body of Laura rub against her. The woman was applying a towel to dry her now baldpate.

"As smooth as an eight ball," Joe commented. "The surgeon will have no difficulty finding the place where he has to cut."

The word 'cut' sent alarm into the girl. What did Joe mean by that word? Slowly, Thora was returning to the world. She was not an anonymous watcher from a distance any longer. She was starting to realize that she was a player in what was taking place, a vital player. In fact all of this centered on her. They had shaved her hair from her head. Why? It did not make any sense.

She once again opened her eyes. This time they were prepared for the onslaught of bright light and they were able to penetrate through it to take a glimpse of her surroundings. She was in a hospital room. The walls were wainscoted. The top half was a bland cream color while the bottom half was painted lime green. There was a window in the room that just looked out onto the sky. In the distance there were some apartment buildings. Thora took this information as an affirmation that she was on a higher-level floor of a psychiatric institution in Pittsburgh.

She saw a male and female, both clad in white uniforms, going about their business. Joe and Laura were relatively young. They could be no more than in their twenties. Neither seemed aware that their patient was now watching them.

"I wonder if Dr. Strayne will still do the operation?" Joe said.

"Of course, he will. He is the only one here that is qualified to do a lobotomy," Laura answered, as she was emptying Thora's hair into a garbage can. She was not going to keep it for a wig afterall. "What makes you wonder?"

"I've heard that Dr. Strayne likes to play the stock market and that he has thousands of dollars tied into it."

"Yes, so?"

"The stock market crashed Laura!" Joe raised his voice. He was standing over the sink cleaning the straight razor. "Dr. Strayne could have lost every penny of his investment. If that happened he would be in no condition to perform such a delicate operation. I know that I would not be able to concentrate if I lost all of my money."

"Dr. Strayne is a sensible man. He would not let the loss of a few dollars affect his job," Laura answered as if it would be only a minor setback to the surgeon.

Thora's eyes continued to wander the contours of her hospital room. She saw the leather straps wrapped around her legs. They were restraining her for some reason. Then she saw a mirror hanging on the wall. If she lifted her head high enough she should be able to see her reflection in it. She began squirming in her bed trying to lift herself high enough to have a look. When she finally managed to prop herself up, the mirror presented to her a terrible image of a bald, emaciated visage that did not look anything like herself. Her cheeks had sunken into her mouth. Her eyes were dark and protruding. The freshly shaved scalp made her appear ghoulish. The image in the mirror could not be her, she thought. It could not be her. Yet, she knew that it had to be her. What happened to her? How did the once pretty Thora Meadowford descend into such an abomination of herself? How did she become a frail, living skeleton? She realized that she did not look after herself very well on her journey into Canada. She hardly ate. She rarely slept. It all had taken a toll upon her and had reshaped her into that pathetic thing that she saw in the mirror. She started to cry and saw the tears slip down the cheeks of the vile creature in the mirror.

"She's awake!" Laura said out loud. She ran up to Thora and put her arms around her head while Joe took the girl by the legs and pulled her back into her bed.

"Let go of me!" Thora cried out. She wanted to grab Laura and jerk her away from her but she could not do so because of the restraining straps on her wrists.

"There, there, my child!" Laura said softly. "Everything is okay. You just need some rest."

"I want to see my mommy!" Thora blurted. "I want to see my mom!" She did not know why she said it. She knew in her deepest levels that her mother would be the last place that she would ever find solace.

"Your mother is just outside of the door. If you want I can call her in," Laura answered as she stroked her hand over Thora's bald scalp.

"My mom is outside of the door?" Thora said through her sobs and her dismay. She could not believe that her mother would actually be here for her.

"Your dad is too," Laura added. "Shall I let them in?"

Almost immediately Thora's instincts were to say no. They said that she was going to be very hurt by what would happen if she were to see her mother and her father. Yet despite this, the girl agreed to allow them in.

"I'll go get them," Laura said.

Chapter 67

When Birds Do Not Migrate

As the door opened, Thora could hear her parents whispering to each other as if they were doing some last second rehearsals of what they were going to say to their daughter. It had been months since the last time that she saw them. She wondered how her father had fared in his murder trial. Was that nightmare over or was it still being dragged out? Was her mother still a victim to the bottle? How were they going to react when they see the grotesque monstrosity on the bed that was posing as their flesh and blood?

And then they stepped into view. Her mother seemed like she put on weight. All that soda mix she added to her drinks was taking a toll on her. Her father looked heavier as well but he still managed to look good whereas her mother's appearance had vastly deteriorated. There was a grimace on Langley's face when he beheld the freak on the bed. Her father was never any good at cloaking his feelings and bestowing an atmosphere of dignity even if it were false dignity upon those he believed undignified. Cora, for her part, looked askance and would not directly place her eyes on her daughter although Thora knew full well that her mother was hawking her out of her periphery. The girl sensed that her mother was equally as appalled as her father at the sight of her.

Despite this, Thora decided to be brave and said cheerfully to the both of them, "Mom! Dad! It is so good to see you."

The utterance of those words had such a cathartic effect upon the girl that she could feel her eyes well up with tears as if she were greeting parents that were actually loving and not these two wretched loveless characters that possessed such a paucity of genuine affection that the girl might as well have given her fealty and devotion to whomever passed by in the open doorway behind them.

"It is good to see you too Thora," Cora said as she stepped towards the window and looked out. The woman still had not set direct eyes on her daughter.

"Can you see our car parked down there?" Langley said to his wife. "I don't want anybody mucking around with it." He too went to the window to take a glimpse.

"Who's going to muck around with the Motorized Egg?" Thora asked. "That car is falling apart!" She chuckled uncomfortably. Her parents were here visiting her but they were ignoring her and would not engage in any meaningful conversation.

"We don't have that jalopy any more," Langley said. "We got rid of it and bought ourselves a Bentley just like the one that Uncle Thaddeus has."

"Really?" Thora said with a degree of enthusiasm. "Things are going well for the family now?"

She heard her mother groan. "Things are going well for the banks," she said. "They are liable to lend money to any old fool that comes asking."

Langley smacked his lips at the comment. His skin reddened a few degrees. But he chose not to respond. "Pittsburgh, Pennsylvania," he said as he looked out over the city. "I never liked it here. There's no refinement or elegance to this city. There's nothing to entertain the educated mind."

"So this is Pittsburgh," Thora said. "I thought it was but was not entirely sure." Maybe by getting involved in a petty conversation with her parents it could evolve into something meaningful and something that would give her the support that she so desperately needed. She was about to have an operation that would radically change her life. She needed to know that this was all for the best and that when she comes out of it she would have something there to come out to. She was going to have a lobotomy. She did not know what the word meant and what it entailed. It had a frightening ring to it and she desperately needed someone's hand to hold. She hoped that this hand would belong to one of her parents.

"They don't have loony bins back home," Langley answered curtly, displaying his ineptitude at being compassionate and understanding. "If they did, you can be sure that you would be there rather than here. Thank God, we ran into that inheritance or we would not be able to afford any of this."

"I thought that you did not get that much from Grandfather's estate?" Thora stated.

"This is not Grandfather's inheritance, dear," Cora said. "This is from Uncle Thaddeus. We received a quarter of a million dollars from him."

"Most of which I have tied into the stock market," Langley boasted. "I want to convert that quarter million into a full million and then put it all into the company. I got all of Thaddeus' shares as well."

"Step back a pace," Thora said with dismay. "You said that you got the money from Uncle Thaddeus? When did he die?"

"That's right, you would not know," Cora said. "You weren't home when that happened."

"You were gallivanting across the country on your trek into insanity when Uncle Thaddeus' heart gave out and he died in the courthouse while he was making his testimony during my case," her father said. "Thank God that he did. He was damning me up there in the witness stand but in the end he was the one that got the damnation."

It was just like her father to find no pity for a man that had helped him financially all of those years. He had not changed at all since she had disappeared. He was still the same old greedy self-centered character that possessed all the trite traits of a parasite.

"He got the damnation and you got his money," Thora found herself smirking. Uncle Thaddeus was dead. Even though the man was not much higher on the evolutionary scale than her boorish father, the man still deserved to have some dignity bestowed upon him. Thaddeus received in death what he reaped in life. He led a loveless life and now he had a loveless death. His wife and children deserted him. All that he truly had in life after his marriage broke apart was Dearborn Cable and even that company was not there for him as his existence waned. It withered along with him. He died a morally bereft man and his legacy afterwards would be a depiction of a miserly old codger fit for playing the bad guy in children's literature. Thora's heart went out to Uncle Thaddeus. She remembered that night that she spent at his house and when he visited her room and for the first time had revealed to her that there was something more to him than just a cold, analytical disposition.

"Yes, if Grappling Haven had a mental institution, you can be sure that we would have you in there," Langley said as he walked away from the window and seated himself in a chair. He looked up at his daughter in bed for a moment. His face puckered up in an expression of disgust. "What the hell did you do to yourself, little girl? You sure don't look like the daughter that I had!"

"They cut off my hair for the operation," Thora responded. She could sense the condemnation in his gaze. He was divorcing himself from her. She could feel it and she intuited that it was going to be forever. "Why am I having this operation? This lobotomy?" she asked her parents.

"You are having it for your own good, my dear," Cora answered. She was sitting at the foot of her daughter's bed. "You proved that you were too dangerous for yourself and society at large during your adventure."

"The State wanted to try you in adult criminal court," Langley added. "If the DA got his way you would have received the death sentence."

"If it had not been for James Whattam I think that that the DA would have gotten his way," Thora's mother said. "Despite the bad feelings between him and your father, I think that we could all be thankful that Mr. Whattam managed to convince the judge that you were not mentally able to stand trial and that it was much better for you that you be placed in psychiatric care for the rest of your life."

Thora could feel herself crumble as her mother spoke. It dawned on her that she was never going to get out of here. They have determined that she was crazy. No one saw things the way that she saw them. She thought of Officer Bombino. That policeman knew the ghosts exist and that they and Bewdley Beacon were responsible for any crime that took place during her flight to Pioneer Lake. Bombino obviously did not say anything. He allowed her to go down. He allowed her to go down without her even being aware of any of it. "How come I don't remember any of this?" she asked her mother.

"They kept you heavily sedated my dear," Cora said. "Your hallucinations had taken over every aspect of your life and as long as these visions governed you you were too dangerous to yourself and others. The medication saved your life, if you ask me."

"They might have saved her life but they have been steadily eating away at my savings," Langley sniped from his chair. "Do you know how expensive it is to keep you from killing yourself?"

"This operation will mean that we would no longer have to worry about that cost," Cora said. "Once the procedure is completed you will no longer represent a danger to anybody."

"So you are having a part of my brain sliced away just so that you can save a few dollars!" Thora cried out. It was just like her parents to act so ruthlessly.

"Don't you say such a thing!" Cora suddenly rasped. "If it were a matter of money we could have let you stand trial and go to the electric chair! We are still going to incur a prohibitively large medical expense by keeping you in institutions after the operation. None of this comes for free Thora dear." Her hands gestured to show the room that she was in. "You have a private room. You are not in a ward with all of the other mental cases. Don't you ever imply that your father and I have not provided for you. You've had the finest upbringing any child could ever have had! But something went wrong. It wasn't our fault and it might not even be your fault. But something did go wrong and this is what fate doled out to you. We've got to accept it and make the best of it."

"Besides, it was not our decision to give you the operation," her father said. "It was the decision of the hearing that you were to have it and since it was their choice they are the ones that are going to pay for the procedure."

"I had a hearing? Who spoke in my defense?" Thora peeped. She felt very small in a world that was conspiring against her. She was being brushed under the rug and being left for forgotten. "How come I could not have stated my case? I'm not crazy! I'm not dangerous!"

"You couldn't speak because you were incapacitated by the medication. Believe me dear, this is all for your own good!" Her mother patted her feet. Not once did she even show any trace of guilt in not defending her child. Mothers in the natural world have a strong reputation of being very fierce in defending their young. A mother bear would fight male bears twice her size to keep them away from her brood. Cora Meadowford was no mother bear. Cora Meadowford showed no maternal instincts. She kowtowed to expediency and always chose the easiest path and there was no path easier than the one to her liquor decanter.

"I think that if you were allowed to speak at your hearing things would have gone even worse for you," Langley added. "Once you start talking about ghosts, they would have immediately earmarked you for committal to the mental hospital."

"But that is what I got in the end anyway, isn't it?" Thora said, staring at the buffoon in this room that had the audacity to think that he was a caring father. Langley Meadowford was a charlatan and a disgrace to his father and grandfather. How did they go so wrong in shaping the character of this newest heir to the Meadowford dynasty? It might have been the only flaw in their reputation.

"Girl, soon it will all be over with and you won't have to worry about any of this," Langley answered. "The only thing that you will care about is if supper will be served on time."

"You are going to have a carefree existence, my child! Never will you have to concern yourself with anything ever again, even supper. I am told that in these places that all the meals go down like clockwork and that they will never be late," Cora added to her husband's comment. "I envy you that, little Thora. Even though things are going better for your father and I, we still have to constantly live with the trials and tribulations that everyday life presents. Even though most of these are rather insignificant in the bigger scheme of things they do add up and take a toll on a person's nerves."

Her parents were trying to rationalize what they were permitting to happen to their daughter. It was the feeblest of silver linings to a cloud that Thora had ever heard. But what made it painful to her was that they did not feel saddened about what was going to happen her. They almost seemed like they were anxious to have it all over and done with so that they could go on with their lives and forget the vegetable in the psychiatric hospital that at one time was their daughter. "If getting a lobotomy is all that good then why don't the two of you get one too!" she said to them.

"Now, now Thora! There is no reason to get hostile at us!" Langley retorted. "We're not the ones that are a menace to society. We are good citizens and upstanding members of the community."

"Some fine upstanding members of the community you are!" Thora blasted. "You are a murderer. I know it. Bewdley Beacon told me what you said to him in jail. I don't know how you finagled yourself out of the electric chair. You fooled the courts but you don't fool me. You killed those people on that road. And as for you," Thora turned to her mother. "The only thing that you care about is that precious bottle of yours. As long as the march of bottles remains unbroken, you will always turn a blind eye on the deeds of your undisciplined husband. Tell me Dad, do I have a new brother or sister yet?" She was referring to her father's affair with Lena Taylor, the eighteen year-old maid that Langley kept in New Hampshire. The last that she heard Lena was pregnant with Langley's child.

"Miss Taylor had the baby and regretfully gave her up to the adoption agency up there in New England," Cora answered. The woman had remained remarkably stoic after her daughter's tirade. Any other woman would have thrown a philandering husband out of the door but not Cora. She accepted his adventures outside of their marriage. The woman was too weak to stand up to her husband. Was it because she feared losing out on the family fortune or was she satisfied that as long as she was kept in alcohol and was not rebuked for this habit that anything that Langley did was all right by her? Thora did not know. Nor did she care. Going into the oblivion of her post-operation world did have a silver lining. It would rid her once and for all of this pair of socially maladroit cretins. She would much rather deal with the foggy unknown than be focused upon the latest misadventures of Mr. and Mrs. Langley Meadowford. In a way as well Thora was glad for her new stepsister. That child will never have to know what a buffoon her natural born father was. The little baby might have a chance to grow up normal and not have to hide her head in shame whenever Cora or Langley did something embarrassing in public.

"That's a good thing," Thora said. "At least the baby will not have to run away later in life."

"That is a closed topic in our house, girl," Langley said. "It is over and done with and I do not want to ever broach that subject again." He spoke as an authoritarian as if his words and wishes were to be respected. Thora just did not want to give that man such a courtesy. Respect has to be earned. If Langley ever earned any, he had long ago squandered it.

"More rules, eh Dad?" Thora sighed. "You are such a wise man and you know what is best for all of us." Her tongue burned with the sarcasm. "Do you think that you will ever have a child that will actually love you?"

Langley's face dropped momentarily at the acidic comment. His eyes seemed hurt but only for a moment. "It doesn't matter if they love me or not," he said. "Because what is important is that I love them and I will do whatever it takes to make sure that they are looked after and don't have to struggle in life."

"Doing what it takes? Does that include placing them in a loony bin as you called it for the rest of their lives?" Thora spat. "I don't believe for a second that either of you truly love me or Rebecca. You don't even care for each other. You live separate lives under the same roof. You each have a thing that you prize. You, the bottle," Thora said to her mother. "And you, your greed," she eyed her father. "Rebecca and I never were in the running. You didn't try to find Becky when she left. You didn't try to find me. If it hadn't been for Officer Bombino, I would have been long ago forgotten."

"Now, you hold your horses young lady!" Langley burst in. "Where do you get off saying such things? Would your mother and I be here today if we did not care? We could have let the doctor go on with the operation that will turn you in a vegetable without being here. But we wanted to be here to say goodbye to you." There were actually tears in the man's eyes that Thora could not quite understand.

"Your father is right dear!" Cora said. Her eyes were tearless but there was lament clearly expressed in her face. "We did not have to be here. We chose to be here to be with you one last time. Don't you think for a minute that we are nothing but horrible wicked ogres out of a fairy tale with the sole purpose to make the lives of our daughters miserable! We genuinely do care and love you and Rebecca and even the newborn that we will never know! We might not be saints but we are real people with real troubles and we do what we can to make life good for not only us but our children as well!"

"When we learned that you were missing we were beside ourselves with worry and fret," Langley said. "But our hands were tied. I could not go out after you because of the conditions of my bail. And your mother, she can't drive so she was forced to stay at home."

"When we learned that you were found, we were greatly relieved," Cora added. "But then we learned that you suffered with what the doctors call dementia praecox or schizophrenia as we call it, we did everything that we could to find something that could help you overcome this condition. Sadly, the only current treatments are rather harsh."

"Electric shock therapy, hydrotherapy, chemotherapy and lobotomy," Langley recited the treatments. "They are all very intrusive and are not the easiest things in the world to withstand but we are told that sometimes they do work and help rid the patient of their demons. We want to get rid of your ghosts, Thora. We want you to live as comfortable a life as possible."

Thora listened to her parents finally open up to her and show their human sides. She always instinctively knew that these sides were present in them but when they scarcely reveal themselves it was understandable for her to slip into believing that they were the wicked parents of fairy tales. They were very hurting individuals, her parents. It must have been hard for them to deal with children that went out on the lam and children that rarely showed any appreciation for the things that they did for them. Yet, she still had to wonder if they were doing everything that they could for her. Langley had said that after the operation the girl would be nothing more than a vegetable. Vegetables don't have personalities. Without a personality, all those characteristics that when joined together comprise Thora Meadowford would be gone. In essence, even though her body would go on and live, she, herself, would die today on the operating table. She started to get very very scared.

"This is really it for me, isn't it?" she said to her parents. She felt new tears pouring down her face. "After today, I will never be back!"

She saw her father swallow a lump in his throat. That told her that what she said was true. He was openly and unashamedly crying. "Thora," he said through a choked voice. "I want you to know that your mother and I love you and will always love you. We will be here for you for the rest of our days."

Thora felt her mother's hand take hers. "This is the worst day in my life, my child," the woman said. Her eyes were glistening through a coating of tears. "I would give anything to have things differently. There is nothing more that I want than to have you and Rebecca home with us. But it can't be that way!" she sobbed.

"Why?" Thora cried out. "Why can't it be that way?"

"Because the law has ordered that this operation takes place and the doctors have stated that it would be well beyond the capacity of your mother and I to provide you with the proper home care after all is said and done," Langley said.

"Caring for a lobotomized patient requires the services of a full time fully trained professional around the clock," Cora said, her hand still holding Thora's. "We can't afford such home care. It is better for you to be in an institution."

"But don't worry Thora, you won't spend out the rest of your life in this sad place," Langley said. "I've been studying the brochures of several reputable hospitals and I do believe that your mother and I have decided that as soon as it is safe to do so we are going to have you transferred to a facility in Colorado."

"Colorado? That is way out west!" Thora exclaimed. In the back of her mind she recalled what a voice had said to her through her grandfather's coffin. 'If birds do not migrate north and south then you shall nest in the west.' The prophecy was going to come true. Birds migrate north and south through instinct. After the lobotomy, she would no longer have any instincts. And she would spend the rest of her days out west.

"It's not that far away Thora. We could be there in the space of a couple of days by train or automobile," Langley said. "The institution that I have in mind is up in the mountains. You will be treated every day to spectacular scenery and clean air. Who knows nature might find a cure for you that humans just can't provide."

"We promise to be there as often as we can!" Cora added. "You won't be alone!"

Even though Thora sensed the earnestness in her parents' pledges, she knew that the reality would be that she would be forgotten in her Rocky Mountain asylum. Cora and Langley would never have the time available to them to make the visits. Life would just keep on getting in the way.

At that moment, the two hospital aides, Joe and Laura peeked through the door. "I'm afraid that time is up," Joe said. "The anesthesiologist is ready for the patient."

A surge of sudden fright flooded Thora's veins. This was it. Her time had come. She saw the eyes of her parents' grow wide and frightened. Her mother's hand began trembling erratically as it tried to grip her hand tighter. Her parents seemed as helpless and inept to stop the inevitable as she felt. This was her last moment with them. After this moment was gone she would not know them again. There was so much that she wanted to say to them. She no longer wanted to condemn them for what they had done to her. She just wanted them to know that despite everything, they were a blessing in her life and that she would hold them in the highest of esteem for what little time that she had left.

"We will be there for you Thora," her father said. He had come to the side of the bed and wrapped his arms around her and held her tighter than he had ever held her before.

"I love you Dad," Thora cried into his shoulder. "I will always love you."

"And I love you too, my beautiful daughter!" Langley whispered in her ear and then he let her go.

A moment later Thora found herself in her mother's hug. There was the scent of stale liquor on her breath and clothing but the girl did not allow that to interfere with the honesty of the moment. "I love you Mom!" she said. "I don't want you to worry about me. I will be all right."

"We will all be together again in Heaven," Cora said. "I just know it and I dream for that day to come." She released herself from her daughter. Mascara was running down her face.

"I dream for that day too!" Thora answered.

She was gazing at her parents for the last time that she would recall. They were standing by her bedside, Langley's arm wrapped over Cora's shoulder. Thora no longer saw self-serving miscreants. She saw loving, caring parents going through a very agonizing moment. There was no doubt that they loved her and there was no doubt that she was somebody significant and important. She did matter after all.

"All right now," Joe said, as he walked in the space between the parents and the child. "It is time." He started to push Thora's bed towards the exit.

The last thing that Thora saw of her parents was her mother silently mouthing the words, "I love you" to her.

Chapter 68

Thora the Thunder

She was wheeled upon her bed through the musty corridors of the asylum. She went past several people congregated haphazardly here and there along the way. There was something different about these humans. There was an absence in their faces that spoke loudly of their conditions. These were mental patients Thora realized. They have parted with the conventional reality supported by all those that live outside of the walls of this building and have found their own terms and conditions to conduct themselves. In essence, they lived in their own little worlds and had built barriers from the outside world to keep it from impinging on theirs. The outside world sought means to break through those barriers and forcibly rearrange the private little worlds into something that would be of benefit to it.

Theirs was a fate that she would not share. They still waged battle trying to sustain their world. In her fate the battle would be over. The radical treatment that she was about to experience will annihilate everything that comprised Thora Meadowford. She would be reduced to a vegetative state where she would be unable to do even the most rudimentary activity to look after herself. She would be nothing more than a slab of breathing meat left in storage with other breathing slabs of meat. There would be no interaction with them. There would be no contacts and conduits to the world beyond her skin. She would be just left with her thoughts but these would not truly be her thoughts as those parts of the brain that created and conjugated these thoughts would be removed or mutilated. All that would remain and function would be those centers that would tell the slab of meat to inhale and exhale and to digest the food that would be force-fed through her oral cavity. This could go on for years, far more years than she already lived. She just spent a meager thirteen years as a member of society. She was liable to live the next eighty years as breathing meat and nothing more.

They came to a stop in front of an elevator. Joe pushed the 'Up" button.

"I'm glad you pushed up rather than down," Thora said.

"Why's that?" Laura smiled looking down at the girl from behind the bed that she pushed.

"That means that I'm going to Heaven rather than that other place," Thora joked.

Laura laughed uncomfortably and said, "You are not going to either place as of yet. You've got many years ahead of you here on Earth."

"As a vegetable!" Thora asserted. "I guess I should be satisfied that I am a perennial rather than an annual seeing that I have a lot of years ahead of me then, right?"

"You won't be a vegetable," Laura responded.

"You may have limited cognitive function for a period of time," Joe said, "But these are modern times and there have been such great strides in psychiatric treatments that I am almost certain that before your life is through, you will be fully restored to a healthy mental state."

The man spoke with such optimism but it was optimism that Thora just could not share. She did not have faith in future developments in psychiatry. As far as she was concerned, she held no future at all.

The elevator door opened and the two attendants pushed the bed inside. The lift was empty save for one old man standing in the corner. This fellow wore a hat that he kept tilted forward so that his face would not be exposed. Yet, even though his eyes were hidden Thora sensed that the man was looking at her. His hands were held together in front of him. They bore many liver spots and showed the weathered wrinkling of someone that spent a great deal of time outdoors. There was something vaguely familiar about those hands. She got the idea that she had seen them before.

The surge of the upward motion of the elevator came to a stop and the doors to the new floor opened. Joe and Laura pushed the bed out and Thora found herself in a brightly lit hallway that exuded a very pharmacological aroma. This was a floor where real medicine was practiced. This was unlike the floor that she came from. That one was choking with old lingering smells of tobacco and human waste.

There were signs hanging from the ceiling. These were painted green and bore white lettering that tended to spell out long exotic words that she could not be bothered trying to sound out. All that she knew was that they had a very health science orientation to them.

Her bed was pushed through several corridors on this new floor. She immediately noticed that the mental patients that she saw lounging about on her previous floor were not to be found here. There was a hustle and bustle here with many people going to and fro in light blue loose-fitting outfits. This was the floor of the outside world trying to force its values onto those that lived in their private little worlds. They would be soon exerting their muscle upon her.

The bed took an abrupt right turn halfway down yet another corridor and suddenly Thora was no longer in a hallway. She was wheeled into a large room where there were other beds lined up against the tiled walls. Upon these beds were comatose patients. From what she could see of these people they were all beyond elderly. These were very old people at the edge of life's exit door. "What kind of room is this?" she asked her escorts.

"It's the common waiting room for the hospital's operating theaters," Joe answered her. "You will wait here until the anesthesiologist is ready for you." He was pushing her bed into an available spot flanking the wall.

"How long will that be?" Thora was looking about at the morbid occupants waiting along with her. If she had previously resigned herself to her fate that resignation was rescinded. The other patients in this room looked barely to be alive. She could almost swear that some of them might be dead already.

"It shouldn't be too long," Laura replied for Joe. "There is a bit of a backlog this morning but that is because there has been an unexpectedly huge influx of patients in Admitting and a lot of the doctors normally assigned up here are downstairs helping with the processing."

"Is it because of the stock market crash?" Thora asked. If there were that many attempted suicides today as she had heard reported then it was highly likely that some of these attempts failed. The first place that an attempted suicide goes is to the mental hospital.

"You've heard about it, eh?" Joe responded. "You are very astute this morning. I think that your system has effectively eliminated the toxins from your medication and that you have nothing to worry about regarding undergoing the anesthetic. There will be no side effects."

"That's good news!" Laura said exuberantly. "This should be a breeze for you!"

"There will be a breeze in my head after they cut that hole in it," Thora joked darkly. Maybe it would have been better for her to die on the operating table rather than to live on in a continuous state of catatonia. This was hardly good news at all.

Laura did not appreciate her comment. "Child," she said. "We are doing everything we can to make you healthy again but the first step towards health has to be taken by you. And that first step is to take a healthy, positive attitude towards your treatment."

Joe was filling in something on the chart at the foot of Thora's bed. "There, that is it," he said. "We've done our part. Good luck to you, Miss. I look forward to seeing you again a little later on today."

"Promise me that you will take a positive outlook on all of this," Laura said. She was holding Thora's hand. "I know that you can make it. I have faith in you."

Thora could see a tear forming in the young woman's eye. She realized that she had touched something in the woman's heart. Somehow she got the feeling that Laura felt that this operation was unjust and that there was no need for her to be given such an invasive treatment. "Thank you," she said to Laura, squeezing her hand a little tighter. "Promise me that you will look well after me in the years to come and I promise you that if I ever come back to my senses that I will do my best to make you feel proud for the kindness that you have shown me."

"Good luck Thora!" Laura pulled her hand away and gave the girl one last smile before she walked away with her partner Joe.

Thora was now alone in the waiting room with the half dozen out cold patients. Her moments were waning. She heard these unconscious patients breathing in and out through the oxygen masks that they were provided. There was something peculiarly comforting about the sound of life. These people were so old yet they continued to survive. What made them want to do so, she wondered. They had absolutely nothing to look forward to yet they clung to life and would not let it go. Maybe it was because life is the most precious gift and it is something that should not be discarded even when the act of continuing to be alive was filled with misery, pain and despair. With life there is always hope. Hope dies when the body perishes. Despite the appallingly terrible prognosis about her future the one thing that practically everybody promised her was that she would still somehow be alive and that even though she might be nothing more than a vegetable to the outside world she would still be breathing. As long as she was breathing, she would be fostering hope. Maybe there would one day be a breakthrough and she would be restored to being a functioning member of society. But even if that day never does come she would still have life and that to her was a thought that was very uplifting.

She heard some commotion in the room. A pair of men with their faces obscured by operating masks came toward her bed. One of them lifted the chart and read it. "It's this one over here," he said to his partner who was looking around at the other charts on the other beds.

"Man, there's a lot of them this morning," the other one said. "It's going to be a long time before we get a break today."

"Be thankful that you have got a job," the operating room attendant at the foot of Thora's bed said. "I heard on the radio that thousands of people lost their jobs today because of what happened on Wall Street."

"I sure hope that our jobs are safe," the other man expressed. "I just bought a house and need to pay the mortgage."

"You've got nothing to worry about. Take a look around you at all of the customers! And I hear that Admitting is just jammed pack full. There'll be plenty of work for us until you burn your mortgage papers and then after. Take a look at this kid here. She'll never leave this hospital. Someone is going to have to look after her for at least the next fifty years!"

Thora's bed started to roll. She heard how these attendants had reduced her to an object, to a commodity that was nothing more than some unit of production just like she was being mass engineered at Dearborn Cable. Already she had lost her personhood in society and she had not even had her operation as of yet. She told herself not to listen. She told herself to cling on to hope.

"She is young," the other attendant said as he stepped forward to assist his partner. "I wonder what she did to get herself into this mess?" Even though Thora's eyes were open the two attendants did not bother to address her. She could have answered the question for him.

"She's the notorious Thora Meadowford," the man pushing Thora's bed said. "You must have heard about her. She is the one that killed all those pilots and others to boot. She's a real dangerous one. She says that ghosts made her do it."

"I've heard about her, Thora the Thunder, that is what they called her in the papers, wasn't it?" The attendant looked down onto the bed. His eyes were scrutinizing the restraints on Thora's wrists and body. He wanted to make certain that this homicidal terror did not suddenly lunge up and attack him.

"Yeah, something like that," the other agreed. "You wouldn't think that someone so young would be capable of such atrocities."

"The devil in sheep's clothing," answered the second attendant. "I'm surprised that they are not sending her to the electric chair."

"If ever there was one that deserves it, it is this one. But the bloody legal system is so damned gullible these days. The judge must have looked into her big, sad eyes and just could not bring himself around to give her the chair. If I were the judge I would have had her executed so fast. I don't swallow that this one is innocent. She's evil incarnate."

"You're pretty worked up over this one, aren't you?" the second attendant asked. He was now at the foot of Thora's bed guiding it along.

"I've got a brother that is a pilot with the Coast Guard in Boston. She killed men just like him," the first attendant seethed underneath his operating mask.

They were now in a smaller room that was teeming with equipment and hoses that dangled from the ceiling. "Maybe the doctors will screw up and lose her on the operating table," the other attendant suggested.

"I can only hope so," the first attendant said.

"At any rate once the operation is through, she will be a vegetable and no longer a menace to society," the second attendant said.

"I'll be sure to look her up now and then and use her as a punching bag. I've got to stay in shape, you know."

"You still haven't given up on boxing, have you?"

"There's lots of money in it," the first attendant said as he started to walk away from Thora's bed. "You can make as much money in one fight as you could by working twenty years in this joint. I've got a match coming up at the end of November. If I win that one they are going to give me a shot at the Pennsylvania Welterweight title."

The two attendants' voices faded. They left Thora feeling sick about her prospects. That man was going to beat her up. It frightened her even though she was not going to be aware of it when it happens. She would be in her vegetative state.

A nurse suddenly was standing by her bed. She held in her hand Thora's chart. She read it and then stooped over and placed her thumb on the girl's eyelid and lifted it up. The bright light stung Thora's eyes. Then the nurse checked into her other eye. Once through, she scribbled something onto the chart.

Another nurse appeared. She pulled down Thora's top and held an icy stethoscope to the girl's chest and listened.

"How's the patient?" a man with a deep voice said from beyond Thora's field of vision.

"As healthy as any of us could ever hope to be," replied one of the nurses.

"What are her serotonin levels?" the doctor asked.

"Ideal," the same nurse answered.

"That's good. This should go off with no hitches," the doctor responded. He had now stepped into Thora's field of view. He was a relatively young man with very penetrating and appealing eyes. He bent over and reexamined her eyes using an intense light. "There's some hesitation in the pupils to refract. That means that her system has not entirely flushed out the psychotropic agents but that should be of no concern. Let's put it into gear."

Thora felt a tingling start in her toes and move through the length of her body. This was it, she realized. These were her last moments. Her eyes were wide with fright and they darted about the room in a frenzy to take in as much of the world as they could before they would cease to provide information to a brain that could comprehend. As they skirted about, they detected that same old man that she had seen in the elevator. He was standing at the foot of her bed. His hat was still obscuring his face yet there was enough of his mouth and chin to give the girl an accurate reading as to his identity. To see him again gave the girl such comfort that she no longer was worried about what was about to happen to her.

She lost sight of him when a mask attached to hoses was lowered down to her face.

"I'm going to count backwards from ten," the anesthesiologist said. "I want you to breathe in the mask."

The mask clamped around her mouth and for an instant the girl believed that she was going to suffocate until she saw the old man step closer so that she would be able to see him.

"Ten, nine, eight…"

It was Sambo, her grandfather. She did not know how he had stepped beyond the grave to be here with her but he was here and she gathered such strength from his presence that she no longer cared for her life here on Earth. He represented the eternal and it was to the eternal that she was heading.

"Six, five, four…"

"Have faith in yourself Thora. You shall overcome," Sambo said to her. He was holding her hand and smiling gently into her face. His caring eyes glowing with warmth and love was the last thing that went through Thora's mind before the anesthetic put it to sleep.

Chapter 69

Summer of '74

"You have a visitor," the young attendant tapped the woman on the shoulder. The gray-haired lady scowled and curled herself up into a tighter ball on her corner of the sofa. She hated being interrupted while she watched television. It was hard enough to pay attention as it was, being cooped in a long, rectangular room with a couple of dozen geriatrics that babbled and cackled like a seagull colony at dusk. But when someone actually physically touched her, it was enough to throw her off the deep end. Thora swatted the attendant's hand and firmly clamped her mouth shut in a stubborn pout that said that she wanted to be shut away from the world.

"I said that you have a visitor, Miss Meadowford," the longhaired attendant repeated. He was leaned forward in front of her face. He entirely blocked her view of the ceiling-mounted color television set. This infuriated the woman. Nobody was permitted to do this. Although she had no idea whatsoever of the program that she was watching, she still spent almost every free waking hour in front of the set and took in the electronic images as if they were the center stage of her life. They mesmerized her. They intrigued her. They filled a vacuum within her where a life should have been.

"Get out of my way!" she hissed at the man. She despised this fellow. She despised all the attendants here. They were forever frustrating her with their petty demands. They conspired to keep her from her television when they dragged her out of the recreation area and made her sit in a dining room and forced her to feed on bland meals for which she had no appetite whatsoever. They would not let her get up from the table until she had eaten everything on her plate. Afterwards they would make her attend silly classes where she along with the ninnies of the ward would have to carry out physical activities that were supposed to keep them invigorated and healthy. All that she wanted to do was to sit and watch television and be left alone. They were taking her away from what was important to her.

"Thora, you have a visitor. You are not going to sit here and rot in front of the T.V.!" the man shouted directly in her face. There was strain and exasperation in his cheeks as he tried to persuade her to get up.

"Can't you see that the television is on!" she responded. This should have been reason enough for him to go away and allow her to watch.

"It is, isn't it?" the attendant remarked mockingly, stepping out of Thora's line of view. At once, Thora's eyes honed in on the set the way a moth takes to light. The image on the screen was of a gray haired man sitting slumped in a musty old chair. Beside him on an upright chair was a mousy haired middle-aged woman. On the couch were a young blonde woman and a pudgy-cheeked man with a moustache. They were all yelling at each other. Then the image suddenly changed to the head of a stately fellow talking while over his shoulder in the background was a scene of soldiers cautiously moving through a jungle setting. Then the screen changed once more to several contestants jumping up and down as they guessed the price of a fancy crystal chandelier. And then once more the image altered to a lop-eared cowboy trading quips with a miserable old doctor while a red-haired saloon woman laughed at the remarks.

"See!" the attendant cried. "You are not watching any of this! I'm changing the channels and it is not even fazing you." He held the brown box with the pushdown buttons in his hands. "Now get off your fanny! You have a visitor!" He depressed one of the keys on the box and the picture on the television disappeared. There were sudden complaints from other seats and sofas in the room where other patients were watching the TV set with the same hypnotic trance as Thora.

"For God's sakes, all of you!" the attendant moaned. "Look outside of the window and see the Rocky Mountains! That is what should be interesting you and not what is on the boob tube! Now Miss Meadowford, come with me. There is someone waiting to see you!" He took Thora by the wrist and pulled hard, forcing her out of her chair and onto her feet. "I promise you that you can watch TV again once your visit is over."

Thora fought him every inch of the way from sitting in the chair to standing on her feet but he was stronger than she was and she was fighting a losing battle. Once on her feet, she looked outside of the bank of windows onto the yard that stretched out to the forest on the mountainside. Whenever a visitor was announced to her in the past, it came in the form of something furry that dared to step out from the trees and timidly begin grazing on the green grasses of the lawn. She could see no such creature out there today. "There is no visitor," she said and moved towards her customary chair.

The attendant did not let go of her wrist. "No, not that kind of visitor, Miss Meadowford," he chuckled. "You have a human visitor today."

"A human visitor?" Thora queried. She never had that kind of visitor in her life. She saw some of the others in here have such visitors now and then. These visitors would come onto the ward, look around at the other denizens here, try to make conversation with whomever they were here to see and then invariably go, leaving the visited wondering what that was all about. The patients here much preferred the animal visitors from the forest to these human visitors. Thora liked animals better herself.

The attendant walked in front of her leading the way to a corridor where the rooms had no televisions. She rarely came into this quarter of the ward on her own accord. This was where they held those stupid therapy sessions and where the doctors would talk to the patients. As she followed the man she noted the way that his long locks lifted up and down with the cadence of his gait. It seemed to her that she remembered a time when men would never have such long hair but that was in a very foggy past that she never tried to penetrate. Something about the long ago frightened her and she instinctively avoided thinking about it.

"It's in this room here," the attendant said. "Your visitor wanted privacy so that the two of you can talk." He scratched his head. "For the life of me, I don't know how she is ever going to conduct any conversation with you at all. You have as much to say as this door knob."

Thora looked down at the doorknob in the man's hand. She never knew that such devices were able to talk. You learn something new every day.

He opened the door, revealing a room with a settee décor. There was a small floral divan along one wall with a coffee table before it. Upon this table was a tea service complete with silver pot, cups and saucers, sugar cubes and a creamer. There were half a dozen store bought cookies sitting on the tray as well. The sight of the shortbread cookies set Thora's mouth watering. She loved sweets and could never get enough of them. She rushed towards them, walking past and almost knocking over a woman with flaming red hair.

"Thora! Behave yourself!" the attendant squawked, reaching out and taking hold of the patient by the back of her collar. "You will have plenty of time to eat the cookies. First you must say hello to your guest."

Thora had her mouth full of cookies and had another one in her hand as she turned around to face her guest. The woman was middle-aged if not older. There was something very familiar about her face. It was almost the same face that Thora saw everyday in the mirror except this one was made up and possessed no scar and was framed by well-kept dark auburn hair with red highlights in it. This was in stark contrast to the scraggy grey hair on the face in the mirror. The woman held a bemused expression in her eyes despite the tears that were pouring out of them.

"I can stay here if you like," the attendant said to the woman. "Some of our guests prefer that because some of our patients can get unruly and unmanageable."

"No, I think that I will be fine," the woman said to the attendant. "But thank you, anyway."

"Well, if you need me, just call. I will be not that far away," the attendant said as he left.

The woman nodded. After the man left the room, the woman turned to Thora and asked, "You don't know who I am, do you?"

Thora smiled at the woman and did not answer the question. Her mind was set on getting another cookie in her stuffed mouth. They never gave out this much cookies at evening snack time. This was a feast and she meant to enjoy every single crumb of it.

"I know who you are Thora," the woman said. "I have known you a long, long time. In fact, there is nobody that I have known longer than you. Does that help you in identifying me?"

Thora was reaching for another cookie from the tray. She heard the woman speaking but she paid no attention to her. All that she wanted was to feel the shortbread cookie melt sweetly in her mouth.

"I remember a time when Mother baked for five days straight just before we left for the season at the lake. There must have been two hundred cookies that she made and she placed them in the icebox underneath the blocks of ice. She thought that we would not find them there but you have always had a nose for finding sweets and on the night before we left you dug them out and cracked a tooth on one of them, they were so hard," the woman laughed. "But that did not stop you. You ate at least a dozen of them before we were caught. I can see that you have not changed that much."

What the woman said conjured up a vague recollection in Thora. She put her hand to her mouth where she had cracked that tooth. It had smarted for weeks after that and had to be pulled by the dentist. Her tongue found the spot where the tooth had been. In that gap was some of the broken down shortbread cookie. It nudged the moist chunk forward where her remaining teeth could further chew it.

"Do you remember that Thora?" the woman asked brightly. There was a glint in her eyes as she suspected that she might have made some mental connection with her.

Once more Thora remained silent. She had eaten half of the cookies and was starting to lose interest in them. Her mouth was feeling dry. She spotted the milk sitting in the small container. She took hold of it and brought it up to her mouth and began pouring it into her throat.

"Oh Thora, I wish that you would say something!" the woman moaned. "I know that you understand me and I do believe that you know who I am. You must be curious about whatever became of me as I was and am about you. I heard all about your exploits that summer. I could not have missed it. It was all over the newspapers and the radio. When they finally caught you and brought you back to Grappling Haven for your hearing, I thought that I should have come out of hiding to be there with you. But Rory advised me not to because he believed that they would have put me through the same thing that they were putting you through. He said that there was a lot of evidence to show if one twin was diagnosed with madness that the other twin was likely to suffer from it too. So I stayed hidden at Rory's Aunt Dorothy's farm just outside of Hawkins Corners."

The woman was making no sense to Thora. She heard her babbling in the background but her attention was fixed upon what was happening outside of the window. A rabbit had come out of the forest and was sauntering nervously upon the lawn. It stopped periodically to lift up its ears and listen for any impending danger. Once it was satisfied that there was nothing imminent about to happen it would hop a few steps forward before caution would force it to make the same reconnaissance once more.

"I stayed at Aunt Dorothy's for the summer and did not leave there until the fall after the Stock Market crash. Then with Rory, we headed south for the winter. We went to Florida, vagabonding on the trains that went in that direction. When we reached Miami we soon took advantage of an opportunity to work on the sugar plantations in Cuba. So we were in Havana by Christmas and we stayed in Cuba for almost the next ten years. We were married by the time that I was fifteen and I had my first child before I turned sixteen. That would be your niece June. Yes, we named her after our grandmother. Would you believe that June is now forty-three years old and is a grandmother herself! That makes me a great grandmother at the age of fifty-eight. I find it so unbelievable especially when I see you. Seeing you again takes me back to when we were just thirteen years old." The woman stopped to assess Thora's reactions to this news.

There were no reactions to assess. Thora was staring out of the window at the rabbit on the lawn. She was wriggling her nose at the creature in response to the rabbit's exhibition of the same behavior. Despite this apparent lack of attention, the woman continued with her story.

"We came back to the U.S.A. in 1938. The news from Europe made us uncomfortable in Cuba. There were a lot of Germans in Havana and we feared that they would topple the government there and make it a Nazi outpost in the new world. So we hurried back to America with our three children in tow. We headed directly to Grappling Haven. We had no contact with anybody there for over a decade and both Rory and I were anxious to hear news concerning our respective families." The woman stopped and sighed. "That was a mistake," she said. She looked up at Thora.

Thora was crouched down on the floor and attempting to hop in the manner of the rabbit outside of the window. She was very clumsy and possessed a poor sense of balance. She could not sustain the position any longer than a few seconds before she would tilt to the side and fall over to the floor.

"You are not fooling me, sister," the woman said. "I know that you are listening. You have to remember that I can always read your mind and see past your little games."

Thora fell to the floor once more. She lay on her side there, catching her breath. When she felt strong enough, she got up to her knees to take a peek through the window to see what the rabbit was doing. It had moved closer to the building and had discovered a flowerbed with succulent leaves. It began to nibble at the fronds.

"Yes, it was a mistake to go back to Grappling Haven," the woman continued. She was no longer seeking any indication that Thora was paying attention. "So much had changed in the decade since we left. The Great Depression had come and gone and had left a very ugly scar on the town. All the snobby, upper crust people were long gone. They had either died in reaction to the crash or moved elsewhere to try and sustain whatever fortune they had left. What remained in Grappling Haven were the working class, my husband Rory's family and their ilk. His parents, brothers and sisters and their broods were still in town and were finally finding jobs as the nation was climbing out of the Depression and preparing for war. It seemed to me that our family however was no longer part of Grappling Haven. I could not find hide or hair of any of them for nearly a month until one day I was in the market and ran into Aunt Faye. She did not recognize me at first but I certainly recognized her. She was older but she still retained that elegance that only she could possess.

"Once we struck up a conversation I learned that her name was now Mrs. Gibson. She had remarried and had a new child, a daughter. She no longer lived in the fancy part of town. In fact, the great and haughty Faye Meadowford Thurston had descended down the social ladder to become part of the servile class, if you could believe that! She cleaned houses for a living. Thora, don't do that!"

The woman pulled a leaf from a rubber plant out of Thora's mouth. The patient was mimicking the rabbit. "You can get sick, eating that!" she cried.

Thora looked up at her in shock that she could be rebuked in that manner. The guest was acting like an attendant. Thora hated attendants.

"Please sit still and listen to my story," she said. "I don't know if it means anything to you but it is having a great relieving effect upon me just being able to tell you about what had become of me. You must have wondered."

Thora climbed into a chair that was beside the window and was looking desperately outside. She could not see the rabbit any more and this distressed her. She was about to cry out her anxiety when she saw the creature's tail sticking out through the foliage of the garden. It had buried itself deeper within the leaves and was mawing down on the vegetation with great delight.

"I asked Aunt Faye what had become of the rest of the family. To this point I knew nothing of the fate of our parents. They were nowhere to be found around Grappling Haven. Aunt Faye began by telling me about what happened to Uncle Thaddeus. I did not know that he had died of a heart attack, the news of which did not surprise me at all. I never had any love for that man and even now all these years later I still shudder if I conjure up his memory in my mind.

"When I asked Faye about Mom and Dad the first thing she told me about was a girl called Brenda. This was Dad's illegitimate child that he had with the maid, Lena Taylor, in New Hampshire. Aunt Faye told me that Brenda, our half-sister, had come to live with her for a period of time and that afterwards she was adopted by Helen and James Whattam. That couple never could have children of their own and they were both very eager to be parents."

At the mention of the name Helen Whattam, Thora suddenly stopped mimicking the rabbit. She turned her head towards the woman and actually appeared like she was listening. There was something about Helen Whattam that shone a light into the distant past. Suddenly, there were bleak images in Thora's mind of a musty dark room where evil seemed to be lurking from every corner. It was too much for her to bear. She put her hands to her hair and started screaming frenetically.

"Easy sister," the startled woman cried out, rushing to Thora and trying to comfort her. The woman had no idea what had just happened.

At the same time the longhaired attendant came through the door. In his hand was a needle.

Chapter 70

Nest in the West

"I don't think that there is any need for that," the woman said to the attendant. "I think that I have her settled down." She held Thora tightly in her arms. The heavy expansive breathing seemed to ease somewhat and the patient's trembling was dying off.

"What happened?" the attendant asked. He still held the hypodermic needle in his hand.

"I must have said something to upset her," the woman responded.

The attendant looked from the woman to Thora. "The only time that I see her react explosively is when she is denied her T.V. privileges. You must have hit a nerve from her past. That might be a good thing. It might mean that she is finally breaking out of her shell."

"I don't know if it is a good thing or not," the woman said, gently patting Thora on her shoulder blades. "She's older now and she does not need to have to address any of the foibles of her past any more. She should be allowed just to live peacefully for the rest of her years."

At that moment Thora saw the rabbit come out of the flower garden. It hopped several yards before it stopped and reared up onto its hind haunches. It was surveying its surroundings. Its big eyes roamed the lawn until they stopped and were looking directly into hers. It was like it was trying to tell her something. Thora broke loose from the hold the woman had on her and ran to the window to get closer to the rabbit. Her motion scared the rabbit and it dashed away. But before it reached the forest's edge, it halted and stood up once more. It was still staring back toward the building.

"Come back bunny rabbit!" Thora moaned. "Come back bunny rabbit!"

The woman came to Thora's side and once more placed a hand on her. "There, there, Thora. The rabbit is not going to go away," she said. "The rabbit is here to listen to my story as well." She turned her head back towards the attendant. "I think that we will be okay now," she said to him.

"You know where to find me," the attendant said and closed the door once more on the patient and the visitor.

"Look Thora! The rabbit has come closer so that he can hear better with those big ears of his!" the woman said.

Thora pulled her hair back. "See, I've got big ears too! I want to hear your story too!"

"Are you sure?" the woman said. "I don't want to scare you again."

"I won't get scared Becky!" Thora said, saying the woman's name.

At the sound of her sister saying her name, Rebecca's eyes welled up with tears. It was proof that Thora knew who she was.

"I asked Aunt Faye about Mom and Dad," Rebecca started. "Aunt Faye told me that it had been years since the last time that she interacted with either one. It seems that the fight that they had on Pioneer Lake the last day that we were there was one that was never resolved and that they remained bitter enemies from that day onward. But even though Aunt Faye had not been personally involved with Mom and Dad, she had received regular scuttlebutt on them to keep apprised of their adventures."

The rabbit dropped down from its haunches and began foraging upon the long grasses in the yard. Upon seeing the creature eating, Thora too felt the urge to feed. She reached over and took hold of a cookie and began nibbling at its edges rabbit-style.

"The first thing that Aunt Faye said was that she was surprised that Cora and Langley Meadowford's marriage had survived all of the travails that were thrust upon it, all of the lies, deceit, cheating, and substance abuse. Langley and Cora possessed something between them that Aunt Faye never had with Tom Thurston. She did not know if it was true love or whether it was some neurotic need of the weak to cling to anything that was thrown their way, which would include each other. Whatever trouble either one of our parents could get into they always had the support of the other one." Rebecca stopped and mused on her statement. "In a way I guess they are like us, eh Thora? We've always had each other and we always stood behind what the other one did."

Thora bit into her cookie. Her eyes drifted from the rabbit in the yard to the woman in the room. Something about what Rebecca said just did not ring true to her but she had no idea what it was. When she gazed upon her sister, she could not help but feel the presence of an emptiness that should not have been there.

Rebecca averted her eyes. "Anyway," she sighed. "Aunt Faye told me that our parents sent you here to this institution in Colorado. She said she heard that the reason was financial and not out of any genuine care for your well-being. It was better for them to have you out of their hair and out of their minds rather than to have you nearby in Pittsburgh or some other Pennsylvania institute. Somehow or other our parents were able to survive the Stock Market crash even though our father lost all of his investments in the market. He still had Uncle Thaddeus' house and he sold it to keep his head above water.

"Then the Depression came and our parents moved from Grappling Haven to Dearborn, Michigan where Langley liquidated the family's cable company. He sold it to one of the big three, I am not sure which one, and he had himself quite a little nest egg. Mom and Dad did not suffer during the Thirties at all like the rest of the nation did. That was how they were able to keep you here instead of having you placed in a state-run hospital.

"The last thing Aunt Faye had heard about our parents was that Langley was pursuing government contracts in munitions and that he was likely to become rich beyond his dreams with the looming war in Europe." Rebecca stopped again to see what her sister thought of this news.

Thora seemed not to be paying attention. The rabbit was once again occupying her. The creature was moving back onto the lawn once more. But this time, it was not alone. There were five baby rabbits that appeared out of the forest and they were nervously coming out onto the grass to be with their progenitor. At the sight of the young rodents, Thora began moaning, "Bunny! Bunny!" She was pressed up against the glass of the window. Her nose was bent and her breath created a vapor on the pane.

"Before I parted company with Aunt Faye in that supermarket she asked me about my life and when she learned that I had married Rory McQuoid she chided me and told me that I had thrown away my future by giving it over to that hooligan. She said that I had shown such promise as a child and that she had always believed that I would be the redemption for our line of the family. I defended my choice and my husband as best as I could telling Aunt Faye that there could not be a better father in the world than Rory. He did everything for the kids and would often work two jobs just to make ends meet. This meant nothing to her. She told me that her first husband, Uncle Tom, was always a magnificent father but parenting is only one part of what makes up a fine character. Uncle Tom lacked the other qualities as she was sure Rory did as well. She said that I was in for a life of suffering if I chose to stay with Rory. Then, she had the audacity to say that if I did stay with Rory then she would do everything that she could to make sure that we would not live in Grappling Haven. She did not want us around to muddy the fine reputation that she had in this town." Rebecca sighed once again and shook her head.

"She was true to her word. Nobody in town would hire Rory or me even though FDR's New Deal was in full swing and there was work available. It really hurt because both Rory and I so much wanted to raise our children in the same place where we grew up. But it was not to be, thanks to Aunt Faye. Within two months, we were on our way to Dearborn, Michigan to find Mom and Dad and hopefully get work in one of Dad's enterprises.

"When we got to Dearborn we quickly learned that Aunt Faye had everything all wrong about Mom and Dad. They were not in any fancy mansion living the high life. They were in a small clapboard house in the industrial sector of town. Dad had been unemployed for several years living frugally on his inheritance from Uncle Thaddeus before he got himself a job in one of the car factories. When he had liquidated Dearborn Cable, he had actually gone bankrupt. The creditors took any of the assets that were available there and they were after his inheritance as well. But Mom and Dad changed their names and were living under a different identity. They were now Mr. and Mrs. Samuel Johnson. If you were wondering how I ever found them, well that is a story in itself," Rebecca paused and chuckled. "Well, it was not that much of a story. Rory bumped into Dad at a bowling alley. Dad did not recognize him but Rory was sure that it was Langley. He followed him home that night and the next day we paid Mr. and Mrs. Johnson a visit.

"They were quite taken aback to see their long lost daughter finally come home and to be honest, they had changed for the better. Mom had put away the bottle years ago and Dad had become quite humble and no longer aspired to lofty get rich schemes. He had finally found work and he rather enjoyed actually earning money rather than squandering it. He said that he believed that he could get Rory a job at the factory as well. And he was true to his word for within a week Rory was working alongside his father-in-law on the motor line in Detroit.

"They were tickled pink to learn that they were grandparents and whatever shortcomings they had in raising you and I, dear sister, they more than made up for in being the grandparents to my children. We moved in with them for the first few months, while Rory was getting onto his feet and then would you believe that Rory and I purchased the house next door to them and that we were neighbors. I got work myself as a waitress at a diner and Mom acted as our babysitter. Those were very happy times indeed. The only sorrow that we experienced was that you were not there to share it with us. We often talked about all of us driving out to Colorado to visit you but before we knew it, the Japanese invaded Pearl Harbor and the country was dragged into a war."

Rebecca stopped once again to see what her sister thought of all of this. Thora was still leaning against the window watching the rabbits. She had not said a thing either to Rebecca or to the rabbits. There almost seemed to be a tear in her eyes but that could have been the reflection of the sun on them.

"With the advent of war Rory enlisted into the Army almost immediately and he was overseas within a few months. Dad wanted to join up as well despite Mom's pleadings to stay home. Dad said that he had to do it. His family came from a long line of naval men and that he always felt that he never measured up to his father and grandfather because he had stayed a civilian all of his life. Finally Mom relented and Dad joined the Navy. By the middle of 1942 he was on the Pacific Ocean assigned to a destroyer as Ensign Johnson.

"While our men were gone, Mom and I did our effort for the war as well. Mom became a hostess at the USO where she was the coat check girl while I got a job at the factory assembling armed vehicles. All was going well until I got the telegram in 1943 from the Army. My husband, Rory, was killed in Tunisia when Rommel's forces retook Tripoli." Rebecca had sobbed the final words. "It's been over thirty years and it still feels like yesterday. Rory might have been a smart aleck in his younger days but he grew up to be a fine man. Even Dad liked him.

"Two years later more bad news came to our family. Dad was on the USS Indianapolis. They had just delivered the bomb and were on their way back when the Japanese sub shot its torpedoes. Dad was put into the water where the sharks got him. Langley Meadowford a.k.a. Samuel Johnson was no more." Rebecca was bawling her eyes out.

Thora looked to her sister and saw the tears. She left the window and took Rebecca's head into her arms. "Don't cry Becky. Don't cry!" she muttered, doing her best to comfort the woman.

Rebecca pulled back out of Thora's arms. "Dad proved himself to be a Meadowford like the two Samuel Angus's before him. He even went one step further. He died for his country. Mom never got over his loss. After the war was over and her services were not needed at the USO any more, Mom returned to babysitting. Once my kids no longer needed babysitters, Mom took to taking in children from the neighborhood. Despite this, she could not shake off the depression caused by her husband's loss. She slowly started to deteriorate. By 1951, she was diagnosed with cancer and died six months later. She is buried beside an empty grave that bears her husband's name in Dearborn. Dad's remains were never found."

The rabbits had hopped up to be directly under the windowsill. Thora abandoned her sister and rushed to the window. Her movement this time did not startle the creatures. They just looked up at her and then returned their attention to the flowers that sat in the little garden there.

"When the estate of our parents was settled, there was nothing left for me after the burial expenses. One thing that I noted was that in all of the paperwork there was no mention about who was paying for you here in this institution. Mom and Dad never talked about it and I had never asked. I was under the assumption that what Aunt Faye said was true, that Mom and Dad were paying for you. I started to make enquiries on this. I decided to telephone James Whattam in Grappling Haven. He had been the family attorney and perhaps he was able to give me some insight on it. At first, he was reluctant to talk but he said that if I really wanted to know that maybe I should call his wife, Margaret. She was hard to reach. She was never at home. It took me nearly a week of trying but finally I got her at her house.

I asked her the same question I asked her husband and she told me that she and James had been paying for your care ever since you were placed in Colorado and that they had come out here to visit you a number of times. They said that you were not in very good condition and that it was not a very smart idea for me to come out and see you. It would not only upset me too much to see what had become of my sister but that it might have devastating effects upon you.

"And so I stayed away. I listened to them," Rebecca sighed. "But I promised myself that as soon as they died, I would come out here to visit you. In the meantime I met someone else, a man from Detroit who happened to be the son of a cousin to Art Rozelle. Can you believe that! What a small world! His name is John but everybody calls him Jack. We've been married almost twenty years now. We live in Northern Michigan on some land that is very reminiscent of Pioneer Lake. I love it up there, especially the fall. We never got to see what Black Island looked like in October. We were always back home long before then but if it is anything like it is like in Northern Michigan then maybe we chose the wrong season for our stays. The colors of the leaves are glorious. They make you think that you have stepped into a new world where everything has a new beginning. And to be up on the lake at dawn and watch the migrating fowl prepare for another day of flight just stirs the soul. There is nothing so beautiful. Oh Thora, how I wish that you can see it!"

Thora lifted her head at the mention of her name. She had been trying to stick her hands out through the window to pick up one of the baby rabbits. It was only feet away from her but the glass kept her from carrying through with her desires.

Her sister laughed and then said, "You would love it up there. I wish that I could take you home with me so that you could enjoy it too. But I could never take care of you. I see that now," she allowed a large painful exhalation escape from her lips. "I'm afraid that you are going to have to stay in institutions the rest of your life. As you can guess if you were listening carefully to me, Margaret and James Whattam are both dead now. James died in the late 1960's when an unsatisfied client that he was defending knifed him. Margaret succumbed to a heart attack this spring. In her will, she set aside money to look after you and she made me the executor of that endowment. When I looked at the amount of money that she gave me and

I compared it to the actual monthly expenses in keeping you here, I determined that the money would run out in a decade. I started doing comparisons with other institutions and discovered that if we move you to a facility back in Pittsburgh, Margaret's funding would last another thirty years. And that is why I am here." Rebecca leaned forward toward her sister who was sitting on the floor gawking out of the window at the rabbits.

Thora seemed like she had not heard a word that was said. She was preoccupied with the furry creatures in the yard and garden.

"I know that you love it here and that it has been your home for most of your life but you will like Pittsburgh as well. It is where your roots are. They have lovely grounds there and I imagine that there are rabbits there as well. There is a vacancy there now that I have placed a deposit on. You will be moved to Pittsburgh at the start of September. Oh Thora, I really wish that I did not have to do this but I have no option. I cannot afford to keep you here and I am all that you have in the world. Nobody else is going to pay your bill."

At that moment, the rabbits started to scurry away in a panic. One of the hospital's attendants had come out onto the yard and began chasing the rodents away so that they would not eat up all of the flowers. Upon seeing this, Thora became very agitated. She began screaming, "No bunny come back! No bunny come back!" She was growing hysterical. "Come back! Come back! Leave the bunnies alone!"

The longhaired attendant came through the door to the sitting room where the two twin sisters were having their visit. "What's wrong?" he inquired of Rebecca.

Rebecca had been trying to mollify her sister but was unsuccessful. "She's upset about the rabbits!" the woman responded.

"Thora's always upset about something or other," the man said, taking hold of Thora by the shoulders and leading her towards the door. "I'm going to take her back to the TV room. That should settle her down. I'm afraid that your visit has come to an end, Mrs. Rozelle."

"So it seems," Rebecca sighed. She watched her sister being dragged through the door and taken away from her. It was the last time that the twins Rebecca and Thora ever saw each other.

In another month, Thora left Colorado. Her nest in the west was taken away from her. She was brought to Pittsburgh to the same institution where she had first been placed after being apprehended by Officer Bombino. The first few days there were unsettling for her and she threw up such a commotion that she had to be bound to her bed but afterwards she started to grow accustomed to the place and quickly established herself as one of the mainstays in the TV room where she could be left the entire day without having to be attended to. She was lost in the images of the screen and did not exist beyond them. She had forgotten the real world and the real world forgot her.

Chapter 71

A Distant Ally

A canoe stroked its way through the annals of time and into the new millennium. It did not hesitate to ford the gap between the past and the present. It blazoned through, growing more triumphant with every intrepid stroke its pilot took through the temporal milieu. It sensed that fruition was on hand and that the dark waters of the dark days were drawing to an end and that a new beginning was about to be born. Paddling the canoe was a man that had bore witness to it all from the early times when the prophecy took shape through the long eons where the prophecy remained frozen and inert and all but forgotten save for within his drive alone. Never was there a quietude in his heart; never was what came to pass not inscribed upon his brow. The man all along carried the realization that he was the sculptor of the events and that if he did not fashion the causes and the effects then the prophecy would remain unrealized and the child that slept would never arise and the dark days would go onward with never an end in sight.

But Madoqua never forgot. He had vowed to his people and kin that the boy claimed by Jibatigon would be liberated from the bewitchment that had seized him. To this end he became an apprentice to the medicines of the shamans and the enchantments of the Manitou. He learned through observation. He learned through application. He learned through intuition and experiment. His road to discovery came with many setbacks and heartbreaks. Yet he persevered through the tests and the ordeals and when all else was at its darkest, he clung to his vow and would not let it go even when all indications pointed to the futility, if not folly, of his quest.

He became seasoned at the arts of man and an astute student of the minds that frothed in the various realms and echelons that held residence in his world. From the soundings of the amphibians in the evening marshland to the long, low laments of lost wandering souls, Madoqua developed an understanding of each as individuals and as a complex interplay when all were thrust together. He knew that the whole was not greater than its parts but that it was different from its parts. He learned how to manipulate the constituents. He learned how to manipulate the amalgam. It was a slow and tedious process, fraught with error and painful misjudgments that would have broken any man that did not have the firm resolve and commitment that Madoqua possessed.

His focus had always been the mystical turtle-backed island that was amongst the Tears of Chendos on the sacred lake. It was here that the shaper of destiny slept in seeming eternity in the form of a boy by the name of Rautooskee. Time had gone awry when the spirits of the water had usurped his soul and imprisoned him and set out the conditions of his release. These terms seemed impossible to ever come out of Time that was not nudged or provoked. Madoqua had to learn how to nudge Time and how to provoke it so that the events would fall into order and create the conditions required to free Rautooskee from his state.

For the boy to be awakened his slumbering spirit had to be harkened in the face of a looming disaster by a kindred being whose life had paralleled the disheartening circumstances and conditions of those that etched the biography of the boy. More than this, the kindred spirit must have been reared by those that the sleeper's people would consider enemies. The boy's name must be cried out as a weapon against adversity and it must be uttered in defiance to the will of fate.

Yet to set this into motion the name crier had to be educated and come to possess an understanding, and moreover an acceptance, of his existence and not be sullied into its denial. The fates that inflict the definitions of experience for the crier had to be nudged so that they would sculpt a similar set of memories in the crier to those of the sleeping spirit. Others would have to be enlisted and twisted to carry out the roles that would shape the crier's life so that the crier would be prepared. Conflict and despair had to be summoned in these others so that when the time came they would play out their functions flawlessly and acutely so that the crier would receive the final shaping that would make him capable of carrying out his vital role.

All had been set into place. An enemy people had come to possess the sacred lands. Within their fold a child was born that would be shaped to fulfill destiny. Others in his midst were taken and set upon courses that would see to it that the child would parallel the life of the sleeper. The enemy child, the crier, would know the anguish of losing those that were close to him but afterwards he would meet and confront their departed spirits. These would now possess a dangerous animosity towards him and they would try to tempt him into taking a path that would assure his final destruction.

To help him in that final moment when fate could go either way, a distant ally had to be rallied that would perform the ascribed ritual at precisely the right instant in time that would incite the tumblers of causation that would invoke the crier and awaken the sleeper and steer them clear of the impending peril.

It was now time for Madoqua to prompt the distant ally. He set his canoe onto the course to that faraway land. The distant ally was now ready to play out her role.

Chapter 72

Indestructible

She woke up. She did not open her eyes as she felt the heavy fatigue of a long slumber still gripping her brain. It seemed like it was unwilling to let go. It would have been easy enough for her to succumb to it and drift off back into its mesmerizing aura. But she decided against giving in. She had slept enough. It was time to wake up.

As she opened her eyes, she felt the painful intensity of artificial light impinging upon her pupils and making them hostile towards accepting the stimuli that would come their way. Nonetheless, she forced them open. Her eyes gave a total disregard to her brain. They would not provide it with anything meaningful for it to comprehend and process. But her brain was a powerful organ and it was a willful agent. It mustered the light that came in through the eyes and arranged it into meaningful patterns that gave her an indication of what was out there beyond her skin.

The first thing that she saw was a calendar on the wall. For a moment she thought that maybe her eyes had won the battle for the calendar displayed the month of July in the year 2000. She rubbed them so that they would properly focus. When they were ready to take on the light again the date July 2000 still showed on the calendar.

How could it be such a date? The last year that she recalled was 1929. Had she been asleep for over seventy years? That seemed entirely impossible.

Nobody can sleep that long. Perhaps the calendar was somebody's practical joke. Her sister Rebecca was notorious for pulling gags and Thora quickly suspected her twin as the one behind the prank.

Yet, as she started to smile at Becky's little amusement, she took note that this was not her bedroom in her parents' house, as she had believed when she first woke up. This room was larger than that quaint snug upstairs parlor that she had there.

Someone coughed.

Thora turned around. There were others in this setting with her. She saw three other beds in the room. On one of them was an old woman who was holding her balled up fist to her mouth while her chest was hacking up phlegm that was trying to settle in her lungs. Thora did not recognize the woman at all. She was dressed in a filthy nightshirt and her gray hair fell down in unkempt tussles to her shoulders.

"Who are you?" Thora snapped more than asked. She felt that her privacy had been invaded. How dare someone share the same bedroom as her!

The old woman took her hand away from her mouth and turned to face Thora. The woman's face was as haggard as the rest of her. Some sputum still dangled from her dried lips as she opened them to say, "I'm my daddy's little princess!" There were no teeth in her mouth and her small gray eyes carried an emptiness that told Thora immediately that the little princess was not entirely there.

"What are you doing in this room?" Thora barked. She felt severely agitated by the presence of the little princess. She did not know where she was but she felt some territorial imperative come over her that wanted to immediately oust the little princess from the room.

"I'm grooming myself so that I will look presentable at my birthday party," the woman said, as she started running her hands through her hair. "I want Daddy to be proud of me."

Thora watched with abhorrence as the liver-spotted fingers got stuck in the frayed knots and the old woman began to wince and cry. "Daddy is going to be so upset with me! I should have washed my hair last night like I promised him. But I was naughty and played on the swing instead with the girls from next door."

The old woman continued to babble but Thora had shut her out. She was taking note of the room where she found herself. It did not have the atmosphere that one associates with a bedroom or even a hotel room. There was only one kind of room that possessed the antiseptic smell that this one carried; there was only one kind of room that had beds with side railings. This was a hospital room.

How did she end up in a hospital? She tried to augur into her mind to dig up her most recent memories before she went to sleep. Then as she delved into what shady remnants there were there, she felt that an ancient stone castle tumbled down on her. She had been on Pioneer Lake and she was trying to desperately escape from Officer Bombino as well as her grandmother's ghost. Their faces along with the faces of others exploded in her mind. She saw her Mom and Dad, Becky, the Whattams, Bewdley Beacon, and Captain Buck. Superimposed upon them were the apparitions of the old Dutch ghosts, the Nells, and her great grandfather, Samuel Angus Meadowford the First. All these faces filled her mind and all tried to tell her a story simultaneously. She was not ready to hear any of them. She screamed, "Shut up!"

The little princess looked up at her. "That is not a nice thing to say. Daddy always told me that you have to be polite no matter what you feel inside."

Thora lifted her eyes to the old woman and found herself hissing, "You are nuts!"

She threw her legs over the side of the bed. All at once a pair of knobby, bony knees caught her sight. These were not the legs that she was accustomed to seeing at the bottom end of her body. They looked like the legs that belonged to an old woman. They were meatless, ghostly white and had etched upon them a series of blue veins. A thirteen year-old girl does not normally have such lower limbs. "What happened to my legs!" she gasped.

The little princess stopped her bantering and looked over at Thora. She was staring at Thora's legs. She held a curious expression as if she did not understand what Thora was talking about. But Thora was not paying any attention to her. Thora was holding her arms in front of her face. These, too, looked like they were on the other side of life as well. Her eyes flitted back to the calendar on the wall. July 2000. It couldn't be. She started looking along the wall for another object that usually is suspended upon them. She could not find one amongst the cheerless paintings of country settings and fruit baskets.

"Is there a mirror here?" she cried. At the same time she noted that the little princess had one lying on her bed beside her. Thora put her weight onto her legs and felt pain race up and down the pair of them. Her hips sagged. They were not used to supporting the weight of her upper body. Was she really old? Was the calendar right?

It just could not be. This had to be an elaborate joke by Becky. Becky must have somehow snuck her into a hospital while she slept and made things seem the way that they were. Her old appendages were articles from a costume store. They were not real. But in her foggy memory she seemed to recall that her sister had run away and could not have possibly been behind the prank. And in her misty recollections she could hear Officer Bombino telling her that she was going to jail. Competing with him was the dimmest trace of her parents, Cora and Langley Meadowford, explaining to her that she was going to a psychiatric hospital and that some complicated procedure was going to be performed upon her.

"No!" she said to herself in defiance of these dark memories. She had dreamt all of that. None of it actually happened in her real life. Her hips were gaining control of her balance and she started towards the little princess' bed. Her legs felt chunky and wooden. They did not move with any smooth canter. They thumped along, her knees unbending. The effort just to amble the dozen feet to the other bed was taxing her to the limit. She could feel that her breath was short. Her body was behaving as if it truly was the body of someone in her eighties. In the back of her mind, there was growing the ugly realization that this was no hoax or prank and that it was the real thing.

She finally made it to the other bed. Upon reaching it, she fell forward onto it and immediately felt the relief in her hips and legs, as they no longer were required to do any work. Her mouth was open and she was gasping for air to revitalize her rubbery lungs. They felt as if they had been calcified and could no longer function properly. As she lie there trying to recuperate from the ordeal, she felt something crawl into her hair.

"It is so thin!" the little princess said. "That's what happens if you don't take care of it! I try to wash my hair at least once a week and that way it won't fall out. I should have washed it last night. Daddy is going to be so upset with me! He wanted me to look like a china doll for my birthday party today. Are you going to come to my party?" The old woman spoke like an eight year-old girl as her enfeebled hands stroked Thora's head.

When Thora felt sufficiently strong enough she reached upward and pushed the old woman's hands away. "Get your filthy paws off of me!" she growled as she tried to locate the mirror on the bed. Her fingers caught hold of it and she drew it towards her face. She never gave herself a chance to mentally prepare for what she might see.

In the looking glass glancing back at her with a horrified expression was the face of an ancient, wrinkled figure that time had not been gentle upon. Under the wispy gray hair was a two-inch scar that ran from the hairline to almost halfway to the thick bushy eyebrows. Beyond the terror in the slate eyes there was another emotion that revealed itself and that was sadness on a monumental scale. What had these eyes seen in the last seventy years that it was not telling her brain?

Thora dropped the mirror from her hand. It bounced on the bed and then slipped off its side and cracked on the floor beneath.

"You broke my mirror!" the little princess gasped as she lifted the article. "How am I going to make myself presentable for my party now!"

"There isn't going to be a party for you, you old fool!" Thora mumbled. The little princess was suffering from the same delusion that had possessed her before she took a gander in the looking glass. The old woman believed that she still was in her youth and that time had not stormed into her life and destroyed everything. Thora no longer held onto that delusion. The mirror told all. The mirror verified those deep dark fears that were at the back of her mind. She had spent a lifetime in a mental hospital and was entirely unaware of it. She had been robbed of time. She had just got through the entrance door when she was abruptly taken to the exit door. She never got a chance to look around at what sat in between.

"You are going to have seven years bad luck!" the little princess harped at her.

"I've already had ten times that much!" Thora responded. Her chest was beginning to throb as she tried to cope with such a massive shock to her mind. Her body had lived an entire lifetime yet her soul was not there for the majority of it. Where was it in all of that time? The only images that her mind would give her were the images of her childhood and her brief interlude in adolescence. Anything past that point was a blank slate. "Do you know who I am?" she found herself asking the old woman.

"Yes, I do!" the little princess answered. She was looking at her image in the cracked mirror. How come she did not see an old woman in it? Her mind must have been even further gone than hers. "You're Thora Thunder. Everybody knows that!"

Thora Thunder? She had heard that term before although she could not place where she had heard it.

"You're the crazy woman that murdered all of those people long ago," the little princess continued. "But I'm not scared of you because you had your brain removed. That has made you as gentle as a lamb."

The scar on her head must have been the remnants of the operation, the lobotomy. Thora's fingers started rubbing it. They felt the tiny groove in her forehead and the parallel holes where the stitching took place. How could they have done such a thing to a thirteen-year old girl? Especially an innocent thirteen-year old girl? She was not responsible for the deaths that took place. Bewdley Beacon and the ghosts had done them. And even if she did kill those people it would have been far better for the authorities to give her the electric chair rather than slicing away a piece of her brain and allowing her to wake up decades later to discover that life had been taken away from her anyways.

Her chest still hurt. The pain, if anything, was increasing rather than subsiding. Something started to tell Thora that she was going to die soon and that the only reason that she was now awake was to say goodbye to it all. It was the final cruelty. She wished that she had not woken up. She wished that she had drifted off into death while she was in that other state where nothing registered in her mind.

"Good morning ladies!" a woman's voice hailed from behind her.

"Good morning Miss Laura!" the little princess regaled. "Today is my birthday party!"

"Everyday is your birthday party Mary!" the woman answered. "Why is Thora on your bed?" Thora could hear the woman's feet approaching.

"She came over here and broke my mirror!" the little princess named Mary responded.

"Give me that at once!" the woman named Laura shouted. From where Thora was lying on the bed, she saw an arm wrapped in a navy blue sleeve reach across her and take the mirror from Mary. "There's broken glass in it. I don't want you cutting yourself Mary!"

"But I need a mirror to do my hair!" Mary protested.

"We'll get you another one," Laura promised. "Now Thora, I'm going to put you back in your bed and you stay there. I don't want you wandering about with that hip of yours. I don't want you breaking it again like you did last winter."

Thora felt an arm slip underneath her neck and a hand take hold of one of hers. She was gently lifted and led back to the bed that was hers. Everything in her body was in agony. Her heart was producing sharp pains that reverberated everywhere inside of her. But even through all of the pain, Thora was able to take notice of the window in the room and what sat beyond it.

It was a city that she recognized. It was Pittsburgh. A lot of it had changed from what her memories of the steel town had been yet a lot of it had remained the way that it was. On the hills that climbed out from the city she could see the blast furnaces still at work producing the steel for the nation. But overtop of these hills, there was something else that was familiar to the woman. It was a cloud that bore the shape of a giant canoe. In that canoe was an Indian warrior who was steadily paddling his vessel forward towards her.

"Now lie down Thora and stay put," the woman called Laura said. Her face was now filling Thora's line of sight. Laura was also a very old woman but unlike Mary or the woman in the mirror, Laura managed to keep herself groomed and retained a very professional demeanor.

Thora suddenly realized that she recognized this woman. She was the young woman that had been an attendant along with a fellow named Joe. They had prepped her for her operation seventy years ago. This Laura was on the other side of life as well. Had she been here all of this time and cared for her while she was in her vegetative state?

"You're Laura, aren't you?" she asked the woman as the woman was tucking her into her bed.

There was great surprise on Laura's face. It was as if she was shocked that the vegetable could say something comprehensible. "Yes, I am, my dear!" Laura answered. There were some tears showing in the corners of her old eyes.

"It was you and Joe that got me ready for my operation, wasn't it?"

"Yes it was Thora. That was so long ago. I am taken aback that you remember!" Laura was leaned forward as she gazed softly down into Thora's face.

"It seems like yesterday to me," Thora said. "Have you been here all of this time looking after me?"

"Not for all of it," Laura said. "You spent over forty years in a facility in Colorado."

Colorado? There was something vaguely familiar about that state. Didn't her parents say that they were going to send her there? "I was out west?" Thora asked.

"Yes, you were Thora dear. You were there until your benefactor died and then your sister had you brought back here to Pennsylvania." Tears were streaming down Laura's cheeks.

Thora reached up to wipe them away. Inside her thoughts, she felt warmth at the notion that this caring woman had been with her through the years. Laura was a beautiful person. "My sister knows what happened to me and that I am in a mental hospital?"

"We don't call these care facilities by that archaic term any more, but yes, your sister Rebecca has been here to visit you many times before she passed away." Laura suddenly pulled away from the bed. Her face reddened.

"Becky is dead?" Thora could now understand the significance of why Laura reacted the way that she did. She had made a mistake in revealing this information to her. And then the significance of what Laura said began to strike Thora. "Becky is dead?" Her twin sister whom she used to sit at the piano in the parlor on Pioneer Lake had perished? It was a cold, cold item to register in a mind that was craving nothing but warmth.

She saw Laura compose herself and saw that the woman was determined to be forthright in what she was going to say. "Your sister Rebecca passed away in 1993 when she was hit by a snowmobile in Northern Michigan where she made her home with her husband. Had that accident not happened, I am sure that Rebecca would still be alive and would still be coming here to visit you. She was very healthy and very happy save for her concern for you."

"Becky is dead," Thora repeated. She could feel herself start to disintegrate. She remembered the last time that she saw her sister on that morning back in Grappling Haven when the family was having yet another of its endless fights. Becky had had enough of it and decided to run away. Before she left she had told Thora that if she wanted to she could meet her at their secret place. Now, seventy-one years later, Thora still did not know where that secret place was. How she wished that she had known! She might have led a life that she remembered rather than have one comprised of a great emptiness.

"I'm afraid that she is, Thora. I should not have told you that!" Laura lamented.

"What about the others in my family? My mom and Dad?"

Laura shook her head back and forth. "I'm sorry." Then before Thora could react or make any comment, the hospital woman added, "You have to remember what year it is Thora. We are in the new millennium now. Your parents, had they lived, would have been over a hundred years old."

"They are all dead then?" Thora began to experience an icy detachment to everything. She had woken up to a world and time that she did not belong.

"Not all of them Thora," Laura said. "Your sister had children of her own and they had children and they had children. Rebecca was a great grandmother when she died. There are lots of people alive that can claim you as a relative."

"But they are all people that I don't know!" Thora exclaimed. Her heart was starting to grow extremely painful. Her hands began to clutch at it.

"There is one that still lives that you do know," Laura answered. She appeared to be unaware that the old woman on the bed was in the early stages of a massive heart attack.

"Who is that?" Thora asked through a jaw that was so tight that it could barely open.

"Faye Gibson," Laura said. "You would know her as your Aunt Faye. She has been paying your bill here ever since Rebecca died."

"Aunt Faye is still alive?" It was news that shocked her but still she was not surprised. Aunt Faye was a survivor and always appeared to be indestructible. Thora, herself, was not feeling indestructible any longer. Her heart was exploding in her chest.

"She is alive," Laura nodded.

"Are you going to get me my new mirror or not!" Mary, the little princess, demanded. "I have a birthday party to get ready for, you know!"

"It is time to dance," a voice said from the window.

CHAPTER 73

Time to Dance

"It is time to dance."

Thora could barely concentrate and get past all of the immense upheaval that was taking place inside of her body. But even as her heart was spasming and taking away her senses of her extremities she could feel him there, looking through the window. It was the Great Indian Spirit, the one named Madoqua.

"What's wrong Thora?" Laura cried out. She finally recognized the crisis painfully written abundantly over her patient's face.

"Why are you here?" Thora said to the window. Only Madoqua's eyes could be seen peering in. He was of such a proportion that the window would not reveal any more of him.

"You know why I am here," the spirit answered. "Your time has come and you must fulfill your promise while you are still alive."

"What promise did I make to you? I don't remember making any promise!" Thora cried. She had said it in a shrill manner yet her ears only reflected back half whispers to her mind.

"You promised that you would dance and say the name of the Sleeper."

"Nurse!" Laura rasped out loud, while pushing a button at the head of Thora's bed.

"What about my mirror!" Mary, the little princess, matched the hospital woman's volume and sense of urgency. "I want my mirror. I have to get my hair done for my party!"

"I know no name of any sleeper and I don't know how to dance!" Thora answered the Great Indian Spirit.

"Yes, you know his name. It came to you in a dream long ago," Madoqua responded gently.

"I can't remember! Tell me his name!"

"The name has to come from your tongue unprompted. I cannot reveal it to you."

"Drat! Nobody listens to me around here any more!" Laura growled and started towards the door.

"That's because you are one of us now Miss Laura. You are not the boss," Mary answered. "You retired as the boss a long time ago."

Laura stopped. "That isn't true Mary! You are just saying that!"

"And why do I have to say his name?" Thora said to the pair of eyes in the window. Her head was beginning to swim. It seemed like her mind was starting to lose its latches to her body.

"You must say his name for you are the Daughter of the Usurper and it is only you that can carry out this role."

"I don't know what you are talking about!" Thora protested. "Can't you see that I am dying? Can't you give me peace in my last moments of life!"

"It is so true!" Mary railed at Laura. "You are as crazy as the rest of us, Miss Laura! You were retired for only a year before you went bananas and they brought you back here where you were the administrator for fifteen years! Now you are one of us!"

"I don't know what you are talking about!" Laura protested. "And stop getting in the way, Birthday Girl! Thora Thunder is dying and we have to get a nurse here at once!"

"Thora Thunder died the day they took her brain away!" Mary shouted. "Now get me my mirror, please!" The little princess was raving.

Thora heard the argument in the background but she could not pay it any attention. She had her own argument to contend with and she wanted both to be resolved so that she could die in a modicum of peace. She understood already that there was not going to be any serenity in her dying.

"You must say the name for your cousin Jack!" Madoqua said.

"Jack's dead!" Thora retorted. "He died a long time ago!"

"Jack's spirit lives on, Thora! He is at this moment in the gravest of danger and only you can save him from it! You must dance the Dance of Petition for him, for me, and for the Sleeper! You must fulfill the prophecy or the prophecy will never come to pass."

"You sound like you belong in here too!" Thora said. "What happens if I don't dance?"

"Then the curse that has fallen on your family will go on forever. Your cousin Jack will become like your grandmother and his brother. They will endlessly crave to draw innocent souls into the jaws of Jibatigon. They will be demented and never receive any rest."

"The curse on my family, where all Meadowfords will walk the Earth after dying? Am I to shortly commence my walk, Madoqua?"

"There will be no walk for you Thora! You will be cast into the realm of demons. You have met some of these already at the Bianco house."

The image of the beast that first told her about the family curse sprang to Thora's mind. She recalled how the lovely Mrs. Bianco had transformed herself into that godless creature and the absolute terror that she felt upon beholding it. "That is my fate, if I don't dance?"

"Whether I am crazy or not, Thora Thunder is dying!" Laura shouted at Mary. "I have to get a nurse for her at once! Your mirror can wait!"

"But Daddy will be here any minute! If he sees the tangles in my hair, he is liable to give me such a swatting that my face will sting for a week! Please get the mirror first!"

"It is not only your fate that is on the line but the fate of others as well," Madoqua said to Thora.

"What others?"

"Your sister Rebecca, your mother and father, and the woman named Margaret Whattam. If you don't fulfill your promise then they will rise from their graves and become vagabonds of the wind and be endlessly blown over desolate lands where they will be in a constant state of despair and ceaseless hunger that cannot be staved. They will be without any hope of finding restitution. They will be forlorn and bitter and curse you eternally."

"They'll be the Meadowford walking dead?" Had Thora not experienced firsthand the walking dead of her family, she would have thought Madoqua's declarations to be false and contrived. But she had seen her great grandfather, her grandmother, and her cousin. She had seen the pain in their eyes that twisted fate had thrust upon them. She held no desire to expose her parents, her sister and Mrs. Whattam to such devastation. But Thora did have difficulty with the concept that she was going to become a demon. She recognized no evil in her heart and her intentions towards anybody and everybody had never been tainted with malignant intent.

"Yes, you will be a demon in the eyes of time, Daughter of the Usurper. You held the power to liberate the suffering yet you chose to allow them to continue suffering. Does not your Satan in your people's teachings do the same thing?" Madoqua was able to read her mind. "You will grow ugly like him and be shunned by all others who carry the belief that the universe can be a good place."

"But I don't understand any of this!" Thora whimpered. "What does it all have to do with me? Couldn't the Sleeper awake and Jack be liberated without me? What do I have to do with it?"

"You're talking to yourself Thora Thunder!" Mary said from her bed. "They'll never let you out of this place if you talk to yourself. Daddy always said that he would bring me home the day that I stop doing that. And I tried to listen. I tried not to talk to myself but sometimes I just don't have anybody else to talk to. You've never talked to me. You always act like I am not here. But not today Thora Thunder, not today. Today is my birthday and today I am the one that is special."

The Great Indian Spirit looked at the carping old woman on her bed. "Her body lives but her spirit has never blossomed," he said. "Her name is Mary Rose. She was born the same year as you and lived in a town not too far away. Her mother died in childbirth when Mary was two years old. Her father lost his job in the Depression and directed his pain upon the little girl and her baby sister. When her eighth birthday came her father in a burst of alcoholic rage severely beat the girl before taking his own life. Little Mary Rose never recuperated from the incident and has been in institutions ever since. Don't feel anger towards her, Thora. Pity her for she will never get past this moment."

Laura returned to the room. Behind her came a pair of nurses that immediately rushed to Thora's bed. One began pulling the robe from over Thora's head while the other clutched at her wrist and was checking for a pulse. "She's having a heart attack!" the pulse-reader said. "We've got to get her into ICU at once. Call the attendants!"

One nurse began monitoring Thora's heart through a stethoscope while the other placed a small pill under Thora's tongue and began massaging her throat to invoke the swallowing reflex. "Thank you Laura for calling our attention to Thora," the nurse said in a patronizing manner as the nasty little pill went down Thora's throat.

In the meantime two men dressed in hospital whites appeared at the door with a gurney. They allowed the nurses to finish their prep work. Thora was in excruciating agony. Every part of her felt as rigid as a rock with sheering pain racing up and down all of her many arteries. Yet, despite this, all that she wanted was to hear the Great Indian Spirit's reply to her question regarding her role in all of this. He was still at the window watching. She realized that she would be soon wheeled away from him and then she might not see him again. She wanted to comply with his wishes but she needed better instructions. She did not know what to do. She wanted to free Jack. She did not want to condemn the spirits of her parents and Rebecca to walk the Earth. But she could not remember the Sleeper's name and she did not know how to dance.

The two attendants hoisted her onto the gurney.

"Goodbye Thora Thunder," Mary said to her. "I guess you are not coming to my birthday party after all."

Out of the corner of her eye Thora saw Laura step across the room and give the woman a hand mirror that she must have got somewhere along the way. "This is my birthday present to you Mary," Laura said.

Mary held up the mirror in delight and then saw the state of her hair. At once her hands began clawing at the knots and tangles. "How did it get into such a mess? I'm never going to work it all out before Daddy comes!"

One of the nurses took Thora's arm and began to attach a catheter to it. This was attached to a tube that led to a sac filled with clear liquid. Inside that bag as clear as day there was a miniature demon that was no more an inch in height yet it had the same grotesque face as she saw back at Mrs. Bianco's homestead in the forest. It was ranting and raving but its words were lost in the liquid medium that surrounded him. It was flinging its arms and kicking its feet yet it could not cause a ripple in the sac. It did however cause a wave of fright in Thora and she began clawing at the catheter with her free arm. She would not have the demon slither through the tube to enter her system.

The two male attendants had to work hard to subdue her. She was in a frenzy. Madoqua said that she was going to become a demon and now she understood how this transformation was going to take place. She fought back against the attendants, flailing her arms and legs despite all of the pain within them. She was fighting for her soul. She would not have it cast into damnation.

And even as she fought, she could hear the Great Indian Spirit in the background. "The Sleeper can only be awakened by hearing his name being called from a distant place by someone who desperately needs him to clear a new path for her. This someone can only be someone who knows not of the People's traditions and comes from a culture that disdains the ways of the People. Yet, at the time of crisis for this someone, this someone shirks the history of her culture and eagerly accepts the ways of the People. She will cry out the Sleeper's name and she will dance the Dance of the Petition for him, his harbinger and his sentinel. She will dance even though she does not know the steps. She will dance because her heart already knows."

Thora kicked out her leg. It struck the pole that carried the clear sac where the little demon was swirling about in a tantrum of rage and hate. The pole and the sac crashed to the floor. One of the attendants slipped on it and temporarily lost his hold on her.

At once Thora took this opportunity to spring from the bed. The catheter tube dangled from her arm. Below her on the floor the sac of fluid had split open and the little demon was crawling out of the fissure. He was growing rapidly. He now was nearly three inches in height; nearly triple what he was when she first noticed him. Instinctively Thora began stomping her feet, trying to crush the hideous tiny monster with them. At the same time, she was throwing out her arms in unabashed attempts to keep the attendants at bay. As she struggled, Thora thought that she could hear a drum beating from somewhere and a song being sung by a savage soul. She could not understand the words being sung. They were lilting Indian chants with long drawn out vowels and cries that came from the deepest place within the human spirit. They were done in cadence to the drumbeats and they evoked some other time when Nature and not Man ruled the Earth.

The little demon avoided her stomps and was trying to find a hole in her defense so that it could climb up her. She repeatedly crashed her feet to the floor. The rhythm of her pounces was set in time to the drumbeats. She found herself crying out her frustration in missing him and her extreme pain from her dying body. These too came in accord to the beat of the drum and in harmony with the voice of the singer.

The two hospital attendants gave her her space. Her flinging arms and the whiplash of the catheter kept them at bay.

The creature had grown to almost six inches in height now. It had menacing teeth that it liberally used at chomping at her heels. It did not say anything but its message was loud and clear. It meant to possess her, to own her, and to take her to some very dark and horrible place.

Thora's foot crashed down onto it. It was as sharp and hard as a rock. Its pointed skull stabbed all the way through the center of Thora's foot. It started to crawl out of the mangled hole. It was unscathed by the stomp. It reached forward and took hold of Thora's ankle. The woman could feel the needle-like tentacles on the growing creature's finger pads. They were digging into the skin and using it as leverage to haul itself further up her.

She swept at it with her hands, trying to knock it loose. As she made contact, the incredibly swift reflexes of the beast latched onto her wrists and drew itself onto her forearm. From there it grinned through its hideous mouth and eyes at the woman. Although it did not say anything, Thora could hear what it said. It was going to possess her and take her to the realm of its master where she would suffer eternally for the evil that she proliferated on this world. Thora cried out in terror. Her scream matched the wailing notes coming from Madoqua's song. As her scream abated, she was lost in the creature's eyes. It was taking hold of her through some hypnotic glare.

But it could not wholly possess her for she was aware of the beating drum that thumped slowly in Madoqua's hands. It was in time with her heartbeat. Each pulsed in perfect time. Her focus was leaving the demon. It was falling onto the drum and onto her heart.

Without thinking it, she called out a name that she had once heard in a dream. It was a name that should have been foreign to her but it was not. It was a very personal name; one that engendered the positive forces that she witnessed through her artificially abbreviated life. It came from her lips, loud and clear. "Rautooskee!" she cried. Her voice rang out through the room. It touched upon the nurses and the attendants. It touched upon Laura and Mary. They all stood mesmerized by what she was doing. Thora Thunder was coming to life.

The drum beat. The Indian sang.

Thora's thin age-riddled leg moved forward. It carried with it elegance and art. It came down to the floor, only to be followed by the other leg that paralleled the beautiful motion of the first. And then the first leg repeated itself. She was working a circle around the room. Her waist bent in half with the first step and then straightened itself with the second step.

Her eyes never left the demon that sat upon her forearm. Its head was turning to and fro trying to understand what was happening. This was not the way it was supposed to be according to its script. It tried to reassert its dominance by revitalizing its gaze of aggression but it found that it could no longer take on a hideous mask. It began to collapse on Thora's arm as the woman continued to dance around the room to the beat of Madoqua's drum. It fell into a wrapped ball on her arm but it did not vanish.

It transformed itself. It now took on an aura of innocence. And it slowly got up and yawned. It was now a little Indian boy waking up to a new day. "I dance for you," Thora said to the child.

Then the boy's face lost its Hendorun features. A familiar face that Thora at one time believed she would never see again replaced them. It was the face of her cousin Jack. "I dance for you," Thora said to Jack.

And then Jack's body grew and his face gradually evolved into the proud and noble mien of a Great Indian Spirit. It was Madoqua. "And I dance for you!" Thora said.

She continued her dance through the room, weaving her path between the beds and the dressers, between the staff and the patients. She danced even when the drum stopped beating. She danced until her body was no longer able to sustain her and keep her in motion. She danced until there was only a fading ember left in her mind and all else was dark around her. She danced until the ember died out.

CHAPTER 74

Passenger

She was in the bow of an enormous canoe. The birch bark gunwales of the vessel were so high that she could not see beyond them to the terrain that she was passing. Anything that was above them was blanketed in darkness. She could only see forward and that too was draped in an impenetrable blackness.

She could hear her companion behind her. She could hear his breath. It was musical. It still hummed the song that it sang only moments before. She felt no need to turn around and gaze upon him. She felt no fear in his company. She trusted him. He was a good man and he would not steer her wrong.

He was taking her somewhere, in that she was sure. But what that destination was she could not make a conjecture. There was no sense of anticipation in her. When they get there, they will get there and until they get there, they will travel in the canoe, he, fast at the helm and she, the quiet passenger, absorbing anything that impinges upon her. It did not matter if anything impinges on her because the way that she felt nothing could improve the moment. She was at peace. She had finally taken off the robe that had made her Thora Meadowford, Thora Thunder. She was now whoever she was and nothing else. She did not need to become anybody else. She did not need to be herself. She just was and that was it. Nothing more. Nothing less. A passenger in a canoe idling away the time.

Something was taking on light beyond the bow of the canoe. It started like a tiny speck of illumination, like a mote of dust caught in the beam of a flashlight. But it began to grow and take on dimension and description as it encapsulated more of the space ahead of her.

The helmsman behind her continued to sing his soft song and did not bother to provide her with detail about what she was seeing. Nor did she want him to do so. What she was witnessing was solely up to her to interpret and provide definition. It had nothing to do with him. It only had to do with her.

And as they drew closer, her mind was exacting detail upon the manifestation. She saw that it was a shoreline upon a northern lake in the Canadian arboreal wilderness. Leading away from this shoreline was a bare rock that crept upward towards a structure on its summit. The building was not in immaculate shape but Thora did not want it to be in such shape. She wanted it to be as it was, an icon to the process of becoming rather than being. She sensed that becoming was actually being and that the two concepts were one in the same. She would have it no other way.

As the canoe moved forward through the weave of slipstreams that separated it from shore, Thora saw that the land was not uninhabited. There were people there. She could count three of them. It was still too early to tell whom they were but she already knew in her heart precisely their identities. They were coming down towards a great dock along the shore. They were coming to greet her.

The helmsman slowed the vessel and steered it towards the wooden pier. Upon the pier standing proudly looking out at her was her father, the man known as Langley. Never before had Thora recognized how handsome he was. Never before had she seen that kind of smile on his face. It was an honest one, one that was not hiding behind crossed purposes and ulterior motives. He had finally outgrown them and become the man that he was destined to be.

Behind him was Cora Meadowford. She was waving one hand towards her while her other hand was tucked into the grip of her husband. Her eyes were bright and her complexion rosy. Nothing was her master any longer.

And approaching the dock was someone who was an exact replica of her.

She was full of cheer and excitement about finally being reunited with her sister. She could not wave however because her hands were full. She was carrying a cat that even from out in the water Thora could hear mew. It was Capers.

The family was finally back together and Thora could feel her eyes cloud with tears. She had to turn around to thank her Indian guide, the great Madoqua. But as her neck bent to the rear of the canoe, she saw that he was not there. Taking his place were two men, her grandfather Sambo and his father Samuel Angus Meadowford the First.

They nodded simultaneously to her and said together, "Welcome home."